A Treasury of
Hans Christian Andersen

A Treasury of
HANS
CHRISTIAN
ANDERSEN

❖

*Translated from the Danish
by Erik Christian Haugaard*

NELSON DOUBLEDAY, Inc.
Garden City, New York

My gift to the world

—Hans Christian Andersen

This translation is dedicated to the memory of
Ruth Hill Viguers,
who knew that the leather outlasts the gilding.

Acknowledgments

ONE DAY in September 1967, I translated a very short Andersen tale, which she did not know, for Ruth Hill Viguers; and then the whole idea of a new Andersen translation came into being. A few months later Peter Hyun took the initiative and set out to make the possibility into a project. Virginia Haviland, Harriet Quimby, Paul Heins, and George Woods were so kind as to lend their good names on an application for a grant to the Chapelbrook Foundation; the response of this foundation was generous and immediate and, thanks to them, the two years that this work has been in progress has not been a time of need. When the translation was nearing completion, Dr. Bo Gronbech told me many interesting and important facts about Hans Christian Andersen. Valborg Lauritzen typed the enormous manuscript; and for her ability, good nature, and patience in trying to make out the many corrections, I am, indeed, grateful. The Jubilee Fund of the Danish National Bank kindly provided a small grant so I could pay my faithful typist. To Sharon Steinhoff I owe my thanks for many an hour's necessary but tedious labor. Most of all, I am indebted to my wife, without whose assistance and help the translation would not have been done at all.

Erik Christian Haugaard
Veksebo, Denmark
September 1972

Contents

Introduction

AFTER having worked for more than two years on the translation of Andersen's fairy tales, I have come to be on intimate terms with him. It has been said that intimacy breeds contempt; and I am sure it does for those who search for idols. But I think one can love a person for his faults as well as his virtues. Man is made from clay and clay is fragile. But maybe it is its frailty that makes us look with double wonder at an ancient Greek vase: it is so delicate, so brittle, and yet it has survived.

Andersen lived seventy years; and I believe his fairy tales will live forever. He had innumerable weaknesses, which I shall not recount, for most of them all men possess; but he had that great courage that poets must have; and that made it possible for him to be totally aware of his own faults and virtues. A poet's laboratory is himself, and Andersen made use of those traits for which he would have been laughed at or censored, as well as those that might earn him applause.

He had an enormous pride, a faith in his own talent, and a belief in his own particular genius; and this brought him into conflict with the intellectuals of his time. What his critics did not understand was that his pride was also the guardian of his talent. He was a very careful writer. Many of his stories were rewritten many times. It was of great concern to him that his tales should be able to be read aloud as if they were being told.

The fairy tale speaks to all of us; that is its particular charm. The beggar and the prince pause in the market place to hear the storyteller; and for the moment they are merely men, subject to the passions that rule us all. Again and again, in his notes and his autobiography, Andersen refers to the stories he had heard as a child. It is a strange irony that our all-embracing modern forms of communication have killed the storyteller, and may end by making us all mute.

These stories that Andersen heard as a child were all very simple tales, and their characters were probably more archetypes than they were individuals. They were not meant to surprise—let alone shock—the listener. Indeed, their attraction lay in the fact that they were familiar. The mean, the petty, the evil, the good, and the kind were so in the manner that one was used to; it was the plot itself that held one's interest. We of the twentieth century, who are so used to plotless novels with heroes so infinitely complex that, after having read the book, it is easier for us to describe the characters' nervous systems than to tell what the story was about, hardly ever come into contact with this early form of literature. Yet these stories, stripped as they are of the fashionable and the modish, give us—at least for a moment—that peace which is necessary for survival. Man must live in his own time—he has no choice—but for the sake of his sanity he must sometimes escape its tyranny—if only to be able to recognize it. *Once upon a time* denies time and thus curtails its power over us.

Once upon a time is a definite point in the infinite. It exists somewhere but has no particular date, which is a feat that is hardly explainable—and yet, maybe it is. We have divided time into precise periods. "Was *once upon a time* in the Iron Age, the Bronze Age, or the thirteenth century?" we ask, for we are enlightened. But the peasant who heard a fairy tale in the market place and retold it to his family when he came home had no such conceptions. Time, for him, stretched from the creation till that moment which can best be described as *now*. And though he knew that raiment and customs changed, he did not believe they had very much influence on people. He knew the Bible well, yet it did not disturb him to see the Virgin portrayed as if she were a rich Florentine lady. Were not Saul and David like the kings he knew? Was Eve much different from his own wife? *Once upon a time* was not magic or poetic, as it is to us. But then, the twentieth century has produced no fairy tales.

Andersen was the last great teller of fairy tales. We may create tales of imagination and fantasy, but they are not fairy tales. The fairy tale and the folk tale take place in the real world, no matter how exotic and strange their backgrounds may be. Witches, trolls, or mermaids may appear; but they are not figments of anyone's imagination; they are as real as the princess or the peasant. We who are manacled by a belief in progress and theories of natural behavior find it hard to understand this. We prefer to escape into fantasy, into worlds that are safe because they never have existed and never will.

"Once upon a time there was a boy who was so very, very poor that all he owned was the suit of clothes that he was wearing; and that was too small for him. . . ." That could have been the opening of a fairy tale or a description of Hans Christian Andersen setting out from his native Odense to seek his fortune in Copenhagen. Did he see witches, fairy godmothers, and trolls? He did indeed, as certainly as Odysseus heard the Siren sing. Like the heroes of the fairy tales, Andersen went out into the wide world, with a good deal of naïveté, curiosity, and lust for life as ballast. He sought the princess and half the kingdom. Nothing less would do, for he was a real poet. And he did win, if not the princess and half the kingdom, then something even better: fame in half if not the whole world. Did it make him happy? I think it did, for it meant that his suffering had not been in vain. Out of his personal grief and unhappiness, beauty had been born. Yet it was not Andersen but we who gained most from this struggle. The artists, musicians, and poets are the richest of all human beings, for they can leave a legacy that will last as long as men breathe.

Andersen adopted the most ancient literary forms—the fairy tale and the folk tale—and changed them into something that was his own. He was not a collector of folklore, a reteller of what had already been told, as were the brothers Grimm, whom he admired very much.

A translator is a servant of what he is translating; it is, after all, reduced to sentences and even single words, whose double he has to find. He must try not only to translate the sense but the spirit as well. This is his art, this is what he should and will be judged by. He must be faithful to the original and yet produce a fluent, readable version in another language. But these demands of fluency and readability must not be excuses for changing the author's literary style. Andersen's prose in Danish is not smooth, it is choppy and abrupt; and that is part of his charm. I hope that I have "translated" this as well.

The translator must not let his own personal opinions, or those of his times, influence him. Unfortunately, many of the early translators of Hans Christian Andersen were Victorians, and they had a tendency to make a kiss on the mouth, in translation, land on the cheek. Passion had to be ethereal rather than sensual; and it was so easy and desirable, considering the audience of the time, to change sentiment into sentimentality. I shall not judge these early translators too harshly; for I, too, have been tempted to cut a little here and there to please my audience.

As far as I have been able, I have been faithful to the original text, even when I knew that certain ideas might offend people of my own times, or might—which is far worse—appear ridiculous in their eyes. I have tried to be loyal to only one person, Hans Christian Andersen; and I hope most fervently that I have succeeded.

E.C.H.

A Treasury of
Hans Christian Andersen

1
❊◇❊

The Tinderbox

A SOLDIER came marching down the road: Left . . . right! Left . . .
right! He had a pack on his back and a sword at his side. He had
been in the war and he was on his way home. Along the road he met
a witch. She was a disgusting sight, with a lower lip that hung all the
way down to her chest.

"Good evening, young soldier," she said. "What a handsome
sword you have and what a big knapsack. I can see that you are a
real soldier! I shall give you all the money that you want."

"Thank you, old witch," he said.

"Do you see that big tree?" asked the witch, and pointed to the
one they were standing next to. "The trunk is hollow. You climb up
to the top of the tree, crawl into the hole, and slide deep down inside
it. I'll tie a rope around your waist, so I can pull you up again when
you call me."

"What am I supposed to do down in the tree?" asked the soldier.

"Get money!" answered the witch and laughed. "Now listen to me.
When you get down to the very bottom, you'll be in a great passageway where you'll be able to see because there are over a hundred
lamps burning. You'll find three doors; and you can open them all
because the keys are in the locks. Go into the first one; and there on
a chest, in the middle of the room, you'll see a dog with eyes as big as
teacups. Don't let that worry you. You will have my blue checkered
apron; just spread it out on the floor, put the dog down on top of it,
and it won't do you any harm. Open the chest and take as many
coins as you wish, they are all copper. If it's silver you're after, then

go into the next room. There you'll find a dog with eyes as big as millstones; but don't let that worry you, put him on the apron and take the money. If you'd rather have gold, you can have that too; it's in the third room. Wait till you see that dog, he's got eyes as big as the Round Tower in Copenhagen; but don't let that worry you. Put him down on my apron and he won't hurt you; then you can take as much gold as you wish."

"That doesn't sound bad!" said the soldier. "But what am I to do for you, old witch? I can't help thinking that you must want something too."

"No," replied the witch. "I don't want one single coin. Just bring me the old tinderbox that my grandmother forgot the last time she was down there."

"I'm ready, tie the rope around my waist!" ordered the soldier.

"There you are, and here is my blue checkered apron," said the witch.

The soldier climbed the tree, let himself fall into the hole, and found that he was in the passageway, where more than a hundred lights burned.

He opened the first door. Oh! There sat the dog with eyes as big as teacups glaring at him.

"You are a handsome fellow!" he exclaimed as he put the dog down on the witch's apron. He filled his pockets with copper coins, closed the chest, and put the dog back on top of it.

He went into the second room. Aha! There sat the dog with eyes as big as millstones. "Don't keep looking at me like that," said the soldier good-naturedly. "It isn't polite and you'll spoil your eyes." He put the dog down on the witch's apron and opened the chest. When he saw all the silver coins, he emptied the copper out of his pockets and filled both them and his knapsack with silver.

Now he entered the third room. That dog was big enough to frighten anyone, even a soldier. His eyes were as large as the Round Tower in Copenhagen and they turned around like wheels.

"Good evening," said the soldier politely, taking off his cap, for such a dog he had never seen before. For a while he just stood looking at it; but finally he said to himself, "Enough of this!" Then he put the dog down on the witch's apron and opened up the chest.

"God preserve me!" he cried. There was so much gold that there was enough to buy the whole city of Copenhagen; and all the gingerbread men, rocking horses, riding whips, and tin soldiers in the whole world.

Quickly the soldier threw away all the silver coins that he had in his pockets and knapsack and put gold in them instead; he even filled his boots and his cap with money. He put the dog back on the chest, closed the door behind him, and called up through the hollow tree.

"Pull me up, you old witch!"

"Have you got the tinderbox?" she called back.

"Right you are, I have forgotten it," he replied honestly, and went back to get it. The witch hoisted him up and again he stood on the road; but now his pockets, knapsack, cap, and boots were filled with gold and he felt quite differently.

"Why do you want the tinderbox?" he asked.

"Mind your own business," answered the witch crossly. "You have got your money, just give me the tinderbox."

"Blah! Blah!" said the soldier. "Tell me what you are going to use it for, right now; or I'll draw my sword and cut off your head."

"No!" replied the witch firmly; but that was a mistake, for the soldier chopped her head off. She lay there dead. The soldier put all his gold in her apron, tied it up into a bundle, and threw it over his shoulder. The tinderbox he dropped into his pocket; and off to town he went.

The town was nice, and the soldier went to the nicest inn, where he asked to be put up in the finest room and ordered all the things he liked to eat best for his supper, because now he had so much money that he was rich.

The servant who polished his boots thought it was very odd that a man so wealthy should have such worn-out boots. But the soldier hadn't had time to buy anything yet; the next day he bought boots and clothes that fitted his purse. And the soldier became a refined gentleman. People were eager to tell him all about their town and their king, and what a lovely princess his daughter was.

"I would like to see her," said the soldier.

"But no one sees her," explained the townfolk. "She lives in a copper castle, surrounded by walls, and towers, and a moat. The king doesn't dare allow anyone to visit her because it has been foretold that she will marry a simple soldier, and the king doesn't want that to happen."

"If only I could see her," thought the soldier, though it was unthinkable.

The soldier lived merrily, went to the theater, kept a carriage so he could drive in the king's park, and gave lots of money to the poor. He remembered well what it felt like not to have a penny in his purse.

He was rich and well dressed. He had many friends; and they all said that he was kind and a real cavalier; and such things he liked to hear. But since he used money every day and never received any, he soon had only two copper coins left.

He had to move out of the beautiful room downstairs, up to a tiny one in the garret, where he not only polished his boots himself but also mended them with a large needle. None of his friends came to see him, for they said there were too many stairs to climb.

It was a very dark evening and he could not even buy a candle. Suddenly he remembered that he had seen the stub of a candle in the tinderbox that he had brought up from the bottom of the hollow tree. He found the tinderbox and took out the candle. He struck the flint. There was a spark, and in through the door came the dog with eyes as big as teacups.

"What does my master command?" asked the dog.

"What's this all about?" exclaimed the soldier. "That certainly was an interesting tinderbox. Can I have whatever I want? Bring me some money," he ordered. In less time than it takes to say thank you, the dog was gone and back with a big sack of copper coins in his mouth.

Now the soldier understood why the witch had thought the tinderbox so valuable. If he struck it once, the dog appeared who sat on the chest full of copper coins; if he struck it twice, then the dog came who guarded the silver money; and if he struck it three times, then came the one who had the gold.

The soldier moved downstairs again, wore fine clothes again, and had fine friends, for now they all remembered him and cared for him as they had before.

One night, when he was sitting alone after his friends had gone, he thought, "It is a pity that no one can see that beautiful princess. What is the good of her beauty if she must always remain behind the high walls and towers of a copper castle? Will I never see her? . . . Where is my tinderbox?"

He made the sparks fly and the dog with eyes as big as teacups came. "I know it's very late at night," he said, "but I would so like to see the beautiful princess, if only for a minute."

Away went the dog; and faster than thought he returned with the sleeping princess on his back. She was so lovely that anyone would have known that she was a real princess. The soldier could not help kissing her, for he was a true soldier.

The dog brought the princess back to her copper castle; but in the morning while she was having tea with her father and mother, the king and queen, she told them that she had had a very strange dream that night. A large dog had come and carried her away to a soldier who kissed her.

"That's a nice story," said the queen, but she didn't mean it.

The next night one of the older ladies in waiting was sent to watch over the princess while she slept, and find out whether it had only been a dream, and not something worse.

The soldier longed to see the princess so much that he couldn't bear it, so at night he sent the dog to fetch her. The dog ran as fast as he could, but the lady in waiting had her boots on and she kept up with him all the way. When she saw which house he had entered, she took out a piece of chalk and made a big white cross on the door.

"Now we'll be able to find it in the morning," she thought, and went home to get some sleep.

When the dog returned the princess to the castle, he noticed the cross on the door of the house where his master lived; so he took a piece of white chalk and put crosses on all the doors of all the houses in the whole town. It was a very clever thing to do, for now the lady in waiting would never know which was the right door.

The next morning the king and queen, the old lady in waiting, and all the royal officers went out into town to find the house where the princess had been.

"Here it is!" exclaimed the king, when he saw the first door with a cross on it.

"No, my sweet husband, it is here," said his wife, who had seen the second door with a cross on it.

"Here's one!"

"There's one!"

Everyone shouted at once, for it didn't matter where anyone looked: there he would find a door with a cross on it; and so they all gave up.

Now the queen was so clever, she could do more than ride in a golden carriage. She took out her golden scissors and cut out a large piece of silk and sewed it into a pretty little bag. This she filled with the fine grain of buckwheat, and tied the bag around the princess' waist. When this was done, she cut a little hole in the bag just big enough for the little grains of buckwheat to fall out, one at a time, and show the way to the house where the princess was taken by the dog.

During the night the dog came to fetch the princess and carry her on his back to the soldier, who loved her so much that now he had only one desire, and that was to be a prince so that he could marry her.

The dog neither saw nor felt the grains of buckwheat that made a little trail all the way from the copper castle to the soldier's room at the inn. In the morning the king and queen had no difficulty in finding where the princess had been, and the soldier was thrown into jail.

There he sat in the dark with nothing to do; and what made matters worse was that everyone said, "Tomorrow you are going to be hanged!"

That was not amusing to hear. If only he had had his tinderbox, but he had forgotten it in his room. When the sun rose, he watched the people, through the bars of his window, as they hurried toward the gates of the city, for the hanging was to take place outside the walls. He heard the drums and the royal soldiers marching. Everyone was running. He saw a shoemaker's apprentice, who had not bothered to take off his leather apron and was wearing slippers. The boy lifted his legs so high, it looked as though he were galloping. One of his slippers flew off and landed near the window of the soldier's cell.

"Hey!" shouted the soldier. "Listen, shoemaker, wait a minute, nothing much will happen before I get there. But if you will run to the inn and get the tinderbox I left in my room, you can earn four copper coins. But you'd better use your legs or it will be too late."

The shoemaker's apprentice, who didn't have one copper coin, was eager to earn four; and he ran to get the tinderbox as fast as he could; and gave it to the soldier.

And now you shall hear what happened after that!

Outside the gates of the town, a gallows had been built; around it stood the royal soldiers and many hundreds of thousands of people. The king and the queen sat on their lovely throne, and across from them sat the judge and the royal council.

The soldier was standing on the platform, but as the noose was put around his neck, he declared that it was an ancient custom to grant a condemned man his last innocent wish. The only thing he wanted was to be allowed to smoke a pipe of tobacco.

The king couldn't refuse; and the soldier took out his tinderbox and struck it: once, twice, three times! Instantly, the three dogs were before him: the one with eyes as big as teacups, the one with eyes as big as millstones, and the one with eyes as big as the Round Tower in Copenhagen.

"Help me! I don't want to be hanged!" cried the soldier.

The dogs ran toward the judge and the royal council. They took one man by the leg and another by the nose, and threw them up in the air, so high that when they hit the earth again they broke into little pieces.

"Not me!" screamed the king; but the biggest dog took both the king and the queen and sent them flying up as high as all the others had been.

The royal guards got frightened; and the people began to shout: "Little soldier, you shall be our king and marry the princess!"

The soldier rode in the king's golden carriage; and the three dogs danced in front of it and barked: "Hurrah!"

The little boys whistled and the royal guards presented arms. The princess came out of her copper castle and became queen, which she liked very much. The wedding feast lasted a week; and the three dogs sat at the table and made eyes at everyone.

2
✳◇✳

Little Claus and Big Claus

ONCE upon a time there lived in a village two men who had the same name; they were both called Claus. But one of them owned four horses, while the other had only one; so to tell them apart the richer man was called Big Claus and the poorer one Little Claus. Now let's hear what happened to the two of them because that's a real story!

Six days a week Little Claus had to work for Big Claus and loan him his horse; and in return Big Claus had to let Little Claus borrow his four horses on Sunday. One day a week Little Claus felt as if all the horses belonged to him, and he would crack his whip in the air and shout orders to them merrily.

One morning when the sun was shining brightly and the villagers, all dressed up in their Sunday best, with their prayer books under their arms, were passing his field, Little Claus cracked his whip in the air, whistled, and called out very loudly, "Gee up, all my horses!"

"You may not say that!" exclaimed Big Claus. "Only one of the horses is yours."

But Little Claus forgot very quickly what Big Claus had said, and the next time someone went by and nodded kindly in his direction, he shouted, "Gee up, all my horses!"

Big Claus turned around and shouted! "I beg you for the last time not to call all those horses yours because if you do it once more I'll take the mallet that I use to drive in the stake for tethering my four horses and hit your one horse so hard that it will drop dead on the spot."

"I promise never to say it again," said Little Claus meekly. But the words were hardly out of his mouth when still another group of churchgoers stopped to watch him plow. They smiled and said good morning in a very friendly way. "What a fine figure I must cut, driving five horses," he thought; and without realizing what he was doing, he cracked the whip and cried, "Gee up, all my horses!"

"I'll give your horse gee up!" screamed Big Claus in a rage; and he took his tethering mallet and hit Little Claus's only horse so hard on the forehead that it fell down quite dead.

"Poor me!" cried Little Claus. "Now I don't have any horse at all!" And he sat down and wept. But as there was nothing else to do he flayed the horse and hung the hide up to dry. When the wind had done its work, Little Claus put the hide in a sack and set off for town to sell it in the market place.

It was a long way and the road led through a forest. The weather turned bad and among the dark shadows Little Claus lost his way. He turned first in one direction and then in another. Finally he did find his way again; but by then it was late afternoon and too late to reach town before nightfall.

Not far from the road he saw a farmhouse. The shutters were closed but above them there shone tiny streams of light. "There I may ask for shelter for the night," Little Claus thought, and made his way to the front door and knocked.

The farmer's wife answered the door, but when she heard what he wanted she shook her head. "You'll have to go away," she ordered. "My husband isn't home and I cannot allow a stranger to come in."

"Then I'll have to sleep outside," said Little Claus. The farmer's wife shut the door without another word; and Little Claus looked about him. Near the house was a haystack, and between that and the dwelling there was a shed with a flat thatched roof.

"I'll stretch out on that," Little Claus mumbled, looking at the roof. "It will make a fine bed and I doubt that the stork will fly down and bite me." The latter was said in jest because there was a stork's nest on the roof of the farmhouse.

Little Claus climbed up on the roof of the shack; and while he was twisting and turning to make himself comfortable, he realized that from where he lay he could see right into the kitchen of the farmhouse because, at the top, the shutters did not close tightly.

A fine white linen cloth covered the large table and on it were not only a roast and wine but a platter of fish as well. On one side of the table sat the farmer's wife and on the other the deacon; and while she filled his glass with wine, he filled himself with fish because that was his favorite food.

"If only I had been invited too!" Little Claus sighed, and pushed himself as near to the window as he could without touching the shutters. There was a cake on the table too; this was better than a party, it was a feast!

He heard someone galloping on the road; he turned and saw the rider: it was the farmer coming home.

Now this farmer was known for two things: one, that he was a good fellow, and the other, that he suffered from a strange disease; he couldn't bear the sight of a deacon. One glance and he went into a rage. And that, of course, was the reason why the deacon had come visiting on a day when the farmer wasn't at home; and that too was why the farmer's wife had made the most delicious food she could for her guest.

When they heard the farmer riding up to the door of his house, both the farmer's wife and the deacon were terrified; and she told him to climb into a large empty chest that stood in the corner. The poor man, trembling with fear, obeyed her. Then the woman hid all the food and the wine in the oven, for she knew that if her husband saw all the delicacies he was certain to ask her why she had made them.

"Ow!" groaned Little Claus when he saw the last of the food disappear into the bread oven.

"Is there someone up there?" the farmer called, and when he saw Little Claus lying on the roof of the shed he told him to come down. "What were you doing up there?"

Little Claus explained how he had lost his way in the forest and asked the farmer to be allowed to spend the night in his house.

"You are most welcome," said the farmer, who was the kindest of men, as long as there was no deacon in sight. "But first let's have a bite to eat."

The farmer's wife greeted them both very politely, set the table, and served them a large bowl of porridge. The farmer, who was very hungry, ate with relish; but Little Claus kept thinking of all the delicious food in the oven and couldn't swallow a spoonful.

At his feet under the table lay the sack with the horse hide in it. He stepped on the sack and the horse hide squeaked. "Shhhhhhhh!"

whispered Little Claus to the sack; but at the same time he pressed his foot down on it even harder and it squeaked even louder.

"What have you got in the bag?" asked the farmer.

"Oh, it's only a wizard," Little Claus replied. "He was telling me that there's no reason for us to eat porridge when he has just conjured both fish and meat for us, and even a cake. Look in the oven."

"What!" exclaimed the farmer; and he ran to the oven and opened it. There he saw all the good food that his wife had made for the deacon; and she—not daring to tell him the truth—silently served the roast, the fish, and the cake.

After he had taken a few mouthfuls, Little Claus stepped on the sack again so that the hide squeaked.

"What is the wizard saying now?" asked the farmer eagerly.

"He says that he has conjured three bottles of wine for us and that you will find them in the corner next to the oven."

The farmer's poor wife brought out the wine, which she had hidden, and poured it for Little Claus and her husband, who made so many toasts to each other's health that they were soon very merry. Then the farmer began to think about Little Claus's sack and what a wonderful thing it must be to have a wizard.

"Do you think he could conjure the Devil?" the farmer asked. "For now that I have the courage I wouldn't mind seeing what he looks like."

"Why not?" replied Little Claus. "My wizard will do anything I tell him to. . . . Won't you?" he added, stepping on the sack so that it squeaked. Turning to the farmer, Little Claus smiled. "Can't you hear that he said yes? But the Devil has such an ugly face that he's not worth looking at."

"I'm not afraid," said the farmer, and hiccupped. "How terrible can he look?"

"He looks just like a deacon!"

"Pooh!" returned the farmer. "That's worse than I thought! I must confess that I cannot stand the sight of a deacon; but now that I know that it is only the Devil I will be looking at, maybe I can bear it. But don't let him come too near me and let's get it over with before I lose my courage."

"I'll tell my wizard," said Little Claus and stepped on the hide; then he cocked his head as if he were listening to someone.

"What is he saying?" asked the farmer, who could only hear the hide squeak.

"He says that if we go over to the chest in the corner and open it up we shall see the Devil sitting inside. But we must be careful when we lift the lid, not to lift it too high, so the Devil can escape."

"Then you must hold onto the lid while I lift it," whispered the farmer to Little Claus as he tiptoed to the chest in which the deacon was hiding. This poor fellow had heard every word that Little Claus and the farmer had said and was quaking with fear.

The farmer opened the chest no more than an inch or two and peeped inside. "Ah!" he screamed and jumped up, letting the lid fall back into place. "I saw him! He looked exactly like our deacon! It was a dreadful sight!"

After such an experience you need a drink; and Little Claus and the farmer had many, for they drank late into the night.

"You must sell me that wizard," the farmer finally said. "Ask whatever you want for it. . . . I'll give you a bushel basket full of money, if that's what you'd like."

"I wouldn't think of it," replied Little Claus. "You have seen for yourself all the marvelous things that wizard can do."

"But I want it with all my heart," begged the farmer; and he kept on pleading with Little Claus until at last he agreed.

"I cannot forget that you gave me a night's lodging," Little Claus said. "Take my wizard, but remember to fill the bushel basket to the very top."

"I shall! I shall!" exclaimed the farmer. "But you must take the chest along too. I won't have it in my house. Who knows but that the Devil isn't still inside it?"

And that's how it happened that Little Claus gave the farmer a sack with a horse hide in it and in return was given not only a bushel full of money and a chest but a wheelbarrow to carry them away.

"Good-by!" called Little Claus, and off he went.

On the other side of the forest there was a deep river with a current that flowed so swiftly that you could not swim against it. But the river had to be crossed and so a bridge had been built. When Little Claus reached the middle of that bridge, he said very loudly—so the deacon, who was still inside the chest, could hear him—"What's the point of dragging this chest any farther? It's so heavy, you'd think it was filled with stones. I'm all worn out. I know what I'll do, I'll dump

the chest into the stream and if the current carries it home to me, all
well and good; and if not, it doesn't matter." Then he took hold of
the chest and pushed it, as if he were about to lift it out of the wheelbarrow and let it fall into the water.

"No, stop it!" cried the deacon from inside the chest. "Let me out!
Please, let me out!"

"Oh!" shouted Little Claus as if he were frightened. "The Devil is
still in there. I'd better throw the chest right into the river and drown
him."

"No! No!" screamed the deacon. "I'll give you a bushel of money
if you'll let me out!"

"That's a different tune," said Little Claus, and opened the chest.
The deacon climbed out and shoved the chest into the river. Together
Little Claus and the deacon went to the deacon's home, where he
gave Little Claus the bushel of coins that he had promised him. Now
Little Claus had a whole wheelbarrow full of money.

"That wasn't bad payment for my old horse," he said to himself as
he dumped all the coins out on the floor of his own living room.
"What a big pile it is! It will annoy Big Claus to find out how rich I
have become, all because of my horse. I won't tell him but let him
find out for himself."

A few minutes later a boy banged on Big Claus's door and asked
him if he could borrow his grain measure for Little Claus.

"I wonder what he is going to use that for," thought Big Claus;
and in order to find out he dabbed a bit of tar in the bottom of the
measuring pail, which was quite clever of him because when it was
returned he found a silver coin stuck to the spot.

"Where did that come from?" shouted Big Claus, and ran as fast
as he could to Little Claus's house. When he saw Little Claus in the
midst of his riches, he shouted even louder, "Where did you get all
that money from?"

"Oh, that was for my horse hide, I sold it last night."

"You were certainly well paid!" said Big Claus; and hurried home
where he took an ax and killed all four of his horses; then he flayed
them and set off for town with their hides.

"Hides for sale! Hides for sale! Who wants to buy hides?" Big
Claus shouted from street to street.

All the shoemakers and tanners came out of their workshops to
ask him the price of his wares.

"A bushel full of coins for each hide," he replied.

"You must be mad!" they all shouted at once. "Do you think we count money by the bushel?"

"Hides for sale! Hides for sale!" Big Claus repeated. And every time that someone asked him the price he said again, "A bushel full of coins."

"Are you trying to make fools of us?" the shoemakers and the tanners shouted. And while the crowd continued to gather around them, the tanners took their leather aprons and the shoemakers their straps and began to beat Big Claus.

"Hides . . ." screamed one of the tanners. "We'll see to it that your hide spits red!"

"Out of town with him!" they shouted. And certainly Big Claus did his best to get out of town as fast as he could; never in his whole life had he gotten such a beating.

"Little Claus is going to pay for this!" he decided when he got home. "He is going to pay with his life."

But while Big Claus was in town, something unfortunate had occurred: Little Claus's grandmother had died. And although she had been a very mean and scolding hag, who had never been kind to Little Claus, he felt very sad. Thinking that it might bring her back to life, he put his old grandmother in his own warm bed and decided to let her stay there all night, even though this meant that he would have to sleep in a chair.

It was not the first time that Little Claus had tried sleeping in a chair, but he could not sleep anyway; so he was wide awake when Big Claus came and tiptoed across the room to the bed in which he thought Little Claus was sleeping.

With an ax Big Claus hit the old grandmother on top of the head as hard as he could. "That's what you get for making a fool out of me," he explained. "And now you won't be able to do it again," he added and went home.

"What a wicked man!" thought Little Claus. "If my grandmother hadn't already been dead, he would have killed her."

Very early the next morning he dressed his grandmother in her Sunday best; then he borrowed a horse from his neighbor and harnessed it to his cart. On the small seat in the back of the cart, he put the old woman in a sitting position with bundles on either side of her, so she wouldn't fall out of the cart while he was driving. He went through the forest and just as the sun was rising he reached an inn. "I'd better stop to get something to keep me alive," he said.

It was a large inn, and the innkeeper was very rich. He was also very kind, but he had a ferocious temper, as if he had nothing inside him but pepper and tobacco.

"Good morning," he said to Little Claus. "You're dressed very finely for so early in the morning."

"I'm driving to town with my grandmother," he replied. "She's sitting out in the cart because I couldn't persuade her to come in here with me. I wonder if you would be so kind as to take a glass of mead out to her; but speak a little loudly because she is a bit hard of hearing."

"No sooner said than done," answered the innkeeper; and he poured a large glass of mead which he carried out to the dead woman.

"Here is a glass of mead, which your son ordered for you," said the innkeeper loudly but politely; but the dead woman sat perfectly still and said not a word.

"Can't you hear me?" he shouted. "Here is mead from your son!"

He shouted the same words again as loud as he could, and still the old woman sat staring straight ahead. The more he shouted, the madder the innkeeper got, until finally he lost his temper and threw the mead, glass and all, right into the woman's face. With the mead dripping down her nose, she fell over backward, for Little Claus had not tied her to the seat.

"What have you done?" shouted Little Claus as he flung open the door of the inn. "Why, you have killed my grandmother!" he cried, grabbing the innkeeper by the shirt. "Look at the wound she has on her head!"

"Oh, what a calamity!" the innkeeper exclaimed, and wrung his hands. "It is all because of that temper of mine! Sweet, good Little Claus, I will give you a bushel full of money and bury your grandmother as if she were my own, as long as you'll keep quiet about what really happened, because if you don't they'll chop my head off; and that's so nasty."

And that was how Little Claus got another bushel full of coins; and the innkeeper, true to his word, buried the old woman as well as he would have had she been his own grandmother.

As soon as he got home Little Claus sent his boy to borrow Big Claus's grain measure.

"What, haven't I killed him?" Big Claus exclaimed. "I must find out what's happened. I'll take the measure over there myself."

When he arrived at Little Claus's and saw all the money, his eyes grew wide with wonder and greed. "Where did you get all that from?" he demanded.

"It was my grandmother and not me that you killed, and now I have sold her body for a bushel full of money."

"You were certainly well paid," said Big Claus, and hurried home. When he got there he took an ax and killed his old grandmother; then he dumped the poor old woman's body in his carriage and drove into town. He went at once to the apothecary and asked if he wanted to buy a corpse.

"Who is it and where did you get it from?" the apothecary inquired.

"Oh, it is my grandmother, and I have killed her so I could sell her body for a bushel of money," Big Claus said.

"God save us!" cried the apothecary. "You don't know what you're saying. . . . If you talk like that you'll lose your head." And the apothecary lectured him, telling him how wicked a crime murder was and that it was committed only by the most evil of men, who deserved the severest punishment. Big Claus was terrified and leaped into his carriage. He set off in the direction of his home, wildly whipping his horses. But no one tried to stop him, for everyone believed that he had gone mad.

"I'll make you pay for this!" Big Claus cried as soon as he was well out of town. "Little Claus is going to pay for this," he repeated when he got home. Then he took a large sack and went to see Little Claus.

"So you fooled me again!" he shouted. "First I killed my horses and then my grandmother; and it's all your fault. But you have fooled me for the last time!" Grabbing Little Claus around the waist, he shoved him into the sack. As he flung the sack over his shoulder he said loudly, "And now I am going to drown you!"

It was quite far to the river, and as he walked the sack with Little Claus in it seemed to grow heavier and heavier. The road went past the church, and Big Claus heard the organ being played and the congregation singing. "It would be nice to hear a hymn or two before I go on," he thought. "Everybody's in church and Little Claus can't get out of the sack." So Big Claus put down the sack near the entrance and went into the church.

"Poor me! Poor me!" sighed Little Claus. He twisted and turned but he could not loosen the cord that had been tied around the opening of the sack.

At that moment an old herdsman happened to pass. He had snow-white hair and walked with a long crook. In front of him he drove a large herd of cows and bulls. One of the bulls bumped into the sack and Little Claus was turned over.

"Poor me! Poor me!" cried Little Claus. "I am so young and am already bound for heaven."

"Think of poor me; I am an old man," said the herdsman, "and am not allowed to enter it."

"Open up the sack!" shouted Little Claus. "You get inside it, instead of me, and then you will get to heaven right away!"

"Nothing could be better," said the old man. He untied the sack and Little Claus crawled out at once.

"Take good care of my cattle," the herdsman begged as he climbed into the sack. Little Claus promised that he would and tied the sack securely. Then he went on his way, driving the herd before him.

A little later Big Claus came out of the church and lifted the sack onto his back. He was surprised how much lighter it was now, for the old man weighed only half as much as Little Claus.

"How easy it is to carry now; it did do me good to hear a hymn!" he thought.

Big Claus went directly down to the river that was both deep and wide and dumped the sack into the water, shouting after it: "You have made a fool of me for the last time!" For of course he believed that Little Claus was still inside the sack that was disappearing into the river.

On his way home he met Little Claus with all his cattle at the crossroads.

"What!" exclaimed Big Claus. "Haven't I drowned you?"

"Oh yes," answered Little Claus. "You threw me in the river about half an hour ago."

"But where did you get that huge herd of cattle?" Big Claus demanded.

"They are river cattle," replied Little Claus. "I'll tell you everything that happened to me. But, by the way, first I want to thank you for drowning me. For now I shall never have anything to worry about again, I am really rich. . . . Believe me, I was frightened when you threw me over the bridge. The wind whistled in my ears as I fell into the cold water. I sank straight to the bottom; but I didn't hurt myself because I landed on the softest, most beautiful green grass you can imagine. Then the sack was opened by the loveliest maiden. She was all dressed in white except for the green wreath in her wet hair. Taking my hand, she asked, 'Aren't you Little Claus?' When I nodded she said, 'Here are some cattle for you and six miles up the road there is an even bigger herd waiting for you.' Then I realized that to the water people the streams and rivers were as roads are to us. They use them to travel on. Far from their homes under the oceans, they follow the streams and the rivers until they finally become too shallow and come to an end. There are the most beautiful flowers growing down there and the finest, freshest grass; the fish swimming around above your head remind you of the birds flying in the air. The people are as nice as they can be; and the cattle fat and friendly."

"Then tell me why you came up here on land again?" asked Big Claus. "I never would have left a place as wonderful as that."

"Well," said Little Claus, "that is just because I am smart. I told you that the water maiden said that another herd of cattle would be waiting for me six miles up the road. By 'road,' she meant the river; and I am eager to see my cattle. You know how the river twists and turns while the road up here on land is straight; so I thought that if I used the road instead of the river I would get there much faster and save myself at least two miles of walking."

"Oh, you are a lucky man!" exclaimed Big Claus. "Do you think that if I were thrown into the river I would be given cattle too?"

"I don't know why not," replied Little Claus. "But I cannot carry you, as you did me, you're too heavy. But if you'll find a sack and climb into it yourself I'll be glad to go to the bridge with you and push you into the water."

"Thank you very much," said Big Claus. "But if I don't get a herd of cattle when I get down there I'll beat you as you have never been beaten before."

"Oh no! How can you think of being so mean!" whimpered Little Claus as they made their way to the river.

It was a hot day and when the cattle spied the water they started running toward it, for they were very thirsty. "See how eager they are to get to the river," remarked Little Claus. "They are longing for their home under the water."

"Never mind them!" shouted Big Claus. "Or I'll give you a beating right here and now." He grabbed a sack that was lying on one of the bulls' backs and climbed up on the bridge. "Get a rock and put it in with me, I'm afraid that I might float."

"Don't worry about that," said Little Claus. But he found a big stone anyway and rolled it into the sack next to Big Claus before he tied the opening as tightly as he could. Then he pushed the sack off the bridge.

Splash! Plop! Down went Big Claus into the river and straight to the bottom he went.

"I am afraid that he will have trouble finding his cattle," said Little Claus, and drove his own herd home.

❊✧❊

The Princess and the Pea

ONCE upon a time there was a prince who wanted to marry a princess, but she would have to be a real one. He traveled around the whole world looking for her; but every time he met a princess there was always something amiss. There were plenty of princesses but not one of them was quite to his taste. Something was always the matter: they just weren't real princesses. So he returned home very sad and sorry, for he had set his heart on marrying a real princess.

One evening a storm broke over the kingdom. The lightning flashed, the thunder roared, and the rain came down in bucketfuls. In the midst of this horrible storm, someone knocked on the city gate; and the king himself went down to open it.

On the other side of the gate stood a princess. But goodness, how wet she was! Water ran down her hair and her clothes in streams. It flowed in through the heels of her shoes and out through the toes. But she said that she was a real princess.

"We'll find that out quickly enough," thought the old queen, but she didn't say a word out loud. She hurried to the guest room and took all the bedclothes off the bed; then on the bare bedstead she put a pea. On top of the pea she put twenty mattresses; and on top of the mattresses, twenty eiderdown quilts. That was the bed on which the princess had to sleep.

In the morning, when someone asked her how she had slept, she replied, "Oh, just wretchedly! I didn't close my eyes once, the whole night through. God knows what was in that bed; but it was something hard, and I am black and blue all over."

Now they knew that she was a real princess, since she had felt the pea that was lying on the bedstead through twenty mattresses and twenty eiderdown quilts. Only a real princess could be so sensitive!

The prince married her. The pea was exhibited in the royal museum; and you can go there and see it, if it hasn't been stolen.

Now that was a real story!

Little Ida's Flowers

"WHAT a pity, all my flowers are dead!" said little Ida. "Last night they were so beautiful, and now all their leaves have withered. Why does that happen?" she asked the student who had come visiting.

The young man was sitting on the sofa. Ida was very fond of him because he knew the most marvelous stories, and with a pair of scissors could cut out of paper the most wonderful pictures: flowers, hearts, little dancing ladies, and castles with doors that could open. He was a happy young man and fond of children.

"Why do my flowers look so sad today?" she asked again, and showed the student her bouquet of dying flowers.

He looked at them a moment before he said, "I know what is wrong with them, they have been dancing all night and that is why they look so tired and hang their heads."

"But flowers can't dance," said little Ida.

"Sure they can," replied the student. "When darkness comes and we go to bed and sleep, then the flowers jump about gaily enough. Nearly every night they hold a grand ball."

"Are children allowed to come to the ball too?" asked little Ida, who was eager to know how flowers brought up their children.

"Oh yes, both the little daisies and the lilies of the valley are allowed to come," smiled the student.

"Where do the most beautiful of the flowers dance?"

"You have been in the park near the king's summer castle, the one that has the splendid garden. You've been there to feed the swans.

Remember how they swim toward you when you throw bread crumbs? That's where the grand ball is held; and very grand it is."

"I was there yesterday with my mother," little Ida said, and looked pensive. "But there wasn't a leaf on any of the trees, and not a flower anywhere. There were a lot this summer. Where are they now?"

"As soon as the king and all his courtiers move into town, then the flowers move up to the castle. There they live a merry life; I wish you could see it. The two most beautiful roses sit on the throne; they are the king and queen. The big red tiger lilies are lords in waiting; they stand behind the throne and bow. Then in come all the most beautiful flowers and the grand ball begins. The blue violets are midshipmen. They dance with the hyacinths and the crocuses, and call them Miss. The tulips and the big yellow lilies are the old ladies, they see to it that everyone behaves and dances in time to the music."

"But," interrupted little Ida, "are the flowers allowed to dance in the king's castle?"

"No one knows they are there," continued the student. "Sometimes the old night watchman, who is supposed to take care of the castle when the king is away, does walk through it. He carries a great bunch of keys, one for every door in the castle; and as soon as the flowers hear the rattle of the keys they hide. The old night watchman can smell them but he has never seen them."

"Oh, how wonderful!" little Ida clapped her hands. "Wouldn't I see the flowers either if I were there?"

"I think you could," said the student. "Next time you are in the park, look in through the windows of the castle and you will probably see them. I was out there today, I saw a long yellow daffodil, she was lying stretched out on a sofa. She was a lady in waiting."

"What about the flowers in the botanical garden; are they allowed to attend the ball too? And how do they get out there? It is a very long way from where they live to the castle."

"Oh sure, they can come!" exclaimed the student. "When flowers want to, they can fly. You have seen butterflies. Don't they look like yellow, red, and white flowers? That is exactly what they were once. They are flowers who have jumped off their stems and have learned to fly with their petals; and when they first get a taste for it, they never return to their stems, and their little petals become real wings.

"There's no way of knowing whether the flowers from the botanical garden know about what goes on in the castle. The next time you are there, you can whisper to one of the flowers that there will be a grand ball that night in the castle, and see what happens. Flowers can't keep a secret, so that flower will tell it to the others; and when night comes, they will all fly to the castle. That will certainly surprise the professor who is in charge of the garden. The next day when he takes his morning walk, there won't be a single flower left in the whole botanical garden; and I am sure he will write a paper about it."

"But how will the flower I tell it to talk to the others? I am sure that I have never seen a flower speak," said little Ida.

"They mime. It's a regular pantomime. You have seen how, when the wind blows, all the flowers shake their heads and rustle their leaves; what they are saying to each other is just as plain as what we say with our tongues is to us."

"Does the professor understand what they are saying?" asked little Ida.

"Sure he does. One morning when he came into the garden he saw a large nettle rustle its leaves at a carnation. It was saying, 'You are so beautiful that I love you.' But that kind of talk the professor doesn't like, so he hit the nettle across the fingers—that is, its leaves. But the nettle burned him, and since then the professor has never dared touch a nettle."

"That is very funny!" little Ida laughed.

"I don't think that it's the least bit funny," said the old chancellor, who had just come into the room and had overheard the last part of the conversation; but he never found anything funny. "Such fantastic ideas are nonsense; they are harmful to a child and boring for grown-ups."

The old chancellor did not like the student, especially when he found him cutting pictures out of paper with a pair of scissors. The student had just finished cutting a hanged man holding a heart; he'd been condemned for stealing hearts. Now the young man had started on another. It was the picture of a witch who was riding on a broom and was carrying her husband on the end of her nose.

Little Ida thought that everything the student did was amusing; and she thought a great deal about what he had said about her flowers. "My flowers are tired from dancing," she thought, and carried her bouquet over to the little table on which her playthings were. She had a whole drawer full of toys too, and even a doll that lay in its own bed.

The doll's name was Sophie. Little Ida picked her up and explained, "Please, be a good doll and sleep in the drawer tonight. The flowers are sick and have to sleep in your bed, so they can get well."

The doll didn't answer; she was angry because someone else was to sleep in her bed.

Little Ida put the flowers in the bed and pulled the covers up around them. She promised them that if they would be good and lie still she would make them a cup of tea. "You will be well enough to be up and around tomorrow morning," she added. Then she drew the curtains around the bed so the sun wouldn't shine in their eyes.

All that evening she could not think about anything but what the student had told her. When her bedtime came, she ran over to the window and pulled aside the drapes to look at her mother's plants, which were sitting in flowerpots on the window sill. She whispered to both the tulips and the hyacinths, "I know where you are going tonight." The flowers acted as though they hadn't heard her. They moved neither a petal nor a leaf; but little Ida believed what she had been told.

When she got into bed, little Ida lay awake thinking about how beautiful it must have been when all the flowers danced in the royal castle. "I wonder if my flowers have really been there," she muttered; and then she fell asleep.

Late at night she woke; she had dreamed about the flowers and the student, who the chancellor had said was filling her head with nonsense. It was very quiet in the bedroom. On the table beside her parents' bed, the night light burned.

"I wonder if my flowers are still lying in Sophie's bed," she whispered. "Oh, God, how I would love to know!"

She sat up in bed and looked toward the door. It was ajar; in the next room were her flowers and all her playthings. She listened; someone was playing the piano softly and more beautifully than she had ever heard it played before.

"Now all the flowers are dancing. Oh, God, how I would love to see it," she whispered. But she didn't dare get up, for she was afraid she would wake her father and mother.

"If only the flowers would come in here," she thought. But the flowers didn't come, and the music kept on playing.

Finally she climbed out of bed, tiptoed over to the door, and looked into the living room.

There was no night light burning in there, but she could see anyway, for the moon shone in through the windows onto the floor. It was so bright that it was almost as light as day. All the tulips and the hyacinths stood in two long rows on the floor; on the window sill stood only their empty flowerpots. The flowers danced so gracefully, holding onto each other's leaves. They formed chains and swung each other around, just as children do when they dance.

A big yellow lily sat at the piano and played. Little Ida remembered that she had seen it in the garden that summer. The student had said, "Why, it looks like Miss Line!" Everybody had laughed at him then; but now little Ida thought that the slender yellow flower really did look like Miss Line; and behaved just as she did when she played. There the flower was, turning its yellow face from side to side and nodding in time to the music.

None of the flowers noticed little Ida. Suddenly a big blue crocus jumped up on the table where her playthings were, went right over to the doll's bed, and drew the curtains. There lay the sick flowers. But they didn't seem sick any more. They leaped out of bed. They wanted to dance too. The little porcelain man, whose chin was chipped, bowed to the flowers. They jumped down onto the floor; and what a good time they had!

Now in Denmark at Shrovetide little children are given a bunch of birch and beech branches tied together with ribbons, and fastened to their twigs are paper flowers, little toys, and candies. It is an old custom for the children to whip their parents out of bed with these switches on Shrove Monday. The switches are pretty and most of the children keep them. Little Ida's had been lying on the table among her other toys. Bump! Down they jumped with their ribbons flying; they thought they were flowers. A handsome little wax doll, with a broad-brimmed hat just like the one the chancellor wore, was tied to the top of the longest branch.

The switches danced the mazurka, for they were stronger than the flowers and could stamp their feet. All at once the wax doll began to grow. It became taller and bigger and started screaming at the paper flowers: "What a lot of nonsense to tell a child! What a lot of nonsense!"

Now the wax doll looked exactly like the chancellor; for he, too, wore a broad-brimmed hat and had a yellow complexion and a sour expression. The ribbons started to hit the wax doll across the legs, and he had to pull himself together till he was only a little wax doll again.

It was all so funny that little Ida could not help laughing. The switches kept on dancing, and the chancellor had to dance too—when he was as big and tall as a man and when he was only a little wax doll. He was given no rest, until the flowers begged the switches to stop; the flowers who had lain in the doll's bed felt especially sorry for the little wax doll.

As soon as the switches stopped dancing there came a knocking from the drawer where the doll Sophie lay. The little porcelain man went carefully to the edge of the table, leaned over the side of it, and pulled the drawer open as much as he could—which wasn't very much. Sophie stuck out her head. "I see there is a ball. Why hasn't anyone told me about it?"

"Would you like to dance with me?" asked the porcelain man.

"Pooh! You are chipped," said Sophie, and sat down on the edge of the drawer, with her back to the poor little porcelain man. She thought that one of the flowers would come and ask her to dance, but none of them did. The porcelain man danced by himself and he didn't dance badly at all.

Since none of the flowers seemed to notice her, Sophie jumped down upon the floor. She landed with a crash and all the flowers came running over to ask her whether she had hurt herself; the flowers who had lain in her bed were especially considerate.

But Sophie hadn't hurt herself. Little Ida's flowers thanked her for having been allowed to sleep in her bed, and they told her that they loved her; then they took her out to the middle of the floor, where there was a great splash of moonlight, and danced with her. All of the other flowers made a circle around them, and Sophie was so happy that she told the flowers they could keep her bed, even though she didn't like sleeping in the drawer.

"Thank you," the flowers replied. "It is most kind of you, but our life is short. Tomorrow we shall be dead. Tell little Ida to bury us out in the garden where the canary is buried; and next year we shall come to life again and be even more beautiful than we are now."

"You mustn't die!" cried the doll, and kissed the flowers.

At that moment the door of the dining room opened and the most beautiful flowers came dancing in. Little Ida could not imagine where they had come from, unless they were the flowers from the park near the king's castle.

First entered two roses who wore gold crowns. They were the king and the queen. Behind them came the carnations and the lilies, bowing and waving to the other flowers.

There was music. Big poppies and peonies blew on the pods of sweet peas with such vigor that their faces were red. The bluebells tingled. It was a funny orchestra both to watch and to listen to. At last came all the other flowers, dancing: violets, daisies, and lilies of the valley; as they finished their dance, they kissed each other. It was lovely to see.

The flowers said good night to each other, and little Ida climbed back into her little bed and dreamed about everything she had seen.

The next morning when she woke, she ran right over to the doll's bed to see if the flowers were still there. There they were, but now they were all shriveled and dead. Her doll Sophie was in the drawer; she looked awfully sleepy.

"Can you remember what you are supposed to tell me?" little Ida asked. Sophie didn't say a word.

"You are not a good doll," scolded little Ida. "Remember how all the flowers danced with you!" Then she took a paper box that had a lovely picture of a bird on its lid and laid the flowers in it.

"That will be your honorable coffin," she said. "And when my cousins come from Norway, then we'll have a funeral and bury you, so you can come again next summer and be more beautiful than you are now."

The cousins from Norway were two strong boys. Their names were Jonas and Adolph. Their father had given them each a bow and some arrows; and these they had brought along to show little Ida.

She told them about the poor flowers that had died and allowed them to attend the funeral. It was almost a procession. First came the boys with their bows slung over their shoulders, then little Ida, carrying the pretty little paper box. In the corner of the garden they dug a little grave. Ida kissed the flowers before she buried them. Jonas and Adolph shot an arrow above the grave, for they didn't have a gun or a cannon.

Inchelina

ONCE upon a time there was a woman whose only desire was to have a tiny little child. Now she had no idea where she could get one; so she went to an old witch and asked her: "Please, could you tell me where I could get a tiny little child? I would so love to have one."

"That is not so difficult," said the witch. "Here is a grain of barley; it is not the kind that grows in the farmer's fields or that you can feed to the chickens. Plant it in a flowerpot and watch what happens."

"Thank you," said the woman. She handed the witch twelve pennies, and she went home to plant the grain of barley. No sooner was it in the earth than it started to sprout. A beautiful big flower grew up; it looked like a tulip that was just about to bloom.

"What a lovely flower," said the woman, and kissed the red and yellow petals that were closed so tightly. With a snap they opened and one could see that it was a real tulip. In the center of the flower on the green stigma sat a tiny little girl. She was so beautiful and so delicate, and exactly one inch long. "I will call her Inchelina," thought the woman.

The lacquered shell of a walnut became Inchelina's cradle, the blue petals of violets her mattress, and a rose petal her cover. Here she slept at night; in the daytime she played on the table by the window. The woman had put a bowl of water there with a garland of flowers around it. In this tiny "lake" there floated a tulip petal, on which Inchelina could row from one side of the plate to the other, using two white horsehairs as oars; it was an exquisite sight. And Inchelina could sing, as no one has ever sung before—so clearly and delicately.

One night as she lay sleeping in her beautiful little bed a toad came into the room through a broken windowpane. The toad was big and wet and ugly; she jumped down upon the table where Inchelina was sleeping under her red rose petal.

"She would make a lovely wife for my son," said the toad; and grabbing the walnut shell in which Inchelina slept, she leaped through the broken window and down into the garden.

On the banks of a broad stream, just where it was muddiest, lived the toad with her son. He had taken after his mother and was very ugly. "Croak . . . Croak . . . Croak!" was all he said when he saw the beautiful little girl in the walnut shell.

"Don't talk so loud or you will wake her," scolded the mother. "She could run away and we wouldn't be able to catch her, for she is as light as the down of a swan. I will put her on a water-lily leaf, it will be just like an island to her. In the meantime, we shall get your apartment, down in the mud, ready for your marriage."

Out in the stream grew many water lilies, and all of their leaves looked as if they were floating in the water. The biggest of them was the farthest from shore; on that one the old toad put Inchelina's little bed.

When the poor little girl woke in the morning and saw where she was—on a green leaf with water all around her—she began to cry bitterly. There was no way of getting to shore at all.

The old toad was very busy down in her mud house, decorating the walls with reeds and yellow flowers that grew near the shore. She meant to do her best for her new daughter-in-law. After she had finished, she and her ugly son swam out to the water-lily leaf to fetch Inchelina's bed. It was to be put in the bridal chamber. The old toad curtsied and that is not easy to do while you are swimming; then she said, "Here is my son. He is to be your husband; you two will live happily down in the mud."

"Croak! . . . Croak!" was all the son said. Then they took the bed and swam away with it. Poor Inchelina sat on the green leaf and wept and wept, for she did not want to live with the ugly toad and have her hideous son as a husband. The little fishes that were swimming about in the water had heard what the old toad said; they stuck their heads out of the water to take a look at the tiny girl. When they saw how beautiful she was, it hurt them to think that she should have to marry the ugly toad and live in the mud. They decided that they would not let it happen, and gathered around the green stalk that held the leaf anchored to the bottom of the stream. They all nibbled on the stem, and soon the leaf was free. It drifted down the stream, bearing Inchelina far away from the ugly toad.

As Inchelina sailed by, the little birds on the shore saw her and sang, "What a lovely little girl." Farther and farther sailed the leaf with its little passenger, taking her on a journey to foreign lands.

For a long time a lovely white butterfly flew around her, then landed on the leaf. It had taken a fancy to Inchelina. The tiny girl laughed, for she was so happy to have escaped the toad; and the stream was so beautiful, golden in the sunshine. She took the little silk ribbon which she wore around her waist and tied one end of it to the butterfly and the other to the water-lily leaf. Now the leaf raced down the stream—and so did Inchelina, for she was standing on it.

At that moment a big May bug flew by; when it spied Inchelina, it swooped down and with its claws grabbed the poor girl around her tiny waist and flew up into a tree with her. The leaf floated on down the stream, and the butterfly had to follow it.

Oh God, little Inchelina was terrified as the May bug flew away with her, but stronger than her fear was her grief for the poor little white butterfly that she had chained to the leaf with her ribbon. If he did not get loose, he would starve to death.

The May bug didn't care what happened to the butterfly. He placed Inchelina on the biggest leaf on the tree. He gave her honey from the flowers to eat, and told her that she was the loveliest thing he had ever seen, even though she didn't look like a May bug. Soon all the other May bugs that lived in the tree came visiting. Two young lady May bugs—they were still unmarried—wiggled their antennae and said: "She has only two legs, how wretched. No antennae and a thin waist, how disgusting! She looks like a human being: how ugly!"

All the other female May bugs agreed with them. The May bug who had caught Inchelina still thought her lovely; but when all the others kept insisting that she was ugly, he soon was convinced of it too. Now he didn't want her any longer, and put her down on a daisy at the foot of the tree and told her she could go wherever she wanted to, for all he cared. Poor Inchelina cried; she thought it terrible to be so ugly that even a May bug would not want her, and that in spite of her being more beautiful than you can imagine, more lovely than the petal of the most beautiful rose.

All summer long poor Inchelina lived all alone in the forest. She wove a hammock out of grass and hung it underneath a dock leaf so that it would not rain on her while she slept. She ate the honey in the flowers and drank the dew that was on their leaves every morning.

Summer and autumn passed. But then came winter: the long, cold winter. All the birds that had sung so beautifully flew away. The flowers withered, the trees lost their leaves; and the dock leaf that had protected her rolled itself up and became a shriveled yellow stalk. She was so terribly cold. Her clothes were in shreds; and she was so thin and delicate.

Poor Inchelina, she was bound to freeze to death. It started to snow and each snowflake that fell on her was like a whole shovelful of snow would be to us, because we are so big, and she was only one inch tall.

She wrapped herself in a wizened leaf, but it gave no warmth and she shivered from the cold.

Not far from the forest was a big field where grain had grown; only a few dry stubbles still rose from the frozen ground, pointing up to the heavens. To Inchelina these straws were like a forest. Trembling, she wandered through them and came to the entrance of a field mouse's house. It was only a little hole in the ground. But deep down below the mouse lived in warmth and comfort, with a full larder and a nice kitchen. Like a beggar child, Inchelina stood outside the door and begged for a single grain of barley. It was several days since she had last eaten.

"Poor little wretch," said the field mouse, for she had a kind heart. "Come down into my warm living room and dine with me."

The field mouse liked Inchelina. "You can stay the winter," she said. "But you must keep the room tidy and tell me a story every day, for I like a good story." Inchelina did what the kind old mouse demanded, and she lived quite happily.

"Soon we shall have a visitor," said the mouse. "Once a week my neighbor comes. He lives even more comfortably than I do. He has a drawing room, and wears the most exquisite black fur coat. If only he would marry you, then you would be well provided for. He can't see you, for he is blind, so you will have to tell him the very best of your stories."

But Inchelina did not want to marry the mouse's neighbor, for he was a mole. The next day he came visiting, dressed in his black velvet fur coat. The field mouse had said that he was both rich and wise. His house was twenty times as big as the mouse's; and learned he was, too; but he did not like the sun and the beautiful flowers, he said they were "abominable," for he had never seen them. Inchelina had to sing for him; and when she sang *"Frère Jacques, dormez vous?"* he fell in love with her because of her beautiful voice; but he didn't show it, for he was sober-minded and never made a spectacle of himself.

He had recently dug a passage from his own house to theirs, and he invited Inchelina and the field mouse to use it as often as they pleased. He told them not to be afraid of the dead bird in the corridor. It had died only a few days before. It was still whole and had all its feathers. By chance it had been buried in his passageway.

The mole took a piece of dry rotten wood in his mouth; it shone as brightly as fire in the darkness; then he led the way down through the long corridor. When they came to the place where the dead bird lay, the mole made a hole with his broad nose, up through the earth, so that light could come through. Almost blocking the passageway was a dead swallow, with its beautiful wings pressed close to its body, its feet almost hidden by feathers, and its head nestled under a wing. The poor bird undoubtedly had frozen to death. Inchelina felt a great sadness; she had loved all the birds that twittered and sang for her that summer. The mole kicked the bird with one of his short legs and said, "Now it has stopped chirping. What a misfortune it is to be born a bird. Thank God, none of my children will be born birds! All they can do is chirp, and then die of starvation when winter comes."

"Yes, that's what all sensible people think," said the field mouse. "What does all that chirping lead to? Starvation and cold when winter comes. But I suppose they think it is romantic."

Inchelina didn't say anything, but when the mouse and mole had their backs turned, she leaned down and kissed the closed eye of the swallow. "Maybe that was one of the birds that sang so beautifully for me this summer," she thought. "How much joy you gave me, beautiful little bird."

The mole closed the hole through which the daylight had entered and then escorted the ladies home. That night Inchelina could not sleep; she rose and wove as large a blanket as she could, out of hay.

She carried it down in the dark passage and covered the little bird with it. In the field mouse's living room she had found bits of cotton; she tucked them under the swallow wherever she could, to protect it from the cold earth.

"Good-by, beautiful bird," she said. "Good-by, and thank you for the songs you sang for me when it was summer and all the trees were green and the sun warmed us."

She put her head on the bird's breast; then she jumped up! Something was ticking inside: it was the bird's heart, for the swallow was not really dead, and now the warmth had revived it.

In the fall all the swallows fly to the warm countries. If one tarries too long and is caught by the first frost, he lies down on the ground as if he were dead, and the cold snow covers him.

Inchelina shook with fear. The swallow was huge to a girl so tiny that she only measured an inch. But she gathered her courage and pressed the blanket closer to the bird's body. She even went to fetch the little mint leaf that she herself used as a cover and put it over the bird's head.

The next night she sneaked down to the passageway again; the bird was better although still very weak. He opened his eyes just long enough to see Inchelina standing in the dark with a little piece of dry rotten wood in her hand, as a lamp.

"Thank you, you sweet little child," said the sick swallow, "I feel so much better. I am not cold now. Soon I shall be strong again and can fly out into the sunshine."

"Oh no," she said. "It is cold and snowing outside now and you would freeze. Stay down here in your warm bed, I will nurse you."

She brought the swallow water on a leaf. After he had drunk it, he told her his story. He had torn his wing on a rosebush, and therefore could not fly as swiftly as the other swallows, so he had stayed behind when the others left; then one morning he had fainted from cold. That was all he could remember. He did not know how he came to be in the mole's passageway.

The bird stayed all winter. Inchelina took good care of him, grew very fond of him, and breathed not a word about him to either the mole or the field mouse, for she knew that they didn't like the poor swallow.

As soon as spring came and the warmth of the sun could be felt through the earth, the swallow said good-by to Inchelina, who opened the hole that the mole had made. The sun shone down so pleasantly. The swallow asked her if she did not want to come along with him; she could sit on his back and he would fly with her out into the great forest. But Inchelina knew that the field mouse would be sad and lonely if she left.

"I cannot," she said.

The bird thanked her once more. "Farewell. . . . Farewell, lovely girl," he sang, and flew out into the sunshine.

Inchelina's eyes filled with tears as she watched the swallow fly away, for she cared so much for the bird.

"Tweet . . . tweet," he sang, and disappeared in the forest.

Poor Inchelina was miserable. Soon the grain would be so tall that the field would be in shade, and she would no longer be able to enjoy the warm sunshine.

"This summer you must spend getting your trousseau ready," said the field mouse, for the sober mole in the velvet coat had proposed to her. "You must have both woolens and linen to wear and to use in housekeeping when you become Mrs. Mole."

Inchelina had to spin by hand and the field mouse hired four spiders to weave both night and day. Every evening the mole came visiting, but all he talked about was how nice it would be when the summer was over. He didn't like the way the sun baked the earth; it made it so hard to dig in. As soon as autumn came they would get married. But Inchelina was not happy; she thought the mole was dull and she did not love him. Every day, at sunrise and at sunset, she tiptoed to the entrance of the field mouse's house, so that when the wind blew and parted the grain, she could see the blue sky above her. She thought of how light and beautiful it was out there, and she longed for her friend the swallow but he never came back. "He is probably far away in the wonderful green forest!" she thought.

Autumn came and Inchelina's trousseau was finished.

"In four weeks we shall hold your wedding," said the field mouse.

Inchelina cried and said she did not want to marry the boring old mole.

"Fiddlesticks!" squeaked the field mouse. "Don't be stubborn or I will bite you with my white teeth. You are getting an excellent husband; he has a velvet coat so fine that the queen does not have one that is better. He has both a larder and kitchen, you ought to thank God for giving you such a good husband."

The day of the wedding came; the mole had already arrived. Inchelina grieved. Now she would never see the warm sun again. The mole lived far down under the ground, for he didn't like the sun. While she lived with the field mouse, she at least had been allowed to walk as far as the entrance of the little house and look at the sun.

"Farewell. . . . Farewell, you beautiful sun!" Inchelina lifted her hands up toward the sky and then took a few steps out upon the field. The harvest was over and only the stubbles were left. She saw a little red flower. Embracing it, she said: "Farewell! And give my love to the swallow if you ever see him."

"Tweet . . . Tweet . . ." something said in the air above her.

She looked up. It was the little swallow. As soon as he saw Inchelina he chirped with joy. And she told the bird how she had to marry the awful mole, and live forever down under the ground, and never see the sun again. The very telling of her future brought tears to her eyes.

"Now comes the cold winter," said the swallow, "and I fly far away to the warm countries. Why don't you come with me? You can sit on my back; tie yourself on so you won't fall off and we will fly far away from the ugly mole and his dismal house; across the great mountains, to the countries where the sun shines more beautifully than here and the loveliest flowers grow and it is always summer. Fly with me, Inchelina. You saved my life when I lay freezing in the cold cellar of the earth."

"Yes, I will come," cried Inchelina, and climbed up on the bird's back. She tied herself with a ribbon to one of his feathers, and the swallow flew high up into the air, above the forests and lakes and over the high mountains that are always snow-covered. Inchelina froze in the cold air, but she crawled underneath the warm feathers of the bird and only stuck her little head out to see all the beauty below her.

They came to the warm countries. And it was true what the swallow had said: the sun shone more brightly and the sky seemed twice as high. Along the fences grew the loveliest green and blue grapes. From the trees in the forests hung oranges and lemons. Along the roads the most beautiful children ran, chasing many-colored butterflies. The swallow flew even farther south, and the landscape beneath them became more and more beautiful.

Near a forest, on the shores of a lake, stood the ruins of an ancient temple; ivy wound itself around the white pillars. On top of these were many swallows' nests and one of them belonged to the little swallow that was carrying Inchelina.

"This is my house," he said. "Now choose for yourself one of the beautiful flowers down below and I will set you down on it, it will make a lovely home for you."

"How wonderful!" exclaimed Inchelina, and clapped her hands. Among the broken white marble pillars grew tall, lovely white flowers. The swallow sat her down on the leaves of one of them; and to Inchelina's astonishment, she saw a little man sitting in the center of the flower. He was white and almost transparent, as if he were made of glass. On his head he wore a golden crown. On his back were a pair of wings. He was no taller than Inchelina. In every one of the flowers there lived such a tiny angel; and this one was the king of them all.

"How handsome he is!" whispered Inchelina to the swallow.

The tiny little king was terrified of the bird, who was several times larger than he was. But when he saw Inchelina he forgot his fear. She was the loveliest creature he had ever seen; and so he took the crown off his own head and put it on hers. Then he asked her what her name was and whether she wanted to be queen of the flowers.

Now here was a better husband than old mother toad's ugly son or the mole with the velvet coat. Inchelina said yes; and from every flower came a lovely little angel to pay homage to their queen. How lovely and delicate they all were; and they brought her gifts, and the best of these was a pair of wings, so she would be able to fly, as they all did, from flower to flower.

It was a day of happiness. And the swallow, from his nest in the temple, sang for them as well as he could. But in his heart he was ever so sad, for he, too, loved Inchelina and had hoped never to be parted from her.

"You shall not be called Inchelina any longer," said the king. "It is an ugly name. From now on we shall call you Maja."

"Farewell! Farewell!" called the little swallow. He flew back to the north, away from the warm countries. He came to Denmark; and

there he has his nest, above the window of a man who can tell fairy
tales.

"Tweet . . . tweet," sang the swallow. And the man heard it and
wrote down the whole story.

6

❋❖❋

The Naughty Boy

ONCE upon a time an old poet—a really nice and kind old poet—was sitting cozily by his potbelly stove toasting apples. Outside a storm was raging and the rain was coming down by the bucket.

"Anyone caught out tonight won't have a dry stitch on," remarked the poet, and sighed.

"Open the door! I am wet and freezing!" cried a little child, and banged on the poet's door, while the wind made all the windows rattle.

"Poor little fellow!" exclaimed the poet, and hurried to open the door. There stood a little boy; he was stark naked and the water was streaming down his golden hair. He was so cold that he was trembling all over; and had he not been let in, he certainly would have died that night out in the awful storm.

"You poor little boy." The poet took him by the hand. "Come in and sit down by the stove and get dry. I'll give you wine and toasted apples. You are a beautiful child!"

And that he was. His eyes shone like two stars, and even though his golden hair was wet, it curled most becomingly. He looked like an angel as he stood there pale and shivering. In his hands he had a bow and some arrows, which were much the worse for having been out in the rain, for all the colors on the pretty arrows had run into each other.

The old poet sat down next to the stove with the child in his lap. He dried his hair and warmed his hands in his own; then he gave him a toasted apple and a glass of mulled wine. The boy soon recovered.

The color returned to his cheeks. He jumped down from the poet's knees and began to dance around his chair.

"You are a lively child," said the old poet, and smiled. "What is your name?"

"I am called Cupid," answered the boy. "Don't you know me? There are my bow and arrows. I am good at shooting. Look, the moon has come out; the weather is fine now."

"But I am afraid your bow and arrows are spoiled," the poet said.

"That is too bad!" The boy picked up the bow and glanced at it. "Now that it's dry it looks all right," he argued. "Look, the string is taut. No harm has come to it." Cupid slipped an arrow into the bow and bent it. He took aim and the arrow pierced the old man's heart! "There, you can see for yourself, my bow is fine," the naughty, ungrateful boy said laughingly to the poor old poet who had taken him into his warm living room and given him mulled wine and the very best of his toasted apples.

The old poet lay on the floor, weeping. He had really been hit, right in the heart. "Oh . . . oh . . ." he moaned. "The mischievous child! I am going to tell all the other boys and girls to beware of Cupid and never to play with him, so he cannot do them any harm."

All the boys and girls who were warned by the old poet did their best to be on the alert against Cupid; but he fooled them anyway, because he is very cunning.

When a student is returning from a lecture at the university, Cupid runs along beside him, wearing a black robe and with a book under his arm. The student cannot recognize him; he mistakes him for another student and takes his arm; then Cupid shoots an arrow into his heart. The girls are not safe from him, even in church when they are being confirmed. In the theater, he sits astride the chandelier and nobody notices him up there among the burning candles, but they feel it when he shoots his arrows at them.

He runs about in the royal parks and on the embankment where your parents love to go for a walk. He has hit their hearts with his arrows once, too. Ask them, and see what they say.

Cupid is a rascal! Don't ever have anything to do with him! Imagine, he once shot your poor old grandmother, right through the heart; it's so long ago that it no longer hurts, but she hasn't forgotten it. Pooh! That mischievous Cupid! Now you know what he is like and what a naughty boy he is.

7

The Traveling Companion

Poor Johannes was miserable; his father was ill and there was no hope of his recovering. It was late in the evening; they were alone together. The lamp on the table was burning low.

"You have been a good son," whispered the father. "I am sure that God will help you and protect you." The dying man looked kindly and earnestly at his son, then he breathed very deeply and died.

He looked as if he were asleep. Johannes wept, for now he was alone in the world. He had neither father or mother, nor brothers or sisters. He kneeled down and kissed his father's hand. Many a tear ran down his cheeks before he finally fell asleep with his head resting against the hard board of the bedstead.

He dreamed a strange dream, in which the sun and the moon curtsied before him. He saw his father, too, alive and well. He heard him laugh as he always did whenever something amused him. A lovely girl, with long beautiful hair and a gold crown on her head, took his hand in hers; and his father said to him, "This is your bride: the most beautiful girl in the world." Then he woke, the dream was over. His father was dead. There lay his cold body. He was all alone, poor Johannes!

Next week his father was buried. Johannes walked behind the coffin. He could no longer see his father, whom he loved so much. He heard the earth fall on the coffin lid. He peered down into the grave. He could see the corner of the burial chest; another shovelful of earth and that, too, was out of sight. At that moment Johannes felt that his heart would break from sorrow. A psalm was sung and it sounded so beautiful that he burst out crying, and the tears relieved his grief. The sunlight played on the leaves of the trees; it was as if the sun wanted to say, "Do not be sad, Johannes! Can't you see how beautiful the blue sky is? Your father is up there and he is begging God to help, so that all may go well for you."

"I will try always to be good," thought Johannes. "Then I, too, will go to heaven when I die and see my father again. I will have so much to tell him, and he will teach me about all the beautiful things in heaven, as he taught me about all that is beautiful here on earth. Oh, how wonderful it will be!" For a moment, as the words became a picture in Johannes' mind, he smiled though tears ran down his face.

The little birds in the chestnut tree sang, "Tweet . . . Tweet . . ." They were happy even though they were attending a funeral; or maybe they were happy because they knew that the dead man now had wings more beautiful than theirs, for he had been good while he lived on earth. Johannes saw how the little birds flew from the branches of the tree far out into the world, and he wanted to fly with them. But first he must carve a wooden cross to put on his father's grave.

In the evening when he was finished, he returned to the church-yard and found the grave covered with sand and decorated with flowers. The people of the village had wanted to show that they, too, loved his father and felt sorrow at his death.

Early the next morning Johannes packed his few belongings into a small bundle and put his inheritance of fifty silver marks in a purse which he hid under his belt. Now he was ready to go out into the world, but first he went to his father's grave to pray and say good-by. "I shall always be good, Father," he promised, "so that you may, without shame, bid God to protect me."

As he walked across the fields, leaving the village behind him, the flowers nodded as the wind blew over them and said, "Welcome, Johannes! Welcome to our green world, is it not beautiful?" But Johannes could not hear them; he turned to look once more at the old church where he had been baptized and where every Sunday he had attended service with his father and sung hymns. High up in one of the little windows of the tower he saw the church pixy with his red woolen hat. The pixy was shading his eyes with his hand, the sun was shining right in his face. Johannes waved good-by to him and the pixy took off his hat and swung it over his head; then he put his hand on his heart and blew kisses toward Johannes, to show that he wished him good luck and a happy journey.

Johannes thought about all the beautiful things he would see in the big marvelous world as he walked on, farther and farther away from all that he knew. Soon he no longer recognized the countryside. He passed through villages and towns he had never seen before, and all the people he met were strangers.

The first night he slept in a haystack and thought it was as fine a bed as anyone could have, that a king could not have offered him one more comfortable. The fields, the little river, the haystack, and the blue heaven above him. What a lovely bedchamber! The green grass dotted with red and white flowers was a carpet; the hedge of wild roses and the elderberry bushes were better than bouquets of flowers in vases; and the river, with its clear water, was his washing basin. The reeds that grew along its edge nodded to say both good morning and good night to him, and the moon was an excellent night lamp that couldn't set fire to the curtains. Here Johannes could sleep peacefully and he did, and only woke after the sun had risen and all the little birds started singing, "Good morning! Good morning! Aren't you up yet?"

The bells rang from the church tower; it was Sunday. The people were going to church and Johannes went too; he sang a hymn and listened to the minister preach. Everything was just as it was in the church where he had been baptized and attended service with his father.

In the churchyard there were many graves where the grass grew high, for there was no one to tend them. Johannes thought of his own father's grave which soon would look like these, now that he was not there to weed and plant flowers on it. He pulled up some of the grass and straightened the wooden crosses that had fallen; then he took the wreaths that the wind had blown from the graves and put them back where he thought they belonged, hoping that some stranger would do the same for his father's grave.

Outside the church stood a beggar. Johannes gave him a silver coin and then walked on, happy and content, out into the wide, wide world.

Toward evening a storm began to gather. Johannes looked for shelter but the landscape was bare and uninhabited; finally, when night had already fallen, he saw a little church on a hill. The door to the church was ajar; here he would seek shelter until the storm was over.

"I will just sit in a corner," he thought. "I am tired and need some rest." He sat down, folded his hands, and said his prayers; then he fell asleep and dreamed, while the storm broke and lightning flashed and the thunder roared.

When he woke it was past midnight, the storm was over, and the moonlight shone through the windows into the church. Near the altar stood a coffin; it was open and in it lay a dead man who was to be buried the next day. Johannes was not afraid, for he had a good conscience, and he knew that the dead cannot do anyone any harm. It is living, evil human beings one has to fear. Two such worthless men were now standing before the open coffin. They wanted to harm the dead man; they were preparing to take him out of his coffin and throw him out of the church. Poor dead man!

"What are you doing?" cried Johannes. "It is sinful to disturb the dead. Let the poor man sleep in Jesus' name!"

"Nonsense!" screamed one of the wicked men. "He has cheated us. He owed us money, which he couldn't pay back, and now he has died, on top of it, and we shan't ever see a penny of our money again. But we shall have our revenge. We shall throw him in front of the church door and there he can lie like a dog."

"I have only fifty marks," said Johannes, "it is my inheritance from my father. I will give it to you if you will promise me to let the dead man lie in peace. I can get along without money, I am strong and God will help me."

"Yes," sneered the wicked men, "if you will pay his debts, we shan't harm him." They took Johannes' money and, laughing at his goodness, went on their way. Johannes put the dead man back into his coffin, folded the cold hands, and then as happily as ever entered the dark forest just beyond the church.

The moonlight shone down through the leaves of the trees and Johannes saw the little elves playing, for they did not mind his coming. They knew he was a good and innocent human being; only from evil and dishonest people do the elves hide. Some of them were no bigger than Johannes' finger. Their long yellow hair was held in place by golden combs. Two by two, they would swing on the drops of dew that clung to the leaves and the tops of the high grass. Sometimes the dewdrops would roll down in among the grass and how the elves would laugh. Oh, it was a joy to watch them! They sang all the songs that Johannes had learned when he was a child. Colorful spiders, with silver crowns on their heads, spun palaces and bridges from bush to bush, which caught the dew and looked like glass in the moonlight. The elves played the whole night through; only when the sun rose did they climb back into their flowers. Then the wind grabbed their bridges and palaces and carried them high into the air as flying spider webs.

Johannes had just come out of the forest when he heard someone call behind him, "Wait, where are you going?"

"Out into the wide world," answered Johannes. "I am a poor fellow who has neither father nor mother, but I am sure that God will help me."

"I want to go out in the wide world too," said the stranger. "Let's be traveling companions."

"That's a good idea," agreed Johannes, and so they went on together.

It took no time for them to become fond of each other, for they were both good and kind. Johannes soon realized that the stranger was much wiser than he; he seemed to be able to talk about everything and to have been everywhere. There was hardly anything that existed that he did not know something about.

The sun was high in the sky when they stopped to rest under a large tree. There they ate their lunch. Just as they were finishing, an old woman came hobbling along. Her back was bent and she had a crutch under one arm. Strapped to her back was a bundle of firewood, which she had gathered in the forest; and in her apron, which she had tied together to make a little sack, there were three bunches of birch switches. Suddenly she slipped and fell. She screamed, for she had broken her leg. The poor woman!

Johannes suggested that they carry her to her home, but the stranger opened his knapsack and took out a little jar. In this there was a salve which he said could cure her leg, make it whole and well again, so that she could walk home by herself, as if her leg had never been broken. As payment he wanted the three bunches of birch switches she carried in her apron.

"You want to be well paid," said the old woman, and nodded very strangely. She did not want to give up her switches, yet it was not pleasant to lie there on the road with a broken leg, so she gave the switches to the stranger. As soon as he had rubbed a little salve on her leg she was up and walking better than she had before. It was an unusual salve, not the kind that you can buy at the pharmacy.

"What will you do with the switches?" asked Johannes.

"Oh, I just took a fancy to them because I am a strange fellow, I suppose," said the wayfarer, and they walked on in silence.

"Look at those heavy, dark clouds," remarked Johannes, pointing to the horizon. "We are in for a storm."

"No," laughed his companion, "they are not clouds, they are mountains. Beautiful high mountains which one can climb right up into the sky, where the air is always fresh. They are marvelous, believe me. Tomorrow we shall reach that far out in the wide world."

But the mountains were farther away than they thought; it was the next evening before they came to the foothills. Here started the great black forests that covered most of the mountainsides. There were boulders as large as whole villages. It would not be easy to cross these mountains; therefore Johannes' traveling companion suggested that they stay at an inn for the night to be fresh for the morning's climb.

In the public room of the inn a crowd had gathered; a traveling puppet theater was just about to give a performance. The spectators sat in rows facing the little stage. In the first row was a fat old butcher. He had taken the best seat and next to him sat his dog, a ferocious-looking bulldog.

The comedy began. It was a very nice play with a king and a queen in it. They sat on a throne and had golden crowns on their heads. The queen had a long dress that trailed behind her; it was expensive but she could afford it. Wooden dolls with handlebar mustaches and glass eyes stood at the doors, opening and closing them in order to air the room. It was a lovely comedy with nothing tragic about it at all; but just as the queen was crossing the stage the bulldog—God knows what the dog was thinking; his master, in any case, was not holding onto him—jumped right up on the stage and grabbed the queen by her waist with his great jaws. Crunch! Crack! It was a tragedy after all!

The poor man who owned the puppet theater and had played all the parts was beside himself with misery. The queen was the most beautiful of all his dolls and now the bulldog had beheaded her.

When all the rest of the audience had gone, Johannes' traveling companion said that he would repair the doll. He took out his little jar and put some salve on it. It was the same salve that had helped the poor woman when she broke her leg. As soon as the salve had been smeared on the doll she was whole again, but that was not all! The doll could move her little limbs by herself. The puppeteer was delighted; now he didn't have to pull her strings any more. The queen could dance by herself and that was more than any of the other dolls could do.

When night came and everyone at the inn had gone to bed, deep and sorrowful sighs were heard. The lamenting kept on, and finally they all got up to see what was the matter. The sighing came from the theater. The puppeteer opened the box that was also the small stage. All the wooden dolls were lying in a great heap. There were the king and his followers, and it was they who were sighing so mournfully. They stared with their glass eyes out into the darkness; they wanted to be rubbed with the magic salve so they, too, would be able to move and dance like the queen.

The queen kneeled down and held out her golden crown, while she spoke: "Please take this in return for putting some salve on my husband and his courtiers."

The puppeteer, who owned the theater and all the dolls, felt so sad that he cried, and promised the wayfarer that he would give him all the money he received the following night if only he would smear a little salve on four or five of the other dolls. Johannes' friend said he cared not for money; what he wanted was the old sword that the theater director had hanging from his belt. As soon as it was given to him, he rubbed a little salve on six of the dolls. They started instantly to dance so prettily that all the real people, who had been standing about watching them, began to dance too. The coachman danced with the cook, and the waiters with the maids. The poker tried to dance with the little brass shovel that stood by the fireplace; but they didn't dance far: they fell with a clatter after they had taken their first step. It was an exciting night!

The next day Johannes and his friend left the inn and started to climb the mountains. Upward they went through the dark forest of fir trees, until the church steeples in the valley looked like little red berries amidst all the greenery below them. They could see far and wide; before them were views of dozens of places where they had not been.

Johannes had never seen so much of the beautiful world all at once. The sun shone down from a cloudless blue sky. From the valleys they heard the sound of the hunters' horns; the melody was so beautiful that tears came into his eyes and he could not help saying out loud: "Oh, God, I could kiss you for your kindness to us all, for having given us such a beautiful world to live in!"

His companion had also folded his hands and was looking out over the forest and the towns. All at once they heard a strange but pleasant sound above them; they looked up. There was a great white swan and the beautiful bird was singing as they had never heard a bird sing before. But its voice grew weaker and weaker; and finally it bent its head toward its body and fell to the ground, right at their feet. There the lovely bird lay, dead.

"What wonderful wings!" cried the wayfarer. "A pair of wings as white and large as those must be worth a lot. I shall have them! It is fortunate I have a sword." With a single stroke he cut off both of the dead swan's wings, and now they were his.

They traveled mile after mile, and yet they still were in the mountains. At last they came to a large town. More than a hundred towers shone as if they were made of silver, while the sunlight played upon them. In the middle of the town there was a great marble castle with a roof of gold, and that was where the king lived.

Johannes and his friend stopped at an inn outside the walls because they wanted to wash and change their clothes before entering the city. The innkeeper told them that the king was a very kind and friendly man who never did anyone any harm; but what a daughter he had! Oh, God preserve us, she was a horrible princess! Oh, she was beautiful enough. There was no one lovelier to look at; but what good was that when she was as cruel and wicked as any witch, and had already caused the death of many a fine prince? She had proclaimed that anyone could propose to her—prince or beggar alike. She didn't care who her suitor was; all he had to do to win her hand and become king when her father died was to answer correctly three questions that she asked him; but if he failed, then he must have his head chopped off or be hanged—that's how heartless the beautiful princess was.

Her poor old father was very sad indeed, but he could do nothing about it, for once, long ago, he had promised her never to interfere in the manner she chose a husband. Every prince who had come to woo the princess had failed to guess the correct answers to her questions and had been either beheaded or hanged; but there was not one who had not been warned beforehand, and he need not have proposed. Still the old king was so upset and sorry about all the suffering that once a year he spent a whole day on his knees and ordered his whole army to do the same. They prayed that the princess would become good, but she didn't. The old ladies who drank schnapps colored it black to show that they were in mourning, and that was the most they could do.

"What a horrible princess," said Johannes. "She should be switched, that is what she deserves. If I were the old king, I would beat her until I drew blood."

Just at that moment they heard the people outside shouting, "Hurrah!" The princess was riding by. She was so beautiful that anyone who looked at her forgot how wicked she was; and that's why everyone was now shouting, "Hurrah!" Twelve lovely maidens in white silk dresses, with golden tulips in their hands, riding on jet-black horses, were with her. The princess herself rode a milk-white horse; its bridle was set with rubies and diamonds. Her dress was of the purest gold, and the whip she carried in her hand looked like a sunbeam. The golden crown on her head was like the stars of heaven, and her cape was made out of thousands of butterfly wings; and yet she was far more beautiful than all her clothes.

When Johannes saw her, his face became as red as blood dripping from a wound and he could not utter a word. The princess looked like the girl with a golden crown that he had dreamed about the night his father died. She was so beautiful, and he already loved her so much, that he could not believe that she was an evil witch who ordered men to be beheaded or hanged, because they could not guess the answers to the questions she asked them.

"Anyone can propose to her, even a poor man like me. I will go to the castle, for nothing can stop me from going," Johannes announced.

Everyone begged him not to go, for they all agreed that he would fare no better than the others who had tried; even his traveling companion advised him against it, but Johannes was not to be dissuaded. He brushed his clothes, polished his shoes, and combed his yellow hair; then he went alone into the town and straight up to the castle.

"Come in!" called the old king when Johannes came knocking.

Johannes opened the door to the castle, and the old king, wearing a dressing gown and embroidered slippers, welcomed him. The king had his golden crown on his head, his scepter in one hand, and the golden apple of state in the other. "Wait a moment," he said, while he tucked the apple under his arm so that he could shake hands with Johannes. But as soon as he heard that it was another suitor who had come, he started to cry so bitterly that both the apple and the scepter fell on the floor, and he had to dry his eyes with his dressing gown. Poor old king!

"Don't do it!" he begged. "You will be no more fortunate than any of the others. Come and see!" And he led Johannes into the princess' private garden. Ugh! It was a horrible sight! In every tree were hanging the bodies of three or four princes who had proposed marriage to the princess but had not been able to answer the three questions she asked. When the wind blew, their skeletons rattled and made such a racket that they frightened all the birds, so that none ever flew into the garden. The vines wound themselves around human bones, and grinning skulls filled the flowerpots instead of flowers. Wasn't that a fine garden for a princess!

"Look around you," said the king. "You will end up like all the others. So please, please don't propose to my daughter; it really makes me very unhappy, I am very sensitive on that point."

Johannes kissed the old king's hand and said that he was sure everything would be all right, for he was very much in love with the lovely princess.

At that moment the princess came riding into the castle yard followed by all her ladies in waiting. The king and Johannes went out to greet her. How beautiful she was as she gave Johannes her hand. Now he was even more in love than he had been before; surely, she could not be a cruel and wicked witch. They all went up into the great hall and there the page boys served cookies and jam. But the old king was so sad that he didn't eat anything; besides, he thought the cookies were too hard.

It was decided that Johannes was to come to the castle the next morning and there in front of the judges and the king's council answer the question the princess would ask. If he could answer it, then he would have to come back and answer two more questions on the two following days, but no one as yet had ever answered the princess' first question, so the day she asked it had been the last of their lives.

Johannes was not worried or frightened about what was going to happen. He was happily dreaming about the beautiful princess. He was confident that God would help him, though he didn't know exactly how; nor did he give it much thought as he skipped through the streets on his way back to the inn, where his friend was waiting for him.

Johannes could not stop talking about how beautiful the princess was and how kindly she had received him. He longed for the next day when he would see her again and try his luck at guessing the answer to her question.

His friend shook his head; he was not happy. "I am very fond of you," he said. "We could have remained together a long time yet, and now I have to lose you. Poor, dear Johannes, I feel like crying but shan't do it. It would spoil our last evening together, so let us be happy. Let's be gay; tomorrow when you are gone there will be time for my tears."

The whole town had heard that the princess had a new suitor, and they all went into mourning. The theater was closed, and the little old ladies who sold candy put black crepe around their chocolate pigs. The king and all the priests went to church and prayed on their knees. Everyone was miserable, for no one believed that poor Johannes would fare better than all the other suitors had.

Late in the evening the wayfarer ordered a bowl of punch and said to Johannes that now they ought to drink to the health of the princess. When Johannes had drunk his second glass, he was so tired that he no longer could keep his eyes open and fell asleep. His friend lifted him gently from the chair and laid him on the bed.

When the darkest hour of the night had almost come, Johannes' friend tied the swan's wings on his back and stuck into his pocket the largest bunch of switches that he had got from the old lady for curing her leg. He opened the window and flew out over the town to the royal castle, where he landed on the balcony of the princess and hid in a corner next to her window.

The clock in the tower struck the quarter before the hour; it would soon be midnight. The whole town was still. Suddenly the princess' window opened and out she flew, her white cape trailing behind her; on her back were a pair of large black wings. The wayfarer made himself invisible so that no one could see him. Behind the princess he flew, whipping her so hard that he drew blood. She was flying toward the big black mountain beyond the city. The wind took hold of her cape and spread it out like the sail of a ship, and the moon shone through it.

"Oh, how it is hailing! How it is hailing!" moaned the princess every time the switches hit her back.

Finally, when she reached the mountain, she knocked on it as if it were a door. The mountain rumbled like thunder and opened itself so the princess could enter. Right behind her was Johannes' friend, though she could not see him, for he was invisible.

They were walking through a long, high corridor. The walls were lighted curiously by the glow of red spiders who ran up and down like little flames. Now they were in a great hall built of silver and gold. Along the walls was a row of blue and red flowers, as large as sunflowers; but one could not pick them, for their stems were snakes and their faces were the fire shooting out of the snakes' mouths. The ceilings were studded with glowworms and sky-blue bats whose thin, fragile wings beat constantly. What a strange sight! In the middle of the hall stood a throne, which rested on the skeletons of four horses; their bridles were made of red spiders. The seat of the throne itself was milk-white glass, and the pillows were little black mice who were biting each other's tails. Above it was a canopy made of pink spider webs, decorated with little green flies that shone like precious stones. On the throne sat an old troll with a crown on his ugly head and a scepter in his hand. He kissed the princess on the forehead and invited her to sit down beside him on the throne.

Now the music began. Big black grasshoppers played on mouth organs. Owls beat themselves on their stomachs: they were the drums. It was a funny concert. Small black trolls with jack-o'-lanterns in their hats were dancing. No one could see the wayfarer, who was standing behind the throne watching and listening to everything. The courtiers entered; they were very elegant and distinguished. But anyone who looked at them carefully could see what they really were: cabbage heads attached to broomsticks, which the troll had made alive by witchcraft, and then dressed in beautifully embroidered robes. But they were of no importance: courtiers are only for show.

After the dancing had gone on for a while, the princess told the troll about her new suitor and asked him what question she should ask him the next morning.

"Listen," said the troll, "ask him to guess what you are thinking about, and then think about something very commonplace, because he will never guess that. Just think of your shoes. Then have his head cut off, but don't forget to bring me his eyes tomorrow night, I love to eat them."

The princess curtsied most humbly and said that she wouldn't forget the eyes. Then the troll commanded the mountain to open itself again and the princess started her flight back to the castle. Johannes' friend was flying right behind her, and he beat her so severely with his switches that she moaned loudly about the terrible hailstorm and was glad when she finally reached the window of her bedchamber. The wayfarer flew back to the inn, where Johannes was still sleeping. He took off his wings and went to bed, for he had a right to be tired.

Very early the next morning, when Johannes awoke, his friend told him that he had had a strange dream. He had dreamed about the princess and her shoes. "So when the princess asks you what she is thinking about, do remember to say, her shoes," he said. Of course, that was what he had heard the troll tell the princess that she should be thinking about; but the wayfarer did not tell Johannes about his visit to the mountain.

"Well, I can just as well say one thing as the other," said Johannes, "and maybe you have dreamed the true answer, for I am sure that God wants to help me. Still, I think we should say good-by to each other, for if I guess wrong I shall never see you again."

They kissed and Johannes went into the town and straight up to the castle. The big hall was filled with people; all the judges sat in easy chairs and had eiderdown pillows on which to rest their heads, for they had grave matters to think about. The king paced the floor with a white handkerchief in his hands and constantly dried his eyes. The princess entered; she was even more beautiful than she had been the day before. She greeted everyone graciously and kindly, and took Johannes' hand in hers and said: "Good morning, dear friend."

Now Johannes had to guess what she was thinking about. She looked ever so kindly toward him, but when she heard the word "shoes," her face grew as white as chalk and her body shook. She couldn't hide that Johannes had given the right answer.

Glory be, how happy the old king was! He turned a somersault, and the people clapped both for him and for Johannes, who had guessed the answer to the first question.

Johannes' friend was pleased when he heard how well everything had gone. But Johannes folded his hands and thanked God, for he was certain that it was He who had helped him and would probably help him with the other questions. The following morning he would have to answer the second one.

The second evening passed just like the first. As soon as Johannes slept, his traveling companion tied the swan's wings on his back and followed the princess. But he now brought along two of the bundles of switches and beat her even harder. Again no one saw him and he heard everything that was said. This time the princess was to think about her gloves. Early the next morning he told Johannes that he had dreamed that the princess would think of her gloves.

When Johannes guessed correctly the whole court turned somersaults, as they had seen the king do the day before. But the princess had to lie down on her divan and wouldn't speak to anyone.

Now everything depended on what Johannes said the next morning. If he guessed right the third time, she would have to marry him and he would inherit the kingdom when her father died; but if he didn't he would lose his life and the troll would eat his pretty eyes.

That evening Johannes went to bed early, said his prayers, and slept peacefully; while the wayfarer tied the swan's wings on his back, stuck his sword in his belt, and taking all three bundles of switches with him, flew to the castle.

It was pitch-dark. There was such a storm that the tiles were blown off the roofs, and the trees in the princess' garden, in which the skeletons hung, swayed as reeds do in the wind. Every minute the lightning flashed, and the thunder roared continually, as if it were one great thunderclap that lasted the whole night through.

The window opened, the princess flew out. Her face was as white as death, but she laughed at the storm, which was not wild enough for her taste. Her white cape whirled around her like a great sail. Johannes' friend beat her so hard with the three bundles of birch branches that blood dripped down on the earth far below and the princess could hardly fly.

At last she reached the mountain. "It is hailing! What a storm!" she said to the troll. "I have never been out in weather like that before."

"Yes, you can get too much of a good thing," said the troll.

Now the princess told him that Johannes had guessed what she had been thinking a second time. "If he guesses right again tomorrow, then he will have won. I shall never visit this mountain again and never be able to do any more magic. Oh, it is so sad!"

"He will not be able to guess your thoughts tomorrow, not unless he is a greater wizard than I am! I shall think of something that he has never seen. Now let us be merry!" The troll took the princess by the hand and they danced among the little trolls and the jack-o'-lanterns. On the walls the glowing red spiders ran up and down like tiny tongues of fire. The owls beat the drums. The crickets sang. The black grasshoppers blew on their mouth organs. It was a grand ball!

They danced until it was very late and the princess had to return or she would be missed at the castle. The troll said he would follow her home: that would give them a little more time together.

As they flew through the storm, Johannes' friend wore out his three bundles of switches on their backs. Never before had the troll experienced such a hailstorm. Outside the castle he said good-by to the princess and whispered to her, "Think of my head."

The wayfarer had heard what the troll said. Just as the princess had disappeared into her bedchamber and the troll turned to fly home, he grabbed him by his long black beard and with one stroke of his sword cut off the troll's head. He threw the body into the lake for the fishes to eat, but the ugly head he wrapped in his silk handkerchief and took it with him to the inn; then he went to bed and to sleep.

The next morning he gave the handkerchief to Johannes but told him that he must not untie it before the princess had asked him to guess what she was thinking about.

The big hall in the castle was so crowded with people that they stood as close together as radishes do when they have been bound in bunches by a farmer. The judges and the king's council were sitting in their easy chairs, resting their heads on eiderdown pillows. The king had put on brand-new robes and had had his crown and his scepter polished, which made them look very nice. But the princess was very pale and dressed in black; she looked as if she were attending a funeral.

"What am I thinking about?" she asked.

Johannes untied the handkerchief. He was shocked and frightened when he saw the horrible head of the troll. All the people shuddered, for it was a terrifying sight, but the princess sat as still as a stone statue and did not utter a word. At last she rose. Without looking at anyone or at anything, without turning to the right or the left, she sighed deeply, gave Johannes her hand, and said: "Now you are my master. Tonight we shall be married."

"That's what I like to hear!" shouted the king. "That's the way it ought to be!"

Everyone shouted, "Hurrah!" The royal guards marched down the streets with a band in front of them. The church bells rang; the old ladies who sold the candy took the black crepe off their chocolate pigs. Three oxen, stuffed with ducks and chickens, were roasted on the town square for everyone to eat. The fountains splashed the finest wine; and if you bought two pennies' worth of pretzels, then the baker gave you six muffins with raisins as part of the bargain.

When evening came, the whole town was illuminated; the soldiers fired their cannons, and little boys shot off firecrackers. In the castle all the most elegant people in the country were gathered; they ate and drank and toasted each other and all the young people danced; one could hear the young girls singing far away:

> "So many a fair maiden
> Calls for a dance so gay.
> The air with music is laden.
> Beautiful maiden, turn about,
> Stamp your feet, and whirl,
> Until your shoes are worn out.

But the princess was still a witch and didn't love Johannes at all. The wayfarer had not forgotten this, so he gave Johannes three feathers from the swan's wings and a little bottle filled with liquid, and said to him: "Tonight, next to the marriage bed place a large tub of water and throw these feathers and empty this liquid into it. When the princess starts to get into bed, push her into the tub and duck her three times under the water; then she will no longer be a witch and will love you dearly."

Johannes took his friend's advice. When he shoved the princess underneath the water the first time, she screamed and changed into a black swan with fiery eyes, who wiggled and strained in his grasp. The second time she was plunged into the water, she became a white swan with a black ring around her neck. Johannes prayed to God as he pushed her under the third time; and instantly she changed into the most beautiful princess. She was even lovelier than before; and she thanked him, with tears in her eyes, for having broken the evil spell.

The next day the king came visiting; so did the court and half of the people of the town. They all wanted to pay their respects to the bridal couple. Last of all came Johannes' traveling companion. He had a knapsack on his back and a walking stick in his hand. Johannes kissed him and begged him not to leave. "All my good fortune is your doing!" he cried.

But his friend shook his head; then he spoke softly and gently. "No, my time on earth is over. I have paid my debt. Do you remember the dead man whom the evil men wanted to harm? You gave everything you owned so that he could rest in his coffin. I am the dead man." With these words he disappeared.

The wedding celebration lasted a month. Johannes and the princess loved each other ever so much. The old king lived for many years and enjoyed having his grandchildren sit on his knee and play with his scepter, while Johannes ruled the whole kingdom.

The Little Mermaid

FAR, far from land, where the waters are as blue as the petals of the cornflower and as clear as glass, there, where no anchor can reach the bottom, live the mer-people. So deep is this part of the sea that you would have to pile many church towers on top of each other before one of them emerged above the surface.

Now you must not think that at the bottom of the sea there is only white sand. No, here grow the strangest plants and trees; their stems and leaves are so subtle that the slightest current in the water makes them move, as if they were alive. Big and small fishes flit in and out among their branches, just as the birds do up on earth. At the very deepest place, the mer-king has built his castle. Its walls are made of coral and its long pointed windows of amber. The roof is oyster shells that are continually opening and closing. It looks very beautiful, for in each shell lies a pearl, so lustrous that it would be fit for a queen's crown.

The mer-king had been a widower for many years; his mother kept house for him. She was a very intelligent woman but a little too proud of her rank: she wore twelve oysters on her tail; the nobility were only allowed six. Otherwise, she was a most praiseworthy woman, and she took excellent care of her grandchildren, the little princesses. They were six lovely mermaids; the youngest was the most beautiful. Her complexion was as fine as the petal of a rose and her eyes as blue as the deepest lake but, just like everyone else down there, she had no feet; her body ended in a fishtail.

The mermaids were allowed to play all day in the great hall of the castle, where flowers grew on the walls. The big amber windows were kept open and the fishes swam in and out, just as the swallows up on earth fly in through our windows if they are open. But unlike the birds of the air, the fishes were not frightened, they swam right up to the little princesses and ate out of their hands and let themselves be petted.

Around the castle was a great park where there grew fiery-red and deep-blue trees. Their fruits shone as though they were the purest gold, their flowers were like flames, and their branches and leaves were ever in motion. The earth was the finest sand, not white but blue, the color of burning sulphur. There was a blue tinge to everything, down on the bottom of the sea. You could almost believe that you were suspended in mid-air and had the blue sky both above and below you. When the sea was calm, the sun appeared like a crimson flower, from which all light flowed.

Each little princess had her own garden, where she could plant the flowers she liked. One of them had shaped her flower bed so it resembled a whale; and another, as a mermaid. The youngest had planted red flowers in hers: she wanted it to look like the sun; it was round and the crimson flowers did glow as though they were so many little suns. She was a strange little child: quiet and thoughtful. Her sisters' gardens were filled with all sorts of things that they had collected from shipwrecks, but she had only a marble statue of a boy in hers. It had been cut out of stone that was almost transparently clear and had sunk to the bottom of the sea when the ship that had carried it was lost. Close to the statue she had planted a pink tree; it looked like a weeping willow. The tree was taller than the sculpture. Its long soft branches bent toward the sand; it looked as if the top of the tree and its root wanted to kiss each other.

The princesses liked nothing better than to listen to their old grandmother tell about the world above. She had to recount countless times all she knew about ships, towns, human beings, and the animals that lived up on land. The youngest of the mermaids thought it particularly wonderful that the flowers up there had fragrance, for that they did not have on the bottom of the sea. She also liked to hear about the green forest, where the fishes that swam among the branches could sing most beautifully. Grandmother called the birds "fishes"; otherwise, her little grandchildren would not have understood her, since they had never seen a bird.

"But when you are fifteen, then you will be allowed to swim to the surface," she promised. "Then you can climb up on a rock and sit and watch the big ships sail by. If you dare, you can swim close enough to the shore to see the towns and the forest."

The following year, the oldest of the princesses would be fifteen. From one sister to the next, there was a difference in age of about a year, which meant that the youngest would have to wait more than five whole years before she would be allowed to swim up from the bottom of the sea and take a look at us. But each promised the others that she would return after her first day above, and tell about the things she had seen and describe what she thought was loveliest of all. For the old grandmother could not satisfy their curiosity.

None of the sisters longed so much to see the world above as the youngest, the one who had to wait the longest before she could leave her home. Many a night this quiet, thoughtful little mermaid would stand by the open window, looking up through the dark blue waters where the fishes swam. She could see the moon and the stars; they looked paler but larger down here under the sea. Sometimes a great shadow passed by like a cloud and then she knew that it was either a whale or a ship, with its crew and passengers, that was sailing high above her. None on board could have imagined that a little beautiful mermaid stood in the depths below them and stretched her little white hands up toward the keel of their ship.

The oldest of the sisters had her fifteenth birthday and swam up to the surface of the sea. When she returned she had hundreds of things to tell. But of everything that had happened to her, the loveliest experience by far, she claimed, had been to lie on a sandbank, when the sea was calm and the moon was out, and look at a great city. The lights from the windows and streets had shone like hundreds of stars; and she had been able to hear the rumbling of the carriages and the voices of human beings and, best of all, the sound of music. She had seen all the church towers and steeples and heard their bells ring. And just because she would never be able to enter the city, she longed to be able to do that more than anything else.

How carefully her youngest sister listened to every word and remembered everything that she had been told. When, late in the evening, the little mermaid would stand dreaming by the window and look up through the blue water, then she imagined that she could see the city and hear the bells of the churches ringing.

The next year the second of the sisters was allowed to swim away from home. Her little head had emerged above the water just at the moment when the sun was setting. This sight had been so beautiful that she could hardly describe it. The whole heaven had been covered in gold and the clouds that had sailed above her had been purple and crimson. A flight of wild swans, like a white veil just above the water, had flown by. She had swum toward the sun, but it had set, taking the colors of the clouds, sea, and sky with it.

The third of the sisters, who came of age the following year, was the most daring among them. She had swum way up a broad river! There she had seen green hills covered with vineyards, castles, and farms that peeped out through the great forests. She had heard the birds sing and the sun had been so hot that she had had to swim under the water, some of the time, just to cool off. In a little bay, she had come upon some naked children who were playing and splashing in the water. She had wanted to join them, but when they saw her they got frightened and ran away. A little black animal had come: it was a dog. But she had never seen one before. It had barked so loudly and fiercely that she became terrified and swam right back to the sea. What she never would forget as long as she lived were the beautiful forest, the green hills, and the sweet little children who had been able to swim even though they had no fishtails as she had.

The fourth of the sisters was timid. She stayed far away from shore, out in the middle of the ocean. But that was the most beautiful place of all, she asserted. You could see ever so far and the sky above was like a clear glass bell. The ships she had seen had been so far away that they had looked no bigger than gulls. But the little dolphins had turned somersaults for her and the great whales had sprayed water high up into the air, so that it looked as though there were more than a hundred fountains.

The fifth sister's birthday was in the winter and, therefore, she saw something none of her sisters had seen. The ocean had been green, and huge icebergs had been floating on it. Each of them had been as lovely as a pearl and yet larger than the church towers that human beings built. They had the most fantastic shapes and their surface glittered like diamonds. She had climbed up on the largest one of them all; the wind had played with her long hair, and all the ships had fearfully kept away. Toward evening a storm had begun to blow; dark clouds had gathered and bolts of lightning had flashed while the thunder rolled. The waves had lifted the iceberg high up on their shoulders, and the lightning had colored the ice red. The ships had taken down their sails; and on board, fear and terror had reigned. But the mermaid had just sat on her iceberg and watched the bolts of lightning zigzag across the sky.

The first time that any of the sisters had been allowed to swim to the surface, each had been delighted with her freedom and all she had seen. But now that they were grownups and could swim anywhere they wished, they lost interest in wandering far away; after a month or two the world above lost its attraction. When they were away, they longed for their father's castle, declaring it the most beautiful place of all and the only spot where one really felt at home.

Still, many evenings the five sisters would take each other's hands and rise up through the waters. They had voices far lovelier than any human being. When a storm began to rage and a ship was in danger of being wrecked, then the five sisters would swim in front of it and sing about how beautiful it was down at the bottom of the sea. They begged the sailors not to be frightened but to come down to them. The men could not understand the mermaids' songs; they thought it was the wind that was singing. Besides, they would never see the beauty of the world below them, for if a ship sinks the seamen drown, and when they arrive at the mer-king's castle they are dead.

On such evenings, while her sisters swam, hand in hand, up through the water, the youngest princess had to stay below. She would look sadly up after them and feel like crying; but mermaids can't weep and that makes their suffering even deeper and greater.

"Oh, if only I were fifteen," she would sigh. "I know that I shall love the world above, and the human beings who live up there!"

At last she, too, was fifteen!

"Now you are off our hands," said the old dowager queen. "Let me dress you, just as I dressed your sisters." She put a wreath of white lilies around her hair; each of the petals of every flower was half a pearl. She let eight oysters clip themselves onto the little mermaid's tail, so that everyone could see that she was a princess.

"It hurts," said the little mermaid.

"One has to suffer for position," said her old grandmother. The little mermaid would gladly have exchanged her heavy pearl wreath for one of the red flowers from her garden (she thought they suited her much better) but she didn't dare.

"Farewell," she said and rose, light as a bubble, up through the water.

The sun had just set when she lifted her head above the surface. The clouds still had the color of roses and in the horizon was a fine line of gold; in the pale pink sky the first star of evening sparkled, clearly and beautifully. The air was warm and the sea was calm. She saw a three-masted ship; only one of its sails was unfurled, and it hung motionless in the still air. Up on the yards the sailors sat, looking down upon the deck from which music could be heard. As the evening grew darker, hundreds of little colored lamps were hung from the rigging; they looked like the flags of all the nations of the world. The little mermaid swam close to a porthole and the swells lifted her gently so that she could look in through it. The great cabin was filled with gaily dressed people; the handsomest among them was a young prince with large, dark eyes. He looked no older than sixteen, and that was, in truth, his age; that very day was his birthday. All the festivities were for him. The sailors danced on the deck, and as the young prince came up to watch them, a hundred rockets flew into the sky.

The night became as bright as day and the little mermaid got so frightened that she ducked down under the water. But she soon stuck her head up again; and then it looked as if all the stars of the heavens were falling down on top of her. She had never seen fireworks before. Pinwheels turned; rockets shot into the air, and their lights reflected in the dark mirror of the sea. The deck of the ship was so illuminated that every rope could clearly be seen. Oh, how handsome the young prince was! He laughed and smiled and shook hands with everyone, while music was played in the still night.

It grew late, but the little mermaid could not turn her eyes away from the ship and the handsome prince. The colored lamps were put out. No more rockets shot into the air and no more cannons were fired. From the depth of the ocean came a rumbling noise. The little mermaid let the waves be her rocking horse, and they lifted her so that she could look in through the porthole. The ship started to sail faster and faster, as one sail after another was unfurled. Now the waves grew in size and black clouds could be seen on the horizon and far away lightning flashed.

A storm was brewing. The sailors took down the sails. The great ship tossed and rolled in the huge waves that rose as though they were mountains that wanted to bury the ship and break its proud mast. But the ship, like a swan, rode on top of the waves and let them lift her high into the sky. The little mermaid thought it was very amusing to watch the ship sailing so fast, but the sailors didn't. The ship creaked and groaned; the great planks seemed to bulge as the waves hit them. Suddenly the mast snapped as if it were a reed. It tumbled into the water. The ship heeled over, and the sea broke over it.

Only now did the little mermaid understand that the ship was in danger. She had to be careful herself and keep away from the spars and broken pieces of timber that were being flung by the waves. For a moment it grew so dark that she could see nothing, then a bolt of lightning illuminated the sinking ship. She looked for the young prince among the terrified men on board who were trying to save themselves, but not until that very moment, when the ship finally sank, did she see him.

At first, she thought joyfully, "Now he will come down to me!" But then she remembered that man could not live in the sea and the young prince would be dead when he came to her father's castle.

"He must not die," she thought, and dived in among the wreckage, forgetting the danger that she herself was in, for any one of the great beams that were floating in the turbulent sea could have crushed her.

She found him! He was too tired to swim any farther; he had no more strength in his arms and legs to fight the storm-whipped waves. He closed his eyes, waiting for death, and he would have drowned, had the little mermaid not saved him. She held his head above water and let the waves carry them where they would.

By morning the storm was over. Of the wrecked ship not a splinter was to be found. The sun rose, glowing red, and its rays gave color to the young prince's cheeks but his eyes remained closed. The little mermaid kissed his forehead and stroked his wet hair. She thought that he looked like the statue in her garden. She kissed him again and wished passionately that he would live.

In the far distance she saw land; the mountains rose blue in the morning air. The snow on their peaks was as glittering white as swan's feathers. At the shore there was a green forest, and in its midst lay a cloister or a church, the little mermaid did not know which. Lemon and orange trees grew in the garden, and by the entrance gate stood a tall palm tree. There was a little bay nearby, where the water was calm and deep. The mermaid swam with her prince toward the beach. She laid him in the fine white sand, taking care to place his head in the warm sunshine far from the water.

In the big white buildings bells were ringing and a group of young girls was coming out to walk in the garden. The little mermaid swam out to some rocks and hid behind them. She covered her head with seaweed so that she could not be seen and then peeped toward land, to see who would find the poor prince.

Soon one of the young girls discovered him. At first she seemed frightened, and she called the others. A lot of people came. The prince opened his eyes and smiled up at those who stood around him —not out at the sea, where the little mermaid was hiding. But then he could not possibly have known that she was there and that it was she who had saved him. The little mermaid felt so terribly sad; the prince was carried into the big white building, and the little mermaid dived sorrowfully down into the sea and swam home to her father's castle.

She had always been quiet and thoughtful. Now she grew even more silent. Her sisters asked her what she had seen on her first visit up above, but she did not answer.

Many mornings and evenings she would swim back to the place where she had last seen the prince. She watched the fruits in the orchard ripen and be picked, and saw the snow on the high mountains melt, but she never saw the prince. She would return from each of these visits a little sadder. She would seek comfort by embracing the statue in her garden, which looked like the prince. She no longer tended her flowers, and they grew into a wilderness, covering the paths and weaving their long stalks and leaves into the branches of the trees, so that it became quite dark down in her garden.

At last she could bear her sorrow no longer and told one of her sisters about it; and almost at once the others knew as well. But no one else was told; that is, except for a couple of other mermaids, but they didn't tell it to anyone except their nearest and dearest friends. It was one of these friends who knew who the prince was. She, too, had seen the birthday party on the ship, and she could tell where he came from and where his kingdom was.

"Come, little sister," the other princesses called, and with their arms around each other's shoulders they swam.

All in a row they rose to the surface when they came to the shore where the prince's castle stood. It was built of glazed yellow stones and had many flights of marble stairs leading up to it. The steps of one of them went all the way down to the sea. Golden domes rose above the roofs, and pillars bore an arcade that went all the way around the palace. Between the pillars stood marble statues; they looked almost as if they were alive. Through the clear glass of the tall windows, one could look into the most beautiful chambers and halls, where silken curtains and tapestries hung on the walls; and there were large paintings that were a real pleasure to look at. In the largest hall was a fountain. The water shot high up toward the glass cupola in the roof, through which the sunbeams fell on the water and the beautiful flowers that grew in the basin of the fountain.

Now that she knew where the prince lived, the little mermaid spent many evenings and nights looking at the splendid palace. She swam nearer to the land than any of her sisters had ever dared. There was a marble balcony that cast its shadow across a narrow canal, and beneath it she hid and watched the young prince, who thought that he was all alone in the moonlight.

Many an evening she saw the prince sail with his musicians in his beautiful boat. She peeped from behind the tall reeds; and if someone noticed her silver-white veil, they probably thought that they had only seen a swan stretching its wings.

Many a night she heard the fishermen talking to each other and telling about how kind and good the prince was; and she was so glad that she had saved his life when she had found him, half dead, drifting on the waves. She remembered how his head had rested on her chest and with what passion she had kissed him. But he knew nothing about his rescue; he could not even dream about her.

More and more she grew to love human beings and wished that she could leave the sea and live among them. It seemed to her that their world was far larger than hers; on ships, they could sail across the oceans and they could climb the mountains high up above the clouds. Their countries seemed ever so large, covered with fields and forests; she knew that they stretched much farther than she could see. There was so much that she wanted to know; there were many questions that her sisters could not answer. Therefore she asked her old grandmother, since she knew much about the "higher world," as she called the lands above the sea.

"If men are not so unlucky as to drown," asked the little mermaid, "then do they live forever? Don't they die as we do, down here in the sea?"

"Yes, they do," answered her grandmother. "Men must also die and their life span is shorter than ours. We can live until we are three hundred years old; but when we die, we become the foam on the ocean. We cannot even bury our loved ones. We do not have immortal souls. When we die, we shall never rise again. We are like the green reeds: once they are cut they will never be green again. But men have souls that live eternally, even after their bodies have become dust. They rise high up into the clear sky where the stars are. As we rise up through the water to look at the world of man, they rise up to the unknown, the beautiful world, that we shall never see."

"Why do I not have an immortal soul!" sighed the little mermaid unhappily. "I would give all my three hundred years of life for only one day as a human being if, afterward, I should be allowed to live in the heavenly world."

"You shouldn't think about things like that," said her old grandmother. "We live far happier down here than man does up there."

"I am going to die, become foam on the ocean, and never again hear the music of the waves or see the flowers and the burning red sun. Can't I do anything to win an immortal soul?"

"No," said the old merwoman. "Only if a man should fall so much in love with you that you were dearer to him than his mother and father; and he cared so much for you that all his thoughts were of his love for you; and he let a priest take his right hand and put it in yours, while he promised to be eternally true to you, then his soul would flow into your body and you would be able to partake of human happiness. He can give you a soul and yet keep his own. But it will never happen. For that which we consider beautiful down here in the ocean, your fishtail, they find ugly up above, on earth. They have no sense; up there, you have to have two clumsy props, which they call legs, in order to be called beautiful."

The little mermaid sighed and glanced sadly down at her fishtail.

"Let us be happy," said her old grandmother. "We can swim and jump through the waves for three hundred years, that is time enough. Tonight we are going to give a court ball in the castle."

Such a splendor did not exist up above on the earth. The walls and the ceilings of the great hall were made of clear glass; four hundred giant green and pink oyster shells stood in rows along the walls. Blue flames rose from them and not only lighted the hall but also illuminated the sea outside. Numberless fishes—both big and small—swam close to the glass walls; some of them had purple scales, others seemed to be of silver and gold. Through the great hall flowed a swiftly moving current, and on that the mermen and mermaids danced, while they sang their own beautiful songs. Such lovely voices are never heard up on earth; and the little mermaid sang most beautifully of them all. The others clapped their hands when she had finished, and for a moment she felt happy, knowing that she had the most beautiful voice both on earth and in the sea.

But soon she started thinking again of the world above. She could not forget the handsome prince, and mourned because she did not have an immortal soul like his. She sneaked out of her father's palace, away from the ball, from the gaiety, down into her little garden.

From afar the sound of music, of horns being played, came down to her through the water; and she thought: "Now he is sailing up there, the prince whom I love more than I love my father and mother: he who is ever in my thoughts and in whose hands I would gladly place all my hope of happiness. I would dare to do anything to win him and an immortal soul! While my sisters are dancing in the palace, I will go to the sea witch, though I have always feared her, and ask her to help me."

The little mermaid swam toward the turbulent maelstrom; beyond it the sea witch lived. In this part of the great ocean the little mermaid had never been before; here no flowers or seaweeds grew, only the gray naked sea bed stretched toward the center of the maelstrom, that great whirlpool where the water, as if it had been set in motion by gigantic mill wheels, twisted and turned: grinding, tearing, and sucking anything that came within its reach down into its depths. Through this turbulence the little mermaid had to swim, for beyond it lay the bubbling mud flats that the sea witch called her bog and that had to be crossed to come to the place where she lived.

The sea witch's house was in the midst of the strangest forest. The bushes and trees were gigantic polyps that were half plant and half animal. They looked like snakes with hundreds of heads, but they grew out of the ground. Their branches were long slimy arms, and they had fingers as supple as worms; every limb was in constant motion from the root to the utmost point. Everything they could reach they grasped, and never let go of it again. With dread the little mermaid stood at the entrance to the forest; her heart was beating with fear, she almost turned back. But then she remembered her prince and the soul she wanted to gain and her courage returned.

She braided her long hair and bound it around her head, so the polyps could not catch her by it. She held her arms folded tightly across her breast and then she flew through the water as fast as the swiftest fish. The ugly polyps stretched out their arms and their fingers tried to grasp her. She noticed that every one of them was holding, as tightly as iron bands, onto something it had caught. Drowned human beings peeped out as white skeletons among the polyps' arms. There were sea chests, rudders of ships, skeletons of land animals; and then she saw a poor little mermaid who had been caught and strangled; and this sight was to her the most horrible.

At last she came to a great, slimy, open place in the middle of the forest. Big fat eels played in the mud, showing their ugly yellow stomachs. Here the witch had built her house out of the bones of drowned sailors, and there she sat letting a big ugly toad eat out of her mouth, as human beings sometimes let a canary eat sugar candy out of theirs. The ugly eels she called her little chickens, and held them close to her spongy chest.

"I know what you want," she cackled. "And it is stupid of you. But you shall have your wish, for it will bring you misery, little princess. You want to get rid of your fishtail, and instead have two stumps to walk on as human beings have, so that the prince will fall in love with you; and you will gain both him and an immortal soul." The witch laughed so loudly and evilly that the toad and eels she had had on her lap jumped down into the mud.

"You came at the right time," she said. "Tomorrow I could not have helped you; you would have had to wait a year. I will mix you a potion. Drink it tomorrow morning before the sun rises, while you are sitting on the beach. Your tail will divide and shrink, until it becomes what human beings call 'pretty legs.' It will hurt; it will feel as if a sword were going through your body. All who see you will say that you are the most beautiful human child they have ever seen. You will walk more gracefully than any dancer; but every time your foot touches the ground it will feel as though you were walking on knives so sharp that your blood must flow. If you are willing to suffer all this, then I can help you."

"I will," whispered the little mermaid, and thought of her prince and how she would win an immortal soul.

"But remember," screeched the witch, "that once you have a human body you can never become a mermaid again. Never again shall you swim through the waters with your sisters to your father's castle. If you cannot make the prince fall so much in love with you that he forgets both his father and mother, because his every thought concerns only you, and he orders the priest to take his right hand and place it in yours, so that you become man and wife; then, the first morning after he has married another, your heart will break and you will become foam on the ocean."

"I still want to try," said the little mermaid, and her face was as white as a corpse.

"But you will have to pay me, too," grinned the witch. "And I want no small payment. You have the most beautiful voice of all those who live in the ocean. I suppose you have thought of using that to charm your prince; but that voice you will have to give to me. I want the most precious thing you have to pay for my potion. It contains my own blood, so that it can be as sharp as a double-edged sword."

"But if you take my voice," said the little mermaid, "what will I have left?"

"Your beautiful body," said the witch. "Your graceful walk and your lovely eyes. Speak with them and you will be able to capture a human heart. Have you lost your courage? Stick out your little tongue, and let me cut it off in payment, and you shall have the potion."

"Let it happen," whispered the little mermaid.

The witch took out a caldron in which to make the magic potion. "Cleanliness is a virtue," she said. And before she put the pot over the fire, she scrubbed it with eels, which she had made into a whisk.

She cut her chest and let her blood drip into the vessel. The steam that rose became strange figures that were terrifying to see. Every minute, the witch put something different into the caldron. When the brew reached a rolling boil, it sounded as though a crocodile were crying. At last the potion was finished. It looked as clear and pure as water.

"Here it is," said the witch, and cut out the little mermaid's tongue. Now she was mute, she could neither speak nor sing.

"If any of the polyps should try to grab you, on your way back through my forest," said the witch, "you need only spill one drop of the potion on it and its arms and fingers will splinter into a thousand pieces."

But the little mermaid didn't have to do that. Fearfully, the polyps drew away when they saw what she was carrying in her hands; the potion sparkled as though it were a star. Safely, she returned through the forest, the bog, and the maelstrom.

She could see her father's palace. The lights were extinguished in the great hall. Everyone was asleep; and yet she did not dare to seek out her sisters; now that she was mute and was going away from them forever. She felt as if her heart would break with sorrow. She sneaked down into the garden and picked a flower from each of her sisters' gardens; then she threw a thousand finger kisses toward the palace and swam upward through the deep blue sea.

The sun had not yet risen when she reached the prince's castle and sat down on the lowest step of the great marble stairs. The moon was still shining clearly. The little mermaid drank the potion and it felt as if a sword were piercing her little body. She fainted and lay as though she were dead.

When the sun's rays touched the sea she woke and felt a burning pain; but the young prince stood in front of her and looked at her with his coal-black eyes. She looked downward and saw then that she no longer had a fishtail but the most beautiful, little, slender legs that any girl could wish for. She was naked; and therefore she took her long hair and covered herself with it.

The prince asked her who she was and how she had got there. She looked gently and yet ever so sadly up at him with her deep blue eyes, for she could not speak. He took her by the hand and led her up to his castle. And just as the witch had warned, every step felt as though she were walking on sharp knives. But she suffered it gladly. Gracefully as a bubble rising in the water, she walked beside the prince; and everyone who saw her wondered how she could walk so lightly.

In the castle, she was clad in royal clothes of silk and muslin. She was the most beautiful of all, but she was mute and could neither sing nor speak. Beautiful slave girls, clad in silken clothes embroidered with gold, sang for the prince and his royal parents. One sang more beautifully than the rest, and the prince clapped his hands and smiled to her; then the little mermaid was filled with sorrow, for she knew that she had once sung far more beautifully. And she thought, "Oh, if he only knew that to be with him I have given away my voice for all eternity."

Now the slave girls danced, gracefully they moved to the beautiful music. Suddenly the little mermaid lifted her hands and rose on the tips of her toes. She floated more than danced across the floor. No one had ever seen anyone dance as she did. Her every movement revealed her loveliness and her eyes spoke far more eloquently than the slave's song.

Everyone was delighted, especially the prince. He called her his little foundling. She danced again and again, even though each time her little foot touched the floor she felt as if she had stepped on a knife. The prince declared that she should never leave him, and she was given permission to sleep in front of his door on a velvet pillow.

The prince had men's clothes made for her, so that she could accompany him when he went horseback riding. Through the sweet-smelling forest they rode, where green branches touched their shoulders and little birds sang among the leaves. Together they climbed the high mountains and her feet bled so much that others noticed it; but she smiled and followed her prince up ever higher until they could see the clouds sail below them, like flocks of birds migrating to foreign lands.

At night in the castle, while the others slept, she would walk down the broad marble stairs to the sea and cool her poor burning feet in the cold water. Then she would think of her sisters, down in the deep sea.

One night they came; arm in arm they rose above the surface of the water, singing ever so sadly. She waved to them, and they recognized her, and they told her how much sorrow she had brought them. After that they visited her every night; and once she saw, far out to sea, her old grandmother. It had been years since she had stuck her head up into the air; and there, too, was her father the mer-king with his crown on his head. They stretched their hands toward her but did not dare come as near to the land as her sisters.

Day by day the prince grew fonder and fonder of her; but he loved her as he would have loved a good child, and had no thought of making her his queen. And she had to become his wife or she would never have an immortal soul, but on the morning after his marriage would become foam on the great ocean.

"Don't you love me more than you do all others?" was the message in the little mermaid's eyes when the prince kissed her lovely forehead.

"Yes, you are the dearest to me," said the prince, "for you have the kindest heart of them all. You are devoted to me and you look like a young girl I once saw, and will probably never see again. I was in a shipwreck. The waves carried me ashore, where a holy temple lay. Many young girls were in service there; one of them, the youngest of them all, found me on the beach and saved my life. I saw her only twice, but she is the only one I can love in this world; and you look like her. You almost make her picture disappear from my soul. She belongs to the holy temple and, therefore, good fortune has sent you to me instead, and we shall never part."

"Oh, he does not know that it was I who saved his life," thought the little mermaid. "I carried him across the sea to the forest where the temple stood. I hid behind the rocks and watched over him until he was found. I saw that beautiful girl whom he loves more than me!" And the little mermaid sighed deeply, for cry she couldn't. "He has said that the girl belongs to the holy temple and will never come out into the world, and they will never meet again. But I am with him and see him every day. I will take care of him, love him, and devote my life to him."

Everyone said that the young prince was to be married; he was to have the neighboring king's daughter, a beautiful princess. A magnificent ship was built and made ready. It was announced that the prince was traveling to see the neighboring kingdom, but that no one believed. "It is not the country but the princess he is to inspect," they all agreed.

The little mermaid shook her head and smiled; she knew what the prince thought, and they didn't.

"I must go," he had told her, "I must look at the beautiful princess, my parents demand it. But they won't force me to carry her home as my bride. I can't love her. She does not look like the girl from the temple as you do. If I ever marry, I shall most likely choose you, my little foundling with the eloquent eyes." And he kissed her on her red lips and played with her long hair, and let his head rest so near her heart that it dreamed of human happiness and an immortal soul.

"Are you afraid of the ocean, my little silent child?" asked the prince as they stood on the deck of the splendid ship that was to sail them to the neighboring kingdom. He told the little mermaid how the sea can be still or stormy, and about the fishes that live in it, and what the divers had seen underneath the water. She smiled as he talked, for who knew better than she about the world on the bottom of the ocean?

In the moonlit night, when everyone slept but the sailor at the rudder and the lookout in the bow, she sat on the bulwark and looked down into the clear water. She thought she saw her father's palace; and on the top of its tower her old grandmother was standing with her silver crown on her head, looking up through the currents of the sea, toward the keel of the ship. Her sisters came; they looked at her so sorrowfully and wrung their white hands in despair; she waved to them and smiled. She wanted them to know that she was happy, but just at that moment the little cabin boy came and her sisters dived down under the water; he saw nothing but some white foam on the ocean.

The next morning the ship sailed into the harbor of the great town that belonged to the neighboring king. All the church bells were ringing, and from the tall towers trumpets blew, while the soldiers stood at attention, with banners flying and bayonets on their rifles.

Every day another banquet was held, and balls and parties followed one after the other. But the princess attended none of them, for she did not live in the palace; she was being educated in the holy temple, where she was to learn all the royal virtues. But at last she came.

The little mermaid wanted ever so much to see her; and when she finally did, she had to admit that a more beautiful girl she had never seen before. Her skin was so delicate and fine, and beneath her long dark lashes smiled a pair of faithful, dark blue eyes.

"It is you!" exclaimed the prince. "You are the one who saved me, when I lay half dead on the beach!" And he embraced his blushing bride.

"Oh, now I am too happy," he said to the little mermaid. "That which I never dared hope has now happened! You will share my joy, for I know that you love me more than any of the others do."

The little mermaid kissed his hand; she felt as if her heart were breaking. His wedding morning would bring her death and she would be changed into foam of the ocean.

All the churchbells rang and heralds rode through the streets and announced the wedding to the people. On all the altars costly silver lamps burned with fragrant oils. The priests swung censers with burning incense in them, while the prince and the princess gave each other their hands, and the bishop blessed them. The little mermaid, dressed in silk and gold, held the train of the bride's dress, but her ears did not hear the music, nor did her eyes see the holy ceremony, for this night would bring her death, and she was thinking of all she had lost in this world.

The bride and bridegroom embarked upon the prince's ship; cannons saluted and banners flew. On the main deck, a tent of gold and scarlet cloth had been raised; there on the softest of pillows the bridal couple would sleep.

The sails were unfurled, and they swelled in the wind and the ship glided across the transparent sea.

When it darkened and evening came, colored lamps were lit and the sailors danced on the deck. The little mermaid could not help remembering the first time she had emerged above the waves, when she had seen the almost identical sight. She whirled in the dance, glided as the swallow does in the air when it is pursued. Everyone cheered and applauded her. Never had she danced so beautifully; the sharp knives cut her feet, but she did not feel it, for the pain in her heart was far greater. She knew that this was the last evening that she would see him for whose sake she had given away her lovely voice and left her home and her family; and he would never know of her sacrifice. It was the last night that she would breathe the same air as he, or look out over the deep sea and up into the star-blue heaven. A dreamless, eternal night awaited her, for she had no soul and had not been able to win one.

Until midnight all was gaiety aboard the ship, and the mermaid danced and laughed with the thought of death in her heart. Then the prince kissed his bride and she fondled his long black hair and, arm in arm, they walked into their splendorous tent, to sleep.

The ship grew quiet. Only the sailor at the helm and the little mermaid were awake. She stood with her white arms resting on the railing and looked toward the east. She searched the horizon for the pink of dawn; she knew that the first sunbeams would kill her.

Out of the sea rose her sisters, but the wind could no longer play with their long beautiful hair, for their heads had been shorn.

"We have given our hair to the sea witch, so that she would help you and you would not have to die this night. Here is a knife that the witch has given us. Look how sharp it is! Before the sun rises, you must plunge it into the heart of the prince; when his warm blood sprays on your feet, they will turn into a fishtail and you will be a mermaid again. You will be able to live your three hundred years down in the sea with us, before you die and become foam on the ocean. Hurry! He or you must die before the sun rises. Our grandmother mourns; she, too, has no hair; hers has fallen out from grief. Kill the prince and come back to us! Hurry! See, there is a pink haze on the horizon. Soon the sun will rise and you will die."

The little mermaid heard the sound of her sisters' deep and strange sighing before they disappeared beneath the waves.

She pulled aside the crimson cloth of the tent and saw the beautiful bride sleeping peacefully, with her head resting on the prince's chest. The little mermaid bent down and kissed his handsome forehead. She turned and looked at the sky; more and more, it was turning red. She glanced at the sharp knife; and once more she looked down at the prince. He moved a little in his sleep and whispered the name of his bride. Only she was in his thoughts, in his dreams! The little mermaid's hand trembled as it squeezed the handle of the knife, then she threw the weapon out into the sea. The waves turned red where it fell, as if drops of blood were seeping up through the water.

Again she looked at the prince; her eyes were already glazed in death. She threw herself into the sea and felt her body changing into foam.

The sun rose out of the sea, its rays felt warm and soft on the deathly cold foam. But the little mermaid did not feel death, she saw the sun, and up above her floated hundreds of airy, transparent forms. She could see right through them, see the sails of the ship and the blood-red clouds. Their voices were melodious, so spiritual and tender that no human ear could hear them, just as their forms were so fragile and fine that no human eye could see them. So light were they that they glided through the air, though they had no wings. The little mermaid looked down and saw that she had an ethereal body like theirs.

"Where am I?" she asked; and her voice sounded like theirs—so lovely and so melodious that no human music could reproduce it.

"We are the daughters of the air," they answered. "Mermaids have no immortal soul and can never have one, unless they can obtain the love of a human being. Their chance of obtaining eternal life depends upon others. We, daughters of the air, have not received an eternal soul either; but we can win one by good deeds. We fly to the warm countries, where the heavy air of the plague rests, and blow cool winds to spread it. We carry the smell of flowers that refresh and heal the sick. If for three hundred years we earnestly try to do what is good, we obtain an immortal soul and can take part in the eternal happiness of man. You, little mermaid, have tried with all your heart to do the same. You have suffered and borne your suffering bravely; and that is why you are now among us, the spirits of the air. Do your good deeds and in three hundred years an immortal soul will be yours."

The little mermaid lifted her arms up toward God's sun, and for the first time she felt a tear.

She heard noise coming from the ship. She saw the prince and the princess searching for her. Sadly they looked at the sea, as if they knew that she had thrown herself into the waves. Without being seen, she kissed the bride's forehead and smiled at the prince; then she rose together with the other children of the air, up into a pink cloud that was sailing by.

"In three hundred years I shall rise like this into God's kingdom," she said.

"You may be able to go there before that," whispered one of the others to her. "Invisibly, we fly through the homes of human beings. They can't see us, so they don't know when we are there; but if we find a good child, who makes his parents happy and deserves their love, we smile and God takes a year away from the time of our trial. But if there is a naughty and mean child in the house we come to, we cry; and for every tear we shed, God adds a day to the three hundred years we already must serve."

The Emperor's New Clothes

MANY, many years ago there was an emperor who was so terribly fond of beautiful new clothes that he spent all his money on his attire. He did not care about his soldiers, or attending the theater, or even going for a drive in the park, unless it was to show off his new clothes. He had an outfit for every hour of the day. And just as we say, "The king is in his council chamber," his subjects used to say, "The emperor is in his clothes closet."

In the large town where the emperor's palace was, life was gay and happy; and every day new visitors arrived. One day two swindlers came. They told everybody that they were weavers and that they could weave the most marvelous cloth. Not only were the colors and the patterns of their material extraordinarily beautiful, but the cloth had the strange quality of being invisible to anyone who was unfit for his office or unforgivably stupid.

"This is truly marvelous," thought the emperor. "Now if I had robes cut from that material, I should know which of my councilors was unfit for his office, and I would be able to pick out my clever subjects myself. They must weave some material for me!" And he gave the swindlers a lot of money so they could start working at once.

They set up a loom and acted as if they were weaving, but the loom was empty. The fine silk and gold threads they demanded from the emperor they never used, but hid them in their own knapsacks. Late into the night they would sit before their empty loom, pretending to weave.

"I would like to know how they are getting along," thought the emperor; but his heart beat strangely when he remembered that those who were stupid or unfit for their office would not be able to see the material. Not that he was really worried that this would happen to him. Still, it might be better to send someone else the first time and see how he fared. Everybody in town had heard about the cloth's magic quality and most of them could hardly wait to find out how stupid or unworthy their neighbors were.

"I shall send my faithful prime minister over to see how the weavers are getting along," thought the emperor. "He will know how to judge the material, for he is both clever and fit for his office, if any man is."

The good-natured old man stepped into the room where the weavers were working and saw the empty loom. He closed his eyes, and opened them again. "God preserve me!" he thought. "I cannot see a thing!" But he didn't say it out loud.

The swindlers asked him to step a little closer to the loom so that he could admire the intricate patterns and marvelous colors of the material they were weaving. They both pointed to the empty loom, and the poor old prime minister opened his eyes as wide as he could; but it didn't help, he still couldn't see anything.

"Am I stupid?" he thought. "I can't believe it, but if it is so, it is best no one finds out about it. But maybe I am not fit for my office. No, that is worse, I'd better not admit that I can't see what they are weaving."

"Tell us what you think of it," demanded one of the swindlers.

"It is beautiful. It is very lovely," mumbled the old prime minister, adjusting his glasses. "What patterns! What colors! I shall tell the emperor that it pleases me ever so much."

"That is a compliment," both the weavers said; and now they described the patterns and told which shades of color they had used. The prime minister listened attentively, so that he could repeat their words to the emperor; and that is exactly what he did.

The two swindlers demanded more money, and more silk and gold thread. They said they had to use it for their weaving, but their loom remained as empty as ever.

Soon the emperor sent another of his trusted councilors to see how the work was progressing. He looked and looked just as the prime minister had, but since there was nothing to be seen, he didn't see anything.

"Isn't it a marvelous piece of material?" asked one of the swindlers; and they both began to describe the beauty of their cloth again.

"I am not stupid," thought the emperor's councilor. "I must be unfit for my office. That is strange; but I'd better not admit it to anyone." And he started to praise the material, which he could not see, for the loveliness of its patterns and colors.

"I think it is the most charming piece of material I have ever seen," declared the councilor to the emperor.

Everyone in town was talking about the marvelous cloth that the swindlers were weaving.

At last the emperor himself decided to see it before it was removed from the loom. Attended by the most important people in the empire, among them the prime minister and the councilor who had been there before, the emperor entered the room where the weavers were weaving furiously on their empty loom.

"Isn't it *magnifique?*" asked the prime minister.

"Your Majesty, look at the colors and the patterns," said the councilor.

And the two old gentlemen pointed to the empty loom, believing that all the rest of the company could see the cloth.

"What!" thought the emperor. "I can't see a thing! Why, this is a disaster! Am I stupid? Am I unfit to be emperor? Oh, it is too horrible!" Aloud he said, "It is very lovely. It has my approval," while he nodded his head and looked at the empty loom.

All the councilors, ministers, and men of great importance who had come with him stared and stared; but they saw no more than the emperor had seen, and they said the same thing that he had said, "It is lovely." And they advised him to have clothes cut and sewn, so that he could wear them in the procession at the next great celebration.

"It is magnificent! Beautiful! Excellent!" All of their mouths agreed, though none of their eyes had seen anything. The two swindlers were decorated and given the title "Royal Knight of the Loom."

The night before the procession, the two swindlers didn't sleep at all. They had sixteen candles lighting up the room where they worked. Everyone could see how busy they were, getting the emperor's new clothes finished. They pretended to take the cloth from the loom; they cut the air with their big scissors, and sewed with needles without thread. At last they announced: "The emperor's clothes are ready!"

Together with his courtiers, the emperor came. The swindlers lifted their arms as if they were holding something in their hands, and said, "These are the trousers. This is the robe, and here is the train. They are all as light as if they were made of spider webs! It will be as if Your Majesty had almost nothing on, but that is their special virtue."

"Oh yes," breathed all the courtiers; but they saw nothing, for there was nothing to be seen.

"Will Your Imperial Majesty be so gracious as to take off your clothes?" asked the swindlers. "Over there by the big mirror, we shall help you put your new ones on."

The emperor did as he was told; and the swindlers acted as if they were dressing him in the clothes they should have made. Finally they tied around his waist the long train which two of his most noble courtiers were to carry.

The emperor stood in front of the mirror admiring the clothes he couldn't see.

"Oh, how they suit you! A perfect fit!" everyone exclaimed. "What colors! What patterns! The new clothes are magnificent!"

"The crimson canopy, under which Your Imperial Majesty is to walk, is waiting outside," said the imperial master of court ceremony.

"Well, I am dressed. Aren't my clothes becoming?" The emperor turned around once more in front of the mirror, pretending to study his finery.

The two gentlemen of the imperial bedchamber fumbled on the floor, trying to find the train which they were supposed to carry. They didn't dare admit that they didn't see anything, so they pretended to pick up the train and held their hands as if they were carrying it.

The emperor walked in the procession under his crimson canopy. And all the people of the town, who had lined the streets or were looking down from the windows, said that the emperor's clothes were beautiful. "What a magnificent robe! And the train! How well the emperor's clothes suit him!"

None of them were willing to admit that they hadn't seen a thing; for if anyone did, then he was either stupid or unfit for the job he held. Never before had the emperor's clothes been such a success.

"But he doesn't have anything on!" cried a little child.

"Listen to the innocent one," said the proud father. And the people whispered among each other and repeated what the child had said.

"He doesn't have anything on. There's a little child who says that he has nothing on."

"He has nothing on!" shouted all the people at last.

The emperor shivered, for he was certain that they were right; but he thought, "I must bear it until the procession is over." And he walked even more proudly, and the two gentlemen of the imperial bedchamber went on carrying the train that wasn't there.

10

❋◈❋

The Steadfast Tin Soldier

ONCE there were five and twenty tin soldiers. They were all brothers because they had been made from the same old tin spoon. With their rifles sticking up over their shoulders, they stood at attention, looking straight ahead, in their handsome red and blue uniforms.

"Tin soldiers!" were the first words they heard in this world; and they had been shouted happily by a little boy who was clapping his hands because he had received them as a birthday gift. He took them immediately out of the box they had come in and set them on the table. They were all exactly alike except one, who was different from the others because he was missing a leg. He had been the last one to be cast and there had not been enough tin. But he stood as firm and steadfast on his one leg as the others did on their two. He is the hero of our story.

Of all the many toys on the table, the one you noticed first was a pasteboard castle. It was a little replica of a real castle, and through its windows you could see right into its handsomely painted halls. In front of the castle was a little lake surrounded by trees; in it swans swam and looked at their own reflections because the lake was a glass mirror. It was all very lovely; but the most charming part of the castle was its mistress. She was a little paper doll and she was standing in the entrance dressed like a ballerina. She had a skirt of white muslin and a blue ribbon draped over her shoulder, which was fastened with a spangle that was almost as large as her face. The little lady had her arms stretched out, as if she were going to embrace someone.

She stood on one leg, and at that on her toes, for she was a ballet dancer; the other, she held up behind her, in such a way that it disappeared under her skirt; and therefore the soldier thought that she was one-legged like himself.

"She would be a perfect wife for me," he thought. "But I am afraid she is above me. She has a castle and I have only a box that I must share with twenty-four soldiers; that wouldn't do for her. Still, I would like to make her acquaintance." And the soldier lay down full length behind a snuffbox; from there he could look at the young lady, who was able to stand on the toes of only one leg without losing her balance.

Later in the evening, when it was the children's bedtime, all the other tin soldiers were put back in the box. When the house was quiet and everyone had gone to bed, the toys began to play. They played house, and hide-and-seek, and held a ball. The four and twenty tin soldiers rattled inside their box; they wanted to play too, but they couldn't get the lid open. The nutcracker turned somersaults, and the slate pencil wrote on the blackboard. They made so much noise that the canary woke up and recited his opinion of them all in verse. The only ones who didn't move were the ballerina and the soldier. She stood as steadfast on the toes of her one leg as the soldier did on his. His eyes never left her, not even for a moment did he blink or turn away.

The clock struck twelve. Pop! The lid of the snuffbox opened and out jumped a troll. It was a jack-in-the-box.

"Tin soldier," screamed the little black troll, "keep your eyes to yourself."

The tin soldier acted as if he hadn't heard the remark.

"You wait till tomorrow!" threatened the troll, and disappeared back into its box.

The next morning when the children were up and dressed, the little boy put the one-legged soldier on the window sill. It's hard to tell whether it was the troll or just the wind that caused the window to open suddenly and the soldier to fall out of it. He dropped down three stories to the street and his bayonet stuck in the earth between two cobblestones.

The boy and the maid came down to look for him and, though

they almost stepped on him, they didn't see him. If only the tin soldier had shouted, "Here I am!" they would have found him; but he thought it improper to shout when in uniform.

It began to rain; first one drop fell and then another and soon it was pouring. When the shower was over two urchins came by. "Look," said one of them, "there is a tin soldier. He will do as a sailor."

The boys made a boat out of a newspaper, put the tin soldier on board, and let it sail in the gutter. Away it went, for it had rained so hard that the gutter was a raging torrent. The boys ran along on the sidewalk, clapping their hands. The boat dipped and turned in the waves. The tin soldier trembled and quaked inside himself; but outside, he stood as steadfast as ever, shouldering his gun and looking straight ahead.

Now the gutter was covered by a board. It was as dark as it had been inside the box, but there he had had four and twenty comrades. "I wonder how it will all end," thought the soldier. "I am sure it's all the troll's doing. If only the ballerina were here, then I wouldn't care if it were twice as dark as pitch."

A big water rat that lived in the gutter came up behind the boat and shouted, "Have you got a passport? Give me your passport!"

The tin soldier didn't answer but held more firmly onto his rifle. The current became stronger, and the boat gathered speed. The rat swam after him; it was so angry that it gnashed its teeth. "Stop him! Stop him!" the rat shouted to two pieces of straw and a little twig. "Stop him! He hasn't got a passport and he won't pay duty!"

The current ran swifter and swifter. The tin soldier could see light ahead; he was coming out of the tunnel. But at the same moment he heard a strange roaring sound. It was frightening enough to make the bravest man cringe. At the end of the tunnel the gutter emptied into one of the canals of the harbor. If you can imagine it, it would be the same as for a human being to be thrown down a great waterfall into the sea.

There was no hope of stopping the boat. The poor tin soldier stood as steady as ever, he did not flinch. The boat spun around four times and became filled to the brim with water. It was doomed, the paper began to fall apart; the tin soldier was standing in water up to his neck. He thought of the ballerina, whom he would never see again, and two lines from a poem ran through his mind.

> Fare thee well, my warrior bold,
> Death comes so swift and cold.

The paper fell apart and the tin soldier would have sunk down into the mud at the bottom of the canal had not a greedy fish swallowed him just at that moment.

Here it was even darker than it had been in the sewer; the fish's stomach was terribly narrow, but the soldier lay there as steadfast as he had stood in the boat, without letting go of his rifle.

The fish darted and dashed in the wildest manner; then suddenly it was still. A while later, a ray of light appeared and someone said, "Why, there is a tin soldier." The fish had been caught, taken to the market, and sold. The kitchen maid had found the soldier when she opened the fish up with a big knife, in order to clean it. With her thumb and her index finger she picked the tin soldier up by the waist and carried him into the living room, so that everyone could admire the strange traveler who had journeyed inside the belly of a fish. But the tin soldier was not proud of his adventures.

How strange the world is! He was back in the same room that he had left in the morning; and he had been put down on the table among the toys he knew. There stood the cardboard castle and the little ballerina. She was still standing on one leg, the other she had lifted high into the air. She was as steadfast as he was. It touched the soldier's heart and he almost cried tin tears—and would have, had it not been so undignified. He looked at her and she at him, but never a word passed between them.

Suddenly one of the little boys grabbed the soldier, opened the stove, and threw him in. The child couldn't explain why he had done it; there's no question but that the jack-in-the-box had had something to do with it.

The tin soldier stood illuminated by the flames that leaped around him. He did not know whether the great heat he felt was caused by his love or the fire. The colors of his uniform had disappeared, and he could not tell whether it was from sorrow or his trip through the water. He looked at the ballerina, and she looked at him. He could feel that he was melting; but he held on as steadfastly as ever to his gun and kept his gaze on the little ballerina in front of the castle.

The door of the room was opened, a breeze caught the little dancer and like a sylph she flew right into the stove. She flared up and was gone. The soldier melted. The next day when the maid emptied the stove, she found a little tin heart, which was all that was left of him. Among the ashes lay the metal spangle from the ballerina's dress; it had been burned as black as coal.

The Wild Swans

FAR, far away where the swallows are when we have winter, there lived a king who had eleven sons and one daughter, Elisa. The eleven brothers were all princes; and when they went to school, each wore a star on his chest and a sword at his side. They wrote with diamond pencils on golden tablets, and read aloud so beautifully that everyone knew at once that they were of royal blood. Their sister Elisa sat on a little stool made of mirrors and had a picture book that had cost half the kingdom. How well those children lived; but it did not last.

Their father, who was king of the whole country, married an evil queen, and that boded no good for the poor children. They found this out the first day she came. The whole castle was decorated in honor of the great event, and the children decided to play house. Instead of the cakes and baked apples they usually were given for this game—and which were so easy to provide—the queen handed them a teacup full of sand and said that they should pretend it was something else.

A week later little Elisa was sent to live with some poor peasants; and the evil queen made the king believe such dreadful things about the princes that soon he did not care for them any more.

"Fly away, out into the world with you and fend for yourselves! Fly as voiceless birds!" cursed the queen; but their fate was not as terrible as she would have liked it to be, for her power had its limits. They became eleven beautiful, wild swans. With a strange cry, they flew out of the castle window and over the park and the forest.

It was very early in the morning when they flew over the farm where Elisa lived. She was still asleep in her little bed. They circled low above the roof of the farmhouse, turning and twisting their necks, to catch a glimpse of their sister, while their great wings beat the air. But no one was awake, and no one heard or saw them. At last they had to fly away, high up into the clouds, toward the great dark forest that stretched all the way to the ocean.

Poor little Elisa sat on the floor playing with a leaf. She had no toys, so she had made a hole in the leaf and was looking up at the sun through it. She felt as though she were looking into the bright eyes of her brothers; and when the warm sunbeams touched her cheeks, she thought of all the kisses they had given her.

The days passed, one after another, and they all were alike. The wind blew through the rosebush and whispered, "Who can be more lovely than you are?"

The roses shook their heads and replied: "Elisa!"

On Sundays the old woman at the farm would set her chair outside and sit reading her psalmbook. The wind would turn the leaves and whisper, "Who can be more saintly than you?"

The psalmbook would answer as truthfully as the roses had: "Elisa!"

When Elisa turned fifteen she was brought back to the castle. As soon as the evil queen saw how beautiful the girl was, envy and hate filled her evil heart. She would gladly have transformed Elisa into a swan at first sight; but the king had asked to see his daughter, and the queen did not dare to disobey him.

Early the next morning, before Elisa was awake, the queen went into the marble bathroom, where the floors were covered with costly carpets and the softest pillows lay on the benches that lined the walls. She had three toads with her. She kissed the first and said, "Sit on Elisa's head that she may become as lazy as you are." Kissing the second toad, she ordered, "Touch Elisa's forehead that she may become as ugly as you are, so her father will not recognize her." Then she kissed the third toad. "Rest next to Elisa's heart, that her soul may become as evil as yours and give her pain."

She dropped the toads into the clear water and, instantly, it had a greenish tinge. She sent for Elisa, undressed her, and told her to step into the bath. As she slipped into the water, the first toad leaped onto Elisa's head, the second touched her forehead, and the third snuggled as close to her heart as it could. But Elisa did not seem to notice them.

When Elisa rose from the bath, there floating on the water were three red poppies. If the toads had not been made poisonous by the kiss of the wicked queen, they would have turned into roses; but they had become flowers when they touched Elisa. She was so good and so innocent that evil magic could not harm her.

When the wicked queen realized this, she took the juice from walnut shells and rubbed Elisa's body till it was streaked black and brown; then she smeared an awful-smelling salve on the girl's face and filtered ashes and dust through her hair. Now it was impossible for anyone to recognize the lovely princess.

Her father got frightened when he saw her, and said, "She is not my daughter." Only the watchdog and the swallows recognized her; but they were only animals and nobody paid any attention to them.

Elisa wept bitterly and thought of her eleven brothers who had disappeared. In despair, she slipped out of the castle. She walked all day across fields and swamps until she came to the great forest. She did not know where she was going; she only knew that she was deeply unhappy and she longed more than ever to see her brothers again. She thought that they had been forced out into the world as she had; and now she would try to find them.

As soon as she entered the forest, night fell. She had come far away from any road or path. She lay down on the soft moss to sleep. She said her prayers and leaned her head against the stump of a tree. The night was silent, warm, and still. Around her shone so many glowworms that, when she touched the branch of a bush, the little insects fell to the ground like shooting stars.

That night she dreamed about her brothers. Again they were children writing on their golden tablets with diamond pens; and once more she looked at the lovely picture book that had cost half the kingdom. But on their tablets her brothers were not only doing their sums, they wrote of all the great deeds they had performed. The pictures in the book became alive: the birds sang, and the men and women walked right out of the book to talk to Elisa. Every time she was about to turn a leaf, they quickly jumped back onto the page, so as not to get in the wrong picture.

When she awoke, the sun was already high in the heavens; but she couldn't see it, for the forest was so dense that the branches of the tall trees locked out the sky. But the sun rays shone through the leaves and made a shimmering golden haze. The smell of greenness was all around her, and the birds were so tame that they almost seemed willing to perch on her shoulder. She heard the splashing of water; and she found a little brook, and followed it till it led her to a lovely little pool that was so clear, she could see the sand bottom in a glance. It was surrounded by bushes; but at one spot the deer, when they came down to drink, had made a hole. Here Elisa kneeled down.

Had the branches and their leaves not been swayed gently by the wind, she would have believed that they had been painted on the water, so perfectly were they mirrored. Those upon which the sun shone glistened, and those in the shade were a dark green.

Then Elisa saw her own face and was frightened: it was so dirty and ugly. She dipped her hand into the water and rubbed her eyes, her cheeks, and her forehead till she could see her own fresh skin again. She undressed and bathed in the clear pool, and a more beautiful princess than she, could not have been found in the whole world.

When she had dressed, braided her long hair, and drunk from the brook with her cupped hand, she wandered farther and farther into the forest without knowing where she was going. She thought about her brothers and trusted that God would not leave her. There ahead of her was a wild apple tree. Hadn't God let it grow there so that the hungry could eat? Its branches were bent almost to the ground under the weight of the fruit. Here Elisa rested and had her midday meal; before she walked on, she found sticks and propped up the heavily laden branches of the apple tree.

The forest grew darker and darker. It was so still that she could hear her own footsteps: the sound of every little stick and leaf crumbling under her foot. No birds were to be seen or heard, no sunbeams penetrated the foliage. The trees grew so close together that when she looked ahead she felt as if she were imprisoned in a stockade. Oh, here she was more alone than she had ever thought one could be!

Night came and not a single glowworm shone in the darkness. When she lay down to sleep she was hopelessly sad; but then the branches above her seemed to be drawn aside like a curtain, and she saw God looking down at her, with angels peeping over His shoulders and out from under His arms. And in the morning when she awoke, she did not know whether she had really seen God or it had merely been a dream.

Elisa met an old woman who was carrying a basket full of berries on her arm, and she offered the girl some berries. Elisa thanked her and then asked if she had seen eleven princes riding through the forest.

"No," the old woman replied. "But I have seen eleven swans with golden crowns on their heads, swimming in a stream not far from here."

She said she would show Elisa the way and led her to a cliff. Below it a little river twisted and turned its way through the forest. It seemed to be flowing in a tunnel, for the trees that grew on either side stretched their leafy branches toward each other and then intertwined. Where the branches were not long enough to span the stream, the trunks had pulled up part of their roots, in order to lean farther out over the water so the branches could meet.

Elisa said good-by to the old woman and followed the stream until its water ran out into the sea.

Before her lay the beautiful ocean. There was not a sail to be seen nor any boat along the shore. She could not go any farther. How would she ever be able to find her brothers? She looked down. The shore was covered with pebbles: all the little stones were round; they had been made so by the sea. Iron, glass, stones, everything that lay at her feet had been ground into its present shape by water that was softer than her own delicate hand. "The waves roll on untiringly, and grind and polish the hardest stone. I must learn to be as untiring as they. Thank you for the lesson you have taught me, waves; and I am sure that one day you will carry me to my dear brothers."

Among the dried-out seaweed on the beach she found eleven swans' feathers. She picked them up; to each of them clung a drop of water, whether it was dew or a tear she did not know.

Although she was alone, Elisa did not feel lonely for she could watch the ever changing scene before her. The sea transforms itself more in an hour than a lake does in a year. When the clouds above it are dark, then the sea becomes as black as they are; and yet it will put on a dress of white if the wind should suddenly come and whip the waves. In the evening when the winds sleep and the clouds have turned pink, the sea will appear like the petal of a giant rose. Blue, white, green, red: the sea contains all colors; and even when it is calm, standing at the shore's edge, you will notice that it is moving like the breast of a sleeping child.

When the sun began to slide down behind the sea, Elisa saw eleven wild swans, with golden crowns on their heads, flying toward the beach. Like a white ribbon being pulled across the sky, they flew one after the other. Elisa hid behind some bushes. The swans landed nearby, still flapping their great white wings.

At the moment when the sun finally sank below the horizon, the swans turned into eleven handsome princes, Elisa's brothers. She shrieked with joy when she saw them. Although they had grown up since she had seen them last, she recognized them immediately and ran out from her hiding place to throw herself in their arms. They were as happy to see her as she was to see them. They laughed and cried, as they told each other of the evil deeds of their wicked stepmother.

"We must fly as wild swans as long as the sun is in the sky," explained the oldest brother. "Only when night has come do we regain our human shape; that is why we must never be in flight at sunset, for should we be up among the clouds, like any other human beings, we would fall and be killed. We do not live here, but in a country on the other side of the ocean. The sea is vast. It is far, far away; and there is no island where we can rest during our long journey. But midway in the ocean, a solitary rock rises above the waves. It is so tiny that we can just stand on it; and when the waves break against it, the water splashes up over us. Yet we thank God for that ragged rock, for if it were not there we should never be able to visit again the country where we were born. As it is, we only dare attempt the flight during the longest days of the year. We stay here eleven summer days and then we must return. Only for such a short time can we fly over the great forest and see our father's castle, and circle above the church where our mother is buried. It is as if every tree, every bush, in our native land were part of us. The wild horses gallop across the plains today as they did yesterday when we were children, and the gypsies still sing the songs we know. That is why we must come back —if only once a year. And now we have found you, our little sister. But we can only stay here two more days; then we must fly across the ocean to that fair land where we live now. How shall we be able to take you along? We have neither ship nor boat!"

"What can I do to break the spell that the queen has cast?" asked Elisa.

They talked almost the whole night through; only for a while did they doze. Elisa was awakened by the sound of wings beating the air.

Her brothers had turned into swans again. They flew in circles above her and then disappeared over the forest. But her youngest brother had stayed behind. He rested his white head in her lap, and she stroked his strong white wings. Just before sunset, the others returned; and when twilight came, they were princes once more.

"Tomorrow we must begin the flight back to our new homeland," said the oldest brother. "We dare not stay longer; but how can we leave you behind, Elisa? It will be a whole year before we can return. My arms when I am a man are strong enough to carry you through the forest; wouldn't the wings of all of us be strong enough to carry you over the sea when we are swans?"

"I'll go with you!" exclaimed Elisa.

They worked all night, weaving a net of reeds and willow branches. Just before sunrise, Elisa lay down upon it; and she was so tired that she fell asleep. When the sun rose, and the princes changed into swans again, they picked up the net with their bills and flew up into the clouds with their sleeping sister. The burning rays of the sun fell on her face, so one of the swans flew above her, to shade her with his great wings.

They were far out over the ocean when Elisa awoke. So strange did it feel to be carried through the air that at first she thought she was dreaming. Some berries and roots lay beside her. Her youngest brother had collected this provision for her journey, and it was he who now flew above her and shaded her from the sun.

The whole day they flew as swiftly as arrows through the air; yet their flight would have been even faster had they not been carrying Elisa. Soon the sun would begin to set. Dark clouds on the horizon warned of a coming storm. Elisa looked down; there was only the endless ocean; she saw no lonely rock. It seemed to her that the wings were beating harder now. She would be the cause of her brothers' deaths. When the sun set, they would turn into men again; then they would fall into the sea and be drowned. She prayed to God, but still there was no rocky islet to be seen. Black clouds filled the sky; soon the breath of the storm would be upon them. The waves seemed as heavy as lead, and in the clouds lightning flashed.

The rim of the sun touched the sea. Elisa trembled with fear. Suddenly the swans dove down so fast that she thought that they were falling; but then they spread out their wings again.

Half of the sun had disappeared when Elisa saw the little rock.

Looking down from the air, she thought that it looked more like a seal who had raised his head above the water. Just as the sun vanished they landed on the rock; and when the last of its light, like a piece of paper set aflame, flared up and then was gone, her brothers stood around her arm in arm.

The island was so tiny that they had to stand holding onto each other all night. The lightning made the sky bright and the thunder roared. They held each other's hands and sang a psalm, which comforted them and gave them courage.

At dawn the storm was over and the air was fresh and clear. The swans flew away from the rock, carrying Elisa. The sea was still turbulent. The white surf looked like millions of swans swimming on a raging green ocean. When the sun was high in the sky, Elisa saw a strange landscape. There was a mountain range covered with ice and snow. Halfway down the mountainsides was a huge palace, miles long, made of arcades, one on top of the other. And below that was a forest of gently waving palm trees, in which there were flowers with faces as large as millstones. She asked if that were the country where they lived, and the swans shook their heads. What she was seeing was a fata morgana: a mirage, an ever changing castle in the air to which no human being could gain admittance. As Elisa stared at it, the mountains, the castle, and the forest disappeared. It melted together and now there were twenty proud churches, every one alike, with high towers and tall windows. She thought she heard their organs playing, but it was the sound of the sea beating far below. The churches, in turn, changed into ships with towering sails. She was just above them; but when she looked down, she saw only fog driven by wind over the waves. The world of the sea and the air is always changing, ever in motion.

At last she saw the shores of the real country that was their destination. The mountains, which were covered with forests of cedar, were blue in the afternoon light; and she could see castles and towns. Before the sun had set, the swans alighted in front of a cave; its walls were covered with vines and plants that had intertwined and looked like tapestries.

"Tomorrow you must tell us what you have dreamed," said her youngest brother, showing her the part of the cave that was to be her bedchamber.

"May I dream how I can break the spell that the wicked queen cast," she said fervently; and that thought absorbed her so completely that she prayed to God and begged Him to help her; and while she was falling asleep she kept on praying.

Elisa felt as though she were flying into the fata morgana, the castle in the air; and a fairy came to welcome her who was young and beautiful, and yet somehow resembled the old woman whom Elisa had met in the forest and who had told her about the eleven swans with golden crowns on their heads.

"Your brothers can escape their fate," began the fairy, "if you have enough courage and endurance. The waves of the ocean are softer than your hands, yet they can form and shape hard stones; but they cannot feel the pain that your fingers will feel. They have no hearts and therefore they do not know fear: the suffering that you must endure. Look at the nettle that I hold in my hand! Around the cave where you are sleeping grow many of them; only those nettles or the ones to be found in churchyards may you use. You must pick them, even though they blister and burn your hands; then you must stamp on them with your bare feet until they become like flax. And from that you must twine thread with which to knit eleven shirts with long sleeves. If you cast one of these shirts over each of the eleven swans, the spell will be broken. But remember, from the moment you start your work until it is finished, you must be silent and never speak to anyone—even if it takes you years, you must be mute! If you speak one word, that word will send a knife into the hearts of your brothers. Their lives depend on your tongue: remember!"

The fairy touched Elisa's hand with the nettle. It felt like fire and she woke. It was bright daylight. Near her lay a nettle like the one she had seen in her sleep. She fell on her knees and said a prayer of thanks; then she walked outside to begin her work.

Her delicate hands picked the horrible nettles, and it felt as if her hands were burning and big blisters rose on her arms and hands. But she did not mind the pain if she could save her brothers. She broke every nettle and stamped on it with her bare feet until it became as fine as flax and could be twined into green thread.

When the sun set, her brothers came. At first they feared that some spell had been cast upon their sister by their evil stepmother, for Elisa was silent and would not answer their questions. But when they saw her hands covered with blisters, they understood the work she was doing was for their sake. The youngest of her brothers cried and his tears fell on her hands; the pain ceased and the burning blisters disappeared.

That night she could not sleep; she worked the whole night through. She felt that she could not rest until her brothers were free. The following day she was alone, but time passed more swiftly. By sunset the first of the nettle shirts was finished.

The next day she heard the sound of hunters' horns coming from the mountains. They came nearer and nearer and soon she could hear dogs barking. Frightened, she bound the nettles she had collected into a bundle with the thread she had already twined and the finished shirt; then she fled into the cave and sat down on the nettle heap.

Out of the thicket sprang a large dog; then came another and another. Barking, they ran back and forth in front of the entrance to the cave. Within a few minutes the hunters followed. The handsomest among them was the king of the country. He entered the cave and found Elisa. Never before had he seen a girl lovelier than she.

"Why are you hiding here, beautiful child?" he asked. Elisa shook her head. She dared not speak because her brothers' lives depended upon her silence. She hid her hands behind her back so that the king might not see how she suffered.

"You cannot stay here," he said. "Follow me, and if you are as good as you are beautiful, then you shall be clad in velvet and silk, wear a golden crown on your head, and call the loveliest of my castles your home."

He lifted her up on his horse. Elisa cried and wrung her hands. The king would not set her down again. "I only want to make you happy," he said. "Someday you will thank me for what I have done." Then he spurred his horse and galloped away with Elisa. The other hunters followed him.

By evening they reached the royal city with its many churches and palaces. The king led her into his castle with its lofty halls, where the waters of the fountains splashed into marble basins, and where the ceilings and the walls were beautifully painted. But none of this did Elisa notice, for she was crying so sorrowfully, so bitterly.

Silently but good-naturedly, she let the maids dress her in regal gowns, braid her hair with pearls, and pull long gloves over her blistered hands. When she entered the great hall, dressed so magnificently, she was so beautiful that the whole court bowed and curtsied. The king declared that she was to be his queen. Only the archbishop shook his head and whispered that he believed the little forest girl to be a witch who had cast a spell over the king.

The king did not listen to him. He ordered the musicians to play and the feast to begin. Dancing girls danced for Elisa; and the king showed her the fragrant gardens and the grand halls of his castle. But neither her lips nor her eyes smiled. Sorrow had printed its eternal mark on her face. Finally the king showed her a little chamber. Its walls and floor were covered by costly green carpets. It looked like the cave where she had been with her brothers. In a corner lay the green thread which she had spun from the nettles, and from the ceiling hung the one shirt that she had already knitted. One of the hunters had taken it all along as a curiosity.

"Here you can dream yourself back to your former home," remarked the king. "Here is the work you used to do; it will amuse you amid present splendor to think of the past."

A sweet smile played for a moment on Elisa's lips when she saw what was nearest and dearest to her heart restored to her. The color returned to her cheeks. She thought of her brothers, and she kissed the king's hand. He pressed her to his breast and ordered that all the church bells be rung and their wedding proclaimed. The silent girl from the woods was to become the queen.

The archbishop whispered evil words in the king's ear, but they did not penetrate his heart. The marriage ceremony was held, and the archbishop himself had to crown the queen. He pressed the golden band down on her head so hard that it hurt. But she did not feel the pain, for sorrow's band squeezed her heart and made her suffer far more.

She must not speak a word or her brothers would die. But her eyes spoke silently of the love she felt for the king, who did everything he could to please her. Every day she loved him more. If only she could tell him of her anguish. But mute she must be until her task was finished. At night while the king slept, she would leave their bed and go to the chamber with the green carpets, and make the nettle shirts for her brothers. But when she had finished the sixth shirt she had no more green thread with which to knit.

She knew that in the churchyard grew the nettles that she needed. She had to pick them herself. But how was she to go there without anyone seeing her?

"What is the pain in my hands compared to the pain I feel in my heart?" she thought. "I must attempt it and God will help me."

As if it were an evil deed she was about to perform, she sneaked fearfully out of the castle late at night. She crossed the royal park and made her way through the empty streets to the churchyard. The moon was out; and on one of the large tombstones she saw a group of lamias sitting. They are those dreadful monsters with the bodies of snakes and the breasts and heads of women. They dig up the graves of those who have just died, to eat the flesh of the corpses. Elisa had to walk past them. She said her prayers, and though they kept their terrible gaze upon her, they did her no harm. She picked her nettles and returned to the castle.

Only one person had seen her: the archbishop, for he was awake when everyone else was sleeping. Now he thought that what he had said was proven true: the queen was a witch who had cast her spell on the king and all his subjects.

When next the king came to confession, the archbishop told him what he had seen and what he feared. He spoke his condemning words so harshly that the carved sculptures of the saints shook their heads as though they were saying: "It is not true. Elisa is innocent!"

But that was not the way the archbishop interpreted it; he said that the saints were shaking their heads because of their horror at her sins.

Two tears rolled down the king's cheeks, and with a heavy heart he returned to the castle. That night he only pretended to sleep and, when Elisa rose, he followed her. Every night she went on with her work; and every night the King watched her disappear into the little chamber.

The face of the king grew dark and troubled. Elisa noticed it, though she did not know its cause; and this new sorrow was added to her fear for her brothers' fate. On her royal velvet dress fell salt tears, and they looked like diamonds on the purple material, making it even more splendid. And all the women of the court wished that they were queens and could wear such magnificent clothes.

Soon Elisa's work would be over. She had to knit only one more shirt; but she had no more nettles from which to twine thread. Once more, for the last time, she would have to go to the churchyard. She shook with fear when she thought of walking alone past the horrible lamias, but she gathered courage when she thought of her brothers and her own faith in God.

Elisa went; and secretly the king and the archbishop followed her. They saw her disappear through the gates of the churchyard. The same terrifying lamias were there, and they were sitting near the place where the nettles grew. The king saw her walk toward them, and he turned away as his heart filled with repulsion, for he thought that Elisa, his queen—who that very night had rested in his arms—had come to seek the company of these monsters.

"Let the people judge her," said he. And the people judged her guilty and condemned her to the stake.

She was taken from the great halls of the castle and thrown into a dungeon, where the wind whistled through the grating that barred the window. Instead of a bed with silken sheets and velvet pillows, they gave her the nettles she had picked as a pillow and the shirts she had knitted as a cover. They could have given her no greater gift. She prayed to God and started work on the last of the shirts. Outside in the streets, the urchins sang songs that mocked and scorned her, while no one said a word of comfort to her.

Just before sunset, she heard the sound of swan's wings beating before her window. It was her youngest brother who had found her. She wept for happiness, even though she knew that this might be the last night of her life. Her work was almost done and her brothers were near her.

The archbishop had promised the king that he would be with Elisa during the last hours of her life. But when he came, she shook her head and pointed toward the door, to tell him to go. Her work must be finished that night or all her suffering, all her tears, all her pain would be in vain. The archbishop spoke some unkind words to her and left.

Poor Elisa, who knew that she was innocent but could not say a word to prove it, set to work knitting the last shirt. Mice ran across the floor and fetched the nettles for her; they wanted to help. And the thrush sang outside the iron bars of the window, as gaily as it could, so that she would not lose her courage.

One hour before sunrise, her brothers came to the castle and demanded to see the king. But they were refused, for it was still night and the guards did not dare wake the king. Elisa's brothers begged and threatened; they made so much noise that the captain of the guard came and, finally, the king himself. But at that moment the sun rose; the brothers were gone but high above the royal castle flew eleven white swans.

A stream of people rushed through the gates of the city. Everyone wanted to see the witch being burned. An old worn-out mare drew the cart in which Elisa sat. She was clad in sackcloth; her hair hung loose and framed her beautiful face, which was deadly pale. Her lips moved; she was mumbling a prayer while she knitted the last shirt. The other ten lay at her feet. Even on the way to her death she did not cease working. The mob that lined the road jeered and mocked her.

"Look at the witch, she is mumbling her spells!" they screamed. "See what she has in her hands! It is no hymnbook; it is witchcraft! Get it away from her and tear it into a thousand pieces!"

And the rabble tried to stop the cart and tear Elisa's knitting out of her hands. But at that moment eleven white swans flew down and perched on the railing of the cart; they beat the air with their strong wings. The people drew back in fear.

"It is a sign from heaven that she is innocent," some of them whispered; but not one of them dared say it aloud.

The executioner took her hand to lead her to the stake, but she freed herself from him, grabbed the eleven shirts, and cast them over the swans. There stood eleven princes, handsome and fair. But the youngest of them had a swan's wing instead of an arm, for Elisa had not been able to finish one of the sleeves of the last shirt.

"Now I dare speak!" she cried. "I am innocent!"

The people, knowing that a miracle had taken place, kneeled down before her as they would have for a saint. But Elisa, worn out by fear, worry, and pain, fainted lifelessly into the arms of one of her brothers.

"Yes, she is innocent!" cried the oldest brother; and he addressed himself to the king and told of all that had happened to himself, his brothers, and their sister Elisa. While he spoke a fragrance of millions of roses spread from the wood that had been piled high around the stake. Every stick, every log had taken root and set forth vines. They were a hedge of the loveliest red roses, and on the very top bloomed a single white rose. It shone like a star. The king plucked it and placed it on Elisa's breast. She woke; happiness and peace were within her.

The church bells in the city started to peal, though no bell ringers pulled their ropes, and great flocks of birds flew in the sky. No one has ever seen a gayer procession than the one that now made its way to the royal castle.

The Garden of Eden

ONCE there lived a prince who had a library far greater than anyone else has ever had, either before him or since. All his books were very beautiful; and in them he could read about and see portrayed in pictures, everything that had ever happened in the whole world. There was no country, no people whom he could not learn about; but where the garden of Eden lay was not mentioned in any of his books. This made the prince very sad, for it was paradise that interested him most.

His grandmother had told him, when he was still a little boy just starting school, that in the garden of Eden all the flowers were cakes. On each of them was written, in the finest of sugar: history, geography, addition, subtraction, or the multiplication tables; and all children had to do was to eat the right cakes and they knew their lessons at once. The more cakes they ate, the better educated they became. Then, he had believed his grandmother's story; but as he grew up and became wiser, he understood that the beauty of paradise was far greater and more difficult to conceive.

"Oh, why did Eve pluck the apple and why did Adam eat the forbidden fruit? If I had been Adam, man would never have fallen and sin would not have conquered the world." This he had said to his grandmother when he was a little boy. Now, at seventeen, he felt no differently; and thoughts about the garden of Eden still filled his mind.

His favorite diversion was to take solitary walks in the woods. One day when he had ventured farther than usual a storm overtook him.

Though it was not yet evening, the day grew as dark as night and the rain came down in torrents. Soon he lost his way. He slipped in the wet grass and stumbled over the rocks. The poor prince was wet to the skin. Exhausted, he climbed up the side of the cliff, pressing his body against the water-drenched moss. He was about to give up when he heard a strange whistling noise near him; then he came upon a cavern in the cliff wall. Inside the cave was a fire so great that a whole deer could be roasted over it; and that was exactly what was being done. A woman who was so big and strong that she looked like a man, who had put on skirts, was turning a spit on which was a buck, antlers and all.

She put another log on the fire; then she turned and called to the prince, "Come in! Sit down by the fire and dry your clothes."

"It's drafty in here," the prince said. He was shivering as he sat down on the floor near the fire.

"It's going to be a lot draftier when my sons come home," said the woman. "You are in the cave of the winds. The four winds of the world are my sons, do you understand?"

"Where are they now?" asked the prince, who had understood her well enough.

"If a question is stupid, how can one give a clever answer?" grumbled the woman. "My sons are out on their own, playing ball with the clouds, somewhere up there." She pointed upward and toward the entrance to the cave.

"I see," nodded the prince. "You speak more roughly than the women I am used to talking to."

"Well, they are not mothers of sons like mine." The woman grinned. "I have to be tough to keep my sons in tow. But I can take care of them, however stiff-necked they are. See those four leather bags hanging on the wall? They are just as afraid of them as you were of the switch in the corner. I am stronger than they are, and if they don't behave, then I pick any one of them up and put him in a bag, and there he can stay until I let him out again. There is one of them coming now."

It was the north wind. He was clad in bearskin with a sealskin cap pulled down over his ears. He brought hail and snow in with him; and icicles were hanging from his beard.

"You'd better not go near the fire just yet," said the prince, "or you will get frostbite on your hands and your face."

"Frostbite!" laughed the north wind as loud as he could. "Why, frost and coldness are what I love. How has such a little weakling as you found your way to the cave of the winds?"

"He is my guest," said the old woman, "and if you are not satisfied with that explanation, then I will put you in your bag. You know that I mean what I say."

That quieted the north wind down, and he began to tell about where he had been and what he had seen during the month that he had been away.

"I have just come from the Arctic Ocean," he began. "I have been visiting the Barents Sea with Russian whalers. I sat sleeping on their tiller when they rounded the North Cape. Fulmars flew around my legs. They are strange birds. They flap their wings once or twice and then hold them out straight, gliding along at a good speed."

"Don't be so long-winded," interrupted his mother. "What was it like on the Barents Sea?"

"Oh, it was beautiful. Flat as a dance floor. The snow was melting and the moss was green. Skeletons of walrus and polar bears lay among the sharp stones. They looked like the limbs of giants and were covered with green mold. One would think that the sun had never shone on them. I blew the fog away so that I could see a little better. Someone had built a shed from the wreckage of stranded ships, with walrus skin stretched over it; it had turned strange green and red colors. A polar bear sat on the roof and growled. I went down to the beach and had a look at the birds' nests there. They were filled with little naked offspring who were screaming with their bills open. I blew down into them; that taught them to keep their mouths shut. Down at the water's edge lay the walruses, looking like giant maggots with pigs' heads and teeth more than a yard long."

"You describe it well," admitted his mother. "My mouth waters, hearing about it."

"The Russians began to hunt the walruses. They thrust their harpoons into the animals, and the blood spouted like geysers high up in the air and spattered the white ice red. It made me think of playing a little game myself. I blew, and brought my own ships, the great icebergs, down to squeeze their boats. You should have heard them whimper and whine; but I whistled higher than they did. I held their ships in my vise of ice; they got so frightened that they started to unload the dead walruses and everything else they had aboard onto the ice. Then I sent them a snowstorm and let them drift south, for a taste of salt water. They will never return to the Barents Sea."

"Then you have done evil," said his mother.

"What good I do, I will let others tell about," said the north wind and grinned. "But there is my brother, the west wind. I like him better than the others, there is a smell of the salt sea about him and he brings some blessed coldness with him."

"Is that the gentle zephyr?" asked the prince.

"It is the zephyr, all right," said the old woman, "but he is not so gentle any more. When he was young he was a sweet-looking boy, but that is all gone now."

The west wind looked like a savage. He wore a helmet on his head. In his hand he held a big club that he had cut from a tree in one of the great mahogany forests of America.

"Where are you coming from?" asked his mother.

"From the great primeval forest," he answered, "where thorny liana stretches itself from tree to tree, where the water snake lives and man has never set foot."

"And what did you do there?"

"I looked at the deep river that fell from the cliffs down into the valley, sounding like thunder, and made a spray great enough to bear a rainbow. I saw a buffalo swim in the river; the currents caught it and carried it, among a flock of ducks, down toward the waterfall. When they came to the rapids, the ducks flew up; but the buffalo couldn't fly, it had to follow the water down the turbulent falls. Oh, I liked that sight so much that I blew a storm great enough to fell trees that have stood a thousand years and break them into kindling."

"Is that all you have done?" asked the old woman.

"I have turned somersaults on the savannah, patted wild horses, and blown down a coconut or two. I have a couple of stories I could tell; but it is best not to tell everything one knows. That you know well enough, old thing." He kissed his mother so that she almost fell over backward. Oh, he was a wild boy!

The south wind arrived; he wore a turban and a Bedouin's cape. "It's cold in here," he said, and threw more wood on the fire. "You can tell that the north wind came home first."

"It is so hot in here that you could fry polar bears," grumbled the north wind.

"You are a polar bear yourself," retorted the south wind angrily.

"Do you want to be put in the bag?" asked the old woman, and sounded as if she meant it. "Sit down, and tell us about the places you have been."

"In Africa, Mother," began the south wind, crestfallen. "I have been hunting lions with the Hottentots in the land of the Kaffirs; the great plains were olive green; here the antelopes danced, and I ran races with the ostriches, and won every time. I visited the desert, its yellow sand looked like the ocean's floor. There I met a caravan; they had just slaughtered the last of their camels, to get a little to drink. The sun burned down upon them from above, and the hot sand fried them. The great borderless desert stretched all around them. Then I played with the fine dry sand, I whirled it up in pillars, toward the sky. Oh, that was a dance. You should have seen the face of the merchant; he pulled his caftan up over his head to protect himself and then threw himself down in front of me, as if I were Allah, his God. I buried them all in a pyramid of sand. Next time I come I shall blow it away and let their bones be bleached by the sun, so that other travelers can see that which is hard to believe in the loneliness of the desert: the fact that other men have been there before them."

"You have only been evil," scolded his mother; "into the bag you go." She grabbed the south wind around his waist, bent him in half, and stuffed him into one of the leather bags. But the south wind wouldn't keep still and the bag jumped all over the floor; then his mother took it and, using it as a pillow, she sat down upon the bag and he had to lie quietly.

"You have got lively sons," said the prince.

"They are plucky enough; but I can manage them," answered the mother. "Here comes my fourth son."

It was the east wind; he was dressed as a Chinese.

"Oh, that is where you have been," said the mother, and nodded. "I thought you had been in the garden of Eden."

"No, that is where I fly tomorrow," replied the east wind. "Tomorrow it is exactly a hundred years since I was there last. Now I am coming from China. I have danced around the porcelain tower so swiftly that all the little bells rang. Down in the streets the state officials were getting a beating. I didn't count how many bamboo canes were worn out on their backs. All the officers from the first to the ninth grades were being punished. Every time they were hit, they screamed: 'Thank you, thank you, our father protector!' But they didn't mean a word of it, and I rang the bells of the tower, and sang: 'Tsing, tsang, tsu!' "

"You are getting a little too frisky," laughed his mother. "I am glad you are visiting paradise tomorrow; it always improves your manners. Remember to drink from the spring of wisdom, and to bring a bottle full of the water back to your mother."

"I certainly will," said the east wind, "but why have you put my brother from the south in his bag? Let him out. I want him to tell me all about the bird phoenix. The princess in the garden of Eden asks to hear about that bird whenever I visit her. Please let him out, and I shall give you two pocketfuls of tea. I picked it myself and it is fresh and green."

"In appreciation of the tea and because you are my favorite, I will let him out." The old woman untied the bag and the south wind climbed out; he looked embarrassed because the prince had seen his punishment.

"I have a palm leaf." The south wind carefully avoided looking at the prince while he spoke. "You can give it to the princess. On it, the bird phoenix has carefully written, with his bill, his whole life story, all that happened to him during the hundred years he lived. She can read it herself. I saw the bird phoenix set fire to its own nest, as if it were the wife of a Hindu. The dry branches crackled and the smoke had a strange fragrance. At last the bird itself burned with a clear flame and became ashes; and the egg lay red hot among the embers. The shell cracked with a bang like a cannon shot, and the young bird flew up. Now he is king of all the other birds; and the only phoenix in the whole world. He has bitten a mark in the palm leaf; that is his way of sending a greeting to the princess."

"No more talk, let us eat," said the mother of the winds, and started to carve the deer. The prince sat down next to the east wind and they were soon fast friends.

"Tell me," begged the prince, "who is this princess that you are all talking about, and where lies the garden of Eden?"

"Ah! Ha!" laughed the east wind. "Would you like to come along tomorrow? You must remember that no man has been there since Adam and Eve were thrown out. I assume you know about them from the Bible."

"Certainly," said the prince gravely.

"Well, when they were banished, the garden of Eden sank down underground, but it kept its beauty, its warmth and mild air. The queen of the fairies lives there, and there lies the Island of Bliss, where death can never come. If you will climb up on my back tomorrow, then I shall take you there. That is enough talking for tonight, I am tired."

Soon they all fell asleep. It was still early in the morning when the prince awoke, but to his surprise, he found himself flying high up among the clouds. The east wind was carrying him and had a good grasp on him so that he wouldn't fall. They were up so high that the earth below him with its forests and fields looked like a colored map.

"Good morning," said the east wind. "You could have slept a little longer yet. There is not much to look at, all the land below us is flat. But if you want to count the churches you can; they look like chalk marks on the green board down there." It was the fields and meadows the east wind referred to as the "green board."

"It wasn't very polite of me not to say good-by to your mother and your brothers."

"Never mind, a man who is asleep is excused!" grumbled the east wind, and flew even faster. As they passed over the treetops, all the leaves and branches rustled. When they crossed the sea, the waves grew white and the big ships curtsied deeply like swans.

When evening came, they flew in darkness over a great city. The thousands of lights burning below reminded the prince of the sparks that fly from a piece of paper when it has been set on fire. It was so lovely that the prince clapped his hands. But the east wind scolded him and said that he could make better use of his hands by holding on, or he might end up hanging from a church spire.

With grace the great eagles fly over the black forests, but the east wind flies more gracefully. Swift is the horse of the Cossacks, but the east wind is swifter.

"There are the Himalayas," said the east wind. "It is the highest mountain range in Asia; soon we shall be in the garden of Eden."

The wind turned in a southeasterly direction, and soon the prince could smell the fragrance of spices and flowers. Figs and pomegranates grew wild as did a vine that bore both red and blue grapes. Here they rested for a while and stretched themselves out in the soft grass. The flowers nodded to the wind as if they were saying, "Welcome back."

"Are we not in the garden of Eden?" asked the prince.

"Not yet," answered the wind, "but it won't be long now before we are there. Can you see the cave up on the side of that cliff? The grapevines almost hide it. We have to fly through it. Wrap your cape tightly around you. Here the sun is burning hot, but in there it is as cold as ice. The birds that fly past the opening of the cave have one wing in the warm summer and the other in the coldest of winters."

"So this is the gate of paradise," thought the prince as he wrapped himself in his cape. In they went, and cold it was; but the distance was short. The east wind spread out his wings, and they burned like fire, lighting the caves through which they flew. There were great blocks of stones, wet from the water endlessly dropping. They had the strangest shapes; some looked like organ pipes and others like banners. Sometimes the room was so large that the ceiling was lost in darkness; other times, the passages were so narrow that they had to crawl on all fours to get through them. The prince thought they looked like burial chambers.

"Are we taking Death's road to paradise?" he asked.

The east wind did not answer. He pointed toward a radiantly blue light ahead of them. The rocks gave way to a mist, which finally looked like a white cloud in the moonlight. It was no longer cold. The air was mild and fresh like mountain air, and yet filled with the fragrance of the roses that grew in the valley.

Below them was a river; its water was as transparent as air. Gold and silver fish swam in it; and so did scarlet eels. Each time they twisted their bodies, blue sparks flew and illuminated the water. The leaves of the water lilies were all the colors of the rainbow, and the flower itself was a flame that drew its substance from the water, as oil lamps draw theirs from oil. A marble bridge carved as intricately as if it had been ivory led to the Island of Bliss, where the garden of Eden lay.

The east wind carried the prince in his arms, across the river to the island, and set him down among the flowers. The leaves and the petals of the flowers sang to him all the songs he had heard as a child, but their voices were far more beautiful than human voices.

The prince could not recognize any of the trees. Were they palm trees or giant water plants? Certainly, he had never before seen any trees so succulent and tall. Long garlands of wonderful vines, like the ones that decorate old holy books and twist themselves around the gilded first letter on their pages, hung between the trees. Around him he saw the strangest mixtures of animals and plants. In the grass stood some peacocks with their great colorful tail feathers spread out. He drew nearer and touched them. They were not animals but giant burdock leaves as splendid as peacocks' tails. Lions and tigers jumped about among the bushes, tame as kittens. Doves as white as pearls beat their wings so near the lions that they touched their manes. Shy antelopes, with dark eyes as deep as pools, nodded their heads as if they, too, wanted to join the game.

There was the fairy, the princess of the garden of Eden. Her clothes were brighter than the sun, and her face as happy as a mother's when she looks at her sleeping child. She was young and beautiful; a train of lovely girls, each with a star in her hair, followed her.

The east wind gave her the palm leaf, the gift from the bird phoenix, and her eyes sparkled with joy. She took the prince by the hand and led him into her castle. The walls had the same transparency that you see when you hold a tulip petal up toward the sun and look through it. The ceiling was a shining flower and the longer you looked at it, the more magnificent it became.

The prince stepped over to one of the windows, looked out through it; and there he saw the tree of knowledge, the snake, and Adam and Eve. Surprised, he turned to the fairy and asked, "Have they not been banished?"

She smiled and explained to him that what he saw were pictures burned into the glass by Time itself. They were not like any painting he had seen, for they were alive: the leaves of the trees moved and the people portrayed in them came and went as in a mirror. He stood before another window and there he saw Jacob's ladder stretching far up into heaven, and he saw the angels, with their great wings, flying around it. Everything that had ever happened still lived inside these glass paintings. Such curious and wonderful works of art only Time could create.

The fairy smiled at his amazement and led the prince into another great hall in the castle, where the walls were transparent paintings of millions and millions of happy faces: all of them laughing and singing; and their laughter merged with the songs into one melodious hymn to happiness. The faces nearest the ceiling were as tiny as rosebuds, or the point you can make with a sharpened pencil on paper. In the middle of the hall grew a large tree and golden apples the color of oranges hid among its greenery. It was the tree of knowledge, the tree of good and evil, whose fruits Eve had picked and Adam eaten. From its leaves fell red dewdrops, as though the tree shed tears of blood.

"Come down into my little boat," bade the fairy. "It rocks as though it were floating on the swelling waters, and that is a most delightful feeling; but it never moves, though all the countries of the world will pass by for us to look at."

And they did; first the prince saw the snow-clad mountains of the Alps, with their black forests of fir trees and lace collars of clouds. He heard the melancholy sound of the hunters' horns and the herdsmen yodeling. The scene around them changed; banana palms bent their long leaves down toward them and coal-black swans swam near them; beyond the beach the most fantastic flowers bloomed. They were in the Dutch East Indies, the fifth continent. They heard the priests of the savages chant and saw them dance their wild dances. The islands and their blue mountains disappeared, and in their place rose the great pyramids of Egypt, the endless desert, the sphinx and ancient ruins of temples half buried beneath yellow sand. At last, northern lights burned above them, nature's fireworks, far more splendid than any man could construct. The prince was ever so happy; but then, he had seen a great deal more than I have described.

"Can I stay here forever?" he whispered.

"That depends upon yourself," answered the fairy. "If you do not let that which is forbidden tempt you, as Adam did, then you can live here forever."

"I won't touch the apples of the tree of knowledge," said the prince hastily. "There are so many other fruits as lovely as they."

"Examine your own heart, and if there is courage enough in it, then stay. But if you find doubt and weakness there, then ask the east wind to take you with him. He is leaving now and he will not be back for a hundred years. The years here pass like hours, but even a hundred hours are long enough for both temptation and sin. Every evening I shall leave you; and as I go I shall cry out to you to follow me. I shall wave my hand to beckon you to come. But do not obey me. Every step you take toward me will make it more difficult for you to turn back. If you follow me, you will enter the hall where the tree of knowledge grows; underneath its sweet-smelling branches I sleep. As you bend over me I shall smile, but if you kiss my mouth, then Eden's garden will sink down farther into the earth and will forever be lost for you. The cruel wind of the desert will enfold you and cold rain drip from your hair; and sorrow and care will be your lot."

"I will stay," said the prince.

The east wind kissed him on his forehead and said, "Be strong! And I shall see you again when a hundred years have passed. Farewell, farewell!" The east wind spread out his great wings that shone like the lightning of summer or the northern lights of winter.

"Farewell, farewell!" shouted all the flowers and the bushes; and the birds of the air followed him as far as the gate of the garden.

"Now begins our dance," whispered the fairy. "When it is over and the sun begins to set, I shall cry out, begging you to follow me. But do not do it. Every night for a hundred years this will happen; but each time you refuse me makes it easier for you to do it the next time, until at last it will give you no pain. This is the first night and I have warned you."

The fairy led him into a chamber made of white, transparent lilies; their yellow stamens were little golden harps and from them came the most delightful music. The loveliest young maidens, light and slender, danced around him; their gauzelike clothes, like mist, half concealed their beautiful bodies. They sang while they danced a hymn to life: to their own eternal life in paradise.

The sun was setting; the heavens became like gold and the lilies turned the color of roses. The maidens handed the prince a cup of wine; he drank it and felt even more intensely happy than he had before. The back wall of the chamber disappeared and he looked into the great hall where the tree of knowledge grew. Its beauty blinded him. The song coming from the countless faces on the wall sounded like his mother's voice singing to him: "My child, my dearest child."

The fairy waved to him, beckoned to him, and cried lovingly, "Follow me, follow me." He forgot all his promises and ran toward her, on this his very first evening in the garden of Eden. The fragrance of all the strange spices of the world that came from the garden grew stronger, and the music of the harps even more beautiful. In the hall of the tree, it seemed to him that all the millions of happy faces nodded yes, and sang, "One must know and experience everything; man is the master of the world." The dewdrops falling from the leaves of the tree of good and evil no longer looked like tears but like red shining stars.

"Follow me, follow me," whispered a voice, and for each step the prince took, his cheeks grew redder and his blood pulsed even faster through his veins.

"I must," he breathed, "it is no sin to follow beauty and happiness. I just want to see where she sleeps, I shall not kiss her. Nothing is lost unless I do that, and I shall not. I am strong, I am not weak!"

The fairy threw off her beautiful robes and disappeared in among the branches.

"I have not sinned yet," muttered the prince, "and I shall not do it." But he pulled the branches apart to look. There she lay sleeping, as beautiful as only the fairy in the garden of Eden can be. She smiled in her sleep; he bent over her and saw a tear hanging from her long eyelashes.

"Are you crying because of me?" he whispered. "Do not cry, fairest, most beautiful woman! Now I understand the happiness of paradise. It flows with my blood through my veins into my brain, my thoughts. I feel the strength of the angels' eternal life within my mortal body. Let everlasting night come, the riches of one moment like this are enough for me." He kissed away her tear, he kissed her eyes, and his mouth touched hers.

A fearful clap of thunder was heard, deeper, more frightening than any ever heard before. The fairy vanished and the garden of Eden sank into the earth: deep, deep down. The prince saw it disappear into the dark night like a far distant star. He felt a deathly coldness touch his limbs; his eyes closed, and he fell down as though he were dead.

The sharp lashes of the wind whipped his face and the cold rain drenched him, then he awoke. "What have I done?" he sighed. "I have sinned as Adam did. Sinned and caused paradise to sink deeper into the earth." He opened his eyes and saw a star blinking far away, sparkling as the garden of Eden had when it disappeared. It was the morning star.

He rose. He was in the forest near the cave of the winds; their mother was sitting on a tree stump. She looked at him with anger and disgust.

"Already the first evening," she scolded. "I thought so. If you were my boy, then I would put you in a bag."

"That is exactly what will happen to him," said Death, who was standing in the shadow of one of the big trees. He was a strong old man with a scythe in his hands and large black wings on his back.

"In a coffin I shall put him, but not now. Let him first wander about on earth, atoning for his sins, becoming good if he can. Then I shall come, when he least expects it, and put him in a black coffin. I shall carry him on my head to the stars, for there, too, blooms the garden of Eden; and if he has learned to be kind and good, then he shall live there forever. But if his heart and thoughts are filled with sin, then he shall sink in his coffin deeper into the earth than the garden of Eden sank. Only once every thousand years shall I come to fetch him, to find out whether he must be sent even deeper into the earth or be taken to the bright and sparkling star."

❋❖❋

The Flying Trunk

ONCE there was a merchant who was so rich that he could easily
have paved a whole street with silver coins and still have had enough
left over to pave a little alley as well. But he didn't do anything so
foolish, he made better use of his money than that. He didn't give out
a copper coin without getting a silver one in return; that's how good a
merchant he was, but he couldn't live forever.

His son inherited all his money, and he was better at spending than
at saving it. Every night he attended a party or a masquerade. He
made kites out of bank notes; and when he went to the beach, he
didn't skim stones; no, he skimmed gold coins. In that way, the
money was soon gone, and finally he had nothing but four pennies, a
pair of worn-out slippers, and an old dressing gown. He lost all his
friends; they didn't like to be seen with a person so curiously dressed.
But one of them was kind enough to give him an old trunk and say to
him, "Pack and get out." That was all very well, but he had nothing
to pack, so he sat down inside the trunk himself.

It was a strange trunk; if you pressed on the lock, then it could fly.
That is what the merchant's son did, and away it carried him. Up
through the chimney, up above the clouds and far, far away. The
trunk creaked and groaned; its passenger was afraid that the bottom
would fall out, for then he would have a nasty fall. But it didn't, the
trunk flew him directly to the land of the Turks and landed.

The merchant's son hid the trunk beneath some leaves in a forest
and started to walk into town. No one took any notice of him, for in
Turkey everyone wears a dressing gown and slippers.

He met a nurse carrying a babe in her arms. "Hey, you Turkish nurse," he said, "what kind of a castle is that one, right outside the city, with windows placed so high up the walls that no one but a giant could look through them?"

"That is where the princess lives," replied the nurse. "It has been prophesied that a lover will cause her great suffering and sorrow, that is why no one can visit her unless the king and the queen are present."

"Thank you," said the merchant's son. He ran back into the forest where he had hidden the trunk, climbed into it, and flew up to the roof of the palace; then he climbed through a window, in to the princess.

She was sleeping on a sofa and looked so beautiful that the merchant's son had to kiss her. She woke up and was terrified at the sight of the strange man, but he told her that he was the God of the Turks and that he had come flying through the air to visit her. That story didn't displease her.

They sat next to each other on the settee and he told her stories. He made up one about her eyes being the loveliest dark forest pools in which thoughts swam like mermaids. He told her that her forehead was a snow mountain filled with grand halls, whose walls were covered with beautiful paintings. And he told her about the storks that bring such sweet little children. Oh, they were delightful stories; then he proposed and she said yes.

"Come back on Saturday," she said, "then the king and queen come for afternoon tea. They will be proud that I am going to marry the God of the Turks. But make sure, sir, that you have some good fairy tales to tell them. My mother likes noble and moral stories, and my father lively ones that can make him laugh."

"Stories are the only wedding gift I shall bring," said the merchant's son, and smiled most pleasingly. Before they parted, the princess gave him a sword with a whole lot of gold coins attached to the hilt; and these he was in need of.

The merchant's son flew away and bought himself a new dressing gown. When he returned to the forest he started to compose the fairy tale that he would tell on Saturday. And that wasn't so easy. But finally he was finished and Saturday came.

The king, the queen, and the whole court were having tea with the princess. They greeted him most kindly.

"Now you must tell us a fairy tale," said the queen, "and I want it to be both profound and instructive."

"But at the same time funny," added the king.

"I will try," said the merchant's son.

Here is his story; if you listen carefully, you will understand it: "Once upon a time there were some sulphur matches who were extremely proud because they came of such good family. Their family tree, of which each of them was a tiny splinter, had been the largest pine tree in the forest. The matches lay on a shelf between a tinderbox and an old iron pot; and to them they told the story of their childhood and youth:

" 'Then we lived high, so to speak. We were served diamond tea every morning and evening; it is called dew. Whenever the sun was out it shone upon us, and all the little birds had to tell us stories. We knew that we were rich, for we could afford to wear our green clothes all year round, whereas the poor beeches and oaks had to stand quite naked in the winter and freeze. Then the woodcutter came, it was a revolution! The whole family was split. The trunk of our family tree got a job as the mainmast on a full-rigged ship; he can sail around the whole world if he feels like it. We are not sure what happened to the branches, but we got the job of lighting fires for the mean and base multitudes; that is how such noble and aristocratic things as we are ended up in the kitchen.'

" 'My life has been quite different,' said the iron pot that stood on the shelf beside the matches. 'From my very birth I have been scrubbed and set over the fire to boil. I have lost count of how many times that has happened. I do the solid, the most important work here, and should be counted first among you all. My only diversion is to stand properly cleaned on the shelf and engage in a dignified conversation with my friends. We are all proper stay-at-homes here, except for the water bucket, which does run down to the well every so often, and the market basket. She brings us news from the town, but as far as I am concerned it is all disagreeable. All she can talk about are the people and the government. Why, the other day an old earthen pot got so frightened that it fell down and broke in pieces. The market basket is a liberal!'

" 'You talk too much!' grumbled the tinderbox. 'Let us have a pleasant evening.' And the steel struck the flint so that sparks flew.

" 'Yes, let us discuss who is the most important person here,' suggested the matches.

" 'I don't like to talk about myself,' said an earthenware pot. 'Let's tell stories instead. I will begin with an everyday story, the kind that could have happened to any of us. I think that kind of story is the most amusing: *"By the Baltic Sea where the Danish beeches mirror their—"* '

" 'That is a beautiful beginning,' exclaimed the plates. 'We are sure we will love that story.'

" 'There I spent my youth in a quiet home,' continued the earthenware pot. 'The furniture was polished each week, the floors washed every second day, and the curtains were washed and ironed every fortnight.'

" 'How interestingly you describe it,' interrupted the feather duster. 'One can hear that a woman is talking, there is an air of cleanliness about it all.'

" 'How true, how true!' said the water bucket, and jumped, out of pure joy, several inches into the air.

"The earthenware pot told its story; and both the middle and the end were just as interesting as the beginning had been.

"All the plates clattered in unison as applause; and the feather duster took some parsley and made it into a garland with which to crown the pot. She knew it would irritate the others; besides, she thought, 'If I honor her today, she will honor me tomorrow.'

" 'We will dance,' said the big black pair of tongs; and so they did! Goodness, how they could stretch their legs. The cover on the old chair, over in the corner, split right down the middle just trying to follow them with his eyes. 'Where are our laurel leaves?' demanded the tongs when they had finished; and they were crowned with a garland too.

" 'Vulgar rabble,' thought the matches; but they didn't say it out loud.

"The samovar was going to sing; but it had caught cold—at least so it claimed, but it wasn't true. She was too proud; she would only sing in the dining room, when the master and mistress were present.

"Over on the window sill was an old pen that the maid used to write with. There was nothing special about it except that it had been dipped a little too deeply in the inkwell. The pen thought that this was a distinction and was proud of it. 'If the samovar won't sing,' remarked the pen, 'we shouldn't beg it to. Outside the window hangs a bird cage with a nightingale in it; why not let him sing? True, his voice is untrained and he is quite uneducated; but his song has a pleasing naïve simplicity about it.'

" 'I object. I think it is most improper,' complained the teakettle, who was a half sister of the samovar. 'Why should we listen to a foreign bird? Is that patriotic? Let the market basket judge between us.'

" 'I am annoyed and irritated,' shouted the market basket. 'It is most aggravating; what a way to spend an evening! Let's put everything back in its right place, then I'll rule the roost, as I ought to. And you'll see what a difference that will make.'

" 'Let's make noise! Let's make noise!' screamed all the others.

"At that moment the door opened and the maid entered. Instantly, they stood still and kept quiet, every one of them. But even the smallest earthenware pot thought to herself, 'I am really the most important person here in the kitchen and, if I had wanted to, I could have made it into a most amusing evening.'

"The maid took a match, struck it, and lighted the fire. 'Now everyone can see,' thought the match, 'that we are the true aristocrats here. What a flame we make. What glorious light!' And that was the end of the match, it burned out."

"That was a lovely fairy tale," said the queen. "I feel just as if I had been in the kitchen with the matches. You shall have our daughter."

"Certainly," said the king. "We will hold the wedding on Monday," and he patted the merchant's son on the back, for now he was part of the family.

On Sunday evening the whole town was illuminated in honor of the impending marriage. Buns and pretzels were given away to everyone; and the street urchins whistled through their fingers. It was a moving sight.

"I'd better add to the festivities," thought the merchant's son. He went out and bought all the fireworks he could, put them in the trunk, and flew up in the air.

Ah! how high he flew and the fireworks sputtered, glittered, and banged. Such a spectacle no one had seen before. All the Turks jumped a foot up into the air and lost their slippers. Now they knew it was the God of the Turks who would be marrying their princess.

When the merchant's son had returned in his trunk to the forest, he decided to go back into town in order to hear what everyone was saying about his performance—and it's quite understandable that he should want to.

And the things that people said! Everyone had seen something different, but they all agreed that it was marvelous.

"I saw the God himself," said one man. "He had eyes like stars and a beard like the foaming ocean."

"He flew wearing a cloak of fire," said another, "and the prettiest cherubs were peeping out from under its folds."

It was all very pleasing to hear; and tomorrow was his wedding day!

He hurried back to the forest to sleep the night away in his trunk. But where was it?

It had burned to ashes. A little spark from one of the fireworks had ignited it; and that was the end of the trunk, and the merchant's son too! Now he could not fly to his bride.

She waited for him on the roof all day. She is still waiting for him, while he is wandering around the world, telling fairy tales; but they are not so lighthearted as the one he told about the sulphur matches.

The Storks

ON the roof of the last house at the edge of the town, storks had built their home. The mother stork was sitting in the nest. Her four little ones stuck their heads up and peeped out over the edge. Their bills were still black, for they were so young that they had not yet turned red. A few feet away on the ridge of the roof stood their father, as rigidly as a soldier on guard. He was standing on one leg, as still as a wooden statue.

"It looks very distinguished to have a sentry at the nest," he thought. "No one knows that it is my own family; people passing by will believe that I am here on duty. It looks most noble." So he stayed where he was without blinking an eyelid.

Some children were playing down in the street. They looked up at the storks, and the boldest boy among them began singing the old nursery rhyme about the storks. Soon the other joined him:

> "Stork, stork, with legs so long,
> And wings so broad and strong,
> Fly home to your wife and your nest.
> The four young ones you love best:
> The first shall be hanged from the gallow,
> The second shall be dipped in tallow,
> The third shall be plucked and burned,
> The fourth upside down shall be turned."

"Listen to what the boys are singing," said the young storks. "They say we are going to be hanged and burned."

"Don't listen to them," advised their mother. "What one does not hear cannot hurt one."

But the little boys kept singing and pointing their fingers at the storks. Only one of them—his name was Peter—said it was a shame to make fun of the birds, and he wouldn't join the others in their naughty game.

The mother tried to comfort her young ones. "Don't pay any attention to them," she said. "Look how calmly your father is standing guard on one leg."

"We are still afraid," squeaked the young storks, and hid beneath their mother.

The next day the children were playing in the street again, and when they saw the storks they began to sing the song once more:

> "The first shall be hanged from the gallow,
> The second shall be dipped in tallow,
> The third shall be plucked and burned,
> The fourth upside down shall be turned."

"Are we really to be hanged and burned?" asked the young storks again.

"Nonsense!" said their mother. "You are going to learn to fly, then we will visit the meadow and the lake. The frogs will give us a concert, Croak . . . Croak! Afterward we eat them, it is a marvelous amusement!"

"What happens after that?" asked her young ones.

"Then comes the harvest maneuvers, when all the storks in the whole district gather together. It is of great importance to be able to fly well then, for if you can't the general kills you. He sticks his bill right into your heart. So pay attention and learn your lessons."

"So we are going to be killed after all," exclaimed the young storks. "Listen, the boys are singing that song again."

"Listen to me and not to those bad boys," grumbled their mother. "After the great maneuvers, we fly to the hot countries. They are far from here. We have to fly over forests and mountains. We travel to Egypt, where they have triangular stone houses so high that their tops reach the clouds; they are called pyramids. They are so ancient that no stork can remember when they were built. Near them flows a river with muddy banks; one walks in mud and eats frogs all day."

"Oh," sighed her young ones.

"Yes," continued their mother, "one does nothing else but eat all day. While we are living in comfort, it is so cold up here that there is not a green leaf left, and all the clouds freeze to pieces and fall down as little white flakes."

"Do the naughty children freeze to pieces too?" asked the young storks.

"Not quite, but almost. They have to stay inside, in little dark rooms, while you are free to fly about among the flowers in the warm sunshine."

Time passed and the young storks were old enough to stand up in the nest and look about them. Their father came every day with frogs, little snakes, and other goodies that he found. He was fond of his children and did his best to amuse them. He twisted his long neck and made noise with his bill and told them stories about the swamp.

"Now I will have to teach you to fly," said their mother one day, and commanded all four of them up on the ridge of the roof. There they stood, and none too steadily; they used their wings to balance themselves, but they almost fell down.

"Now look at me," commanded their mother. "This is the way you must hold your head, and this the way to keep your legs. One . . . two, one . . . two. You flap your wings; they will bring you ahead in this world."

The mother stork flew in a little circle around the house and landed again. The young ones made some clumsy hops and one of them almost fell off the roof.

"I don't want to learn to fly," said the one that had almost fallen, and climbed back into the nest. "I don't care about the warm countries."

"Do you want to freeze to death when winter comes? Shall I call the boys, so that they can come and hang or burn you?"

"Oh no," said the little stork, and jumped out on the roof again.

By the third day of their training they could really fly. One of them thought that he could sit down in the air as in the nest; but then he fell and learned that to stay in the air you have to use your wings. The boys down in the street were still singing their stupid song.

"Shouldn't we fly down and prick out their eyes?" suggested one of the young storks.

"No nonsense here!" called the mother. "Listen to me, that is more important than anything else. One . . . two . . . three. First we circle to the left around the chimney, then we turn and fly the opposite way around. . . . That was fine! You have been so good that tomorrow I am going to take you all down to the swamp. You will meet some other distinguished families of storks there. Now make sure you behave yourselves better than all the other children there. Remember to hold your heads high and walk straight. It not only looks fine but makes the others respect you."

"But aren't we to avenge ourselves on the naughty children?" asked the young storks.

"Let them scream as loudly as they wish. You will fly high above the clouds, and see the pyramids, while they will stay and freeze here, where there is not a green leaf anywhere or a sweet apple for them to eat."

"We want our revenge anyway," the young ones whispered, though not so loud that their mother could hear them.

The child who had started singing the song and mocked the storks most was only six years old and small for his age at that. But the young storks thought he was a hundred, for he was much bigger than their father and mother. They had no real idea of the difference between children and grownups, and all their hate and wish for revenge were directed toward this particular little boy. He had started it and was the worst child, as far as they were concerned. As the storks grew their anger against the children grew too; and at last their mother had to promise them that they would have their vengeance, but she wanted them to wait until one of the days just before they left.

"I have to see first how you get along on the great harvest maneuver. If your flying is too poor, then the general will put his bill right through you and pierce your heart, and then, after all, the boys will be proven right and you can't blame them."

"We will do our best," said the young storks, and they did. They trained every day, and soon flew so well in formation that it was a pleasure to watch them.

The harvest began and all the storks gathered in preparation for the long flight down to Africa. It was a grand maneuver; in great flocks, they flew over the forests and the towns, and the general observed each one's flight closely. The young storks in this story did particularly well; they were given the grade: A plus frogs and snakes!

That was the best grade one could get, and they were allowed to eat the frogs and snakes and that they quickly did.

"Now is the time for our revenge," they demanded.

"Yes," said their mother. "I have thought about it and now I know how it shall be done. There is a pond where all the little children lie until the stork comes and gets them for delivery to their parents. There they lie dreaming far more pleasantly than they ever will later in their lives. All parents love and desire such little sweet babes and all children want a little sister or little brother. Now we will fly to that pond and bring all the good children who didn't sing the ugly song a little brother or sister; but the bad ones shan't ever get any."

"But the one who started it all, that ugly, horrible little boy," screamed all the young storks, "what shall we do to him?"

"In the pond there is a dead child," said the mother. "He has dreamed himself to death. We will bring that baby to the boy and he will cry because we have brought him a dead little brother. But in all your anger, have you forgotten the good little boy who shamed the others when they made fun of you? Him we will bring both a brother and a sister; and since his name is Peter, you shall all be called Peter."

All that the mother said came true, and the storks in Denmark are still called Peter, even to this day.

The Sandman

IN ALL the world there is no one who knows so many stories as the sandman, and he knows how to tell them, too.

When it is evening and children are sitting around a table or in a corner on a stool, then he comes sneaking up the stairs; he walks on his stocking feet and makes no noise. Quietly he opens the door and slips into the room and throws a little sand into the eyes of the children; then they find it difficult to keep them open. He stands behind them and blows softly down their necks; and their heads seem, oh, so heavy! But it doesn't hurt, for the sandman loves children. He just wants them to get into bed and lie there quietly, so that he can tell them stories.

When the children have fallen asleep, the sandman sits on their beds. He wears very strange clothes; his suit is made out of silk, but it is quite impossible to tell what color it is, for it changes all the time. One moment it is green, the next it's red, and then it may turn blue. Under each arm he has an umbrella: one of them is all covered with pictures, and that he puts on the headboards of the beds of good children, so that they will dream wonderful stories all the night through. The other umbrella has no pictures at all; that is the one bad children get. They toss and turn all night; and when they wake in the morning, they haven't dreamed anything at all.

Now I want to tell you the stories that the sandman told a little boy named Hjalmar during one week. There are seven stories, for there are seven days in a week.

MONDAY

"Now look," said the sandman that evening after he had gotten Hjalmar into bed, "I think I'll fix up your room a little."

At once all the potted plants grew into huge trees that reached all the way to the ceiling. They stretched their limbs across it, and up and down the walls. The room became the loveliest green arbor. On all the branches flowers bloomed; every one of them was more beautiful and fragrant than a rose; and if you ate them, they tasted sweeter than jam. There were fruits on the trees that shone like gold, and buns bursting with raisins. Oh, it was quite marvelous! But amidst all this splendor, someone was unhappy. The sound of sighing and whimpering came from the table drawer where Hjalmar kept his schoolbooks.

"Now what is the matter?" said the sandman as he opened the drawer.

It was the slate that was sighing; Hjalmar had done his sums on it, and added everything up wrong. The slate pencil, which hung from a piece of string at the corner of the slate, was jumping about in agony as a little dog does on a leash. It wanted to help but it couldn't. Hjalmar's exercise book was sobbing too; it was heartrending to hear. On the top of each page were printed the most exquisite letters, models for the student to copy. Hjalmar had tried, but his letters did not resemble the printed ones: they didn't stand up straight, but more or less dragged themselves along the lines; they looked as if they were fainting or having fits.

"Stand up straight!" screamed the printed letters. "Look at us!"

"Oh, we would love to," sighed Hjalmar's letters. "But we can't, we are not feeling well."

"You should have cod-liver oil," said the sandman.

That helped; the letters that Hjalmar had written got so frightened that they immediately straightened themselves.

"I see there won't be any time for stories tonight; I'd better drill them!" said the sandman as he looked severely at the poor letters. They, in turn, blushed; and all the A's appeared really ashamed.

"Left . . . right . . . left . . . right," he commanded. And the letters obeyed him as if they were soldiers. Soon they stood as straight and handsome as their printed brothers. But the next morning, when Hjalmar peeped at them, they looked just as wretched as they had the day before.

TUESDAY

As soon as Hjalmar had got into bed the sandman touched all the furniture in the room with his magic wand; and they began to talk. They all talked about themselves except for the spittoon; it stood silently in its corner, it was so disgusted by the vanity and egocentricity of all the others, who only thought about themselves and never —not even for a moment—of poor creatures like himself, who had to stand in a corner and be spit at.

On the wall above the chest of drawers hung a painting of a landscape, with trees, flowers, and a meadow. In the background there were several castles; it was a very pretty painting, framed in gold. The sandman touched the painting and everything within it became alive. The birds began to sing and the branches of the trees swayed in the wind. The clouds sailed in the sky, casting their shadows upon the grass in the meadow.

The sandman lifted the sleeping Hjalmar out of his bed and held him up to the picture. The boy took a step, and there he was, inside the painting. The sun was shining through the leaves of the trees. He ran down to the river; there was a little sailing ship moored to the bank. It was painted red and white. The sails shone like silver; and six swans, with golden crowns on their heads, drew it through the water. Hjalmar sailed past the forest and the trees told him stories about robbers, witches, the little elves that lived in flowers, and the tales that they—the trees—had heard from the butterflies.

The most wonderful fish, with silver and gold scales, swam around the boat; they jumped out of the water into the air and then fell with a splash back down into the river. Birds of all colors and sizes flew above him. All the animals, even the mosquitoes and flying beetles, wanted to get near Hjalmar; and each one had a little story to tell him.

It was a real voyage. At one moment Hjalmar was sailing through a dense, dark forest, and the next, through a beautiful garden filled with sunlight and flowers. He sailed past marble castles, and on their balconies stood the loveliest princesses; and the strangest part of it was that they looked exactly like the girls he played with every day. The princesses were holding sugar pigs that were better than the ones you could buy in the market place. The girls offered to share them with Hjalmar. When he took hold of an end of a pig, it broke off and he always received the larger piece and the princess the smaller one. In front of every castle a little prince with a golden sword stood guard; and when Hjalmar sailed by, they ordered it to rain tin soldiers and raisins—for they were real princes.

Sometimes he seemed to be sailing through the halls of great mansions, and at other times, right through fantastic towns. He visited the one where the nursemaid lived, who had taken care of him when he was a baby. Hjalmar loved her dearly. There she stood on the square waving to him and singing a little verse about him, which she had composed herself:

> "Oh, my little boy, how I do miss
> The sight of your sweet face,
> The little mouth that I did kiss,
> Your trusting, innocent gaze.
> I shared your laughter, your mirth;
> And yet we had to part.
> May God bless you on this earth,
> And keep pure your loving heart."

And all the birds joined her song. The flowers danced and the trees nodded, as if they, too, had been told stories by the sandman.

WEDNESDAY

It was pouring outside. Hjalmar could hear the rain beating on the roof, even though he was sleeping. The sandman opened the window. The street had become a lake and right below Hjalmar's window a great ship was moored.

"Come for a sail, Hjalmar," said the sandman. "This ship will take you far away; and yet, when you wake up tomorrow, you will be back in your bed."

Hjalmar stood up and got dressed in his Sunday suit. Once he was on the deck of the ship, it was no longer raining, the sun was shining. A wind gently filled the sails. The ship tacked around the church and through the streets. Soon it was out on the ocean. As far as the eye could see stretched the wild sea. Hjalmar saw a flock of storks; they were on their way to the hot countries. One of the storks flew low and far behind the others. They had been flying for days, and this stork was ever so tired. Its great wings beat slower and slower, as it came nearer and nearer to the surface of the sea. It tried to gain height but it couldn't; then it collided with the sail of the ship, falling with a loud bump, down on the deck.

The cabin boy picked it up and put it in the little hen coop amidships. There it stood looking very bedraggled and sad among the hens, ducks, and turkeys.

"What a creature!" cackled all the hens.

The turkey cock rustled his feathers and made himself look twice as big as he was; then he spoke to the stork, asking him who he was and where he came from.

The ducks nudged each other and said, "Quack . . . quack!"

The stork told them about the hot countries, about Egypt with its pyramids, and the ostrich that can run across the desert sands faster than a horse.

The ducks didn't understand a word he said and, therefore, remarked to each other, "Let us agree that he is stupid."

"Certainly he is stupid," gobbled the turkey cock, making so much noise that the stork stopped talking. He just stood in a corner of the coop and thought about Africa.

"What beautiful long thin legs," gobbled the turkey. "What do they cost a yard?"

"Quack quack quack!" laughed all the ducks, while the stork pretended that he hadn't heard the insult.

"You ought to join in the merriment," said the turkey, "for it was very witty indeed. Or do you find it too low a joke? I mean for someone like you who has such high legs? Gobble! Gobble!" laughed the turkey. "You have no sense of humor. The rest of us have both wit and intellect; we are most interesting!"

The turkey gobbled and the ducks quacked, for they found themselves ever so amusing.

Hjalmar walked over to the hen coop, opened the door, and let the stork out. Now that it was rested, the stork could fly again. It nodded to Hjalmar as though it were saying thank you; and then it spread its great wings and flew south toward Egypt.

The hens clucked; the ducks quacked; and the turkey cock got all red in the face.

"Tomorrow we are going to cook soup of you," said Hjalmar, and then he woke up. He was back in his little bed. That certainly had been a strange journey the sandman had taken him out on.

THURSDAY

"Now!" began the sandman. "Don't be afraid, here is a little mouse." And he held a little sweet furry animal up to Hjalmar. "It has come to invite you to a wedding; two of the little mice who live beneath the floor of your mother's larder have decided to marry. They have a beautiful apartment down there."

"But how will I get down through the mousehole?" asked Hjalmar.

"Let me see," said the sandman thoughtfully. "I will have to make you smaller." He touched Hjalmar with his magic wand. Instantly the boy began to grow smaller, until finally he wasn't larger than your forefinger. "Now you can borrow the tin soldier's uniform; it is always nice to wear a uniform when you are invited out."

"I will," said Hjalmar; and in a moment he had the uniform on and looked like the nicest little tin soldier.

"Please, sir, would you be so kind as to sit down in your mother's thimble? That will be your carriage and I will be your horse," said the little female mouse.

"Am I to be pulled by a girl? Won't it be too hard work?" asked Hjalmar politely; but he was already on his way to the mouse wedding. They were driving in a long corridor that was just wide enough for the mouse and her guest to pass through. It wasn't dark at all. Little pieces of dry rotten wood illuminated the way.

"Doesn't it smell lovely here?" asked the mouse. "The hall has been greased with lard, and that of the best quality."

Now they entered the chamber where the wedding was to take place. To the right stood all the female mice; they were whispering to each other and making faces. To the left stood the male mice; they were stroking their whiskers but didn't say much. In the middle of the room were the bridal couple; they sat on a cheese rind and kissed each other all the time, which was permissible in public, for they were engaged and soon would be married.

More and more guests arrived. The room was soon so crowded that the smaller mice had to stay in the corners or they would have been trampled to death. It didn't help that the bridal couple were now standing in the doorway and nearly blocking it. The room had been greased with lard, just like the corridor: that was the wedding feast, which the guests could munch on whenever they wished. As dessert a pea was served; in it, a member of the family had bitten the bridal couple's initials. It was most extraordinary!

All the mice declared that it had been a marvelous wedding and that the conversation had been extremely intelligent.

When it was over, the little female mouse drove Hjalmar back. It had certainly been a distinguished feast he had been invited to attend. But he had had to make himself small and put on a tin soldier's uniform.

FRIDAY

"There are so many grownups who plague me to come and visit them," said the sandman, "especially those who have a bad conscience. 'Oh, kind sandman,' they beg, 'please come. We can't sleep; our eyes won't close. We have to lie awake all night and look at our bad deeds. They sit like little trolls at the end of our beds and throw boiling water on us to keep us awake. Won't you come and tell them to go away so that we can sleep?' And then they sigh so deeply and say, 'We will pay you for it. Just come and say good night to us, sweet sandman. We have put the money on the window sill.' But that kind of favor you can't buy for money," explained the sandman.

"What is going to happen tonight?" asked Hjalmar.

"Would you like to go to another wedding?" laughed the sandman. "It will be a little different from the one you went to last night. Your sister's doll—the one that is dressed as a man and whom you all call Herman—wants to marry the doll named Bertha. It is Bertha's birthday today and she's expecting a lot of presents."

"Oh, I know all about that." Hjalmar sounded bored. "My sister is always making birthday parties or holding weddings for her dolls, especially when they need new clothes. I think she has done it a hundred times."

"But tonight is the hundred and first time, and that is an anniversary that doesn't take place often. When that is over, everything is over. Come take a look!"

Hjalmar glanced toward the table where his playthings were. There was light in the window of the little paper dollhouse; and outside it stood all his tin soldiers and presented arms. The bridal couple sat on the floor. They were leaning their backs against the leg of the table and looking pensively at each other—and that was not so strange; after all, they were getting married.

The sandman had put on Hjalmar's grandmother's skirt and was busy performing the marriage ceremony. As soon as it was over all the furniture sang this beautiful song, which the pencil had written especially for the occasion; he didn't care whether the words made sense so long as they rhymed.

> Wedding one hundred and one
> Has only just begun.
> He is proud as a pin,
> She is made of skin.
> Hurrah for pin, hurrah for skin
> Whose married life does now begin!

Then it was time to give presents, but the two dolls had declared they didn't want anything eatable, they were going to live on love.

"Should we go to the country or travel abroad for our honeymoon?" asked the groom.

This was a weighty problem; and therefore both the swallow, who had traveled widely, and the old hen from the farmyard, who had hatched five broods of chickens, were asked to give their opinions. The swallow told all about the countries of the south, where grapes hung in clusters on the vines and the air was mild and warm. He described the mountains and their strange and beautiful colors, so different from those one can see in the north.

"Ah, but they don't have any kale!" clucked the hen. "I spent one summer out in the country, I had my little chickens with me. We vacationed in a gravel pit. Sand is so delightful to scratch and scrape in. And we were allowed to visit the part of the garden where the kale grew. It had a lovely green color; I am sure that nothing has a more beautiful color."

"But one kale plant looks just like all the others," said the swallow, "and besides, the weather is always so bad here."

"We are used to that," replied the hen.

"But it is always cold, I am freezing," shivered the swallow.

"That is good for the kale," cackled the hen. "Besides, sometimes the weather is hot here too. I remember a summer four years ago; it lasted almost five weeks. It was so hot you could hardly breathe. Besides in foreign lands they have all sorts of creepy poisonous things, and bandits. I think that people who don't love their native land are ungrateful scoundrels who shouldn't be allowed to live here." And the hen began to cry, though she continued to talk. "I have traveled myself once, twelve miles in a wooden crate. Believe me, traveling is no pleasure."

"I think the hen is a very sensible woman," said the doll called Bertha. "I don't like to travel in mountains myself. What is it but up one side and down the other? No, let us move out to a gravel pit and go for walks among the kale stalks."

And that was what they decided to do.

SATURDAY

"Are you going to tell me a story?" asked Hjalmar as soon as he had gotten into bed.

"No, tonight I haven't got time for one," said the sandman, and opened his most beautiful umbrella over Hjalmar's bed. "But you can look at this. It is all Chinese."

Suddenly the umbrella looked like a Chinese bowl. Inside it there was a whole world: blue trees and blue bridges, with little Chinese men and women standing on them and nodding their heads at Hjalmar.

"Today I have to see to it that the whole world is properly cleaned, for tomorrow is Sunday, you know. I have to go to the church towers to find out whether the church elves have remembered to polish the bells, so they won't sound false. Then I have to go out into the fields and inspect them, to make sure that the wind has dusted all the flowers and trees. But the most important work is to take down all the stars and polish them. I put them in my apron; but first I have to number all the holes so that I can put them back in the right place again. If I don't, some of them might not fit correctly; then they might slip out and there would be too many shooting stars, falling down one after the other."

"Now look here, Mr. Sandman," said the old portrait of Hjalmar's great-grandfather, which hung on the wall opposite Hjalmar's bed. "I am the boy's great-grandfather, and I am pleased that you tell Hjalmar stories, but you must not confuse the child. One cannot take down stars and polish them; the stars are planets like our earth; and that is exactly what is so exciting about them."

"Thank you, thank you, old Great-grandfather," said the sandman; but he didn't look the least bit grateful. "You are the head of the family, the great head, the grand head. But I am a great deal older than you are; I am a heathen. The Romans and the Greeks worshiped me and called me the God of Dreams. I have visited the grandest palaces and am still a welcome guest anywhere. I know how to please both children and grownups. But why don't you tell a story?" With these words the sandman left, taking his umbrella with him.

"These days, one is not even allowed to express an opinion," grumbled Great-grandfather's portrait. And then Hjalmar woke up.

SUNDAY

"Good evening," said the sandman.

Hjalmar nodded his head as a greeting, then jumped out of bed, ran over to Great-grandfather's portrait and turned his face to the wall so he couldn't interrupt as he had done yesterday.

"Now tell me the story about the five peas in the pod, the tale of the cock that crowed too loud, and the one about the darning needle that was so proud that she thought she was a sewing needle," demanded Hjalmar.

"That was a lot," said the sandman. "You know, you can get too much of a good thing. Besides, I like to show you things rather than tell you stories. I think I will let you see my brother; he is also called the sandman, but he only visits you once and then he carries you away on his horse. He tells you a story, but he only knows two. One is the loveliest story ever told, so beautiful that you cannot imagine it; the other is so ugly and terrifying that it, too, is indescribable." The sandman lifted little Hjalmar up so that he could see out the window. "There rides my brother, the other sandman who is called Death. He is not really as frightening or horrible as he is portrayed in books. He is not a skeleton. That is just the silver embroidery on his uniform. Being in the cavalry, he rides a horse. Look at his lovely velvet cape fluttering in the wind behind him as he gallops by."

And Hjalmar saw how Death rode and dismounted to take away the people who had died; some were old, but others were young. Some he placed in front of him and others behind him. He asked everyone the same question: "How is your report card?"

And all of them replied: "Oh, it is fine!" But he was not satisfied with their answers, he had to look himself. Everyone who had good marks he put in front of him, and to them he told the loveliest story in the world; but those who had bad marks he put behind him, and they were told a terrible story. They cried and wanted to jump down from the horse but they couldn't.

"I think Death is a nice sandman," said Hjalmar. "I am not afraid of him."

"Oh, there is no reason to be," smiled the sandman. "Just make certain that you have a good report card."

"Now that is what I call a very instructive story," mumbled Great-grandfather's picture. "You see, it helps to complain and express one's opinion." Now he was satisfied.

Now you have heard the story of the sandman. You can ask him to tell you stories, himself, when he comes tonight.

16

❖

The Rose Elf

IN THE middle of the garden grew a rosebush; it was filled with flowers, and in the most beautiful of them all lived an elf. He was so small that he could not be seen by the human eye. Within every petal of the rose he had a bedchamber. He was wonderfully well proportioned and as lovely as any child. From his shoulders to his heels stretched his beautiful wings. Oh, what fragrant air there was where he slept; and how clear and transparent were the walls, for they were the delicate pink petals of a rose.

All day the little elf flew about in the warm sunshine. He visited all the flowers in the garden, rode on the backs of butterflies, and just for fun he counted how many steps long all the roads and paths on a linden leaf were. What he called roads and paths we call the veins of the leaf; but he was so tiny that they seemed to him like endless roads. The sun set before he was finished, for he had started the work too late.

It was chilly. The dew was falling, and the evening breeze began to blow. The elf hurried home as fast as he could but the rose had already closed itself for the night. He couldn't get in. He flew around the bush but not one of the flowers was open. The poor little elf became frightened. He had spent every night of his life sleeping sweetly within the petal of a rose. Never before had he been out in the dark. "Oh, this will be my death!" he muttered.

At the end of the garden there was an arbor whose latticework was covered with honeysuckle. The flowers looked like painted trumpets; and inside one of these, the elf hoped he would be able to sleep.

He flew toward the shaded nook but someone was there: two human beings, a beautiful young woman and a handsome young man. They sat close to each other on the little bench and wished never to be separated, for they loved each other, even more than the best little child loves his father and mother.

"We must part," the young man said, and sighed. "Your brother frowns on our love and that is why he is sending me away. I am going on a business trip far, far away, across the mountains. Farewell, my sweet bride! For my bride you are!"

They kissed and the young girl wept. She picked a rose for him, but before she handed it to the young man, she kissed it so passionately that the flower opened. The elf flew into the rose and leaned his head up against one of the fragrant, soft walls: at last, he had got inside! Through the petals of the rose he could hear the two young people saying good-by to each other. The young man pinned the rose on his chest. Oh, how his heart beat! The little elf couldn't sleep for all the noise.

As the young man walked through the dark forest he took the rose in his hand. Again and again he kissed it, so fervently that he almost crushed the elf to death. He could feel how the young man's lips burned; and the rose opened itself as if it were midday.

Another man was also afoot in the forest that night: the young girl's evil brother. In his hand he had a long sharp knife. While the young man kissed his rose, the evil man stabbed him to death. He cut off his head; and then buried both head and body in the soft earth under a linden tree.

"Now he is gone and soon he will be forgotten," thought the evil man. "He was supposed to go on a long journey across the mountains. On such a trip one can easily lose one's life, and that is what will have happened to him. He will never return and my sister will never dare ask me why."

He covered the newly dug earth with leaves and twigs and walked home through the dark night. But he was not as alone as he thought he was, for the little elf was with him. He was inside a rolled-up, withered linden leaf that had fallen into the evil man's hair, while he made the grave. Afterward the murderer had put his hat on again; and in the darkness the poor little elf shook both with fear and with anger, thinking of the ugly deed he had witnessed.

At sunrise the evil man returned to his house. He took his hat off and went into his sister's bedchamber. The beautiful young girl was still asleep, dreaming about the young man she loved, who she thought had started on his long journey across the mountains. Her evil brother bent over her and laughed: the laughter of a devil. The leaf fell from his hair without his noticing it. He tiptoed out of his sister's room and went to his own, to sleep.

The little elf rushed out of the leaf and into the sleeping girl's ear. He told her of the evil deed he had seen. To the girl it was like a dream. He described how her brother had murdered the young man she loved and buried him under a flowering linden tree; then he explained where in the forest the linden tree was. Finally he remarked, "You will find on your bed a wizened linden leaf and then you will know that this is not a dream."

The girl woke and there was the leaf! Oh, how she cried! How many salt tears she shed. And there was no one to comfort her, no one she could tell of her misery. The window was open; the elf could have flown out to his rose in the garden; but he could not bear to leave the girl all alone. On the window sill was a plant, and there on a flower he spent the rest of the day.

Several times the evil brother came. He joked and laughed boisterously. The poor girl did not dare show her sorrow.

As soon as night came, she sneaked out of the house and went to the forest to find the linden tree. Beneath it she dug up the corpse of the young man she loved. She cried and lamented and prayed to God that she, too, soon would die.

She would have liked to take his body back to have it properly buried, but that was impossible. She held the head in her hands and kissed the cold, pale lips; then she shook the earth out of his beautiful hair.

"This shall be mine forever," she said. She covered the dead body; and walked home, carrying her lover's head and the branch of a jasmine bush that grew near the linden tree.

As soon as she returned, she buried the head of the young man in the largest flowerpot she could find, and planted the jasmine branch above it.

"Farewell," whispered the little elf. He could no longer bear to see the girl's sorrow and flew out into the garden to find his rose. Only a few petals clung to the green hip; the flower bloomed no more.

"Soon all that is beautiful will fade and disappear," sighed the elf.

But he did find one rose that still had fragrant petals in which he could live.

Every morning he flew to the poor girl's window. He always found her standing by the flowerpot crying, her tears falling on the branch from the jasmine bush; and as the poor girl grew paler and paler, the jasmine branch grew greener. New leaves unfolded and soon white flower buds appeared. The girl kissed them. Her brother chided her and said she must be crazy or stupid to stand like that, crying before a plant. He did not know whose bright eyes and red lips had become dust beneath the lovely jasmine.

One day the young girl rested her head on the window sill next to the flowerpot and fell asleep. The elf found her slumbering and crawled into her ear to tell her about the evenings in the arbor, when the sweet-smelling roses were in bloom. And while she dreamed, her life ebbed out. She died and went to heaven where she was reunited with the young man whom she loved.

The jasmine flowers, like great white bells, opened and spread their sweet fragrance throughout the room; that was their way of crying for the dead.

When the evil brother saw the beautiful flowering bush he took it into his own bedchamber, as if it were his inheritance. It was so pleasant to look at and smelled so nicely. The little elf followed him and then flew from flower to flower to tell everyone of the evil brother's deed and the poor girl's suffering—for in every flower grew a soul that could understand.

"We know all about it," said the flowers. "We know everything! Haven't we grown from the eyes and lips of the dead man? We know all! We know all!"

The little elf could not understand how the flowers could be so calm. He flew out to the bees, who were collecting honey, and told them the story. They, in turn, told it to their queen; and she declared that they would murder the guilty man on the following morning.

But that night—the very first after the girl's death—while the brother slept, the flowers of the jasmine bush opened. The invisible souls of the flowers, every one carrying a poisoned spear, gathered around his ears and told him stories that gave him terrible dreams. When he screamed in fear, they stuck the deadly points of their spears into his tongue.

"Now we have revenged the dead," they cried, and flew back into their flowers.

In the morning when the window of the bedchamber was opened, the rose elf and the bees, led by the queen, flew into the room to kill the brother. But he was already dead. People were standing around his bed. "The strong smell of the jasmine killed him," one of the men said.

Now the elf understood the flowers' vengeance, and told the queen bee about it. She and all the other bees swarmed about the jasmine bush. The people tried to shoo them out. Finally a man picked up the plant and was going to carry it outside. One of the bees stung his hand. The flowerpot fell to the floor and broke.

All the people looked in horror at the white skull that was loosened from the black earth. Now they knew that the dead man had been a murderer.

The queen bee hummed a song about the flowers' revenge and about the little elf that may live within even the tiniest leaf and can expose and avenge evil.

17

✧

The Swineherd

THERE once was a poor prince. He had a kingdom and, though it wasn't very big, it was large enough to marry on, and married he wanted to be.

Now it was rather bold of him to say to the emperor's daughter: "Do you want me?" But he was a young man of spirit who was quite famous, and there were at least a hundred princesses who would have said thank you very much to his proposal. But the emperor's daughter didn't. Let me tell you the story.

On the grave of the prince's father there grew a rose tree. It was a beautiful tree that only flowered every fifth year; and then it bore only one rose. That rose had such a sweet fragrance that anyone who smelled it forgot immediately all his sorrow and troubles. The prince also owned a nightingale which sang as though all the melodies ever composed lived in its throat—so beautiful was its song. The prince decided to send the rose and the nightingale to the emperor's daughter, and had two little silver chests made to put them in.

The emperor ordered the gifts to be carried into the grand assembly room where the princess was playing house with her ladies in waiting. That was their favorite game and they never played any other. When the princess saw the pretty little silver chests she clapped her hands and jumped for joy.

"Oh, I hope one of them contains a pretty little kitten," she said; but when she opened the chest, she found a rose.

"It is very prettily made," said one of the ladies in waiting.

"It is more than pretty; it is nice," remarked the emperor. Then the princess touched the rose and she almost wept with disappointment.

"Oh, Papa," she shrieked. "It is not glass, it's real!"

"Oh, oh!" shrieked all the ladies in waiting. "How revolting! It is real!"

"Let's see what is in the other chest first, before we get angry," admonished the emperor. There was the nightingale, who sang so beautifully that it was difficult to find anything wrong with it.

"Superbe! Charmant!" said the ladies in waiting. They all spoke French, one worse than the other.

"That bird reminds me of the late empress' music box," said an old courtier. "It has the same tone, the same sense of rhythm."

"You are right," said the emperor, and cried like a baby.

"I would like to know if that is real too," demanded the princess.

"Oh yes, it is a real bird," said one of the pages who had brought the gifts.

"In that case we will let the bird fly away," said the princess; and she sent a messenger to say that she would not even permit the prince to come inside her father's kingdom.

But the prince was not easily discouraged. He smeared his face with both black and brown shoe polish, put a cap on his head, then he walked up to the emperor's castle and knocked.

"Good morning, Emperor," said the young man, for it was the emperor himself who had opened the door. "Can I get a job in the castle?"

"Oh, there are so many people who want to work here," answered the emperor, and shook his head. "But I do need someone to tend the pigs, we have such an awful lot of them."

And so the prince was hired as the emperor's swineherd. There was a tiny, dirty room next to the pigpen, and that was where he was expected to live.

The young man spent the rest of the day making a very pretty little pot. By evening it was finished. The pot had little bells all around it, and when it boiled, they played, ever so sweetly:

> Ach, du lieber Augustin,
> Alles ist weg, weg, weg.

But the strangest and most wonderful thing about the pot was that, if you held your finger in the steam above it, then you could smell what was cooking on any stove in town. Now there was something a little different from the rose.

The princess was out walking with her ladies in waiting, and when she heard the musical pot she stopped immediately. She listened and smiled, for "Ach, du lieber Augustin" she knew. She could play the melody herself on the piano with one finger.

"It is a song I know!" she exclaimed. "That swineherd must be cultured. Please go in and ask him what the instrument costs."

One of the ladies in waiting was ordered to run over to the pigpen, but she put wooden shoes on first.

"What do you want for the pot?" she asked.

"Ten kisses from the princess," said the swineherd.

"God save us!" cried the lady in waiting.

"I won't settle for less," said the swineherd.

"Well, what did he want?" asked the princess.

"I can't say it," blushed the lady in waiting.

"Then you can whisper it," said the princess; and the lady in waiting whispered.

"He is very naughty," said the princess, and walked on. But she had gone only a few steps when she heard the little bells play again, and they sounded even sweeter to her than they had before.

> Ach, du lieber Augustin,
> Alles ist weg, weg, weg.

"Listen," she said, "ask him if he will be satisfied with ten kisses from one of my ladies in waiting."

"No, thank you!" replied the swineherd to that proposal. "Ten kisses from the princess or I keep my pot."

"This is most embarrassing," declared the princess. "You will all have to stand around me so no one can see it."

And the ladies in waiting formed a circle and held out their skirts so no one could peep. The swineherd got his kisses and the princess the pot.

Oh, what a grand time they had! All day and all evening they made the little pot boil. There wasn't a stove in the whole town that had anything cooking on it that they didn't know about. They knew what was served for dinner on every table: both the count's and the cowherd's. The ladies in waiting were so delighted that they clapped their little hands.

"We know who is going to have soup and pancakes and who is eating porridge and rib roast! Oh, it is most interesting."

"Very!" said the imperial housekeeper.

"Keep your mouth shut. Remember, I am the princess," said the emperor's daughter.

And all the ladies in waiting and the imperial housekeeper said: "God preserve us, we won't say a word."

The swineherd—that is to say, the prince whom everyone thought was a swineherd—did not like to waste his time, so he constructed a rattle which was so ingenious that, when you swung it around, it played all the waltzes, polkas, and dance melodies ever composed since the creation of the world.

"It is superb!" exclaimed the princess as she was walking past the pigsty. "I have never heard a more exquisite composition. Do go in and ask what he wants for the instrument, but I won't kiss him!"

"He wants a hundred kisses from the princess," said the lady in waiting who had been sent to speak to the swineherd.

"He must be mad," declared the princess. She walked on a few steps and then she stood still. "One ought to encourage art," she said. "I am the emperor's daughter. Tell him he can have ten kisses from me just as he got yesterday. The rest he can get from my ladies in waiting."

"But we don't want to kiss him," they all cried.

"Stuff and nonsense!" replied the princess, for she was angry. "If I can kiss him, you can too. Besides, what do you think I give you room and board for?"

And one of the ladies in waiting went to talk with the swineherd. "One hundred kisses from the princess or I keep the rattle," was the message she came back with.

"Then gather around me!" commanded the princess. The ladies in waiting took their positions and the kissing began.

"I wonder what is going on down there by the pigsty," said the emperor, who was standing out on the balcony. He rubbed his eyes and put his glasses on. "It is the ladies in waiting. What devilment are they up to? I'd better go down and see." Then he pulled up the backs of his slippers, for they were really only a comfortable old pair of shoes with broken backs. Oh, how he ran! But as soon as he came near the pigsty he walked on tiptoe.

The ladies in waiting were so busy counting kisses—to make sure that the bargain was justly carried out and that the swineherd did not get one kiss too many or one too few—that they didn't hear or see the emperor, who was standing on toptoe outside the circle.

"What's going on here?" he shouted. When he saw the kissing he took off one of his slippers and started hitting the ladies in waiting on the tops of their heads, just as the swineherd was getting his eighty-sixth kiss.

"*Heraus!* Get out!" he screamed, for he was really angry; and both the swineherd and the princess were thrown out of his empire.

There they stood: the princess was crying, the swineherd was grumbling, and the rain was streaming down.

"Oh, poor me!" wailed the princess. "If only I had married the prince. Oh, I am so unhappy!"

The swineherd stepped behind a tree, rubbed all the black and brown shoe polish off his face, and put on his splendid royal robes. He looked so impressive that the princess curtsied when she saw him.

"I have come to despise you," said the prince. "You did not want an honest prince. You did not appreciate the rose or the nightingale, but you could kiss a swineherd for the sake of a toy. Farewell!"

The prince entered his own kingdom and locked the door behind him; and there the princess could stand and sing:

> "Ach, du lieber Augustin,
> Alles ist weg, weg, weg."

For, indeed, everything was "all gone"!

18

The Buckwheat

IT happens often after a thunderstorm that the buckwheat fields appear all black, as if they had been burned. If you ask the farmer, he will say that the buckwheat has been singed by lightning, but he doesn't know why. Let me tell you what I heard from a sparrow, who had the story from an old willow tree. This willow tree grew right next to a buckwheat field, and it's still there if you want to see it. It's a large, dignified tree; but it's ancient and has a knobby bark. It's split down the middle and in the crevice grass and blackberries grow. The trunk leans a little to one side and the branches hang down toward the earth like long green hair.

All around it are fields of grain: rye, barley, and oats. How lovely oats are! The kernels, when they are ripe, look like so many canary birds sitting on a branch. It stands so gloriously as harvest time approaches, for the heavier the oats become, the more humbly they bend their heads toward the ground.

But on the field nearest the old willow tree grew buckwheat; and buckwheat do not bow their heads but hold them high. They always stand stiff and proud.

"We are as fruitful as any of the others," said the buckwheat. "And we are more beautiful, besides. Our flowers are as lovely as the apple tree's. It is a delight to look at us. You, old willow tree, do you know of anything more beautiful than we are?"

The old willow tree nodded its head vigorously, as if it were saying, "Yes, I certainly do!"

The buckwheat were so indignant that they stood even straighter.

"You stupid tree! You are so old that you have grass growing in your stomach."

The weather turned nasty. A storm was brewing and all the flowers of the fields folded their leaves and bent their delicate heads, while the wind tore past them; but the buckwheat proudly tossed their heads.

"Bend your heads as we do," called the flowers.

"I don't need to," replied the buckwheat.

"Bend, bend," screamed the other grains. "In a minute the storm's angel, with its great wings that stretch from the clouds down to the earth, will be here! And he will cut you in two if you do not ask him to be merciful!"

"I will not bow and bend," shouted the buckwheat.

"Close your flowers and fold your leaves," warned the old willow tree. "And do not look at the bolts of lightning that appear when the clouds burst; even man does not dare do that, for through the lightning you can see right into God's heaven and that sight makes men blind. Think what would happen to us if we, who are so much less than man—we who are merely humble plants—should dare to do such a thing."

"Much less?" scowled the buckwheat. "Now I am going to look right into God's heaven!" And it did, confidently and proudly, while the whole sky was aflame with lightning.

When the bad weather was over the grain and the flowers, refreshed by the rain, raised their heads in the still, clear air; but the buckwheat had been singed black; they were dead and useless, not fit for the reaper but only for the plow.

The old willow tree swayed her branches gently in the breeze. Drops of water fell from its leaves, and the little sparrows asked, "Why are you crying? The weather is so glorious now. See how the sun shines and the clouds sail by above us. Can't you smell the sweet fragrance of the flowers and the bushes? Why are you weeping, old willow tree?"

The old tree told the sparrow about the buckwheat's pride, presumption, and its punishment—for punishment always follows presumption.

Now I have told you the story, as the sparrow told it to me, one evening when I asked him to tell me a fairy tale.

19

✳◇✳

The Angel

"WHEN a good child dies, an angel comes down from heaven and takes the dead child in his arms; then the angel spreads out his wings and flies with the child to visit all the places that the little one has loved. They pick a whole armful of flowers and bring them to God; in heaven, these flowers will bloom even more beautifully than they have on earth. God presses all the flowers to His heart; but the one that is dearest to Him, He gives a kiss, and then that flower can sing and join in the hosanna."

This was what one of God's angels was telling to a dead child whom he was carrying up to heaven. The child heard it as though in a dream, while the angel flew with him above all the places where he had played and been happy. At last they came to a garden filled with the most beautiful flowers.

"Which ones shall we take along and plant up in heaven?" asked the angel.

There was a tall rosebush whose stem some evil hand had broken, so that all the branches, with their half-open buds that had already begun to wither, lay limp all around it.

"Oh, the poor bush!" cried the child. "Take it along that it may flower again up with God."

The angel kissed the child for the choice he had made and took the rosebush. They picked other flowers. Some were the most elegant in the garden; but they took some wild pansies and violets too.

"Now we have enough flowers," said the child, and the angel nodded. Now they could fly up to God, but the angel tarried.

Night came, and the town grew still. The angel flew with the child above the narrow streets where the poor lived. The day before had been moving day, and the lanes were filled with old straw, broken pots and plates, rags and garbage. It was a sorry sight.

The angel pointed to a broken earthenware pot; near it lay a dried-out wild flower, to whose roots a clump of soil still clung. It had been thrown out in the street together with the other trash.

"That flower we shall take along," said the angel. "And I shall tell you its story while we fly." The angel picked up the dead wild flower and they flew on their way.

"Down in that narrow street," the angel began, "there lived in a cellar a little poor boy who had been ill from birth and had spent his life in bed. When he was 'well,' he would walk around the room, leaning on two crutches. In the middle of the summer, when the sun was so high in the sky that its rays fell into the little courtyard, a chair would be placed by the door of the cellar, and there the boy would enjoy the warm sunshine. The child had to hold up his hands in front of his face, for his eyes were used to the twilight of the cellar. His hands were white and thin, and beneath the transparent skin one could see the blood pulsing through his veins. After such a day his parents would say: 'Today he has been outside.'

"He knew about the greenness of the forest in spring because the neighbor's children would bring him the first green branch of the beech tree. The sick boy would hold it over his head and pretend that he was out in the woods, where the sun shone and the birds sang. One day one of the children brought him a bouquet of wild flowers. Among them was one flower that still had roots. This was planted in an earthenware pot and placed next to the bed. It grew. Each year it had new shoots and new flowers unfolded. The wild flower became the sick child's garden: his treasure on this earth. He watered it and took care of it, making sure that it always stood where the bit of light that came through the tiny cellar window would fall upon it. The flower became part of his world, not only when he was awake but when he dreamed as well. It bloomed for him alone: to give pleasure to his eyes and send sweet fragrance for him to enjoy. When God called him, the boy turned in death toward the flower.

"He has been with God a year now. A whole year the flower stood in the window forgotten; then it was all dried out, so it was thrown out in the street with the other garbage. We shall take the poor dead flower along in our bouquet, for it has spread more happiness than the grandest flower in any royal garden."

"But how do you know all this?" asked the child whom the angel was carrying up to heaven.

"How do I know?" the angel said, and smiled. "I was myself that sick little boy who could not walk without crutches. Oh, I recognize my flower again!"

The child opened his eyes as widely as he could and looked into the happy face of the angel. Just at that moment they flew into heaven, where all sorrows cease. God embraced the dead child, pressed him to His heart; and he grew wings and flew away, hand in hand, with the angel who had brought him into heaven. God pressed all the flowers that they had given Him to His heart; but the dead wild flower He kissed and it gained a voice and could sing with the angels that flew around God, in ever widening circles out into infinity. All sang with equal bliss and fervor: those who had died when old and those who had come as children, and the little wild flower that had been thrown out among the trash in the dark and narrow lane.

20

The Nightingale

IN China, as you know, the emperor is Chinese, and so are his court and all his people. This story happened a long, long time ago; and that is just the reason why you should hear it now, before it is forgotten. The emperor's palace was the most beautiful in the whole world. It was made of porcelain and had been most costly to build. It was so fragile that you had to be careful not to touch anything and that can be difficult. The gardens were filled with the loveliest flowers; the most beautiful of them had little silver bells that tinkled so you wouldn't pass by without noticing them.

Everything in the emperor's garden was most cunningly arranged. The gardens were so large that even the head gardener did not know exactly how big they were. If you kept walking you finally came to the most beautiful forest, with tall trees that mirrored themselves in deep lakes. The forest stretched all the way to the sea, which was blue and so deep that even large boats could sail so close to the shore that they were shaded by the trees. Here lived a nightingale who sang so sweetly that even the fisherman, who came every night to set his nets, would stop to rest when he heard it, and say: "Blessed God, how beautifully it sings!" But he couldn't listen too long, for he had work to do, and soon he would forget the bird. Yet the next night when he heard it again, he would repeat what he had said the night before: "Blessed God, how beautifully it sings!"

From all over the world travelers came to the emperor's city to admire his palace and gardens; but when they heard the nightingale sing, they all declared that it was the loveliest of all. When they returned to their own countries, they would write long and learned books about the city, the palace, and the garden; but they didn't forget the nightingale. No, that was always mentioned in the very first chapter. Those who could write poetry wrote long odes about the nightingale who lived in the forest, on the shores of the deep blue sea.

These books were read the whole world over; and finally one was also sent to the emperor. He sat down in his golden chair and started to read it. Every once in a while he would nod his head because it pleased him to read how his own city and his own palace and gardens were praised; but then he came to the sentence: "But the song of the nightingale is the loveliest of all."

"What!" said the emperor. "The nightingale? I don't know it, I have never heard of it; and yet it lives not only in my empire but in my very garden. That is the sort of thing one can only find out by reading books."

He called his chief courtier, who was so very noble that if anyone of a rank lower than his own, either talked to him, or dared ask him a question, he only answered, "P." And that didn't mean anything at all.

"There is a strange and famous bird called the nightingale," began the emperor. "It is thought to be the most marvelous thing in my empire. Why have I never heard of it?"

"I have never heard of it," answered the courtier. "It has never been presented at court."

"I want it to come this evening and sing for me," demanded the emperor. "The whole world knows of it but I do not."

"I have never heard it mentioned before," said the courtier, and bowed. "But I shall search for it and find it."

But that was more easily said than done. The courtier ran all through the palace, up the stairs and down the stairs, and through the long corridors, but none of the people whom he asked had ever heard of the nightingale. He returned to the emperor and declared that the whole story was nothing but a fable, invented by those people who had written the books. "Your Imperial Majesty should not believe everything that is written. A discovery is one thing and artistic imagination something quite different; it is fiction."

"The book I have just read," replied the emperor, "was sent to me by the great Emperor of Japan; and therefore, every word in it must be the truth. I want to hear the nightingale! And that tonight! If it does not come, then the whole court shall have their stomachs thumped, and that right after they have eaten."

"*Tsing-pe!*" said the courtier. He ran again up and down the stairs and through the corridors; and half the court ran with him, because they didn't want their stomachs thumped. Everywhere they asked about the nightingale that the whole world knew about, and yet no one at court had heard of.

At last they came to the kitchen, where a poor little girl worked, scrubbing the pots and pans. "Oh, I know the nightingale," she said, "I know it well, it sings so beautifully. Every evening I am allowed to bring some leftovers to my poor sick mother who lives down by the sea. Now it is far away, and as I return I often rest in the forest and listen to the nightingale. I get tears in my eyes from it, as though my mother were kissing me."

"Little kitchenmaid," said the courtier, "I will arrange for a permanent position in the kitchen for you, and permission to see the emperor eat, if you will take us to the nightingale; it is summoned to court tonight."

Half the court went to the forest to find the nightingale. As they were walking along a cow began to bellow.

"Oh!" shouted all the courtiers. "There it is. What a marvelously powerful voice the little animal has; we have heard it before."

"That is only a cow," said the little kitchenmaid. "We are still far from where the nightingale lives."

They passed a little pond; the frogs were croaking.

"Lovely," sighed the Chinese imperial dean. "I can hear her, she sounds like little church bells ringing."

"No, that is only the frogs," said the little kitchenmaid, "but any time now we may hear it."

Just then the nightingale began singing.

"There it is!" said the little girl. "Listen. Listen. It is up there on that branch." And she pointed to a little gray bird sitting amid the greenery.

"Is that possible?" exclaimed the chief courtier. "I had not imagined it would look like that. It looks so common! I think it has lost its color from shyness and out of embarrassment at seeing so many noble people at one time."

"Little nightingale," called the kitchenmaid, "our emperor wants you to sing for him."

"With pleasure," replied the nightingale, and sang as lovely as he could.

"It sounds like little glass bells," sighed the chief courtier. "Look at its little throat, how it throbs. It is strange that we have never heard of it before; it will be a great success at court."

"Shall I sing another song for the emperor?" asked the nightingale, who thought that the emperor was there.

"Most excellent little nightingale," began the chief courtier, "I have the pleasure to invite you to attend the court tonight, where His Imperial Majesty, the Emperor of China, wishes you to enchant him with your most charming art."

"It sounds best in the green woods," said the nightingale; but when he heard that the emperor insisted, he followed them readily back to the palace.

There every room had been polished and thousands of little golden lamps reflected themselves in the shiny porcelain walls and floors. In the corridors stood all the most beautiful flowers, the ones with silver bells on them; and there was such a draft from all the servants running in and out, and opening and closing doors, that all the bells were tinkling and you couldn't hear what anyone said.

In the grand banquet hall, where the emperor's throne stood, a little golden perch had been hung for the nightingale to sit on. The whole court was there and the little kitchenmaid, who now had the title of Imperial Kitchenmaid, was allowed to stand behind one of the doors and listen. Everyone was dressed in their finest clothes and they all were looking at the little gray bird, toward which the emperor nodded very kindly.

The nightingale's song was so sweet that tears came into the emperor's eyes; and when they ran down his cheeks, the little nightingale sang even more beautifully than it had before. His song spoke to one's heart, and the emperor was so pleased that he ordered his golden slipper to be hung around the little bird's neck. There was no higher honor. But the nightingale thanked him and said that he had been honored enough already.

"I have seen tears in the eyes of an emperor, and that is a great enough treasure for me. There is a strange power in an emperor's tears and God knows that is reward enough." Then he sang yet another song.

"That was the most charming and elegant song we have ever

heard," said all the ladies of the court. And from that time onward they filled their mouths with water, so they could make a clucking noise, whenever anyone spoke to them, because they thought that then they sounded like the nightingale. Even the chambermaids and the lackeys were satisfied; and that really meant something, for servants are the most difficult to please. Yes, the nightingale was a success.

He was to have his own cage at court, and permission to take a walk twice a day and once during the night. Twelve servants were to accompany him; each held on tightly to a silk ribbon that was attached to the poor bird's legs. There wasn't any pleasure in such an outing.

The whole town talked about the marvelous bird. Whenever two people met in the street they would sigh; one would say, "night," and the other, "gale"; and then they would understand each other perfectly. Twelve delicatessen shop owners named their children "Nightingale," but not one of them could sing.

One day a package arrived for the emperor; on it was written: "Nightingale."

"It is probably another book about our famous bird," said the emperor. But he was wrong; it was a mechanical nightingale. It lay in a little box and was supposed to look like the real one, though it was made of silver and gold and studded with sapphires, diamonds, and rubies. When you wound it up, it could sing one of the songs the real nightingale sang; and while it performed its little silver tail would go up and down. Around its neck hung a ribbon on which was written: "The Emperor of Japan's nightingale is inferior to the Emperor of China's."

"It is beautiful!" exclaimed the whole court. And the messenger who had brought it had the title of Supreme Imperial Nightingale Deliverer bestowed upon him at once.

"They ought to sing together, it will be a duet," said everyone, and they did. But that didn't work out well at all; for the real bird sang in his own manner and the mechanical one had a cylinder inside its chest instead of a heart. "It is not its fault," said the imperial music master. "It keeps perfect time, it belongs to my school of music." Then the mechanical nightingale had to sing solo. Everyone agreed that its song was just as beautiful as the real nightingale's; and besides, the artificial bird was much pleasanter to look at, with its sapphires, rubies, and diamonds that glittered like bracelets and brooches.

The mechanical nightingale sang its song thirty-three times and did not grow tired. The court would have liked to hear it the thirty-fourth time, but the emperor thought that the real nightingale ought to sing now. But where was it? Nobody had noticed that he had flown out through an open window, to his beloved green forest.

"What is the meaning of this!" said the emperor angrily, and the whole court blamed the nightingale and called him an ungrateful creature.

"But the best bird remains," they said, and the mechanical bird sang its song once more. It was the same song, for it knew no other; but it was very intricate, so the courtiers didn't know it by heart yet. The imperial music master praised the bird and declared that it was better than the real nightingale, not only on the outside where the diamonds were, but also inside.

"Your Imperial Majesty and gentlemen: you understand that the real nightingale cannot be depended upon. One never knows what he will sing; whereas, in the mechanical bird, everything is determined. There is one song and no other! One can explain everything. We can open it up to examine and appreciate how human thought has fashioned the wheels and the cylinder, and put them where they are, to turn just as they should."

"Precisely what I was thinking!" said the whole court in a chorus. And the imperial music master was given permission to show the new nightingale to the people on the following Sunday.

The emperor thought that they, too, should hear the bird. They did and they were as delighted as if they had gotten drunk on too much tea. It was all very Chinese. They pointed with their licking fingers toward heaven, nodded, and said: "Oh!"

But the poor fisherman, who had heard the real nightingale, mumbled, "It sounds beautiful and like the bird's song, but something is missing, though I don't know what it is."

The real nightingale was banished from the empire.

The mechanical bird was given a silk pillow to rest upon, close to the emperor's bed; and all the presents it had received were piled around it. Among them were both gold and precious stones. Its title was Supreme Imperial Night-table Singer and its rank was Number One to the Left.—The emperor thought the left side was more distinguished because that is the side where the heart is, even in an emperor.

The imperial music master wrote a work in twenty-five volumes about the mechanical nightingale. It was not only long and learned but filled with the most difficult Chinese words, so everyone bought it and said they had read and understood it, for otherwise they would have been considered stupid and had to have their stomachs poked.

A whole year went by. The emperor, the court, and all the Chinese in China knew every note of the supreme imperial night-table singer's song by heart; but that was the very reason why they liked it so much: they could sing it themselves, and they did. The street urchins sang: "Zi-zi-zizzi, cluck-cluck-cluck-cluck." And so did the emperor. Oh, it was delightful!

But one evening, when the bird was singing its very best and the emperor was lying in bed listening to it, something said: "Clang," inside it. It was broken! All the wheels whirred around and then the bird was still.

The emperor jumped out of bed and called his physician but he couldn't do anything, so the imperial watchmaker was fetched. After a great deal of talking and tinkering, he repaired the bird, but he declared that the cylinders were worn and new ones could not be fitted. The bird would have to be spared; it could not be played so often.

It was a catastrophe. Only once a year was the mechanical bird allowed to sing, and then it had difficulty finishing its song. But the imperial music master made a speech wherein he explained, using the most difficult words, that the bird was as good as ever; and then it was.

Five years passed and a great misfortune happened. Although everyone loved the old emperor, he had fallen ill; and they all agreed that he would not get well again. It was said that a new emperor had already been chosen; and when people in the street asked the chief courtier how the emperor was, he would shake his head and say: "P."

Pale and cold, the emperor lay in his golden bed. The whole court believed him to be already dead and they were busy visiting and paying their respects to the new emperor. The lackeys were all out in the street gossiping, and the chambermaids were drinking coffee. All the floors in the whole palace were covered with black carpets so that no one's steps would disturb the dying emperor; and that's why it was as quiet as quiet could be in the whole palace.

But the emperor was not dead yet. Pale and motionless he lay in his great golden bed; the long velvet drapes were drawn, and the golden tassels moved slowly in the wind, for one of the windows was open. The moon shone down upon the emperor, and its light reflected in the diamonds of the mechanical bird.

The emperor could hardly breathe; he felt as though someone were sitting on his chest. He opened his eyes. Death was sitting there. He was wearing the emperor's golden crown and held his gold saber in one hand and his imperial banner in the other. From the folds of the curtains that hung around his bed, strange faces looked down at the emperor. Some of them were frighteningly ugly, and others mild and kind. They were the evil and good deeds that the emperor had done. Now, while Death was sitting on his heart, they were looking down at him.

"Do you remember?" whispered first one and then another. And they told him things that made the cold sweat of fear appear on his forehead.

"No, no, I don't remember! It is not true!" shouted the emperor. "Music, music, play the great Chinese gong," he begged, "so that I will not be able to hear what they are saying."

But the faces kept talking and Death, like a real Chinese, nodded his head to every word that was said.

"Little golden nightingale, sing!" demanded the emperor. "I have given you gold and precious jewels and with my own hands have I hung my golden slipper around your neck. Sing! Please sing!"

But the mechanical nightingale stood as still as ever, for there was no one to wind it up; and then, it couldn't sing.

Death kept staring at the emperor out of the empty sockets in his skull; and the palace was still, so terrifyingly still.

All at once the most beautiful song broke the silence. It was the nightingale, who had heard of the emperor's illness and torment. He sat on a branch outside his window and sang to bring him comfort and hope. As he sang, the faces in the folds of the curtains faded and the blood pulsed with greater force through the emperor's weak body. Death himself listened and said, "Please, little nightingale, sing on!"

"Will you give me the golden saber? Will you give me the imperial banner? Will you give me the golden crown?"

Death gave each of his trophies for a song; and then the nightingale sang about the quiet churchyard, where white roses grow, where fragrant elderberry trees are, and where the grass is green from the tears of those who come to mourn. Death longed so much for his garden that he flew out of the window, like a white cold mist.

"Thank you, thank you," whispered the emperor, "you heavenly little bird, I remember you. You have I banished from my empire and yet you came to sing for me; and when you sang the evil phantoms that taunted me disappeared, and Death himself left my heart. How shall I reward you?"

"You have rewarded me already," said the nightingale. "I shall never forget that, the first time I sang for you, you gave me the tears from your eyes; and to a poet's heart, those are jewels. But sleep so you can become well and strong; I shall sing for you."

The little gray bird sang; and the emperor slept, so blessedly, so peacefully.

The sun was shining in through the window when he woke; he did not feel ill any more. None of his servants had come, for they thought that he was already dead; but the nightingale was still there and he was singing.

"You must come always," declared the emperor. "I shall only ask you to sing when you want to. And the mechanical bird I shall break in a thousand pieces."

"Don't do that," replied the nightingale. "The mechanical bird sang as well as it could, keep it. I can't build my nest in the palace; let me come to visit you when I want to, and I shall sit on the branch outside your window and sing for you. And my song shall make you happy and make you thoughtful. I shall sing not only of those who are happy but also of those who suffer. I shall sing of the good and of the evil that happen around you, and yet are hidden from you. For a little songbird flies far. I visit the poor fishermen's cottages and the peasant's hut, far away from your palace and your court. I love your heart more than your crown, and yet I feel that the crown has a fragrance of something holy about it. I will come! I will sing for you! Only one thing must you promise me."

"I will promise you anything," said the emperor, who had dressed himself in his imperial clothes and was holding his golden saber and pressing it against his heart.

"I beg of you never tell anyone that you have a little bird that tells you everything, for then you will fare even better." And with those words the nightingale flew away.

The servants entered the room to look at their dead master. There they stood gaping when the emperor said: "Good morning."

21

The Sweethearts

A TOP and a ball were lying in a drawer among a lot of other toys. One day the top said to the ball, "Shouldn't we become engaged? After all, we are lying right next to each other in the drawer." But the ball, who was made of morocco leather, thought of herself as a very refined young lady and would not even answer a question like that.

The next day the little boy, whose toys they all were, painted the top red and yellow and hammered a brass nail in the middle of it. It looked marvelous when it spun.

"Look at me now!" called the top to the ball. "What do you say, wouldn't we make a fine pair? You can jump and I can dance! How happy we would be together."

"That's what you think," replied the ball. "Are you aware that my mother and father were a pair of morocco slippers, and that I have a cork inside me?"

"But I am of mahogany," boasted the top. "The mayor made me, himself, on a lathe he has in his cellar. It gave him great pleasure."

"How do I know that what you're saying is true?" asked the ball.

"May I never be whipped into a spin again if I am lying," answered the top.

"You speak well for yourself," admitted the ball. "But I have to refuse because I am almost engaged to a swallow. Every time I jump up into the air, he puts his head out of the nest and asks, 'Will you? Will you?' Even though I haven't said yes, I have thought it; and that's almost the same as being engaged. But I promise that I shall never forget you."

"A lot of difference that will make," growled the top. And that was the end of their conversation.

The next day the ball was taken out of the drawer, and the top watched as she was thrown so high up into the sky that she looked like a bird and finally all but disappeared. Every time she hit the ground she bounced up again quite high; and the top could not make up his mind whether she jumped up like that because she wanted to get another glimpse of the swallow, or just because she had cork inside her.

The ninth time the ball went up into the air, it did not return. The boy searched for it everywhere but it was gone.

"I know what's happened to her," said the top, "she's up in the swallow's nest and is getting married to the swallow."

The more the top thought about the ball, the more in love with her he was. And because he couldn't have her, he wanted her all the more. The strangest part of it was that she had preferred another. The top spun and whirled; round and round he went; and all the time he was thinking of the ball. And in his imagination she grew prettier and prettier. Years passed and finally she became an old love.

The top was not young any more; but then one day he was painted all over with gold paint. Now he was a golden top; and he spun and leaped up into the air. . . . Oh, that was something! But then it sprang too high and was gone! Everyone looked for it everywhere, even in the cellar, but it was not to be found. Where was it?

It had jumped into the garbage bin. There all kinds of things were lying: gravel, a cabbage stalk, dirt, dust, and a lot of leaves that had fallen down from the gutter under the roof.

"This is a fine place to be!" thought the top. "I wonder how long my gilding will last here. What a lot of riffraff!" The top glanced at the cabbage stalk and then at a funny round thing that looked like a rotten apple. But it wasn't an apple; it was the old ball who had lain for years in the gutter, where the water had oozed through it.

"Thank God! At last someone of one's own kind has come, someone I need not be ashamed to talk to," said the ball, and looked at the golden top. "I was made from morocco leather by the hand of a fine young lady, and have a cork inside me. Although, I admit, it's hard to see it now. I was just about to marry a swallow when I fell

166 A Treasury of Hans Christian Andersen

into the gutter under the roof. There I have lain and oozed for five years; that's a long time for a young girl."

The top didn't say anything. He was thinking of his old sweetheart; and the more he heard, the more certain he was that it was she.

At that moment a maid came to throw something away. "Hurrah! There's the golden top!" she cried.

The golden top was brought back to the living room, where he was honored and respected. There no one ever talked about the ball, and the top never mentioned his old love again. You get over it when your beloved has lain in a gutter and oozed for five years. You never recognize her when you meet her in the garbage bin.

22

The Ugly Duckling

IT WAS so beautiful out in the country. It was summer. The oats were still green, but the wheat was turning yellow. Down in the meadow the grass had been cut and made into haystacks; and there the storks walked on their long red legs talking Egyptian, because that was the language they had been taught by their mothers. The fields were enclosed by woods, and hidden among them were little lakes and pools. Yes, it certainly was lovely out there in the country!

The old castle, with its deep moat surrounding it, lay bathed in sunshine. Between the heavy walls and the edge of the moat there was a narrow strip of land covered by a whole forest of burdock plants. Their leaves were large and some of the stalks were so tall that a child could stand upright under them and imagine that he was in the middle of the wild and lonesome woods. Here a duck had built her nest. While she sat waiting for the eggs to hatch, she felt a little sorry for herself because it was taking so long and hardly anybody came to visit her. The other ducks preferred swimming in the moat to sitting under a dock leaf and gossiping.

Finally the eggs began to crack. "Peep . . . Peep," they said one after another. The egg yolks had become alive and were sticking out their heads.

"Quack . . . Quack . . ." said their mother. "Look around you." And the ducklings did; they glanced at the green world about them, and that was what their mother wanted to do, for green was good for their eyes.

"How big the world is!" piped the little ones, for they had much more space to move around in now than they had had inside the egg.

"Do you think that this is the whole world?" quacked their mother. "The world is much larger than this. It stretches as far as the minister's wheat fields, though I have not been there. . . . Are you all here?" The duck got up and turned around to look at her nest. "Oh no, the biggest egg hasn't hatched yet; and I'm so tired of sitting here! I wonder how long it will take?" she wailed, and sat down again.

"What's new?" asked an old duck who had come visiting.

"One of the eggs is taking so long," complained the mother duck. "It won't crack. But take a look at the others. They are the sweetest little ducklings you have ever seen; and every one of them looks exactly like their father. That scoundrel hasn't come to visit me once."

"Let me look at the egg that won't hatch," demanded the old duck. "I am sure that it's a turkey egg! I was fooled that way once. You can't imagine what it's like. Turkeys are afraid of the water. I couldn't get them to go into it. I quacked and I nipped them, but nothing helped. Let me see that egg! . . . Yes, it's a turkey egg. Just let it lie there. You go and teach your young ones how to swim, that's my advice."

"I have sat on it so long that I guess I can sit a little longer, at least until they get the hay in," replied the mother duck.

"Suit yourself," said the older duck, and went on.

At last the big egg cracked too. "Peep . . . Peep," said the young one, and tumbled out. He was big and very ugly.

The mother duck looked at him. "He's awfully big for his age," she said. "He doesn't look like any of the others. I wonder if he could be a turkey? Well, we shall soon see. Into the water he will go, even if I have to kick him to make him do it."

The next day the weather was gloriously beautiful. The sun shone on the forest of burdock plants. The mother duck took her whole brood to the moat. "Quack . . . Quack . . ." she ordered.

One after another, the little ducklings plunged into the water. For a moment their heads disappeared, but then they popped up again and the little ones floated like so many corks. Their legs knew what to do without being told. All of the new brood swam very nicely, even the ugly one.

"He is no turkey," mumbled the mother. "See how beautifully he uses his legs and how straight he holds his neck. He is my own child and, when you look closely at him, he's quite handsome. . . . Quack! Quack! Follow me and I'll take you to the henyard and introduce you to everyone. But stay close to me, so that no one steps on you, and look out for the cat."

They heard an awful noise when they arrived at the henyard. Two families of ducks had got into a fight over the head of an eel. Neither of them got it, for it was swiped by the cat.

"That is the way of the world," said the mother duck, and licked her bill. She would have liked to have the eel's head herself. "Walk nicely," she admonished them. "And remember to bow to the old duck over there. She has Spanish blood in her veins and is the most aristocratic fowl here. That is why she is so fat and has a red rag tied around one of her legs. That is the highest mark of distinction a duck can be given. It means so much that she will never be done away with; and all the other fowl and the human beings know who she is. Quack! Quack! . . . Don't walk, waddle like well-brought-up ducklings. Keep your legs far apart, just as your mother and father have always done. Bow your heads and say, 'Quack!'" And that was what the little ducklings did.

Other ducks gathered about them and said loudly, "What do we want that gang here for? Aren't there enough of us already? Pooh! Look how ugly one of them is! He's the last straw!" And one of the ducks flew over and bit the ugly duckling on the neck.

"Leave him alone!" shouted the mother. "He hasn't done anyone any harm."

"He's big and he doesn't look like everybody else!" replied the duck who had bitten him. "And that's reason enough to beat him."

"Very good-looking children you have," remarked the duck with the red rag around one of her legs. "All of them are beautiful except one. He didn't turn out very well. I wish you could make him over again."

"That's not possible, Your Grace," answered the mother duck. "He may not be handsome, but he has a good character and swims as well as the others, if not a little better. Perhaps he will grow handsomer as he grows older and becomes a bit smaller. He was in the egg too long, and that is why he doesn't have the right shape." She smoothed his neck for a moment and then added, "Besides, he's a drake; and it doesn't matter so much what he looks like. He is strong and I am sure he will be able to take care of himself."

"Well, the others are nice," said the old duck. "Make yourself at home, and if you should find an eel's head, you may bring it to me."

And they were "at home."

The poor little duckling, who had been the last to hatch and was so ugly, was bitten and pushed and made fun of both by the hens and by the other ducks. The turkey cock (who had been born with spurs on, and therefore thought he was an emperor) rustled his feathers as if he were a full-rigged ship under sail, and strutted up to the duckling. He gobbled so loudly at him that his own face got all red.

The poor little duckling did not know where to turn. How he grieved over his own ugliness, and how sad he was! The poor creature was mocked and laughed at by the whole henyard.

That was the first day; and each day that followed was worse than the one before. The poor duckling was chased and mistreated by everyone, even his own sisters and brothers, who quacked again and again, "If only the cat would get you, you ugly thing!"

Even his mother said, "I wish you were far away." The other ducks bit him and the hens pecked at him. The little girl who came to feed the fowls kicked him.

At last the duckling ran away. It flew over the tops of the bushes, frightening all the little birds so that they flew up into the air. "They, too, think I am ugly," thought the duckling, and closed his eyes—but he kept on running.

Finally he came to a great swamp where wild ducks lived; and here he stayed for the night, for he was too tired to go any farther.

In the morning he was discovered by the wild ducks. They looked at him and one of them asked, "What kind of bird are you?"

The ugly duckling bowed in all directions, for he was trying to be as polite as he knew how.

"You are ugly," said the wild ducks, "but that is no concern of ours, as long as you don't try to marry into our family."

The poor duckling wasn't thinking of marriage. All he wanted was to be allowed to swim among the reeds and drink a little water when he was thirsty.

He spent two days in the swamp; then two wild geese came—or rather, two wild ganders, for they were males. They had been hatched not long ago; therefore they were both frank and bold.

"Listen, comrade," they said. "You are so ugly that we like you. Do you want to migrate with us? Not far from here there is a marsh where some beautiful wild geese live. They are all lovely maidens, and you are so ugly that you may seek your fortune among them. Come along."

"Bang! Bang!" Two shots were heard and both the ganders fell down dead among the reeds, and the water turned red from their blood.

"Bang! Bang!" Again came the sound of shots, and a flock of wild geese flew up.

The whole swamp was surrounded by hunters; from every direction came the awful noise. Some of the hunters had hidden behind bushes or among the reeds but others, screened from sight by the leaves, sat on the long, low branches of the trees that stretched out over the swamp. The blue smoke from the guns lay like a fog over the water and among the trees. Dogs came splashing through the marsh, and they bent and broke the reeds.

The poor little duckling was terrified. He was about to tuck his head under his wing, in order to hide, when he saw a big dog peering at him through the reeds. The dog's tongue hung out of its mouth and its eyes glistened evilly. It bared its teeth. Splash! It turned away without touching the duckling.

"Oh, thank God!" he sighed. "I am so ugly that even the dog doesn't want to bite me."

The little duckling lay as still as he could while the shots whistled through the reeds. Not until the middle of the afternoon did the shooting stop; but the poor little duckling was still so frightened that he waited several hours longer before taking his head out from under his wing. Then he ran as quickly as he could out of the swamp. Across the fields and the meadows he went, but a wind had come up and he found it hard to make his way against it.

Toward evening he came upon a poor little hut. It was so wretchedly crooked that it looked as if it couldn't make up its mind which way to fall and that was why it was still standing. The wind was blowing so hard that the poor little duckling had to sit down in order not to be blown away. Suddenly he noticed that the door was off its hinges, making a crack; and he squeezed himself through it and was inside.

An old woman lived in the hut with her cat and her hen. The cat was called Sonny and could both arch his back and purr. Oh yes, it could also make sparks if you rubbed its fur the wrong way. The hen had very short legs and that was why she was called Cluck Lowlegs. But she was good at laying eggs, and the old woman loved her as if she were her own child.

In the morning the hen and the cat discovered the duckling. The cat meowed and the hen clucked.

"What is going on?" asked the old woman, and looked around. She couldn't see very well, and when she found the duckling she thought it was a fat, full-grown duck. "What a fine catch!" she exclaimed. "Now we shall have duck eggs, unless it's a drake. We'll give it a try."

So the duckling was allowed to stay for three weeks on probation, but he laid no eggs. The cat was the master of the house and the hen the mistress. They always referred to themselves as "we and the world," for they thought that they were half the world—and the better half at that. The duckling thought that he should be allowed to have a different opinion, but the hen did not agree.

"Can you lay eggs?" she demanded.

"No," answered the duckling.

"Then keep your mouth shut."

And the cat asked, "Can you arch your back? Can you purr? Can you make sparks?"

"No."

"Well, in that case, you have no right to have an opinion when sensible people are talking."

The duckling was sitting in a corner and was in a bad mood. Suddenly he recalled how lovely it could be outside in the fresh air when the sun shone: a great longing to be floating in the water came over the duckling, and he could not help talking about it.

"What is the matter with you?" asked the hen as soon as she had heard what he had to say. "You have nothing to do, that's why you get ideas like that. Lay eggs or purr, and such notions will disappear."

"You have no idea how delightful it is to float in the water, and to dive down to the bottom of a lake and get your head wet," said the duckling.

"Yes, that certainly does sound amusing," said the hen. "You must have gone mad. Ask the cat—he is the most intelligent being I know—ask him whether he likes to swim or dive down to the bottom of a lake. Don't take my word for anything. . . . Ask the old woman, who is the cleverest person in the world; ask her whether she likes to float and to get her head all wet."

"You don't understand me!" wailed the duckling.

"And if I don't understand you, who will? I hope you don't think that you are wiser than the cat or the old woman—not to mention myself. Don't give yourself airs! Thank your Creator for all He has done for you. Aren't you sitting in a warm room among intelligent people whom you could learn something from? While you, yourself, do nothing but say a lot of nonsense and aren't the least bit amusing! Believe me, that's the truth, and I am only telling it to you for your own good. That's how you recognize a true friend: it's someone who is willing to tell you the truth, no matter how unpleasant it is. Now get to work: lay some eggs, or learn to purr and arch your back."

"I think I'll go out into the wide world," replied the duckling.

"Go right ahead!" said the hen.

And the duckling left. He found a lake where he could float in the water and dive to the bottom. There were other ducks, but they ignored him because he was so ugly.

Autumn came and the leaves turned yellow and brown, then they fell from the trees. The wind caught them and made them dance. The clouds were heavy with hail and snow. A raven sat on a fence and screeched, "Ach! Ach!" because it was so cold. When just thinking of how cold it was is enough to make one shiver, what a terrible time the duckling must have had.

One evening just as the sun was setting gloriously, a flock of beautiful birds came out from among the rushes. Their feathers were so white that they glistened; and they had long, graceful necks. They were swans. They made a very loud cry, then they spread their powerful wings. They were flying south to a warmer climate, where the lakes were not frozen in the winter. Higher and higher they circled. The ugly duckling turned round and round in the water like a wheel and stretched his neck up toward the sky; he felt a strange longing. He screeched so piercingly that he frightened himself.

Oh, he would never forget those beautiful birds, those happy birds. When they were out of sight the duckling dove down under the water to the bottom of the lake; and when he came up again he was beside himself. He did not know the name of those birds or where they were going, and yet he felt that he loved them as he had never loved any other creatures. He did not envy them. It did not even occur to him to wish that he were so handsome himself. He would have been happy if the other ducks had let him stay in the henyard: that poor, ugly bird!

The weather grew colder and colder. The duckling had to swim round and round in the water, to keep just a little space for himself that wasn't frozen. Each night his hole became smaller and smaller. On all sides of him the ice creaked and groaned. The little duckling had to keep his feet constantly in motion so that the last bit of open water wouldn't become ice. At last he was too tired to swim any more. He sat still. The ice closed in around him and he was frozen fast.

Early the next morning a farmer saw him and with his clogs broke the ice to free the duckling. The man put the bird under his arm and took it home to his wife, who brought the duckling back to life.

The children wanted to play with him. But the duckling was afraid that they were going to hurt him, so he flapped his wings and flew right into the milk pail. From there he flew into a big bowl of butter and then into a barrel of flour. What a sight he was!

The farmer's wife yelled and chased him with a poker. The children laughed and almost fell on top of each other, trying to catch him; and how they screamed! Luckily for the duckling, the door was open. He got out of the house and found a hiding place beneath some bushes, in the newly fallen snow; and there he lay so still, as though there were hardly any life left in him.

It would be too horrible to tell of all the hardship and suffering the duckling experienced that long winter. It is enough to know that he did survive. When again the sun shone warmly and the larks began to sing, the duckling was lying among the reeds in the swamp. Spring had come!

He spread out his wings to fly. How strong and powerful they were! Before he knew it, he was far from the swamp and flying above a beautiful garden. The apple trees were blooming and the lilac bushes stretched their flower-covered branches over the water of a winding canal. Everything was so beautiful: so fresh and green. Out of a forest of rushes came three swans. They ruffled their feathers and floated so lightly on the water. The ugly duckling recognized the birds and felt again that strange sadness come over him.

"I shall fly over to them, those royal birds! And they can hack me to death because I, who am so ugly, dare to approach them! What difference does it make? It is better to be killed by them than to be bitten by the other ducks, and pecked by the hens, and kicked by the girl who tends the henyard; or to suffer through the winter."

And he lighted on the water and swam toward the magnificent swans. When they saw him they ruffled their feathers and started to swim in his direction. They were coming to meet him.

"Kill me," whispered the poor creature, and bent his head humbly while he waited for death. But what was that he saw in the water? It was his own reflection; and he was no longer an awkward, clumsy, gray bird, so ungainly and so ugly. He was a swan!

It does not matter that one has been born in the henyard as long as one has lain in a swan's egg.

He was thankful that he had known so much want, and gone through so much suffering, for it made him appreciate his present happiness and the loveliness of everything about him all the more. The swans made a circle around him and caressed him with their beaks.

Some children came out into the garden. They had brought bread with them to feed the swans. The youngest child shouted, "Look, there's a new one!" All the children joyfully clapped their hands, and they ran to tell their parents.

Cake and bread were cast on the water for the swans. Everyone agreed that the new swan was the most beautiful of them all. The older swans bowed toward him.

He felt so shy that he hid his head beneath his wing. He was too happy, but not proud, for a kind heart can never be proud. He thought of the time when he had been mocked and persecuted. And now everyone said that he was the most beautiful of the most beautiful birds. And the lilac bushes stretched their branches right down to the water for him. The sun shone so warm and brightly. He ruffled his feathers and raised his slender neck, while out of the joy in his heart, he thought, "Such happiness I did not dream of when I was the ugly duckling."

23

The Pine Tree

OUT in the forest grew a very nice-looking little pine tree. It had plenty of space around it, so that it got both fresh air and all the sunshine it could want. Near it grew some larger pine and other evergreen trees; but the little pine was so busy growing that it took no notice of them, or of the children who came to the forest to pick wild strawberries and raspberries, not even when they sat down near it and said so loudly that anyone could have heard them: "Goodness, what a beautiful little tree!" No, the tree heard nothing, for it was not listening.

The following year it was a little taller and had a new ring of branches; and the next year it had one more. That is the way you can tell the age of a pine tree—by the rings of branches it has.

"Oh, how I wish I were as big as the big trees," moaned the little pine tree. "Then I could spread my branches out, and with my top, I could see far out into the wide world! The birds would come and nest in me; and when the wind blew, then I would bend and sway as elegantly as the other trees."

The warm sunshine gave it no pleasure, nor did the songs of the little birds or the sight of the red clouds that drifted across the sky at sunset.

Winter came. The snow lay white and sparkling. Rabbits came running, and jumped over the little pine tree. "Oh, how mortifying!" it cried every time. But two years passed before the little tree had grown so tall that the rabbits could no longer jump over it but had to run around it instead.

"To grow, to grow," thought the pine tree, "to become tall and old; there's nothing in the world so marvelous!"

In the autumn the woodcutter came to chop down some of the older trees. He came every year and the young tree, now that it was growing up, shook inside itself when the tall, mighty trees fell with a thunderous crash to the ground. Their branches were shorn and there they lay: naked, thin, and long. One could hardly recognize them. They were loaded onto a horse-drawn wagon and carried out of the forest.

Where were they being taken? What would happen to them?

In spring, when the swallows and the storks returned, the young pine put the question to them: "Do any of you know where the trees go and what happens to them?"

The swallows didn't know, but the storks looked thoughtful for a moment. Then one of them said, "I think I know. I have met many tall ships on my way to Egypt. The ships have lofty masts and they smell of pine, so I'm sure they must be pine. I tell you, they stood proudly."

"If only I were old enough to become a mast and sail across the ocean," said the pine tree. "Tell me about the ocean. What does it look like?"

"It's too big for me to try to tell about it," replied the stork, and walked away.

"Be glad that you are young," whispered the sun's rays. "Enjoy your strength and the pleasure of being alive."

The wind kissed the young tree and the dew shed tears over it; but the pine tree noticed neither.

Just before Christmas, some of the trees that were cut down weren't any older or taller than the one who was so dissatisfied. These trees did not have their branches shorn; but they were loaded onto wagons and driven out of the forest just as the other, larger trees had been.

"Where are they going?" asked the pine tree. "None of them was any taller than I am; and I saw one that was at least a foot shorter. Why were they allowed to keep their branches? And where were they going?"

"We know! We know! We know!" chirped the sparrows. "We have been in the town and looked through the windows. We know where they are. They have come to glory. They have been given the greatest honor a tree could wish for. They have been planted right in the middle of the warm living rooms of people's houses. They are decorated with silver and gold tinsel. There are apples and toys and heart-shaped cookies and hundreds of candles on their branches."

The pine tree was so excited that its boughs trembled. "And what else happened to them?"

"We don't know," chirped the sparrows. "We've told you everything we saw."

"Have I been created to become like that?" thought the tree jubilantly. "Will that glory be mine? Why, that is much better than sailing across the oceans. Oh, how I long for it to happen! I wish it soon would be Christmas again. I am as tall and as good looking as the trees that were chosen last year. I wish I were on the wagon already. I wish I were in the warm room being decorated. I wonder what will happen after that? Something even better, even grander will happen, why else should they put gold and silver on me? But what will it be? How I long for it to happen! How I suffer from anticipation. I can hardly understand myself. . . . Oh, how difficult it is to be me!"

"Be happy with us," said the wind and the sunshine. "Be glad that you are young; enjoy your youth and your freedom, here in nature."

But the tree was not happy. It grew and grew; and now it was dark green both in winter and summer, and people who passed by often remarked, "What a lovely tree!"

Then one Christmas, it was the first tree to be cut down. It felt the ax sever it from its roots; and it fell with a sigh to the ground. A feeling of pain, of helplessness, came over it, and never for a moment did it think of the glory that was to come. It only felt the sadness of leaving the place where it had grown. It knew that it would never see again the little bushes and flowers that had grown around it, or hear the songs of the little birds that had sat on its branches. No, parting was no pleasure.

The tree didn't recover before it was being unloaded in town and heard someone say, "What a beautiful tree! We shall have that one and no other."

Two servants in livery carried the tree up to a magnificent hall. Portraits were hanging on the walls, and next to the big tile stove stood two Chinese vases with lions on their lids. There were rocking chairs, and sofas covered with silk; and on a table lay picture books and toys worth more than a hundred times a hundred crowns—so at least the children claimed. The tree was planted in a bucket filled with sand, but nobody could see that it was an old one, for it was covered by a green cloth and stood on a many-colored rug.

The tree shook with expectation. What was about to happen? The servants and the young ladies of the family started to decorate it. On the branches they hung little colored nets that were filled with sweets; and golden apples and walnuts were tied to the tree so that they looked as if they were growing there. A hundred little red, blue, and white candles were fastened on the branches; and among them, on the green needles, sat little dolls that looked exactly like human beings. At last, on the very top of the tree was placed a golden star. It was magnificent, unbelievably magnificent!

"Tonight . . . tonight," everyone said. "Tonight it will be glorious!"

"Oh," thought the tree, "why doesn't night come! The candles will be lit—I wonder what will happen then! Will the other trees come from the forest and look at me? Will the sparrows peep in through the windows? Will I grow roots and stand here both summer and winter?"

The poor tree had a bark-ache from anticipation, which for a tree is as annoying as headache is to a human being.

Finally evening did come, and the candles were lit. Oh, how beautiful it looked. The poor tree trembled with emotion. In fact, it shook so much that one of its branches caught on fire, which smarted and hurt.

"God preserve us!" cried the ladies, and put out the fire.

Now the poor tree didn't even dare tremble; it was horrible! There it stood, rigid and still, and fearing every moment that it might lose some of its decorations. How bewildering everything was! The big doors opened and the children came running in. They were so wild, especially the older ones, they looked as if they wanted to overturn the tree. The little children were so overawed by the tree that they just stood and stared silently. But that didn't last long; soon they were making as much noise as the older ones. The grownups came last; but they had seen the sight many times before. Soon they all were dancing and singing around the tree; then the presents, which had been hung on the tree, were given out.

"What are they doing?" thought the tree. "What is going to happen now?"

The candles burned down and were extinguished, and the children were allowed to plunder the tree. They grabbed the little nets with sweets in them and pulled at the candied fruit and the nuts. They were so rough that they almost broke off the branches; and they would certainly have upset the tree, had it not been for the string with which its top was attached to the ceiling.

Now the children danced and played, and no one but the old nurse paid any attention to the tree; she kept walking around and around it, looking among the branches to see if she could find an apple or a fig which the youngsters might have overlooked.

"A story! A story!" screamed all the children, and pushed a fat man toward the Christmas tree.

He sat down beneath it, for, as he said, he liked sitting among the "greenery," and it wouldn't harm the tree to hear a story. "But I shall tell only one," he declared. "You can choose between 'Willowy, Wollowy' and 'How Humpty-dumpty Fell Down the Stairs but Won the Princess Anyway.'"

" 'Willowy Wollowy'!" screamed several of the children.

" 'Humpty-dumpty'!" screamed the others; and the room was filled with their shouting.

"Isn't there something that I am supposed to do?" thought the tree, not knowing that it had already done everything that it was supposed to do.

The man told the story of "How Humpty-dumpty Fell Down the Stairs but Won the Princess Anyway." When he had finished all the children screamed that they wanted more, for they hoped to be able to persuade him to tell the story of "Willowy, Wollowy" too; but they couldn't. They had to be satisfied with the story about Humpty-dumpty.

The pine tree stood still, deep in its own thoughts. The birds out in the forest had never told a story like that. "No, that's the way of the world," it said to itself. "Humpty-dumpty falls down the stairs but he wins the princess anyway." The tree believed that the story it had heard was true because the man who had told it looked so trustworthy. "Yes, who knows?" it whispered to itself. "Maybe I, too, will fall down the stairs and win the princess." And the tree looked forward to the next day, when it would again be decorated with lights and hung with toys.

"Tomorrow," it thought, "tomorrow I shan't tremble as I did today. I shall really enjoy myself, and hear the story of Humpty-dumpty again; and maybe the one about 'Willowy, Wollowy' too." All night long the tree silently thought of the glory that was to come on the following day.

The next morning the servants came.

"Now it all starts all over again," thought the tree.

But it didn't. The servants dragged the tree up two flights of stairs into the attic, where they threw it in a dark corner which the daylight never reached.

"What is the meaning of this?" the tree asked itself. "Why have I been put here? What will happen now?"

The tree leaned itself up against the wall and thought and thought. It had plenty of time for thinking, because days and nights went by without anyone coming into the attic to disturb it. When finally some-one did come, it was only to put some old boxes up there. The tree was hidden in the corner and quite forgotten.

"Now it is winter outside," thought the tree. "The earth is so hard and covered with snow that they cannot plant me. They are sheltering me here till spring. How considerate man is! I just wish it weren't so dark and so terribly lonely! There isn't even a rabbit here. It was so nice out in the forest when the ground was covered with snow and the rabbits darted about. Though I didn't like it when I was very small and they could jump over me. But here it is so quiet and I am terribly lonely."

"Twick . . . twick," said a little mouse, and nipped its way out of the wall.

"Twick . . . twick . . ." And another, even smaller mouse appeared.

The two little mice sniffed at the tree and then climbed up among the branches.

"It is cold," remarked the mice. "But otherwise it is a quite nice attic. Don't you think so, old pine tree?"

"I am not old," protested the pine tree. "There are lots of trees in the forest much older than I am."

"Where do you come from?" asked one of the little mice. Those little creatures were very curious and they asked the tree one question after another. "What do you know? What can you tell us? Tell us about the most beautiful place in the world. Have you been there? . . . Have you ever been in the larder, by the way? In the larder where there are cheeses lying on shelves, hams hanging from the ceiling, and where you can dance on tallow candles; and where you can come in thin and go out fat?"

"I don't know of any such place," replied the tree. "But I know the forest where the sun shines and the birds sing." And the pine tree told them of its youth in the woods.

The little mice listened quietly, for they had never heard of such a place; and when the tree was finished they said, "Think how much you have seen! How happy you must have been!"

"Happy?" repeated the pine tree, and thought about what it had told the little mice. "Yes, I suppose I had a quite good time," it confessed. Then the tree told about Christmas Eve and how it had been decorated with candles and sweets.

"Oh," sighed the mice, "how fortunate you have been, old pine tree."

"I am not old!" protested the tree. "I have come this very winter from the forest. I am in my prime. I just appear a little stunted because I have been cut down."

"You tell about everything so marvelously," exclaimed the little mice; and the next night they brought along four of their friends.

The pine tree again told the story of its youth in the forest and what had happened to it on Christmas Eve; and the more it told, the more clearly it could remember everything.

"Yes, they were good times; and they can come again. They will come again! Humpty-dumpty fell down the stairs but he won the princess anyway." And the pine tree remembered a little birch tree that had grown nearby it in the forest, for to the pine tree the little birch was a real princess.

"Who was Humpty-dumpty?" asked the little mice.

The pine tree told them the fairy tale it had heard. It could remember every word of it. The little mice were so pleased that they climbed to the very top of the tree to show their appreciation. The next night more mice came; and on Sunday two rats arrived. But they criticized the story and said it wasn't amusing at all. This made the poor little mice sad, for now they thought less of the story too.

"Don't you know any other stories?" asked one of the rats.

"No, I only know that one," admitted the pine tree. "I heard it on the happiest night of my life; but then I didn't know that it was the happiest night."

"It is a particularly uninteresting story. Don't you know any about bacon or candle stumps? No stories that take place in a larder?"

"No," the tree answered.

"Well, in that case you're not worth listening to," said the rats, and left.

The mice stayed away too; and the pine tree sighed in its loneliness. "It was nice when the quick little animals came visiting and listened to what I had to tell. But now that is over too. I must remember to be happy when I am taken out again," the tree muttered. "I wonder when that will be."

Finally, one morning it happened. The servants came up to the attic and started moving boxes about; they were cleaning up. When they found the tree in the corner they handled it roughly and threw it about. At last a young man carried it down the many flights of stairs out into the yard.

"Now life begins again," it thought. There was fresh air and it felt the sun's rays. Everything was happening so fast, and it was so excited at being outside, that the tree looked at the world about it but not at itself. The yard was bordered by a garden where all the bushes and trees were in flower. The roses covered the little fence and smelled so sweetly. The linden tree was in bloom. The swallows flew about singing, "Tweet, tweet. . . . My lover has come." But they didn't mean the pine tree.

"Now I am going to live!" shouted the tree joyously, and spread out its branches. But all its needles were yellow and dead. It was thrown into a corner of the yard where the nettles prospered. The golden star from Christmas Eve was still on its top and the sun reflected in it.

Playing in the yard were two of the children who had danced around the tree on Christmas Eve and had loved it so much then. The younger child now ran over and tore the golden star from the tree.

"Look what I found on this horrid old Christmas tree," he said. He was wearing boots and he kicked the tree's branches so that many of them broke.

The pine tree saw all the greenness about it; then it looked at itself and wished it had been left in the dark corner of the attic. It remembered its youth in the forest, the glory of Christmas Eve, and the little mice who had listened so contentedly to the story about Humpty-dumpty.

"Gone! Gone!" sighed the poor tree. "If I only could have been happy while I had a chance to be. Now it is all over and gone! Everything!"

One of the servants came and cut the tree up for kindling. It became a little pile of wood. The cook used it to light the kitchen range. It flared up instantly and the tree sighed so deeply that it sounded like a shot. The children who were playing in the yard heard it, and they ran in and sat down in front of the stove.

"Bang! Bang!" they cried.

Every time the tree sighed, it thought of a summer day in the forest, or a winter night when the stars are brightest, and it remembered Christmas Eve and Humpty-dumpty: the only fairy tale it had ever heard and knew how to tell. Then it became ashes.

The children returned to the yard to play. The little boy had fastened the golden star to his chest. The star the pine tree had worn on the happiest evening of its life. But that was a long time ago; now the pine tree is no more, just as this story is over; for all stories—no matter how long they are—must eventually come to an end.

24

＊◇＊

The Snow Queen

a fairy tale told in seven stories

THE FIRST STORY, WHICH CONCERNS ITSELF WITH A BROKEN
MIRROR AND WHAT HAPPENED TO ITS FRAGMENTS

ALL RIGHT, we will start the story; when we come to the end we shall
know more than we do now.

Once upon a time there was a troll, the most evil troll of them all;
he was called the devil. One day he was particularly pleased with himself, for he had invented a mirror which had the strange power of
being able to make anything good or beautiful that it reflected appear
horrid; and all that was evil and worthless seem attractive and worth
while. The most beautiful landscape looked like spinach; and the
kindest and most honorable people looked repulsive or ridiculous.
They might appear standing on their heads, without any stomachs;
and their faces would always be so distorted that you couldn't recognize them. A little freckle would spread itself out till it covered half a
nose or a whole cheek.

"It is a very amusing mirror," said the devil. But the most amusing
part of it all was that if a good or a kind thought passed through anyone's mind the most horrible grin would appear on the face in the
mirror.

It was so entertaining that the devil himself laughed out loud. All
the little trolls who went to troll school, where the devil was head-

master, said that a miracle had taken place. Now for the first time one could see what humanity and the world really looked like—at least, so they thought. They ran all over with the mirror, until there wasn't a country or a person in the whole world that had not been reflected and distorted in it.

At last they decided to fly up to heaven to poke fun of the angels and God Himself. All together they carried the mirror, and flew up higher and higher. The nearer they came to heaven, the harder the mirror laughed, so that the trolls could hardly hold onto it; still, they flew higher and higher: upward toward God and the angels, then the mirror shook so violently from laughter that they lost their grasp; it fell and broke into hundreds of millions of billions and some odd pieces. It was then that it really caused trouble, much more than it ever had before. Some of the splinters were as tiny as grains of sand and just as light, so that they were spread by the winds all over the world. When a sliver like that entered someone's eye it stayed there; and the person, forever after, would see the world distorted, and only be able to see the faults, and not the virtues, of everyone around him, since even the tiniest fragment contained all the evil qualities of the whole mirror. If a splinter should enter someone's heart—oh, that was the most terrible of all!—that heart would turn to ice.

Some of the pieces of the mirror were so large that windowpanes could be made of them, although through such a window it was no pleasure to contemplate your friends. Some of the medium-sized pieces became spectacles—but just think of what would happen when you put on such a pair of glasses in order to see better and be able to judge more fairly. That made the devil laugh so hard that it tickled in his stomach, which he found very pleasant.

Some of the tiniest bits of the mirror were still flying about in the air. And now you shall hear about them.

THE SECOND STORY, WHICH IS ABOUT A LITTLE BOY AND A LITTLE GIRL

In a big city, where there live so many people and are so many houses that not every family can have a garden of its own and so must learn to be satisfied with a potted plant, there once lived a poor little girl and a poor little boy who had a garden a little bit larger than a flowerpot. They weren't brother and sister but loved each other as much as if they had been. Their parents lived right across from each other; each family had a little apartment in the garret, but the houses were built so close together that the roofs almost touched. Between the two gutters that hung from the eaves and collected the water when it rained, there was only a very narrow space, and the two families could visit each other by climbing from one gable window to the other.

In front of the windows each family had a wooden box filled with earth, where herbs and other useful plants grew; but in each box there was also a little rose tree. The parents got the idea that, instead of setting the boxes parallel to their windows, they could set them across, so they reached from one window to the other. In that manner, the two gables were connected by a little garden. The peas climbed over the sides and hung down; and the little rose trees grew as tall as the windows and joined together, so that they looked like a green triumphal arch. The sides of the boxes were quite high and since the children could be relied upon not to try to climb over them, they were allowed to take their little wooden stools outside and sit under the rose trees; and there it was pleasant to play.

In winter that was not possible; then the windows were tightly closed and sometimes they would be covered by ice. Then the little children would heat copper coins on the stove and press them against the glass until the roundest of holes would melt in the ice; through each of these peeped the loveliest little eye: one belonged to a little boy and the other to a little girl. His name was Kai and hers was Gerda. In summer they had to take only a few steps to be together; but in the winter they had to run down and up so many stairs and across a yard covered by snowdrifts.

"The white bees are swarming," said the old Grandmother.

"Do they have a queen too?" asked Kai, for he knew that real bees have such a ruler.

"Yes, they have," said the old woman. "She always flies right in the center of the swarm, where the most snowflakes are. She is the biggest of them all, but she never lies down to rest as the other snowflakes do. No, when the wind dies she returns to the black clouds. Many a winter night she flies through the streets of the town and looks in through the windows; then they become covered by ice flowers."

"Yes, I've seen that!" said first one child and then the other; and now they knew that what the Grandmother said was true.

"Could the Snow Queen come inside, right into our room?" asked the little girl.

"Let her come," said Kai. "I will put her right on top of the stove and then she will melt."

The Grandmother patted his head and told them another story. But that night, as Kai was getting undressed, he climbed up on the chair by the window and looked out through his peephole. It was snowing gently; one of the flakes fell on the edge of the wooden box and stayed there; other snowflakes followed and they grew until they took the shape of a woman. Her clothes looked like the whitest gauze. It was made of millions of little star-shaped snowflakes. She was beautiful but all made of ice: cold, blindingly glittering ice; and yet she was alive, for her eyes stared at Kai like two stars, but neither rest nor peace was to be found in her gaze. She nodded toward the window and beckoned. The little boy got so frightened that he jumped down from the chair; and at that moment a shadow crossed the window as if a big bird had flown by.

The next day there was frost; but by noon the weather changed and it thawed. Soon it was spring again and the world grew green; the swallows returned to build their nests and the windows were opened. The little children sat in their boxes, above the eaves and high above all the other stories of the houses.

The roses bloomed particularly marvelously that summer. The little girl had learned a psalm in which roses were mentioned in one of the verses; her own roses reminded her of it, and so she sang, and the boy joined her:

> "In the valley where the roses be
> There the child Jesus you will see."

The two little children held each other's hands, kissed the flowers, and looked up into the blessed sunshine. Oh, these were lovely summer days, and it was ever so pleasant to sit under the little rose trees that never seemed to stop flowering.

One afternoon as Kai and Gerda sat looking at a picture book with animals and flowers in it—it was exactly five o'clock, for the bells in the church tower had just struck the hour—Kai said, "Ouch, ouch! Something pricked my heart!" And then again, "Ouch, something sharp is in my eye."

The little girl put her arms around his neck and looked into his eyes but there was nothing to be seen. Still, it hurt and little Gerda cried out of sympathy.

"I think it is gone now," said Kai. But he was wrong, two of the splinters from the devil's mirror had hit him: one had entered his heart and the other his eyes. You remember the mirror, it was that horrible invention of the devil which made everything good and decent look small and ridiculous, and everything evil and foul appear grand and worth while. Poor Kai, soon his heart would turn to ice and his eyes would see nothing but faults in everything. But the pain, that would disappear.

"Why are you crying?" he demanded. "You look ugly when you cry. There is nothing the matter with me. Look!" he shouted. "That rose up there has been gnawed by a worm; and look at that one, it is all crooked. They are ugly roses, as ugly as the boxes they grew in." Then he kicked the sides of the box and tore off the two roses.

"What are you doing, Kai?" cried the little girl, and when Kai saw how frightened she was, he tore off yet another flower; and then climbed through the window into his parents' apartment, leaving Gerda to sit out there all alone.

Later, when she came inside with the picture book, he told her that picture books were for babies. And when Grandmother told stories he would argue with her or—which was much worse—stand behind her chair with a pair of glasses on his nose and imitate her most cruelly. He did it so accurately that people laughed. Soon he learned to mimic everyone in the whole street. He had a good eye for their little peculiarities and knew how to copy them.

Everyone said, "That boy has his head screwed on right!" But it was the splinters of glass that were in his eyes and his heart that made him behave that way; that, too, was why he teased little Gerda all the time—she who loved him with all her heart.

He did not play as he used to; now his games were more grown up. One winter day when snow was falling he brought a magnifying glass and looked at the snowflakes that were falling on his blue coat.

"Look through the glass, Gerda," he said to his little playmate;

and she did. Through the magnifying glass each snowflake appeared like a flower or ten-pointed star. They were, indeed, beautiful to see.

"Aren't they marvelous?" asked Kai. "And each of them is quite perfect; they are much nicer than real flowers. They are all flawless as long as they don't melt."

A little bit later he came by, with his sled on his back, and wearing his hat and woolen gloves. He screamed into Gerda's ear as loud as he could, "I have been allowed to go down to the big square and play with the other boys!" And away he went.

Now down in the snow-covered square the most daring of the boys would tie their sleds behind the farmers' wagons. It was good fun and they would get a good ride. While they were playing, a big white sled drove into the square; the driver was clad in a white fur coat and a white fur hat. The sled circled the square twice and Kai managed to attach his little sled onto the back of the big one. He wanted to hitch a ride.

Away he went; the sled turned the corner and was out of the square. It began to go faster and faster, and Kai wanted to untie his sled, but every time he was about to do it, the driver of the big white sled turned and nodded so kindly to him that he didn't. It was as if they knew each other. Soon they were past the city gate; and the snow was falling so heavily that Kai could not see anything. He untied the rope but it made no difference, his little sled moved on as if it were tied to the big one by magic. They traveled along with the speed of the wind. Kai cried out in fear but no one heard him. The snow flew around him as he flew forward. Every so often his little sled would leap across a ditch and Kai had to hold on, in order not to fall off. He wanted to say his prayers, but all he could remember were his multiplication tables.

The snowflakes grew bigger and bigger until they looked like white hens that were running alongside him. At last the big sled stopped and its driver stood up and turned around to look at Kai. The fur hat and the coat were made of snow; the driver was a woman: how tall and straight she stood. She was the Snow Queen!

"We have driven a goodish way," she said, "but you look cold. Come, creep inside my bearskin coat."

Kai got up from his own sled and walked over to the big one, where he sat down next to the Snow Queen. She put her fur coat around him, and it felt as if he lay down in a deep snowdrift.

"Are you still cold?" she asked, and kissed his forehead. Her kiss was colder than ice. It went right to his heart, which was already half made of ice. He felt as though he were about to die, but it hurt only for a minute, then it was over. Now he seemed stronger and he no longer felt how cold the air was.

"My sled, my sled, don't forget it!" he cried. And one of the white hens put it on her back and flew behind them. The Snow Queen kissed Kai once more, and then all memory of Gerda, the Grandmother, and his home disappeared.

"I shan't give you any more kisses," she said, "or I might kiss you to death."

Kai looked at the Snow Queen; he could not imagine that anyone could have a wiser or a more beautiful face; and she no longer seemed to be made of ice, as she had when he first saw her outside his window, the time she had beckoned to him. In his eyes she now seemed utterly perfect, nor did he feel any fear. He told her that he knew his multiplication tables, could figure in fractions, and knew the area in square miles of every country in Europe, and what its population was.

The Snow Queen smiled, and somehow Kai felt that he did not know enough. He looked out into the great void of the night, for by now they were flying high up in the clouds, above the earth. The storm swept on and sang its old, eternal songs. Above oceans, forests, and lakes they flew; and the cold winter wind whipped the landscape below them. Kai heard the cry of the wolves and the hoarse voice of the crows. The moon came out, and into its large and clear disk Kai stared all through the long winter night. When daytime came he fell asleep at the feet of the Snow Queen.

THE THIRD STORY: THE FLOWER GARDEN OF THE OLD WOMAN WHO KNEW MAGIC

But how did little Gerda feel when Kai did not return? She asked everyone where he had gone and none could answer. The boys who had been in the square could only tell that they had seen him tie his little sled to the back of a big white sled that had driven out of the city gate.

No one knew where he had gone and little Gerda cried long and bitterly. As time passed people began to say that he must have died; probably he had drowned in the deep, dark river that ran close to the city. It was a long and dismal winter.

Finally spring came with warm sunshine.

"Kai is dead and gone!" sighed little Gerda.

"I don't believe that," said the sunbeams.

"No, he is dead and gone," she repeated, and asked the swallows if that were not true.

"We don't believe it either," they answered; and at last little Gerda was convinced that Kai was not dead.

"I will put on my new red shoes, the ones Kai has never seen," she said one day. "And then I will go down to the river and ask it a few questions."

It was very early in the morning; she kissed the old Grandmother, who was still asleep, put on her new red shoes, and walked out through the city gate and down to the river.

"Is it true that you have taken my playmate? I will give you my new red shoes if you will give him back to me."

She thought that the little waves nodded strangely; so she took her treasure, her new red shoes, and threw them out into the river. They struck the water not far from shore, and the little waves carried them back to her. It was as if the river did not want her little shoes since it had not taken Kai. This little Gerda did not realize, she thought that she just hadn't thrown them far enough out; therefore, she climbed into a rowboat that lay among the reeds, stood up in its stern, and threw the shoes out over the water again. The boat had not been moored and, by stepping into the stern, she loosened the bow from the sand and the rowboat started to drift. Although she noticed it at once and turned around, prepared to leap up onto the bank, the boat was already several feet away from shore and she didn't dare jump.

The boat floated faster and faster downstream with the current. Poor Gerda was so frightened that she just sat down and cried. No one heard her except the sparrows and they could not carry her to shore. But they flew alongside the boat, twittering: "We are here! We are here!" to comfort her.

The boat drifted down the river. Gerda sat perfectly still; she was in her stocking feet; the shoes followed the boat but they were far behind. The landscape was beautiful on both sides of the river. Be-

yond the banks, which were covered with flowers, there were
meadows with cows and sheep grazing upon them; but there was not
a human being to be seen anywhere.

"Maybe the river will carry me to where Kai is," thought Gerda.
And that thought was a great comfort and she felt much happier. For
hours she sat looking at the green shores; then the boat drifted past a
cherry orchard; in the middle of it stood a strange little house with
blue and green windows and a straw roof. Before the doors two
wooden soldiers kept guard and presented arms when a boat glided
by on the river.

Little Gerda, thinking that they were alive, waved and called; but
naturally they did not answer. The current of the river carried the
boat to the shore, and Gerda started to shout for help as loudly as
she could. An old lady came out of the house; she had on a big
broad-brimmed hat with the loveliest paintings of flowers on it.

"Poor little child!" she cried when she saw Gerda. "How did you
get out there on the river, all alone, and sail so far out into the wide
world?" The old lady waded out till she could catch hold of the boat
with her shepherd's crook and drew it into shore. Then she lifted
Gerda out of the boat. The poor child was happy to be on dry land
once again, but she was a little afraid of the old lady.

"Tell me who you are and how you have gotten into such a predic-
ament," the old woman asked.

Gerda told her everything and the old lady shook her head. When
Gerda asked whether she had seen little Kai, all the old lady could
say was that he hadn't gone by her house but that he probably would
arrive there sooner or later. She told little Gerda not to be so sad but
to come and eat some of her cherries and look at her flowers. They
were prettier than any picture book, and every one of them could tell
a story. The old lady took Gerda by the hand, opened the door to her
little house, and led her inside.

The windows were placed high up, and the colored glass gave a
strange light to the room. On the table stood a bowl filled with the
most delicious cherries, and Gerda ate as many of them as she could.
While she ate, the old woman combed Gerda's hair with a gold comb
and her hair curled prettily around her little rosebud face.

"I have longed so much for a little girl like you," said the old
woman. "You just wait and see what good friends we shall become."

While her hair was being combed, Gerda began to forget her

playmate Kai more and more. The old lady knew witchcraft; but she was not an evil witch, she just liked to do a little magic for her own pleasure. She wanted little Gerda to stay with her very much; that was why she went with her shepherd's crook out into the garden and pointed it at all the rosebushes. Immediately, the sweet flowering bushes sank down into the earth and disappeared. One could not even see where they had been. Now she need not fear that when little Gerda saw the roses she would think of Kai and run away.

Then she took Gerda out into the garden and showed it to her. Oh, what a beautiful place it was! All the flowers imaginable were there; and all of them in full bloom, although they belonged to different seasons. Certainly no picture book could be as beautiful as they were. Gerda almost jumped for joy, and she played among them all day until the sun set behind the tall cherry trees. Then she was given the loveliest of beds with a red quilt stuffed with dried violets to cover herself; and there she slept, dreaming sweeter dreams than even a queen on her wedding night.

The next day she played in the warm sunshine with the flowers again; and in this manner many days went by. Gerda, at last, knew every flower in the garden, and though there were so many different kinds, there seemed to be one missing, but she did not know which it was.

One day as she was sitting looking at the old lady's grand hat, with its painted flowers, she saw among them a rose. The old woman had forgotten the one in her hat when she got rid of all the roses—that happens if you are absent-minded.

"What!" exclaimed Gerda. "Are there no roses in the garden?" She ran about the garden, looking and searching, but nowhere did she find a rosebush. She felt so sad that she wept and her tears fell on the very plot of earth where a rose tree had grown. Through the earth, moistened by her tears, the tree shot upward again, blooming just as beautifully as when the old woman had made it vanish. Gerda kissed the flowers and thought of the roses at home and of little Kai.

"I have stayed here much too long," she cried. "I must find little Kai. Do you know where he is?" she asked the roses. "Do you think that he is dead?"

"No, he is not dead," answered the roses. "We have been down under the earth, where the dead are, and Kai was not there."

"Thank you," said little Gerda. She asked the other flowers if they knew where Kai was.

Every flower stood in the warm sunshine and dreamed its own fairy tale; and that it was willing to tell, but none of them knew anything about Kai.

What story did the tiger lily tell her? Here it is:

"Can you hear the drum: boom . . . boom! It has only two beats: boom . . . boom. Listen to the woman's song of lament; hear the priest chant. The Hindu wife is standing on the funeral pyre, dressed in a long red gown. Soon the flames will devour her and her husband's body. She is thinking of someone who is standing among the mourners; his eyes burn even hotter than the flames that lick her feet, his flaming eyes did burn her heart with greater heat than those flames which soon will turn her body into ashes. Can the fire of a funeral pyre extinguish the flame that burns within the heart?"

"That story I don't understand," said little Gerda.

"Well, it is my fairy tale," answered the tiger lily.

Next Gerda asked the honeysuckle; and this is what it said:

"High up above the narrow mountain road the old castle clings to the steep mountainside. Its ancient walls are covered by green ivy; the vines spread over the balcony where a beautiful young girl stands. No unplucked rose is fresher than she, no apple blossom, plucked and carried by the spring wind, is lighter or dances more daintily than she. Hear how her silk dress rustles. Will he not come soon?"

"Is that Kai you mean?" asked little Gerda.

"I tell only my own story, my own dream," answered the honeysuckle.

Now it was the little daisy's turn:

"Between two trees a swing has been hung. Two sweet little girls, with dresses as white as snow and from whose hats green ribbons hang, lazily swing back and forth. Their brother, who is older than they are, is standing up behind them on the swing. He has his arms around the ropes so that he will not fall. In one hand he has a little bowl; in the other, a clay pipe. He is blowing soap bubbles. The swing glides, and the bubbles with their ever changing colors fly through the air. The last bubble clings to the pipe, then the breeze takes it. A little black dog, which belongs to the children, stands on its hind legs barking at the bubble and it breaks. Such is my song: a swing and a world of foam."

"Your tale may be beautiful but you tell it so sadly, and you didn't mention Kai at all," complained little Gerda. "I think I will ask the hyacinth."

"There were three beautiful sisters; they were so fine and delicate that they were almost transparent. One had on a red dress; the second, a blue; and the third, a white one. They danced, hand in hand, down by the lake; but they were not elves, they were real human children. The air smelled so sweet that the girls wandered into the forest. The sweet fragrance grew stronger. Three coffins appeared; and in them lay the three beautiful sisters. They sailed across the lake, and glowworms flew through the air like little candles. Were the dancing girls asleep or were they dead? The smell of the flowers said they were corpses, the bells at vespers ring for the dead."

"Oh, you make me feel so sad," said little Gerda. "And the fragrance from your flowers is so strong that it makes me think of the poor dead girls. Is Kai dead too? The roses, who have been down under the earth, said that he wasn't."

"Ding! dong!" rang the little hyacinth bells. "We are not tolling for Kai, we do not know him. We are singing our own little song, the only one we know."

Gerda approached a little buttercup that shone so prettily between its green leaves.

"You little sun, tell me, do you know where my playmate is?" she asked.

The buttercup's little shining face looked so trustfully back at her, but it too had only its own song to sing and it was not about Kai.

"Into a little narrow yard," began the buttercup, "God's warm sun was shining; it was the first spring day of the year. The sunbeams reflected against the white walls of the neighbor's house; nearby the first little yellow flower had unfolded itself. It was golden in the sunlight; the old grandmother brought her chair outside to sit in the warm sun. Her grandchild, the poor little servant maid, had come home for a short visit. She kissed her grandmother. There was gold in that kiss: the gold of the heart. Gold in the mouth, gold on the ground, and gold in the blessed sunrise. Now that was my little story," said the buttercup.

"Oh, the poor Grandmother," sighed little Gerda. "She must be longing for me and grieving, as she did when little Kai disappeared. But I will soon go back home and bring little Kai with me. There is no point in asking any of the other flowers, each one only sings its own song."

She tied her long dress up so that she could run fast, and away she went. The narcissus hit her leg smartly when she jumped over it and Gerda stopped. "What, do you know something?" she asked, and bent down toward the flower.

"I can see myself, I can see myself," cried the narcissus. "High up in the garret lives the little ballerina; she stands on tiptoe and kicks at the world, for it is but a mirage. She pours a little water from the kettle on a piece of cloth; it is her corset that she is washing, for cleanliness is next to godliness. Her white dress is hanging in the corner; it has also been washed in the teakettle, then it was hung out on the roof to dry. Now she puts it on, and around her neck she ties a saffron-colored kerchief; it makes the dress seem even whiter. She lifts one leg high in the air. She is bending her stem. I can see myself! I can see myself!"

"I don't care either to see you or to hear about you," said Gerda angrily. "Your story is a silly story," and with those words she ran to the other end of the garden.

The door in the wall was closed; she turned the old rusty handle and it sprang open. Out went little Gerda, in her bare feet, out into the wide world. Three times she turned to look back but no one seemed to have noticed her flight.

At last she could not run any farther, and she sat down on a big stone to rest. She looked at the landscape; summer was long since over, it was late fall. Back in the old lady's garden, you could not notice the change in seasons, for it was always summer and the flowers of every season were in bloom.

"Goodness me, how much time I have wasted," sighed Gerda. "It is already autumn, I do not dare rest any longer," and she got up and walked on. Her little feet hurt and she was tired. The leaves of the willow tree were all yellow, the water from the cold, fall mist dripped from it, as its leaves fell one by one. Only the blackthorn bush bore fruits now, and they are bitter. Oh, how somber and gray seemed the wide world.

THE FOURTH STORY, IN WHICH APPEAR A PRINCE AND
A PRINCESS

More and more often did Gerda have to rest. The ground was now covered with snow. A big crow landed near her; the bird sat there a long time, wriggling its head and looking at her. "Caw . . . Caw!" he remarked, which in crow language means "Good day." He was kind, and asked the girl why she was out all alone in the lonely winter world.

The word "alone" Gerda understood only too well; and she told the crow her story and asked him if he had seen little Kai.

The crow nodded most thoughtfully and said, "Maybe, maybe!"

"Oh, he is alive!" screamed little Gerda, and almost squeezed the poor bird to death, while she kissed him.

"Be sensible, be sensible," protested the crow. "It may be little Kai I have seen; but if it is, then I am afraid he has forgotten you for the sake of the princess."

"Does he live with a princess?" asked little Gerda.

"Yes, he does," answered the crow, "but are you sure you don't understand crow language? I much prefer speaking it."

"No, I have never learned it; but Grandmother knows it, I wish now that she had taught it to me."

"Never mind, it can't be helped," said the crow. "I shall do my best, which is a lot more than most people do," and the crow told Gerda all that he knew:

"Now in this kingdom, where we are at present, there lives a princess who is immensely clever; she has read all the newspapers in the whole world and forgotten what was written in them, and that is the part that proves how intelligent she is. A few weeks ago, while she was sitting on the throne—and that, people say, is not such an amusing place to sit—she happened to hum a song which has as its chorus the line 'Why shouldn't I get married?'

" 'Why not, indeed?' thought the princess. 'But if I am to get married it must be to a man who can speak up for himself.' She didn't want anyone who just stood about looking distinguished, for such a fellow is boring. She called all her ladies in waiting and told them of her intention. They clapped their hands, and one of them said, 'Oh, how delightful. I had such an idea myself just the other day.' . . . Believe me, everything I tell you is true," declared the crow. "My fiancée is tame, she has the run of the castle and it is from her I got the story." His fiancée was, naturally, another crow, for birds of a feather flock together.

"The newspapers were printed with a border of hearts and the princess' name on the front page. Inside there was a royal proclamation: any good-looking man, regardless of birth, could come to the castle and speak with the princess, and the one who seemed most at home there and spoke the best, she would marry.

"Believe me," said the crow, and shook his head, "as sure as I am sitting here, that proclamation got people out of their houses. They came thick and fast, you have never seen such a crowd. But neither the first nor the second day did the princess find anyone who pleased her. They could all speak well enough as long as they were standing in the street; but as soon as they had entered the castle gates and saw the royal guards, in their silver uniforms, the young men lost their tongues. They didn't get them back, either, when they had to climb the marble stairs, lined with lackeys dressed in gold; or when they finally arrived in the grand hall with the great chandeliers and had to stand in front of the throne on which the princess sat. All they could do was repeat whatever she said; and that she didn't want to hear once more. One should think every one of them had had his tummy filled with snuff or had fallen into a trance. But as soon as they were down in the streets again they got their tongues back, and all they could do was talk.

"There was a queue, so long that it stretched from beyond the city gate all the way up to the castle. I flew into town to have a look at it. Most of the men got both hungry and thirsty while they waited; the princess didn't even offer them a glass of lukewarm water. Some of the more clever ones had brought sandwiches, but they didn't offer any to their neighbors, for they thought: 'Let him look hungry and the princess won't take him.'"

"But Kai! What about Kai?" asked Gerda. "Did he stand in the queue too?"

"Don't be impatient. We are coming to him. Now the third day a little fellow arrived, he didn't have a carriage nor did he come on horseback. No, he came walking straight up to the castle. He was poorly dressed but had bright shining eyes like yours, and the most beautiful long hair."

"That is Kai!" shouted little Gerda, and clapped her hands in joy.

"He had a little knapsack on his back," continued the crow.

"It wasn't a knapsack," interrupted Gerda. "It was his sled."

"Sled or knapsack, it doesn't matter much," said the crow. "I didn't look too closely at him. But this I know from my fiancée: when he entered the castle and saw the royal guards and all the lackeys, they didn't make him the least bit fainthearted. He nodded kindly to them and said, 'It must be boring to spend your life waiting on the stairs, I think I will go inside.' The big hall with its lighted candelabra, its servants carrying golden bowls, while courtiers stood around dressed in their very best, was impressive enough to take away the courage of even the bravest—and, on top of all that, the young man's boots squeaked something wicked—but he did not seem to notice either the elegant hall or his noisy boots."

"It must be Kai," said Gerda. "His boots were new and I know they squeaked, I have heard them myself."

"Well, squeak they did," said the crow. "But he walked right up to the princess, who was sitting on a pearl as big as a spinning wheel. Behind her stood all her ladies in waiting with their maids and their maids' maids; and all the gentlemen of the court with their servants and their servants' servants, each of whom, in turn, kept a boy. And the servant's servant's boy, who stood next to the door, always wore slippers and was so proud that one hardly dared look at him!"

"It must have been horrible!" Little Gerda shook her head. "But Kai got the princess anyway?"

"If I hadn't been a crow, I would have taken her and that even though I am engaged. My fiancée tells me that he talks as well as I do when I talk crow language. He said that he hadn't come to propose marriage but only to find out whether she was as clever as everybody said she was. He was satisfied that what he heard was true; and the princess was satisfied with him."

"I am sure it was Kai, for he is so clever, he can figure in fractions. Won't you take me to the castle?"

"That is easier said than done," said the crow, and looked

thoughtfully at Gerda. "I will talk to my fiancée about it, she might know how we can do it. For I can tell you, it is not easy for a poor little girl like you to get into the castle."

"But I will get in!" protested Gerda. "As soon as Kai hears that I am here he will come and fetch me himself."

"Wait here by the big stone," commanded the crow, wriggled his head, and flew away.

The crow didn't return before dusk. "Caw! Caw!" he said, and alighted on the stone. "I bring you greetings from my fiancée, she sends you this little piece of bread. She took it in the kitchen where there is bread enough, and you must be hungry. It is quite impossible for you to enter the castle. You have bare feet; the guards in their silver uniforms and the lackeys in their golden ones won't allow it. But don't weep, we will get you in anyway. My fiancée knows where the key is kept to the back stairs, and they lead right up to the royal bedchamber."

They entered the royal garden and watched the lights in the castle being extinguished, one by one. At last the crow led her to a little door in the rear of the castle that was half open. Little Gerda's heart beat both with fear and with longing, she felt as though she were doing something wrong; and yet all she wanted to do was to see whether it was little Kai who had won the princess. She was sure it must be he.

In her mind she saw his lively, clever eyes, his long hair; he was smiling as he did when they sat under the little rose trees at home. He would be happy to see her, and she would tell him of the long journey she had made for his sake. She would tell him, too, how sad everyone had become because he was gone, and how they all had missed him. She felt so happy and so fearful.

They had reached the stairs; a little lamp burned on a chest. In the middle of the floor stood a tame crow, twisting its head about and looked at her quizzically. Gerda curtsied as Grandmother had taught her to do.

"My fiancé has told me so many nice things about you. He has narrated your *vita* as it is called, I have found the story most touching! Will you take the lamp and I shall walk ahead and show the way."

"I think someone is coming," whispered Gerda. There was a whirling, rushing sound; and on the wall were strange shadows of horses with flying manes, dogs and falcons, servants and hunters.

"Oh, they are only dreams," said the crow. "They have come to fetch their royal masters. That is only lucky for us; the easier it will be for you to have a good look at them while they are sleeping. But remember, when you gain honor and position, to be grateful and not forget those who helped you get it."

"That is no way to talk," grumbled the crow from the woods.

Now they entered the first of the great halls. The walls were covered with pink satin and decorated with artificial flowers. The shadows of the dreams reappeared, but they flew past so quickly that Gerda did not even get a chance to see whether Kai was mounted on one of the horses. Each hall they passed through was more magnificent than the one before it. At last they came to the royal bedchamber. The ceiling looked like the top of a large palm tree with glass leaves; from the center of it eight ropes of pure gold hung down, attached to them were the two little beds that the royal couple slept in. Each bed was shaped like a lily; in the white lily slept the princess, and in the red lily the young man who had won her. Gerda peeped into it and saw a head of long brown hair. "It is Kai!" she shouted in her joy. The dreams returned as fast as the wind and the young boy awoke.

He wasn't little Kai!

It was only the long brown hair they had in common, although he was young and handsome too. From the white lily bed the princess raised her head and asked what the commotion was about. Poor Gerda started to cry; and then between sobs, she told her story and explained how the crows had helped her.

"You poor thing!" said the prince. The princess said the same, and they did not scold the crows, on the contrary they praised them; although they warned them not to do it again. Still, they were to have a reward.

"Would you rather be free," asked the princess, "or receive permanent positions as royal court crows, with permission to eat all leftovers?"

Both the crows curtsied and said they preferred permanent positions. After all, they had to think of their old age. "To be secure is better than to fly," they said.

The prince got out of his bed and let Gerda sleep in it; he could hardly do more. She folded her little hands and thought, "How good all animals and human beings are." Then she closed her eyes and slept. This time the dreams looked like little angels. One of them was drawing a sled behind her; and on it sat little Kai; and he nodded to Gerda. But that was only a dream and it was gone as soon as she awoke.

In the morning Gerda was dressed from head to toe in silk and velvet; and the little prince and princess begged her to stay with them. But she asked only for a little carriage and a horse and some boots, so that she could continue on her journey out in the wide world to find Kai.

She was given not only new boots but a muff as well, and good warm clothes. When she was ready to leave, a fine carriage of the purest gold drove up in front of the castle. The coat of arms of the princess was on the door, and not only was there a coachman to drive her, but a servant stood on the back of the carriage and two little soldiers rode in front. The prince and the princess themselves helped her into the carriage and wished her luck. Her friend, the crow from the woods, drove with her the first couple of miles. They sat beside each other, for the crow got sick if he had to ride sitting backward. The other crow stood at the gate and flapped her wings; she had had a headache since she had been given a permanent position, and besides, she had overeaten. The carriage was lined with candy, and on the seat across from Gerda was a basket of fruit.

"Good-by, good-by!" shouted the little prince and princess; and Gerda wept, for she had grown fond of them, and the crow wept too. When they had driven a little way the crow said good-by, and that was even harder to bear. He flew up into a tall tree and sat there waving with his black wings until he could no longer see the carriage that glistened as though it were made of sunlight.

THE FIFTH STORY, WHICH IS ABOUT THE ROBBER GIRL

They were driving through a great dark forest, and the golden carriage shone like a flame right in the robbers' eyes, and they couldn't bear it.

"Gold! Gold!" they screamed as they came rushing out of the woods. They grabbed hold of the horses and killed the coachman, the servant, and the soldiers; then they dragged little Gerda out of the carriage.

"She is lovely and fat, I bet she has been fed on nuts," said an old robber woman; she had a beard and eyebrows so big and bushy that they almost hid her eyes. "She will taste as good as a lamb," and the robber woman took a long shining knife from her belt; it was horrible to look at.

"Ouch!" screamed the old hag, for just at that moment she had been bitten in the ear by her own little daughter, whom she carried on her back. The child was such a wild and naughty creature that it was a marvel. "Ouch!" the woman cried again, and missed her chance to kill Gerda.

"The girl is to play with me!" declared the little robber girl. "But she is to give me her muff and her dress and sleep in my bed with me." And just to make certain that her mother had understood her, she bit her again as hard as she could.

The robber woman turned and jumped into the air from the pain; and all the robbers laughed and said, "Look how she dances with her brat."

"I want to drive in the carriage," cried the little robber girl, and she was allowed to, for she was terribly spoiled. She and Gerda sat inside the carriage while it was being driven along little paths that brought it deeper and deeper into the forest. The little robber girl was as tall as Gerda but much stronger, and her skin had been tanned by the sun. Her eyes were almost black and looked sad. She put her arms around Gerda and said, "I won't allow them to kill you, so long as you don't make me angry. You must be a princess?"

"No, I am not," answered Gerda, and then she told her whole story and how much she loved little Kai.

The robber girl looked very seriously at her, nodded her head, and said: "I won't allow them to kill you even if I do get angry at you, I will do it myself." Then she dried Gerda's eyes and put her own hands inside the warm soft muff.

At last the carriage stopped; they had come to the robber castle. The walls were cracked and the windows were broken. Crows and ravens flew in and out of the big holes in the tower. Big dogs ran about in the courtyard; they looked ferocious enough to be able to eat human beings; they sprang up in the air but they didn't bark, that wasn't allowed.

In the middle of the great hall a fire burned. The smoke drifted up among the blackened rafters; how it ever got out was its own business. A big copper kettle filled with soup hung over the fire, and next to it, on spits, hares and rabbits were being roasted.

"You are going to sleep with me, over here among all my little pet animals," said the little robber girl, and dragged Gerda over to a corner of the hall, where there lay some straw and some blankets. Above them, on poles, sat about a hundred doves; they were asleep, but a couple opened their eyes and turned their heads when the little girls came.

"They are all mine," said the girl, and grabbed one of them by its legs. The dove flapped its wings. "Kiss it," demanded the robber girl, and shoved the frightened bird right up into Gerda's face.

"Up there are two wood pigeons," the robber girl explained as she pointed to a recess in the wall, high above them, that had been turned into a cage by a few wooden bars. "They would fly away if they could, but they can't."

"Here is my old sweetheart, bah!" She took hold of the antlers of a reindeer that stood tied near her bed and gave them a hard pull. "One has got to hold onto him too, or he would leap away. Every evening I tickle his throat with my sharp knife, that frightens him." The little girl pulled a knife out from a crack in the wall and let its sharp point glide around the reindeer's neck; the animal backed as far away as it could, in terror. That made the little robber girl laugh; and she pulled Gerda down into her bed.

"Do you sleep with your knife?" asked Gerda, frightened.

"I always sleep with the knife," answered the little robber girl. "One never knows what might happen. But tell me again the story of little Kai and why you have gone out into the wide world." Gerda told her story once more, and the wood pigeons, up in their cage, cooed; the doves were all asleep. The little robber girl put one of her arms around Gerda—in her other hand, she kept her knife—and fell asleep. She snored loudly.

Poor Gerda didn't dare close her eyes; she didn't know whether she was going to live or die. The robbers all sat around the fire and sang while they drank. The little girl's mother was so drunk that she turned a somersault. Oh, it was a pretty sight for a little girl to see!

Suddenly one of the wood pigeons cooed, "We have seen little Kai. A white hen carried his sled. He sat in the Snow Queen's sled when she flew low over the forest. We had just come out of our eggs and she breathed on us; all the other young ones died. We, alone, survived. Coo! Coo!"

"What is it you are saying?" cried Gerda. "Where was the Snow Queen going? Do you know?"

"I suppose she went to Lapland, where there always are snow and ice, but ask the reindeer that stands tied by your bed."

"Oh yes, ice and snow are always there; it is a blessed place," sighed the reindeer. "There one can jump and run about freely in the great, glittering valleys. The Snow Queen keeps a summer tent there, but her castle is far to the north, near the pole, on an island called Spitsbergen."

"Oh, Kai, little Kai!" mumbled Gerda.

"Lie still," commanded the robber girl, "or I will slit open your stomach!"

In the morning Gerda told her what she had heard from the wood pigeons. The little robber girl looked quite solemn, then nodded her head and said, "I am sure it is he, I am sure." Then she turned to the reindeer and asked him if he knew where Lapland was.

"Who should know that better than I?" answered the poor animal. "There I was born, there I have run across the great snow fields." And his eyes gleamed, recollecting what he had lost.

"Listen," whispered the little robber girl to Gerda. "All the men are gone. Only Mama is here and she won't leave; but in a little while she will take a drink from the big bottle and then she will take a nap. And then . . . I will help you!"

She jumped out of bed, ran over and threw her arms around her mother, pulled her beard, and said, "Oh, my own sweet billy goat, good morning!"

The mother tweaked her daughter's nose, so that it turned both red and blue, but it was all done out of love.

When the mother had drunk from the big bottle, she lay down for her midmorning nap; then the robber girl spoke to the reindeer: "I would have loved to tickle your throat for many a day yet, for you look so funny when I do it. But never mind, I will let you loose so that you can run back to Lapland; but you are to take the little girl with you and bring her to the Snow Queen's palace where her playmate is. I know you have heard everything she said, for you are always eavesdropping."

The reindeer leaped into the air out of pure joy. The robber's daughter lifted Gerda up on the animal's back and tied her on so she wouldn't fall off; and she even gave her a little pillow to sit on. "I don't really care about your boots, you need them," she said. "It is cold where you are going. But the muff I am keeping, for it is so soft and nice. But you shan't freeze, I will give you my mother's great big mittens; they will keep you warm all the way up to your elbows. Here, put them on! Now your hands look as ugly as my mother's."

Gerda cried from happiness and relief.

"I don't like all your tears," scolded the little robber girl. "You should look happy now. Here are two loaves of bread and a ham, so you won't go hungry," she said as she tied the bread and the ham on the back of the reindeer; then she opened the door and called all the big dogs in. She cut the rope that tethered the reindeer and said in parting, "Run along, but take good care of the little girl!"

Gerda waved good-by with her great big mittens, and away they went, through the forest and across the great plains, as fast as they could. They heard the wolves howl and the ravens cry; and suddenly the sky was all filled with light.

"There are the old northern lights," said the reindeer. "Look how they shine!"

Still they went on both day and night: farther and farther north.

The bread was eaten and the ham was eaten; and then they were in Lapland.

THE SIXTH STORY: THE LAPP WOMAN AND THE FINNISH WOMAN

They stopped before a little cottage; it was a wretched little hovel: the roof went all the way down to the ground and the doorway was so low that you had to creep through it on all fours. The only person at home was an old Lapp woman who was busy frying some fish over an oil lamp. The reindeer told her Gerda's story; but first he had told his own, because he thought that was more interesting. Poor Gerda was so cold that she couldn't even talk.

"Oh, you poor things!" said the Lapp woman. "You have far to go yet. It is more than a hundred miles from here to the camp of the Snow Queen. She amuses herself by shooting fireworks off every night. I shall give you an introduction to the Finnish woman who lives up there. She knows more about it all than I do and will be able to help you. Paper I have none of, so I will write on a dried codfish."

When little Gerda had eaten and was warm again, the Lapp woman wrote a few words on a dried codfish and told Gerda not to lose it. Then she tied her on the reindeer's back again and away they ran.

Whish . . . Whish . . . it said up in the sky as the northern lights flickered and flared; they were the Snow Queen's fireworks. At last they came to the Finnish woman's house; they had to knock on the chimney, for the door was so small that they couldn't find it.

Goodness me, it was hot inside! The Finnish woman walked around almost naked. She pulled off both Gerda's boots and her mittens so that the heat would not be unbearable for her. The reindeer got a piece of ice to put on its head. Then the Finnish woman read what was written on the codfish; she read it three times and then she knew it by heart. The fish she put in the pot that was boiling over the fire. It could be eaten, and she never wasted anything. The reindeer told first of his own adventures and then of Gerda's. The Finnish woman squinted her intelligent eyes but didn't utter a word.

"You are so clever," said the reindeer finally. "I know you can tie all the winds of the world into four knots on a single thread. If the sailor loosens the first knot he gets a fair wind; if he loosens the second a strong breeze; but if he loosens the third and the fourth knots, then there's such a storm that the trees in the forest are torn up by the roots. Won't you give this little girl a magic drink so that she gains the strength of twelve men and can conquer the Snow Queen?"

"The strength of twelve men," laughed the Finnish woman. "Yes, I should think that would be enough." Then she walked over to a shelf and took down a roll of skin which she spread out on the table. Strange words were written there, and the Finnish woman read and studied till the perspiration ran down her forehead.

The reindeer begged her again to help little Gerda; and Gerda looked up at her with eyes filled with tears. The Finnish woman winked, then drew the reindeer into a corner, where she whispered to him while she gave him another piece of ice for his head.

"Little Kai is in the Snow Queen's palace and is quite satisfied with being there; he thinks it is the best place in the whole world. This is because he has gotten a sliver of glass in his heart and two grains of the same in his eyes. As long as they are there he will never be human again, and the Snow Queen will keep her power over him."

"But can't you give Gerda some kind of power so that she can take out the glass?" asked the reindeer.

"I can't give her any more power than she already has! Don't you understand how great it is? Don't you see how men and animals must serve her; how else could she have come so far, walking on her bare feet? But she must never learn of her power; it is in her heart, for she is a sweet and innocent child. If she herself cannot get into the Snow Queen's palace and free Kai from the glass splinters in his eyes and his heart, how can we help her? Two miles from here begin the gardens of the Snow Queen. Carry Gerda there and set her down by the bush with the red berries, then come right back here and don't stand about gossiping." The Finnish woman lifted Gerda back on the reindeer's back, and he ran as fast as he could.

"I don't have my boots on, and I forgot the mittens," cried Gerda when she felt the cold making her naked feet smart. But the reindeer did not dare return. He ran on until he came to the bush with the red berries. There he put Gerda down and kissed her on her mouth; two tears ran down the animal's cheeks; then he leaped and ran back to the Finnish woman as fast as he could.

There stood poor Gerda, barefooted and without mittens on, in the intense arctic cold. She entered the Snow Queen's garden and ran as fast as she could in the direction of the palace. A whole regiment of snowflakes advanced against her. They had not fallen from the sky, for that was cloudless and illuminated by northern lights. The snowflakes flew just above the snow-covered earth; and as they came nearer they grew in size. Gerda remembered how they had looked when seen through a magnifying glass, but these were even bigger and horrible to look at. They were the Snow Queen's guard. And what strange creatures they were! Some of them looked like ugly little porcupines, others like bunches of snakes all twisted together, and some like little bears with bristly fur. All of the snowflakes were brilliantly white and terribly alive.

Little Gerda stopped and said her prayers. It was so cold that she could see her own breath; it came like a fine white smoke from her mouth, then it became more and more solid and formed itself into little angels that grew as soon as they touched the ground; all of them had helmets on their heads and shields and spears in their hands. When Gerda had finished saying her prayers a whole legion of little angels stood around her. They threw their spears at the snow monsters, and they splintered into hundreds of pieces. Little Gerda walked on unafraid, and the angels caressed her little feet and hands so she did not feel the cold.

But now we must hear what happened to little Kai. He was not thinking of Gerda—and even if he had been, he could not have imagined that she could be standing right outside the palace.

THE SEVENTH STORY: WHAT HAPPENED IN THE SNOW QUEEN'S PALACE AND AFTERWARD

The walls of the palace were made of snow, and the windows and doors of the sharp winds; it contained more than a hundred halls, the largest several miles long. All were lighted by the sharp glare of the northern lights; they were huge, empty, and terrifyingly cold. Here no one had ever gathered for a bit of innocent fun; not even a dance for polar bears, where they might have walked on their hind legs in the manner of man and the wind could have produced the music. No one had ever been invited in for a little game of cards, with something good to eat and a bit of not too malicious gossip; nor had there ever been a tea party for young white lady foxes. No, empty, vast, and cold was the Snow Queen's palace.

The northern lights burned so precisely that you could tell to the very second when they would be at their highest and their lowest points. In the middle of that enormous snow hall was a frozen lake. It had cracked into thousands of pieces and every one of them was shaped exactly like all the others. In the middle of the lake was the throne of the Snow Queen. Here she sat when she was at home. She called the lake the Mirror of Reason, and declared that it was the finest and only mirror in the world.

Little Kai was blue—indeed, almost black—from the cold; but he did not feel it, for the Snow Queen had kissed all feeling of coldness out of him, and his heart had almost turned into a lump of ice. He sat arranging and rearranging pieces of ice into patterns. He called this the Game of Reason; and because of the splinters in his eyes, he thought that what he was doing was of great importance, although it was no different from playing with wooden blocks, which he had done when he could hardly talk.

He wanted to put the pieces of ice together in such a way that they formed a certain word, but he could not remember exactly what that word was. The word that he could not remember was "eternity." The Snow Queen had told him that if he could place the pieces of ice so that they spelled that word, then he would be his own master and she would give him the whole world and a new pair of skates; but, however much he tried, he couldn't do it.

"I am going to the warm countries," the Snow Queen had announced that morning. "I want to look into the boiling black pots." By "black pots," she meant the volcanoes, Vesuvius and Etna. "I will chalk their peaks a bit. It will do them good to be refreshed; ice is pleasant as a dessert after oranges and lemons."

The Snow Queen flew away and Kai was left alone in the endless hall. He sat pondering his patterns of ice, thinking and thinking; he sat so still one might have believed that he was frozen to death.

Little Gerda entered the castle. The winds began to whip her face, and could have cut it, but she said her prayers and they lay down to sleep. She came into the vast, empty, cold hall; then she saw Kai!

She recognized him right away, and ran up to him and threw her arms around him, while she exclaimed jubilantly: "Kai, sweet little Kai. At last I have found you."

But Kai sat still and stiff and cold; then little Gerda cried and her tears fell on Kai's breast. The warmth penetrated to his heart and melted both the ice and the glass splinter in it. He looked at her and she sang the psalm they had once sung together:

> Our roses bloom and fade away,
> Our infant Lord abides alway.

> May we be blessed his face to see
> And ever little children be.

Kai burst into tears and wept so much that the grains of glass in his eyes were washed away. Now he remembered her and shouted joyfully: "Gerda! Sweet little Gerda, where have you been so long? And where have I been?" Kai looked about him. "How cold it is, how empty, and how huge!" And he held onto Gerda, who was so happy that she was both laughing and crying at the same time. It was so blessed, so happy a moment that even the pieces of ice felt it and started to dance; and when they grew tired they lay down and formed exactly that word for which the Snow Queen had promised Kai the whole world and a new pair of skates.

Gerda kissed him on his cheeks and the color came back to them. She kissed his eyes and they became like hers. She kissed his hands and feet, and the blue color left them and the blood pulsed again through his veins. He was well and strong. Now the Snow Queen could return, it did not matter, for his right to his freedom was written in brilliant pieces of ice.

They took each other by the hand and walked out of the great palace. They talked of Grandmother, and the roses that bloomed on the roof at home. The winds were still; and as they walked, the sun broke through the clouds. When they reached the bush with the red berries the reindeer was waiting there for them. He had brought another young reindeer with him and her udder was bursting with milk. The two children drank from it and the reindeer kissed them. Then they rode on the backs of the reindeer to the home of the Finnish woman, where they got warm, were given a good meal and instructions for the homeward journey.

They visited the Lapp woman. She had sewn warm clothes for them and was getting her sled ready.

The two reindeer accompanied them to the border of Lapland. There the green grass started to break through the snow and they could not use the sled any longer. They said good-by to the reindeer and to the Lapp woman. Soon they heard the twitter of the first birds of spring and in the woods the trees were budding.

They met a young girl wearing a red hat and riding a magnificent horse. Gerda recognized the animal, for it was one of the horses that had drawn her golden carriage. The girl had two pistols stuck in her belt; she was the little robber girl, who had got tired of staying at home and now was on her way out into the wide world. She recognized Gerda immediately and the two of them were so happy to see each other.

"You are a fine one," she said to Kai, "running about as you did. I wonder if you are worth going to the end of the world for?" Gerda touched her cheek and asked her if she knew what had happened to the prince and the princess. "They have gone traveling in foreign lands," answered the robber girl.

"And what about the crow?"

"The crow is dead," said the girl. "His tame fiancée has become a widow, she wears a black wool thread around her leg. She thinks mourning becomes her, but it is all nonsense. But tell me what happened to you and how you managed to find him!"

And both Gerda and Kai told her everything that had happened to them.

"Well, the end was as good as the beginning," said the robber girl, and took each of them by the hand and promised that if she ever came through the town where they lived she would come and visit them. Then she rode away out into the world; and Kai and Gerda walked hand in hand homeward.

It was really spring. In the ditches the little wild flowers bloomed. The churchbells were ringing. Now they recognized the towers; they were approaching their own city and the home they had left behind.

Soon they were walking up the worn steps of the staircase to the old Grandmother's apartment. Nothing inside it had changed. The clock said: "Tick-tack . . ." and the wheels moved. But as they stepped through the doorway they realized that they had grown: they were no longer children.

The roses were blooming in the wooden boxes and the window was open. There were the little stools they used to sit on. Still holding each other's hands, they sat down, and all memory of the Snow Queen's palace and its hollow splendor disappeared. The Grandmother sat in the warm sunshine, reading aloud from her Bible: *"Whosoever shall not receive the Kingdom of Heaven as a little child shall not enter therein."*

Kai and Gerda looked into each other's eyes and now they understood the words from the psalm.

> Our roses bloom and fade away,
> Our infant Lord abides alway.
> May we be blessed his face to see
> And ever little children be.

There they sat, the two of them, grownups; and yet in their hearts children, and it was summer: a warm glorious summer day!

25

The Darning Needle

ONCE upon a time there was a darning needle who was so refined that she was convinced she was a sewing needle.

"Be careful! Watch what you are holding!" she shouted to the fingers who had picked her up. "I am so fine and thin that if I fall on the floor you will never be able to find me again."

"Don't overdo it," snarled the fingers, and squeezed her around the waist.

"Look, I am traveling with a retinue," said the needle. She was referring to the thread that trailed behind her but wasn't knotted. The fingers steered the needle toward the cook's slippers; the leather had split and had to be sewn.

"This is vulgar work," complained the darning needle. "I can't get through it. I shall break! I shall break!" And then she broke. "Didn't I tell you I was too fine?" she whined.

Had it been up to the fingers, then the darning needle would have been thrown away; but they had to mind the cook, so they dipped the needle in hot sealing wax and stuck it into the cook's blouse.

"Now I have become a brooch," exclaimed the darning needle. "I have always felt that I was born to be something better. When you are something, you always become something." Then she laughed inside herself; for you cannot see from the outside when a needle is laughing. There she sat as proudly as if she were looking out at the world from a seat in a golden carriage.

"May I take the liberty of asking you whether you are made of gold?" The darning needle was talking to her neighbor, a pin. "You look very handsome, and you have a head, even though it is small. Take my advice and let it grow a little bigger; not everyone can be so fortunate as to be dipped in sealing wax." The darning needle drew herself up a little too proudly; for she fell out of the blouse and down into the sink, at exactly the moment when the cook was rinsing it out.

"Here we go, traveling!" exclaimed the darning needle. "I hope I won't get lost." But she did get lost.

"I am too fine for this world," she remarked when she finally came to rest at the bottom of a gutter. "But I know who I am and where I come from, and that is always something." And the darning needle kept her back straight and remained cheerful.

All sorts of garbage were floating by above her: twigs, straw, pieces of newspaper. "Look how they sail on," mumbled the needle. "They have no idea what is sticking up right beneath them; and I can stick! Look at that old twig; it does not think about anything else in the whole world but twigs, because it is one. There goes a straw. . . . Look how it turns first one way and then the other. . . . Don't think so much of yourself, or you may get hurt on the curb-stone. . . . There comes a newspaper; everything written in it is already forgotten, and yet it spreads itself out as if it were of great importance. . . . I sit patiently and wait. I know who I am and that I shall never change."

One day something shiny came to rest near the needle. It was a glass splinter from a broken bottle, but the darning needle thought it was a diamond. Since it glittered so nicely, she decided to converse with it. She introduced herself as a brooch. "I presume you are a diamond," she said. And the glass splinter hastily agreed that he was "something of that nature." Each of them believed that the other was valuable, and so they began to discuss how proud and haughty the rest of the world was.

"I have lived in a box belonging to a young lady," began the darning needle. "She was a cook, and she had five fingers on each hand. There never existed creatures so conceited as those fingers; and yet they were only there to take me out of the box and put me back."

"Did they shine?" asked the glass splinter.

"Shine!" sneered the needle. "Oh, they were haughty. They were five brothers: all born fingers; and they stood in a row next to each other, in spite of there being so much difference in their sizes. The one who resembled the others the least was the thumb. He was short and fat and had only one joint in his back, so he could only bend once. He always kept to himself, and said that if he were ever chopped off a man's hand that man could not become a soldier. The other four fingers stuck together. The first one was always pointing at everything, and if the cook wanted to find out whether a sauce was too sour or too sweet, that finger was stuck into the dish or the pot; and it guided the pen when she wrote. The next finger was the tallest and he looked down on the others. The third one wore a gold ring around his stomach; and the fourth one never did anything, and that's what he was proud of. They bragged and boasted day and night! That was all they could do well. And I dived into the sink."

"And here we sit and glitter," said the glass splinter. At that moment the water in the gutter suddenly rose and went over its sides, taking the glass splinter with it.

"Well, he got his advancement," said the darning needle. "I was left behind, but I am too refined to complain. That, too, is a form of pride but it is respectable." And the needle kept her back straight and went on thinking.

"I am almost convinced that a sun ray must have given birth to me. When I think of it, the sun is always searching for me underneath the water; but I am so fine that my own mother cannot find me. If I had my old eye—the one that was broken off—I think I would cry. No, I wouldn't anyway, crying is so vulgar."

One day some street urchins were rummaging in the gutter. They found nails, coins, and the like. They made themselves filthy and they enjoyed doing it.

"Ow!" cried one of the boys. The needle had pricked him. "What kind of a fellow are you?"

"Fellow! I am a lady!" protested the darning needle. The sealing wax had long since worn off and she was black; but black things look thinner, so she thought that now she was even finer than before.

"Here comes an eggshell!" shouted another boy, and stuck the pin into it.

"How well it becomes a black needle to stand before a white sail! Everyone can see me. I hope I shan't get seasick and throw up, that is so undignified.

"There is no remedy against seasickness better than an iron stomach, and the awareness of being just a bit above the common herd. I feel much better. The more refined one is, the more one can bear."

"Crash!" said the eggshell. A wagon wheel had rolled over it.

"Ow!" cried the darning needle. "Something is pressing against me. I think I am going to be seasick after all. I fear I will break!"

But it didn't break, even though a loaded wagon drove over it. There it lay, lengthwise in the gutter; and there we'll leave it.

26

The Bell

IN the narrow streets of the city, at dusk, just as the sun was setting and painting the clouds above the chimney pots a fiery red, people would sometimes hear a strange sound like the knell of a great churchbell. Only for a moment could it be heard, then the noise of the city—the rumbling of the carts and the shouting of the peddlers— would drown it out. "It is the vesper bell, calling folk to evening prayers; the sun must be setting," was the usual explanation.

To those who lived on the outskirts of the town, where the houses were farther away from each other and had gardens around them— some places were even separated by a field—the sunset was much more beautiful and the sound of the bell much louder. It seemed to come from a church in the depth of a fragrant forest, and it made the people who heard it feel quite solemn as they looked toward the darkening woods.

As time passed people began to ask each other whether there wasn't a church in the woods. And it was not far from that thought to the next: "The bell sounds so beautiful, why don't we go out and try to find it?"

Now the rich people got into their carriages and the poor people walked; but to all of them the road to the forest seemed very long. When they finally reached some weeping willows that grew on the edge of the woods they sat down under the trees to rest; and, looking up into the branches, believed that they were sitting in the middle of the forest. One of the bakers from town pitched a tent there and sold cakes. Business was good, and soon there were two bakers. The second one to arrive hung above his tent a bell, which was tarred on the outside to protect it from the rain, but it had no tongue.

When the people came back to town they said that their outing had been very romantic; and that word is not as tepid as a teaparty. Three persons claimed to have penetrated the forest and come out on the other side. They had heard a bell, but they said that the sound seemed to come not from the woods but from the town. One of them had written a sonnet about the bell, in which he compared its sound to that of a mother's voice when she speaks to her lovely, beloved child; the last line declared that no melody could be sweeter than that bell's song.

At last the emperor heard about it, and he promised that whoever found out where the sound came from would be given the title of "Bell Ringer of the World"; and that even if he discovered that it wasn't a bell that made it.

Now many people went out in search of the bell; they did it for the title and for the wages that went with it. But only one returned with an answer: an explanation of a sort. He had been no farther in the forest than the rest—and that hadn't been very far—but he claimed that the bell-like sound came from a great owl who was sitting inside a hollow tree. It was the bird of wisdom and it was incessantly knocking its head against the trunk; but whether the ringing was caused by the bird's head or the tree trunk he had not yet decided. The emperor bestowed upon him the title of "Bell Ringer of the World," and every year he published a paper on the subject, without anyone becoming any wiser.

One Sunday in May, when the children who had reached the age of fourteen were confirmed, the minister preached so movingly that all the young people present had tears in their eyes. It was a solemn occasion; after all, it was expected that they should become grownups; and that as soon as the ceremony was over, their child-souls would enter the bodies of reasonable adults. It was a beautiful day, and after the service all the children who had been confirmed walked, in a flock, to the forest. The sound of the unknown bell was particularly strong that day; and all of them had a great desire to go and search for it. That is, all of them except three: One girl had to hurry home for the final fitting of her new dress, which had been especially sewn for a ball she was to attend that night. The dress and the ball had been her real reasons for being confirmed. Another was a poor boy who had had to borrow both shoes and suit from the son of his parents' landlord; and they were to be delivered back as soon as the ceremony was over. The third was a boy who declared that he never went anywhere without his parents' permission. He had always been a good boy and would continue to be one even after he was confirmed; that is nothing to poke fun at—but all the other children did.

So three of them stayed behind but all the rest went on. The sun was shining, the birds were singing, and the young people who had just been confirmed were singing too. They walked hand in hand, for they hadn't become anything in the world yet, and they could afford to be friendly.

Soon two of the smallest became tired and turned back toward the town; and a couple of girls sat down in a meadow to braid wreaths of wild flowers; so they were four fewer. When the rest of the group reached the weeping willow trees, where the baker's tent was pitched, most of them said, "Well, here we are; you can see that the bell doesn't really exist. It is just something one imagines."

But from deeper in the woods came the sound of the bell: sweet and solemn; and five of the children decided to go on, just a little farther. It was not easy to make one's way through the forest; the trees grew close together, blackberry brambles and other thorny bushes were everywhere. But it was beautiful; the sun rays played and they heard the nightingale sing. It was glorious, but it was no place for girls; their dresses would be torn.

They came to great boulders covered with different kinds of moss. They heard the gurgling of a spring: "Gluck, gluck."

"I wonder if that isn't the bell," said one of the five, and lay down on the ground in order to hear the bubbling of the water better. "I think I ought to investigate this some more," he added, and let the other four go on without him.

They came to a house made of branches and bark. A huge wild apple tree towered above it and roses grew in such abundance up its walls that they covered the roof of the little cottage. On one of the ramblers hung a little silver bell. Was that the bell that they had heard? All but one of the boys agreed that it was. He claimed that this bell was too small and delicate to be heard so far away; besides, it did not produce the kind of music that could touch a man's heart. "No," he said. "It is an entirely different bell that we heard before."

But the youth who had spoken was a king's son, and one of his comrades remarked, "Oh, his kind always wants to think themselves cleverer than the rest of us."

They let him go on alone. When the cottage and his friends were lost from sight, the great loneliness of the forest engulfed the prince. He could still hear the little bell, which had pleased his friends, tingle merrily; and from farther away—borne on the wind's back—came the sound of the people at the baker's tent singing as they drank their tea. But the knell of the great bell of the forest grew stronger and stronger; then it seemed to be accompanied by an organ; he thought the sound of it came from the left where the heart is.

Leaves rustled, twigs snapped; someone else was making his way through the woods. The prince turned; in front of him stood another boy. He had wooden shoes on his feet, and the sleeves of his tunic were too short because he had outgrown it. He was the youth who had had to return the clothes he had worn at confirmation, as soon as the ceremony was over. The landlord's son had got his finery back, and the poor lad had put on his own old clothes, stuck his feet into his clogs, and set off in search of the great bell whose deep clang had called on him so powerfully that he had had to follow it.

"Let us go on together," proposed the prince. But the poor boy looked down at his wooden shoes and pulled at the sleeves of his tunic to make them a little longer. His poverty made him shy, and he excused himself by saying that he feared he could not walk as fast as the prince. Besides, he thought that the bell was to be found on the other side of the forest; on the right, where everything great and marvelous is.

"Then I suppose we shall not meet again," said the prince, and nodded to the poor boy, who walked into the densest part of the forest, where brambles and thorns would tear his worn-out clothes to shreds and scratch his face, legs, and hands till blood streamed down them. The prince did not escape being scratched, but the sun did shine on the path he took, and we shall follow him, for he was a good and courageous boy.

"I will find the bell," he declared, "if I have to go to the end of the world to do it."

On the limbs of a tree sat ugly monkeys; they grinned and screamed to each other: "Throw something at him! Throw something at him. He is a royal child!"

But the prince did not even notice them; he walked on deeper and deeper into the forest. Here grew the strangest flowers: lilies shaped like white stars, with blood-red stamens; tulips as blue as the sky; and apple trees, whose fruit looked like soap bubbles.—How such a tree would have glittered in the sunlight!—He passed green meadows where deer played in the grass underneath solitary oak trees. In every crack and crevice of their trunks grew grass and moss.

There were many lakes in which white swans swam; he could hear the beating of their great wings. He lingered and listened. More than once he wondered whether the knell might not come from somewhere deep inside one of the lakes; but then, when he strained his ears, he understood that the sound came from far away, from the very depth of the forest.

The sun was setting and the sky turned red as fire. The forest became so still that the prince sank down on his knees and said, "I shall never find what I seek! The sun is setting; soon the night will come—the dark, dark night. . . . But maybe I can still get another glimpse of the sun, see it once more before it disappears, by climbing that cliff over there, which is higher than the tallest trees."

His hands grabbed the brambles that grew among the wet stones, and he pulled himself upward. So eager was he to reach the top of the cliff that he noticed neither the slimy snakes nor the toads who barked like dogs.

Just before the sun set he reached the summit. Oh, what splendor! Below him stretched the ocean, that great sea that was flinging its long waves toward the shore. Like a shining red altar the sun stood where sea and sky met. All nature became one in the golden sunset: the song of the forest and the song of the sea blended and his heart seemed to be part of their harmony. All nature was a great cathedral: the flowers and the grass were the mosaic floors, the tall trees and swaying clouds were its pillars and heaven itself was the dome. High above the red color was disappearing for the sun had set. The millions of stars were lighted: the millions of little diamond lamps. The prince spread out his arms toward it all: the forest, the ocean, and the sky. But just at that moment, from the right side of the cliff came the poor boy with his ragged tunic and his wooden shoes. He had arrived there almost as quickly by going his own way.

The two boys ran to meet each other. There they stood, hand in hand, in the midst of nature's and poetry's great cathedral; and far above the great invisible holy bell was heard in loud hosanna.

27

The Hill of the Elves

SOME lizards were darting in and out of the cracks and crevices of an old oak tree. All of them could speak lizard language, so they understood each other.

"Have you heard all the rumbling and grumbling inside the old hill where the elves live?" asked one of the lizards. "I haven't been able to sleep a wink these last two nights. I might as well have had a toothache."

"Oh yes, something is going on up there, for sure," began another lizard. "Last night they put the hill on four red pillars and let it stand like that until it was almost time for the cock to crow. They certainly gave their home a good airing. The elfin maidens have to learn a new dance in which they stamp their feet. There is no doubt about it, something is up."

"I have talked with an acquaintance of mine, an earthworm," declared a third lizard. "I met him as he was coming out of the hill, where he has been digging for the last two days. He has heard a good deal.—The poor creature can't see but he's a master at both hearing and feeling.—The elves are expecting very important guests. The earthworm wouldn't tell me who they were, but that's probably because he didn't know. The will-o'-the-wisps have all been hired to make a torchlight procession, as it's called. All the gold and silver in the whole hill—and there's enough of it—is to be polished and set out in the moonlight."

"Who can the visitors be?" cried all the lizards. "What is going to happen? Listen to the humming! Listen to the buzzing!"

Just at that moment the hill of the elves opened and an old elfin lady came tripping out. She had the same hollow back that all elves have, and she was very respectably dressed. She was the elfin king's housekeeper, and distantly related to him; that was why she wore an amber heart on her forehead. Goodness, how she could run. Away she went down to the marsh where the night raven lived.

"You are invited to the Mount of the Elves this very night," she said. "But you will have to do us the favor of delivering the invitations. Since you have no home of your own and cannot return our hospitality, you will have to make yourself useful instead. We are expecting distinguished guests, trolls of the greatest importance, and the elfin king wants to impress them."

"Whom am I to invite?" asked the night raven.

"Well, to the grand ball, anyone can come," began the old elfin lady. "Even human beings are invited; that is, those who have some small talent akin to ours: such as being able to talk in their sleep. But the party tonight is to be more select; only those of the highest rank are to attend. I argued with the elfin king about the guest list, for in my opinion neither ghosts nor spooks should be on it. . . . The old merman and his daughters, the mermaids, must be the first ones you invite. They don't like to be where it's dry, so tell them that they can count on having a wet stone each to sit on, if not something better. Remember to say that that's a promise; and I don't think they'll refuse. After that call on all the older trolls of the highest rank who have tails, the river spirit, and the gnomes. Then there are the graveyard sow, the Hell horse, and the three-legged church monster; it wouldn't do to forget them. They belong to the clergy; but that is their profession, so I shan't hold it against them. Besides, we are all related, and they visit us regularly."

"Caw!" said the night raven, and flew away to deliver the invitations.

The elfin maidens were already dancing on top of the hill. Over their shoulders were long shawls woven from mist and moonlight. They looked very pretty, if you like that sort of thing.

The great hall in the middle of the mount had certainly been done up. The floors had been washed in moonlight, and all the walls had been waxed with witches' grease till they shone like tulip petals.

Out in the kitchen frogs were being roasted on spits, and snakes stuffed with children's fingers were baking. The salads were made of toadstool seeds, garnished with moist snouts of mice; and for dressing there was hemlock juice. Saltpeter wine that had been aged in tombs and beer from the bog-witch brewery had been poured into decanters. Altogether a festive—though a bit conservative—menu. Rusty nails and bits of colored glass from a church window were the desserts.

The old elfin king's crown had been polished with powder ground from slate pencils. For this purpose only pencils that have belonged to especially studious boys may be used; and those are hard to find. In the bedchambers the newly washed curtains were being made to stick to the walls with the help of snakes' spit. Everywhere, everybody was busy. There were bustle and commotion throughout the hill.

"Now I'll burn some horsehair and swine bristles, and then I shall have done my share," remarked the old elfin lady who was the elfin king's housekeeper.

"Dear . . . dear Father," pestered the youngest of the elfin king's daughters, "won't you tell us who the distinguished guests are?"

"Well, I suppose I have to," began the king. "Two of you had better be prepared to get married because two of you are going to get married. The old troll king of Norway is coming. Dovre—his castle—is made of granite, and it is large and so high that on the roof of the great hall there is always snow. He has a gold mine, too; and that is nothing to sneeze at, even though some people do. He is bringing his sons along, and they are thinking of getting married. The old troll is a real Norwegian: honest, full of life, and straightforward. I have known him a long, long time. We became friends at his wedding. He had come to Denmark for a wife. She was the daughter of the king of the chalk cliffs of Möen; but she's been dead a long time now.

"How I look forward to seeing the old fellow again. I have been told that his sons are a spoiled couple of cubs: cocky and bad-mannered. But who knows, such talk may all be slander. Time will rub the nonsense off them, anyway. Let me see you show them how they ought to behave."

"When are they coming?" asked his oldest daughter.

"That depends upon the wind and the weather," sighed the king. "They are traveling by ship. I wanted them to journey through Sweden, but the old troll is conservative. He doesn't keep up with the changing times, which in my opinion is very wrong of him."

At that moment two will-o'-the-wisps came running into the hall. One ran faster than the other and that was why he came first.

"They are coming! They are coming!" they both shouted.

"Hand me my crown and I shall go out and stand in the moonlight," said the king of the elves and, followed by the elfin maidens, he went to meet the guests.

His daughters lifted their shawls and curtsied all the way to the ground.

There he was: the troll king from Dovre! His crown was made of ice and polished pine cones. He was wearing a bearskin coat and heavy boots. His sons, on the other hand, were lightly dressed: their collars were open and they weren't wearing suspenders. They were two big strapping fellows.

"Is this a hill?" laughed the younger one. "In Norway we would call it a hole in the ground."

"Don't be silly," said the old troll king. "Holes go inward and hills go upward. Don't you have eyes in your head?"

The thing that surprised the two young men most was that they could understand the language; and they said so.

"Don't make fools of yourselves," scolded their father, "or everybody will think that you were born yesterday and put on the stove to dry overnight."

They entered the great hall where all the guests were gathered; they had arrived so fast you would think that the wind had blown them there. The old merman and his daughters were sitting in tubs full of water and feeling right at home. Except for the sons of the troll king, everyone exhibited his or her best table manners, while the two young men put their feet on the table. But they thought that anything they did was becoming.

"Take your feet out of the dishes!" bellowed the old troll king.

His sons obeyed him, but not right away. They tickled their dinner partners—two young elfin maidens—with pine cones that they had brought in their pockets from Norway. In the middle of the dinner they took off their boots to make themselves more comfortable and handed them to the elfin maidens to take care of.

But the old troll king was a different sort than his sons. He described so well the proud mountains of Norway, the rivers and streams that leaped down the cliffs, white and bubbling, and sounded like both a thunderclap and an organ playing, when they plunged into the valleys far below. He told about the salmon that could leap up the swiftest waterfall, while the river nymphs played on their golden harps. He made them imagine a still winter night, when you can hear the sound of sleigh bells and see the young people skate, carrying burning torches, across the glasslike surface of the lakes, when the ice is so transparent that the skaters can watch the fish fleeing, in terror, below them. Yes, he knew how to tell a story well; it seemed to all the other guests that they could hear the buzz of the great sawmills and the singing of the young men and women as they danced the Halling dance.

"Hurrah!" the troll king suddenly cried; and in the midst of his storytelling kissed the old elfin lady so that it could be heard throughout the hall. "That was a brotherly kiss," he explained, in spite of their not being related at all.

Now the young elfin maidens danced. First the simple dances and then the new one in which they stamped their feet. The final one was the most difficult and was called "Stepping Outside the Dance." How they twirled and twisted. One could hardly make out which were legs and which were arms, or which end was up and which was down. The poor Hell horse got so dizzy watching it that he began to feel sick and had to leave the table.

"Whoa!" shouted the old troll king. "They have got legs, and they can dance; but what else can they do?"

"Judge for yourself," said the elfin king, and called his youngest daughter to him. She was as fair as moonlight and the most delicate of the sisters.

She stuck a white wand in her mouth and vanished—that was her accomplishment.

The old troll king said that this was not the kind of talent he would want his wife to have, and he was sure that his sons agreed with him.

The second sister could walk beside herself, so that she looked as if she had a shadow; something that neither elves nor trolls possess.

The third sister's talent lay in an entirely different direction. She had been apprenticed to the bog witch and knew both how to brew beer and how to garnish elder stumps with glowworms.

"She will make a good housewife," said the troll king, and winked at her. He would have drunk a toast in her honor but he thought he had drunk enough already.

Now came the fourth sister. She had a golden harp. When she

struck the first string, they all lifted their left legs—for trolls and elves are left-legged—and when she struck the second string they all had to do exactly what she commanded.

"She is a dangerous woman," said the troll king. His two sons sneaked out of the hall; they were bored.

"And what can the next one do?" asked the troll.

"I have learned to love Norway," she said softly. "And I will only marry a Norwegian."

But the youngest of the elfin king's daughters whispered to the old troll king, "She says that because she once heard a Norwegian verse in which it was prophesied that, when the world went under, the mountains of Norway would stand as a tombstone over it; and she is terribly afraid of dying."

"Ha-ha!" laughed the old troll king. "And you let the cat out of the bag. . . . And what can the seventh and last of them do?"

"The sixth comes before the seventh," said the elfin king, who knew how to count.

The sixth daughter was so shy that she did not want to step forward. "I can only tell people the truth," she finally whispered, "and that no one likes to hear, so I am busy sewing on my shroud."

Now came the seventh; and she was the last of the sisters. What could she do? She could tell fairy tales, as many as anyone wanted to hear.

"Here are my five fingers, tell me a fairy tale for each of them," demanded the troll king.

The elfin maiden took his hand in hers and began. The king of the trolls laughed so hard that he almost split his sides. When she came to the finger that was encircled by a gold ring—it looked as if it knew that there was an engagement in the air—the troll cried, "Hold onto what you have got! My hand is yours. You I shall marry myself!"

But the elfin maiden protested that she still had two stories to tell: one for the ring finger and one for the little finger, which would be short.

"They can wait," said the king of the trolls. "We can hear them next winter. And you shall tell us about the pine trees, the birches, the crinkling frost, and about the gifts that the river nymphs bring; for we do so love a well-told tale in Norway, and no one there knows how to tell them. We shall sit in my granite hall that is lighted by pine pitch torches and drink mead out of golden horns that once belonged to Viking kings. The river nymph has given me a couple of them. The echo—he is a tall, thin fellow—will come and sing for us. He knows all the songs that the milkmaids sing when they drive their herds into the meadows. Oh, we'll have a good time! The salmon will leap and knock on our granite walls, but we won't let him in. Oh, believe me! Norway is a dear old place! . . . But where are my sons?"

Where were his sons? They were racing about on the field blowing out the poor will-o'-the-wisps, who had been peacefully assembling for the torchlight parade.

"What do you mean by running about like this?" scolded their father. "I have chosen a mother for you. Now you can find wives for yourselves among your aunts."

But the boys said they would rather drink toasts and make speeches, for they had no desire to get married. So they made speeches and they toasted each other, and when they were finished they turned their glasses upside down so that everyone could see that they were empty. Then they took off their shirts and lay down on the table to sleep, for, as they said, they didn't "stand on ceremony."

The old troll king danced with his young bride and exchanged boots with her, for that is more refined than exchanging rings.

"Now the cock crows!" shouted the old elfin lady who was the housekeeper and kept an eye on everything. "We have to close the shutters or the sun will burn us all."

And the hill of the elves closed. But outside the lizards were running up and down the old oak tree.

"Oh, I did like that old Norwegian troll king," said one of the lizards.

"I liked his sons best," said the earthworm, but the wretched little creature couldn't see.

28

The Red Shoes

ONCE there was a little girl who was pretty and delicate but very poor. In the summer she had to go barefoot and in the winter she had to wear wooden shoes that rubbed against her poor little ankles and made them red and sore.

In the same village there lived an old widow whose husband had been a shoemaker; and she sat sewing a pair of shoes from scraps of red material. She did her very best, but the shoes looked a bit clumsy, though they were sewn with kindness. They were meant for the poor little girl, whose name was Karen.

Now on that very day that her mother was to be buried, Karen was given the red shoes. Though they weren't the proper color for mourning, she had no others, so she put them on. Raggedly dressed, barelegged, with red shoes on her feet, she walked behind the pauper's coffin.

A big old-fashioned carriage drove by; in it sat an old lady. She noticed the little girl and felt so sorry for her that she went at once to the minister and spoke to him. "Let me have that little girl, and I shall be good to her and bring her up."

Karen thought it was because of her new red shoes that the old lady had taken a fancy to her. But the old lady declared that the shoes looked frightful and had them thrown into the stove and burned. Karen was dressed in nice clean clothes and taught to read and to sew. Everyone agreed that she was a very pretty child; but the mirror said, "You are more than pretty, you are beautiful."

It happened that the queen was making a journey throughout the country, and she had her daughter, the little princess, with her. Everywhere people streamed to see them. When they arrived at a castle near Karen's village, the little girl followed the crowd out there. Looking out of one of the great windows of the castle was the little princess. So that people could see her, she was standing on a little stool. She had no crown on her head but she wore a very pretty white dress and the loveliest red shoes, made from morocco. They were certainly much prettier than the ones the old shoemaker's widow had made for Karen. But even they had been red shoes, and to Karen nothing else in the world was so desirable.

Karen became old enough to be confirmed. She was to have a new dress and new shoes for this solemn occasion. The old lady took her to the finest shoemaker in the nearby town and he measured her little foot. Glass cabinets filled with the most elegant shoes and boots covered the walls of his shop. But the old lady's eyesight was so poor that she didn't get much out of looking at the display. Karen did; between two pairs of boots stood a pair of red shoes just like the ones the princess had worn. Oh, how beautiful they were! The shoemaker said that they had been made for the daughter of a count but that they hadn't fit her.

"I think they are patent leather," remarked the old lady. "They shine."

"Yes, they shine!" sighed Karen as she tried them on. They fit the child and the old woman bought them. Had she known that they were red, she wouldn't have because it was not proper to wear red shoes when you were being confirmed. But her eyesight was failing—poor woman!—and she had not seen the color.

Everyone in the church looked at Karen's feet, as she walked toward the altar. On the walls of the church hung paintings of the former ministers and their wives who were buried there; they were portrayed wearing black with white ruffs around their necks. Karen felt that even they were staring at her red shoes.

When the old bishop laid his hands on her head and spoke of the solemn promise she was about to make—of her covenant with God to be a good Christian—her mind was not on his words. The ritual music was played on the organ; the old cantor sang, and the sweet voices of the children could be heard, but Karen was thinking of her red shoes.

By afternoon, everyone had told the old lady about the color of Karen's shoes. She was very angry and scolded the girl, telling her how improper it was to have worn red shoes in church, and that she must remember always to wear black ones, even if she had to put on an old pair.

Next Sunday Karen was to attend communion. She looked at her black shoes and she looked at her red shoes; then she looked at her red shoes once more and put them on.

The sun was shining, it was a beautiful day. The old lady and Karen took the path across the fields and their shoes got a bit dirty.

At the entrance to the church stood an old invalid soldier leaning on a crutch. He had a marvelously long beard that was red with touches of white in it. He bowed low toward the old lady and asked her permission to wipe the dust off her feet. Karen put her little foot forward too.

"What pretty little dancing shoes!" said the soldier and, tapping them on the soles, he added, "Remember to stay on her feet for the dance."

The old lady gave the soldier a penny, and she and Karen entered the church.

Again everyone looked at Karen's feet, even the people in the paintings on the wall. When she knelt in front of the altar and the golden cup was lifted to her lips, she thought only of the red shoes and saw them reflected in the wine. She did not join in the singing of the psalm and she forgot to say the Lord's Prayer.

The coachman had come with the carriage to drive them home from church. The old lady climbed in and Karen was about to follow her when the old soldier, who was standing nearby, remarked, "Look at those pretty dancing shoes."

His words made her take a few dancing steps. Once she had begun, her feet would not stop. It was as if the shoes had taken command of them. She danced around the corner of the church; her will was not her own.

The coachman jumped off the carriage and ran after her. When he finally caught up with her, he grabbed her and lifted her up from the ground, but her feet kept on dancing in the air, even after he managed to get her into the carriage. The poor old woman was kicked nastily while she and the coachman took Karen's shoes off her feet, so she could stop dancing.

When they got home, the red shoes were put away in a closet, but Karen could not help sneaking in to look at them.

The old lady was very ill. The doctors had come and said that she would not live much longer. She needed careful nursing and constant care, and who else but Karen ought to give it to her? In the town there was to be a great ball and Karen had been invited to go. She looked at the old lady, who was going to die anyway, and then she glanced at her red shoes. To glance was no sin. Then she put them on; that too did no great harm. But she went to the ball!

She danced! But when she wanted to dance to the left, the shoes danced to the right; and when she wanted to dance up the ballroom floor, the shoes danced right down the stairs and out into the street. Dance she did, out through the city gates and into the dark forest.

Something shone through the trees. She thought it was the moon because it had a face. But it was not; it was the old soldier with the red beard. He nodded to her and exclaimed, "Look what beautiful dancing shoes!"

Terrified, she tried to pull off her shoes. She tore her stockings but the shoes stayed on. They had grown fast to her feet. Dance she did! And dance she must! Over the fields and meadows, in the rain and sunshine, by night and by day. But it was more horrible and frightening at night when the world was dark.

She danced through the gates of the churchyard; but the dead did not dance with her, they had better things to do. She wanted to sit down on the pauper's grave, where the bitter herbs grew, but for her there was no rest. The church door was open and she danced toward it, but an angel, dressed in white, who had on his back great wings that reached almost to the ground, barred her entrance.

His face was stern and grave, and in his hand he held a broad, shining sword.

"You shall dance," he said, "dance in your red shoes until you become pale and thin. Dance till the skin on your face turns yellow and clings to your bones as if you were a skeleton. Dance you shall from door to door, and when you pass a house where proud and vain children live, there you shall knock on the door so that they will see you and fear your fate. Dance, you shall dance. . . . Dance!"

"Mercy!" screamed Karen, but heard not what the angel answered, for her red shoes carried her away, down through the churchyard, over the meadows, along the highways, through the lanes: always dancing.

One morning she danced past a house that she knew well. From inside she heard psalms being sung. The door opened and a coffin decked with flowers was carried out. The old lady who had been so kind to her was dead. Now she felt that she was forsaken by all of mankind and cursed by God's angel.

Dance she must, and dance she did. The shoes carried her across fields and meadows, through nettles and briars that tore her feet so they bled.

One morning she danced across the lonely heath until she came to a solitary cottage. Here, she knew, the executioner lived. With her fingers she tapped on his window.

"Come out! Come out!" she called. "I cannot come inside, for I must dance."

The executioner opened his door and came outside. When he saw Karen he said, "Do you know who I am? I am the one who cuts off the heads of evil men; and I can feel my ax beginning to quiver now."

"Do not cut off my head," begged Karen, "for then I should not be able to repent. But cut off my feet!"

She confessed her sins and the executioner cut off her feet, and the red shoes danced away with them into the dark forest. The executioner carved a pair of wooden feet for her and made her a pair of crutches. He taught her the psalm that a penitent sings. She kissed the hand that had guided the ax and went on her way.

"Now I have suffered enough because of those red shoes," thought Karen. "I shall go to church now and be among other people."

But when she walked up to the door of the church, the red shoes danced in front of her, and in horror she fled.

All during that week she felt sad and cried many a bitter tear. When Sunday came she thought, "Now I have suffered and struggled long enough. I am just as good as many of those who are sitting and praying in church right now, and who dare to throw their heads back with pride." This reasoning gave her courage, but she came no farther than the gate of the churchyard. There were the shoes dancing in front of her. In terror she fled, but this time she really repented in the depth of her heart.

She went to the minister's house and begged to be given work. She said that she did not care about wages but only wanted a roof over her head and enough to eat. The minister's wife hired the poor cripple because she felt sorry for her. Karen was grateful that she had been given a place to live and she worked hard. In the evening when the minister read from the Bible, she sat and listened thoughtfully. The children were fond of her and she played with them, but when they talked of finery and being beautiful like a princess, she would sadly shake her head.

When Sunday came, everyone in the household got ready for church, and they asked her to go with them. Poor Karen's eyes filled with tears. She sighed and glanced toward her crutches.

When the others had gone, she went into her little room that was so small that a bed and a chair were all it could hold. She sat down and began to read from her psalmbook. The wind carried the music from the church organ down to her, and she lifted her tear-stained face and whispered, "Oh, God, help me!"

Suddenly the sunlight seemed doubly bright and an angel of God stood before her. He was the same angel who with his sword had barred her entrance to the church, but now he held a rose branch covered with flowers. With this he touched the low ceiling of the room and it rose high into the air and, where he had touched it, a golden star shone. He touched the walls and they widened.

Karen saw the organ. She saw the old paintings of the ministers and their wives; and there were the congregation holding their psalmbooks in front of them and singing. The church had come to the poor girl in her little narrow chamber; or maybe she had come to the church. Now she sat among the others, and when they finished singing the psalm they looked up and saw her.

Someone whispered to her: "It is good that you came, Karen."

"This is His mercy," she replied.

The great organ played and the voices of the children in the choir mingled sweetly with it. The clear, warm sunshine streamed through the window. The sunshine filled Karen's heart till it so swelled with peace and happiness that it broke. Her soul flew on a sunbeam up to God; and up there no one asked her about the red shoes.

29

The Jumping Competition

THE flea, the grasshopper, and the jumping jack decided to hold a competition to see which of them could jump the highest. They invited the whole world, and anyone else who wanted to come, to look at it. Each of them felt sure that he would become the champion.

"I will give my daughter to the one who jumps the highest," declared the king. "Honor is too paltry a reward."

The flea was the first to introduce himself. He had excellent manners; but then he had the blood of young maidens in him and was accustomed to human society, and that had left its mark on him.

Then came the grasshopper. He was stout but not without grace and dressed in a green uniform, which he had acquired at birth. He said he was of ancient family and that his ancestors came from Egypt. He claimed that he was so highly esteemed in this country that he had been brought directly from the fields and given a card house. It was three stories high and all made of picture cards. It had both doors and windows.

"I sing so well," he boasted, "that sixteen native crickets, who have been cheeping since birth—but never have been honored with a card house—grew so thin from envy, when they heard me sing, that they almost disappeared."

Both the flea and the grasshopper gave a full account of their merits. Each of them thought it only fitting that he should marry a princess.

Now came the jumping jack. He was made from the wishbone of a goose, two rubber bands, some sealing wax, and a little stick that was mahogany. He didn't say a word, which made the whole court certain that he was a genius. The royal dog sniffed at him and said that he came of good family. The old councilor, who had received three decorations as a reward for keeping his mouth shut, declared that the jumping jack was endowed with the gift of prophecy. One could tell from looking at its back whether we would have a mild winter or not; and that was more than one could tell from the back of the fellow who wrote the almanac.

The old king merely said, "I don't talk much, but I have my own opinion about everything."

The competition began. The flea jumped so high that one could not see him; and then everyone said he hadn't jumped at all, which was most unfair! The grasshopper only jumped half as high as the flea but landed right in the face of the king and that did not please His Majesty, who said it was repulsive.

Now it was the jumping jack's turn; he sat so still and appeared so pensive that everyone decided that he wouldn't jump at all.

"I hope he hasn't got sick," said the royal hound, and sniffed at him; but just at that moment he jumped. It was a little, slanted jump, but high enough so that he landed in the lap of the princess, who was sitting on a golden stool.

"The highest jump is into my daughter's lap," declared the king. "The jumping jack has shown both intelligence and taste; she shall marry him." And the jumping jack got the princess.

"I jumped highest," said the flea. "But it is of no importance; she can keep him: wishbone, rubber bands, sealing wax, mahogany stick, and all! I don't care! I know I jumped the highest, but in this world it's only appearance that counts."

The flea enlisted in a foreign army and it was rumored that he was killed in battle.

The grasshopper sat down in the ditch and thought about the injustice of the world. "It's appearance that counts! It's appearance that counts!" he said. And then he sang his own sad song. It's from him that we have the story, which, even though it has been printed, may still be a lie.

30

The Shepherdess and the Chimney Sweep

HAVE you ever seen a really old cabinet, the kind whose wood is dark from age and that doesn't have a spot on it that isn't carved, so that it looks like a mass of vines and twirls? Once there stood in a parlor just such an heirloom that had been in the family for four generations. From the bottom to the top there were roses and tulips; everywhere there were curlicues, and little deer heads with numerous antlers peered out from among them. But the most amazing figure was in the center panel. It was a man with a long beard, who had little horns sticking out of his forehead and the legs of a goat. He had a grin on his face—for you could hardly call it a smile. He looked so funny that the children who lived in the house gave him a name. They called him Mr. Goat-legged Commanding-General-Private-War-Sergeant because it was so difficult to say, even for a grownup; and they knew of no one—either living or carved—who could boast of such a fine title.

From his cabinet he was always looking straight across the room at a little table that stood beneath a mirror, for on the table was the loveliest little porcelain shepherdess. She had her skirt pinned up with a red rose; on her feet were golden shoes, on her head she had a golden hat, and in her hand was a shepherd's crook. Oh, she was beautiful! Next to her stood a little chimney sweep, and he was black as coal, except for his face, which was as pink and white as hers. Somehow this seemed wrong; he ought to have had at least a dab of soot on his nose or his cheek. But he was of porcelain too, and his profession was make-believe; he might just as well have been a prince. There he stood with his ladder in his hands looking as delicate as the shepherdess. They had been standing close together, for that was the way they had always been placed; and so they thought it was natural that they be engaged. They had much in common: both were young, both were made from the same clay, both were breakable.

Near them on the table there was another figure; he was three times as big as either of them. He was a Chinese mandarin and he knew how to nod. He was of porcelain too, and insisted that he was the shepherdess' grandfather. Although he couldn't really prove that he was related to her at all, he behaved as if he had as much right over her as her parents and demanded that she obey him. Now Mr. Goat-legged Commanding-General-Private-War-Sergeant had asked for the shepherdess' hand in marriage, and the Chinese mandarin had nodded.

"You will have a husband who I am almost certain is made of mahogany," said the old mandarin. "You will be called Mrs. Goat-legged Commanding-General-Private-War-Sergeant. He has a whole cabinetful of silverware, plus all that he has hidden in the secret compartments."

"I don't want to live in a dark closet!" wailed the shepherdess. "They say that he has eleven porcelain wives in there already."

"Then you shall be number twelve!" declared the Chinese mandarin. "And tonight! As soon as the cabinet creaks, there shall be a wedding, my dear, and that is as certain as it is that I am Chinese!" And he nodded his head back and forth until he fell asleep.

The little shepherdess cried and cried; then she looked up at her beloved, the chimney sweep. "I beg you to go with me out into the world, for we cannot stay here," she sobbed.

"I will do anything that you ask," he replied. "Let's go at once. I must be able to earn a living at my profession."

"If only we were down on the floor already," she said anxiously. "I won't feel safe before we are out in the wide world."

The chimney sweep did his best to console her. He showed her where she should set her little feet along the carved edges of the table and on the leaves of the gilded vines that wound themselves around its legs. He made use of his ladder and soon they had reached the floor. But then they looked up at the cabinet, where there was an uproar. All the carved deer were shaking their antlers in fury; and Mr. Goat-legged Commanding-General-Private-War-Sergeant was jumping up and down. "They're eloping! They're eloping!" he cried as loud as he could over to the Chinese mandarin.

A drawer in the wall, just a little above the floor, was luckily open and the frightened lovers jumped inside it. Here lay three or four incomplete decks of cards and a little puppet theater. The puppets were performing a play. In the front row of the audience sat all the queens: hearts, diamonds, spades, and clubs, fanning themselves with their tulips; behind them sat the knaves and looked both above and below the ladies in the front row, just to show that they had heads at both ends, exactly as they always do in a deck of cards. The play was about two lovers who weren't allowed to be together and reminded the poor shepherdess so much of her own situation that she wept and wept.

"I can't bear it!" she said. "We must get out of here."

By the time they were back down on the floor again, the old Chinese mandarin was awake. He was nodding his head and rocking back and forth with his whole body, which was rounded at the bottom, for he had no legs.

"Here comes the old mandarin!" screamed the little shepherdess, and fell down on her porcelain knees because she was so upset.

"I have an idea," said the chimney sweep. "We could climb down into the potpourri jar, over there in the corner. There we shall be among roses and lavender and we can throw salt in the eyes of anyone who comes."

"It won't do!" cried the shepherdess. "The potpourri jar and the mandarin were once engaged. It's a long time ago but a certain amount of affection always remains for the lovers of one's youth. . . . No, we have no choice, we must go out into the wide world."

"But do you realize what that means?" asked the chimney sweep. "Have you thought about how wide the world is and that we can never come back?"

"I have!" she said determinedly.

The chimney sweep looked steadfastly into her eyes. "The only way I know how to get out is through the chimney. Have you the courage to climb into the belly of the stove and up through the flue into the chimney? From there on, it's upward, ever upward, where no one can reach us, till we come to the opening; and then we shall be out in the wide world."

He led her over to the stove and opened the door. "Oh, how dark it looks," she said. But she followed him into the belly of the stove and crawled with him up the flue, though it was pitch-dark.

"Now we are in the chimney. Look up and you will see a star!"

It was true, there was a star shining through the darkness, as if it wished to guide them on their way. They climbed, they crawled; it was a terrible journey: up, up they went. The chimney sweep hoisted and held onto the shepherdess, showing her where to put her little porcelain feet. Finally they reached the top of the chimney and sat down on the edge of it. They were exhausted and they had every right to be.

The star-filled sky was above them and all the roofs of the city were below them. They could see far and wide, out into the world. The poor little shepherdess had never imagined that the wide world would be so big. She leaned her head on the chimney sweep's shoulder and cried so hard that the gold in her waistband began to chip.

"It's far too much!" she sobbed. "I cannot bear it! The world is much too big. I wish I were back on the table beneath the mirror. I shall never be happy again until I am! I followed you out into the wide world; now you must take me home, if you care for me at all."

The chimney sweep tried to reason with her. He talked about the Chinese mandarin and Mr. Goat-legged Commanding-General-Private-War-Sergeant; but that just made her cry all the more. Finally she kissed him, and then he could only obey her.

And they climbed back down the chimney with great difficulty, crawled through the flue, and entered the belly of the stove; there they peeped out through the door to see what was going on in the parlor.

Not a sound came from the room. In the middle of the floor lay the old Chinese mandarin. He had fallen off the table when he tried to follow them. Now he was in three pieces and his head had rolled over in a corner. Mr. Goat-legged Commanding-General-Private-War-Sergeant stood where he always had been, deep in thought.

"How horrible!" exclaimed the little shepherdess. "Old Grandfather is broken and it's all our fault! I shan't live through it!"

"He can be glued," said the chimney sweep. "He can be put together again. . . . Don't carry on so! . . . All he needs is to be glued and have a rivet put in his neck, and he'll be able to say as many nasty things as he ever did."

"Do you think so?" she asked. They climbed up onto the table and stood where they had before.

"Well, this is as far as we got!" the chimney sweep said. "We could have saved ourselves a whole lot of trouble."

"Do you think it will be expensive to have Grandfather put together again?" asked the shepherdess. "Oh, how I wish it were already done!"

And Grandfather was glued and a rivet was put in his neck; and then he was as good as new, except for one thing: he couldn't nod any more.

"You seem to think so much more highly of yourself since you have been broken," said Mr. Goat-legged Commanding-General-Private-War-Sergeant. "I can't understand why anyone should be proud of being glued. Am I to have her or not?"

The chimney sweep and the little shepherdess looked pitifully at the Chinese mandarin; they were so terrified that he would nod. But he couldn't nod; and he didn't want to admit to a stranger that he had a rivet in his neck and would never be able to nod again. So the two young porcelain lovers stayed together. They blessed the rivet in Grandfather's neck and loved each other until they broke.

31

The Little Match Girl

IT was dreadfully cold, snowing, and turning dark. It was the last evening of the year, New Year's Eve. In this cold and darkness walked a little girl. She was poor and both her head and feet were bare. Oh, she had had a pair of slippers when she left home; but they had been too big for her—in truth, they had belonged to her mother. The little one had lost them while hurrying across the street to get out of the way of two carriages that had been driving along awfully fast. One of the slippers she could not find, and the other had been snatched by a boy who, laughingly, shouted that he would use it as a cradle when he had a child of his own.

Now the little girl walked barefoot through the streets. Her feet were swollen and red from the cold. She was carrying a little bundle of matches in her hand and had more in her apron pocket. No one had bought any all day, or given her so much as a penny. Cold and hungry, she walked through the city; cowed by life, the poor thing!

The snowflakes fell on her long yellow hair that curled so prettily at the neck, but to such things she never gave a thought. From every window of every house, light shone, and one could smell the geese roasting all the way out in the street. It was, after all, New Year's Eve; and this she did think about.

In a little recess between two houses she sat down and tucked her feet under her. But now she was even colder. She didn't dare go home because she had sold no matches and was frightened that her father might beat her. Besides, her home was almost as cold as the street. She lived in an attic, right under a tile roof. The wind whistled through it, even though they had tried to close the worst of the holes and cracks with straw and old rags.

Her little hands were numb from cold. If only she dared strike a match, she could warm them a little. She took one and struck it against the brick wall of the house; it lighted! Oh, how warm it was and how clearly it burned like a little candle. She held her hand around it. How strange! It seemed that the match had become a big iron stove with brass fixtures. Oh, how blessedly warm it was! She stretched out her legs so that they, too, could get warm, but at that moment the stove disappeared and she was sitting alone with a burned-out match in her hand.

She struck another match. Its flame illuminated the wall and it became as transparent as a veil: she could see right into the house. She saw the table spread with a damask cloth and set with the finest porcelain. In the center, on a dish, lay a roasted goose stuffed with apples and prunes! But what was even more wonderful: the goose—although a fork and knife were stuck in its back—had jumped off the table and was waddling toward her. The little girl stretched out her arms and the match burned out. Her hands touched the cold, solid walls of the house.

She lit a third match. The flame flared up and she was sitting under a Christmas tree that was much larger and more beautifully decorated than the one she had seen through the glass doors at the rich merchant's on Christmas Eve. Thousands of candles burned on its green branches, and colorful pictures like the ones you can see in store windows were looking down at her. She smiled up at them; but then the match burned itself out, and the candles of the Christmas tree became the stars in the sky. A shooting star drew a line of fire across the dark heavens.

"Someone is dying," whispered the little girl. Her grandmother, who was dead, was the only person who had ever loved or been kind to the child; and she had told her that a shooting star was the soul of a human being traveling to God.

She struck yet another match against the wall and in its blaze she saw her grandmother, so sweet, so blessedly kind.

"Grandmother!" shouted the little one. "Take me with you! I know you will disappear when the match goes out, just like the warm stove, the goose, and the beautiful Christmas tree." Quickly, she lighted all the matches she had left in her hand, so that her grandmother could not leave. And the matches burned with such a clear, strong flame that the night became as light as day. Never had her grandmother looked so beautiful. She lifted the little girl in her arms and flew with her to where there is neither cold nor hunger nor fear: up to God.

In the cold morning the little girl was found. Her cheeks were red and she was smiling. She was dead. She had frozen to death on the last evening of the old year. The sun on New Year's Day shone down on the little corpse; her lap was filled with burned-out matches.

"She had been trying to warm herself," people said. And no one knew the sweet visions she had seen, or in what glory she and her grandmother had passed into a truly new year.

32

Little Tuck

THIS is a story about a little boy named Tuck. His real name was Carl, but when he was very tiny he had pronounced it "Tuck" and the name had stuck. Such things are always nice to know.

Now Tuck had to take care of his sister Gustava, who was much younger than he was, and study his lessons at the same time. These are two jobs that are not easily combined. The poor boy was singing little rhymes to his sister, who was sitting in his lap, and trying to read his geography book at the same time. The book lay open on the table beside him. He was supposed to learn where all the towns of Zealand were, and everything else that was important about them. The only one that he knew anything about at all was Copenhagen.

At last his mother came home and took little Gustava from him. But now it was almost dark and they could not afford to light a candle just so he could study. Little Tuck sat by the window, trying to read in the fading light.

"There is the old washerwoman from the alley," said his mother, who was looking out of the window. "She can hardly walk and yet she must carry water all the way from the pump in the square. Be a good boy, Tuck, and go and carry it for her."

Little Tuck ran at once to help the old woman. When he got home it was dark; there was no point in even asking for a candle, for it was Tuck's bedtime. His bed was a bench in the living room; and there he lay trying to recall everything the teacher had said about the cities and towns of Zealand. He had put the geography book under his pillow, for someone had told him that this could help him learn his lessons—though that kind of advice one shouldn't put much faith in.

He was thinking as hard as he could, when suddenly it felt as though someone were kissing him gently on his eyes and then on his mouth. He felt as if he were awake and asleep, both at the same time. There was the old washerwoman looking down at him kindly. "It would be a sin and a shame," she said, "if you did not know your lesson tomorrow in school because you helped me. Now I shall help you and the Lord will help us both."

The book under his pillow began to move about as if it were alive; and then a hen crawled out of it.

"Cluck! Cluck!" said the hen. "I come from the town of Køge! Cluck! Cluck!" And the hen told him the number of inhabitants the town had and all about the battle that had been fought there, though she added that it wasn't worth talking about.

"Bang! Bang! Bang!" A parrot made out of wood fell from the sky and landed in little Tuck's bed. It was the popinjay from the fairgrounds of Praestø; the one that the good citizens shot at when they held their famous marksmanship competition. The popinjay claimed that he had as many nails in his body as the town of Praestø had inhabitants; and that he was very proud of. "Thorvaldsen lived right outside me, and my location is superb," the popinjay remarked as if he were the town itself.

All at once little Tuck was no longer in bed; he was riding along on a handsome horse; sitting behind him was a knight who was holding onto him so he wouldn't fall. Away they galloped. The gaily colored plumes on the knight's helmet streamed in the wind; they were riding through the forest toward Vordingborg. Here, in his royal castle, King Valdemar was holding court. The town was filled with people; banners flew from the high towers; and in the great hall musicians were playing; and the king, his courtiers, and the ladies of the court were dancing. Without warning, the sun began to rise; the night was over and the towers of the castle disappeared one after the other, until only one remained standing. The town was no longer a city but had shrunk to being a large hamlet, poor and wretched. Some school children, with books under their arms, were passing in one of the streets. "Two thousand inhabitants," they remarked. But they were bragging; the formerly so important royal city was even smaller than that.

Little Tuck was back in bed: half dreaming, half awake. Someone was approaching his bed.

"Little Tuck, little Tuck," cried a voice. It was a sailor boy who looked young enough to be a cadet or a cabin boy; but he was neither. "I bring you greetings from Korsør. It is a new town, a town that is growing! The mail coach from Copenhagen stops here, and steamships are moored in our harbor. Once people thought that Korsør was a horrid, vulgar place, but that was only prejudice. Listen to what Korsør says about itself: 'I am surrounded by green forests and blue sea. Inside my walls a poet was born, who is amusing to read—which is more than most poets are. I thought of sending a ship around the world. I didn't, but I could have if I had wanted to. My city gate is covered with roses, which smell so sweetly. . . .'"

Little Tuck thought he saw the roses; but then the colors blended and the roses were gone. Green, forest-clad banks rose above a blue fjord. The tall spires of an old cathedral stretched upward toward the sky. On one of the sloping hills, water splashed in broad streams; they came from a spring, and near it sat an old man with long white hair and a golden crown on his head. It was old King Hroar. In olden times the town was called "Hroar's spring"; today the Danes call it Roskilde (*kilde* is the Danish word for "spring"). In the cathedral, all the kings and queens of Denmark are buried. Little Tuck seemed to be able to see them all as they walked hand in hand, with golden crowns on their heads, into the cathedral; and he could hear the organ playing, mixed with the sound of the water rushing from the spring. "Don't forget that here the Estates assemble!" called King Hroar.

Suddenly the cathedral was gone; as if someone had turned the pages of a picture book, a woman now stood before him. She looked like a gardener's helper. Indeed, that's what she must have been, for she was busy weeding the town square of Sorø, where grass grows between the cobblestones. She had draped her gray linen apron over her head. It must have just rained, for she was all wet. "In Sorø it always rains," she commented. She knew stories about both King Valdemar and Bishop Absalon, and could recite long, amusing passages from Holberg's plays. But then, without warning, she hunched her shoulders, her head began to bob, and she looked like a frog. "One has to dress according to the weather. . . . Croak! Croak! . . . It is as wet and as peaceful as the grave in this town. Croak! Croak. . . .

That is, except when the boys from the academy are here reciting Greek, Latin, and Hebrew. . . . Croak! Croak!" And the old woman who was a frog—or the frog who was an old woman—kept making the same sound: "Croak! Croak!" The monotone made Tuck sleep even more deeply.

But still dreams came to him. His little sister Gustava, with her big blue eyes and long, curly, yellow hair, had grown up; and even though neither of them had wings, they were both able to fly. Hand in hand, Tuck and Gustava flew above the fields and green forests of Zealand.

"Listen to the cock crowing, little Tuck," she said. "See the hens fly up from Køge. You shall have a henyard so big, so huge, that you will never know hunger or want. When you aim at the popinjay, you shall hit the mark and become a rich and happy man. Your house shall rise as proudly as King Valdemar's castle once did in Vordingborg; and in your garden there will stand marble sculptures like those of Thorvaldsen near Praestø. Your name will be praised around the world, just as far as the ship from Korsør could have sailed. 'Remember the assembling of the Estates, Little Tuck,' says King Hroar, for there you shall give wise and good counsel. Finally, you will become old and die; then you shall sleep peacefully. . . ."

"As though I were lying in Sorø," said little Tuck, and woke up. It was a lovely morning and all his dreams were immediately forgotten— and that was just as well, for it is not good for us to know the future.

Tuck jumped out of bed and quickly took his geography book out from underneath his pillow and began to study.

The old washerwoman stuck her head in through the door and nodded kindly to him. "Thank you for the help yesterday, little Tuck. May the Lord bless you and make your best dreams come true."

Little Tuck didn't remember what he had dreamed; but Our Lord did.

33

The Shadow

ON the shores of the Mediterranean the sun really knows how to shine. It is so powerful that it tans the people a mahogany brown; and the young scholar who came from the north, where all the people are as white as bakers' apprentices, soon learned to regard his old friend with suspicion. In the south one stays inside during most of the day with the doors and shutters closed. The houses look as if everyone was asleep or no one was at home. The young foreigner felt as if he were in prison, and his shadow rolled itself up until it was smaller than it had ever been before. But as soon as the sun set and a candle lighted the room, out came the shadow again. It was truly a pleasure to watch it grow; up the wall it would stretch itself until its head almost reached the ceiling.

"The stars seem so much brighter here," thought the scholar, and he walked out onto his balcony where he stretched himself just as his shadow had done. And on all the balconies throughout the city people came out to enjoy the cool evening. Had the town appeared dead and deserted at noon, certainly now it was alive! People were flocking into the streets. The tailors and the shoemakers moved their workbenches outside; the women came with their straight-backed chairs to sit and gossip. Donkeys heavily laden with wares tripped along like little maids. Children were everywhere. They laughed, played, and sometimes cried as children will do, for children can run so fast that they are not certain whether it is a tragedy or a comedy they are enacting. And the lights! Thousands of lamps burned like so many falling stars. A funeral procession, led by little choir boys in black and white, passed with mournful but not sad-looking people following the black-draped horse and wagon. The church bells were ringing. "This is life!" thought the young foreigner, and he tried to take it all in.

Only the house directly across from his own was as quiet now as it had been at midday. The street was very narrow and the opposite balcony was only a few yards away. Often he stood and stared at it, but no one ever came out. Yet there were flowers there and they seemed to be flourishing, which meant that they were cared for or else the sun would long since have withered them. "Yes," he concluded, "they must be watered by someone." Besides, the shutters were opened, and while he never saw any light, he sometimes heard music. The scholar thought this music "exquisite," but that may be only because all young northerners think everything "exquisite" the first time they are in the south.

He asked his landlord if he knew who lived across the street, but the old man replied that he did not and, in fact, had never seen anyone enter or leave. As for the music, he could hardly express how terrible he thought it. "It's as if someone were practicing," he said. "The same piece, over and over and over again! And it's never played all the way through! It's unbearable!"

One night the young foreigner, who slept with his balcony door open, awakened with a start. A breeze had lifted his drapes so that he caught a glimpse of the opposite balcony. The flowers were ablaze with the most beautiful colors and in their midst stood a lovely maiden. For an instant the scholar closed his eyes to make sure that he had had them open. In a single leap he was standing in front of the drapes. Cautiously, he parted them; but the girl had vanished, the light had disappeared, and the flowers looked as they always did. The door, however, had been left open, and from far inside he could hear music; its gentle strains seemed to cast a spell over him, for never before had he taken such delight in his own thoughts. How does one get into that apartment? he wondered; and he perused the street below. There was no private entrance whatever, only a group of small shops; surely one could not enter a home through a store.

The next evening the scholar was sitting as usual on his balcony. From his room the lamp burned brightly, and since his shadow was very shy of light, it had stretched itself until it reached the opposite balcony. When the young man moved, his shadow moved. "I believe my shadow is the only living thing over there," he muttered. "See how it has sat down among the flowers. The balcony door is ajar. Now if my shadow were clever, it would go inside and take a look around; then it would come back and tell me what it had seen. Yes, you ought to earn your keep," he said jokingly. "Now go inside. Did you hear me? Go!" And he nodded to his shadow and his shadow nodded back at him. "Yes, go! But remember to come back again." There the scholar's conversation with his shadow ended. The young man rose, and the shadow on the opposite balcony rose; the young man turned around and the shadow also turned around; but then there happened something that no one saw. The shadow went through the half-open door of the other balcony, while the scholar went into his own room and closed the drapes behind him.

The next morning on his way to the café where he had his break-fast and read the newspapers, the scholar discovered that he had no shadow. "So it really went away last night!" he marveled. More than anything else, the young man was embarrassed; people were certain to notice, and might demand that he explain or, worse than that, might make up explanations of their own. He returned at once to his room and there he remained for the rest of the day. That evening he walked out onto his balcony for a bit of fresh air. The light streamed from behind him as it had on the evening before. He sat down, stood up, stretched himself; still there was no shadow, and though it was doubtful that anyone could see him, he hurried inside again almost immediately.

But in the warm countries everything grows much faster than it does in the north, and less than a week had passed before a shadow began to sprout from the scholar's feet. "The old one must have left its roots behind, what a pleasant surprise!" he thought happily. Within a month he walked the streets unconcerned; his shadow, though a little small, was quite respectable. During the long trip, for the scholar was going home, it continued to grow until even a very big man, which the scholar was not, would not have complained about its size.

Settled once more in his own country, the scholar wrote books about all that is true and beautiful and good. The days became years. The scholar was now a philosopher; and the years became many. One evening when he was sitting alone in his room there was a very gentle knock at the door.

"Come in," he called. But no one came, so the philosopher opened the door himself. Before him stood the thinnest man that he had ever seen but, judging from his clothes, a person of some importance. "Whom do I have the honor of addressing?" the philosopher asked.

"I thought as much," replied the stranger. "You don't recognize me, now that I have a body of my own and clothes to boot. You never would have believed that you would meet your old shadow again. Things have gone well for me since we parted. If need be, I can buy my freedom!" The shadow jiggled its purse, which was filled with gold pieces, and touched the heavy gold chain that it wore around its neck. On all of its fingers were diamond rings, and every one was genuine.

"I must be dreaming!" exclaimed the philosopher. "What is happening?"

"Well, it isn't something that happens every day," said the shadow, "but then, you're not an ordinary person. Nobody knows that better than I do, didn't I walk in your first footsteps? . . . As soon as you found that I could stand alone in the world, you let me go. The results are obvious. Without bragging, I can say few could have done better. . . . Of late, a longing has come over me to talk with you before you die—you must die, you know. Besides, I wanted to see this country again, only a rogue does not love his native land. . . . I know that you have a new shadow. If I owe you or it anything, you will be so kind as to tell me."

"Is it really you?" cried the philosopher. "It's so incredible! I wouldn't have believed that one's shadow could come back to one as a human being!"

"Tell me how much I owe you," insisted the shadow. "I hate to be in debt."

"How can you talk like that?" replied the philosopher. "What debt could there be to pay? Be as free as you wish! I am only happy to see you again. And I rejoice in your good luck. Sit down, old friend," he invited most cordially. "Tell me how all this came about, and what you saw that night in the house across the street."

"Yes, I will tell you about it," agreed the shadow, and sat down. "But first you must promise me that you will never tell anyone that I once was your shadow. I've been thinking of becoming engaged; after all, I am quite rich enough to support a large family."

"Don't give it another moment's thought," the philosopher said. "I will never tell anyone who you really are. Here is my hand on it. A man is no better than his word."

"And a word is a shadow," remarked the shadow, because it could not speak otherwise.

It was really amazing, how human the shadow appeared. It was dressed completely in black, but everything was of the finest quality from its patent leather boots to its hat of the softest felt. The gold chain and the rings have already been described, but one's eye fell upon them so often that one cannot help mentioning them again. Yes, the shadow was well dressed, and clothes make the man.

"Now I shall begin," announced the shadow, and it stamped its boots as hard as it could on the philosopher's new shadow, which was curled up like a poodle at the feet of the man. Perhaps it did this because it hoped to attach the philosopher's shadow to itself, or maybe just because it was arrogant; but the new shadow did not appear ruffled. It lay perfectly still and listened, for it too wanted to know how one could be free and become one's own master.

"Do you know who lived in the house across the street?" asked the shadow. "That's the best of all, it was Poetry! I was there for three weeks, and that is just as edifying as having lived three thousand years and read everything that's ever been composed or written. This I say, and what I say is true! I have seen all and I know all!"

"Poetry!" cried the philosopher. "Yes . . . yes. She is often a hermit in the big cities. I saw her myself once, but only for a short moment and my eyes were drowsy from sleep. She was standing on the balcony and it was as if the northern lights were shining around her. . . . Go on, go on! There you were on the balcony; then you walked through the doorway and . . . and . . ."

"I was in the entrance hall. That's what you sat looking at all the time, the vestibule. There was no lamp in there, and that's why from the outside the apartment appeared dark. But there was a door. It opened onto another room, which opened onto another, which opened onto another. There was a long row of rooms and anterooms before one reached the innermost where Poetry lived. And these were ablaze with more than enough light to kill a shadow, so I never saw the maiden up close. I was cautious and patient, and that is the same as being virtuous."

"Come, come," commanded the philosopher curtly. "Tell me what you saw."

"Everything! And I'll tell you about it, but first . . . It has nothing whatever to do with pride, but out of respect to my accomplishments, not to speak of my social position, I wish you wouldn't address me so familiarly."

"Forgive me!" exclaimed the philosopher. "It is an old habit, and they are the hardest to get rid of. But you are quite right, and I'll try to remember. . . . Please do continue, for I am immensely interested."

"Everything! I have seen all, and I know all!"

"I beg you to tell me about the innermost room where Poetry dwelled. Was it like the beech forest in spring? Was it like the interior of a great cathedral? Or was it like the heavens when one stands on a mountaintop?"

"Everything was there!" replied the shadow. "Of course, I never went all the way in. The twilight of the vestibule suited me better, and from there I had an excellent view. I saw everything and I know all. I was at the court of Poetry, in the entrance hall."

"But what did you see?" urged the philosopher. "Did Thor and Odin walk those halls? Did Achilles and Hector fight their battles again? Or did innocent children play there and tell of their dreams?"

"I am telling you that I was there. And you understand, I saw everything that there was to see. You could not have stayed there and remained a human being, but it made a human being of me! I quickly came to understand my innermost nature, that part of me which from birth can claim kinship to Poetry. When I lived with you, I didn't even think about such things. You'll remember that I was always larger at sunrise and at sunset, and that I was more noticeable in the moonlight than you were. Still, I had no understanding of my nature; that did not come until I was in the vestibule, and then I became a human being.

"I was fully mature when I came out; by then you had already left the south. Being human made me ashamed to go around as I was; I needed boots, clothes, and all the other trimmings that make a man what he is. So there was nothing else for me to do but hide. . . . I wouldn't say this to anyone but you, and you mustn't mention it in any of your books. . . . I hid under the skirts of the woman who sold gingerbread men in the market. Luckily, she never found out how much her petticoats concealed. I came out only in the evening; then I would walk around in the moonlight, stretching myself up the walls to get the kinks out of my back. Up and down the streets I went, peeping through the windows of the attics as well as the drawing rooms. And I saw what no one ever sees, what no one ever should see! It's really a horrible world, and I wouldn't be human if it weren't so desirable. I saw things that ought to be unthinkable; and these were not only done by husbands and wives, but by parents and the sweet, innocent children! I saw," said the shadow, "I saw everything that man must not know, but what he most ardently wishes to know—his neighbor's evil! If I had written a newspaper, everyone would have read it; but instead I wrote directly to the persons themselves, and I wreaked havoc in every city that I came to. People feared me so much and were so fond of me! The universities gave me honorary degrees, the tailors gave me clothes, and the women said that I was handsome. In a word, each donated what he could, and so I became the man that I am. . . . But it is getting late, and I must say good-by. Here is my card. I live on the sunnier side of the street and am always home when it rains."

"How strange!" remarked the philosopher after the shadow had left.

The years and the days passed, and the shadow came again. "How are things going?" it asked.

"Oh," replied the philosopher, "I have been writing about all that is true and beautiful and good, but no one cares to hear about anything like that, and I am terribly disappointed because those are the things that are dear to me."

"Well, they aren't to me," said the shadow. "I've been concentrating on gaining weight, and that there's some point in. You don't understand the world, that's what's the matter with you. You ought to travel. I am going on a trip this summer, would you like to join me? If you would like to travel as my shadow it would be a pleasure to have you along. I'll pay for your trip!"

"You go too far!" retorted the philosopher.

"It all depends how you look at it. The trip will do you good and, traveling as my shadow, you'll have all your expenses paid by me."

"Monstrous!" shouted the philosopher.

"But that's the way of the world, and it isn't going to change," said the shadow, and left.

Matters did not improve for the philosopher; on the contrary, sor-

row and misery had attached themselves to his coattails. For the most part, whenever he spoke of the true and the beautiful and the good, it was like setting roses before a cow. Finally he became seriously ill. "You look like a shadow of your former self," people would say, and when he heard these words a shiver went down his spine.

"You ought to go to a health resort," suggested the shadow when it came to visit him again. "There's no other alternative. I will take you along for old time's sake. I'll pay the expenses, and you'll talk and try to amuse me along the journey. I'm going to a spa, myself, because my beard won't grow. That's a disease too, you know, because beards are a necessity. If you're sensible, you'll accept. We'll travel as friends."

And so they traveled, the shadow as master and the master as shadow, for whether they were being driven in a coach, riding horseback, or simply walking, they were always side by side and the shadow kept itself a little in the fore or in the rear, according to the direction of the sun. It knew how to create the impression that it was the superior. The philosopher, however, was not aware of any of this. He had a kind heart, which did not even have a guest room reserved for envy. The journey was not yet over when the philosopher suggested to the shadow, "Now that we're traveling companions—and when you consider the fact that we've grown up together, shouldn't we call each other by first names? It makes for a much pleasanter atmosphere."

"There's something in what you say," began the shadow, who now was the real master. "You have spoken frankly, and what you have said was well meant; therefore, I ought to be honest with you. As a philosopher, you know how strange nature can be. Some people cannot bear to have a rough piece of material next to their bodies, and others can't hear a nail scratching on glass without it upsetting their nervous systems. Well, I would have the same feeling if you were to call me by my first name. I would have the feeling that I was being pressed to the ground, as if my relationship to you had never changed. You understand it's merely a feeling, it has nothing whatever to do with pride. But I could call you by your first name and satisfy half of your request."

From then on, the shadow always spoke and referred to the philosopher by his first name. "He goes too far," thought the man. "He's hardly civil to me." But when one is poor, one does more thinking than speaking.

At last they arrived at the famous resort where people came from all over the world to be cured. Among the guests was a beautiful princess who suffered from seeing too clearly, which is a very painful disease. She noticed at once that one of the new arrivals was very different from everyone else. He had come to make his beard grow, she was told. "But that's not the real reason," she muttered to herself. And to satisfy her curiosity, she went right up and spoke to the stranger, for the daughter of a king need not stand on ceremony with anyone.

"Your trouble is that you cannot cast a shadow," the princess announced.

"Your Royal Highness is getting well!" exclaimed the shadow. "I know that you suffered from seeing too clearly, but you must be getting over it. You show signs of perfect health. . . . I grant you that it is a very unusual one, but I do have a shadow. Other people have just ordinary shadows, but I despise the ordinary. You know how one dresses one's servants so that their livery is finer than one's own clothes; well, I let my shadow pretend that he is human. As you can see, I have even bought him a shadow. It was very expensive, but I am fond of doing the original."

"What!" thought the princess. "Have I really been cured? This is the finest spa there is. How fortunate I am to be born in the time when these marvelous waters were discovered. . . . But just because I am well is no reason to leave. I'm enjoying myself here. That stranger interests me, I hope his beard won't grow too quickly."

That night there was a grand ball that everyone attended, and the shadow danced with the princess. The princess was light on her toes, but the shadow was even lighter; such a graceful partner she had never had before. They discovered that he had once visited her country while she was abroad. There, too, the shadow had peeped through all of the windows, those that faced the street and those that did not. He had seen both this and that; and he knew how to tell about some of what he had seen and how to hint at the rest, which was even more impressive. The princess was astounded. She had never spoken to anyone who was so worldly wise, and out of respect for what he knew, she danced with him again.

The next time they danced together the princess fell in love. The shadow noticed the sudden change with relief. "She's finally been cured of seeing too clearly," he thought.

The princess would have confessed her feelings immediately if she hadn't been so prudent. She thought of her realm and of the people she ruled. "He knows well the ways of the world, that's a good sign," she commented silently. "He dances well, that is also a virtue. But is he really educated, for that is very important? I'd better test him." Then she began to ask the shadow questions so difficult that she herself did not know the answers.

An expression of confusion came over the shadow's face. "You cannot answer!" exclaimed the princess.

"I learned the answers to questions like that in childhood," said the shadow. "I believe that even my shadow, who is sitting over there by the door, could respond correctly."

"Your shadow! That really would be remarkable!"

"I can't say for certain," continued the shadow. "I just wouldn't be surprised if he could. After all, he's never done anything but follow me around and listen to what I say. Yes," he cried in a sudden burst of enthusiasm, "I believe he will be able to answer you! . . . But, Your Royal Highness, if you will allow me to make a suggestion. My shadow is so proud of being thought to be human, if Your Royal Highness wishes to create the right atmosphere, so that the shadow will be able to do his best, please treat him as if he were a man."

"I'd prefer it that way," said the king's daughter, and she joined the philosopher, who was alongside the door. She questioned him about the sun and the moon, and about the human race, both inside and out; and he answered every query both cleverly and politely.

"What must the man be worth, if his shadow is so wise!" thought the princess. "It would be a blessing for my people if I chose him for my husband. I shall do it!"

The shadow was very amenable. It agreed without hesitation that their plans must not be revealed until the princess had returned home. "I will not even tell my shadow," he said, while he thought how admirably the world had been created.

Not long after they came to the land which the princess ruled whenever she was there.

"My good friend," the shadow began to the philosopher. "Now that I am as happy and as powerful as anyone can hope to be, I'd like to share my good fortune with you. You may live with me always, here in the castle; you may drive with me in the royal coach; and you will be paid one hundred thousand gold pieces a year. In return, all I ask is that you let everyone call you a shadow; that you never admit to anyone that you have ever been a human being; and that once a year, when I sit on the balcony so that the people can pay me homage, you lie at my feet as a shadow should. . . . I might as well tell you that I am marrying the princess, and the wedding is tonight."

"No, this cannot happen!" cried the philosopher. "I don't want to do it, and I won't! You are a fraud! I will tell everything! You've fooled both the people and the princess; but now I will tell them that I am a human being and that you are only my shadow, who's been masquerading as a man!"

"No one will believe you," warned the shadow. "Now be reasonable or I'll call the guard."

"I intend to ask for an audience with the princess," replied the philosopher.

"But I will speak with her first," said the shadow, "and you will be imprisoned."

The shadow's threat very quickly became a reality, for the royal sentry knew whom the princess had chosen to be her husband.

"You are shivering," remarked the princess as soon as he entered her chambers. "You must not get sick this evening, not for the wedding!"

"I've just had the most horrible experience that one can have," replied the shadow. "Imagine! . . . Oh, how fragile a shadow's brain must be! . . . Imagine, my shadow has gone mad. He believes he is a man. And that I . . . that I am his shadow!"

"How dreadful!" she exclaimed. "He isn't running around loose, I hope."

"No, no, he's not," he said softly. "I am so afraid he will never get well."

"Poor shadow," continued the princess. "He must be suffering terribly. It would really be kinder to free him from that particle of life he has. Yes, the more I think about it, the more convinced I am that it's necessary for him to be done away with. . . . Quietly, of course."

"It seems so cruel," said the shadow, "when I think of how loyal a servant it was," and a sound resembling a sigh escaped from the shadow's lips.

"How noble you are!" exclaimed the princess.

That night the whole city was brilliantly lighted. The cannons were shot off. Bum! Bum! Bum! The soldiers presented arms. Oh, what a wedding it was! The shadow and the princess came out onto the balcony, and the people screamed, "Hurrah!"

The philosopher heard nothing of all of this, for they had already taken his life.

34

The Old House

ONCE upon a time there stood in a street a very old house; it was nearly three hundred years old. You could tell what year it had been built by reading the date cut into one of the beams; all around it tulips and curling hop vines had been carved. Right above the entrance a whole verse had been inscribed, and above each window appeared a grinning face. The second story protruded out over the first. The lead gutters, which hung under the roof, were shaped like dragons, with the monster's head at either end. The water was supposed to spout out of their mouths, but it didn't; the gutter was filled with holes and the water ran out of the dragons' stomachs.

All the other houses in the street were new and well kept, their walls were straight and smooth, and they had large windows. It was quite reasonable that they should feel themselves superior to the old house. Had they been able to speak they probably would have said: "How long are we to tolerate that old ruin? Bow windows are out of fashion and, besides, they obstruct our view. It must believe itself to be a castle, judging from the size of the steps leading up to the entrance, and that iron railing makes one think of funerals; not to speak of the brass knobs. It's embarrassing!"

Right across from the old house stood a new house; it was of the same opinion as all the other houses in the street. But behind one of its windows sat a little boy, a little red-cheeked child with bright, shining eyes who preferred the old house, and that both in the daytime when the sun shone and at night in the moonlight. When he looked at the walls of the old house, with its cracks and bare spots where the mortar had fallen off, then he could imagine how the street once had looked: in olden times, when all the houses had had broad steps leading up to their doors, and bay windows, and gables with tall pointed roofs. He could see the soldiers marching through the streets armed with halberds. Oh, he found the old house worth looking at and dreaming about.

Its owner was an old man who wore the strangest old-fashioned pants, a coat with brass buttons, and a wig that you could see was a wig. Every morning an old servant arrived to clean and run errands for the old gentleman; otherwise, he was all alone. Sometimes he came to the window and looked out into the street; then the little boy nodded to him and the old man nodded back. In this manner they became acquainted; no, more than that, they were friends, although they had never spoken to each other.

The little boy heard his parents say, "Our neighbor, across the street, must be terribly lonely."

Next Sunday the boy made a little package and, when he saw the servant going by in the street, he hurried down and gave it to him. "Would you please give this to your master?" he asked. "I have two tin soldiers, and I would like your master to have one of them, for I have heard that he is so terribly lonely."

The old servant smiled and nodded and took the little package, with the tin soldier inside it, to his master. Later that day a message arrived, inviting the boy to come and visit the old man. The child's parents gave their permission; and thus he finally entered the old house.

The brass knobs on the iron railing seemed to shine so brightly that one might believe that they had been newly polished in honor of the boy's visit. The little carved trumpeters in the oak doorway seemed to be blowing especially hard on their instruments, for their cheeks were all puffed up. It was a fanfare! "Tra . . . tra . . . trattalala! The boy is coming! Tra . . . tra . . . trattalala!" The door was opened and he stood in the hall. All the walls were covered with paintings portraying ladies in long silk gowns and knights in armor. The boy thought that he could hear the silk gowns rustle and the armor clang. Then there were the stairs; first they went up a goodish way, and then down a little bit, and ended in a balcony. It was wooden and a bit rickety, grass and weeds grew out of every crack, making it look more like a garden than a balcony. Antique flowerpots with human faces and donkey ears stood ranged in a row; the plants grew to suit themselves. One of them was filled with carnations that spread out over the rim in all directions; that is, the green leaves and the stems, the flowers hadn't come yet. One could almost hear the plant saying: "The breeze has caressed me and the sun has kissed me and promised me a flower next Sunday, a little flower next Sunday."

The old servant led the boy into a chamber where the walls did not have paper on them; no, they were covered with leather, which had gilded flowers stamped upon it.

> "Gilding fades all too fast.
> Leather, that is meant to last,"

said the walls.

In the room were high-backed armchairs with carvings all over them. "Sit down, sit down!" they cried. And when you sat down in them they mumbled. "Ugh, how it cracks inside me! I think I got rheumatism like the old cabinet. Ugh, how it creaks and cracks."

At last the little boy entered the room with the bow windows. Here the old master of the house greeted him. "Thank you for the tin soldier, my little friend," said he. "And thank you for coming."

"Thanks, thanks," said all the furniture, although it sounded a little more like: "Crack . . . Crack." There were so many chairs, tables, and cabinets in the room that they stood in each other's way, for they all wanted to see the little boy at once.

In the center of one of the walls hung a picture of a beautiful young girl. She was laughing and dressed in clothes from a bygone time. She did not say "thank you" or "crack" as the furniture had, but she looked down so kindly at the little boy that he could not help asking, "Where did you get her?"

"From the pawnbroker's," replied the old gentleman. "His shop is filled with pictures that no one cares about any more. The people they portray have been dead so long that no one remembers them. But though she has been dead and gone for fifty years, I knew her once."

Under the portrait hung a bouquet of faded flowers, carefully preserved behind glass. They looked old enough to have been picked half a century ago. The pendulum of the grandfather clock swung back and forth, and the hands moved slowly around, telling everything in the room that time was passing and that they were getting older; but that did not disturb the furniture.

"My parents say that you are terribly lonely," said the little boy.

"Oh," the old man smiled, "that is not altogether true. Old thoughts, old dreams, old memories come and visit me and now you are here. I am not unhappy."

Then from a shelf he took down a book that was filled with wonderful pictures. There were processions in which there were golden carriages, knights, and kings who looked like the ones in a deck of cards; and then came the citizens carrying the banners of their trades: the tailors' emblem was a pair of scissors held by a lion; the shoemakers had an eagle with two heads above their banner—for, as you know, shoemakers do everything in pairs. What a picture book that was!

The old man left for a moment to fetch some comfits, apples, and nuts; it was certainly nice to be visiting in the old house.

"But I can't stand it here!" wailed the tin soldier, who was standing on the lid of a chest. "It is so lonely and sad here; once you have lived with a family one cannot get accustomed to being alone. I can't stand it! The days are ever so long and the evenings feel even longer. It is not the same here as in your home, where your parents talked so pleasantly and you sweet children made such a lot of lovely noise. No, that poor old man really is lonely. Do you think anybody ever gives him a kiss? Or looks kindly at him? Here there is no Christmas tree ever, or gifts! The only thing he will ever get will be a funeral! . . . I can't stand it!"

"You mustn't take it so to heart," said the little boy. "I think it is very nice here. All the old thoughts and dreams come to visit, so he said."

"I see none of them and I don't want to either," screamed the tin soldier. "I can't stand it!"

"You will have to," said the little boy just as the old man returned with the comfits, apples, and nuts; and at the sight of them the boy forgot all about the soldier.

Happy and content, the little boy returned home. Days and weeks went by. The boy nodded to the old man from his window, and from the funny bow window of the old house the greeting was returned. Finally the little boy was asked to come visiting again.

The carved trumpeters blew, "Tra . . . tra . . . tratralala. . . .

The boy is here! . . . Tra tra!" The knights in armor clanged with their swords and the silk gowns of the ladies rustled, the leather on the wall said its little verse, and the old chairs that had rheumatism creaked. Nothing had changed, for in the old house every day and hour were exactly alike.

"I can't stand it!" screamed the tin soldier as soon as he saw the boy. "I have wept tin tears! It is much too mournful and sad here. Please, let me go to the wars and lose my arms and legs, that at least will be a change. I can't stand it, for I know what it is like to have old thoughts and old memories come visiting. Mine have been here and that is not amusing. Why, I almost jumped right off the lid of the chest. I saw all of you and my own home as plainly as if I had been there. It was Sunday morning and all you children were standing around the big table singing hymns, as you always do on Sunday. Your parents were nearby, looking solemn. Suddenly the door opened and little Maria, who is only two years old, entered. She always dances whenever she hears music, and she tried to dance to the tune you were singing, but hymns are not made for dancing, they are too slow. She stood first on one leg and flung her head forward, and then on the other and flung her head forward, but it didn't work out. You looked grave, all of you, but I found it too difficult not to laugh —at least inside myself. I laughed so hard that I fell off the table and hit my head so hard that I got a lump on it. I know it was wrong of me to laugh and the lump was punishment for it. That is what the old man meant by old thoughts and memories: everything that has ever happened to you comes back inside you. . . . Tell me, do you still sing your hymns on Sunday? Tell me something about little Maria and about my comrade, the other tin soldier. He must be happy. Oh, I can't stand it!"

"I have given you away," said the little boy. "You will have to stay, can't you understand that?"

The old man brought him a drawer in which lay many wonderful things. There were old playing cards with gilded edges, a little silver piggy bank, and a fish with a wiggly tail. Other drawers were opened and all the curiosities were looked at and examined. Finally the old man opened the harpsichord; on the inside of the lid was a painting of a landscape. The instrument was out of tune but the old man played on it anyway, and hummed a melody.

"Ah yes, she used to sing that," he sighed, and looked up toward the painting he had bought from the pawnbroker and his eyes shone like a young man's.

"I am going to the wars! I am going to the wars!" screamed the tin soldier as loudly as he could, and fell off the chest.

"What could have happened to him?" said the old man. Together he and the boy were searching for the little soldier on the floor. "Never mind, I will find him later," said the old man, but he never did. There were so many cracks in the floor and the tin soldier had fallen right down through one of them; there he lay buried alive.

The day passed and the little boy returned home. Many weeks went by, winter had come. All the windows were frozen over. The little boy had to breathe on the glass until he could thaw a little hole so that he could see out. Across the street the old house looked quite deserted; the snow lay in drifts on the steps. They had not been swept; one would think no one was at home. And no one was. The kind old man had died.

That evening a hearse drew up in front of the old house and a coffin was carried down the steps. The old man was not to be buried in the town cemetery but somewhere out in the country, where he had been born. The hearse drove away. No one followed it, for all his friends and family had died long ago. The little boy kissed his fingers and threw a kiss after the hearse as it disappeared down the street.

A few days afterward an auction was held; the furniture in the old house was sold. The boy watched from the window. He saw the knights in armor and the ladies with their silken gowns being carried out of the house. The old high-backed chairs, the funny flowerpots with faces and donkey ears were bought by strangers. Only the portrait of the lady found no buyer; it was returned to the pawnbroker. There it hung; no one remembered her and no one cared for the old picture.

Next spring the house itself was torn down, "It was a monstrosity," said the people as they went by. One could see right into the room with the leather-covered walls; the leather was torn and hung flapping like banners in the wind. The grass and weeds on the balcony clung tenaciously to the broken beams. But at last all was cleared away.

"That was good," said the neighboring houses.

A new house was built, with straight walls and big windows but not quite where the old house had stood; it was a little farther back from the street. On the site of the old house a little garden was planted, and up the walls of the houses on either side grew vines. A fine iron fence with a gate enclosed it, and people would stop in the street to look in, for it was most attractive. The sparrows would sit in the vines and talk and talk as sparrows do, but not about the old house, for they were too young to remember it.

Years went by and the little boy had become a grown man, a good and clever man of whom his parents could be justly proud. He had just got married and had moved into the new house. His young wife was planting a little wild flower in the front garden. He was watching her with a smile. Just as she finished, and was patting the earth around the little plant, she pricked her little hand. Something sharp was sticking out of the soft earth. What could it be?

It was—imagine it!—the tin soldier! The one that had fallen off the chest and down through a crack in the flooring. It had survived the wrecking of the old house, falling hither and thither as beams and floors disappeared, until at last it had been buried in the earth and there it had lain for many years.

The young woman cleaned the soldier off with a green leaf and then with her own handkerchief. It had perfume on it and smelled so delicious that the soldier felt as though he were awakening from a deep sleep.

"Let me have a look at him," said the young man; then he laughed and shook his head. "I don't believe it can be him, but he reminds me of a tin soldier that I once had." Then he told his wife about the old house and its old master and about the tin soldier that he had sent over to keep the old man company, when he had been a boy, because he had known that the old man was so terribly alone.

He told the story so well that his young wife's eyes filled with tears as she heard about the old house and the old man. "It could be the same soldier," she said. "I will keep it so that I shall not forget the story you have told me. But you must show me the old man's grave."

"I do not know where it is," her husband replied. "No one does; all those who knew him were dead. You must remember that I was a very small boy then."

"How terribly lonesome he must have been," sighed the young woman.

"Yes, terribly lonesome," echoed the tin soldier. "But it is truly good to find that one is not forgotten."

"Good," screamed something nearby in so weak a voice that only the tin soldier heard it. It was a little piece of leather from the walls of the old house. The gilding had gone long ago, and it looked like a little clod of wet earth. But it still had an opinion, and it expressed it.

"Gilding fades all too fast,
But leather, that is meant to last."

But the tin soldier did not believe that.

35
✷◆✷

A Drop of Water

SURELY you know what a magnifying glass is. It looks like one of the round glasses in a pair of spectacles; but it is much stronger, and can make things appear a hundred times larger than they are. If you look at a drop of water from a pond through it, a thousand tiny animals appear that cannot see with the naked eye; but they are there and they are real. They look like a plate of live shrimps jumping and crowding each other. They are all so ferocious that they tear each other's arms and legs off, without seeming to care. I suppose that is their way of life, and they are happy and content with it.

Now there once was an old man whom everybody called Wiggle-waggle, because that happened to be his name. He always made the best of things; and when he couldn't, he used magic.

One day when he looked through his magnifying glass at a drop of ditch water he was shocked at what he saw. How those creatures wiggled and waggled: hopping, jumping, pulling, pushing, and eating each other up—yes, they were cannibals.

"It is a revolting sight!" exclaimed old Wiggle-waggle. "Can't one do anything to make them live in peace, and each mind his own business?" He thought and thought, and when he couldn't find an answer, he decided to use magic.

"I'll give them a bit of color; then they will be easier to study," he decided. He let a drop of something that looked like red wine fall into the ditch water—but it wasn't red wine, it was witch's blood of the very finest type, the one that costs two shillings a drop. All the little creatures immediately turned pink. Now they looked like a whole town of naked savages.

"What have you got there?" asked an old troll who had come visiting. He had no name, which among trolls is distinguished.

"If you can guess what it is," replied Wiggle-waggle, "then I will make you a present of it. But it isn't easy, unless you know it."

The troll who had no name looked through the magnifying glass. What he saw looked like a city with all the inhabitants running around naked. It was a disgusting sight, but even more disgusting to see was the way people behaved. They kicked and cuffed each other; they beat and bit and shoved; those who were on the bottom strove to get to the top, and those on the top struggled to be on the bottom.

"Look, his leg is longer than mine! I will bite it off! Away with you!"

"Look, he has a lump behind his ear. It is small but it embarrasses him and gives him pain. We will really make him suffer!" And they pushed and pulled him; and finally they ate him up, all because he had had a little lump behind his ear.

One little creature sat still, all by herself in a corner, like a modest, sensitive little maiden. She wanted peace and quiet. But she was dragged out of her corner, mistreated, and finally she was eaten up.

"It is most instructive and amusing," said the troll.

"But what do you think it is?" asked Wiggle-waggle. "Have you figured it out?"

"That is easy," answered the troll. "It's Copenhagen or some other big city, they are all alike."

"It's ditch water," said Wiggle-waggle.

36

The Happy Family

THE largest leaves here in Denmark are the burdock leaves. If a little girl holds one in front of her tummy, then it will serve as an apron. If it should rain, one can use one as an umbrella; it is big enough. The burdock plant never grows alone; it is fond of company. Where you find one you will find more, and sometimes a whole forest of them. They look beautiful; and all this beauty is snail food. Those large white snails that the aristocrats and other grand people used to make into fricassee in the old times, and exclaim enthusiastically about how delicious they were—"What a flavor!" they used to cry—well, those white snails live on burdock leaves. And, as a matter of fact, it was for their sake that the burdock was originally planted.

Now there once was an old manor house where no one ate the snails; the custom had died there long ago, as had most of the snails; but the burdock, it thrived. They spread out all over the paths, and some of the lawns, for burdocks are not easy to get rid of. A good part of the park was a jungle of burdock leaves; and if a solitary plum or apple tree had not survived, no one would ever have believed that there once had been a garden there. In the very center of this forest lived the last survivors of the white snails. They were a couple and very, very old.

Exactly how old they were they didn't know, but they could remember that once their family had been numerous, and that their ancestors had come from some foreign land. That the burdock forest had been planted for their sake they knew too; and that they were proud of it. They had never been outside, but they knew vaguely that

there was a world outside; it was called the manor house. There
snails were cooked until they turned black and then they were served
on a silver dish. What happened afterward was not clear to them.
They didn't have any idea either what it was like to be "cooked" or
"served on a silver dish." But that the whole ceremony was extremely elegant and distinguished they had no doubt. Neither the
toad, nor the dung beetle, nor the earthworm—all of whom had been
asked—could tell them anything about it, since none of their family
had ever been "cooked" or "served on a silver dish."

The old white snails knew that they were the most distinguished
beings in the whole world, that the forest of burdocks had been
planted for their sake, and that the manor house stood merely so that
they someday could be brought there, to be cooked and put on a silver dish.

They lived a lonely yet happy life; as they had no children of their
own, they had adopted an ordinary garden snail. They had brought
him up carefully, as though he were their own; their only disappointment had been that he wouldn't grow. However, the mother
snail was always imagining that he was becoming fatter—in spite of
his being just an ordinary snail—and she would beg her husband, who
hadn't noticed it, to just feel their son's house. This the father snail
would do, and then he would agree with her.

One day the rain was pouring down!

"Listen to how it is drumming on the burdock leaves," said the father snail.

"It is raining through," cried his wife. "Look how the water is running down the stalks. Everything will be soaked down here. But we
have our houses and even the little one has his. Certainly, we were
created superior to all other creatures in the world. We are the true
aristocrats, born with houses on our backs, and with a whole forest
of burdock leaves especially sprouting and growing for our sake. I
wonder how far our forest stretches and what is beyond it?"

"Nothing," replied her husband. "There can be no better place
than this, and what is beyond does not interest me."

"Oh, I am not sure of that," argued his wife. "I wouldn't mind
being taken up to the manor house to be boiled and served on a silver
plate. All our ancestors have been; I am sure it is something very special, to have that happen to one."

"I believe it possible that the manor house has fallen apart and be-

come a ruin," said the father snail. "Or possibly the burdocks have
grown so large around it that the people inside it can't get out. But all
that is of no importance! You are always fretting. I am afraid our son
takes after you, he is so restless. For the last three days he has been
crawling up that stalk there, it gives me a headache just to look at
him."

"Don't scold him!" said the mother snail. "He keeps a dignified
pace, I am sure he will be a credit to us. After all, what have we old
people to live for but our children? Have you thought about where
we are going to find a wife for him? I wonder if anywhere in this forest there lives anyone of our own kind."

"Black slugs there are enough of; but they are not real snails, they
have no houses of their own. Although they are common they think a
lot of themselves. But we could ask the ants, they are always running
about as if they had something important to do; they may have come
across a snail that would make a wife for our little son."

"Oh yes! We know of the sweetest one," said the ants. "But it may
be difficult to arrange; you see, she is a queen."

"That is of no importance," said the old snails. "Does she have a
house of her own?"

"She has a castle," replied the ants proudly. "The loveliest ant castle with seven hundred corridors."

"Thank you," said the snail mother but she didn't mean it. "Our
son is not going to live in an anthill. If you have nothing better to
suggest, then we will ask the mosquitoes, they fly about everywhere."

"We have found a wife for him," buzzed the mosquitoes. "About a
hundred yards from here there lives, on a gooseberry bush, a little
snail. She has a house of her own; she lives all alone and is old
enough to get married."

"I think she should come to him," said the father snail. "It is more
fitting, since she only has a gooseberry bush; whereas, our son has a
whole burdock forest."

The mosquitoes flew to make the proposal; it took her a whole
week to come; but that only proved that she was a proper snail.

A wedding was held. Six glowworms shone as brightly as they
could, but otherwise the affair passed off very quietly, for the old
folks could not endure riotous merriment. The mother of the
bridegroom made the speech, for her husband was much too over-
come by emotion to say a word. The young people were given the

burdock forest as their inheritance; and both of the old snails declared that it was the best place in the whole world. The old snail mother promised them that if they lived a decent and upright life, and multiplied, then they and their children would be taken to the manor house to be cooked and served on a silver dish.

After the speech, the two old snails crept inside their houses and slept; and that so deeply that they never came out again.

The young couple reigned over the burdock forest and had a very, very large family. But none of them was ever boiled or served on a silver dish, which made them believe that the manor house had fallen into ruin and that all the human beings in the world had died. Since no one ever contradicted them, it was true. The rain drummed down on the burdock leaves to make music for them, and the sun shone on the forest for their sake; and every little snail in the whole family was very, very happy.

37

The Collar

ONCE upon a time there was a fine gentleman whose only worldly possessions were a bootjack, a comb, and a loose collar; but that was such a fine one that it would have enhanced the best shirt in the world; and this story is about the collar. He was old enough to begin thinking about marriage when, by chance, he found himself being washed in the same tub as a lady's garter.

"Ah," sighed the collar. "Never have I met anyone so soft and dainty, with so slender and lovely a figure. May I ask your name?"

"I won't tell you," snapped the garter.

"Where exactly do you . . . belong?" asked the collar.

The garter, who was by nature shy, found the question indiscreet and didn't answer.

"I think you must be a kind of waistband," continued the collar. "Something that is worn on the inside. I see that you are both useful and decorative, Miss . . . Miss . . ."

"Please don't talk to me!" said the garter. "I have given you neither cause nor permission to do so."

"Your beauty is cause enough and gives its own permission," replied the collar, who thought himself not only gallant but also witty.

"Don't come near me!" screamed the garter. "There is something . . . something masculine about you."

"I am a gentleman. I own both a bootjack and a comb," boasted the collar, but he was lying: the comb and bootjack belonged to his master.

"Don't come near me!" moaned the garter. "I am not used to such treatment."

"Prude!" snapped the collar. Just at that moment he was taken out of the tub; then he was starched and hung over a chair out in the sunshine. A little bit later he was taken in and put on an ironing board.

"Madam," began the collar as soon as he saw the warm iron, "I assume that you are a widow. The very sight of you makes me warm, and all my wrinkles disappear. Be careful not to burn a hole in me. . . . Please, will you marry me?"

"Rag!" snarled the iron as it passed proudly over the collar, imagining that it was a steam engine drawing a whole string of railway cars behind it. "Rag!" repeated the iron on its return journey.

The collar was found to be just a little frayed on the edges and the maid took a pair of scissors to cut off the few loose threads.

"Oh!" exclaimed the collar when he saw the scissors. "You must be a prima ballerina. What leg movement! Never have I seen anything so elegant; no human being could surpass you!"

"I know that," said the scissors.

"You deserve to be a countess!" declared the collar. "All I have is a bootjack, a comb, and a gentleman to wait upon me; I wish I were a count!"

"Is he proposing?" snarled the scissors; she was angry, so she really cut the collar and then it was spoiled.

"I suppose I'd better propose to the comb!" thought the collar, and said, "How pretty your teeth look, miss, and you have not lost one of them. Tell me, have you never thought of marriage?"

"Didn't you know," said the comb, and blushed, "that I am engaged to the bootjack?"

"Engaged indeed!" sneered the collar. Now that there was no one to propose to, he had decided to become a cynic.

Time passed and finally the collar ended in the rag pile of the paper mill. There was a big rag party, and the fine linen stayed in one bunch and the coarse in another, as is the custom in this world. All the rags liked to talk and had a lot to tell, but the collar talked more than anyone else because he so loved to brag.

"I have had so many sweethearts! Women couldn't leave me alone! But then, I was a gentleman and so well starched. I had both a comb and a bootjack though I never used either of them. You should have seen me then, when I was buttoned and lying on my side. I shall never forget my first fiancée. She was a waistband: so soft, so refined and beautiful, I was the cause of her death; she drowned herself in a washtub for my sake. Then there was the widow, she was red hot with passion but I abandoned her. My wound, which you can still see, was given me by a prima ballerina; she was infatuated and fierce. My own comb loved me. She lost all of her teeth because of it—I believe she cried them out. Oh yes, I have lived! And I have a great deal on my conscience. But what troubles me most is to think of the garter—I mean the waistband—and her unhappy end in the washtub. I deserve to be made into paper, that will atone for it."

All the rags were made into paper, but the collar became the particular piece of paper that this story is printed on. This was his punishment for having bragged so much and told so many lies. The collar's fate is worth remembering. How can you be sure that you won't end in the rag pile, be made into paper, and have your whole life's story—even the most intimate and secret parts—printed on you; and then, like the rag, have to run around the world telling everyone about it?

38

The Flax

THE flax was blooming. It had the most beautiful blue flowers; their petals were as soft as the wings of a moth and even more delicate. The sun shone on the flax, and the rain clouds watered it, which is just as pleasant to the flax and just as good for it as it is for a child to be washed by his mother and given a kiss. Both flax and children thrive on such treatment.

"People say that this year's crop will be the best for many a year," said the flax. "They say that we are taller than our parents were, and that fine linen can be woven from our stalks. Oh, how happy I am! None can be happier than I am. I am well and strong and I know I shall become something. The sunshine's kisses make me cheerful, the rain refreshes me. I am the most fortunate of all plants."

"Take it easy," mumbled the old fence. "You don't know the world as I do. I am filled with knots and that is as good as having a memory." Then the old wooden fence creaked a doleful song:

> "Crack and break,
> Snap and bend,
> A song must end."

"No, no!" shouted the flax. "The sun will shine tomorrow as well, and the dew will fall. I can hear myself growing, I can feel every flower. I am happy!"

But one day the farmer and the hired hands came and pulled the flax up, roots and all; and that hurt! Then it was thrown into a tub filled with water, as if they meant to drown it. And when the poor flax was finally taken out, it was only to be toasted over a fire. It was most terrifying.

"One cannot always be fortunate," sighed the flax. "Suffering is a form of experience, and one can learn from it."

But the suffering, the pains and aches grew worse. The flax was beaten and bruised, hacked and hackled, and then finally put on the spinning wheel. That was almost the worst of all: around and around it went, getting dizzier and dizzier, till it was not able to think at all.

"I was happy once," moaned the flax amid all the tortures. "One must learn to appreciate the happy childhood and youth one has had, and be happy! Happy! . . . Oh!"

The flax had now been spun; and the farmer's wife set the loom and wove a lovely large piece of linen out of it.

"Oh, this is truly marvelous! I never imagined that this could happen to me," said the flax. "I am always fortunate! The fence was just talking nonsense with its

> "Crack and break,
> Snap and bend,
> A song must end."

"A song is never over. I think mine is just beginning now. I have suffered but I have also been rewarded for my suffering. I am most fortunate. . . . I am strong yet soft, white and ever so long. This is much superior to being merely an herb, even a flowering one. Then I wasn't taken care of as I am now, I only got water to drink if it rained. Now the maid turns me over each morning so the sun can bleach me on both sides; and she sprinkles me with water when I get too dry. The minister's wife has declared that I am the finest piece of linen in the whole county. I cannot become any happier."

Now the linen was ready to be cut and sewn. Again it hurt; the scissors cut and the needle pricked, it was no pleasure! Well, what did it become? Something that all of us have use for but we never mention: twelve pairs of them.

"Now I have become something," thought the linen. "Now I know what I was meant for. It is a blessing to be useful in this world; it is a true pleasure. Out of one we have become twelve, all alike, a whole dozen. Again how fortunate I am!"

Years went by; and even the strongest linen can't last forever.

"Sooner or later the end must come," said each of the twelve pieces of linen. "I would like to have lasted just a little bit longer, but one must not make impossible demands."

The linen, that had become rags, was torn into tiny pieces, and now it thought that all was over, for it was chopped and hacked and finally boiled. It hardly was aware, itself, of all that it went through, and then it became fine white paper!

"Now that was a surprise . . . a most happy surprise," exclaimed the paper. "Why, now I am whiter and more elegant than I was before! This is too marvelous, I wonder what is going to be written on me?"

A very excellent story was written on the paper, and everyone who heard it or read it became both better and cleverer because of it. They were a real blessing: the words that had been written down on that paper.

"That is more than I ever dreamed possible when I was a little blue flower in the fields. How could I imagine then that I would ever become the messenger of happiness and knowledge to human beings? I can't even understand it now. But it is so, even though God knows I have done little to deserve it; I have only lived. Yet each time that I have thought, 'Now the song is over,' it hasn't been. It has merely started all over again: finer, better, more beautiful than before. I wonder if I shall travel now, be sent all over the world so that everyone can read me? I think it is very probable. For every flower that I used to have, I now have a thought that is equally beautiful. I am the most fortunate, the happiest thing in the whole world."

But the paper was never sent on any journey, except a very short one, down to the printers. Every word written on the paper was set in type and then printed; hundreds of books were made and in each of them you could read exactly the same words as had been written down on the paper. This, after all, was much more sensible. Many more people could read it, while the poor paper would have worn itself out before it had got halfway around the world.

"Yes, I agree," thought the paper, which now had become a manuscript. "It is far more sensible, I never thought about it. I will stay home like an old grandfather who is respected and honored, and the books will run about and do the work. After all, I am the original, it was on me that the words first were written. The ink flew from the pen down on me and penetrated me. I am most happy, most fortunate."

Once the book was printed, the manuscript was put away on a shelf. "It is good to rest after such an achievement," said the paper. "It is well to contemplate what one is and what one has inside one. It is as if I only realize now what is written on me. I am getting to know myself and that is half the way to wisdom. I wonder what will happen to me now? Something even better I am sure, even more wonderful."

One day the manuscript was taken from its shelf to be burned, for the printer was not allowed to sell it to the grocer so that he could use it to wrap his wares in. It made quite a pile next to the fireplace. All the children in the house were there, they wanted to watch, see it flare up high and then slowly die until only a few embers, a few sparks, hopped out of the gray ashes, like school children hurrying home; then, when it was all over, a single last spark would fly past and that was the schoolteacher running after the children.

All the paper was thrown into the fire. *Whish!* the flames shot up, high up into the chimney. Never had the flax been as tall as it was now and never had it shone so brightly—not even when it had been white linen. All the black written letters became for a moment—as thought and words were burned—fiery red.

"Now I will become one with the sun," said a thousand voices within the flame that shot up high above the chimney stack. Lighter even than the flames, too tiny to be seen, flew the little beings. There were as many as there once had been flowers on the flax. As the paper became black ashes, they ran across it, and their footsteps were those last sparks that the children said were "school children going home." The last spark flared; it was the schoolmaster running after his pupils. The children clapped their hands and chanted:

> "Crack and break,
> Snap and bend.
> A song must end."

But the little invisible ones did not agree, they said: "No, the song never ends. That is the most wonderful part of it. We know it and that is why we are the happiest of all."

But the children didn't hear them, nor would they have understood if they had. And that is just as well, for children shouldn't know everything.

39

The World's Most Beautiful Rose

THERE once was a mighty queen in whose garden grew the most beautiful flowers. Every season there were some in bloom, and they had been collected in all the countries of the world. But roses she loved above all flowers, and in her garden were many kinds, from the wild hedge rose with green leaves that smell like apples to the loveliest rose of Provence. Roses grew up the walls of the castle, twined themselves around the marble columns, and even entered the halls and corridors of the castle, where their ramblers crept across the ceilings and filled the rooms with the fragrance of their flowers.

But inside the castle sorrow lived, for the queen was dying. The wisest of all the doctors who were attending her said, "There is only one remedy that can save her. Bring her the world's most beautiful rose, the one that symbolizes the highest and purest love, and when her eyes see that flower, then she will not die."

The young and the old brought their roses—the most beautiful ones that grew in their gardens—but it was not such a flower that could cure the queen. From love's garden the rose must be brought, but which flower would be the symbol of the highest and purest love?

The poets sang of the world's most beautiful rose, and each mentioned a different one. Word was sent to all, regardless of rank and class, whose hearts did beat for love.

"No one has as yet mentioned the right flower," said the wise man. "No one has pointed to that place where it grows, in all its glory and beauty. It is not the rose from Romeo's and Juliet's tomb or Valborg's grave, though those roses will always bloom and shed their fragrance in stories and poetry. Nor is it the rose that blooms on Winkelried's blood-covered lance. From the hero's blood, shed in defense of his native land, the reddest rose springs; and it is said that such a death is sweet, but it is not the most beautiful rose in the world. The magical wonderful rose, which can only be grown under constant care, through days and years and sleepless nights: the rose of science, it is not either."

"I know where it blooms," exclaimed a happy mother who, carrying her babe, had entered the queen's bedchamber. "I know where the world's most beautiful rose is to be found, the rose of the highest and purest love. It blooms on the cheeks of my child, when he wakes from his sleep and laughs up at me, with all his love."

"Yes, in truth, that rose is lovely, but there are those even more beautiful," said the wise man.

"Yes, far more beautiful," said one of the ladies in waiting. "I have seen it, and a more exalted, sacred rose than that does not exist. It is as pale as the petals of a tea rose and I have seen it on our queen's cheeks when, without her golden crown, she walked, carrying her sick child in her arms, back and forth across the room one whole long night. She kissed her babe and prayed to God as only a mother prays in her agony."

"Yes, wonderful and holy is the white rose of sorrow, but that is not the one."

"No, the world's most beautiful rose I saw before the altar of Our Lord," a pious old priest said. "I saw it shine on an angel's face. Among a group of young girls who had come to take communion, there was one who looked with such simple and innocent a love up toward her God that on her face bloomed the rose of the highest and purest love."

"Blessed is that rose too," said the wise man. "But none of you has yet mentioned the world's most beautiful rose."

At that moment into the room stepped a little boy, the queen's son. His eyes were filled with tears and he was carrying a big book with silver clasps and bound in vellum. The book was open.

"Mother!" said the little one. "Listen to what I have read." And the child sat down by his mother's bedside and read about Him who suffered death on the Cross in order to save humanity. "Greater love there cannot be."

The queen's pale cheeks took on a pinkish shade, and her eyes became big and clear, as from the pages of the book grew the world's most beautiful rose, the one that grew from Christ's blood on the Cross.

"I see it," she said. "And those who have seen that rose, the most beautiful in the world, shall never die."

40

The Year's Story

IT was one of the last days in January; there was a horrible snow-storm. The wind was whirling the snow through the streets and lanes of the town. The windows of the houses were so covered with snow that you could not see through them, and from the roofs little ava-lanches fell down into the streets. People could hardly walk against the wind; and if they had it behind them, it was almost worse, for then they had to run. When two people met they held onto each other in order not to fall. All the carriages and horses were covered with snow, it looked as if they had been powdered; and the servants who stood on the backs of the carriages bent their knees, in order not to be so tall that their faces got whipped by the wind. The pedestrians walked as close to the carriages as they could, to get a bit of protec-tion from the wind; they could easily keep up with them, for the vehi-cles could not drive very fast. When the storm finally died down, a narrow path was shoveled along the sidewalks. Every time two peo-ple met, they paused, for the path was too narrow for them to pass each other. Which one was to be polite and step into the snowbank, that was the question. Usually neither of them was willing to get his feet wet in order that the other man could keep his dry. Silently, they faced each other, until by some unspoken agreement both of them would sacrifice one foot by putting it into the deep snow.

Toward evening the wind disappeared completely; the heavens looked as if they had been swept, and the stars shone as if they had been newly minted. Some of them had a blue tinge to them. And it froze. In the morning the snow had formed a crust strong enough to bear the weight of a sparrow. There were enough of them; they hopped around on the snow and on the shoveled path, but they couldn't find much to eat, and all of them were freezing.

"Peep!" said one sparrow to another. "So that is what they call the New Year! Why, it is worse than the old one; we might as well have kept it. I am very dissatisfied and I have good reasons for being so."

"Yes, all the human beings were lighting firecrackers to celebrate the New Year," piped a particularly cold little sparrow. "They were so happy to get rid of the Old Year that I expected that the weather would get warm. But what happened! It is colder now than ever. I think the calendar is not working."

"You are so right," said a third sparrow. He was old and had a tuft of white on top of his head. "It is their own invention, the calendar; they believe that everything obeys it. But they are wrong. I go by nature's calendar and, according to that, the New Year starts when Spring comes."

"But when does Spring come?" asked all the other sparrows.

"Spring comes when the stork comes back. But he is not very dependable. Here in the city he never shows himself, he prefers the country. Let us fly out there and wait for him; Spring is always a little closer out there."

"That is all very well," said a little sparrow that had been peeping all the time without really saying anything. "But in the city one has certain conveniences that I am afraid I shall miss in the country. The family who live in a house near here have hung little wooden boxes on the walls for us to nest in. My husband and I have made our home in one, and there we have brought up our children. I know the family have done it in order to have the pleasure of seeing us fly about; I am sure they wouldn't have done it otherwise. They throw bread crumbs out, too. It amuses them and gives us a living. We feel we are being taken care of. That is why my husband and I will stay here; not that we are satisfied, mind you, we certainly are not! But we will stay."

"And we shall fly out to the country and see if Spring isn't coming soon," said the others; and away they flew.

It certainly was colder out in the country than it had been in the city; at least, a couple of degrees. The wind was as sharp as a knife when it blew across the snow-covered fields. The farmer, driving in his sleigh, would slap his hands on his back to keep them warm, and that even though he had woolen mittens on. The whip lay in his lap and his lean horses ran so fast that steam rose from their sweaty flanks.

The sparrows jumped about in the sleigh track and froze. "Tweet . . . Peep!" they said. "When does Spring come? Why does it take so long?"

"So long, so long." The words seemed to echo across the fields. Where did the voice come from? Were the words spoken by that strange old man who was sitting in the middle of the big snowdrift over there? A long white beard, he had, and frosty silver hair; he was dressed in a white cloak like the ones the peasants used to wear. His cheeks were pale but his eyes were clear.

"Who is that old fellow?" asked the sparrows.

"I know who he is," answered an old raven who was sitting on a fence post. Since we are all small birds in the eyes of God—and the raven knew it—he condescended to answer the sparrows' question. "I know the old man! It is Winter: the old fellow from last year. He didn't die on the first of January, just because the calendar said so. No, he is the guardian of the little prince, Spring. He is the governor. Oh, it is so cold! You little birds must be freezing."

"That is what I said," piped the smallest of the sparrows. "That calendar is only a human invention. It doesn't fit nature. They should have let us figure it out, we are more delicately created."

A week went by and then another. The forest was black and the little lake was frozen. It looked as if it were not water but lead. The clouds were not real clouds but more like frozen bits of fog hanging over the landscape. The crows flew in flocks but did not scream. It was as if the world slept. Suddenly a ray of sunlight fell upon the ice of the frozen lake and the surface looked like melting tin. The snow on the fields and the hills looked a little different; it didn't sparkle any more. But the white figure, the old man, still sat on top of the snowdrift and looked toward the south. He did not seem to be aware that the blanket of snow that covered the ground was slowly melting and seeping into the earth. A little patch of green appeared and here all the sparrows gathered.

"Tweet . . . Peep! Spring is coming!" they shouted.

"Spring, Spring!" The word traveled across the fields and meadows, through the black-brownish woods, where the moss that grew on the tree trunks already was green. From the south, flying through the air, came the first two storks of the year. On the back of each rode a little child: a girl and a boy. They kissed the earth and, wherever they walked, snowdrops bloomed in the snow. Hand in hand, they went over to old man Winter, greeted him and embraced him; at that moment they were all three hidden in a heavy fog. It spread and covered the whole landscape: everything! Then the wind began to blow; first weakly, making the fog dance like a curtain, then more strongly, until it had swept the fog and mist away. Warmly the sun shone. Winter, the old man, had gone; the children of Spring now sat on the throne of the year.

"That is what I call a proper New Year," said the sparrows. "Now we will have our rights back and compensation for all we have suffered this winter."

Wherever the two children went, green buds appeared on the bushes and trees. The grass in the meadows grew taller and taller. The little girl carried flowers in her apron, and these she threw all about her as she walked; but no matter how many she cast, her little apron was as full as ever. In her eagerness she shook her apron over the apple trees, so that they were filled with flowers long before they had green leaves; they looked almost as if they had been covered by snow.

She clapped her hands and the boy clapped his, and birds came, no one knew from where, and they all sang and twittered: "Spring has come!"

It was lovely to watch! Many an old granny came outside in the sunshine; how nice and warm it was. Down in the meadow all the yellow flowers bloomed just as they had when she was a girl. "The world is young again," she thought; and said, "What a blessed day it is!"

The woods were still a brownish green, and every branch was covered with buds. But down among the roots the fragrant woodruff grew, and violets and tender anemones. Each blade of grass was filled with power. Oh yes, the earth was covered by the most elegant carpet, and on it sat Spring's young couple and held hands. They sang and laughed; and grew and grew.

A mild rain fell, but the young ones did not notice it, for who can distinguish between raindrops and the tears of happiness? The bride and the bridegroom kissed each other; and at the moment the buds on the trees burst, and when the sun rose all the woods were green.

Hand in hand, Spring's children walked beneath the new green roof of the forest, where the fleeting shadows caused shadings in the greenness. Each leaf had a maiden's innocence. The river and the brooks sang as their clear water rushed across stones, coloring the gravel. All nature seemed to shout of its own eternity, and the cuckoo and the lark sang. It was a beautiful spring, only the willow tree was cautious; it was wearing woolen mittens on its flowers.

Days passed and weeks passed; great waves of heat came rolling from the south and turned the wheat yellow. In the little lakes in the woods, the big leaves of the northern lotus spread themselves out over the still waters; and the fishes would swim underneath them, enjoying their shade. Ripe, juicy, almost black cherries hung from the trees and all the rosebushes were blooming. The sun baked the cottage walls. There on the south side, on a bench, sat Summer. She was a beautiful woman; maybe even lovelier than she had been, when last we saw her, as the young bride of Spring. She is looking toward the horizon where black clouds are building a mountain range all the way up to the sun. Like a petrified black-blue ocean, the clouds swallow up the sky. In the forest, not a bird is singing. Nature is silent. No breezes blow, everything is still, locked in expectancy. But along roads and paths everyone is hurrying, and that whether they are walking, riding, or driving in a carriage. They have one thought, all of them, and that is to seek shelter.

Suddenly a great light bursts forth, blinding and sharper than the sun's. Then again darkness, followed by the noise of a great thunderclap. The rain pours down. Light and darkness, silence and thunder alternate. In the marshes the young reeds, with their brown featherlike tops, sway and roll like waves on an ocean. The branches of the trees are hidden behind sheets of water, and the grain on the field lies prostrate flat on the ground. It looks as though it could never raise itself up again.

But as suddenly as the thunderstorm came it is gone. A few single drops of rain fall, and then the sun breaks through the clouds. To every straw and leaf pearly drops of water cling. Again the birds are singing, and in the pools in the woods the fishes are leaping, while mosquitoes fly in swarms above the water. On a boulder on the beach sits Summer. He is a powerful man; his arms and legs are muscular. His hair is wet from the shower. He stretches himself; he and all the nature around him seem rejuvenated by the bath. Summer is strength and fertility, the crowning of hopes.

Sweet was the fragrance of the field of flowering clover. The bees flew across it; in the center lay some stones. In Viking times it had been a holy place. Blackberry brambles now covered the altar stone. Here the queen bee and her court built a castle of wax and filled it with honey. Only Summer and his wife saw it; and truly, it was for their sake that the offering was laid on the altar stone.

When the sun set, the evening sky shone more golden than any church cupola, and from the pale darkness of the summer night the moon looked down.

Weeks went by, and days. The farmers began to harvest, and their sharp scythes glistened in the sunlight as they reaped the grain. The branches of the apple trees bent toward the ground, heavy with red and yellow fruit. The hops smelled sweetly. Under the hazelnut bushes, filled with nuts, rested a man and a woman: Summer and his grave and beautiful wife.

"What richness," she sighed, "a blessed homely wealth, and yet I long for something else, I do not know what it is. Rest? Peace? No, it is neither, and more than both, that I wish for! Look, they are plowing again. Man always wants more; he is never satisfied. The storks are flying in flocks now, following the plowman. The bird from Egypt that carried us through the air. Do you remember when we, as children, came here to the north? We brought sunshine and flowers and the green woods. The wind is turning them yellow and brown now, like southern trees; but here they do not bear golden fruits."

"You shall see them," said Summer. "Be happy!" And he spread out his arms toward the woods, and its leaves turned red and golden. The fruit of the wild rose shone red on its brambles and the elderberries hung like black grapes from the trees. The wild chestnuts fell out of their blackish-green shells; and deep in the forest the violets flowered once again.

The queen of the year grew more and more silent and thoughtful. "The evening air is cold," she said, and her cheeks grew pale. "The night mist is damp! I long for the land of my childhood."

She watched the storks fly south, following each one with her eyes until it disappeared. She looked up at the empty nest; a cornflower grew in one of them, as though the nest were there for its protection; then the sparrows came visiting.

"The noble owners have left," they mocked as they searched the nest for something eatable. "I guess they couldn't take a bit of wind;

it was too much for them, and so they left. Well, a pleasant journey is all I can wish them. Tweet!"

The leaves turned more and more yellow, and soon the tree would stand naked again. The harvest was over and the fall storms had begun. On a bed of yellow leaves lay the queen of the year; she looked toward the twinkling stars; the sun had set. Her husband stood near her. The wind rustled the leaves and she was gone. A butterfly, the last of the year, flew through the cold air.

From the sea drifted the wet and cold autumn fogs; the long nights of winter had begun. The king of the year stood with snow-white hair, and the first snow of the year covered the fields. The church bell rang the joyous message of Christmas.

"The bells are ringing to celebrate the birth of the New Year," said the king of the year. "Soon they will come, the new king and queen, and I shall be allowed to rest, as she does now. Rest and find peace in the stars."

Out in the forest, among the pine and spruce trees, walked the Christmas angel; she consecrated those trees that were to take part in the feast.

"May you bring happiness and joy," said the king of the Old Year. The last few weeks had made an ancient man of him; his hair was no longer white but silver, like the frost. "Soon I shall rest. The new rulers are now receiving their scepter and their crown."

"But still the power is yours, not theirs," said the angel of Christmas. "You must rule, not rest. Let the snow lay like a warm blanket over the young grain. Learn to bear the burden it is to rule, while others are praised and honored; and yet you are still master. Learn to be forgotten while you live! The hour of your freedom will come when Spring comes."

"And when does Spring come?" asked Winter.

"When the first storks arrive," answered the angel.

With silver hair and snow-white beard, Winter sat and waited; old but not decrepit, strong as the winter storms and the all-powerful ice. He sat on his snowbank and looked toward the south, as Winter had done the year before.

The ice on lakes and fjords groaned and the snow creaked when you walked on it. The children were skating. The ravens and crows looked very decorative on the white background. Everything was still, not a wind stirred. Winter clenched his hands, and the thickness of the ice grew by inches, every night.

The sparrows came flying out from town and asked, "Who is that old man over there?"

And the raven who sat on the fence post—it was either the same one as last year or his son—answered, "It is Winter. The old fellow is not dead as the calendar says. He is the guardian for the New Year, for Spring, who will soon be here."

"When does Spring come?" asked the sparrows. "Then we will get a decent government, the last one was no good!"

Deep in thought, Winter nodded toward the naked, leafless forest, where every branch, every trunk, showed its graceful forms. An ice-cold mist covered all. Winter, the master of the world, was dreaming of his youth, his manhood. When the sun rose, the forest was clad in ice, the white frost decked each branch, each twig. It was Winter's dream of Summer. The sunlight melted the ice, and it fell from the branches, down onto the snow.

"When is Spring coming?" asked the sparrows.

"Spring, Spring!" came the echo from the drifts of snow; and the sun grew warmer and warmer.

The snow was melting and the birds sang, "Spring is coming!"

The storks flew high in the air: the first of the year. On their backs rode two lovely children; the birds landed on a field. The children kissed the earth and embraced old man Winter, and like a mist he disappeared. The year's story had ended!

"It is all very true," said the sparrows. "And it is a pretty story, but that's not what the calendar says, and that is what counts in this world."

41

It Is Perfectly True!

"IT IS a monstrous story!" said a hen. She lived in a part of the town far away from where the event had taken place. "It is a horrible story and it has happened in a henhouse. I am glad that I am not sleeping alone on the perch tonight. I would not dare close my eyes!"

And then she told the story. The other hens were so shocked that their feathers stood up, and the rooster's comb fell down. It is perfectly true!

But we will start at the beginning and that took place in another corner of the town in a henhouse. The sun had just set and all the hens had flown up on their roost. Among them was a white-feathered hen with stumpy legs; she laid an egg every day and was very respectable. Now as she sat down on her perch she picked at her feathers a bit, and one little feather fell out.

"There it went," she said. "The more I pick myself, the more beautiful I will become." This was said for fun, for she was a cheerful soul, though otherwise—as I have already said—very respectable.

It was dark on the perch; the hens sat roosting side by side, but the hen that sat nearest to the one who had lost a feather wasn't asleep. She had heard what had been said and she hadn't; and that is a very wise thing to do if you want to live in peace with your neighbors. But still she could not help telling the hen next to her what she had heard.

"Did you hear what was said? I won't mention names, but there is a hen among us who is going to pluck her feathers off just to look more attractive. If I were a rooster I would despise her!"

Right above the henhouse lived an owl family; and they have sharp ears. They heard every word that the hen had said and the mother owl rolled her eyes and beat her wings. "Don't listen, but I suppose you couldn't help but hear it. I heard it with my own ears and one has to hear a lot before they fall off. There is one of the hens in the henhouse that has so forgotten all decency and propriety that she is sitting on the perch and picking off all her feathers, while the rooster is looking at her."

"*Prenez garde aux enfants!*" said the father owl. "It is not fit for the children to hear!"

"But I will tell our neighbor about it," said the mother. "She is such a courteous owl. I hold her in the highest esteem." And away she flew.

"Tu-whit! Tu-whoo!" both the owls hooted, and so loudly that the pigeons could not help hearing it. "Have you heard, have you heard! Tu-whoo! There is a hen that has plucked all her feathers off for the rooster's sake. She will freeze to death, if she hasn't already, tu-whoo!"

"Where? Where?" cooed the pigeons.

"In the neighboring yard! I have almost seen it with my own eyes. It is a most indecent story, but it is perfectly true."

"True, true, every word," cooed the pigeons, and repeated the story in their own henhouse. "There is a hen—some say that there are two—that have plucked all their feathers off in order to look different and in that way gain the attention of the rooster. They have played a dangerous game, for one can catch a cold that way and die of fever; and they are dead, both of them!"

"Wake up! Wake up!" crowed the cock, and flew up on the fence. Sleep was still in his eyes, but he crowed anyway. "Three hens have died of unrequited love for a rooster! They have plucked all their feathers off. It is a nasty story. I won't keep it, pass it on!"

"Pass it on, pass it on," piped the bats. And the hens clucked and the roosters crowed: "Pass it on, pass it on." And in this manner the story went from henhouse to henhouse until it arrived back at the very place where it had started.

"There are five hens, so it is said, that have all plucked their feathers off to prove which one of them had become thinnest because of unhappy love for the rooster. Then they pecked each other until blood flowed and they all fell down dead! It's a shame for their families and a great loss to their owner."

The hen who had lost the first little feather naturally did not recognize the story; and as she was a decent and respectable hen, she said, "I despise those hens! But there are more of that kind! Such things must not be kept secret! I will do whatever I can to have it printed in the newspaper, then the whole country will hear about it. And that is what those hens and their families deserve."

And it was published in the newspaper and it is perfectly true that one little feather can become five hens!

42

The Swans' Nest

BETWEEN the Baltic and the North Sea lies an old swans' nest called Denmark. In that have been and will be hatched swans whose fame will never die.

In ancient times one flock of swans flew across the Alps down to the green plains of the land of eternal May, where it is pleasant to live. That flock of swans were called Lombards.

Another flock flew to Byzantium. Shiny white were their feathers and faithful their eyes; around the emperor's throne they gathered and their great wings were like shields that guarded and protected him. They were given the name of Varangians.

From France came screams of terror and fear. Bloodthirsty swans with fiery wings had come from the north and the people prayed: "Free us, O Lord, from the wild Normans."

On the green fields of England, by the open sea, stood the trebly crowned Danish swan, holding his golden scepter out over the country.

The heathens on the coast of Pomerania fell on their knees when the Danish swans came, sword in hand, carrying the flag of the cross.

"That was all in ancient, bygone times!" you may object.

But also in an age not so distant from our own has a swan flown from the nest, and as it flew through the air it illuminated it and the light spread over all countries. It was as if the beat of its wings caused a mist to disperse, and all the stars in the sky became clearer and more visible, as if the heavens had come closer to our earth. That swan was Tycho Brahe.

"That, too, is long ago!" I hear you say. "What about now in our times?" We have seen swans, too, fly with powerful wings high up in the sky. One touched, with his wings, the golden harp, and the music resounded through the north. The stark mountains of Norway rose high in the light from an ancient sun. The gods of the north and the heroes and heroines from the Viking age again walked in the deep green forest.

One swan beat with its wing on the marble cliff so hard that it broke, and the beauty locked in the stone became visible to all.

Another swan tied threads of thoughts from land to land, so that words with the speed of light could travel from country to country.

God still loves the swans' nest that lies between the Baltic and the North Sea. Let giant birds of prey gather to destroy it; it shall survive. Even the little cygnets, with their downless chests, will make a ring around the nest and defend it with their bills and claws, as we have seen them do in our times.

Many centuries will pass and swans will fly from the nest, and be seen and heard around the world, before that time shall come when truthfully it can be said: "That was the last song, the last swan from the swans' nest."

43

The Pixy and the Grocer

THERE once was a proper student; he lived in a garret and didn't own a thing. There once was a proper grocer; he lived on the first floor and owned the whole house. Now the pixy stayed with the grocer, for there on Christmas Eve he was given a whole bowlful of porridge with a lump of butter in it. That the grocer could afford, therefore the pixy lived in his store, and from that a moral can be drawn.

One evening the student came knocking on the grocer's back door. He needed a candle and a piece of cheese for his supper; and he was, as usual, his own errand boy. He was given his wares and paid for them. The grocer wished him good evening and the grocer's wife gave him a friendly nod, though she was a woman who could do more than nod her head: she could talk anyone's ear off. The student nodded back and would have gone, had he not started reading what was written on the paper that the cheese had been wrapped in. It was a page torn from an old book of poetry that deserved a better fate than to be used as wrapping paper.

"Most of the pages of that book are still here," said the grocer. "I gave an old woman some coffee beans for it; you can have the rest for eight pennies."

"Thank you," replied the student. "Let me have what is left of the book instead of the cheese, I can eat plain bread for supper. It would be a pity if all of it were torn to pieces. You are a splendid person, a practical man, but you have no more idea of what poetry is than that old barrel over there."

Now that was not a very nice thing to say, especially about the barrel. But both the grocer and the student laughed; it had been said in fun. It annoyed the pixy though. He had overheard the remark and thought it was an insult to the grocer, who owned the whole house and sold the very best quality butter.

Night fell; the store was closed and everyone had gone to sleep except the student and the pixy. He sneaked into the grocer's bedroom. The grocer's wife was sleeping with her mouth open and the pixy stole her sharp tongue: she didn't use it while she slept. Everything in the whole house that he put the tongue on was given the power of speech. Each of them could express its feelings and formulate its thoughts just as well as the grocer's wife could. But since there was only one tongue, they could only speak one at a time, which was a blessing, I am sure, or they all would have talked at once.

The first thing that was allowed to borrow the tongue was the barrel; it was filled with old newspapers. "Is it really true," asked the pixy, "that you don't know what poetry is?"

"Certainly I know what poetry is," said the barrel. "It's something printed on the back page of a newspaper that people cut out sometimes. I think that I have more poetry inside me than the student has. And what am I compared to the grocer, just a poor old barrel."

Then the pixy put the tongue on the coffee grinder and there it certainly wagged. He also put it on the tub of butter and the cash drawer just to hear their opinions. They agreed unanimously with the barrel, and the opinion of the majority must be respected.

"I will fix that student!" muttered the pixy, and sneaked up the back stairs to the garret where the young man lived. The student was still up, a light was burning in his room. The pixy looked through the keyhole. The young man was sitting reading the old book he had bought for eight pennies.

How bright the room seemed! It was as if a ray of light came from the book, a luminous tree whose branches spread out across the ceiling. The leaves were fresh and green and on each branch flowers bloomed and fruit hung. The flowers were faces of young maidens, some with radiant dark eyes and others with clear blue ones. The fruits were sparkling stars. All the while the most beautiful music could be heard.

Such splendor the little pixy had never seen or even thought possible. He stood on his toes and looked and looked until the light was put out. Even when the student had blown out his candle and gone to bed, the pixy tarried. He could still hear the music, a song so soft and comforting; a lovely lullaby for the student, who was falling asleep.

"But that was fantastic!" mumbled the pixy. "That I had not expected! I think I will move in with the student!" Then he thought—and he thought very sensibly—"But the student does not have any porridge." And he sighed.

Down the stairs he went, down to the grocer. And that was lucky, for the barrel had almost worn out the grocer's wife's tongue. It had lectured, giving all the opinions that were written in the old newspapers inside it. When the pixy came it had just begun to repeat them. He took the tongue and gave it back to its owner. But from that time on the whole store, from the cash drawer to the firewood that lay by the stove, all had the same opinions as the barrel, whom they so honored and respected that when the grocer, in the evening, would read aloud the theater column to his wife, they thought that the barrel had written it.

But the pixy no longer stayed downstairs in the evening to listen to the grocer and his wife. No, as soon as the student had lit his candle, it was as if the light from the garret were an anchor cable that drew him up. He had to go and peek through the keyhole. He experienced greatness. He saw what we see when God, disguised as the storm, walks across the turbulent ocean. He cried without knowing why he cried, but found that in those tears happiness was hidden. "How wonderful it must be," he thought, "to sit under the magic tree together with the student." But that was not possible; he had to be satisfied with looking through the keyhole.

The autumn winds blew; the cold air whistled through the loft and down the corridor where the little pixy was standing, his eyes glued to the keyhole of the student's door. It was cold, wretchedly cold; but the pixy did not feel it before the student had put out his light and the sound of the music that came from the garret had ceased. But then he froze! He hurried down into his own little warm corner that was so cozy and comfortable.

At Christmas when the porridge with the lump of butter in it was served, the pixy acknowledged no other master than the grocer.

One night the pixy was awakened by a terrible noise. People were banging on the shutters of the store, the whole street was as light as day from a fire. Everyone wanted to know whose house was burning. Was it his own or the neighbor's? It was terrible! The grocer's wife got so disconcerted that she took off her gold earrings and put them in her pocket, in order to save something.

The grocer hurriedly collected his bonds and the maid her silk shawl: that was her luxury, the one she could afford. All the people wanted to save what was dearest to them, and so did the pixy. He ran up the stairs and into the student's room. The young man was standing calmly at the window looking at the fire in the house across the street. The little pixy grabbed the book that was lying on the table, put it into his red cap, and ran. He had saved the most valuable thing in the house.

He climbed out on the roof and up on the chimney stack; there, illuminated by the burning house, he sat holding his treasure tightly with both his hands.

Now he finally understood his heart's desire, where his loyalty belonged! But when the fire in the house across the street had been put out, then he thought about it again. "I will share myself between them," he said, "for I cannot leave the grocer altogether. I must stay there for the sake of the porridge."

That was quite human! After all, we, too, go to the grocer for the porridge's sake.

44

The Millennium

THEY will come on wings of steam, the young citizens of America will fly through the air, across the great ocean, to visit old Europe. They will come to see the monuments of bygone ages, the ruins of the great cities, just as we today visit Southeast Asia to stare at the crumbling glories of the past.

Thousands of years hence, they will come.

The Thames, the Danube, and the Rhine will still be flowing; Mount Blanc will stand with its snow-covered peak. The northern lights will be shining above the Scandinavian countries, though generations upon generations will have become dust. Many of those men, who to us seem so mighty, will be as nameless as the Vikings who rest in their grave chambers inside the hills, on top of which the farmers today like to place a bench, so that they can watch the wind make waves in the flat fields of grain.

"To Europe!" cry the young Americans. "To the land of our forefathers! To the wonders of an earlier civilization. To beautiful Europe!"

The airships will be crowded, for it is much faster to fly than to sail. The passengers will have already made their hotel reservations by telegraphing ahead. The first European coast to come into view will be Ireland's, but the passengers will still be sleeping; they will have given orders not to be awakened before the airship is over England. The airship will land in Shakespeare's country, as the more cultured of the passengers call it—others call England the "land of the machine" or the "land of politics."

A whole day will these busy travelers give to England and Scotland; then they will be off via the tunnel under the Channel to France: the country of Charlemagne and Napoleon. The learned among them will discuss the Classicist and Romantic movements that so interested the Frenchmen of the distant past. Molière's name will be mentioned. Heroes, scientists, and poets whom we have never heard of—they have yet to be born in that crater of Europe, Paris!—will be on the lips of these young people.

Then the airship will fly over that country from which Columbus sailed and where Cortes was born: Spain, the home of Calderón, who composed his dramas in perfect verse. Beautiful dark-eyed women will still inhabit its fertile dales; one will hear the names of *el Cid* and the Alhambra in the old songs that people will still be singing.

Through the air, across the sea to Italy, where the Eternal City of Rome once was. It will be gone; the Campagna will be a desert. Only one wall of St. Peter's will still be standing, and there will be doubt as to its authenticity.

To Greece, to sleep one night in a luxury hotel on the top of Mount Olympus, so one will be able to say that one has been there; and then onward to the Bosporus, to rest for a few hours on the site of Byzantium. They will watch poor fishermen repairing their nets, while they listen to tales about Turkish harems of an all but forgotten age.

They will fly above ruins of great cities along the Danube, which in our times are still unknown. They will land to look at impressive monuments—accomplishments that lie in the future, but which will be admired as achievements of the fruitful past.

They will come to Germany, which once was crisscrossed by railroads and canals: the land where Luther spoke, Goethe sang, and Mozart once held the scepter of music. When they speak of science and the arts, they will mention other names that we do not know. One day will be the time they allot to Germany and one for all of Scandinavia: for the fatherlands of Oersted and Linnaeus, and for Norway, the young country of old heroes. Iceland will be visited on the homeward journey; the geyser will spout no longer, and the volcano Hekla will have died; but the cliff-bound island will stand in the turbulent sea as a memorial tablet to the sagas.

"There's so much to see in Europe," the young Americans will say. "And we have seen it all in a week, just as the famous guidebook promised we could." Then they will discuss the author of the book which they all will have read: *Europe Seen in Seven Days*.

45

Under the Willow Tree

THE countryside around Køge is very barren. True, the town is situated on the coast, and the seaside is always lovely, but it can be much prettier than it is there. The city is surrounded by flat fields and it is far to the nearest forest. And yet, if it is the place that you call home, you will find something beautiful about it: something that you will long for when, later on in life, you see places that are truly beautiful.

On the outskirts of Køge there is a little stream that ebbs out in the sands of a beach, and along its banks it is quite lovely, especially in summer. Knud and Johanna thought this place was as beautiful as any place could be. They were two children who lived next door to each other and whose gardens went right down to the stream. Both of the families were very poor, but there was an elderberry tree in one of the gardens and a willow tree in the other. The children had only to crawl under the hedge to be together. Sometimes they played under the elderberry tree but more often under the willow, even though this grew on the bank of the stream. Our Lord looks after all small creatures; otherwise, very few of them would survive. Besides, the children were careful, especially the boy, who was so frightened of the water that even in summer he never waded in the sea as all the other children did. He had had to bear a lot of teasing about it, until little Johanna had a dream that she was out sailing in a boat, on Køge Bay, and Knud walked out to meet her—first the water went up to his throat and then over his head, but he walked on. From then on, whenever the children teased him, he would refer to Johanna's dream as proof of his courage. He was very proud of it; but he went no nearer the water.

The parents of the children often visited each other, and the children played together all the time, either in the gardens or out in the road. Along the sides of the road many willow trees grew, but they were stunted, for they had not been planted there to be looked at but for the sake of their branches, from which fences and baskets could be woven. The willow tree in the garden was allowed to grow as it wanted to, and under its widespread branches the children passed many happy hours.

On market day the great square in the center of Køge became a little city of tents. Here silk ribbons, boots, and many other kinds of wares were sold. There were always big crowds of people and usually there was rain. Every peasant for twenty miles around came to Køge. The smell of the damp woolen clothing blended with the delicious odor of gingerbread. There was a booth where gingerbread alone was sold, and the best part of it was that the man who owned it stayed with Knud's parents whenever he was in town, so the boy was always given a piece of gingerbread which he shared with Johanna. There was another wonderful thing about the gingerbread baker, he knew how to tell stories. He could make them up about almost everything, even his own gingerbread figures.

One evening he told a tale about a gingerbread man and a gingerbread woman that made such a deep impression on the two children that they never forgot it; so maybe it is a good idea that we hear it too, especially since it is short.

"Once there lay on the counter of my booth two gingerbread figures. One of them was a man with a hat on his head, the other a girl, who had no hat but did have a dab of gold for hair. Their faces were on the front of their heads just as human beings' faces are; and they, too, shouldn't be judged by how they look from behind. The man had a bitter almond on the left side of his chest and that was his heart. The gingerbread girl was just plain gingerbread. They were displayed on the counter as samples. And as the days went by they fell in love, but neither of them spoke of their love, and if you don't do that, nothing will ever come of it.

" 'He is a man, it is only proper that he should speak first,' thought the gingerbread girl, though she was dying to know whether her love was returned.

"His thoughts were more ferocious: men's usually are. He dreamed that he was an urchin who had fourpence, so he could buy the little gingerbread girl and eat her up.

"For weeks they lay on the counter and became more and more dried out. The gingerbread girl's ideas became more refined, more womanly. 'It is enough to have lain on the same counter with him,' she thought, and then she broke in two at the waist.

"'If she had known of my love, she might have lasted longer,' thought the gingerbread man.

"That was their story and here they are, both of them," said the baker. "Theirs was an unhappy fate and proves that silent love leads to unhappiness. . . . Now look at them!" And he gave the gingerbread man to Johanna and the two pieces of the gingerbread girl to Knud, but the children were so touched by the story that they couldn't eat the cakes.

The next day the children went to the churchyard. Its walls were so overgrown with ivy that they looked as if the red bricks were covered by a green carpet. Here among the greenery Knud and Johanna leaned the gingerbread man and the gingerbread woman up against the wall and told the other children the story of silent love and what a waste of time it was—the love, that is, not the story, for the children found that very amusing. They were all so absorbed in the tale that they didn't notice that a bigger boy had stolen one of the gingerbread figures. It was the maiden and out of meanness he ate her all up. The children wept when they realized what had happened; and then they ate the gingerbread man—probably so that the poor fellow would not suffer from being alone in the world. They never forgot the story.

The two children were always together either under the elderberry tree or under the willow. Johanna had a voice that was as clear as a silver bell, and she would sing the loveliest songs. Knud had no voice at all, but he knew the words of all the songs by heart—and that is always something. The people of Køge, even the rich grocer's wife, would stop when they passed the gardens, to listen to Johanna sing. "That little brat has a beautiful voice," they would say.

Those were beautiful, happy days but they did not last. Little Johanna's mother died and her father decided to move to Copenhagen. The neighbors had tears in their eyes when they parted, and the two children wept aloud. The grown-ups promised to write to each other at least once a year.

Shortly afterward Knud was apprenticed to a shoemaker—such a big boy could not spend all his time playing. In the autumn he was confirmed in the church in Køge. How Knud would have liked to go to Copenhagen on that solemn day, to see Johanna. He had never been in the capital, though the distance was not more than twenty miles. On a clear day you can see the towers of Copenhagen across the bay; and the morning he was confirmed, Knud saw the golden cross on the top of the steeple of the Church of Our Lady.

How often he thought of Johanna! But did she remember him?

At Christmas a letter arrived from Johanna's father. All had turned out well for him and he had married again; but Johanna had had even greater good luck. Her lovely voice had won her a position in the theater. She sang in the kind of play in which there was music and she already earned quite a bit of money. That was why she was sending her "dear neighbors in Køge a silver mark, to buy wine for Christmas Eve and to toast my health—" that she had written herself; and she added: "My very best regards to Knud!"

They all wept. Everything was so wonderful and their tears came from happiness. Not a day passed without Knud thinking of Johanna, now that he could read in her letter that she thought of him.

The nearer the time came for his apprenticeship to end, the more certain he was that he loved Johanna and that one day she would become his wife.

He would think of Johanna; a smile would play on his lips and he would pull the leather even tighter to the last. Once he stuck the big needle right into his thumb; but it did not matter, he was so happy in his dreams. He was not going to be silent as the two gingerbread figures had been; from that story he had learned a lot.

Finally his apprenticeship was over and he packed his knapsack. He was going to Copenhagen for the first time in his life. He had already got a position there with a shoemaker. How surprised Johanna would be when she saw him. She was now seventeen and he was nineteen.

He had thought of buying a gold ring for her in Køge but had decided that he could probably buy a much more beautiful one in Copenhagen. He said good-by to his parents, took his knapsack on his back, and set out. It was a rainy and windy autumn day; he was wet to the skin by the time he had walked the twenty miles to the big city and found the home of the shoemaker he was to work for.

The very first Sunday he went to the address that he had copied from Johanna's father's letter. He had put on his new suit and was wearing the hat he had bought in Køge. He looked well in it; it was his first hat, until then he had always worn a cap.

He found the house. They lived on the top floor, and it almost made him dizzy to walk up so many flights of stairs. "How strangely people live in the huge lonesome city," he thought, "all on top of each other."

Johanna's father greeted him kindly; his new wife, whom Knud had not met before, shook his hand and offered him coffee. Their apartment was neat and well furnished.

"Johanna will be so pleased to see you," said the father. "You have grown up to be a nice-looking young man. I will call her. She is a girl that a father can be proud of; she has gone far. And with God's help she will go even further. She has her own room and she pays me rent."

Her father knocked on her door as if he were a stranger to his own daughter. They stepped inside. Oh, what a beautiful room she had! Knud felt certain that there was not a room so elegant in all of Køge. The queen could not have a better one. The floor was covered by a rug, and the curtains were so long that they almost reached the floor. There was a little upholstered chair covered with velvet, several pictures on the walls, and a mirror as big as a door. Knud noticed it all and yet he saw only Johanna! She looked quite different from what he had expected; she was much more beautiful than he had imagined she would be. There was not a girl in Køge as lovely as she, or as refined. For a moment she stared at him strangely as if she didn't know him, but then she came running over to him. Knud thought that she was going to kiss him. But she didn't, though she was happy to see him.

She had tears in her eyes when she looked at the friend from her childhood. And she asked so many questions: about Knud's parents and everyone else in Køge, including the elderberry tree and the willow tree. She called them "mother elderberry" and "father willow," and talked about them as if they were human beings. And why shouldn't she? After all, they were as human as the two gingerbread cakes. Of those she talked too; about their silent love and how they lay on the counter beside each other, not daring to speak of it.

She laughed so warmly, so kindly. "No, she hasn't changed," thought Knud. His cheeks blushed and his heart beat so strangely. Knud also sensed that it was for her sake that he was invited to stay all evening.

They had tea. Later she read aloud from a book, and Knud felt that every word she read was about him and his love for her. When she sang a little song for them, the song became more than a song, it was a little story that came from her heart. The tears ran down his cheeks; he could not stop them and to speak was impossible. He thought that he had behaved very stupidly, but when he left she shook his hand warmly and said: "You have a kind heart, Knud. Always stay as you are."

After such a marvelous experience it was difficult to sleep, and Knud did not close his eyes all night. When he said good-by, Johanna's father had remarked, "Now don't let the whole winter pass before you visit us again." Knud thought that this was as good as an invitation and decided to go back on the following Sunday.

In the meantime, every day when he was finished working for his master—and this could be quite late, for they also worked by lamplight—he would walk through the street on which Johanna lived. Beneath her window he would stop and look up. Once he saw her shadow against the curtains and that was a very pleasant evening. The shoemaker's wife complained that he was always running about at night, but his master laughed and said, "Knud is a young man."

"On Sunday I will see her again," thought Knud. "Then I will tell her how she has always been in my thoughts. I will ask her to be my little wife! True, I am only a poor shoemaker, but I will work hard and one day I shall have my own shop. Yes, that is what I will say. Love must have a voice, the silent kind is of no use; that I learned from the gingerbread cakes."

Sunday came and Knud along with it; but unfortunately Johanna and her family were all going out that day. Johanna took his hand in a most friendly way and asked him if he had ever been to the theater. "I will send you a ticket," she said. "Next Wednesday I will be singing. My father knows where your master lives."

That certainly was thoughtful of her. At noon on Wednesday an envelope with a ticket had arrived for him, but there was no note or letter with it. In the evening Knud went for the first time in his life to the theater; and what did he see? He saw Johanna, so beautiful, so lovely. In the play she got married to a stranger; but then, it was only a play, not real life, or Johanna would not have sent him a ticket to come and see it. Knud knew that well enough, so he didn't mind. Everybody clapped and shouted, and so did Knud. He screamed, "Hurrah," as loud as he could.

Even the king, who attended the performance, smiled most kindly down at Johanna; one could see he was pleased. Knud felt himself terribly small among such splendid company, but he loved his Johanna ever so much and felt sure that she cared for him too. A man must say the first words; that was what the little gingerbread girl had thought, and that story Knud had not forgotten.

Next Sunday Knud set off to visit Johanna. He felt as solemn as if he were going to church to receive the sacraments. Johanna was home alone, nothing could have been luckier.

"I am glad you have come," she said. "I nearly sent Father off to fetch you, but I felt sure that you would come. Next Friday I will be leaving Copenhagen. I am going to France. I must, for only there can I learn to be a great singer."

Knud felt as though the whole room were turning around him and that, within him, his heart were breaking, but he did not cry. Even though no tears could be seen in his eyes, it was obvious that he was very sad.

Johanna saw it right away, and she almost cried. "Oh, you poor, faithful, honest soul!" she exclaimed, and her words loosened Knud's tongue. He told her how much he loved her and how much he wanted her to be his wife.

Johanna, who had been holding his hand in hers, let go of it and turned as pale as death. Then she said, seriously, almost mournfully, "Don't make yourself and me unhappy, Knud. I will always be your good sister whom you can trust. But I can never be more." She stroked his moist forehead with her soft hands. "God gives us strength when we ask it of Him."

At that moment her stepmother came into the room.

"Knud is beside himself because I am leaving," said Johanna to her stepmother, and then patted him on the back. "Now be a man," she said smilingly, as if they had only been talking about her journey.

"Child," she added, "you will have to be kind and sensible as you were when we were children and sat under the willow tree."

Knud's world broke into pieces and one piece was lost forever. He felt that his thoughts were like loose threads that the wind could play with. He stayed even though he was not sure whether he had been invited to. But Johanna's father and his wife treated him kindly, and Johanna poured the tea as she had the last time he had been there. She sang, too, but her voice did not sound as sweet; yet it was beautiful enough to break one's heart. When they parted, Knud did not offer her his hand but she took it anyway. "Will you not give your sister your hand when you say good-by? My dear old playmate!" She smiled while tears ran down her cheeks. "Sister," she repeated. That word brought no comfort to Knud; thus they parted.

She sailed to France. Knud stayed in Copenhagen and walked its muddy streets. The young shoemakers asked him what he was brooding about and invited him to come along with them. "To amuse yourself is almost a duty when you are young," one of them explained.

He went with them to a dance. There were many pretty girls, but none as lovely as Johanna. In the midst of all the gaiety, where he had expected to forget her, he remembered her most clearly. "God gives us strength when we ask it of Him," she had said. Knud folded his hands as if he were going to kneel down and pray right there, with the dancing couples all about him, and the violins playing. He was shocked! What had he done? How could he have taken Johanna with him to such a place? For she was with him; didn't he carry her in his heart?

He rushed out into the street and did not stop running till he stood once more before the house where she had lived. The house was dark; everything was dark and lonesome. The world went its way and Knud went his.

Winter came and the Sound froze; it was a real ice winter and all of nature seemed dead and buried.

Finally spring came. The ice thawed and ships from foreign countries came to the harbor of Copenhagen once again. Knud longed to go away, far away, out into the wide world, but not to France.

He packed his knapsack and set out. He wandered along the roads of Germany without purpose or peace. He walked from one city to the next, too restless to remain in any one of them. Only when he reached Nuremberg, far to the south, did his feet begin to drag, so that he felt that he had the power to make himself stay put.

It was a strange city that looked as though it had been cut out of an old-fashioned picture book. Each street went its own way, not one of them was straight; and the houses did not necessarily follow them. Some of the houses jutted out and filled half the sidewalk, and not two of them looked alike. Some had bay windows and little towers, others had gables and carved cornices. Around the crooked roofs ran copper gutters shaped like dragons or strangely elongated dogs.

Here, on the main square, Knud stood one morning with his knapsack on his back. He was looking at one of the old fountains whose waters fell down over marvelous bronze figures depicting scenes from the Bible and history. A pretty servingmaid had come to fetch water; she gave him a rose from the handful of flowers she was carrying. This, Knud decided, was a good omen.

He could hear the music of an organ. He was reminded of home, of the church in Køge. The church here was very large; it was a cathedral. Knud entered. The sunlight shone through the stained-glass windows and between the tall, slender columns. He felt the holiness of the place and for the first time his soul was at peace.

He sought and found a good master; he stayed in Nuremberg and learned the language.

The old moat and defenses around the town had been made into gardens, but the city wall, with its sturdy towers, was still intact. There was a wooden gallery along the outside of the walls where ropemakers twisted their long cords into strong rope. In the cracks and crevices of the old stonemasonry, elderberry trees had taken root; their branches spread out over the low cottages built at the base of the walls. Here the master for whom Knud worked lived; and he had a little garret room in his master's house. The elderberry branches shaded the window of the attic in which Knud slept. He lived there one summer and the following winter, but when spring arrived he could not remain. The smell of the flowering elderberry was too much for him. It reminded him of Køge, of his home. He felt that he was back in the garden of his childhood. Knud found another master and moved farther inside the city where there were no elderberry trees.

His new master lived near one of the old bridges, across from a water mill. The houses were built at the water's edge and they all had

rickety old balconies that hung out over the river. Here were no elderberry trees, not even a single flower could grow; but there was an
old willow tree. It clung to the house, holding onto it so that the raging waters could not uproot it and tear it away. Its branches hung
down over the river just as the willow tree's at home had over the little stream.

He had moved from "mother elderberry" to "father willow." Especially at night in the moonlight the willow tree would make him yearn
for home. At last he could not stand it any longer. And why? Ask the
flowering elderberry tree, ask the willow. He bade his master good-by
and left Nuremberg to travel farther south.

He never talked to anyone about Johanna; he kept his sorrow
locked within himself. But he often thought about the story of the
two gingerbread figures and how the man had had a bitter almond on
his left side. Now he felt he knew its bitter taste. Johanna, who was
always gentle and smiling, was like the girl, gingerbread all the way
through. The straps of his knapsack cut his shoulders and neck, he
felt that he had difficulty breathing; he readjusted them but it did not
help. The world was not whole around him, he carried half of it inside him, and that he could do nothing about.

It was not before he reached the great mountains that the dimen-
sions of the world grew real and his thoughts turned outward, not inward to torture himself.

The sight of the Alps brought tears to his eyes. He thought they
looked like the folded wings of the world. What would happen if the
world spread its wings, with their great feathers of black forests, waterfalls, clouds, and snow fields? "On doomsday it will happen and
the earth will fly toward God and break like a soap bubble! Oh, I
wish doomsday would come!" he sighed.

The countryside he passed through seemed to him like an enormous orchard.

The young girls, sitting on the little wooden balconies of the
houses doing lacework, would nod to the wanderer. The snow on the
tall mountains glowed like embers in the light from the setting sun.
The green lakes, surrounded by dark pine trees, reminded him of the
color of the sea at home in Køge, but the sadness that he felt was
more filled with sweetness than with pain.

Where the Rhine like a gigantic wave rushed forth and its waters
were crushed and transformed into mist where rainbows play, he

thought of the water mill near Køge. There, too, the water roared and was crushed into foam. He would have liked to stay in the little town by the Rhine but there were too many elderberries and willows growing there. So he set out across the great mountains. He walked through narrow passes, along roads that clung to the steep mountainside like swallows' nests. Far below him were clouds which hid the waterfalls that he could hear roaring in the abyss.

Amidst the eternal snow he walked and the summer sun warmed his back. He said farewell to the north and came to the country where chestnut trees spread their crowns between fields of corn and vineyards. The mountains were a wall between himself and his memories, and that was a blessing.

He came to the great city of Milan. There he found a German shoemaker who would hire him. The master and his wife were a kind, elderly couple who soon grew fond of the young journeyman, who, though he was so silent, worked so hard. It was as if God had finally given Knud peace, taken the burden from his heart.

His greatest pleasure was to climb to the top of Milan Cathedral, which seemed to him to have been shaped out of the white snow of his own country. He stood among the spires and arches, with sculptures peeping out at him at every turn. Above him was the blue sky and below him the city and the great plains of Lombardy. Looking toward the north, he could see the snow-covered Alps, and at the sight of them he would recall Køge and its church with ivy-covered walls. But he no longer thought of it with longing. He had decided that here, beyond the great mountains, his grave would be.

It was now three years since he had left Denmark and one whole year since he had come to Milan. One evening his employer, the old German shoemaker, invited him to the opera. What a fantastic theater it was, with its seven balconies, gold leafing, and silk curtains. Every seat was occupied by an elegantly dressed lady or gentleman; they looked as though they were at a ball. The women carried little bouquets of flowers in their hands. So many lamps burned that the huge room was as light as if the sun itself had been the chandelier. The orchestra began to play. It was much larger than the one in the theater in Copenhagen, but that evening Johanna had sung, while here . . .

It was magic! The curtain rose and there stood Johanna clad in gold and silk, with a crown on her head! She sang as beautifully as only one of God's angels can and then she stepped to the front of the stage and smiled—as only Johanna could smile—down at Knud.

Poor Knud grabbed his master's hand and screamed as loudly as he could, "Johanna!" But his cry was drowned in the music.

The old shoemaker nodded and said, "Yes, her name is Johanna," and then he took the program and pointed to the spot where her full name stood.

It was no dream! The audience applauded and shouted her name and the ladies threw their flowers up on the stage. Endless curtain calls were demanded. When she left the opera house the crowd unharnessed the horses of her carriage and drew it in triumph through the city. Knud helped to pull it, and he was the happiest among that happy group. When they came to the brilliantly lit villa where she lived, Knud stood by the door of her carriage. It opened and she stepped out. The light from the many lamps illuminated her dear face. She smiled and thanked them all. She was deeply touched. Knud looked straight into her face and she looked straight into his, but she did not recognize him.

A gentleman wearing a decoration on his chest offered her his arm. She took it. "They are engaged," he heard people behind whisper.

Knud walked straight home and packed his knapsack. Now he wanted to return to the elderberry tree and to the willow tree. Yes, under the willow tree one could dream a whole life in one short hour.

Everyone begged him to stay, but they could not keep him from leaving. They told him that the first snow had already fallen in the mountains. But he only said that he would walk in the wheel tracks of a carriage and cut himself a good stout cane.

He walked toward the mountains. He climbed up and came down on the other side. Weak and tired, he stumbled toward the north.

The stars came out; it was night, no house or town was near. Far down below him, in the valley, stars were shining—it was the lamps in the houses but to Knud it appeared as if there were two heavens: one above him and one below. He felt that he was ill. More and more stars appeared below him. Finally he realized that it was a little village, and he gathered the last of his strength and walked toward it.

He stayed a few days in a little inn. Down here in the valley the snow had already melted and the roads were muddy. One morning someone played a Danish melody on a barrel organ. His restless longing for home returned.

Knud set out again. He walked so fast, as if he feared that if he did not get home soon he would find everyone there dead. To no one had he spoken of his grief, the greatest sorrow that a man can experience. Such misery you cannot tell to the world, for it does not amuse or entertain anyone, even your friends. And poor Knud had no friends. A foreigner in a foreign land, he wandered homeward toward the north.

He had received only one letter from his parents and that had been more than a year ago. In it they had written, "You are not really Danish like we are. We love our country but you love only foreign lands." His parents felt they had a right to write like that because they knew him, because they were his father and mother.

It was evening. He was walking along a broad highway; it began to freeze. The landscape had become more and more flat, there were fields and meadows. At the side of the road stood a big willow tree. Everything looked so homely, so Danish. He sat down under the willow tree. He was terribly tired; his head fell down on his chest and he closed his eyes. He felt that the branches of the tree engulfed him, embraced him. The tree became an old man, "father willow" himself; and he lifted Knud up in his arms and carried his tired son home to the bleak beach of Køge, to the garden of his childhood.

Yes, it was the willow tree from Køge, it had gone out into the world to find him, and now "father willow" had found him and brought him back to the little garden by the stream. And there stood Johanna, dressed in all the beautiful clothes she had had on when last he saw her, and with the golden crown on her head. She shouted to him, "Welcome!"

Beside her stood two strange figures; they looked larger and more human than they had when he was a child. They were the gingerbread man and the gingerbread girl.

"Thank you," they said to Knud. "You have taught us always to speak up and say what one feels, or else nothing will come of it. We have, and now we are engaged."

Then the gingerbread couple walked ahead of them through the town of Køge, and they looked very decent and proper even from behind. They walked right up to the church, and Knud and Johanna followed them; they, too, were walking hand in hand. The church looked as it always had, with green ivy covering its walls. The big doors of the church opened, the organ was playing.

At the entrance the gingerbread couple stepped aside and said,

"The bridal couple must go first." Knud and Johanna walked up to the altar and kneeled down. Ice-cold tears ran from Johanna's eyes. It was his great love that was thawing the ice around her heart; the tears fell on his burning cheeks and woke him.

There he sat under a willow tree in a foreign land on a cold winter evening, while the winds whipped hail into his face.

"That was the loveliest moment of my life," he mumbled. "And it was only a dream. God, let me dream it once more!" He closed his eyes. He slept, and he dreamed.

In the early morning it began to snow, and the wind made a snowdrift that covered his legs and his feet while he slept. At church time the peasants found the journeyman; he had frozen to death underneath the willow tree.

Five Peas from the Same Pod

THERE once were five peas in a pod; they were green and the pod was green, and so they believed that the whole world was green, and that was quite right. Now the peas grew and the pod grew, and each little pea adjusted itself to its accommodations; they sat five in a row, one right next to the other. The sun shone on the pod and the rain washed it. It was warm and cozy inside, light in the daytime and dark at night, just as it is supposed to be. As the peas grew bigger they also reasoned better and thought much more; after all, they had to do something to pass the time away.

"I wonder if we shall sit here forever," said one of them. "I am afraid that I shall grow hard from sitting so long. I have a notion that there is something outside, I can feel it!"

Weeks passed and the peas turned yellow and the pod turned yellow. "The world is turning yellow," they all five said; and that was not an unreasonable thing for them to say.

Suddenly they felt the pod being torn off the plants. They had fallen into the hands of a human being. The pod was stuck down into a pocket where a lot of other pods lay. "Soon they will open up for us," said the peas, and that's what they were waiting for.

"I wonder which one of us will go farthest," said the smallest of the peas. "I am sure something will happen soon."

"Come what will!" said the largest.

"Crack!" The pod was opened; and all five peas rolled out into the sunshine. They were in a little boy's hand. He inspected them and said that they were perfect ammunition for a peashooter. One he shot off right away.

"Now I fly out into the wide world. Catch me if you can!" the pea shouted, and away it went.

"I shall fly right up into the sun, for that is a fitting pod for me!" shouted the second.

"Oh! We shall sleep wherever we end up," said the next two peas. "Rolling is as good as flying." They had fallen out of the boy's hand and were rolling along on the floor; but they were picked up and put in the peashooter anyway. "We will get the farthest," they shouted as they flew.

"Come what will!" said the last of the peas as it soared high into the air. It hit an old rotten board underneath the garret window. The board was filled with cracks; in them earth had collected and moss grew. The pea landed in one of the crevices, the moss closed around it, and it lay hidden but not forgotten by Our Lord.

"Come what will!" it repeated.

In the little garret room lived a very poor woman who did heavy work. She cleaned and polished stoves or chopped wood; she was willing to do anything she could. Strength she had, and hard-working she was; and poor as a church mouse she remained. Living with her was her daughter, who had been lying in bed ill for more than a year. The little girl was thin and delicate; it was as if she could neither live nor die.

"She will soon be going up to her sister," the woman would say. "I had two children once and God saw how difficult it was for me to provide for them; therefore He decided to share the work with me and took one. I would like to keep the other one, but God probably thinks it was a shame to separate them, and now she will be going up to her sister."

But the little sick girl stayed on; patiently, she lay in her bed all alone, while her mother went out to earn money for their keep.

It was spring. Early one morning the sun shone brightly in through the little window and across the floor. The little girl happened to notice something on the other side of the lowest windowpane. She called to her mother, who was just about to leave. "Mother, what's that bit of green? There in the lower pane, it moves in the breeze."

Her mother walked over to the window and opened it. "My!" she said. "It is a little pea. I wonder how that has got up here? Look, it already has green leaves. It will be a little garden for you to look at."

She moved the girl's bed closer to the window so that she could watch the little plant and then she left.

"I think I am getting well, Mother," said the little girl that evening. "The sun has shone so warmly down upon me all day. The little pea has been growing. I think I will soon be out in the sunshine too."

"If only that would happen," said the mother, but she did not believe that it would. Yet she did tie the plant to a stick which she had fastened to the board, so the wind could not break the little pea plant; then she ran a string from the top of the window down to the bottom, giving it something to cling to as it grew. And it certainly did grow; you could see the difference from one day to the next.

"I think it is going to flower," said the woman one morning, and now she, too, began to hope and believe that her little sick girl would get well. She had been aware that the child spoke more lively, and the last few mornings she had sat up in bed by herself in order to see her little garden that consisted of one solitary pea plant.

A week went by and the sick girl was up for the first time; she sat for a whole hour in a chair. The window was opened. Outside in the warm sunshine grew the little pea plant; the flower had opened its red and white petals. The little girl bent down and kissed its fine leaves. That day was a very special day for her, like a birthday.

"God Himself planted that pea and made it thrive for your sake, to give you back your health, my sweet little girl, and to give me joy and hope," the mother said, and smiled toward the flower as though it were an angel sent from God.

But the other peas, what happened to them? The one who had shouted, "Catch me who can," was swallowed by a pigeon. There it lay in the bird's gizzard, like Jonah in the whale. The two lazy peas had not fared any better, they had become pigeon food too. But that is after all a useful and respectable end for a pea. The fourth one, the one that wanted to fly right up to the sun, fell down into a gutter and there it lay for weeks and days in the stagnant water. It grew fat and soggy.

"I am getting nice and plump," it said. "I will get so fat that I burst and that is more than any pea has ever done. I certainly am the most remarkable of the five peas that were in the pod."

And the gutter agreed!

The girl stood at the garret window; her eyes were bright and the color of health was in her cheeks. She folded her hands above the pea flower and thanked God for it.

"I'll stick to my own pea!" said the gutter.

47

The Piggy Bank

THE children's room was filled with toys; on top of the cabinet stood a piggy bank. It was a fat clay pig with a slit in back that had been enlarged with a knife, so that silver crowns could slide through it. Two of those heavy coins had made that journey, besides innumerable pennies. The piggy bank was so filled that it didn't rattle when you shook it; and higher no piggy bank can rise. He stood on top of the cabinet and looked down upon everything in the room; he knew he could buy it all with the money he had in his stomach, and that was a very comfortable feeling.

Everything else in the room knew it, too, though they didn't talk about it. One of the drawers in the chest was open; in it lay a doll. She was old and had once broken her neck, but it had been repaired. Now she sat up and suggested, "Let us play human beings, it is amusing." At once everything started to jump about. The paintings on the wall turned around, in order to show that they had backs as well as fronts. That irritated the doll, who thought they had done it just to be contrary.

It was the middle of the night, but the moon was shining in through the window, giving free illumination. All the toys were invited to join the game, even the old baby carriage, though it didn't really belong. "Everyone has his own good points," it said. "We can't all be aristocrats; some have to work for a living."

The piggy bank was the only one that had received a written invitation; the others feared that he was so far above them that he couldn't hear a spoken one, even if they shouted. He didn't answer. If he were going to watch the game, then he would only do it from his own home. He felt that everyone should comply with his wishes, even when he hadn't expressed them; and everyone did.

The little doll theater was erected in such a place that the piggy bank could watch the performance. They would start the evening by giving a play; later on there would be tea and intelligent conversation. But the rocking horse began talking immediately about the breeding and the breaking of horses; and the baby carriage talked about railroads and steam engines; they were always so professional. The clock on the wall talked politics; it declared that it knew the time, but the other toys said it was slow. The walking cane just stood about admiring its own silver knob, and the two embroidered pillows on the sofa, who were pretty but stupid, giggled.

Finally the play could begin. Everyone had been told that they could applaud or make any noise they wished, such as banging, rumpling, or whistling. The riding whip said it would "crack" for the young people in the play but not for the old: they were so boring.

"I will bang away for anyone," said the firecracker.

The spittoon stood humbly in the corner and mumbled, "One has to be somewhere."

The play was terrible but the acting was marvelous. All the players played in the center of the stage, to make sure their performances were seen.

The doll who once had broken her neck almost lost her head, she was so moved. The piggy bank was touched too, but in his own way; he thought of doing "something" for one of them, such as leaving him a small sum in his will.

All enjoyed themselves so much that they decided to skip the tea and just have the "intelligent conversation." They all felt "just like human beings," and that was not meant satirically. All of them thought their own opinions cleverer than their neighbors', and they all wondered what the piggy bank was thinking about. He was thinking very seriously about wills and funerals: long, slow-moving thoughts. But death and funerals have a habit of coming before one wishes them to come. . . .

"Crash!" Down fell the piggy bank and broke into hundreds of pieces, while the money rolled all over the floor. One of the silver crowns rolled all the way to the door; it wanted to get out into the world and it did, and so did the pennies. The broken pieces of the piggy bank were thrown in the trash can. It wasn't the kind of funeral he had expected.

The next day a new piggy bank stood on the cabinet. He looked just like the other one; and he too couldn't rattle but that was because he was empty. He had just started his career; and with those words we will end our story.

48

Ib and Little Christina

THERE is a river in Denmark called the River of the Gods, the Gudenaa; and not far from its shores, as it flows through the forest of Silkeborg, rises a ridge, on the west side of which was situated a small farm—in fact, it is still there. Even when the rye and barley stand high in the fields, you can see the sandy soil beneath the grain; and the harvest is always meager. This story takes place some years ago; and the farmer who tilled it then had three sheep, a pig, and two oxen. He could have kept a couple of horses but he felt as most farmers in that area did: "Horses eat up their profits themselves." Jeppe was the farmer's name. He farmed in the summer and carved wooden shoes in the winter. He was a skillful carver; but he had a younger helper who was even better than he was, and understood how to make clogs so that they were strong; and yet not heavy and shapeless. They also made other household wares which fetched a good price. Although Jeppe and his family were not rich, no one in that district would have called them poor.

Little Ib was seven years old. He was an only child, and he liked to sit by his father and watch him carve. The boy whittled sticks and sometimes he cut his fingers. One day he did manage to carve two little objects that looked like a pair of tiny wooden shoes. These he wanted to give to Christina, the daughter of the bargeman, who lived in a cottage on the heath. The little girl was very beautiful, and so delicate that she did not look at all like a bargeman's daughter. Had she had clothes to match the loveliness that God had given her, then no one would have guessed that she had been born in a poor cottage on the lonely heath. Her father was a widower who made his living by transporting lumber from the woods down to the locks at Silkeborg. Sometimes he would even sail as far as Randers with his barge. As there was no one at home to take care of little Christina— she was a year younger than Ib—she was always with her father, except on his journeys to Randers. Then her father would bring her to Jeppe's house to stay.

Ib and little Christina never fought, neither when they played nor at table. They would play in the sand, pretend they were making a little garden, or just tumble about. One day they ventured as far as the top of the ridge beyond which was the forest. They found the nest of a snipe with eggs in it; that had been a very exciting adventure.

Ib had never been on the heath, nor had he ever sailed with a barge down the river and through the lakes. But one day Christina's father invited him on a trip, and his parents gave their consent. The evening before they were to set out, the bargeman came to fetch him, and he spent the night in the little cottage on the heath.

Early the next morning the children were sitting on top of the woodpile, in the barge, eating bread and raspberries. Christina's father and his helper were poling the barge down the river; they were following the current, so they sailed along at a good speed. One after another they sailed through the lakes. Every time they entered one, Ib was sure that the river had ended, for bulrushes, reeds, and trees seemed to enclose the lake; but finally a narrow opening would appear that they could sail through. Sometimes the trees leaning out over the narrow river would almost hinder their passing, but always the barge sailed on. Some of the oak trees had naked branches that had lost all their bark and looked as if they had rolled up their sleeves to show their withered old arms. Many of the old alder trees had loosened themselves from the banks and now stood like little islets in the river. White and yellow water lilies floated amid their big green leaves. It certainly was a lovely trip. At last they came to the locks where eels were caught and shipped as far away as Copenhagen. The water rushed over the lock and fell as a waterfall on the other side; and that was something for Ib and little Christina to look at.

At that time no factory or town had been built there yet; there was only the old farm on which not many people lived. The water rushing over the lock and the cry of the wild ducks were the only sounds to be heard. The lumber was loaded onto a bigger barge; and Christina's father bought a little newly slaughtered pig and some eels. Then they were ready for the homeward journey. The pig and the eels were put into a basket. Now they had the current against them, but not the wind; so they hoisted a sail and that was as good as having two horses pull the barge.

When they reached the part of the forest where the bargeman's helper lived, they moored the barge at the bank. Christina's father told the children to stay on board and not to touch anything, while he accompanied his young helper to his home. The bargeman said that he would be back very soon.

The children obeyed him at first, but not for long. They had to peep into the basket that contained the eels and the pig. They took the little pig out; and when they both tried to hold it at once, it fell overboard; and the little dead animal floated away with the current.

It was a terrible calamity! Ib leaped to the shore and soon Christina followed him. "Take me with you!" she cried. They ran in among the trees; and within a few minutes the barge and the river disappeared from their view. Christina fell and began to cry, but Ib calmed her.

"The house is right over there. Come along," he said; but the house was not "right over there," and soon the two children were lost. They walked on and on; the dried leaves rustled and dead branches broke with cracking sound as they stepped on them.

Someone was shouting far away. The children stopped to listen, but then they heard the hoarse frightening cry of an eagle; and they ran. A little while later they came upon a blueberry patch covered with the most delicious large, ripe berries. They were so tempting that they had to sit down and eat them. Their cheeks and lips were stained deep blue. Again they heard someone shouting.

"We will get spanked because of the pig," observed little Christina.

"Let us go home to my parents," said Ib, who was certain that Christina was right. "It is not far from here." The children walked on and finally they came to a road, but it did not lead home. It began to grow dark, and they were very frightened. The terrible stillness of the forest was broken by the terrifying hooting of owls and the cries of other birds that they did not know. Christina cried and Ib cried. They wept for an hour or more before they both lay down under some bushes and fell asleep.

The sun was already high in the sky when they awoke, but they were very cold. They could see the sun shining on top of a nearby hill. Up there they would be able to get warm, and Ib hoped that he would be able to see his home. But they were in another part of the forest, far away from the little farm. When they climbed the hill they found a little pool, and where the sun's rays fell on the water, they could see the fishes swimming. Such a sight they had never seen before. A few minutes later they found some hazelnut bushes and their fears were forgotten. They cracked the nuts and ate them. Although they were far from ripe, they already had little kernels. Then something terribly frightening happened!

A tall woman stepped out from behind the bushes. Her face was brown and her hair was black. She carried a bundle on her back and a big strong cane in her hands; she was a gypsy. At first the children could not understand what she said. She took three nuts out of her apron pocket and told them that they were "wishing nuts," and that each of them contained something marvelous.

Ib looked at the woman for a long time; her expression seemed kind. He asked her if he could have her "wishing nuts," and she gave them to him. Then she picked a whole pocketful of nuts from the bushes for herself.

The two children stared wide-eyed at the "wishing nuts."

"Is there a carriage and horses in one of them?" asked Ib.

"In that one there is a golden carriage with golden horses," answered the woman, and pointed to one of the nuts in the boy's hand.

"Give it to me then," begged little Christina; and Ib gave it to her.

"Is there a pretty little necklace like the one Christina is wearing in this one?" demanded Ib.

"There are ten necklaces," said the woman, "and dresses, stockings, and hats."

"Then I want that one too," shouted little Christina, and Ib gave it to her. The third nut was a little black one. "That one you can keep," said Christina. "It is a pretty one, too."

"And what is in that?" asked Ib.

"What is best for you," said the gypsy.

Ib kept the nut. The gypsy woman said that she would show them the way home; but she led them astray, sending them in the opposite direction from the one they should have gone. But one cannot accuse her of trying to steal the children, and she might have acted in good faith.

In the middle of the forest they met Chris the forester. He knew Ib and he took the children home. Both the bargeman and Ib's parents had been so upset that the children were forgiven, though they deserved a spanking, not only for having let the pig fall in the water but also for running away.

That evening after Christina and her father had returned to their home on the heath, Ib took out the nut that contained what was "best for him." He placed it between the door and its casing and cracked it by closing the door. There was no kernel in it, just some black dirt; it was worm-eaten.

"I thought so!" Ib was not surprised. "How could there be room in a little nut for what was 'best'? Christina will get no carriage or dresses out of her nuts either," Ib muttered.

Winter came; and the years passed by. Finally Ib was old enough to be confirmed. Every Sunday that spring he walked the many miles to the church to receive religious instruction. One day the bargeman came by. He had news to tell: little Christina was old enough to earn her own keep and he had found her a good position in the family of a wealthy innkeeper near Herning. She was to help in the house and they would see to it that she was confirmed.

Ib and little Christina said good-by to each other. "The little sweethearts," they were called. Christina showed Ib the two little "wishing nuts" he had given her, and which he had received from the gypsy that day in the forest; and she told him that the little pair of wooden shoes that he had cut for her were in the bottom of the chest in which she had packed her clothes. Then they parted.

Ib was confirmed but continued living at home, for his father had died and he had to help his mother. He had become as good a carver of wooden shoes as his father had been; and in the summer he took good care of their little farm. Not often did they hear from Christina, but the news that they did get was always good. She wrote to her father about her confirmation and the letter was filled with descriptions of the new clothes she had received from her mistress.

The next spring, on a particularly beautiful day, someone knocked on the door of the little farm. It was the bargeman and Christina; she had been offered a ride in a carriage as far as Tem and back. This had been an opportunity to come home for a visit. Beautiful she was and her clothes were as elegant as any lady's. Ib, who was wearing his work clothes, could hardly utter a word. He took her hand and held it tightly, but his tongue was all tied up in knots. Christina's wasn't: she talked and talked, there was so much to tell, and she kissed Ib boldly on the mouth.

"Don't you know me any more?" she asked.

All he could manage to reply, even though they were alone together, was: "You have become a fine lady and I am so . . . so coarse! But oh, Christina, how I have thought about you and of the time when we were children together!"

Arm in arm, they walked up to the top of the ridge; from there they could see the river and as far as the heath, where Christina's father lived. Ib did not say a word; but as they were returning—and Ib was to go to his home and Christina to her father's—Ib realized how very much he wanted Christina to be his wife. Hadn't they been called "sweethearts" since they were little children? Now he knew that he had always expected that one day they would marry; and he felt as though they were engaged though neither of them had ever spoken a word about it.

Christina could only stay a few hours because she had to be in Tem early the following morning, when the carriage departed that would take her back to the inn at Herning.

Ib and the bargeman accompanied her to Tem. It was a lovely night; the moon was full. All the way, Ib held Christina's hand, and when they finally arrived at their destination he did not want to let go of it. He had great difficulty saying what anyone could have read in his eyes. He spoke only a few words but every one of them came from his heart. "If you have not become used to finer things than I can give you, and if you will be satisfied with living in my mother's house with me as your husband, then I think the two of us should become man and wife. . . . But I will not hurry you."

"Yes, let us wait a little while, Ib," replied Christina, and pressed his hand; then he kissed her on the mouth. "I trust you, Ib," she said. "And I think that I love you! But I would like to have time to think about it."

They parted and Ib told the bargeman that he and Christina were as good as engaged. Christina's father was pleased and not surprised. Although he spent the night at Ib's home, they did not talk any more about it.

A year went by. Two letters had passed between Ib and Christina, and both of them had been signed: "Yours unto death." Then one day the bargeman arrived; he had greetings from Christina. That was easy enough to say. What followed was more difficult and he took his time saying it. Everything went well for Christina; more than well, but then she was a good girl. The innkeeper's son had been home on a visit, he had a good job in an office in Copenhagen. He had taken a liking to Christina and she to him. His parents were not against them marrying, but Christina felt that she had given Ib her word; and therefore she was going to say no. "Even though such a marriage would be fortunate for a poor girl like herself," concluded the bargeman.

At first, Ib did not say a word, but his face turned as white as a newly washed sheet. He shook his head and then mumbled, "I would not wish Christina to say no to good fortune for my sake."

"Write her a few words about it," urged the bargeman.

Ib wrote, but every time he had written a sentence he crossed it out again. All the words seemed wrong to him. **Many** pages he tore up, but by morning the letter to little Christina was finished. Here it is:

I HAVE READ THE LETTER THAT YOU WROTE TO YOUR FATHER. IN IT YOU SAY THAT EVERYTHING GOES WELL FOR YOU AND THAT YOU HAVE AN OPPORTUNITY FOR BETTERING YOURSELF. ASK YOUR OWN HEART, CHRISTINA! IF YOU WANT TO MARRY ME, THEN REMEMBER THAT I AM POOR. DO NOT CONSIDER ME OR MY FEEL-INGS, BUT ONLY YOURSELF. YOU ARE NOT BOUND TO ME; SHOULD YOU FEEL THAT YOU HAVE GIVEN ME YOUR "PROMISE," THEN I RELEASE YOU FROM IT. MAY ALL THE HAPPINESS IN THE WORLD BE YOURS, CHRISTINA. GOD MAY CONSOLE MY HEART.
EVER YOUR DEVOTED FRIEND,
IB

The letter was sent and Christina received it.

A few months later, the banns were read in the little church on the heath and in the big church in Copenhagen. The bridegroom was too busy with his affairs to be able to travel to Jutland. Christina journeyed with her future mother-in-law to the capital, where the young people were to live. Christina had arranged to meet her father in the little village of Funder, which was on the main highway to the south; there they said good-by to each other.

Every once in a while someone would speak about Christina when Ib was present; but Ib himself never mentioned her. He had become so silent, so pensive. He often thought about the nuts that the gypsy woman had given them. Now Christina had got her carriage and all the dresses she could wish for, over across the water in the king's city, Copenhagen. The "wishing nuts" had proven themselves. His nut had been filled with black earth, and the gypsy had said that that was best for him. Now he understood what she had meant: the dark grave was best for him.

Years went by; not many, but to Ib they seemed long. The old inn-keeper and his wife died and their son inherited their wealth: several thousand silver crowns. Now certainly Christina could have her golden carriage and even more dresses than she ever could wear.

Then two years passed during which not even the bargeman received any letters from Christina. Finally one came; it was not a happy one. Poor Christina, neither she nor her husband had been able to handle the sudden richness; it had not been a blessing, for they had not earned it themselves.

The heather bloomed and withered; and many a snowstorm swept across the heath and up over the ridge that protected Ib's little farm-house. Spring came and Ib was plowing his meager fields. Suddenly he felt the plow shake as if it had hit a stone. Something black, shaped like a wood shaving, stuck up from the earth. Ib picked it up; it was metal and, where the plowshare had cut into it, it shone. It was a heavy arm ring of gold from heathen times.

The Viking grave had long ago been leveled. Now its treasure had been found. Ib showed it to the minister, who admired it and told him to take it to the district commissioner.

The official sent a report to Copenhagen and advised Ib to deliver the golden arm ring to the museum himself. "You have found in the earth the finest treasure, the best that could be found," he said.

"The best!" thought Ib. "The best for me, and found in the earth. The gypsy woman was right, my wishing nut, too, has proven true."

Ib sailed from Aarhus to the capital; and since he had never sailed before except with the bargeman up and down the river Gudenaa, it felt like an ocean journey.

In Copenhagen he received the gold value of the arm ring: six hundred silver crowns! Now Ib—who knew so well the forest and the heath—took a walk along the endless streets, lined with stone buildings, of the city.

The evening before he was to sail back, he lost his way, when he was out walking, and ended in one of the poorest quarters of the city, called Christian's Harbor. It was late and the street was deserted. He noticed a little child coming out of one of the most dilapidated of the houses, and he asked her for directions. The little girl looked up at him; she was crying, and said nothing. He asked her what was the matter; and she answered, but he could not understand her.

They were standing under a street lamp. Ib looked down at the child; the light was shining in her face. How strange! He saw with wonder that she looked exactly as Christina had, when she was a child.

He followed the little girl into a miserable house and up the worn, rickety stairs to the garret. They entered a little room right under the roof. The air was foul and it was dark. Ib struck a match. Over in a corner stood a bed; in it lay a woman: the little girl's mother.

"Can I help you?" asked Ib. "This little girl found me down in the street but I am a stranger to the city, myself. Can I call the neighbors?" He stepped closer to the bed and looked down at the woman: it was Christina!

At home, he had not heard her name mentioned in years, because everyone knew that Ib did not like to be reminded of her. Besides, all the rumors had been unpleasant. It was said that the inherited money had made her husband lose his common sense. He had given up his good position and they had traveled in foreign countries. When they returned, they had lived high and got into debt, rather than curtail the luxuriousness of their way of life. It was the old story of the cart going down the hill so fast that it finally overturned. The many merry friends who had dined at their table when wealth decked it now felt no pity. They said he deserved his fate, he had acted like a madman. One morning the body of Christina's husband had been found in a canal near the harbor.

Christina had been pregnant then; her child conceived in wealth was born in poverty. The baby had only lived a few weeks. Now Christina lay ill to death in a garret room more naked and bare than the one she had known as a child on the heath. And now, when she had known luxury, she could not bear her poverty, her wretchedness.

The little girl, who had brought Ib to her, was her daughter, her older and only living child. Her name, too, was Christina.

"I am afraid that I am dying," she mumbled. "What will happen to my child? Where in the world can she find a home?"

Ib lit another match and found a stump of candle; its little flame lighted up the dismal chamber.

Ib looked at the little girl and was again reminded of Christina as she had looked as a child. For her sake he would take the little girl, bring her up, and be kind to her. The dying woman looked up at him; the pupils of her eyes grew larger and larger. Did she recognize him? Ib never knew, for she never spoke again.

We are back in the forest near the River of the Gods as it is called, not far from the heath. It is fall, the western storms have started. The wind is blowing the leaves off the trees. In the bargeman's hut strangers are living. Inside the little farmhouse, so snugly protected from the wind by the ridge, the stove is burning. It is as warm and comfortable as if it were summer; sunshine is here, the kind that shines from a child's eyes. Though it is October, the lark still sings in the little girl's laughter. Here lives gaiety and winter is far away. Little Christina is sitting on Ib's knee; he is both father and mother to her. Her real parents have disappeared, as dreams do to a grownup. The little farmhouse is cozy and neat. The girl's mother sleeps in the churchyard for the poor in Copenhagen.

They say that Ib has a tidy sum put away, gold from the earth; he is rich and he has his little Christina.

49

Clod Hans

An old tale retold

FAR out in the country there was an ancient manor house. The squire who lived in it had two sons. Both of them were so clever that they could answer more questions than anyone would care to ask them. They decided to propose to the princess; this they dared do because the princess had officially proclaimed that she would marry the man in her kingdom who spoke most wittily.

They had only a week to prepare themselves, but that was enough, for they were well educated and that is an advantage. One of them knew by heart the Latin dictionary and the town newspaper for the last three years, and that backward as well as forward. The other one had memorized all the guild laws and regulations, even the ones that most guild masters had never heard about. He felt that this enabled him to discourse on politics; besides that, he could embroider suspenders, for he was artistic.

"I will win the princess!" said both of them.

Their father gave them each a horse; the son who knew the dictionary and the newspapers by heart was given a black one; the embroiderer and expert on guild laws, one as white as milk. Now they greased their jaws with cod liver oil in order to be able to speak even faster than usually; and then they were ready to depart. All the servants were lined up to wave good-by. Just as the two brothers were mounting their horses, their younger brother came running out of the house. I haven't mentioned him before because no one thought anything of him, and he wasn't really considered part of the family.

He was not a scholar like the other two, and that is why they called him Clod Hans.

"You are all dressed up, where are you going?" shouted Clod Hans.

"To the king's castle, to win the princess by our wit. Haven't you heard what the drums have announced and the herald proclaimed?" one of them asked; and the other brother told Hans of the princess' decision to marry the man who could speak most wittily.

"Goodness me! I am going too!" declared Clod Hans while his brothers laughed and rode off.

"Father, let me have a horse!" he shouted. "I have just decided to get married. If she takes me, well and good. If she doesn't, then I will take her."

"Nonsense!" said the father. "I will not give you a horse; you can't speak well; you have no wit. You're not even presentable!"

"Well, if I can't have a horse," laughed Clod Hans, "then I will take the billy goat; that is mine and I can ride it." Up he jumped on the billy goat, dug his heels into its sides, and away he rode. The goat ran as fast as it could and Clod Hans sang and shouted as loud as he could: "Here am I, here am I!"

His two brothers did not say a word to each other. They were too busy getting witty ideas. They rode so sedately you might think they were attending a funeral.

"Hello! Hello!" shouted Hans as soon as he caught up with them. "Here am I! And look what I found in the middle of the road!" He held up a dead crow for them to look at.

"Clod!" they said. "And what are you going to do with that?"

"Give it to the princess!"

"You do just that!" they laughed, and rode on a little bit faster, for they didn't want to be seen in company with their brother.

"Hello, hello, here I am again. Look what I have found! It is not every day that one stumbles across such a treasure!"

The two brothers turned around in their saddles to see what their little brother had now. "Clod!" they said. "It is only an old wooden shoe and broken at that. Are you going to give that to the princess too?"

"I certainly will!" declared Hans, while his brothers laughed and spurred their horses.

"Hello, hello! Here am I!" screamed Clod Hans a little while later. "It is too marvelous, just look!"

"What have you found now?" asked the brothers.

"Oh!" sighed Hans. "Can you imagine how pleased the princess will be?"

"Ugh!" exclaimed his brothers. "Why, it is only mud from a ditch."

"Yes, that is exactly what it is," agreed Hans, "but of the very best quality, the kind that slips right through your fingers. I have filled my pockets with it."

This time the brothers did not laugh, they just rode as fast as they could and arrived at the city gate a whole hour before Clod Hans. Everyone who had come to propose to the princess was given a number and had to line up in a row. They stood so close together that they couldn't move their arms; and that was fortunate, for otherwise they would have torn each other's eyes out, just because one had got there ahead of the other.

All the other citizens of the town crowded around the castle and tried to look through the windows; they wanted to watch the princess receiving her suitors. But as each of them entered the royal hall, he seemed to lose his tongue, for all of them could only stammer and mutter.

"No good!" said the princess every time. "Out!"

The first of the brothers entered, the one who knew the Latin dictionary and the newspapers by heart; but he had forgotten every word of them while he stood in the row with the other suitors. The floor creaked as he walked across it, and the ceiling of the room was an enormous mirror that reflected everything upside down. At one of the windows stood three scribes and an alderman, who wrote down all that was said, so that it could be printed in the newspaper, which would be sold in the streets that very afternoon for twopence. And if that was not frightening enough, the heat would have made anyone uncomfortable; the stoves had red-hot potbellies.

"It is hot in here!" said the unhappy suitor.

"That is because my father is roasting roosters today," said the princess.

"Bah!" That wasn't what he had expected and there he stood with his mouth open. He wanted to say something witty, but he couldn't.

"No good!" said the princess. "Out!"

And outside he had to go. Now came the second brother.

"It is terribly hot," he said.

"Yes, we are roasting roosters," said the princess.

"What did—What?" mumbled the poor man; and all the scribes wrote: "What did—what?"

"No good!" said the princess. "Out!"

Now came Clod Hans. He rode on his billy goat right into the royal hall. "Goodness me, it is hot in here," he said.

"That is because I am roasting roosters today," said the princess.

"That is fine," said Clod Hans, "maybe I can get my crow fried as well."

"That might be possible," laughed the princess. "But do you have anything to fry it in? All our pots and pans are in use."

"Sure, I have," said Clod Hans, and held up the old wooden shoe. "Here is a pot to put it in," and he dropped the crow into the broken shoe.

"Why, it is enough for a meal," said the princess, "but where are you going to get the gravy?"

"I've got pockets full of it! So much that I have some to spare." And Clod Hans showed her the mud.

"That is what I like!" exclaimed the princess. "Somebody who can speak up for himself. I will marry you! But do you know that every word we have said has been written down and will be printed in the newspaper? At one of the windows stand three scribes and an old alderman, and he is the worst, because he does not understand a word of what anyone says." The princess said this to frighten Clod Hans, and the scribes neighed like horses and shook their pens, so blots of ink sprayed onto the floor.

"Well, if the alderman is the most important, then he deserves the best!" shouted Clod Hans, and took all the mud out of his pockets and threw it in the old man's face.

"That was nobly done!" laughed the princess. "I couldn't have done it, but I am sure I will learn how!"

Clod Hans married the princess and became king. He sat on a throne with a crown on his head. I got the story straight out of the alderman's newspaper and that cannot be trusted.

50

The Bottle

IN a crooked alley, among other ill-repaired houses, stood one that was particularly narrow and tall. It was a half-timbered house, and many of the beams were rotten. Only very poor people lived there. Outside the garret window hung a bird cage; it was as decrepit as the house, and its inhabitant did not even have a proper bath: the neck of a broken bottle, corked and hung upside down, had to suffice. The old maid who lived in the garret was standing by the open window, enjoying the warm sunshine. She had just fed the little linnet, and the songbird was hopping back and forth in the cage, singing merrily.

"Yes, you may sing," said the bottleneck. It didn't really speak, for bottlenecks can't talk, but it thought all this inside itself, as we all do sometimes. "Yes, you can sing. You are healthy and well, not an invalid like me. You don't know what it's like to lose your whole lower parts and be left with only a neck and mouth; and then, on top of it, to have a cork stuffed into you. Then you wouldn't sing so loud! But it is good that someone is happy. I have nothing to sing about, and I can't sing. But I have lived an exciting life! I remember when the tanner took me along on a picnic and his daughter got engaged. I was a whole and proper bottle then. Goodness me, it seems just like yesterday. . . . Oh yes, I have experienced a lot. I was created in fire and heat, have sailed across the ocean, lain in the dark earth, and been higher up in the sky than most people. Now I am perched above the street in the sunshine; yes, my story bears repeating. But I am not going to tell it out loud, because I can't."

But the bottleneck could reminisce and it did. The bird sang, and the passers-by down in the alley thought about their own problems or didn't think at all, while the bottleneck reflected upon its life.

It remembered the great oven in the factory, where it had been blown into life. As soon as it had been formed, while it was still burning hot, it had been able to look into the burning red oven. It had felt a desire to jump back into it and be melted down again, but as it cooled that fancy had disappeared. The bottle had stood in a row together with all his sisters and brothers; there had been a whole regiment of them. They had all come from the same oven, but some had been blown into champagne bottles and others into beer bottles, and that makes a difference. Although later on, after they have come out into the world and the beer or the champagne has been drunk, then a beer bottle can be refilled with the costly wine from Vesuvius, Lachryma Christi, and the champagne bottle with boot blacking. But birth still counts and that you can tell from the shape. Nobility remains nobility, even when it contains only boot blacking.

All the bottles were put into cases, and so was the bottle that this story is about. It never occurred to him then that he would end as a useless bottleneck, and then have to work his way up to becoming a bird's bath—for that is better than being nothing at all.

He saw daylight again when the cases of bottles were unpacked in the wine merchant's cellar. Now he was rinsed for the first time, that was a strange experience; then he was put on a shelf. There he lay empty and without a cork, he felt awkward; something was missing but he did not know quite what it was. Then the bottle was filled with wine, corked, and sealed. A label was pasted on it which said, "very fine quality." The bottle felt as though he had passed an examination and received the highest grade. The wine was young and the bottle was young; and the young tend to be lyrical. All sorts of songs about things, that the bottle couldn't possibly know a thing about, seemed to be humming inside him. He saw clearly the green sunlit mountains, where the grapes had grown, as well as the maidens and young men who had kissed each other while they picked the fruit. Oh yes, it is lovely to live! The bottle was filled with passion and love, just as young poets are before they know much about either.

One morning the bottle was sold. The tanner's apprentice had been sent down to buy a flask of the "very best wine." It was put into the picnic basket together with ham, cheese, sausage, the best-quality butter, and the finest bread. It was the tanner's daughter who packed the basket. She was young and lovely, with a smile in her brown eyes and laughter on her lips. Her hands were soft and white, but the skin on her neck was even whiter. She was one of the most beautiful girls in the town and not yet engaged.

She had the picnic basket on her lap, while they drove out into the forest. The bottle peeped out through the snowy white tablecloth that covered the basket; his cork was covered by red sealing wax. He could look right into the face of the young girl and he saw, too, the young seaman who was sitting beside her. They had been friends since childhood. He was the son of a portrait painter. He had just received his mate's license and was to sail the following day on a long voyage to foreign lands. While preparing the basket for the picnic they had talked about the voyage; and there had been no joy or laughter to be seen in the young girl's face.

When they arrived in the forest the young couple went for a walk alone, and what did they talk about? Well, the bottle never knew, for he had stayed in the picnic basket. A very long time seemed to pass before he was taken out. But when it finally happened, something very pleasant seemed to have taken place. Everyone was smiling and laughing, the tanner's daughter too. She didn't say much, but two red roses were blooming on her cheeks.

The tanner took out his corkscrew and grabbed the bottle! It was a strange experience to be opened for the first time. The bottleneck had never forgotten that solemn moment when the cork was drawn and the wine streamed into the glasses.

"To the engaged couple!" toasted the tanner. They all emptied their glasses, and the young mate kissed his bride-to-be.

"Happiness and contentment!" exclaimed the old couple to the young.

The glasses were filled once more. "A happy homecoming and a wedding, a year from now!" shouted the young man. When they had drunk this toast, he grasped the now empty bottle. "You have been part of the happiest day of my life, you shall serve no one after that!"

The young mate threw the bottle high into the air. The tanner's daughter followed it with her eyes; she could not know then that she would see the very same bottle fly through the air once more during her life. The bottle landed in a little pond in the woods. The bottleneck remembered it all very clearly; he could even recall what he had thought when he lay in the water! "I gave them wine, and they gave me swamp water in return, but they meant well." The poor bottle could no longer see the picnic party, but heard them laughing and singing. Finally two little peasant boys came by, looked in among the reeds, noticed the bottle, picked it up; and now he had an owner again.

In the house in the woods, the oldest son had been home the day before; he was a seaman and was about to set out on a long voyage. His mother was making a package of one thing and another that she thought might be useful on so long a journey. His father would take it to the ship and give it to the lad together with his parents' blessings. A little bottle of homemade liquor had already been filled; but when the boys entered with the larger and stronger bottle, the woman decided to put the liquor in that one instead. It was brewed from herbs and was especially good for the stomach. So the bottle was filled once more, this time not with red wine but with bitter medicine, and that was of the "very best" quality too.

Lying between a sausage and a cheese, it was delivered to Peter Jensen, who was the older brother of the two boys who had found the bottle. Now the ship's mate was the very young man who had just become engaged to the tanner's daughter. He did not see the bottle; and if he had, he would not have recognized it, or imagined that the very bottle that had contained the wine with which he had toasted to a happy homecoming could be on board his ship.

True, the bottle was no longer filled with wine, but what it contained was just as desirable to Peter Jensen and his friends. They called Peter the "apothecary," for it was he who doled out the medicine that cured stomach-aches so pleasantly. Yes, that was a good period in the bottle's life; but at last it was empty.

It had stood forgotten in a corner a long time; then the terrible tragedy occurred. Whether it happened on the journey out or on the return voyage was never clear to the bottle, since he had not gone ashore. The ship was caught in the midst of a storm; great heavy black waves broke over the railing and lifted and tossed the vessel; the mast broke; and a plank in the hull was pressed loose. The water poured in so fast that it was useless to try to pump it out. It was a dark night. In the last few minutes before the ship sank, the young mate wrote on a piece of paper, "In Jesus' name, we are lost." Then he added the name of the ship, his own name, and that of his sweetheart. He put the sheet of paper into an empty bottle he had found, corked it, and threw it into the raging sea. He did not know that he had once before held that bottle in his hands, on the day of his engagement.

The ship sank, the crew was lost, but the bottle floated like a gull on the waves. Now that he had a sad love letter inside him, he had a heart. The bottle watched the sun rise and set, thought that the red disk was like the opening of the oven in which he had been born; he longed to float right into it. Days of calm were followed by a storm. The bottle was not broken against a cliff-bound shore, nor was it swallowed by a shark.

For years it drifted, following the currents of the ocean toward the north and then toward the south. He was his own master, but that, too, can become tiresome in the long run.

The note, the last farewell from a bridegroom to his bride, would only bring pain if ever it were held by the hand it had been meant for. Where were they now, those little white hands that had spread the tablecloth on the green moss the day of the picnic? Where was the tanner's daughter? Where was the country where it had happened? The bottle didn't know, he just drifted with the waves and the wind. Although he was thoroughly tired of it; after all, that wasn't what he was meant for. He had no choice in the matter, but finally he floated to shore. It was a foreign country, the bottle didn't understand a word of what was said; and that was most irritating. You miss so much when you don't understand the language.

The bottle was picked up, opened, and the note was taken out to be read. But the finder did not understand what was written on it; he turned the note both upside down and right side up, but he could not read it. He realized that the bottle had been thrown overboard and that the note was a message from a ship, but what it said remained a mystery to him. The note was put back in the bottle and the bottle put away in a closet.

Every time there were visitors the note was shown in the hope that someone could read it, but no one who came ever could. The note that had been written with pencil was made less and less legible by the many hands that held it. Finally the letters could no longer be seen and the bottle was put up in the attic. Spider webs and dust covered him, while he dreamed about the past: the good old days when he had been filled with wine and had been taken on a picnic. Even the days on the ocean seemed pleasant now; the years when he had floated on the sea and had had a secret inside him: a letter, a sigh of farewell.

It remained in the attic twenty years and would have stayed there even longer had not the owner decided to enlarge his house. The whole roof was torn down. The bottle was brought out and the story of how it was found told once more. The bottle did not understand what was being said, for you don't learn a language by standing twenty years in an attic. "If only they had allowed me to stay in the closet downstairs, then I would probably have learned it," thought the bottle.

Once more he was washed and rinsed—and he certainly needed it. The bottle was so clean and transparent that he felt young in his old age; but the note had been lost in the process.

Now the bottle was filled up with seeds: what kind they were the bottle didn't know. Again he was corked, and then wrapped in paper so tightly that not a bit of light came through. He could see neither the sun nor the moon; and the bottle felt that this was a great shame, for what is the point of traveling if you don't see anything? But travel it did; and it arrived safely at its destination and was unpacked.

"They certainly have been careful"—the bottle heard someone say —"but I suppose it has broken anyway." But the bottle was whole, and he understood every word that was said. They spoke his own language, the first one he had heard when he came red hot out of the melting pot: the language that had been spoken at the wine merchant's, at the picnic, and on the ship—his native tongue, the one he understood! The bottle had come home! Oh, what a lovely welcome sound! The bottle nearly jumped for pure joy out of the hands that had picked him up. He hardly felt the cork being drawn and the seeds being shaken out, so happy was he!

He was put down in a cellar, again to be hidden and forgotten by the world. But it's good to be home even when one has to stay in the cellar. The bottle did not even count the years and days he stayed there. Finally somebody came and removed all the bottles, himself included.

The garden outside the house had been decorated. Colored lamps hung from all the trees and bushes; they looked like shining tulips. It was a lovely evening, perfectly still, and the sky was filled with stars. There was a new moon, a tiny sliver of silver surrounding a pale disk; it was a beautiful sight for those who look at beauty.

The paths at the edges of the garden were illuminated too—at least, enough so you could find your way. In the spaces between the bushes of the hedge, bottles with candles in them had been placed. Here, too, stood the bottle that was fated to end as a birdbath. He found the whole affair marvelously to his taste; here he stood, among the greenery, attending a party; he could hear laughter and music and all the sounds of gaiety. True, it came mostly from another part of the garden, where the colored lamps were hung. He had been placed in the more lonesome area; but that gave the bottle more time for reflection. He felt that he stood there not only for amusement and beauty but also because he was useful. Such a combination is superior and can make one forget the twenty years one has spent in the attic—and that sort of thing it is best to forget.

A young couple came walking by, arm in arm, just as the other young couple, on the day of the picnic, had: the tanner's daughter and the mate from the ship. The bottle felt that he was reliving something that had happened once before. Among the guests were some who had not been really invited but were allowed to come and look at the festivities. One of these was an old maid; she had no kin but she had friends. She was having exactly the same thoughts as the bottle; she was also recalling an afternoon spent in the woods, and a young couple walking arm in arm. She had been half of that sight and those had been the happiest moments of her life, and they are not forgotten, regardless of how old one becomes. She did not recognize the bottle nor he her.

That is the way of the world, we can pass each other unnoticed until we are introduced to each other again. And those two were to meet once more, now that they lived in the same town.

From the garden, the bottle was taken to the wine merchant, rinsed, and then once more filled with wine. It was sold to a balloonist, who, on the following Sunday, was to ascend into the sky in a balloon. A great crowd of people gathered to see the event and the regimental band played. The bottle saw all the preparations for the air voyage from a basket, where he lay together with a rabbit who was to be dropped down with a parachute on. The poor bunny, who knew its fate, looked anything but happy. The balloon grew and grew and finally rose from the ground when it couldn't grow any fatter; then the ropes that held it down were cut and it slowly ascended into the sky, carrying the basket with the balloonist, the bottle, and the frightened rabbit up into the air. The crowd below cheered and screamed: "Hurrah!"

"It is a strange feeling," thought the bottle. "It is another way of sailing but, at least, up here you can't run aground."

Many thousands of people were watching the balloon and the old maid in the garret was looking at it too. She was standing at her window, where the bird cage with the little songbird hung; at that time it did not have a glass birdbath but only a cracked cup that had lost its handle. On the window sill was a myrtle bush; the flowerpot had been moved a little out of the way so that the woman could lean out of the window and get a better view of the balloon.

She could see everything clearly: how the balloonist threw the rabbit out and its tiny parachute unfolded.

Now he was taking the bottle and uncorking it. He drank a toast to all the spectators. But he did not put the bottle back; instead he cast it high into the air. The old maid saw that too, but she did not know that this was the very bottle she had seen fly once before: in the springtime of her life, on that happy day in the green forest.

The bottle had hardly the time to think half a thought, not to talk of a whole one. The high point of his life had come and so unexpectedly! Far below him were the towers and roofs of the city; the people looked so tiny.

The bottle descended with quite a different speed than the rabbit had. The bottle performed somersaults as he fell; he had been half filled with wine, but soon that was gone. He felt so young, so joyful and gay. What a journey! The sun reflected in him and every person below was following him with their eyes.

The balloon was soon out of sight and so was the bottle; it fell on a roof and splintered. It hit with such force that all the little pieces danced and jumped, and did not rest before they had fallen all the way down into a yard. The neck of the bottle was whole; it looked as if it had been cut from the rest of the bottle with a diamond.

"It would do as a birdbath," said the man who found it. He lived in a cellar. But since he had neither cage nor bird, he thought it a little expensive to buy them just because he had an old bottleneck that could be used as a birdbath. He remembered the old maid who lived up under the roof, she might find it useful.

A cork was put in the bottleneck, and it was hung upside down in the cage of the little bird that sang so beautifully. Now it was filled with fresh water instead of wine; and what used to be "up" was "down," but that is the sort of change that sometimes does happen in this world.

"Yes, you can sing," sighed the bottleneck, who had had so many adventures. The bird and the old maid knew only of the most recent one when he had been up in a balloon.

Now the bottle had become a birdbath; he could hear the rumble of the traffic down in the street and the voice of the mistress talking to an old friend. They were not talking about the bottleneck but about the myrtle bush in the window.

"There is no reason for you to spend two crowns on a bridal bouquet for your daughter," the old maid was saying. "I will cut you a beautiful one from my bush. You remember the myrtle bush you gave me the day after I had become engaged? Well, the little bush over in the window is a cutting from that one. You hoped that I would cut my bridal bouquet from it, but that day never came. Those eyes are closed that should have shone for me and been the happiness of my life. On the bottom of the sea he sleeps now, my beloved. The bush you gave me became old, but I became even older. When it was just about to die, I cut a branch from it and planted it. Look how it has thrived; finally, it will attend a wedding: your daughter's."

There were tears in the old woman's eyes as she talked about the young man who had loved her when she was young. She recalled his toast and the first kiss he had given her; but that she did not tell about, for she was truly an old maid. No matter how much she thought about the past, it never occurred to her that just outside the window, in the bird cage, hung a witness to those times: the neck of the very bottle that had contained the wine with which her engagement had been celebrated. The bottleneck did not recognize her either, nor did he listen to what she was saying, but that was mostly because the bottleneck never thought about anyone but himself.

51

✧

The Old Oak Tree's Last Dream

A Christmas Story

ON the outskirts of the forest, on a bank above the beach, grew an old oak tree. It was three hundred and sixty-five years old, but to the tree those years did not seem longer than as many days and nights would to a human being. We are awake during the day and sleep at night, and it is then we have our dreams. But the oak tree is awake three seasons of the year and only sleeps during the fourth. It is only in the winter that it rests; that is its night after that long day that is called spring, summer, and autumn.

Many a warm day the mayflies danced around its leaves and branches, soared on their fragile wings to the very crown of the tree. Ever happy were the little insects and, when they grew tired, they rested on a broad green oak leaf. Then the tree could not help saying, "Poor little you, one day is your whole life. How short, how sad is your fate!"

"Sad," the mayfly always replied. "What do you mean by that? Everything is so beautiful, so warm, and so lovely; and I am so happy."

"But only one day and then all is over."

"Over," said the mayfly. "What is over? Are you over too?"

"No, I live many thousands of your days, and my days are so long that they last almost a year, which is so long that you cannot even figure it out."

"I do not understand you. You live thousands of my days, but I have thousands of moments to be happy in. Do you think that all the beauty in the world will die when you do?"

"No," answered the tree. "That will last much longer than even I can imagine."

"Well there, you see, we live equally long; it is just our ways of figuring that are different."

And the little mayfly flew away again, up into the air, and rejoiced that it had been given such lovely fine wings. The air was filled with the scent of flowering clover from the fields, wild roses from the hedges, elder trees, honeysuckle, woodruff, primroses, and wild mint. The fragrance was so strong that the mayfly felt quite drunk from it. The day was long and beautiful, so filled with happiness, so full of joy. When finally the sun did set, the little fly felt tired from all it had experienced so intensely. The wings were no longer strong enough to carry it. Ever so gently it sank down among the soft grass, nodding its head as if it were saying yes. It slept so peacefully, so happily, and that was death.

"Poor little mayfly," said the oak tree, "its life was much too short."

Every summer the mayflies repeated their dance and the oak held the same conversation with them. Generations upon generations of mayflies died, and yet each new insect born was just as happy, just as carefree, as all those that had gone before it. The oak tree was awake through its spring morning, its summer noon, and its fall evening. It felt that soon it was time to sleep; the oak tree's night, winter, was coming.

Already the storms were singing: "Good night, good night! We pluck your leaves. See, there one fell. We pluck, we pluck! We sing you to sleep. We undress you and shake your old branches; they creak but it does them good. Sleep now, sleep, it is your three hundred and sixty-fifth night, which means you are young yet. Sleep. From the clouds snow is falling, it is a warm blanket around your feet. Sleep and dream sweet dreams!"

The oak tree stood nude with its bare branches against the sky, ready to sleep through its long night, ready to dream many a dream just as human beings do.

It, too, had been tiny once: an acorn had been its cradle. By human reckoning it was now in the fourth century of its life. It was the biggest tree in the forest, and its crown rose up high above the others. Sailors used it as a landmark to navigate by, and the wood pigeons built their nests in it. In the fall the migrating birds would rest among its bronze leaves before they flew south. But now in the winter its branches were naked, and only crows and jackdaws used them; they sat there discussing hard times and complaining about how difficult it was to find food, now that winter was here.

It was at the holy Christmastime that the oak tree dreamed the most beautiful dream it had ever dreamed. We shall hear it:

The tree felt that something holy, something solemn and yet joyful, was happening. From every direction it heard church bells ringing. In its dream, it was not winter but the loveliest warm summer day. The branches in its great crown spread themselves out green and fresh, the sun rays played upon its leaves, and the air was filled with the fragrance of flowering trees and bushes. Colorful butterflies played hide-and-seek and the mayflies danced as if the whole world had been created just for their enjoyment. Everything the tree had seen and experienced through its long life passed by in an endless parade. It saw knights with their ladies; they were riding out to hunt, with feathers in their caps and falcons on their hands. And the tree heard the dogs bark and the sound of the hunters' horns. Then strange soldiers camped beneath its branches; they pitched their tents and made fires. The sun reflected in their shining weapons; they ate and drank and sang as if they had conquered time as well as the country. Two shy lovers came and cut their names in its bark; they were the first to do it but others would follow. Once an aeolian harp had been hung in the oak's branches by a happy youth. That had happened so many years ago, yet it hung there again in the dream; and the wind blew through it and made music. The wood pigeons cooed, and the cuckoo called out once for each year that the oak tree had left of its life; but the cuckoo is not to be trusted.

The tree felt as if a great wave of strength, of life, were passing through it. From its tiniest root, deep down in the ground, to its topmost little twigs, it experienced an awareness of life and warmth. It felt its strength increase, it was growing taller and taller. Its great crown was now enormous. As it grew, its feeling of happiness became more and more intense, and it had such a great longing for the sun that it wanted to grow right up into that golden warm sphere.

In its dream, the tree had grown so tall that its top branches were above the clouds; flocks of birds were flying below them; even the swans could not fly above its crown.

Every leaf had become an eye that could see. All the stars were out, even though it was day, and they looked so clear, so bright, and shone as brilliantly as the eyes of children or of the lovers who met beneath the old oak tree.

What a wonderful moment, so full of joy! Yet in the midst of all its happiness the tree felt a longing for other trees and the bushes that grew far below it. It wished that they, too—as well as the little flowers and herbs—could lift themselves high up in the sky as it was doing, and experience its joy. The great oak tree wanted to share its godlike ecstasy. It felt that unless everyone took part in this great dream of happiness it would not be complete. This wish ran through it from root to leaves and was as strong as a human being's desires.

The crown of the tree swayed as its branches turned to look downward. It smelled the odor of woodruff and the stronger fragrance of violets and honeysuckle, and thought that it could hear the cuckoo call.

The top branches of the other trees of the forest now peeped through the clouds; they, too, were growing, lifting themselves up to the sky, toward the sun. Bushes and flowers followed; some of them had freed themselves from the earth and were flying. The birch, like a bolt of white lightning, passed the old oak. The whole forest was flying up toward the sky, even the brown reeds from the swamp were coming. The birds had followed the plants. On a blade of grass sat a grasshopper and played with his wings on his hind legs. Beetles and bees and all the other insects had come, and all of them shared the old oak tree's joyous ecstasy.

"But where are the little blue flowers from the pond?" shouted the oak tree. "And the red harebell and the little primrose?" The old oak did not want anyone to be forgotten.

"We are here, we are here!" sang voices all around it.

"But the woodruff from last summer and all the lilies of the valley from the summer before that, where are they? I remember the year when the wild apples bloomed so beautifully. Oh, so much beauty do I recall through all the years of my life! If it only were all alive now and could be with us!"

"We are, we are," came cries from somewhere higher up; they must have flown there earlier.

"That is the most marvelous of all," rejoiced the old oak tree. "Everything that I have known is here. Nothing has been forgotten, not the tiniest flower or the smallest bird. How is such joy possible? Where is such happiness conceivable?"

"In heaven it is possible," sang the voices.

And the tree felt its roots loosen their grasp on the earth.

"Yes, that is best!" the oak cried. "Now no bands hold me down. I can fly up into the everlasting light, the eternal glory! And all that I held dear is with me. None has been forgotten, all are here with me, all!"

That was the oak tree's dream; and while it was dreaming a great storm blew across the sea and the land. The waves rushed toward the shore and were crushed on the beach, and the wind tore at the old oak tree's branches. Just at the moment when it dreamed that its roots gave way, in its flight toward heaven, it was torn from the ground by the wind and fell. Its three hundred and sixty-five years of life were now as a day is for the mayfly.

Christmas morning the sea had calmed and the storm was over. The church bells were gaily ringing, and above each house, even the smallest and poorest cottages, a blue ribbon of smoke rose from the chimney, like the smoke at a Druid feast of thanksgiving. The sea grew calmer and calmer, and on board the big ships, which the night before had been so hard pressed by the storm, the sailors hoisted gay colorful flags in the rigging to celebrate the holy day.

"The big tree is gone! The old oak tree we used as a landmark!" the sailors shouted, amazed. "It fell in the storm. What shall we use now? There is none that can replace it."

That was the old oak tree's funeral sermon; it was short but well meant. The tree itself lay stretched out on the snow-covered beach. From the ship came the sound of the sailors singing a carol about the joyful season, when Christ was born to save mankind and give us eternal life. The sailors were singing of the same dream, the beautiful dream that the old oak tree had dreamed Christmas Eve: the last night of its life.

52

The Bog King's Daughter

THE storks tell their young ones many stories and fairy tales. All of them take place in the swamps and bogs where storks like to live. They usually choose stories that fit the ages of their children. The smallest are satisfied if their parents say: "Muddle, duddle . . . cribble crabble"; that is plot and morality enough for their taste. But the older ones are not so easily satisfied; they demand something with a deeper meaning or at least a story about their own family. The storks know two stories that are very ancient and very long: one of them is the story of Moses, who was set sailing out upon the waters of the Nile by his mother and was found by a princess. He was carefully brought up and well educated and became a great man. Where he is buried no one knows. That story every child has heard. The other tale is not well known, possibly because it is a bit provincial. It is a fairy tale that has been told by stork mothers for a thousand years; each one of them has told it a little better than her mother, and we shall tell it best of all.

The first storks who told it had experienced it themselves, they had been part of it. They had their summer residence on top of the roof of the wooden house of a Viking chieftain who lived near the great bog in the north of Jutland, which is called Vendsyssel. If one were to describe it learnedly—as it is described in a Danish geography book —then one must explain that once this was an ocean bed, but the waters departed and the land rose. Today the bog is very large, but once it was even larger; there were miles and miles of swamp, marshland, and stretches of peat. There were no trees worth talking about, and over the bog hovered, almost always, a dense fog. At the turn of the eighteenth century there were still wolves there; and it was even wilder a thousand years ago. Yet the landscape was the same; the reeds were no taller, and they had the same feathery flowers and slender leaves. The birch tree's bark was as white as it is now, and the branches with their fine green leaves hung toward the earth as gracefully. The animal life, too, has not changed. The flies, then, were as troublesome as they are now; and the storks wore the same black and white livery with red stockings. But the human beings were dressed differently, though their fate was the same, if they stepped out upon the surface of the great bog: a thousand years ago—as today—they would slowly sink into the muddy ooze down to the bog king. That was the name given to the ruler of the great bog. Some called him the swamp king, but we prefer the bog king and the storks agree with us, for that is what they called him. Very little is known about his rule, which may be just as well.

Near the bog, on the shores of the fjord, a Viking chief had built a big house. It had a stone cellar, three floors and a tower, constructed of logs. On top of the roof a pair of storks had built their nest. The mother stork, who was brooding, was convinced that every one of her eggs would hatch.

One evening the father stork was away from the nest longer than usual, and when he finally returned he looked upset and unhappy. "I have something horrible to tell you," he said.

"Don't!" exclaimed his wife. "Remember I am brooding. If you upset me, it might harm the eggs!"

"You must know what has happened!" insisted the male stork. "She has come, the daughter of our landlord in Egypt, and now she has disappeared!"

"The girl who is related to the fairies? Tell me, tell me! Don't keep me in suspense, that is not good for me when I am sitting on eggs!"

"You know, my dear, that she believed the doctors who said that the water lilies, here in the north, would cure her father. She has flown up here. She was wearing a swanskin and came together with the two other princesses who fly up here every year to bathe—they believe the waters make them retain their youth. The young princess was here and now she is gone!"

"You are so long-winded, get to the point!" complained his wife. "The eggs may catch cold; I can't stand being kept in suspense."

"You know I keep an eye on everything," the male stork continued. "Last night I was down in the reeds, where the mud is solid enough for me to stand, and I saw three swans. There was something about their flight that said: 'Look out, they are not swans, they are something else wearing swanskins.' You know as well as I, how one can feel that a thing just isn't right."

"Yes, yes!" His wife was getting very impatient. "Tell me about the princess and never mind the swanskins, they bore me!"

"You know that right in the center of the bog there is a lake—you can see part of it from here if you stand up. Near the reeds at the shore, there lay the trunk of an old alder tree, and the three swans landed on it. They flapped their wings and looked around. Then one of them cast off her swanskin and I recognized her. She was the princess from the palace in Egypt. She had nothing to cover herself with but her long black hair. She asked the other two to guard her swanskin, while she dived down into the water to pluck the flower that she thought she had spied underneath the water. The other two swans flew up, taking the princess' swanskin with them in their bills. I wondered what they wanted to do with it; and I am sure the princess would have liked to ask the same question. We were answered soon enough.

" 'Dive down into the dark water!' cried the swans. 'Never again shall you see Egypt, you shall stay here in the wild bog forever!' Then, with their beaks, they tore her swanskin into hundreds of pieces. The feathers flew around them; it looked like a snowstorm. Then the two evil princesses flew away."

"It is horrible!" exclaimed the mother stork. "I can't bear hearing stories like that. I am sure it is not good for me. . . . But tell me what happened afterward, please tell me!"

"The princess cried and her tears fell on the trunk of the old alder tree. It began to move! It wasn't an alder tree, it was the bog king himself! The one who lives in the bog and rules it. I saw the tree trunk turn in the water, and then it no longer looked like a tree trunk. Its long branches were not branches but arms! The poor girl got frightened. She tried to jump up onto the shore, but she was too heavy to stand in the muddy bog. At that place the ooze can't even bear me. She sank down into the bog and at the same moment the bog king disappeared. I think he pulled her down. Some big black bubbles rose to the surface, burst, and were gone. Now she is buried in the bog and she will never return to Egypt and bring her father the flower. You couldn't have borne seeing it, I am sure!"

"I don't think you should even have told me about it now; it may spoil the eggs! The princess will take care of herself, I am sure; there is always someone who is ready to help her kind. Now if it had been you or I who had been sucked down into the mud, then everything would have been over."

"Still, I will keep an eye on the place," said the male stork, and he did.

A long time passed; then one day a green stalk shot up through the water. When it reached the surface a leaf unfolded, and in the center of it was a bud. The leaf grew bigger and bigger, and so did the bud. One morning when the stork flew above it he saw that the bud was opening in the warm sunshine. In the flower lay a little girl, a beautiful child; she looked so much like the princess from Egypt that the stork thought it might be she, grown smaller. But on second thought he found it more reasonable that the child was her daughter with the bog king, and that was why she was lying in a water lily.

"She can't stay there," thought the stork. "There is no room in my nest, we are already crowded. But the Viking chief's wife has no child, and I know she wants one badly. I have heard her sighing. Since they claim that I bring children I might as well do it for once. I will give it to our landlady; it will make her happy."

The stork took the little girl in his bill and flew up to the house. There he pecked a hole in the window—that was easy, for it was only covered by a pig's bladder. He lay the baby beside the sleeping woman, then he flew back up to his wife to tell her all about it. The children were allowed to listen; after all, they were almost grown up.

"You see, the princess isn't dead, she must have sent the little girl up with the water lily. And I found a home for her."

"I told you all the time that, if she couldn't take care of herself, then someone else would take care of her," said the mother stork. "But you should think a little more about your own family and less about others. It will soon be time to leave; my wings are itching. The cuckoo and the nightingale have already left, and the quails are saying that the wind will soon blow just right for flying south. I am sure our children will do well on the maneuver; I know them, I am their mother."

The Viking chieftain's wife was ever so happy when she awoke and found the little girl. She kissed and fondled the little baby, but the child did not seem to like it, she kicked and screamed and cried. Finally she fell asleep and no child has ever looked lovelier than she did then. The Viking woman felt so happy and lighthearted that she was sure that her husband and his men would be home soon: they would come just as unexpectedly as the child had. She got busy putting the house in order. She ordered the slaves to polish the old shields that hung on the walls and told her maid to bring out the tapestries that had pictures of their gods woven in them: of Odin, Thor, and Freya. Skins were placed on the wooden benches and dry firewood on the great central fireplace, so that it could be lit as soon as the voyagers returned. The mistress worked along with the others; by evening she was very tired, and she slept well throughout the night.

Just before the sun rose she awoke. The child was gone! She got terribly frightened and jumped out of bed to look for it. She lit a bit of kindling and then she saw at the foot of her bed not the child but a big ugly frog. She felt sick at the sight of it and grabbed a large piece of firewood to kill it. But the toad looked up at her with such infinitely sad eyes that she couldn't. She looked around the room. The frog gave a pathetic little croak, and the woman shivered at the sound. Then she ran and opened up the shutters. Just at that moment the sun rose. Its first rays came in through the opening and fell on the bed, where the big frog was sitting. Its broad mouth became small; its ugly limbs straightened and took on the lovely shape of her little child. The ugly frog was gone.

"What has happened!" she cried. "I must have had an evil dream. There is my lovely fairy child!" She picked up the little girl, kissed her, and pressed her to her heart. But the baby acted more like an angry kitten; she scratched and bit.

The Viking chief did not return that day or the next. He was on his way home but had the wind against him. It blew toward the south for the storks' sake. Fair winds for one are foul for another.

The next night the Viking woman realized how things were with her little child; she was bewitched. By day she was as beautiful as a fairy but her character was wild and evil; at night she was an ugly frog with sad sorrowful eyes and sat whimpering quietly. These transformations in the girl, whom the stork had brought, were caused by the two natures within her. In the daytime she had the shape and appearance of her lovely mother but the soul of her father. At night her kinship with the bog king could be seen in her body, but then she had the sweet character and heart of her mother.

The chieftain's wife was frightened and sorrowful: who could break such a curse? Yet she loved the unfortunate creature that fate had brought to her. She was determined not to tell her husband about the child being bewitched, for she feared that he would set her out in the wilderness to be eaten by wolves, as this was the Viking custom with babies that were deformed. She vowed—poor woman—that her husband would never see the child except by day.

One morning the sound of the wings of storks could be heard. They were resting after the big maneuver and were now ready for the flight south. There were more than two hundred of them.

"Everybody ready!" was the command. "Children and wives stay with your husbands!"

"I feel so light," said one of the stork children. "It creeps and crawls inside me right down into my legs, as if I were filled with living frogs. How wonderful it is to travel!"

"Keep in your places," admonished their mother and father, "and don't talk too much, it is bad for the breathing."

And away they flew!

Right at that moment a horn was blown. The Vikings had landed. Their ships were loaded with rich booty. They had come from the coasts of Gaul, where the people—just as they did in England—prayed: "Free us from the wild Norsemen."

A great celebration took place in the Viking hall near the great bog. A vat of mead was carried in and the great fire was lit. Horses were butchered, and the warm horse blood was sprayed on the new slaves, in honor of Odin: a heathen baptism. The smoke drifted from the fire up to the roof, soot dripped from the great beams; but no one took any notice.

The house was filled with guests and everyone received a costly present. All old disagreements and broken promises were forgotten. They drank and they ate, and they threw the gnawed bones in each other's faces—that was considered amusing. The poet of the time, who was called a *skjald,* was a warrior too; he had been on the voyage, so he knew what he was composing verses about. He sang ballads about their adventures, recalling every battle each Viking had fought in. His verses always ended with the same words! "Richness vanishes and friends die, as one must die oneself; only the fame of greatness never dies." Then they would all bang with their knives or hit their shields with their gnawed bones, so the noise could be heard far away.

The chieftain's wife sat on the women's bench, dressed in a silken gown; she wore gold bracelets and an amber necklace. The *skjald* did not forget to mention her in his verses; he sang about the golden treasure she had brought her rich and famous husband. In truth, the chieftain was pleased with his child, whom he had only seen while the sun was in the sky. She was beautiful, and as for her temper, he liked it. "She will become a valkyrie, who will fight as well as any man and not be frightened by the sound of a sword as it cleaves the air," he said proudly.

The vat of mead was empty and another one was carried into the hall. Oh yes, these were people who could drink. The Vikings had a proverb: "Cattle know when it is best to stop grazing, but a fool never realizes the size of his own stomach." Although all of them knew these words, they seemed to have forgotten them. Just as they did not remember another proverb from that time: "A good friend becomes a bore if he stays too long in another man's house." For weeks the guests stayed, for the sake of the meat and the mead.

Once more that year the Vikings went on a raid, but only across the waters to England. The Viking woman was again alone with her little girl. By now she loved more deeply the sighing frog with the sad lovely eyes than the beautiful girl who bit and tore at her.

The raw and cold autumn fog, which, although it has no mouth, gnaws the leaves of the trees, now covered the landscape. The first snowflakes had followed each other down from the clouds. Winter was not far away. The sparrows had moved into the storks' nest and were criticizing endlessly the departed owners. But where were the father and mother stork and all their children?

They were in Egypt, where the sun in winter shines as warmly as it does in Denmark in the summer. Tamarisks and acacias were in bloom there, and above the temple dome shone Mohammed's moon. On the tops of the tall, slender towers many stork couples sat resting from their long journey. Whole flocks of them had built their nests in the ruins of the other temples; those once busy places that were forgotten now. The date palms lift their leaves high up in the air like gigantic parasols. The whitish-gray pyramids look as if they had been drawn on the clear air of the desert. There the ostrich demonstrates that, although it cannot fly, it at least can run; and the lion, with its sad and knowing eyes, contemplates the marble sphinx that stands half buried in the sand. The waters of the Nile were low and the muddy river bed was alive with frogs. For a stork that was the most pleasant sight of all. The young ones, who had not been in Egypt before, thought it was all an optical illusion, so marvelous was it.

"No, it is real, and that is the way it always is here in our winter residence!" said the stork mother.

"Aren't we going any farther?" asked the young ones. "Aren't we going to see even more?"

"There isn't much more to see," answered their mother. "The part that is fertile is a little too wild. The trees grow too close together in the jungle, and among their branches are thorny vines; only the elephants with their thick skins and broad feet can make their way through there. The snakes are too big to eat and the lizards too agile to catch. And if you go in the other direction, toward the desert, you will get sand in your eyes, and that is not pleasant. No, it is best to stay here, where there are plenty of frogs and grasshoppers. I will stay here, and so will you!"

And they stayed. The old ones had a nest on top of a minaret; there they rested, while they smoothed down their feathers and polished their bills on their long red legs. They would lift their heads and nod gravely toward other storks, as they looked out over the landscape with their brown eyes that seemed to shine with intelligence. The young female storks would wander about in the swamp, making friends and eating a frog for every third step they took. Often they would walk around with a little snake dangling in their bills; they thought it looked attractive, and besides, it tasted good. The young males fought with each other; they would flap their wings and fight such duels with their beaks that sometimes blood would flow.

After a while they all got engaged, which was only natural; then they built nests of their own, and argued and fought some more. In the hot countries everyone has a hot temper, but it was all very entertaining. The older storks found it amusing to watch; they thought anything their own offspring did most marvelous and unique. Every day the sun shone, and every day there was enough to eat; the only thing left to do was to enjoy oneself.

But inside the great castle life was not amusing at all. The great powerful ruler of the country lay as still as a mummy on his couch in the great hall of the castle. The walls were all covered with murals; it looked as if he were lying in the center of an enormous tulip. Servants and relations flocked around him. He wasn't dead, but he wasn't alive either. The water lily from the north that could have saved him would never be found. His young and beautiful daughter who had flown in a swanskin over the ocean and the great mountains, far to the north, to fetch it would never return. "She is dead and gone," said the two princesses who had accompanied her on the journey. Listen to the pretty story they told:

"We were flying, all three of us, high up in the air when a hunter saw us; he shot an arrow and it hit our friend. She sank down toward a little lake, while she sang her good-by: her swan song. By the shore of the lake, under a birch tree, we buried her! We took revenge. We tied burning tinder under the wings of the swallow that lived underneath the hunter's roof. It flew home to its nest and set fire to his house. The hunter died in the fire and the flames could be seen as far as the birch tree under which the princess rests, where she has become dust in the dust. She will never come back to Egypt."

Then they cried, both of them; and the father stork, who heard it all, clattered with his bill, he was so angry.

"Lies and more lies," he said. "I felt like running my beak right through them!"

"And breaking it!" replied his wife. "You would be a sight then! Think a little more about yourself and your family. What is outside it shouldn't concern you."

"I will fly over to the great dome and listen tomorrow, when all the wise men assemble to discuss the king's illness. Maybe they will get a little nearer to the truth."

The learned and the wise gathered, and talked and talked; but the stork couldn't understand their chatter. It did not help the sick man either, or his daughter who was lost in the great bog. We could listen a little to what was said; one has to hear an awful lot of that kind of talk before one dies. But since this is a story and we are free to travel in time as well as space, let's hear about the first assembly of the wise and learn what happened when the king became ill, a year before. We ought to know at least as much as the stork could understand.

"Love breeds life, and the highest form of love breeds the highest form of life. Only through love can our sick king be brought back to life." This had been said at the first assembly, and the learned and the wise had all agreed that it was true.

"It is a beautiful thought," the stork had explained as soon as he came home to the nest.

"I don't quite understand it," his wife had said, "and I don't believe the fault is mine. It is unclear! But it doesn't matter, I have enough to think about already."

The learned and the wise had then gone on to discuss the different forms of love: the one between lovers, and the one that parents feel for their children, besides the more complicated forms, such as the one between light and the plants—how the sun rays kiss the black earth, making the seeds sprout. That part of the discussion was so learned and so filled with long and difficult words that the stork could understand almost none of it, let alone be able to repeat it when he got home. He became very morose, half closed his eyes, and stood on one leg for a whole day. Excessive learning is very hard to bear.

But one thing he did know, for he had heard it said often enough, both by the courtiers and the ordinary people—and they had talked from their hearts: it was a disaster to the whole country that the king was sick, and it would be a great blessing to the people if he got well.

"But where grows the flower that can give him back his health?" That was the question everyone had asked last year. They had studied old learned books, the stars, the weather, and the clouds, and used every possible detour to get at the truth. The wise and the learned—as we know—had agreed upon the maxim, "Love breeds life, life to our father." They repeated it over and over again and wrote it down as a prescription: "Love breeds life." But how the prescription was to be filled, that no one knew. At last they had agreed that the princess, who loved her father so much, must be the one to find the answer. And the wise men even decided how she was to go about it. At night, when the new moon had disappeared from the sky, she was to go out in the desert to the marble sphinx. There she should cast away the sand from the half-buried door at its base and walk through the long corridors that led to the center of one of the great pyramids. Here lay buried one of the great kings from ancient times. The princess was to enter this chamber of death and splendor, and lean her head against the decorated casing that contained the mummy. The dead king would then reveal to her how her father could be saved.

She had done what had been demanded of her, and in a dream she had learned that in the wild bog in the north—the place had been very accurately described—there grew a lotus flower that would bring back her father's health. She was to dive into the black water and pick the first flower that touched her breast.

This had all happened a year and a day before, and that was why the princess had flown in a swanskin from Egypt north to Denmark. The storks knew all about this; and now we know it, which makes the whole story easier to understand. We know, too, that the bog king took her down to his castle and that everyone in Egypt thought she was lost forever—that is, everyone but the wisest of all the wise; he was of the same opinion as the mother stork: "The princess will take care of herself."

"I think I will steal the swanskins from the two evil princesses," proposed the father stork, "then they won't be able to fly north and do more harm. I will hide the swanskins up there until there will be a use for them."

"What do you mean by up there?" asked his wife.

"In our nest up by the bog, in Denmark. Our children can help me carry them. Should they be too heavy, then we can find a hiding place along the way and carry them the rest of the way next year. One swanskin is enough for the princess, but you know how it is when you travel in the north, you can never have clothes enough along."

"Nobody is going to thank you for it," grumbled his wife. "But you are the master; no one listens to me except when I am laying eggs."

In the Viking hall by the great bog, the young girl had been given a name. She was called Helga. A name too soft to fit her character. Years passed; each spring the storks traveled north and each fall they returned to Egypt. Helga grew, became a big girl, and then a maiden sixteen summers old. Beautiful was the shell, but the kernel was hard and cruel; she was wilder and more ferocious than most people in those grim and brutal times.

She found pleasure in seeing the red blood of the horses that were offered to Odin stain her white hands. And once, in a fit of temper, she had bitten the head off a black cock that was to be offered to Thor. To her father she said—and she meant it—"Should your enemies come and tear the roof off the hall while you slept, I should not

368 A Treasury of Hans Christian Andersen

wake you. I would not warn you, for my cheeks are still burning from the time, years ago, when you slapped my face."

But the Viking chieftain did not believe her; his daughter's beauty blinded him to all her faults. He did not know how Helga's soul and body changed when night fell. When she rode, she sat on the horse as if she and the animal were one; and if sometimes the horse got into a fight with another horse, she stayed on its back, laughing while the animals kicked and bit each other. When the Vikings returned from a raid, she would throw herself into the waters of the fjord and swim out to the boat to greet them. From her beautiful long hair she cut strands and with them she made bowstrings.

"Self-made is well made," she would say, and laugh.

Her foster mother—the Viking woman—according to the times and habits of the country, was a strong-willed and capable woman; but toward her daughter she was soft and frightened, for she knew the curse that rested on the poor child.

To make her mother miserable—as if she enjoyed seeing the poor woman's terror—Helga would throw herself over the side of the well when her mother was nearby. The wretched woman would watch while, froglike, she swam in the freezing well water; then, more agilely than a cat, she would climb the steep stone sides of the well and rush into the hall, while her clothes were still dripping wet, so that she dampened the fresh leaves that had been strewn on the floor.

But at twilight, just before the sun set, Helga changed; she became quiet and thoughtful. Then she was obedient and would listen to what was said to her. She would draw close to her mother and, when the sun went down and her appearance and nature were transformed, she would sit still and sorrowful in her frog shape. Her body was much larger than any frog's, and therefore she was all the uglier; she looked like a horrible dwarf with a frog's head and webbed hands and feet. Her eyes alone were lovely with their infinite sadness. Of voice she had none. All she could manage was a hollow croak that sounded like a child sobbing in its dreams. Then her foster mother would take her on her lap and, disregarding her ugly body, she would look into her sad eyes and say, "I could almost wish that you always would be my silent frog child, for you are far more frightening to look at when your outside is beautiful and your inside ugly."

And the poor woman wrote magic runic letters on birch bark and put them on her frog child to break the spell, but none of them worked.

"One wouldn't think she had ever been so small that she could lie in a water lily," said the father stork. "She is a real woman now and the image of her mother, the Egyptian princess. We have never seen her again. And you, my dear, and the Egyptian wise man were wrong, she couldn't take care of herself. Through all these years, ever since she disappeared, I have flown back and forth across the bog but I have seen no sign of her. Once, when I came up here a few days before you and the young ones, in order to repair the nest and put things in order, I flew all night—as if I were an owl or a bat—above the place where she disappeared, but I didn't see a thing. The swanskins that it took us three years to bring up here will never be used. Now they have lain on the bottom of the nest these many years; and if this log house burns down, they will be lost."

"And so will our good nest!" said his wife angrily. "You are less concerned about that than those toys made of feathers, and that precious bog princess of yours. Why don't you dive down and stay with her! You are neither a good father nor a good husband; that I said the very first time that I laid eggs. We will be lucky if that Viking hussy doesn't send an arrow through our own children. She is a madwoman and doesn't know what she is doing. But she ought to remember that we are of an ancient family and have lived here a lot longer than she has. We pay our taxes—and that is only right—one feather, one egg, and a young one, every year. When she is around, then I stay in the nest. Don't think that I fly down in the yard as I used to, and still do in Egypt, where I am friends with almost everyone and even take a look into the pots and pans. No, here I stay at home, and grow more and more irritated over that wench and over you, too! You should have let her stay in the water lily, then we would have been rid of her."

"You are more respectable than your speech shows," said her husband. "I know you even better than you know yourself."

He made a little jump, beat the air twice with his wings, and sailed upward on the breeze. When he had risen, he again flapped his wings as he turned and made a circle. The sunlight shone upon his white feathers; his long neck and bill were stretched straight forward, it was a lovely sight.

"He is the handsomest of the lot of them," said his wife, "but that I will never tell him."

The Vikings returned from their raids abroad early that autumn. Among the prisoners was a Christian priest, one of those who were enemies of Odin and Thor. This new religion, which had already won so many converts in the south, was often discussed among the warriors, as well as among the women of the house. A man called the holy Ansgarius was preaching it, no farther away than Hedeby near Slien. Even Helga had heard about Christ, who for love of humanity gave up his life. But it had gone in one ear and out the other. The word "love" did not seem to have any meaning to her, except at night when, in the wretched shape of a frog, she sat silently in a tiny locked room. But her foster mother had been deeply moved when she listened to the legends told about this strange man who was the Son of God.

The Vikings, who had been abroad, described the great temples built of costly stones for this God whose message was love. Once they had brought back with them two big vessels made of gold; they were richly decorated and had smelled of strange spices. They were censers, which the Christian priests swung in front of their altars, where blood never flowed, although bread and wine were changed into the blood of Him who had sacrificed Himself for the sake of generations yet unborn.

Down into the deep stone cellar of the house the young Christian was carried. His hands and feet were bound. He was handsome. "As handsome as the God Balder," the chieftain's wife claimed.

His plight did not move Helga. She suggested that his legs should be pierced, a rope pulled through them and tied to the tail of a bull. "Then let the dogs loose, and the bull will run as fast it can across the meadows toward the heath, dragging him behind it. That would be an amusing sight and it would be fun to follow on horseback!" she suggested.

Such a horrible death the Vikings would not make him suffer, but because he had offended the gods, he would be offered to them. In the little copse where the stone altar to Odin stood, he was to be killed; and this would be the first time a human being had been sacrificed there.

Young Helga begged to have the privilege of spraying the warm blood on the statues to the gods. She sharpened her knife and when a dog—of which there were so many around the house—ran by her she stuck her knife into it and said with a laugh, "That was to test it."

With horror her mother looked at the evil girl. When night came, and Helga's body and soul changed, then she spoke to her of her sorrow and misery. The ugly frog with the troll-like body stood in front of her and looked up at her with sad eyes and seemed to understand what she was saying.

"Never, even to my husband, have I admitted how doubly you have made me suffer," said the Viking chieftain's wife. "I have more pity for you than I even knew I had. Great is a mother's love; but you, you have never felt love for anything. Your heart is made from the black cold mud of the bog! Why did you ever come to my house!"

The pathetic creature shook, it was as if the words had touched the invisible cord that connects soul and body; great tears formed in its eyes.

"But dark times will come for you," her foster mother continued, "and they will be hard for me too. Better would it have been if you had been set out as a babe on the heath and the cold night air had lulled you to sleep." The woman cried bitterly, then she rose and walked to her bed, which stood on the other side of the leather curtain that divided the room. She was angry and in despair.

The miserable frog sat forlorn in its corner. Every once in a while a sound like a stifled sigh was heard; full of pain was this muffled cry that came from the heart of the poor creature. She seemed to be listening as if she were waiting for someone; then she waddled over to the door and with great difficulty she removed the bar that locked it. Her webbed hand grabbed the tallow lamp, then she drew the iron bar that closed the trap door that led to the cellar. Noiselessly she descended the stairs. In a corner of the underground room she found the helpless prisoner sleeping. She touched him with her cold and slimy hand. He awoke and, seeing the horrible creature in front of him, he shivered with fright, for he thought that she was an evil spirit. The frog took a knife and cut the ropes that bound the man, then she waved her hand to make him understand that he was to follow her.

He mumbled all the holy names that he could remember and crossed himself, but still the creature in front of him stood unchanged. Then he quoted a line from the psalms: " 'Blessed is he that considereth the poor, the Lord will deliver him in time of trouble.' . . . Who are you? Why have you, who are so filled with mercy, the shape of an animal?"

The frog beckoned and led the priest through a corridor out into the stable. She pointed to a horse; he led it outside and swung himself onto its back. With surprising agility, the big frog mounted the animal too; she sat in front of the priest and held onto the horse's mane. The priest understood that his strange companion wanted to guide him, and followed the directions that the frog indicated by a nod or a movement with its webbed hands. Soon they were out on the heath, far away from the Vikings' hall.

The priest felt that the grace and mercy of Our Lord manifested themselves through the strange creature who had saved him. He prayed and sang a hymn. The frog trembled. Was it the prayer that touched the monster's soul? Or did she shiver because it soon would be morning? What did she feel? Suddenly the frog straightened itself and grabbed the bridle to stop the horse; she wanted to dismount. But the priest would not let go of his strange companion. He held onto it while he sang another hymn, hoping that this might break the magic spell that the poor creature so obviously was suffering under.

The horse galloped on. The horizon turned pink, and soon the first ray of the sun broke through the low clouds of morning. With it came the transformation of soul and body: the frog with the sad eyes became the beautiful girl with the evil heart. The priest was horrified when he realized that he held not a giant frog but a beautiful girl in his arms. He jumped down from the horse; he was convinced that the powers of evil were playing some terrible trick upon him. Helga dismounted as quickly as he had and, drawing the knife that hung from her belt, she attacked the shocked and confused young priest.

"Let the blade of my knife reach you," she screamed. "Let it draw blood! You look pale, slave! Beardless fool!"

The two of them wrestled, but it was as if unseen powers gave the young priest strength. The roots of an old tree that grew on the bank of the tiny stream helped him, for Helga's feet got caught in one of them and she fell. The priest dipped his hand in the clear water and, spraying it on her forehead and chest, he bade the unclean spirit leave her and baptized her in the name of Our Lord Jesus Christ. But the water of baptism only has strength when those it falls upon have faith.

Yet had she not the faith herself, it was that very attribute in the young priest that gave him power over her. His strength fascinated her, and she let her arms fall to her sides and stopped fighting with him. To her he seemed a mighty magician: pale and amazed, she looked at this man who knew so many enchantments and charms. To her, his prayers and psalms sounded like magic and the sign of the Cross looked like witchcraft. Had the young man swung a knife or a sharp ax in front of her face, she would not have blinked; but, when he drew with his finger the sign of the Cross on her forehead, she shuddered and closed her eyes. There she sat like a tame bird, with her head bowed.

He spoke to her gently about that deed of love she had performed herself when, in her frog shape, she had come and cut the ropes that held him and led him back to freedom and to life. She was still bound by bands far stronger than those a knife could cut. But also she could gain her freedom and learn to love the eternal light of God. He would take her to Hedeby, the town where the holy Ansgarius lived and worked. He would be able to break the spell.

Although she was willing to ride in front of him, he would not allow her to. "You must sit behind me on the horse, for your magic beauty comes from the Evil One, I fear it!" said the young priest, paused and then added: "But the victory was mine, in Christ!"

He fell on his knees and prayed most piously. The whole forest became a holy church; the birds sang as if they belonged to the congregation, and the wild mint smelled so fragrantly that one could believe it was trying its best to pretend that it was incense. The young priest said aloud the words from the Gospel: " 'To give light to them that sit in the darkness and in the shadow of death, to guide our feet into the way of peace.' "

Then he preached about the nature of God and His love for all; and while he spoke the horse stood still as if it, too, were listening.

Patiently, Helga let the young priest help her up on the animal's back and there she sat like a sleepwalker. The young man tied two twigs together in the form of a cross and, holding the sign before him, they rode deeper and deeper into the forest. The trees grew close together, the road became narrower and narrower; soon it was hardly a path. Sharp brambles grew everywhere and scratched the travelers as they forced their way through them. They followed a stream that soon became a swamp and they had difficulty finding their way around it.

The young priest talked while they rode. His words were not without power, for his faith in the mild God of love, Whom he followed, was great, and he was earnest in his wish to save this young girl's soul. Drops of water will hollow out the hardest stone and the surf of the ocean will wear down the sharpest reefs. Now the dew of God's grace was wearing down the hardness in Helga's soul. She did not know it, any more than the seed in the earth knows that the warm sun and the rain are bringing forth its green sprouts and its flower.

As the mother's lullaby enters the baby's mind and the child can repeat the sounds without understanding their meaning, so did the young priest's words enter Helga's soul.

The forest gave way to open country but not for long; the green woods soon closed around them again. Just before sunset they met a band of robbers.

"Where have you stolen that beautiful maid!" one of them cried as he grabbed the bridle, while the others forced the riders down from their horse.

They were many and the priest had no other weapon than the knife he had taken from Helga. He defended himself well with it; one of the robbers flung an ax at him but he sprang aside and the ax made a deep wound in the neck of the horse. The blood spouted out of the gash and the animal fell to the ground. Then Helga, who had seemed to be in a trance, suddenly awoke and threw herself upon the dying beast. The young priest stood in front of her to protect her, but one of the robbers swung his heavy iron hammer and hit the young man's head so hard that his skull was split. Blood and brain spattered all around him as he fell to the ground, dead.

The robbers grabbed Helga's white arms, but just at that moment the sun set; the last ray of its light disappeared and she changed into an ugly frog. A whitish-green mouth covered her whole face, her arms became thin and slimy, her fine hands became broad with webs between the fingers. The robbers let go of her in horror; there she stood as an ugly monster in their midst. True to her frog nature, she jumped high above the robbers' heads and disappeared in the greenery. The robbers thought that what they had seen was the secret magic of the evil demigod Loke, and they hurried away.

The full moon had risen in the sky when Helga in her pitiful frog shape climbed out of the thicket. She stopped by the bodies of the priest and the dead horse and looked down at them with eyes in which there almost were tears. She made the same sobbing sound a child makes just before starting to cry, and threw herself down over one and then the other of the still bodies. She carried water from a nearby stream and sprayed it on them in the hope of reviving them. But dead they were and dead they would remain. The thought that the wild animals of the woods would eat them was too horrible to bear. She began to dig in the earth, but she had no spade, only a stick: a thick branch of a tree. The webs between her fingers burst and bled.

Soon she realized that she would never be able to dig a hole deep enough. She washed the blood from the dead priest's face and covered it with fresh leaves; then she took the biggest branches she could find and piled them over the bodies of the man and the horse. She knew that even this would not keep the wolves or foxes away, and therefore she looked for the biggest stones that she could carry, and placed them on top of the branches. When the mound was finished she stuffed moss between the stones, and only then did she believe that the grave would be undisturbed.

It had taken her the whole night to finish her work. Now the sun rose, and in its first rays Helga stood as beautiful as ever, but her fine hands were bleeding and for the first time tears ran down her blushing, youthful cheeks.

Now the two natures within her fought. She trembled as if she had had a fever. She looked about with fear and wonder in her eyes. She appeared like a person that had just awakened from a nightmare. She rushed over to a birch tree and held onto it to support herself; then suddenly she climbed up the tree agilely as a squirrel. There in the top of the tree she remained all day sitting perfectly motionless.

All around her reigned the stillness of the forest—thus it is often described, although if one listens carefully and looks closely enough, nature is never still. Two butterflies flew in circles around each other: were they fighting or playing? At the foot of the tree in which the frightened Helga sat were some anthills, and hundreds of tiny creatures moved unceasingly in and out of their homes. In the air danced clouds of little flies and mosquitoes, and big dragonflies flew about on their golden wings. Earthworms crawled out of the wet ground, and moles emptied the earth from their burrows, making little hills. But no one saw little Helga or paid any attention to her, except for a couple of magpies. They landed on the branch on which Helga was sitting. She did not move and the birds, as filled with curiosity as only magpies can be, hopped a little closer to her. The girl blinked and that was enough to frighten the birds. They flew away no wiser than they had come.

When the sun was near setting, Helga felt herself beginning to transform and she slid down the trunk of the tree. When the sun disappeared beneath the horizon, she stood as an ugly frog once more, her webbed hands still torn from the work of the night before. But her eyes had changed, they were not a frog's but the lovely eyes of a young girl, the mirror of a human soul.

Near the grave lay the cross that the young priest had made, the last work of his own hands. Helga picked it up and planted it among the stones that covered the dead priest and the horse. The act brought back the memory of the day before, and she burst into tears. In grief, she decided to make a border of crosses around the graves to decorate them. As she drew the crosses the webs between her fingers fell off: like a torn glove, they lay in the dust. She walked down to the stream and washed; with wonder she looked at her fine white hands. She made the sign of the Cross in the air in the direction of the grave. Her broad frog mouth quivered; her tongue tried to form a word, and that name she had heard so often on that ride through the forest came from her lips. Clearly and distinctly she spoke: "Jesus Christ."

The frog skin fell from her body and there she stood in all her youthful, girlish beauty. But her head was bent; she was tired and she lay down on the moss by the stream and slept.

Toward midnight she awoke. In front of her stood the dead horse; little flames played in the wound on its neck and its eyes glowed. Close by the horse stood the young priest. "More beautiful than Balder," would the Viking woman have said, if she had seen him. Like the horse, he was strangely luminous.

He looked at Helga with eyes so sad and serious and yet so gentle, she felt that she was being judged justly and that there was no corner of her heart that he did not see. With that sharpness of memory that the souls will have on the Day of Judgment, Helga remembered her life. Every kindness performed toward her, every loving word spoken to her, became terribly real. She understood that it was love that had fought and been victorious in the struggle within her, between her soul and the mire from the bog. She realized that she had followed a will greater than her own and that she herself had not been the maker of her own fate. She had been guided and led. She bent her head humbly in front of Him who can see into the most secret compartment of our hearts. And in that moment she felt a flame that purified her, the flame of the Holy Ghost.

"You, daughter of the bog," said the ghost of the priest, "of earth were you made and from the earth you shall be resurrected. The sunbeam within you shall return to its Maker, not to the sun but to God. No soul is doomed, but earthly life can be long and the flight into eternity can seem endless. I come from the land of the dead, where the radiant mountains are, and where all perfection lives. You, too, shall one day travel through the dark valleys to that land. I cannot lead you to Hedeby and a Christian baptism now, for you have a duty to perform back in the bog. You must return and break the shield of water that covers and hides the living root from which you grew."

He lifted her up on the horse and gave her a golden censer to hold like the ones she had seen in the Vikings' hall. A strong, sweet fragrance came from it. The wound in the young priest's head shone like a jewel as he picked up the cross and, holding it high, mounted the horse. The horse galloped but not along the paths—no, they flew through the air, high above the forest. Far down below them, Helga could see the mounds where Viking chiefs had been buried mounted on their horses. Now they rose, these giant specters of man and horse, and stood on top of their grave-hills. In the moonlight the golden bands around their foreheads shone, while their capes fluttered in the wind. The monstrous lind-worm that guards buried treasure stuck its ugly head out of its cave and looked about. Tiny dwarfs ran back and forth carrying lanterns; they looked like sparks from the ashes of burned paper.

Above the heath, the forest, the lakes, and streams they flew, toward the great bog. They circled it and the priest held high the cross, and in the moonlight the two sticks looked like gold. He chanted the mass, and when he sang a hymn, Helga sang too, like a child copying her mother. She swung the censer, and the fragrance of incense spread across the bog and became so strong that the reeds in the swamp shot forth blossoms, and from the muddy depth water lilies sprouted and grew. Everything alive responded, and the dark waters of the bog became covered by a colorful tapestry of water lilies. In the center of it lay a sleeping woman, young and beautiful. Helga thought that she was seeing her own reflection in the water; but it was the bog king's wife, the princess from Egypt.

The dead priest ordered that the sleeping woman be lifted up on the horse, but the burden was too great, the body of the horse was now like a shroud in the wind. The priest made the sign of the Cross and the phantom horse gained strength enough to carry all three of them onto the shore.

Just as they reached solid ground the cock crowed. The priest and the horse became a mist that was borne away by the wind. Helga and her mother stood facing each other, alone.

"Is this my own image I see, reflected in the deep waters?" asked the mother.

"Is that myself I see mirrored in the lake's shiny shield?" exclaimed the daughter.

The two drew near to each other and embraced. The mother understood who it was she held in her arms. "My daughter, the flower of my heart! The lotus of the deep waters," she said, and cried. Her tears were like a baptism of love for Helga.

"In a swanskin I came here and I shed it by the dark lake," the mother explained. "Then I sank down into the deep mire of the bog and it closed around me like a dark wall. Something drew me down, ever downward. I felt a pressure on my eyes, as if sleep were closing them. And I did sleep, I dreamed. I was back in Egypt in the stone chamber of the pyramid. In front of me stood the trunk of the alder tree that had frightened me so, when I stood on the shores of this lake. I looked closely at the cracks and clefts in its bark, and they gained color and became the hieroglyphic writing on a casket such as mummies are laid in. As I stared at it, it opened and out stepped the ancient king: a mummy, black as pitch, glittering like the black slugs that creep in the forest. Whether it was the bog king or the mummy from the pyramids, I did not know. He flung his arms around me, and I felt that now I would die. But life did not desert me. I felt a warmth in my chest. The bog king was gone and a little bird was singing and flapping its wings. It flew from my chest up toward the dark ceiling: a long green string connected the bird to me. I heard its

song and understood its message: 'Freedom! Sunshine!' A longing for
the father of things! I thought of my own father, far away in the sun-
drenched land of Egypt. I loosened the string and freed the bird, let it
fly home to my father. A deep, heavy sleep came over me and I
dreamed no more, until a fragrance and chanting voices woke me and
drew me up from the dark."

The green string from the mother's heart to the bird's wing, where
was it now? Thrown away among other useless things. Only the stork
had seen it. It was the green stalk that had shot up through the water
to form the flower that had made a cradle for the child who now
stood beside her mother.

While they stood there embracing, the stork saw them and flew in
circles above them. Then he flew back to the nest to get the
swanskins he had kept there so faithfully. He threw one to each of the
women. The feathery skins covered them, and they rose from the
ground as two white swans.

"Now we can talk together," said the stork, flying beside them.
"True, we have not the same shaped bills, but we will understand
each other. It was lucky that you came this morning. If you had
waited a day longer we would have been gone. My wife and I and the
young ones will be going south today. . . . Yes, look at me, I am an
old friend of yours from the Nile. So is my wife. Her heart is softer
than her bill; she was always of the opinion that the princess would
take care of herself. My children and I have carried the swanskins up
here. . . . Oh, it makes me happy to see you! It is so lucky that we
are still here. As soon as the sun is high in the sky we will be gone.
We are not flying alone, there is a whole party of storks going. We
will fly ahead and you can follow, then you won't lose your way; but
don't worry, my youngsters and I will keep an eye on you."

"The lotus flower that I was to bring will fly beside me," said the
Egyptian princess. "The flower of my heart I bring and the riddle has
been solved. Homeward! Homeward!"

But Helga insisted that she could not leave before she had bade
good-by to her foster mother, the Viking chieftain's wife. She remembered every kind word, every tear her foster mother had shed because
of her; and at that moment she loved her more than she loved her
real mother.

"Yes," said the stork. "Let us fly to the Vikings' hall. There my
wife and children are waiting. They will open their eyes wide and

clatter their bills when they see you. Not that my wife is one for idle clatter; she talks in short sentences, but she means every word she says. I will make a clatter so they know we are coming."

And the stork clattered loudly with his long bill, and away they flew to the Viking hall.

There everybody was still asleep. Helga's foster mother had lain awake until late, worrying about what could have happened to her daughter who had disappeared together with the Christian priest three days before. She realized that Helga must have helped him to escape, for it was her horse that was missing in the stable. What strange powers had been the cause of this? The Viking woman had pondered long about it. She had heard that Christ had performed miracles for those who followed him. These thoughts stayed with her in her sleep and became real in her dreams. She dreamed that she was awake, sitting up in her bed; outside the world was dark and a horrible storm was brewing. Now the winds gathered, she could hear the surf breaking on the beaches; the great Midgard-worm which encircles the earth was racked by convulsions. The days of the old gods were over, their night had come: Ragnarok, the last battle of the gods, was being fought. The end of the world was near; now the gods would die. The horns blew, and over the rainbow rode the gods, clad in armor, on their way to fight their last battle. In front of them flew the valkyries and behind them walked the Viking chiefs, whom fame had brought to Odin's hall. The northern lights glittered as they illuminated the sky and yet darkness was victorious. It was a fearful sight.

Close to the frightened woman sat little Helga in her frog shape; she also seemed filled with fear, she drew closer to her foster mother. And the Viking woman dreamed that she took the frog on her lap and held it close; in spite of its horrible shape she pressed it with love to her heart. Outside the hall the sound of a furious battle could be heard. The arrows flew like hailstones. The time had come when the earth and the heavens would burst and the stars fall from the sky. All would be destroyed in the great fire, but from its ashes a new earth and heaven would rise. She knew it would come, and that grain would grow where now the waves of the salt sea rolled over the desolate sand. Balder, the gentle loving God, would be released from the Kingdom of the Shadows and rise into the heavens. He came! In her dream the Viking woman saw him, and she recognized him. Balder the God was the Christian priest.

"Jesus Christ!" she cried to him, and kissed the frog-child on her lap. At that moment the frog disappeared and Helga stood before her, as beautiful as ever; but kind and gentle as she had never been before. Helga kissed the hands of her foster mother and thanked her for all the love and care that she had given her. She blessed her for the thoughts that she had sown in her heart, which now bore fruit. The Viking woman said aloud, once more, the name of the "New God," as people called him in the north: "Jesus Christ." Helga became a great swan. She spread out her wings and flew away and the beat of her wings woke the sleeping woman.

As she opened her eyes, she heard still the sound of the feathered blows from her dream. She knew that now was the time that the storks flew south. She rose from her bed and walked outside to see them fly and wish them farewell. The air was filled with storks, flying in great circles; but in the yard by the well, where Helga had frightened her so often with her wild tricks, stood two swans. They looked at her and the dream was still real within her; she recalled how she had seen Helga change into a swan. Then she remembered the face of the young priest as she had seen it in her dream, and she felt a sudden joy that she could not explain.

The swans flapped their big wings and bent their slender necks as if they were greeting her. The Viking woman spread out her arms toward them and smiled, though tears ran from her eyes.

At that moment the last of the storks flew up. The whole sky resounded with the noise of their wings beating and the clatter of their bills.

"We won't wait for the swans," declared the mother stork. "If they want to come along it has to be now. We can't wait any longer. I think it is very cozy to fly together in a family. The way the finches fly, males and females separately, is, in my eyes, indecent! And I don't like the way the swans flap their wings. What formation do they fly in?"

"Everyone flies in his own manner," said her husband patiently. "The swans fly in a slanted line, the cranes in a triangle, and the plover in a winding line, like a snake."

"Don't mention the word 'snake' while we are in the air," admonished his wife. "It will awaken desires in the young ones that can't be satisfied!"

"Are those the high mountains that I have heard about?" asked Helga, who was flying in her swanskin.

"They are thunder clouds drifting by underneath us," answered the mother.

"What are those tall white clouds ahead?" Helga asked a little while later.

"They are the tops of the great mountains where the snow never melts," said her mother; and they flew over the Alps and across the blue Mediterranean.

"Africa, Egypt!" Jubilantly the daughter of the Nile said the words as she, in the feathered dress of a swan, saw below her the yellow-white sandy coast of her home. The storks, too, flew faster when they saw it.

"I can smell the mud of the Nile and the frogs!" said the mother stork to her young ones who were seeing Egypt for the first time. "It tickles my stomach! Oh! You'll see how good everything is going to taste! You will meet the marabou, cranes, and the ibis. They all belong to our family, but they are not nearly as handsome or beautiful as we are. They believe that they are something, especially the ibis, who has been spoiled by the Egyptians. They make a mummy out of him when he dies, and stuff him full of spices, so he won't smell. I prefer stuffing myself with live frogs, and so will you, my children. Better a full stomach while one is alive than a lot of glory after one is dead. That is my opinion and I am always right!"

"Now the stork has come," the servants said in the palace by the Nile.

On a couch covered by leopard skins their royal master lay, neither dead nor alive, waiting, hoping for the lotus flower from the north that would bring his health back to him. Into the great hall flew two white swans; they had come with the storks. They cast off their shiny feathers and there stood instead two beautiful women, as alike as two drops of dew. They bent over the withered shape of the old man on the couch, and as Helga touched her grandfather, blood flowed to his cheeks, his eyes gained luster again, and his lifeless limbs moved. He stood up, well and rejuvenated, and embraced his daughter and his grandchild, like a man happily greeting the dawn after a long dark dream.

There was great joy in the palace and in the storks' nest, too; but in the latter it was mostly over the food: the place was swarming with frogs. While the learned and wise men quickly wrote down the story of the two princesses and the flower of health, which was such a blessing for the royal house and the whole country, the two storks told the story in their own way to their family and friends. But not before everyone had eaten their fill; after all, that was more important than listening to stories.

"Now you must become something," whispered the mother stork to her husband. "You deserve a reward!"

"What should I become?" said her husband. "And what have I really done? It was nothing!"

"You have done more than anyone else. Without you and our youngsters, the princesses would never have seen Egypt again. I am sure you will become something! I think they will give you a doctor's degree, and our children will inherit it, as will their children in turn. You already look like a doctor of philosophy—in my eyes!"

The learned and wise men developed the fundamental idea and moral that ran through the story: "Love breeds life!" It could be explained in several ways: "The warm sunlight was the Egyptian princess and she entered the darkness of the bog; in the meeting between light and dark—the latter being the bog king—the flower sprang . . ."

"I can't remember it word for word," said the father stork, who had been listening from the top of the roof to the learned and wise men discuss the matter, and now was telling about it at home in his nest. "Everything that was said was very complicated and so intelligent that they all were decorated immediately by the king. Even the cook got a medal, but I think that was because of the soup."

"And what did you get?" asked his wife. "Don't tell me they have forgotten the most important person of all, namely, you? The learned ones have only clattered their bills. But maybe they will remember you later?"

When night fell and the peace of sleep reigned over the house there was one who was still awake. It was not the stork who stood guard on one leg at his nest, for he was sleeping soundly. No, it was Helga who was not asleep; she was standing on the balcony of her room, looking up at the stars. They seemed so much clearer and brighter here than in the north, and yet they were the same. She thought about her foster mother, the Viking woman, who lived near the great bog. She remembered her sweet, gentle eyes and the tears they had shed over the wretched frog-child who had now become a princess and was standing in the warm night by the waters of the Nile and dreaming. She thought about how full of love that woman's heart must have been, for her to be able to feel affection for a creature so miserable that when she wore a human shape she was an evil beast, and when she became an animal was ugly to look at and repulsive to touch. A bright star reminded her of how the wound in the dead priest's head had glittered when they rode through the night. She thought of the words he had spoken on their first ride together, how he had talked of the origin of love and its greatest expression, which is the love of all living things.

So much had been given her, so much had she won, so much had she accomplished. Helga's thoughts dwelled both day and night upon this great sum of her good fortune. She was like a child who quickly turns from the giver to the gift. She felt certain that even greater happiness would come, gifts even more splendid than the ones she had already received. Was she not fortune's child for whom miracles had been performed? One day these feelings of exuberance became so overwhelming that she forgot the giver completely. The arrogance of youth possessed her, and her eyes sparkled with a wild courage. Suddenly she heard a great noise from the courtyard below her. She saw two ostriches running in circles around each other. She had never seen this animal before, this great bird, so plump and heavy with its short wings that looked as though they had been clipped. She wondered whether some misfortune might have happened to it and asked someone why it looked like that. And she heard, for the first time, the old Egyptian legend about the ostrich.

Once he had been a very beautiful bird with big strong wings. One evening the other big birds of the forest had said to him: "Brother, should we not tomorrow—if God wills—fly down to the river to bathe and drink?"

And the ostrich had answered, "Yes, I will it!"

Next morning they flew high up in the sky toward the sun, which is the eye of God. Higher and higher they went. The ostrich flew faster and higher than all the others. Arrogantly he flew toward the light, trusting his own strength and not the Superior Being who had given it to him. He would not say "if God wills." The chastising angel drew the veil from the fiery sun and the hot flames burned the wings of the ostrich. The wretched bird sank down to the earth. Never again would his wings carry him high up in the air. He and his kind were condemned to stay forever on the ground. Frightened, the ostrich runs in meaningless circles to remind us human beings to say, as we set out on a journey: "If God wills."

Helga bent her head thoughtfully; then she looked down at the running bird. She sensed its fear and foolish joy in seeing its own shadow cast on the sunlit white wall. In her mind—in her soul—grave, serious thoughts struck root. A life so rich, so happy, had been won, what would the future bring? The best—"if God wills."

In the early spring, when the storks got ready to fly north, Helga took a golden ring and scratched her name in it. She beckoned to the stork and he came. She asked the stork to take it to her foster mother, that the Viking woman might know that the child she had cared for was still alive and well, and had not forgotten her.

"It is uncomfortable," said the stork who was wearing the ring around his neck, "but gold and honor one does not throw in the ditch. Now they will know, up there in the north, that the stork brings good luck."

"You lay gold and I lay eggs," said his wife, "but see if we get any thanks for it. I think it is humiliating!"

"But one has one's good conscience, my dear!" answered her husband.

"You can't hang that around your neck," replied his wife. "And no one has ever grown fat on it."

And away they flew!

The little nightingale that sang among the tamarisk bushes would soon be leaving for the north too. Near the wild bog, Helga had often heard it sing. She would send a message with it; the language of the birds she knew because she had once flown in a swanskin. She had kept in practice by talking to the storks and the swallows. The nightingale would surely understand her. She asked him to fly to the place in the forest in Jutland where the grave of branches and stones was, and there to sing a song and ask the other little birds to do the same.

And the nightingale flew; and so did time!

At harvest the eagle, from the top of a pyramid, saw a caravan of richly loaded camels traveling across the desert. Magnificently clad soldiers, on white Arabian horses, with pink soft muzzles and nostrils, and long manes and tails, guarded it. Important guests were coming. A royal prince from Arabia, who was as handsome as princes ought to be, was making his way to the royal palace.

The stork nests were empty, for the owners had not returned yet, but they were expected. And by chance and good fortune, they did arrive later that day. It was a day of festivity and joy. A wedding was to take place, and Helga was the bride. Clad in silk and jewels, she sat at the head of the table with her bridegroom, the young prince of Arabia. On one side of them sat Helga's mother, and on the other her grandfather.

Helga was not looking at her bridegroom's brown handsome face, nor did she notice his passionate glances. She was looking through the big window out at the night sky where the bright stars sparkled in the heavens.

Suddenly the air was filled with the sound of the beating of storks' wings. Although the old stork couple were tired from their long flight and certainly deserved to rest, they flew first to the balcony of Helga's room and perched there on the railing. They had already heard about the feast and knew in whose honor it was being held. They had also been told, as soon as they entered the country, that they had been depicted in a mural that told the story of Helga's life.

"That was very thoughtful of them," said the male stork.

"I don't think it was so much," disagreed his wife. "They could hardly have done less."

Helga rose from the table and went to her balcony. She knew the storks would be there. Affectionately, she stroked their backs, and the old storks bent their necks. Their young children, who had come with them, felt themselves greatly honored.

Helga looked again up at the clear, star-filled sky. She saw a figure floating near her. It was the dead young priest. He had also wanted to see her on this her wedding day; he had come from paradise.

"The splendor, the glory, is far greater than anything found on this earth," he said.

Helga pleaded so sweetly and so fervently—as she never before had begged for anything—to be allowed to look into paradise—if only for a moment, to see the face of God.

The young priest lifted her up into the glory which cannot be described, to see that which cannot be imagined. And she herself felt transformed so that the splendor which she saw before her was also within her.

"Now we must return," said the young priest.

"Just one more glance," begged Helga. "One short minute more."

"We must return to the earth, all the guests are leaving," he warned.

"One last glance, the very last!"

Helga was back on the balcony, but all the lights had been put out. The great hall was empty and the storks were gone. Where was her bridegroom? In three short minutes, everything had disappeared.

Frightened, Helga walked through the great hall into the smaller room next to it. There she found some strange foreign soldiers sleeping. She opened another door, which should have led to her own room, but now it led out into the garden. The sun was just rising. Three minutes and a whole night was gone!

She saw some storks and called to them in their own language. A male stork looked at her and came nearer.

"You speak our language," he said, "but who are you and where do you come from?"

"It is me, it is Helga! Don't you know me? We spoke together three minutes ago up on the balcony."

"You are mistaken," said the stork. "It must have been something you dreamed."

"No! No!" protested Helga, and reminded him of the Viking hall near the great bog, and how he had brought her the swanskins.

The stork blinked with its eyes. "That is an old, old story. It happened so long ago that my great-great-great-grandmother was alive then. It is true that such a princess once lived here in Egypt, but she disappeared on her wedding night and never returned. It happened hundreds of years ago. You can read the story on the monument in the garden. There are pictures of swans and storks, and on top stands a statue of the princess herself." Finally Helga understood what had happened and she fell on her knees.

The sun was ascending in the sky and its strong rays fell on the kneeling girl; and just as the rays of the sun in time past had changed the ugly frog into the beautiful princess, so did they now change Helga into one single beautiful ray of light, that shot upward to God.

Her body disappeared, became dust; and where she had knelt lay a withered lotus flower.

"That was a new ending to an old story," said the male stork. "I hadn't expected it, but I rather liked it."

"I wonder what the children will think of it?" asked his wife.

"Yes, that is most important," agreed her husband.

53

The Girl Who Stepped on Bread

I SUPPOSE you have heard about the girl who stepped on the bread in order not to get her shoes dirty, and how badly she fared. The story has been both written down and printed.

She was a poor child, but proud and arrogant; she had what is commonly called a bad character. When she was very little it had given her pleasure to tear the wings off flies, so they forever after would have to crawl. If she caught a dung beetle, she would stick a pin through its body; then place a tiny piece of paper where the poor creature's legs could grab hold of it; and watch the insect twist and turn the paper, round and round, in the vain hope that, with its help, it could pull itself free of the pin.

"Look, the dung beetle is reading," little Inger—that was her name —would scream and laugh. "Look, it is turning over the page."

She did not improve as she grew up; in fact, she became worse. She was pretty, and that was probably her misfortune; otherwise, the world would have treated her rougher.

"A strong brine is needed to scrub that head," her own mother said about her. "You stepped on my apron when you were small, I am afraid you will step on my heart when you grow older."

And she did!

A job was found for her as a maid in a house out in the country. The family she worked for was very distinguished and wealthy. Both her master and mistress treated her kindly, more as if she were their daughter than their servant. Pretty she was and prettily was she dressed, and prouder and prouder she became.

After she had been in service for a year her mistress said to her, "You should go and visit your parents, little Inger."

She went, but it was because she wanted to show off her fine dresses. When she came to the entrance of her village, near the little pond where the young men and girls were gossiping, she saw her mother sitting on a stone. The woman was resting, for she had been in the forest gathering wood, and a whole bundle of faggots lay beside her.

Inger was ashamed that she—who was so finely dressed—should have a mother who wore rags and had to collect sticks for her fire. The girl turned around and walked away, with irritation but no regret.

Half a year passed and her mistress said again, "You should go home for the day and visit your old parents. Here is a big loaf of white bread you can take along. I am sure they will be very happy to see you."

Inger dressed in her very best clothes and put on her new shoes. She lifted her skirt a little as she walked and was very careful where she trod, so that she would not dirty or spoil her finery. That one must not hold against her; but when the path became muddy, and finally a big puddle blocked her way, she threw the bread into it rather than get her shoes wet. As she stepped on the bread, it sank deeper and deeper into the mud, carrying her with it, until she disappeared. At last, all that could be seen were a few dark bubbles on the surface of the puddle.

This is the manner in which the story is most often told. But what happened to the girl? Where did she disappear to? She came down to the bog witch! The bog witch is an aunt of the elves, on their father's side. The elves everyone knows. Poems have been written about them and they have been painted, too. But about the bog witch most people don't know very much.

When the mist lies over the swamps and bogs, one says, "Look, the bog witch is brewing!" It was into this very brewery that Inger sank, and that is not a place where it is pleasant to stay. A cesspool is a splendidly light and airy room in comparison to the bog witch's brewery. The smell that comes from every one of the vats is so horrible that a human being would faint if he got even a whiff of it. The vats stand so close together that there is hardly room to walk between them, and if you do find a little space to squeeze through, then it is all filled with toads and slimy snakes. This is the place that Inger came to. The snakes and toads felt so cold against her body that she shivered and shook. But not for long. Inger felt her body grow stiffer and stiffer, until at last she was as rigid as a statue. The bread still stuck to her foot, there was no getting rid of it.

The bog witch was at home that day; the brewery was being inspected by the Devil's great-grandmother. She is an ancient and very venomous old lady who never wastes her time. When she leaves home, she always takes some needlework with her. That day she was embroidering lies and crocheting thoughtless words that she had picked up as they fell. Everything she does is harmful and destructive. She knows how to sew, embroider, and crochet well, that old great-grandmother!

She looked at Inger, and then took out her glasses and looked at her a second time. "That girl has talent!" she declared. "I would like to have her as a souvenir of my visit. She is worthy of a pedestal in the entrance hall of my great-grandson's palace."

The bog witch gave Inger to the Devil's great-grandmother. And that is the way she went to hell. Most people go straight down there, but if you are as talented as Inger, then you can get there via a detour.

The Devil's entrance hall was an endless corridor that made you dizzy if you looked down it. Inger was not the only one to decorate this grand hall; the place was crowded with figures all waiting for the door of mercy to open for them, and they had long to wait. Around their feet, big fat spiders spun webs that felt like fetters and were as strong as copper chains, and they would last at least a thousand years. Every one of these immovable statues had a soul within it that was as restless as its body was rigid and stiff. The miser knew that he had forgotten the key to his money box in its lock and he could do nothing about it. Oh, it would take me much too long to explain and describe all the torments and tortures that they went through. Inger felt how horrible it was to stand there as a statue, her foot locked to the bread.

"That is what one gets for trying to keep one's feet clean," she said to herself. "Look how they are all staring at me!" That was true, they were all looking at the latest arrival, and their evil desires were mirrored in their eyes and spoken without sound by their horrible lips. It was a monstrous sight!

"I, at least, am a pleasure to look at," thought little Inger. "I have a pretty face and pretty clothes on." She moved her eyes; her neck was too stiff to turn. Goodness me, how dirty she was! She had forgotten all the filth and slime she had been through in the bog witch's brewery. All her clothes were so covered with mire that she looked as if she were dressed in mud. A snake had got into her hair and hung down her neck. And from the folds of her dress big toads looked up at her and barked like Pekinese dogs. It was all very unpleasant. But she comforted herself with the thought that the others didn't look any better than she did.

But far worse than all this was the terrible hunger she felt. She couldn't bend down and break off a piece of the bread she was stepping on. Her back was stiff and her arms and legs were stiff, her whole body was like a stone statue; only her eyes could move. They could turn all the way around, so that she looked inside herself and that, too, was an unpleasant sight. Then the flies came; they climbed all over her face, stepped back and forth across her eyes. She blinked to scare them away, but they couldn't fly; their wings had been torn off. That was painful too, but the hunger was worse. Inger felt as if her stomach had eaten itself. She became more and more empty inside, horribly empty.

"If this is going to last long, then I won't endure it!" she said to herself. But it didn't stop, it kept on; and she had to endure it.

A tear fell on her head, rolled down her face and chest, and landed on the bread; and many more tears followed. Who was weeping because of little Inger? She had a mother up on earth, it was she who was weeping. Those tears that mothers shed in sorrow over their bad children always reach the children, but they do not help them, they only make their pain and misery greater. Oh, that terrible hunger did not cease. If only she could reach the bread she was stepping on. She felt as if everything inside her had eaten itself up, and she was a hollow shell in which echoed everything that was said about her up on earth. She could hear it all, and none of it was pleasant, every word was hard and condemning. Her mother wept over her, but she also said: "Pride goes before a fall! That was your misfortune, Inger! How you have grieved your poor mother!"

Everyone up on earth—her mother, too—knew about the sin she had committed, how she had stepped on the bread and disappeared into the mire. A shepherd had seen it happen, and he had told everyone about it.

"You have made me so miserable, Inger!" sighed her mother. "But that is what I expected would happen."

"I wish I had never been born," thought Inger. "That would have been much better. But it doesn't help now that my mother cries."

She heard her master and mistress, who had been like parents to her, talking. "She was a sinful child," they said. "She did not appreciate God's gifts but stepped on them; it will not be easy for her to find grace."

"They should have been stricter," thought Inger, "and shaken the nonsense out of me."

She heard that a song had been made up about her, "The haughty girl who stepped on the bread to keep her pretty shoes dry." It was very popular, everyone in the country sang it.

"Imagine that, one has to have it thrown in one's face so often, and suffer so much for such a little sin," thought Inger. "The others should also be punished for their sins. Then there would be a lot to punish! Uh! How I suffer!"

And her soul became as hard as or even harder than her shell. "How can one improve in such company as there is down here?" she thought. "But I don't want to be good! Look how they stare!" And her soul was filled with hatred against all other human beings. "Now they have something to talk about up there. Oh, how I suffer!"

Every time that her story was told to some little child, Inger could hear it; and she never heard a kind word about herself, for children judge harshly. They would call her the "ungodly Inger" and say that she was disgusting, and even declare that they were glad that she was punished.

But one day, as hunger and anger were tearing at her insides, she heard her story being told to a sweet, innocent little girl, and the child burst out crying. She wept for the haughty, finery-loving Inger. "But won't she ever come up to earth again?" she asked.

And the grownup who had told her the story said, "No, she will never come up on earth again."

"But if she said she was sorry and she would never do it again?"

"But she won't say she is sorry," answered the grownup.

"I wish she would," cried the little girl. "I would give my dollhouse, if she only could come back up on earth again. I think it must be so terrible for poor Inger."

Those words did reach Inger's heart and, for a moment, relieved her suffering. For this was the first time someone had said "poor Inger" and not added something about her sin. A little innocent child had cried for her sake and begged that she should be saved. She felt strange and would have liked to cry herself, but she could not weep, and that, too, was a torment.

As the years passed she heard little from the earth above her; she was talked about less and less. Down in hell's entrance hall nothing ever changed. But one day she did hear a sigh and someone saying, "Inger! Inger! How you have made me suffer, but I thought you would." That was her mother, she was dying.

Sometimes she heard her name mentioned by her old master and mistress; but they spoke kindly, especially her mistress. "I wonder if I will ever see you again, Inger! After all, one cannot be certain where one will go."

But Inger was pretty certain that her kind old mistress would not end where she herself was.

Time passed: long and bitter years. When Inger, finally, again heard her name, she seemed to see above her, in the darkness of the endless hall, two bright stars shining; they were two kind eyes up on earth that now were closing. So many years had gone by that the little child who once had wept so bitterly because of "poor Inger" now was an old woman whom God had called up to Him. At that last moment when all her memories and thoughts of a long life passed through her mind, she remembered, too, that as a little child she had cried bitterly when she heard the story of Inger. In the moment before death, that which had happened so long ago was re-experienced so vividly by the old woman that she said aloud, "Oh, my Lord, have I not, like Inger, often stepped on Your gifts, and not even been aware that I have done it? Have I not, too, felt pride within me, and yet You have not deserted me. Do not leave me now!"

As the old woman's eyes closed, the eyes of her soul opened for all that before had been hidden. Since Inger had been in her thoughts as she died, she now could see her in all her misery. At that sight, she burst into tears just as she had done as a child; in paradise she stood weeping because of Inger. Her tears and prayers echoed in the shell of the girl who stood as a statue in the Devil's entrance hall. Inger's tortured soul was overwhelmed by this unexpected love from above: one of God's angels was crying for her. Why had this been granted her? Her tortured soul thought back upon its life on earth and remembered every deed it had done. The soul trembled and wept the tears that Inger had never shed. The girl understood that her folly had been her own; and in this moment of realization she thought, "Never can I be saved!"

No sooner had she had this thought than a light far stronger than that of a sunbeam shone from heaven down upon her. Far faster than the sun rays melt the snowman, or the snowflake disappears when it lands on a child's warm mouth, did the statue of Inger melt and vanish. Where it had stood, a little bird flew up toward the world above.

Fear-ridden and full of shame, the bird hid in the darkest place it could find, a hole in an old crumbling wall. Its little body shivered. The bird was afraid of every living thing. It could not even chirp, for it was voiceless. It sat in the dark for a long time before it dared peek out and see the glory around it—for the world is, indeed, gloriously beautiful.

It was night; the moon was sailing in the sky and the air was fresh and mild. The bird could smell the fragrance of the trees and bushes. It glanced at its own feather dress and realized how lovely it was; everything in nature had been created with loving care. The bird would have liked to be able to express her thoughts in song; gladly would she have lifted her voice as the nightingale or the cuckoo does in spring, but she couldn't. But God, who hears the silent worm's hymn of praise, heard and understood hers, as He had David's when they only existed in the poet's heart and had not yet become words and melody.

Through days and weeks these soundless songs grew within the little bird; although they could not be expressed in words or music, they could be asserted in deeds.

Autumn passed and winter came, and the blessed Christmas feast drew near. The farmers hung a sheaf of oats on a pole in the yard so that the birds of the air should not go hungry on this day of Our Saviour's birth.

When the sun rose Christmas morning, it shone on the sheaf of oats and all the twittering little birds that flew around it. At that moment the little lonesome bird that did not dare go near the others, but hid so much of the time in the little hole she had found in the old wall, uttered a single "Peep." A thought, an idea, had come to her! She flew from her hiding place, and her weak little peep was a whole song of joy. On earth she was just another sparrow but up in heaven they knew who the bird was.

The winter was hard and harsh. The lakes were covered with ice, and the animals in the forest and the birds knew lean times; it was difficult to find food. The little bird flew along the highway. In the tracks made by the sleds she sometimes found a few grains of oats. At the places where the travelers had rested, she would sometimes find little pieces of bread and crumbs. She ate very little herself but called the other starving sparrows, so that they could eat. In town, she looked for the yards where a kind hand had thrown bread and grain for the hungry birds, and when she found such a place she would eat only a few grains and give all the rest away.

Through the winter, the little bird had collected and given away so many crumbs that they weighed as much as the bread that Inger had stepped on, in order not to dirty her shoes. As the last little tiny piece of bread was found and given away, the wings of the little bird grew larger and their color changed from gray to white.

"Look! There's a sea gull flying out over the lake," said the children as they followed the flight of the white bird that dived down toward the water and then swung itself up high into the sky. The white wings glittered in the sunshine and then it was gone. "It has flown right into the sun," the children said.

54

The Pen and the Inkwell

IT was once remarked by someone who was looking at the inkwell on an author's desk: "Isn't it strange, all that can come out of an inkwell? I wonder what will come from it next? Oh, it is a wonder!"

"That it is," agreed the inkwell. "It is very hard to understand. And that has always been my opinion." The inkwell was talking to the pen and everything else that happened to be on the desk. "It is, indeed, strange and wonderful what can come out of me! Why, I would call it almost unbelievable! Sometimes I don't even know myself what will come next—what will happen when human beings dip into me. One drop of me is enough to cover half a page of paper, and what cannot be written on that! I am someone quite extraordinary. From me springs all poetry; descriptions of people who have never lived, and yet are more alive than those who walk around on two legs; the deepest feelings; the greatest wit; and the loveliest word paintings of nature. How can all that be inside me—I who do not even know nature—but nonetheless it is! All of these gallant knights on their magnificent horses and all the beautiful young girls who live in books have, in fact, been born in me. Yes, I cannot even understand it myself."

"There you spoke the truth!" said the quill pen. "You do not understand because you cannot think; if you could, you would realize that you contain merely liquid. You exist so that I can express upon paper the thoughts that are within me, so that I can write them down. It is the pen that writes! This no man doubts, and I can assure you that most human beings have a great deal more insight into poetry than an old inkwell."

"You have not had much experience yet," said the inkwell. "You are young in the service, though already half used up, I am afraid. Do you really believe that you are the poet? You are only a servant, and I have had many of them before you arrived. Both English steel pens and those who can claim geese as their family. I have known all kinds of pens. I cannot even count the number that have been in my service; and more will come, I am sure. He wears them out, the human being who does the manual labor, he who writes down what is inside me. I wonder what he will lift out of me next."

"Ink tub!" sneered the pen.

Later in the evening the poet came home. He had attended a concert where he had heard an excellent violinist play. He was still very excited about what he had heard. The musician had enticed such marvelous sounds out of his instrument. At one moment it sounded like drops of water falling from the trees, one pearly drop after another; and the next, like a storm riding through a pine forest. The poet had thought he had heard his own heart weeping, so captured had he been by the music. It was not only the strings that had sung but the whole instrument, wood and all. And all the while it had looked so easy: the bow had danced so lightly across the strings. One was almost convinced that anyone could have done it, so effortless had the performance appeared. The violin sang by itself and the bow moved by itself; the two were one. One almost forgot their master: the musician who played upon them and gave to these two dead objects a soul. But the poet had not forgotten him; he pondered over it and wrote down his thoughts.

"How absurd it would seem if the bow and the violin should be proud and haughty about their accomplishments. Yet we, human beings, often are; the poets, the artists, the scientists, and even the generals often boast in vain pride. Yet they are all but instruments that God plays upon. To Him alone belongs all honor. We have nothing to pride ourselves upon!"

Later the poet wrote a parable and called it "The Genius and His Instrument."

"Well, madam, that put you in your place," said the pen to the inkwell when the two of them again were alone. "I suppose you heard him read aloud what I had written down?"

"You wrote what I ordered you to write," retorted the inkwell. "It was especially your silly arrogance and pride that made me think of it, I am sure. But I suppose you can't even understand when you are being made fun of! That whole thing was meant for you and it came from the very depth of me. Don't you think I can recognize my own sarcasm?"

"Ink skirt!" screamed the pen.

"Scribble pin!" shouted the inkwell.

Each of them thought his own repartee the cleverer, and there is nothing so satisfying as the feeling that one has had the last word. It makes for pleasant slumber, and both the inkwell and the pen went to sleep. But the poet was not asleep; like tones from a violin, thoughts upon thoughts came to him. They fell like pearls and rode through the forest as the storm; he felt the cry of his own heart and the spark of the Eternal Master.

To Him alone belongs the honor and the glory!

55

The Dead Child

THE house was in mourning, and sorrow lived in every heart. The youngest child in the family, a four-year-old boy, had died. The parents' pride and hope, their only son. They had two daughters. One of them was to be confirmed that year; they were kind and good girls, both of them. But the child one loses is always closest to one's heart, and this child had been the youngest, and their only son. It was a time of trial. The two young sisters mourned, as young hearts do; they were especially moved by the sorrow of their parents. The father walked as if he were bent by sorrow, but their mother was completely beside herself with grief.

Night and day she had sat beside the bed of her sick child, she had lifted him in her arms, carried him, and nursed him. The child had become an inseparable part of her; and now she could not believe that he was dead and had to be placed in a coffin and hidden in a grave.

How could God take her child from her? But it had happened; and when she could no longer say that it was not so, then in her grief and distress she cried: "God does not know about it. His servants are heartless and do what pleases them. They do not listen to a mother's prayers."

Her pain was so great that she let go of God; and dark thoughts came, thoughts about eternal death—that all was over when our bodies became dust in the dust. With such thoughts, she could hold onto nothing, and she fell into the deepest despair.

She could no longer cry. She paid no attention to her daughters, nor did she notice the tears in her husband's eyes. All her thoughts were with her dead child. She tried to remember everything he had done, every childish, innocent word he had uttered.

The day of the funeral came. The night before she had not slept, except for an hour in the early morning when tiredness had overwhelmed her. During that time the coffin was moved to the most distant room in the house and the lid was nailed down.

When she woke she wanted to see her child again, but her husband, with tears in his eyes, said, "We have closed the coffin, we had to."

"If God is hard and cruel toward me, why should I expect better treatment from you?" she said, sobbing.

The coffin was carried to its grave. The mother, who could find consolation nowhere, sat with her daughters but she did not see them. Her thoughts were homeless, she had abandoned herself to her grief; she was floundering now in a dark ocean, like a ship that has lost its rudder. Thus passed the day of the funeral, and the days that followed were as uniformly filled with suffering. With eyes red from weeping, her family looked at her. They tried to console her but she did not hear them; and maybe they could not find the right words, for they were grieving too.

She and sleep had parted company, although he could have been her best friend, for she needed rest to strengthen her body and give peace to her soul. Her husband persuaded her that she must lie down; and she did. She was not asleep; she only pretended to be by lying very still. Her husband, who was listening to her breathing, was convinced that she had finally fallen asleep. He closed his own eyes and soon slept deeply. He did not hear his wife rise and dress herself. Silently, she let herself out of the house and hurried to that place which her thoughts did not leave, neither day nor night: her son's grave. She saw no one on her way along the path that crossed the meadows to the churchyard; and no one saw her.

The sky was clear and all the stars were out; it was in the beginning of September and the air was warm. The little grave of her child was still covered with flowers; their perfume smelled strongly in the still night. She sat down and bent her head, as if she hoped to be able to see down through the earth to her little boy.

Everything about him was still alive to her. She remembered his smile, the expression of love for her in his face. How could anyone forget how eloquently his little face had spoken as he lay on his sickbed? She remembered how she had bent down over him and taken his hand when he was so weak he could not move it. As she had sat by his bed, she now sat by his grave, but here she could weep freely and her tears fell on his grave.

"Do you want to go down to your child?" asked a voice near her. It sounded so deep and clear, as if her own heart had spoken to her. She turned her head and saw standing beside her a man dressed in a long black cloak with a hood that hid his face. As he looked down at her, she caught a glimpse of his features. He looked austere and yet inspired confidence rather than fear, and his eyes sparkled like a young man's.

"Down to my child," she repeated, and her words sounded like a desperate prayer.

"Do you dare follow me?" asked the man. "I am Death!"

She nodded and suddenly all the stars seemed to shine with the power and glory of the full moon. She noticed the splendor of the flowers that covered the grave, as the earth grew soft under her and she sank slowly down into it. Death covered her with his cape and it was night, and dark as death. She sank deeper than the gravedigger's spade ever will reach; the churchyard became a roof over her head.

Death's cape fell away from her and she was standing in a great hall. Although it was twilight all about her, the place was more comforting than frightening.

There was her child! She pressed him to her heart. He smiled and laughed and looked even more beautiful than he had when he was alive. She shouted for joy but was aware at the same moment that no sound came from her lips. From far away beautiful and strange music reached her ears; it seemed to come nearer and nearer, only to recede again. It came from somewhere beyond the great curtain, black as night, that divided the hall from the land of eternity.

"My sweet mother, my own mother!" she heard her little boy say. Oh, it was his voice, the voice she loved. Kiss followed kiss, in one unending joy.

The little boy pointed toward the curtain and said: "It is not as beautiful up on earth as it is here. Look, Mother! Do you see them all? Such is heavenly bliss."

The mother looked in the direction her son was pointing, but she saw nothing except the curtain dark as night. Her eyes belonged still to the earth, and she could not see what he saw. She heard the music and the singing that came from beyond, but she could not understand the words that were sung.

"I can fly now, Mother," said the child, "fly together with all the other happy children, right up to God. I would like to so much, but your tears hold me back. When you weep I cannot leave you, and I want to. Please let me go, may I? After all, it is but so short a time, and then you will be with me."

"No, stay, stay!" cried the mother. "Only a little while longer. Let me look at you just once more, and kiss you and hold you in my arms!"

And she held onto the child and she kissed him. Mournfully her name was called by someone up above. Who could it be?

"Do you hear?" asked the child. "It is Father who is calling you."

Then she heard deep sobs, like those children make when they have cried too long.

"Hear my sisters," said the boy. "You have forgotten them!"

Suddenly she remembered all that she had left behind. She saw shades fly by her, through the hall of death, and thought that she recognized some of them. What if one of those shades should prove to be her husband or her daughters! No, she could still hear their sighs and their weeping. She had forgotten them for the sake of her dead child.

"Now all the bells of heaven ring," said the little boy. "Mother, the sun is rising!"

A blinding light engulfed her, the child was gone, and she rose upward. She felt bitterly cold and lifted her head to see where she was. She was in the churchyard; she had been lying on the grave of her dead child. But in her dream God had guided her and taught her to understand. She fell on her knees and prayed, "Forgive me, Lord, that I would keep a soul from its flight toward you, and forgive me for forgetting my duties toward the living."

In these words her heart found peace. The sun rose; a bird sang above her head and she heard it. The bells of the church rang for morning prayers. She felt the holiness of everything around her, and that sacred holiness was in her heart as well. She knew again her God and her duties. Longingly she ran toward her home. She bent over her sleeping husband and woke him with a kiss; and they talked, words that came from their hearts. And she was strong and yet at the same time gentle, as a wife should be. Her strength she found in the belief that God's will is always for the best.

Her husband asked her, "Where did you get the strength to comfort others?"

She kissed him and she kissed her children. "From God," she said, "and from my dead child in his grave."

56

The Cock and the Weathercock

THERE were two cocks on the farm, one on the roof and one on the manure heap. They were vain and proud, both of them. But which one had the greater right to be? Tell us your opinion—it won't make any difference, we will stick to our own anyway.

The henyard was divided from the manure heap by a wooden fence and in the manure grew a cucumber; it knew that it was a vegetable and it was proud of being one.

"That is something one is by birth," the cucumber mumbled to herself. "We can't all be born cucumbers; there must be other species as well. Hens and ducks and the other animals on the farm had to be created too. The cock I look up to; he is always sitting on the fence crowing. He is of a great deal more importance than the weathercock, who is placed a little too high up and can't even say, 'Peep,' not to speak of crowing. He has no hens or chickens of his own, and when he sweats, it is green. He never thinks about anyone but himself. Now the cock on the farm, he is something else! When he struts about, it is a dance, a ballet. When he crows, it is music! Wherever he goes, people know how important a trumpeter is! If he came in here and ate me up, leaves and stalk and all, I would call it a blessed death. My body would become his!" said the cucumber.

Toward night there was a horrible storm. The hens, the chickens, and the cock sought shelter. The wooden fence fell, which made a frightening noise. Several tiles flew off the roof, but the weathercock stayed where he was, he did not even turn. He couldn't, which was really strange since he was quite new and had been cast recently. But he was the kind that was born old; steady and sober-minded from birth. He resembled in no way the fluttering birds of the air, the swallows or the sparrows; as a matter of fact, he despised them. "Small birds, common and ordinary," he called them. As for shape and coloring, he found the pigeons more to his taste; their feathers shone like mother-of-pearl, they could almost pass for weathercocks. But he declared that they were fat and stupid and never thought about anything except filling their stomachs. They were uninteresting company. Most of the migrating birds had visited the weathercock and told him fantastic stories about foreign lands, where there were eagles and great birds of prey. The tales had been amusing and interesting the first time he heard them, but the birds always repeated themselves and that the weathercock found tedious. They were tiresome, and life was boring. There was no one worth associating with, everything was flat and dull!

"The world is no good!" he declared. "Twaddle and nonsense: all of it!"

The weathercock was oversophisticated. The cucumber would have found him very interesting and attractive, but she didn't know him, so she admired the cock from the henyard; and now that the fence had blown down, he came visiting.

"What did you all think of that cock's crow?" he asked the hens and the chickens—he was referring to the storm. "I found it a bit raw, it lacked elegance."

Then he stepped up on the manure pile with the determined step of a hussar—he was wearing spurs. All the hens and chickens followed him.

"Vegetable," he said to the cucumber; and in that one word she found such breeding and refinement that she did not even notice that the cock pecked at her and ate her up.

"A blessed death!"

The hens gathered around and the chickens came too, for where one ran the others followed. They clucked and they peeped and they all looked at the cock and admired him, for he was one of their own kind.

"Cock-a-doodle-doo," he crowed. "All the chickens become hens in the henyards of the world, if and when I say so!"

The hens and the chickens clucked and peeped in agreement, all of them. Then the cock crowed some news to the world: "A cock can lay eggs! And do you know what is in such an egg? In it lies a basilisk! No one dares or can stand to look at such a monster. Human beings know it and now you know it too. Now you understand what I am capable of! What a fantastic creature I am!"

The cock flapped his wings, raised his red cockscomb, and crowed once more. All the hens and chickens were a little scared, and very thrilled that someone they knew so well should be such an incredibly important creature. They clucked and peeped so loud that the weathercock could hear them.

And he did; but he pretended that he hadn't, and didn't move. "Nonsense, all of it!" he said to himself. "Henyard roosters cannot lay eggs; and I can't be bothered to lay one. If I wanted to, I am sure I could, but the world is not worthy of an egg. Everything is tiresome, life is a bore! I can't even be bothered to sit here any longer!"

And at that moment the weathercock broke and fell down into the yard. It didn't hit the rooster and kill it. "Though that was its intention," declared all the hens.

Here is the moral of the story: "It is better to boast and crow than to be blasé and break."

57

The Dung Beetle

THE emperor's horse had been awarded golden shoes, one for each hoof. It was such a beautiful animal, with strong legs and a mane that fell like a veil of silk over its neck. Its eyes were sad, and when you looked into them you felt certain that if the horse could speak it would be able to answer more questions than you could ask. On the battlefield it had carried its master through a rain of bullets and a cloud of gun smoke. It was a true war horse, and once when the emperor was surrounded by the enemy, it had bit and kicked their horses and then, when all seemed lost, it had leaped over the carcass of an enemy steed to carry the emperor to safety. The horse had saved his master's golden crown and his life, which was worth a great deal more to the emperor than all the crown jewels. And that was why the blacksmith had been given orders to fasten a golden shoe on each of its hoofs.

The dung beetle climbed to the top of the manure pile to watch. "First the big and then the small," he said. "Not that size is important," he added as he lifted one of his thin legs and stretched it up toward the blacksmith.

"What do you want?" the man asked.

"Golden shoes," replied the dung beetle while balancing on five legs.

"You must be out of your mind to think that you should have golden shoes," the blacksmith exclaimed, and scratched himself behind his right ear.

"Golden shoes!" repeated the dung beetle crossly. "Am I not as good as that big clumsy beast that needs to have a servant to groom it, and even to see to it that it doesn't starve? Do I not belong to the emperor's stable too?"

"But why does the horse deserve golden shoes, have you any idea about that?"

"Idea!" cried the dung beetle. "I have a very good idea of how I deserve to be treated and how I am treated. Now I have been insulted enough; there is nothing left for me to do but go out into the wide world."

"Good riddance," said the smith.

"Brute!" returned the dung beetle, but the blacksmith, who had already returned to his work, did not hear him.

The dung beetle flew from the stable to the flower garden; it was a lovely place that smelled of roses and lavender.

"Isn't it beautiful here?" a ladybug called to him. She had just come for a visit and was busy folding her fragile wings beneath her black-spotted armor. "The flowers smell so sweet that I think I shall stay here forever."

The dung beetle sniffed. "I am used to something better. Why, there isn't even a decent pile of dung here."

The dung beetle sat down to rest in the shadow of a tiger lily. Climbing up the flower's stem was a caterpillar. "The world is beautiful," the caterpillar said. "The sun is very warm and I am getting quite sleepy. When I fall asleep—or die as some call it—I am sure that I shall wake up as a butterfly."

"Butterfly, indeed! Don't give yourself airs. I come from the emperor's stable, and no one there—not even the emperor's horse—has any notions like that. Those who can fly, fly. . . . And those who can crawl, crawl." And then the dung beetle flew away.

"I try not to let things annoy me; but they annoy me anyway," the dung beetle thought as it landed with a thud in the middle of a great lawn, where it lay quietly for a moment before falling asleep.

Goodness, it was raining. It poured! The dung beetle woke with a splash and tried to dig himself down into the earth but he couldn't. The rain had formed little rivers, and the dung beetle swam first on his stomach and then on his back. There was no hope of being able to fly. "I shan't live through it," he muttered, and sighed so deeply that his mouth filled with water. There was nothing to do but lie still where he was, and so he lay still.

When the rain let up for a moment the dung beetle blinked the water out of his eyes and looked about. He saw something white and crawled through the wet grass toward it. It was a piece of linen that had been stretched out on the grass to bleach. "I am used to better but it will have to do," he thought. "Though it's neither as warm nor as comfortable as a heap of dung; but when you travel you have to take things as they come."

And he stayed under the linen a whole day and a whole night; and it rained all the time. Finally, the following morning, the dung beetle stuck his head out from the fold of the linen and, seeing the gray sky, he was very annoyed.

Two frogs sat down on the linen. "What glorious weather," said one to the other. "It's so refreshing and this linen is soaking wet; to sit here is almost as pleasant as to swim."

"I would like to know," began the other frog, "if the swallow, who travels a good deal in foreign countries, ever has been in a land that has a better climate than ours. As much rain as you need; and a bit of wind, too—not to talk of the mist and the dew. Why, it is as good as living in a ditch. If you don't love this climate, then you don't love your country."

"Have you ever been in the emperor's stable?" the dung beetle asked. "There the wetness is spicy and warm. I prefer that kind of climate because I am used to it; but when you travel you can't take it along, that's the way things are. . . . Could you tell me if there is a hothouse in this garden, where a person of my rank and sensitivity would feel at home?"

The frogs either couldn't or wouldn't understand him.

"I never ask a question more than once," said the dung beetle after he had repeated his query the third time without getting an answer.

He walked along until he came upon a piece of a broken flowerpot. It shouldn't have been lying there but the gardener hadn't seen it, so it provided a good home for several families of earwigs. Earwigs do not need very much room, only company, especially lady earwigs, who are very motherly. Underneath the piece of pottery there lived several lady earwigs; and each of them thought that her children were the handsomest and most intelligent in the whole world.

"My son is engaged," one of them announced. "That innocent joy of my life . . . His most cherished ambition is to climb into the ear of a minister. He is charmingly childish, and being engaged will keep him from running about, and that is a great comfort to a mother."

"Our son," began another mother earwig, "came straight out of the egg. He is full of life and that is a joy. He is busy sowing his wild oats, and that, too, can make a mother proud. Don't you agree with me, Mr. Dung Beetle?" She had recognized him by his shape.

"You are both right," remarked the dung beetle; and the earwigs invited him to come into their home and make himself comfortable.

"Now you must meet my children," said a third mother earwig.

"And mine!" cried a fourth. "They are so lovable and so amusing, and they only misbehave when they have stomach aches and it's not their fault that you get one so easily at their age."

All the mothers talked and their children talked; and when the little ones weren't talking, they were pulling at the dung beetle's mustache with the little tweezers that each of them had in his tail.

"Always up to something! Aren't they darling?" the mothers said in a chorus, and oozed mother love. But the dung beetle was bored and asked for directions to the nearest hothouse.

"It is far, far away, nearly at the end of the world, on the other side of the ditch," explained one of the lady earwigs. "If one of my children ever should think of traveling so far away I would die. I am sure of it."

"Well, that is where I am going," said the dung beetle, and to show that he was really gallant, he left without saying good-by.

In the ditch he met many relatives: all of them dung beetles. "This is our home," they said. "It is quite comfortable: warm and wet. Please step down into the land of plenty. You must be tired after all your travels."

"I am!" replied the dung beetle. "I have lain a whole day and a whole night on linen. Cleanliness wears you out so. Then I stood under a drafty flowerpot until I got arthritis in my wings. It is a blessing to be with my own kind again."

"Do you come from the hothouse?" one of the older dung beetles asked.

"Higher still. I was born in the emperor's stable with golden shoes on. I am traveling incognito on a secret mission. And no matter how much you coaxed, I wouldn't tell you about it." With these words the dung beetle crept into the mud and made himself comfortable.

Nearby sat three young lady dung beetles. They were tittering because they didn't know what to say.

"They are not engaged, though they are beautiful," remarked their mother. The young ladies tittered again, this time because they were shy.

"Even in the emperor's stable I have never seen anyone more beautiful," agreed the dung beetle, who had traveled far and wide.

"They are young and virtuous. Don't ruin them! Don't speak to them unless you have honorable intentions. But I see you are a gentleman, and therefore I give you my blessings!"

"Hurrah!" cried all the other dung beetles, and congratulated the foreigner on his engagement. First engaged, then married; there was no reason to put it off.

The first day of married life was good, and the second was pleasant enough, but on the third began all the responsibilities of providing food for his wives, and soon there would probably be offspring.

"They took me by surprise," thought the dung beetle. "Now I shall surprise them."

And so he did. He ran away. All day the wives waited, and all night too; then they declared themselves widows. The other dung beetles were angry and called him a ne'er-do-well, because they feared that now they would have to support the deserted wives.

"Just behave as if you were virgins again," said their mother. "Come, you are still my innocent girls. But shame on the tramp who abandoned you."

In the meantime, the dung beetle was sailing across the ditch on a cabbage leaf. It was morning and two human beings who happened to be passing noticed him and picked him up. They turned the dung beetle over and looked at him from all sides, for these two men were scholars.

The younger of the two, who was the most learned, said, " 'Allah sees the black scarab in the black stone that is part of the black mountain.' Isn't it written thus in the Koran?" Then he translated the dung beetle's name into Latin and gave a lecture in which he explained its genealogy and history. The older scholar remarked that there was no reason to take the dung beetle home with them, because he already had a much more beautiful scarab in his collection.

The dung beetle's feelings were hurt and he flew right out of the scholar's hand, high up into the sky. Now that his wings were dry he was able to make the long journey to the hothouse in one stretch. Luckily, a window was open and he flew straight in and landed on a pile of manure that had been delivered that morning.

"This is sumptuous," he said as he dug himself down into the dung, where he soon was asleep. He dreamed that the emperor's horse was dead and that he—the dung beetle—had not only been given its four golden shoes but had been promised two more. It was a pleasant dream and when the dung beetle awoke he climbed out of the manure to look about him. How magnificent everything was!

There were slender palm trees, whose green leaves appeared transparent when the sun shone on them; and below the trees were flowers of all colors. Some were red as fire, and some were yellow as amber, and some were as pure white as new-fallen snow. "What a marvelous display!" exclaimed the dung beetle. "And think how delicious it all will taste as soon as it is rotten. It is a glorious larder. I must go visiting and see if I can find any of my family living here. I cannot associate with just anybody. I have my pride, and that I am proud of." Then he crawled on, recalling as he did so, his dream and how the horse had died and he was given its gold shoes.

Suddenly a little hand picked him up, and again he was pinched and turned over. The gardener's son and one of his playmates had been exploring in the hothouse and, when they saw the dung beetle, they decided it would be fun to keep it. They wrapped it in a leaf from a grapevine, and the gardener's son stuck it in his pocket.

The dung beetle tried to creep and to crawl, and the boy closed his hand around him and that was most uncomfortable.

The boys ran to the big pond at the other end of the garden. A worn-out wooden shoe with a missing instep became a ship. With a stick for a mast and the dung beetle, who was tied to the stick with a piece of woolen thread, as the captain, the ship was launched.

The pool was large and the dung beetle thought he was adrift on an ocean. He got so frightened that he fell over on his back and there he lay with all his legs pointing up toward the sky.

There were currents in the water and they carried the wooden shoe along. When it got out too far, one of the boys would roll up his trousers—both boys were barefooted—and wade out to bring the shoe nearer the shore. Suddenly, while the shoe was quite far out, almost in the center of the pond, someone called the boys, called them in so stern a voice that they forgot all about the shoe and ran home as fast as they could. The wooden shoe drifted on and on. The dung beetle shuddered with fear, for he couldn't fly away, tethered as he was to the mast.

A fly came to keep him company. "Lovely weather, don't you agree? I think I'll rest here for a moment in the sun. A very comfortable place you have here."

"Nonsense!" cried the dung beetle. "How can I be comfortable when I am tied to the mast? You talk like an idiot, so I'm sure you must be one."

"I'm not tied to anything," said the fly, and flew away.

"Now I know the world," muttered the dung beetle. "It is cruel and I am the only decent one in it. First they refused to give me golden shoes, then they made me lie on wet linen and stand for hours in a draft. Finally, I am tricked into marriage; and when I show my courage by going out into the world to find out what that's like and see how I will be treated there, I am captured by a human puppy who ties me to a mast and sets me adrift on a great ocean. And all the while the emperor's horse runs about with golden shoes on; and that's almost the most annoying part of it all. In this world you must not ask for sympathy. My life has been most interesting. . . . But what difference does that make if no one ever hears about it? . . . But does the world deserve to hear my story? . . . If it did, I would have been given the golden shoes. Had I got them, it would have brought honor to the stable. The stable missed its chance, so did the world, for everything is over."

But everything was not over; some young girls who were out rowing on the pond saw the little ship.

"Look, there is a wooden shoe," one of them said.

"Someone has tied a beetle to the mast," said another; and she leaned over the side of the boat and grabbed the wooden shoe. With a tiny pair of scissors she carefully cut the woolen thread, so that no harm came to the dung beetle. When they returned to shore the girl let him go in the grass. "Crawl or fly, whichever you can, for freedom is a precious gift," she said.

The dung beetle flew straight in through an open window of a large building and landed in the long, soft, silken mane of the emperor's horse, who was standing in the stable where they both belonged. He held on tightly to the mane, then he relaxed and began to think about life.

"Here I am, sitting on the emperor's horse. I am the rider. . . . What am I saying?" The dung beetle was talking out loud. "Now everything is clear to me! And I know it is true! Didn't the blacksmith ask me if I didn't have some idea why the emperor's horse was being shod with golden shoes? Now I understand that it was for my sake that the horse was given golden shoes."

The dung beetle was in the best of humors. "It is traveling that did it!" he thought. "It broadens your horizon and makes everything clear to you."

The sun shone through the window. Its rays fell upon the horse and the dung beetle. "The world is not so bad," remarked the dung beetle. "It all depends on how you look at it." And the world, indeed, was beautiful, when the emperor's horse was awarded golden shoes because the dung beetle was to ride it.

"I must dismount," he thought, "and go and tell the other dung beetles how I have been honored. I will tell them of my wonderful adventures and how I enjoyed traveling abroad. And I'll tell them, too, that I have decided to stay at home until the horse wears out his golden shoes."

58

❄✧❄

What Father Does Is Always Right

Now I want to tell you a story that I heard myself when I was a very little boy, and every time that I have thought of it since, it has seemed to me to be more beautiful. For stories are like people: some —though not all—improve with age, and that is a blessing.

Have you ever been in Denmark and seen the countryside? If you have, then you must have seen one of those really old cottages that has a thatched roof that is overgrown with moss and a stork's nest perched on its ridge. The walls are crooked. The windows are small, and only one of them has a hasp and hinges so that it can be opened. The oven for baking bread juts out of the wall like a well-filled stomach. There are a hedge of elderberries and a tiny pond surrounded by willow trees, where a duck and some ducklings swim. In the yard there is an old dog that barks at everyone who goes by.

In such a cottage, far out in the country, there once lived a farmer and his wife. They had little that they could get along without, but they did have something, and that was a horse that had to graze at the edge of the road because they didn't have a paddock. Sometimes the farmer rode on the horse when he went to town; and sometimes his neighbor borrowed it, and that was to the farmer's advantage, for country people believe that one good turn deserves another. But one day the farmer realized that he'd be doing himself a better turn if he sold the horse or traded it for something which he had more use for, though he didn't know what it could be.

"That you'll find out soon enough," said his wife. "You know best, Father. There's a market in town today. Why don't you ride in on the horse, and there you can sell it or trade it for something else. Whatever you do, I am sure it will be right."

She tied his cravat, which she knew how to do better than anybody else. She made a double bow because that made him look more gallant. She brushed his hat with the palm of her hand, and then she kissed him warmly on the lips. Off he rode on the horse that was to be sold or traded, just as he saw fit; for striking a bargain was something he knew how to do.

The sun was shining and there wasn't a cloud in the sky. The dusty road was filled with folk on their way to market; some in wagons, others on horses, and many on their own poor legs. It was terribly hot and there was not a scrap of shade along the road.

The farmer noticed a man who was leading a cow that was as beautiful as any cow could be; and he thought, "I'll bet that cow gives a lot of good milk." Then he called to the man, "Listen—you with the cow—I'd like to talk with you!" And when the other man turned around, he continued: "I know that a horse is worth more than a cow. But a cow would be more useful to me. Shall we trade?"

"Why not?" said the man.

Now here is where the story should have ended but then it wouldn't have been worth telling. The farmer had done what he had set out to do, and so he should have turned around and gone back home with his new cow. But he thought that, since he had meant to go to the market, it was a pity to miss seeing it.

He walked quickly and the cow walked quickly, and pretty soon they had caught up with a man who was leading a sheep. It was a fine animal with a heavy coat of wool. "A sheep like that I wouldn't mind owning," he thought. "In the winter when it gets too cold you can always take a sheep inside with you. Besides, I don't have enough grazing for a cow, and a sheep is satisfied with what it can find on the side of the road." And the more he looked at the sheep, the better he liked it.

"How would you like to trade your sheep for my cow?" he finally asked. And that bargain was made.

He hadn't gone far with his sheep when he spied a man who was sitting and resting on a big stone. He had good reason for wanting to rest: he was carrying a goose that was bigger than most ganders.

"A fine fat goose!" the farmer cried as he lifted his hat. "How pretty it would look in our pond and then Mother would have someone to give the potato peelings to. How often has she said that we ought to have a goose. And now she can have one! What about trading? I'll give you a sheep for a goose and throw a thank you into the bargain."

"A sheep for my goose?" said the stranger. "Why not? And you can keep your thank you, for I don't like to drive too hard a bargain."

The farmer tucked the goose under his arm and walked on. As he came nearer the town the traffic became greater and greater. All about him were people and animals. There wasn't space for them all on the road; they walked in the gutters and the embankments, and even on the fields. The town's gatekeeper had tethered his hen in his potato patch for fear that she might get frightened by all the confusion and run away. The hen's tail was as finely feathered as a cock's, and as she said, "Cluck! Cluck . . ." she winked. What that meant I cannot tell you, but I do know what the farmer thought: "That hen is as good as the minister's best hen, the one that won the prize at the fair. I wish it were mine. A hen can always find a grain of corn by itself; besides, it can lay eggs. I think I will strike a bargain."

From thought to action is no further than the tongue can travel in a few seconds. The gatekeeper got the goose and the farmer the white hen.

The farmer had done a lot that morning and traveled far. He was thirsty and hungry. The sun was baking hot, as if it had been hired by the innkeeper.

As he was entering the inn, the farmer collided with one of the servants, who was carrying a sack over his shoulder. "What have you got in the sack?" the farmer asked.

"Rotten apples," the other man replied, "and I am on my way to the pigpen with them."

"A whole sackful, what an awful lot that is! I wish Mother could see it. Last year, on our old apple tree next to the woodshed, there was only one single apple. Mother put it in the cupboard and there it lay till it was all dried up and no bigger than a walnut. 'It makes me feel rich just to look at it,' she used to say. Think how she would feel if she had a sackful."

"What will you give me for it?" asked the servant.

"My hen," the farmer replied; and the words were no sooner said than he found he had a sack of rotten apples in his hands instead of a hen.

He went into the taproom, which was crowded with people. There were butchers, farmers, merchants, horse dealers, and even a couple of Englishmen, who were so rich that their pockets were bursting with gold coins. All Englishmen like to gamble, that's a tradition in their country. Now just listen to what happened.

The taproom was next to the kitchen, and the stove that was used for cooking extended right through the kitchen wall into the taproom. Innkeepers are economical and this kind of stove is a great saving in winter. The farmer, without giving it a thought, put his sack of apples down on the stove, and soon they began to simmer and sputter.

"Suss! Suss!" the apples said, and aroused the curiosity of one of the Englishmen.

"What's that?" he asked.

And the farmer told him the whole story of how he had traded his horse for a cow, his cow for a sheep, his sheep for a goose, his goose for a hen, and finally the hen for a sack of rotten apples.

"Your wife will beat you with a rolling pin when you get home. She'll raise the roof," the Englishman commented.

"Beat me?" exclaimed the farmer. "She'll kiss me and say that what Father does is always right."

"I'll make you a wager," said the two Englishmen both at once. "A barrel of gold and a sackful of silver."

"The barrel of gold is enough and, if I lose, I'll fill a barrel with rotten apples and you can have Mother and me for good measure."

"Done! Done!" cried the Englishmen, for betting is in their blood.

They hired the innkeeper's horses and his carriage, and off they went, rotten apples and all. When they came to the farmer's house they drove right up to the door; the old dog barked, and the farmer's wife came out to greet them.

"Good evening, Mother," said the farmer.

"Thank God you arrived home safely," his wife replied.

"Well, I traded the horse."

"Trading is a man's business," she said and, in spite of the strangers, she threw her arms around him.

"I traded it for a cow."

"Thank God for the milk," she exclaimed. "Now we'll have both butter and cheese. That was a good bargain."

"But I traded the cow for a sheep."

"How clever of you," she said happily. "We have just enough grass for a sheep; and sheep's milk is good and the cheese is good, too. I can knit socks and a nightshirt from the wool; and I wouldn't have been able to do anything with cow's hair. A cow just sheds her hair and that's all. What a wise and thoughtful husband you are!"

"But I traded the sheep for a fat goose."

"Oh, my good husband, are we really going to have goose on St. Martin's Eve? You are always thinking of ways to please me. We will tether the goose in the ditch and by November she'll be even fatter."

"I traded the goose for a hen," he said proudly, for now he realized how very well he had done that day.

"That was a good exchange," said the wife. "Hens lay eggs and from eggs come little chicks. Soon we shall have a real henyard and that is something I have always wanted."

"I traded the hen for a sackful of rotten apples."

"Now I must kiss you, my dear husband! While you were away I thought that I should like to make a fine supper for you to eat when you got home; and I decided to make an omelet with chives. I had eggs but no chives. Our neighbor, the schoolmaster, has chives; but, as all the world knows, his wife is a stingy old crow, and when I asked her whether I could borrow some chives, 'Borrow!' she squawked. 'Nothing grows in your garden, not even a rotten apple.' Now I can lend her ten rotten apples, or even a whole sackful, if she wants them. That was the best bargain of all; and now I must give you a kiss." And she kissed him full on the mouth.

"I like that!" cried one of the Englishmen, while the other laughed. "From bad to worse, and they do not even know it! Always happy, always contented. That was worth the money!" And they gave a barrel full of gold coins to the farmer whose wife gave him kisses instead of blows.

Yes, it pays for a wife to admit that her husband is cleverer than she is.

Well, that was that story. I heard it when I was a boy and now you have heard it too; and now you know that what Father does is always right.

59

The Snowman

"It crackles and creaks inside of me. It is so cold that it is a pleasure," said the snowman. "When the wind bites you, then you know you're alive. Look how the burning one gapes and stares." By "the burning one" he meant the sun, which was just about to set. "But she can't make me blink; I'll stare right back at her."

The snowman had two triangular pieces of tile for eyes, and a children's rake for a mouth, which meant that he had teeth. His birth had been greeted by the boys with shouts of joy, to the sound of sleigh bells and the cracking of whips.

The sun set and the moon rose, full and round, beautiful in the blue evening sky.

"There she is again, just in another place. She couldn't stay away." The snowman thought that the sun had returned. "I guess that I have cooled her off. But now she's welcome to stay up there, for it is pleasant with a bit of light, so that I can see. If only I knew how to move and get about, then I would go down to the lake and slide on the ice as the boys do. But I don't know how to run."

"Out! Out! Out!" barked the old watchdog, who was chained to his doghouse. He was hoarse and had been so ever since he had been refused entrance to the house. That was a long time ago now; but when the dog lived inside, it had lain next to the stove. "The sun will teach you to run. I saw what happened to last year's snowman and to the one the year before last. . . . Out! Out! Out! . . . They are all gone."

"What do you mean by that, comrade?" asked the snowman.

"How can that round one up there teach me to run?" By "that round one," he meant the moon. "She ran when I looked straight into her eyes. Now she is trying to sneak back from another direction."

"You are ignorant," said the watchdog. "But you have only just been put together. The round one up there is called the moon. The other one is the sun and she will be back tomorrow. She will teach you how to run, right down to the lake. I've got a pain in my left hind leg and that means the weather is about to change."

"I don't understand him," thought the snowman, "but I have a feeling that he was saying something unpleasant. The hot one—the one that was here a moment ago and then went away, the one he called the sun—is no friend of mine. Not that she's done me any harm; it's just a feeling I have."

The weather did change. In the morning there was a heavy fog. During the day it lifted, the wind started to blow, and there was frost. The sun came out and what a beautiful sight it was! The hoarfrost made the forest appear like a coral reef; every tree and bush looked as if it were decked with white flowers. In the summer when they have leaves, you cannot see what intricate and lovely patterns the branches make. But now they looked like lace and were so brilliantly white that they seemed to radiate light. The weeping birch tree swayed in the wind as it did in summer. Oh, it was marvelous to see. As the sun rose higher in the sky its light grew sharper and its rays made everything appear as if it were covered with diamond dust. In the blanket of snow that lay upon the ground were large diamonds, blinking like a thousand small candles, whose light was whiter than snow.

"Isn't it unbelievably beautiful?" said a young girl who was taking a walk in the garden with a young man. "I think it's even lovelier now than it is in summer." And her eyes shone, as if the beauty of the garden were reflected in them.

They stopped near the snowman to admire the forest. "And a handsome fellow like that you won't see in the summer either," remarked the young man, pointing to the snowman.

The girl laughed and curtsied before the snowman, then she took the young man's hand in hers and the two of them danced across the snow, which crunched beneath their feet as if they were walking on grain.

"Who were they?" the snowman asked the dog. "You've been here on the farm longer than I have. Do you know them?"

"Certainly," answered the old dog. "She has patted me and he has given me bones. I would never bite either of them."

"Why do they walk hand in hand? I have never seen boys walk like that."

"They are engaged," the old dog sniffed. "Soon they will be moving into the same doghouse and will share each other's bones."

"Are they as important as you and I?" asked the snowman.

"They belong to the house and are our masters," replied the dog. "You certainly know precious little, even if you were only born yesterday. I wouldn't have believed such ignorance existed if I hadn't heard it with my own ears. But I have both age and knowledge, and from them you acquire wisdom. I know everyone on the farm; and I have known better times, when I didn't have to stand here, chained up and frozen to the bone. . . . Out! Out! Get out!"

"I love to freeze," said the snowman. "Tell me about the time when you were young, but stop rattling your chain like that, it makes me shudder inside."

"Out! Out!" barked the old dog. "I was a puppy once. 'See that lovely little fellow,' they used to say, and I slept on a velvet chair. I lay in the lap of the master of the house and had my paws wiped with embroidered handkerchiefs. They kissed me and called me a sweetheart, and their little doggy-woggy. When I grew too big to lie in a lap they gave me to the housekeeper. She had a room in the cellar.— You can look right into her window from where you are standing.— Down there I was the master. It wasn't as nicely furnished as upstairs, but it was much more comfortable. I had my own pillow to lie on, and the housekeeper gave me just as good food and more of it. Besides, upstairs there were children and they are a plague, always picking you up, squeezing you, and hugging you, and carrying you about as if you had no legs of your own to walk on. . . . Then there was the stove. In winter there is nothing as lovely as a stove. When it was really cold I used to crawl all the way under it. I still dream of being there, though it's a long time since I was there last. . . . Out! Out! Out!"

"Is a stove a thing of beauty?" asked the snowman. "Does it look like me?"

"You're as much alike as day and night. The stove's as black as coal; it has a long black neck with a brass collar around it. The fire's in the bottom. The stove lives on wood, which it eats so fast that it breathes fire out of its mouth. Ah! To lie near it or, better still, underneath it; until you have tried that you have no idea what comfort is. . . . You must be able to see it from where you are. That window, there, just look in."

And the snowman did and he saw the stove: a black, polished metal figure with brass fixtures. The little door at the bottom, through which ashes could be removed, had a window in it; and the snowman could see the light from the fire. A strange feeling of sadness and joy came over him. A feeling he had never experienced before. A feeling that all human beings know, except those who are made of snow.

"Why did you leave her?" The snowman somehow felt certain that the stove was of the female sex. "How could you bear to go away from such a lovely place?"

"I had to," answered the old watchdog. "They threw me out, put a chain around my neck, and here I am. And all I had done was to bite the youngest of the children from upstairs. I was gnawing on a bone and he took it away. A bone for a bone, I thought, and bit him in the leg. But the master and the mistress put all the blame on me. And ever since then I have been chained. The dampness has spoiled my voice. Can't you hear how hoarse I am? . . . Out! Out! Get out! . . . And that is the end of my story."

The snowman, who had stopped listening to the watchdog, was staring with longing through the cellar window into the housekeeper's room, where the stove stood on its four black legs. "She is exactly the same height as I am," he thought.

"It creaks so strangely inside of me," the snowman muttered. "Shall I never be able to go down into the cellar and be in the same room with her? Isn't it an innocent wish, and shouldn't innocent wishes be granted? It is my greatest, my most earnest, my only wish! And it would be a terrible injustice if it were never fulfilled! I shall get in, even if I have to break the window to do it."

"You will never get down into the cellar," the old dog said. "And if you did manage it, then the stove would make sure that you were out in a minute. . . . Out! Out!"

"I am almost out already!" cried the snowman. "I feel as if I were about to break in two."

All day long the snowman gazed through the window. In the evening the housekeeper's room seemed even more inviting. The light from the stove was so soft. It was not like the moonlight or the sunlight. "Only a stove can glow like that," he thought. Every so often, when the top door of the stove was opened to put more wood in, the bright flames would shoot out, and the blaze would reflect through the window and make the snowman blush from the neck up.

"It's more than I can bear!" he exclaimed. "See how beautiful she is when she sticks out her tongue."

The night was long, but not for the snowman, who was daydreaming happily. Besides, it was so cold that everything seemed to tingle.

In the morning the cellar window was frozen; the most beautiful white flowers decorated the glass, which the snowman did not appreciate because they hid the stove from his view. It was so cold that the windows couldn't thaw and the running nose on the water pump in the yard grew an icicle. It was just the kind of weather to put a snowman in the best of moods, but it didn't. Why, it was almost a duty to be content with weather like that; but he wasn't. He was miserable. He was suffering from "stove-yearning."

"That is a very serious disease, especially for a snowman to get." The old watchdog shook his head. "I have suffered from it myself, but I got over it. . . . Out! Out! Get out! . . . I have a feeling that the weather is going to change."

And it did. It became warmer and the snowman became smaller. He didn't say a word, not even one of complaint, and that's a very telling sign.

One morning he fell apart. His head rolled off and something that looked like the handle of a broom stuck up from where he had stood. It was what the boys had used to help hold the snowman together and make him stand upright.

"Now I understand why he longed for the stove," said the old watchdog. "That's the old poker he had inside him. No wonder. Well, now that's over. . . . Out! Out! Out!"

And soon the winter was over, and the little girls sang:

> "Come, anemones, so pure and white,
> Come, pussy willows, so soft and light,
> Come, lark and cuckoo, and sing
> That in February we have spring."

And no one thought about the snowman.

60

The Ice Maiden

CHAPTER ONE: LITTLE RUDY

LET us visit Switzerland. Let us travel a little in that marvelous land of mountains where forests spread themselves up walls of granite. Let us climb the mountains until we come to the great fields of snow; and then descend to the green meadows, where rivers and streams run so swiftly that one would think they were afraid of missing their chance to meet the ocean and disappear. Down in the valleys the sun feels burning hot, but it also makes its strength felt on the mountaintops. There it shines on heavy masses of snow, melting them through the years into huge, shining blocks of ice, into glaciers.

Two such glaciers have been formed beneath the pinnacles of Schreckhorn and Wetterhorn, filling the wide clefts near the little mountain village of Grindelwald. They are strange and awesome, and in the summer travelers come from all over the world to see them. Either the strangers cross the snow-clad mountains or they come from the valleys far below, climbing for many hours. As they ascend, the valley below them seems to descend, and they look back at it as if they were looking down from a balloon. Often the very tops of the mountains are hidden in what looks like a curtain of smoke, while in the valley with its little brown houses the sun is still shining. Its rays make the greenness of the meadows so brilliant as to appear transparent. Water splashes, gurgles, and sputters below; water tinkles and chimes above, and looks like silver bands as it falls down the sides of the cliffs.

On both sides of the road there are log chalets, each with its own potato patch. The potato patch is necessary, for in every little chalet live large families, and even small stomachs can be very hungry.

As soon as a stranger is spied on his way up the mountain, a flock of children will be there to greet him. Little tradesmen they are, selling charmingly carved toy houses that look just like the ones they live in themselves. About twenty years ago there could sometimes be seen among these children a boy who kept a little apart from the others. He appeared so serious and held the plain box containing his wares so tightly that he looked as if he were unwilling to part with them. Although the boy himself could never have guessed it, it was his very lack of eagerness for his task that attracted buyers; and this very young boy with his very solemn expression sold more than the other children.

Farther up the mountain lived the boy's grandfather, and it was he who carved the lovely little houses that the boy sold. In the old man's house there was a whole chest full of the finest wood carvings: nutcrackers, knives, forks, prancing mountain antelopes, and little boxes covered with vine leaves. Everything that could please the eye of a child was there, but little Rudy—for that was the boy's name—looked with greater interest and longing toward the rifle that hung from the rafters, for his grandfather had promised him that it would be his when he grew strong enough to use it.

Though Rudy was still very young he was set to taking care of the goats; and if a goatherd is to be judged by the way he keeps up with his animals, then Rudy was an excellent goatherd, for he could climb even higher than the goats. Up the trees he would go to fetch the birds' nests. He was daring and brave, but he never smiled except when he stood near the great waterfall or heard in the distance the sound of an avalanche. He did not play with the other children and was to be seen among them only when his grandfather sent him down to sell wood carvings. This work was a real chore for Rudy. He preferred climbing in the mountains or sitting at home with his grandfather. The old man told the boy stories of bygone days. He told him about his ancestors, the people of Meiningen.

"They have not always been Swiss," he explained. "In ancient times they migrated from the north, and there are people living up there to whom you are related; they are called Swedes."

Rudy learned much from his grandfather, but he had other teachers as well, and perhaps what they taught him was even more valuable. They were the dog, Ajola, that Rudy had inherited from his father; and the tomcat, whom Rudy loved especially because he had taught him how to be a climber.

"Come up here on the roof," the cat had said to him when he was yet so young that he could not talk himself. Rudy had understood the cat, as all small children understand the languages of hens, ducks, dogs, and cats.

Animals speak to children as plainly as their parents do; and to very young children even Grandfather's cane can talk. It can neigh and become a horse with swift legs and a flying mane. Some children retain this gift longer than others, and then grownups shake their heads and say that they are slow in developing and start remarking about it being time for them to start growing up. Grownups are always talking, but they are not always worth listening to.

"Come up here, up on the roof," were the first words that the cat said to Rudy and he had understood them at once. "Don't be afraid. All that about falling is all the way you look at it; and if you don't imagine what it's like to fall, you won't fall. You only fall if you're afraid of falling. Come follow me, first one paw and then the other, eyes straight ahead. And when you come to a gap, you leap; and hold on with your claws when you get to the other side. That's the way I do it!"

And that's what Rudy did; and he spent many hours with the tomcat on top of the roof or in the uppermost branches of a tree. Later Rudy learned to climb higher than his friend, to the very edges of the cliffs where the cat never came.

"Higher! Higher!" exclaimed the trees and bushes. "Look how we climb, how near the sky we reach! See how we hang on with our roots to the ledges of the cliffs."

Often Rudy would be on the mountaintop before the sun was up there; then he would be given his breakfast drink, that draft that only God can brew, though man knows the recipe. It is made up of the fragrance of mountain herbs mixed with the smell of mint and thyme from the valleys. All that is heavy, the clouds absorb; then the wind drives the clouds across the tops of the pine trees, to comb and card them. The very essence of all these aromas becomes air, fresh and light; and this was Rudy's first drink in the morning.

The daughters of the sun, its rays, kissed his cheeks, and Dizziness, though she stood nearby, waiting, did not dare to touch him. The swallows from his grandfather's houses, where there were never less than seven nests, joined Rudy and his herd of goats. "You and we . . . You and we!" they sang, bringing messages from all the animals back at the house, even from the hens, the only birds to whom little Rudy paid no attention.

Rudy had traveled much for a child of his tender years. Born in the canton of Valais, he had been carried across the mountain range to his grandfather's house, and recently he had gone by foot to visit Staubbach, that mountain which stands in front of its greater sister, who is called "The Maiden," and covers part of its bright white face with a silver veil as the face of an Arabian woman is concealed. During his first trip Rudy had crossed the great glacier near Grindelwald, but that had been a journey of sorrow, for his mother had died, and as his grandfather once explained: "It was on the glacier that Rudy had his child's merriment stolen from him."

When Rudy was a baby his mother had described him in a letter to her father as a baby who laughed more than he cried. "I think his soul has been changed. While he was imprisoned in the cleft all his laughter froze," his grandfather had been heard to say, though as a rule he seldom spoke about this event.

Yet everyone knew the story of Rudy's life. His father had been a postman and, with a dog as his only companion, had carried the mail across the Simplon Pass. That was in the canton of Valais, and there in the valley of the Rhone, Rudy's father's brother still lived and was a well-known hunter and guide.

When Rudy's father died, Rudy's mother decided that she would return with her year-old son to her father's home in the Bernese Oberland, a few hours' walk beyond Grindelwald. One June day she set out for her father's house, carrying her little boy in her arms. She did not travel alone but went with two hunters who were returning to Grindelwald.

They had traveled the greatest part of their journey and had reached the great snow fields on the mountain ridge, from where Rudy's mother could see her father's house and the green mountainside where she had played as a child. The only difficulty left was the crossing of the upper part of the glacier. Newly fallen snow hid a crevasse—not a deep cleft with a raging river at the bottom but a narrow split in the ice that was deeper than a man's height. The young woman, with her babe in her arms, slid, fell, and was gone. She had not screamed or even uttered a sound, but from below them in the glacier her companions heard a baby cry.

More than an hour passed before the hunters were able to return with ropes and a ladder, so that they could climb down into the crevasse. With great difficulty they brought up the two bodies. The baby was still alive, but though they tried, they could not bring the mother back to life.

So it was that the woodcarver who had lost a daughter received a son. But the little boy had changed. No more could it be said of him, as his mother had, that he laughed more than he cried. His visit to the cold, ice world—where the Swiss mountain people believe the souls of the condemned are frozen till Doomsday—had altered him.

Not unlike raging water frozen and crushed into green blocks of glass is the glacier, one gigantic block tipped on top of another. Far below—deep, deep down—flows a raging river of melted snow and ice; its waters twist themselves through the glacier, making deep caves and great caverns, a wonderful palace of ice. This is the home of the Ice Maiden. She, who kills and crushes all living things that come near her, is both a child of the air and a ruler of the mighty rivers. That is why she can reach, swifter than the mountain goat, the highest peaks, where mountain climbers must wearily cut steps in the ice to gain a foothold; and why she can sail on a twig down a great river, or leap from cliff to cliff with her snow-white hair and her blue-green dress, which glistens like water, streaming behind her.

"Mine is the power!" she exclaims. "I crush anything that comes within my grasp and never let it go! A lovely boy was stolen from me. I had kissed him but not so hard that he died from it. Now he is again among human beings. He herds goats in the mountains. Upward, ever upward, he climbs, away from everyone else, but not from me. He is mine and I claim him."

And she called upon Vertigo to obey her. It was too humid for the Ice Maiden down in the meadows where the mint thrives. Vertigo stretched herself and came swimming up the river. Two of Vertigo's sisters had come with her. Their family is a large one. The Ice Maiden chose the one who has power both inside and out of doors to help her. She is the one who can sit on the top of a flight of stairs or perch herself on the railing of a church tower. She is as agile as a squirrel and can tread air as a swimmer treads water. She tempts her victims to climb too high and then pushes them down into the abyss.

The Ice Maiden and Vertigo are like the polyp that lives in the sea: they grasp anything that comes within their reach; and now Vertigo was ordered to capture Rudy.

"I cannot catch him," Vertigo answered. "I have already tried, but the cat has taught him his own tricks. Besides, that human child has a power of his own, he can push me away. I cannot reach him, even when he hangs from the topmost branches of the tree. If only I could tickle him under the soles of his feet or give him a ducking in the air, but I can't."

"We can do it!" shouted the Ice Maiden. "You and I together."

"No! No!" came the answer, and it sounded like a mountain echo of the tolling of church bells, but it was a song. Other spirits of nature, those that are mild, loving, and good, had joined in a chorus, to have their say. They were the rays of the sun, its daughters, who when night comes retire to the highest mountaintops and there fold their rose-colored wings, which turn a deeper and deeper red as the sun sets.—Man sometimes calls that sight "rose of the evening."—When the sun finally disappears its daughters sleep until their mother again rises above the horizon. The rays of the sun love flowers, butterflies, and human beings, and among the latter, they especially loved little Rudy.

"You will never catch him! You will never catch him!" they said.

"Bigger and stronger men have I caught and carried away!" replied the Ice Maiden.

Then the daughters of the sun sang a song about a wanderer in the mountains and how the whirlwind had robbed him of his cape. "The covering of the man, the wind could take and fly away with, but not the man himself. For man is powerful, more powerful even than we are. His spirit can soar even higher than our mother, the sun. He knows the magic words that make him master of both winds and sea, so that they are his servants and must obey him." Theirs was a lovely song.

Every morning the sun rays shone through the only little window in Rudy's grandfather's house and rested on the sleeping child. The daughters of the sun kissed him, for they hoped to thaw and destroy that kiss of ice which the royal ruler of the glacier, the Ice Maiden, had pressed upon his forehead while he was lying in his dead mother's lap, that time he fell into the crevasse in the glacier and was saved as if by a miracle.

CHAPTER TWO: JOURNEY TO A NEW HOME

When Rudy was eight years old, his uncle who lived in the Rhone Valley sent for him. Here the boy could get better schooling and, when he was grown, would have more opportunity for earning his living. His grandfather had to admit that this was true, and therefore he let the boy go.

It was the day that Rudy was to depart and there were many to say good-by to besides his grandfather. First of all there was the old dog, Ajola.

"Your father was the postman and I was the post dog," said Ajola. "We have climbed both up and down. I know the people and the dogs on the other side of the mountains. I am not in the habit of speaking, but now, when we shall not have the opportunity of talking with each other much longer, there is something I would like to say. I want to tell you a story. It is one I have given much thought to; I don't understand it and you probably won't either. Not that it matters whether we understand it or not, but it has set me to thinking that everything is not right, either among men or among dogs.

"Once I saw a puppy that was traveling by stagecoach. It had a seat for itself like a regular passenger. Its mistress—whether she was a lady or a maid, I cannot tell—had taken a little bottle of milk along for the dog to suck on. She offered the puppy cake, but it only sniffed at the cake and wouldn't eat it; then the woman ate it herself. I was running along beside the coach. It was spring and the road was filled with mud. I was hungry—hungry as only a dog can be. I saw it, and I have thought about it since, and somehow I do not think it's right. I hope that someday you will be able to drive in your own carriage, little Rudy. They tell me that such things are up to yourself. I am not sure. I have never been able to, no matter how loud I barked."

That was Ajola's speech. Rudy kissed the old dog on the wet tip of his nose, then he picked the cat up in his arms, but cats don't like to be carried.

"You are getting too strong, don't squeeze me. You know that I will never use my claws against you. Go and climb over the mountains; haven't I taught you how to climb? Believe that you can't fall, and you won't." And the cat ran away before Rudy could see the look of sorrow in its eyes.

His grandfather's two hens were running about at Rudy's feet. One of them had lost its tail. It had been shot off by a tourist who had mistaken it for an eagle.

"Rudy is going across the mountains," said one of the hens.

"He is always in a hurry," said the other. "I cannot bear saying good-by, I am too sensitive." And both the hens scurried outside to look for something to eat.

Rudy said good-by to the goats, and their braying sounded melancholy and sad.

Two of the guides from the district who were going across the mountains took Rudy with them. It was a long march for so small a boy, but Rudy was strong and his courage was tireless.

The swallows flew above him during the first part of the journey. "You and we! You and we!" they sang. The road led across the Lütschine River, which emerges as several small streams from the dark caves of the Grindelwald glacier. The only bridge across the raging waters were steppingstones and fallen trees, which had been carried downstream by the river and now were locked among the rocks.

Near a thicket of alders they began to ascend the side of the mountain, then, when it seemed safe, they walked out on the glacier itself. Sometimes they climbed over the great blocks of ice and sometimes they encircled them. Sometimes they crawled and sometimes they walked. Rudy's eyes shone with delight and he strode forward, stepping so hard that his boots with the iron taps on his heels made marks in the ice, leaving a trail behind him.

Black earth, which had been carried and deposited by the water coming from the melted snow higher up the mountains, covered much of the surface of the glacier, but here and there its blue-green glasslike ice shone through. There were little pools among the ice packs that one had to skirt. At one point Rudy and his companions saw a big boulder that was tottering at the edge of an ice sheet suddenly break loose, roll, and fall into a crevasse in the ice. They heard the echo come from the dark tunnels of the glacier as it continued its descent.

Upward, ever upward they went. The glacier seemed to be trying to stretch itself as high as the mountain peaks, a wild frozen river with towers of ice caught between craggy cliffs. Rudy remembered what he had been told about how he and his mother had been down at the bottom of one of the frost-breathing crevasses. But the story was no more real to him than so many other stories that he had been told, and he soon stopped thinking about it. When the men thought that the climb was getting particularly difficult, one of them would stretch out his hand to help Rudy. But the boy was not tired and he ran across the slippery ice like a mountain goat.

Soon they were walking among barren rocks, then they reached low, wind-swept forest; next they came to a green pasture. The landscape was ever changing, always different, except for its sentinels, the great snow-covered peaks, which Rudy—like all the other children of the district—knew by name: "The Maiden," "The Monk," and "Eiger." Rudy had never before been up so high, never before set foot on that sea of snow with its immobile waves that the wind sweeps across, raising only the fine powder of the surface, as it blows foam on a turbulent ocean. Up here the glaciers hold hands—if one may say that of glaciers—each one of them a palace for the Ice Maiden, whose power and pleasure it is to imprison and bury all.

The sun was hot and the snow blinding to look at, as if it had just been sown with blue-white, glittering diamonds. Innumerable insects, bees, and butterflies had been brought up here by the wind and now lay dead on the snow. Around the top of Mount Wetterhorn rested a dark cloud; it looked as if it were a wad of black cotton. Hidden inside it was a foehn wind, which could spread terror if it were let loose.

Rudy never forgot that day's journey, or the scene high up there at dusk, with a view of the road he had yet to travel and the deep ravines made by water rushing down the mountains for so many thousands of years that it made one feel lost just to think about how many there must have been.

On the other side of the ocean of snow an abandoned stone building was their shelter for the night. Here they found charcoal and kindling. The men lighted a fire and sat down before it to smoke and drink hot spiced wine. Rudy was given his share of the wine, and he listened to the men, who were talking of the mysteries and secrets of the Alps. They told of the great snakes that lived in the deep lakes, of the gypsies, of ghosts who carried sleeping travelers through the air to a strange floating city called Venice. Then they began to talk about the strange, wild shepherd who drove his black sheep across the pastures at night. Many, though they had not seen him, had heard the sheep bells and the ghostly bleating of the ram. While the men spoke, Rudy listened with curiosity but not fear—for he was frightened of nothing—and in the distance he thought he did hear a hollow, weird animal cry. It became clearer and clearer. The men grew silent; they had heard it too. They warned Rudy that he must not fall asleep.

It was the foehn wind that was speaking: that tempest that casts itself from the mountain peaks down into the valleys with such force that it can snap full-grown trees as if they were reeds, and move houses as if they were pawns in a chess game.

The storm lasted only an hour, then the men told Rudy that he could close his eyes. The boy was so tired that he fell asleep at their command.

Early the next morning they broke camp. The sun now shone on new fields of ice, new glaciers, and new mountains, whose names Rudy did not know. They had entered the canton of Valais on the other side of the mountains and great snow peaks lay between them and Grindelwald; still they had far to go before Rudy would reach his new home, a long journey through valleys, forests, and meadows. Rudy looked eagerly at everything.

As the travelers approached, people came rushing out of their houses to stare at them. Rudy had never seen such strange-looking folk before. They all seemed to be deformed. They were disgustingly fat; below their pale, sallow faces, their yellow flesh sagged in rolls. Their eyes were vacant and told of their stupidity. They were Cretins. The women seemed even more monstrous than the men.

"Are these the kind of people I will find in my new home?" Rudy thought.

CHAPTER THREE: RUDY'S UNCLE

Happily, the people who lived in Rudy's uncle's house looked like the kind of human beings whom Rudy was used to seeing. All of them, that is, except one. Here, too, was one of those poor silly creatures whom you find in the canton of Valais, clothed in loneliness and poverty, whose lot it is to spend a few months of each year with different members of the family. Just at the time when Rudy came, it was his uncle's turn to house and feed poor Saperli.

Rudy's uncle was still a mighty hunter, and besides, he was skilled in barrelmaking. His wife was a tiny, lively woman with a birdlike face. She had the eyes of an eagle and a long neck that was covered with fine hair like down.

Everything was new to Rudy: clothes, habits, and even the language; but a child's ear picks things up easily and he soon would learn to understand it. Rudy's uncle seemed rich in comparison to his grandfather. The rooms in the house were large and the walls were covered with polished guns and the horns of chamois that Rudy's uncle had killed. Over the entrance was a picture of the Blessed Mother. Beneath it a little lamp burned and there was a bouquet of rhododendron.

Rudy's uncle was known not only as the best hunter of the chamois in the district but also as the most experienced and trusted guide. In his house Rudy was now to be the favorite, the one whom the grownups spoiled a little. True, he had a rival: an old hunting dog, useless now but honored and petted for all the use he had once been. Everyone remembered and talked about his former feats, and that is why he was treated like a member of the family who was entitled to spend his old age in leisure. Rudy tried to be friendly and pet the dog, but it did not respond to strangers. Rudy did not remain a stranger long; he soon grew roots in house and heart.

"Life is not so bad in the canton of Valais," his uncle said. "We still have the chamois, and that won't die out as the mountain goat did. Things are much better now than they were—though you'll hear a lot of boasting about the 'good old times.' There is a hole in the sack now. There is fresh air in the valleys; we are not as closed in as we used to be. The new bud is always better than the fallen leaf."

Sometimes Rudy's uncle was very talkative. Then he would tell of his childhood, of the time when his own father was in his prime, when the canton of Valais was "closed tight as a sack" that was full of many unpleasant things, among them the poor unfortunate Cretins.

"When the Frenchmen came, they killed many people, but they killed the sickness as well. Oh, the French can fight in more ways than one. They fought the mountains, the rocks were forced to give up; we have a road across the Simplon. I can say to a three-year-old child, 'Go to Italy.' And if he keeps to the road he will get there. . . . Frenchwomen are good at fighting too." Rudy's uncle laughed and nodded toward his wife, who had been born in France; then he sang a French song and shouted hip-hip-hurrah for Napoleon Bonaparte.

This was the first time that Rudy had heard of France and of the great town on the Rhone River, called Lyon, which his uncle had once visited.

"It won't be long before the boy becomes a good hunter. He has a natural bent for it," Rudy's uncle said more than once, as he taught the boy how to hold a rifle, take aim, and shoot.

During the hunting season he took him up in the mountains and gave him the blood of chamois to drink, for Swiss hunters and guides believe this is an antidote against vertigo. He taught him how to judge when an avalanche would take place—whether it would happen in the morning or the evening—by observing the conditions of the snow and the strength of the sun. He told Rudy to take the chamois as teacher in the art of climbing, to watch how it could leap and land on its feet without sliding. He explained what he should do when there was no foothold on the face of a cliff: how he could hold onto the rock with his elbows or use the muscles of his legs and thighs— even his neck—to prevent himself from falling.

The chamois are clever; they even post guards to tell the flock when a hunter is approaching. The hunter must be cleverer; he must walk against the wind so that the animal cannot pick up his scent. Sometimes Rudy's uncle would fool the chamois by hanging his hat and his tunic on a cane. The chamois, mistaking the clothing for the hunter, would expect an attack from the wrong direction.

One day Rudy and his uncle were out hunting. His uncle had spied a chamois on the side of a mountain. The snow was wet and slippery. The path along the face of the cliff was so narrow that it soon disappeared and became only a thin ledge above a deep abyss, so he lay down and crawled.

Rudy was standing on more solid ground, about a hundred feet below him. Suddenly the boy saw a vulture, the kind that can take a half-grown sheep and fly away with it; it was circling in the air above Rudy's uncle. The boy knew what it intended to do. Any moment it would sweep down on the man and with its wings hurl him into the valley, where it could later feed on his corpse. Rudy's uncle had eye only for the chamois, which could be seen running with its kid. Rudy took aim and was about to shoot the vulture. Just at that moment the chamois leaped up to the ridge of the cliff. Rudy's uncle fired and the antelope was dead. The kid fled; all its life had been spent in training for this moment of flight. The echo from the shot frightened the vulture and it flew away. Rudy's uncle did not know about the danger he had been in until he was told about it later by Rudy.

As they were returning home in high spirits—Rudy's uncle whistling a tune from his childhood—they heard a terrifying but familiar noise coming from not far away. They looked about them and then they looked upward. There above them they saw a part of the snow field being lifted as if it were a linen tablecloth that the wind had caught. It snapped in two, like a gigantic slab of marble breaking. Stones, snow, and ice tumbled down the mountainside. There was a sound like a thunderclap. It was an avalanche! They would not be buried by it, but it would pass much too near them.

"Hold on, Rudy!" his uncle screamed. "Hold on with all your might!"

Rudy threw his arms around the trunk of a tree, while his uncle climbed up into the branches above him. The landslide passed several yards away from them, but the turbulence caused winds of such strength that trunks and branches of trees were broken as if they were dry reeds. Rudy lay pressed to the ground. The tree trunk that he held onto was now a stump, as if it had been sawed in half. The wind had broken off the crown and thrown it a distance away. There among the splintered branches lay his uncle. The man's head was smashed, his face was unrecognizable, although his hand holding onto the branch was still warm. Pale and trembling, Rudy looked at him; this was the first time the boy had become acquainted with fear, the first time he had experienced horror.

Late that night he returned home, bearing the message of death to the house that now belonged to sorrow. His aunt was silent; she did not cry until the following day when her husband's body was carried to the house.

The poor Cretin stayed in bed the whole day, but in the evening he got up and approached Rudy. "Will you write a letter for me? Saperli cannot write, but Saperli can go to the post office."

"Whom do you want to write a letter to?" Rudy asked.

"To our Master Christ," replied the Cretin.

"What are you talking about?"

The half-wit, as they called him, looked with pleading eyes at Rudy, folded his hands, and said very solemnly and piously but in a gentle voice, "Jesus Christ. Saperli wants to beg him to let Saperli lie dead and not the master of this house."

Rudy took Saperli's hands in his. "Such a letter would never be delivered, and it would not bring him back to us." It was difficult for Rudy to explain to the Cretin why what he was asking was impossible.

"Now you are master of the house," Rudy's aunt said to him. And Rudy became the master.

CHAPTER FOUR: BABETTE

"Who is the best hunter in the canton of Valais?" The chamois could answer that question. "Watch out for Rudy," they would say.

"Who is the handsomest hunter?"

"Rudy is the handsomest," the girls would reply, but they did not add, "Watch out for Rudy." Not even the strictest mothers said that, for he nodded as pleasantly to them as he did to their daughters.

He was always happy, with a smile on his lips. His cheeks were tanned bronze by the sun, his teeth were white, and his eyes were dark as coal. A handsome lad and only twenty years old. The ice water in the lakes did not seem freezing to him, he swam like a fish. He could hang onto the sheer, granite mountainside as if he were a snail; no one could climb as well as he. His sinews and his muscles were good. How to leap and to jump he had learned first from the cat and later from the chamois.

With Rudy as a guide any traveler was safe, and he could have made a fortune that way. Barrelmaking he had learned from his uncle, but he never thought of making a living that way either. Rudy was a hunter, and to stalk the chamois was his greatest pleasure. Good hunters weren't poor, and everyone in the district agreed that Rudy was a good match, as long as he did not set his eyes on those above him.

"He kissed me while we were dancing," said the schoolmaster's daughter Annette to her dearest friend. But Annette should never

have told such a thing to her dearest friend, for a secret like that is as
hard to keep as it is to stop sand from running out of a bag with a
hole in it. Soon everyone knew that Rudy, in spite of being so honest
and good-natured, could steal a kiss while he was dancing—and yet
he had never kissed the girl whom he wanted most to kiss.

"Keep an eye on him," said an old hunter. "He has kissed Annette, and since he has started with *A,* he'll kiss through the whole al-
phabet."

A kiss during a dance was as yet all the gossips could bring to
market. He had kissed Annette and yet she was not the flower his
heart pined for.

Down at Bex, between two great walnut trees and beside a rushing
mountain stream, lived a rich miller. His house was large: three stories high with small towers at each corner, and roofed with shingles
that were held fast by strips of lead that reflected the light of both the
sun and the moon. The highest of the towers had a weather vane in
the form of an apple with a golden arrow piercing it, in honor of
William Tell. The mill looked prosperous and decorative, and with a
bit of skill one could describe it or sketch it; but the miller's daughter
was another matter. In any case, Rudy would have said that you
could not possibly draw or tell about such beauty in words. Yet her
picture was in his heart, and there her eyes shone with such brilliance
that they had set his heart afire. Like all fires, it had broken out suddenly; and the strangest part of it was that the miller's daughter
Babette did not even know about it, for she and Rudy had never exchanged a single word.

The miller was rich, and his wealth put Babette a good many
notches above a hunter. "But nothing is up so high that it cannot be
reached," thought Rudy. "All you have to do is climb, and you never
fall unless you believe that you are going to." This was his philosophy
and he had learned it at home.

Now it happened that Rudy had business in Bex. In those days it
was quite a journey, for the railroad hadn't reached there yet. From
the Rhone glacier along the foothills of the Simplon, surrounded by
mountains of varying heights, stretches the valley of Valais, and
through it runs the mighty Rhone River. The river is master of the
valley, and often in spring it swells over its banks to flood the fields
and ruin the roads. Between the towns of Sion and St. Maurice the

valley turns sharply, and at St. Maurice it becomes so narrow there is only room for the river and the road that connects the two towns.

An ancient tower stands guard on the mountainside and looks out across the bridge to the customs house on the other side of the river. Here the canton of Valais ends and the canton of Vaud begins. The nearest town is Bex; from there on the valley seems to grow wider with every step, and as it broadens it grows richer and more fertile. It becomes a garden with walnut, chestnut, and tall cypress trees. Here even the pomegranate will ripen, and it is so warm that you might think you were as far south as Italy.

Rudy soon finished his errand at Bex and walked about the town. But he did not even see any of the apprentices from the mill, let alone Babette. Luck, which was usually kind to him, seemed to frown upon him that day.

It was evening. The air was filled with the fragrance of flowering thyme and the blossoms of the linden trees. A blue veil seemed to cover the forest-clad mountains. The world was silent, not with the silence of sleep or death, but rather as if Nature were holding her breath because she was about to be photographed.

Across the valley ran the telegraph lines; the poles could be seen among the trees. Something was leaning against one of them. At a distance you would have mistaken it for a log because it looked so motionless, but it was Rudy. He was as completely still as his surroundings, and he, too, was neither dead nor asleep. As you cannot tell by looking at a telegraph line that the news it is carrying may change the course of a person's life—or even shake the world—so you could not have guessed by looking at Rudy how overwhelming his thoughts were. He was thinking about happiness, life, and the purpose of existence, and he was wondering what would become of his "constant thought": that thought which from now on would never leave him.

His glances rested on a light in the miller's house where Babette lived. Rudy was standing as still as he did when he took aim before shooting a chamois, but at that moment he resembled the antelope itself, which can stand so motionless that it appears to be made of stone, only to leap and vanish if it hears a tiny pebble fall. And this was exactly what Rudy did when, like a falling pebble, a thought came to him.

"Don't give up," he said aloud. "I will visit the mill and say good

evening to the miller and good day to Babette. Believe that you can't
fall and you won't. After all, Babette has to meet me sooner or later
if I am to be her husband."

Rudy laughed. His spirits rose as he made his way to the mill. He
knew what he wanted, he wanted Babette.

The path followed the river with its turbulent yellowish water. The
willow and linden trees grew along the banks and their branches hung
like tresses above the edges of the rapid flowing water. Rudy walked
as it says in the nursery rhyme:

> . . . till he came to the miller's house
> Where no one was home
> But a cat and a mouse.

The cat was on the steps that led to the front door. It stretched itself, arched its back, and meowed. But Rudy paid no attention; he
went straight up to the door and knocked. "Meow," said the cat
again. Had Rudy been still a child, he would have understood that
the cat said, "There is no one at home." But now Rudy was a
grownup, so he had to ask one of the workers in the mill to learn why
the miller's house was empty.

They had gone to Interlaken: *inter lacus,* as Annette's father, the
schoolteacher, called it, "among the lakes." There on the following
day were to begin the competitions for marksmanship, and people
would be there from all the German-speaking cantons to watch them.
The contests would last a whole week. Poor Rudy, he had not timed
his visit to Bex very well and now there was nothing for him to do
but start on the long road home: back over the mountains via St.
Maurice and Sion, to his own valley; and that's what he did. But the
next morning, by the time the sun had risen, his spirits had risen too.

"Babette is at Interlaken," he thought. "It is far from here, several
days' journey, if you follow the road. But not if you go over the
mountains, then it's not nearly as far. And that's the way for a hunter
to travel, by climbing the mountains. Haven't I done it before? Don't
I come from there? Didn't I live there with my grandfather? I will
win the competition at Interlaken just as I will win Babette's heart
. . . as soon as she gets to know me, that is."

He packed his Sunday suit in a small knapsack, slung his hunting
bag across his shoulders, and with his rifle in his hand set out to

climb the mountains that separated him from Interlaken. But even this short route was long enough. However, the competition would only begin today, and he had been told that Babette and the miller were staying with relatives at Interlaken for the whole week. Rudy decided to cross the great glacier Gemmi because he wanted to descend the mountains near his old home at Grindelwald.

Healthy and happy, he was a fine sight, if anyone had been there to look at him. As he strode along, the valley disappeared and the horizon broadened. First one and then another of the snow-capped mountains came into view. Rudy knew them all. He walked toward Schreckhorn, which stretched upward into the blue sky like a snow-covered stone finger.

Finally, he had crossed the mountains and the green meadows of his childhood stretched themselves toward him. His soul was as light as the mountain air. The valleys were green and filled with the flowers of spring, and in his heart was the wisdom of youth: One cannot die! One cannot age! Live! Live and enjoy! Be free as a bird. Light as a bird he was, walking and dancing along the path, the swallows singing above him as they had when he was a child: "You and we! You and we!"

Below on the velvet green meadow, he saw the little brown wooden houses and the Lütschine River. He saw the glacier covered with dirty gray snow, and its clear green glass borders, lined with deep crevasses, for he could see both the top and the bottom of the great field of ice. The bells of the village rang to greet him and welcome him home. For a moment the memories of childhood so filled his heart that he forgot Babette.

Again he was walking the road alongside which, as a child, he had stood waiting to sell the little wooden toy houses his grandfather had carved. Up among the pine trees was his grandfather's house, but strangers were living in it. Children came. They wanted him to buy their parents' handicraft. Rudy smiled and one of the children gave him a rhododendron. "The rose of the mountains," he whispered. "It is a good omen." And at that moment Babette came back into his mind.

He crossed the bridge where the two streams meet to become the river Lütschine. The evergreens gave way to the birch and oak and elm, and finally he was walking in the shade of the walnut tree. In the distance he saw flags flying: a white cross on a red background, the national banners of both Switzerland and Denmark. Spread out in front of him lay Interlaken.

Rudy thought it was one of the most beautiful sights he had ever seen, a Swiss town dressed up for Sunday. It was not like any other city. It was not a collection of big stone buildings: stodgy, forbidding, and important. No, it was as if all the small wooden houses from the mountainsides had decided to move down into the green valley and had lined themselves up as they pleased, in not too straight rows along the banks of the clear river.

The houses looked exactly like the ones his grandfather had carved, the ones that had stood in the closet of his childhood home. For a moment Rudy imagined that it was so, that the toy houses had grown up like the old chestnut trees that lined the streets.

Each house had intricately carved woodwork around its windows and balconies; the latter were protected by overhanging roofs from rain and snow. On the loveliest street all the houses were new; they had not been there when Rudy, as a boy, visited Interlaken. They were hotels, every one; each had a flower garden in front of it and the road was macadamized. Here there were buildings only on one side of the street, so as not to hide from view the green meadow with its grazing cows, who wore bells around their necks just as they did in the mountains. The pasture was encircled by mountains. In the middle of the chain towered the snow-capped "Maiden," and it was as if the other mountains had stepped aside to give the onlooker a better view of this shining white mountain that is the most beautifully shaped of all the mountains of Switzerland.

How many elegantly dressed foreigners one saw in the streets, which were already crowded with hunters and farmers from the different cantons. The hunters who were participating in the competition wore ribbons with numbers on them in their hats. The houses and bridges were draped with banners, and on some of them there were verses. There was music—trumpets and horns and barrel organs. There were the screams of children and the shouts of adults as they hailed old friends and new acquaintances. Yet all the while could be heard shooting, one shot after another. The sound of the guns was the most inspiring music to Rudy's ears, and once more he forgot Babette and why he had come to Interlaken.

Rudy joined the men competing at target shooting. Every time he fired, his bullet hit the little dark spot at the center of the shield.

"Who is that very young hunter?" people began to ask each other.

"He talks French as if he came from the canton of Valais," someone remarked. "Yet he can speak German as we do here."

"They say," someone else explained, "that when he was a child he lived near Grindel."

Yes, Rudy was full of life! His hands were strong and steady, his eye sharp, so his bullets always hit their mark. Happiness is the mother of courage, and Rudy was always courageous. He made friends easily and soon was surrounded by a group of admirers wherever he went. Everyone knew who he was and spoke well of him; he had no time to think of Babette.

Suddenly a firm hand grasped his shoulder and a man asked him in French, "Are you from the canton of Valais?"

Rudy turned around and saw a fat man with a cheerful red face: it was the rich miller from Bex. He was so heavy-set that he almost hid his daughter Babette, who was standing on tiptoe behind him to get a better view of the young hunter.

The rich miller had been pleased when he heard that it was a hunter from a French-speaking canton who was winning all the competitions, and he had made up his mind to meet him. Fortune certainly was smiling on Rudy, when what he had set out to seek now sought him.

When you are in a strange place and you meet someone from home, you talk to him as if you had always been friends. Rudy was now a man of importance at Interlaken because of his skill at marksmanship just as the miller was a man of importance in Bex because of his mill and his money. They shook hands as equals, which under other circumstances they might never have done. Babette, too, offered Rudy her hand, and as he took it in his he looked so intently into her eyes that she blushed.

The miller told Rudy about their journey, of the many towns they had passed through, and how they had traveled by steamer, railroad, and stagecoach in order to reach Interlaken.

"I took a shorter route," Rudy said. "I went over the mountains; they aren't so high that you can't climb them."

"If you are willing to risk breaking your neck," replied the miller. "And you may well break yours, if you are as daring as you look."

"You can't fall if you don't believe you can," Rudy said.

The miller's relatives at Interlaken, at whose home he and Babette were staying, invited Rudy to visit them—after all, he came from the same district as their own family. Rudy accepted readily. Luck was with him, as she always is with those who have confidence in themselves and remember the proverb: "God provides the nuts but He does not shell them for us."

Rudy sat at the dinner table as if he were already a member of the family. A toast was made to the best marksman at Interlaken. They all lifted their glasses to Rudy, even Babette; and he made a short speech of thanks.

In the late afternoon they all went out for a walk along the beautiful street where all the hotels were. Here there was so much going on and such a throng that Rudy had to offer Babette his arm.

"I am so happy to have met someone from the canton of Vaud," he declared. "The cantons of Vaud and Valais have always been such good neighbors."

Babette thought that he sounded so sincere that she must hold his hand. Soon they were talking as if they had known each other for ever so long. And Rudy thought that he had never heard anyone speak so charmingly, so sweetly, as she pointed out to him how ridiculously the foreign women dressed and carried themselves.

"You mustn't think I am making fun of them. Foreigners can be honest and very kind. And no one knows that better than I because my godmother is an English lady. She was visiting Bex when I was born."

Babette was wearing a gold pin that her godmother had given her. "She has written to me twice, and I have been expecting her at Interlaken this year. She is supposed to come with her daughters. They are unmarried and quite old—nearly thirty." Babette herself was only eighteen.

She gave her little mouth no rest and everything that she had to say seemed to Rudy of great importance. When his turn came, he told her everything that he could tell. He said that he had been in Bex often and knew her father's mill. He admitted that he had seen her many times, though she probably had not noticed him. Finally he confided the thoughts he had had that night when he went to Bex and was told that Babette and her father had gone to Interlaken. "You were far, far away. But there are two ways to get around a wall, and the shorter is to climb over it."

Yes, he said that and he said other things, too. He told her how much he cared for her and that he had come to Interlaken for her sake, and not to prove his skill as a marksman.

While he talked Babette grew very quiet; his confession was almost more than she could bear.

As they walked the sun set and the snow-capped "Maiden," framed by the forest-clad mountains, showed herself in all her glory. For a moment everyone stood still and looked at the majestic sight, even Rudy and Babette.

"Nowhere is it as beautiful as here!" said Babette.

"Nowhere!" echoed Rudy, who was looking at Babette. "Tomorrow I must leave," he said a little while later.

"Come and visit us in Bex," she whispered. "I am sure it will please my father."

CHAPTER FIVE: THE WAY HOME

How many things Rudy had to carry on his way home the next day! There were three silver cups, two quite good rifles, and a silver coffeepot that would come in handy when he settled down. And he was carrying something else that was even more valuable, something that was not a burden and seemed almost to carry him over the high mountains.

The weather was far from pleasant. It was gray, rainy, and raw. Heavy clouds rested on the mountains like veils of grief, obscuring their peaks. From far below, Rudy heard the woodman's ax, and the trees as they rolled down the mountainside looked like toothpicks, though many were tall and stout enough to become the masts of ships. The Lütschine River continuously struck its single chord, and the wind sang its monotonous song as the clouds sailed by overhead.

Just ahead of Rudy a girl suddenly appeared, walking in the same direction as he was, on her way across the mountains. Her eyes seemed to have a strange power. Rudy found himself looking into them; they were clear as glass and fathomlessly deep.

"Have you a sweetheart?" Rudy asked, for those in love can think only of love.

"I have no one!" she exclaimed, and laughed, but something in her voice made him think that she was lying. "Let's not take the longest way," she said. "Here we must go more to the left; it's a shorter way."

"Yes, to the bottom of an ice crevasse," said Rudy. "If you don't know the mountains better than that, you shouldn't play guide."

"Oh, I know the way," she replied. "I have my wits about me. You seem to have left yours down in the valley. Watch out, when you are in the mountains you must think about the Ice Maiden. Men believe that she is no friend of human beings."

"I am not afraid of her," Rudy said with confidence. "She had to let me go when I was child; now that I am a man she will not dare to touch me."

It grew darker. There was a heavy rain that finally turned to snow, a white blinding world.

"Come, take my hand. I will help you climb," the girl offered, and stretched out her hand toward him. Her fingers were cold as ice.

"You help me!" Rudy exclaimed. "I do not need a girl's help to climb."

He walked faster, away from her. The snowstorm swept around him like a blanket. Through the whirling of the wind he could hear a girl's laughter and singing. "She must be a servant of the Ice Maiden," he thought; and he remembered the tales he had heard from the guides on his journey across the mountains when he was a boy.

It almost stopped snowing. He had climbed above the clouds. Still he heard laughter and singing below him, but the voices did not sound human.

When Rudy reached the top of the pass, where the way begins to descend into the Rhone Valley, he saw a patch of clear sky in the direction of Chamonix. Two brilliant stars appeared. He thought of Babette and himself, and of how lucky he had been.

CHAPTER SIX: A VISIT TO THE MILL

"You will bring honor to our family. You will rise above both your father and your uncle," Rudy's aunt said; and her strange eaglelike eyes gleamed, while she moved her long neck more quickly than usual in the peculiar birdlike way she had. "You are fortunate, Rudy.

Come, let me kiss you, for you are as good to me as any son could have been."

Although he submitted and let his aunt kiss him, Rudy's expression told that he considered it a duty.

"How handsome you are!" the old woman sighed.

"That's just something you tell yourself," he replied, and laughed; but her words had pleased him.

"I'll repeat it. You are lucky," his aunt said, and smiled.

"There I agree with you!" Rudy exclaimed, for he was thinking of Babette. Never before in his life had he longed for the valley as he did now. "They must have come home by now. They have probably been home two days already. I must go to Bex."

When Rudy arrived in Bex he found the miller at home. He even seemed glad to see him, and mentioned that he had regards for him from his family in Interlaken. Babette hardly spoke. She seemed to have become so silent, but her eyes talked and their message was eloquent enough for Rudy.

The miller, who was used to being the center of attention, to having people laugh at his jokes and listen to his stories, took an interest in what Rudy had to say. He enjoyed hearing about the life of a hunter, of the difficulties and dangers that one had to endure to hunt the chamois. It was exciting to listen to Rudy tell how he had to make his way along a narrow ledge, high up where the mountainside was a sheer cliff, and how he sometimes had to make use of the bridges nature furnished to cross many a cleft, bridges made only of ice and snow that might give way beneath his foot at any moment, hurling him to his death far below. Rudy looked bold and his eyes shone as he spoke of hunting the chamois. He told, too, about the animal itself: the chamois, that goatlike antelope that lives in the Alps. He described how clever it could be and how courageous it was. He talked of the foehn wind, of avalanches, of landslides that could bury a whole village. And all the while he was speaking he knew that, the better the miller liked his stories, the fonder he would grow of the storyteller.

The miller appeared to be most interested in hearing about buzzards, falcons, hawks, and eagles. Rudy told him about an eagle's nest. It was not far away in the canton of Valais. It had been built very cleverly, on a tiny ledge underneath an overhanging cliff. In the nest there was a young eagle. Only a few days ago an Englishman had offered Rudy a handful of gold coins for the live eaglet.

"But that's too dangerous even for me," laughed Rudy. "That young eagle is quite safe. It would be madness to try to climb up there and get it."

As the wine flowed freely, tongues were loosened, and the evening seemed very short to Rudy, even though it was after midnight when he walked homeward after his first visit to the mill.

It was a while before the last candle in the miller's house was put out. From a little window in the roof the parlor cat stepped out for a bit of fresh air, and in the gutter beneath the eaves she met the kitchen cat.

"Something new has happened at the mill, do you know what it is?" the parlor cat asked. "Someone is secretly engaged in this house, and Father doesn't know about it yet! Rudy and Babette sat all evening stepping on each other's paws under the table. Twice they stepped on my tail, but I didn't meow for fear of attracting attention."

"I would have," said the kitchen cat.

"What can pass for manners in the kitchen is improper behavior in the parlor. I wonder what the miller is going to say when he hears about the engagement."

Yes, what would the miller say? Rudy wanted to know that too, so before many days had passed he was seated in a stagecoach on his way to Bex. He was filled with confidence as the vehicle rumbled over the Rhone bridge, which separates the canton of Valais from that of Vaud. He was imagining the scene when he would be officially engaged that very evening.

When the coach returned later that evening, Rudy was again on it; this time he was going home. Down at the mill the parlor cat ran all over the house spreading the news.

"You there, kitchen cat. . . . Do you want to know what's happened? . . . The miller knows everything. Rudy came early this evening, and he and Babette stood out in the hall, near the miller's room, and whispered and whispered. I heard everything they said, for I was lying at their feet.

" 'I am going straight in to your father,' Rudy said.

" 'Shall I come with you to bolster your courage?' Babette asked.

" 'I have courage to spare; but come along anyway, because when your father sees you he cannot help but look upon us kindly, whether he wants to or not,' he answered. Then into the miller's room the two of them went.

"Rudy's a clumsy fellow. He stepped on my tail and I meowed as loud as I could, but it was as if they had all lost their ears. But I was first in the room and I jumped up on a chair. It's dangerous to get anywhere near Rudy's feet, for you might get kicked. But I needn't have worried about that because it was the miller who did the kicking. He gave Rudy a good kick right out the door and back up into the mountains. Now he can aim at chamois and not at our Babette."

"But tell me how it happened. What did they say to each other?" demanded the kitchen cat.

"Say? . . . They said everything that you have to say when you are courting: 'I love her and she loves me. . . . When there is milk enough in the pail for one, then it will do for two.'

"But the miller replied, 'You aim too high! Babette is sitting on a whole pile of grain sacks, sacks filled with golden grain! You can't get up there.'

" 'Nothing is so high that you cannot reach it if you want to badly enough,' Rudy said, for he is very bold.

"The miller smiled. 'What about the eagle you told me about the last time you were here? That was too high for you, you admitted that; well, Babette is even higher.'

" 'I will reach them both!' Rudy exclaimed.

" 'All right. I will give Babette to you when you give me the little eagle alive.' Then he laughed till tears streamed down his face. 'But thank you for calling all the same. Come again tomorrow and we'll be sure not to be home. Good-by, Rudy.' Babette said good-by too, but she sounded as miserable as a kitten that cannot find its mother.

" 'Don't cry, Babette,' Rudy consoled her. 'A word is a word, and a man is a man. I will bring back the eaglet.'

"The miller stopped laughing and said, 'I hope you will break your neck, so that we will be spared the sight of you here again.' Now that was a kick, wasn't it?

"Rudy is gone. Babette is crying, and the miller is singing a German song that he learned at Interlaken. I wouldn't have cried. What's the point of it? It doesn't help."

"But it keeps up appearances," said the kitchen cat.

CHAPTER SEVEN: THE EAGLE'S NEST

Someone was yodeling as he came up the mountain, yodeling as if he did not have a care in the world. It was Rudy on his way to visit his friend Vesimand.

"You must help me. I will get Ragli to join us. There's an eagle's nest on a tiny ledge near the top of the canyon and I must have the eaglet."

"Why don't you try to fetch the dark of the moon instead? It would be easier." Vesimand smiled. "What makes you so happy today?"

"I am thinking of getting married. But seriously, let me tell you what has happened."

Less than an hour later both Vesimand and Ragli knew why Rudy wanted the eaglet. "You are too daring," they said. "It can't be done. You will break your neck."

"You cannot fall if you don't believe you can," Rudy replied.

At midnight they set out, carrying staves, ropes, and ladders. The path led through brushwood and over huge boulders, ever upward in the dark night. Far below they heard the voice of the river and above them the songs of the tiny waterfalls. Clouds heavy with rain sailed by. Finally they reached a crag on the side of a cliff; they could climb no farther. Above them the granite sides of the cleft almost met, leaving only a sliver of the sky visible. The night seemed to grow darker. They sat down on the narrow ledge to wait for morning to come. In the ravine, far below, the water was rushing. Silently and patiently they waited for dawn. First they must shoot the eagle before making any attempt to capture the eaglet. Rudy sat on his haunches, as motionless as the rock he was sitting on. His gaze rested on that part of the bluff that jutted out and hid the tiny ledge on which the eagle had built its nest. His gun was ready. But the three hunters had long to wait.

At last they heard that terrible whizzing sound of the eagle's great wings beating the air. Against the tiny patch of sky between the cliffs of the crevice they could clearly see the shape of the huge bird. Two of the hunters had their rifles trained on the eagle, but only one shot rang out.

For a moment the wings continued to flap, then they stopped and the bird fell slowly downward. So large did the bird seem, so great the span of its wings, that the hunters suddenly feared that there might not be space enough in the narrow canyon for the bird to fall without brushing against them in its descent, so that one or even all of them might be pushed into the abyss. But the bird did not touch them and soon they heard the breaking of branches below them.

Now the hunters had to get busy. Believing that three ladders, when tied together, would reach the eagle's nest, they began tying the top of one to the bottom of another. Resting the lowest ladder on the very edge of the crag, they leaned the ladders up against the side of the cliff. They were not long enough! Above the top rung of the third ladder the granite continued to rise and it was as straight as a man-made wall for several feet before it curved outward, and thereby protected the eagle's nest.

The young hunters decided that there was only one way to reach the nest. They must retrace their steps and find a place where they might ascend to the top of the canyon, and from there lower two ladders and somehow attach them to the other three.

It was only with the greatest difficulty that they managed to carry the ladders up to the highest point of the precipice. They tied them together and slowly lowered them into the abyss. On the lowest rung of the second ladder sat Rudy.

It was an ice-cold morning. The bottom of the canyon far below him was hidden in vapors. Rudy was like a fly sitting on a piece of straw that some bird while nest building had dropped and that had alighted on the rim of a tall factory chimney; the difference being that, should the straw fall, the fly would take flight, but Rudy had no wings, he could only break his neck. The wind blew around him. He heard the voice of the rushing river in the depths below; it carried the water from the melting snow of the glacier that was the palace of the Ice Maiden.

Rudy swung on the ladders as a spider dangles on a single thread, searching for a place to fasten her web. The fourth time that his fingertips touched the ladders that were leaning against the side of the cliff he managed to get a good grasp. With steady hands he bound the two sets of ladders together, then, as his friends slackened their ropes from above, he forced the two new additions to his giant ladder to rest against the granite wall.

The five ladders were like a reed that at any moment might begin to sway, but they appeared to reach up high enough for Rudy to climb from their topmost rung into the eagle's nest. Now came the most dangerous part of the expedition. Rudy must climb as well as a cat, but he knew how, for a cat had been his teacher. The Ice Maiden's servant, Vertigo, reached out her arms like a sea anemone, but Rudy did not feel her touch.

Rudy's ladder was, after all, not long enough; he could reach the nest by stretching his arms upward but he could not see into it. With his hands he explored the outermost layer of branches that had been braided by the eagle to form its nest. Finding a particularly heavy bough that did not give way when he pulled on it, Rudy swung from the ladder to the nest. His head and shoulders were above its rim. A stench of rotten meat greeted him: half-consumed carcasses of chamois, lambs, and birds were strewn everywhere. Vertigo, who had not been able to disturb him before, now gently blew the odious smell into his face, hoping that the fumes would make him dizzy. Down in the waters of the rushing river waited the Ice Maiden with her white-green hair and her deadly eyes which, like the muzzles of a gun, were trained on Rudy. "Now I shall catch you!" she exclaimed.

Near the rim sat the eaglet. Although it could not fly, it was large, almost full grown. Rudy stared intently at the bird. Holding onto the branch with one hand, he cast a noose around the feet of the eaglet with the other. He pulled the string and the bird was captured. He flung the captive over his shoulder; because of the length of the cord, it hung down below Rudy's feet. Now his other hand was free to grasp the rope that held the ladders, until his feet were on the rungs once more.

"Hold on! Don't believe that you can fall and you won't." That was the wisdom that he had taken with him as he scaled the shaking ladders and cleaved to the wall of granite. He had not believed that he could fall, and he hadn't fallen.

Through the canyon the happy sound of yodeling could be heard. Rudy was again standing on solid earth and he had the eaglet with him.

CHAPTER EIGHT: WHAT THE PARLOR CAT KNEW

"Here is what you asked for," Rudy announced. As he stepped into the miller's house at Bex, he put a large covered basket down on the floor. When he lifted the cloth two savage yellow eyes, rimmed in black, stared wildly at first one thing and then another, as if those eyes burned to attack everything they saw. Its short but strong bill was half open, prepared to bite. Its red neck was covered with down.

"The eaglet!" shouted the miller.

Babette screamed and stepped back, but she did not take her eyes away from Rudy or the bird.

"You do not frighten easily." The miller looked at Rudy and the hunter returned his gaze.

"And you, sir, always keep your word. Each of us has a trait that he likes to be known by."

"Why didn't you break your neck?" the miller asked, but he smiled at the same time.

"Because I held on—and I am still holding on—to Babette."

Now the miller laughed, and Babette knew that this was a good sign. "You haven't got her yet," he said. "But we'd better take the eaglet out of the basket. Look how it stares! Now you must tell me how you captured it."

And Rudy told of his adventure so well that the miller's eyes grew larger and larger. "With your courage and your luck, you can support three wives."

"Thank you, thank you!" Rudy said quickly.

The miller slapped Rudy on the back and again he reminded him, "You haven't got her yet."

"Do you want to hear the latest news from the parlor?" the parlor cat asked the kitchen cat. "Rudy brought the eaglet and exchanged the bird for Babette. They kissed each other while the miller looked on, and that's as good as announcing your engagement. The old man didn't kick this time. He drew in his claws. He let the young couple be alone together while he took his afternoon nap. They sat and purred. They seemed to have so much to say to each other that they won't be finished by Christmas."

And they weren't finished by Christmas. The wind blew and undressed the trees. The snow came to the valleys as well as to the mountains. The Ice Maiden sat in her proud castle which enlarged itself in the winter. The cliffs glistened with ice, and where in summer waterfalls had leaped down the mountainside there now hung elephant-heavy icicles that a man could not encircle with his arms. Snow crystals decorated the branches of the evergreens. The Ice Maiden rode on the wind through the deep valleys. Down at Bex lay a blanket of snow, so she could come there and peek through the windows of the mill and see Rudy, who had never before spent so much time indoors, sitting close to Babette. When summer came, they were to be married; and if their ears were ringing, it was quite understandable because their coming marriage was much discussed among their friends. Finally the sun gained strength, flowers bloomed, but not more beautifully than the happy, laughing Babette, for she was like the spring; and all the birds sang of summer to come and their wedding day.

"How those two can just sit about, hanging onto each other's words, is more than I can understand," said the parlor cat. "I'm bored. . . . Meow."

CHAPTER NINE: THE ICE MAIDEN

Spring had come. The chestnut and the walnut trees formed garlands of greenness from the bridge at St. Maurice to the Lake of Geneva and all along the Rhone, that river which rushes headlong from its source, deep down underneath the green glacier, where the palace of the Ice Maiden is. From there she rides on the wind up to the fields of everlasting snow, to stretch herself in the sunlight and look down into the valleys where human beings are scurrying about like ants on a sun-brightened boulder.

"Reasonable beings you are called by the sun's children; you are nothing but vermin! One rolling ball of snow and that is the end of you, your houses, and your towns. All of them I can crush!" The Ice Maiden lifted her proud head and gazed with eyes as cold as death far and wide. From one of the valleys came the sound of an explosion, the work of men who were blasting to make way for a new railroad line by cutting tunnels through the mountains.

"They are playing mole, digging passages through the earth, that's why it sounds like small stones cracking. If I made one of my castles move, then you would hear a din greater than thunder."

From one of the valleys smoke appeared, like the feathered plume of a hat, streaming out of the funnel of the engine that drew the train along the newly constructed track: a bending, whistling snake of swiftly moving cars.

"They are playing that they are masters, those reasonable beings, but the power of nature commands them." And the Ice Maiden laughed and sang so it echoed throughout the valleys.

"Avalanche!" exclaimed the people of the valley.

The children of the sun—its golden rays—sang their song about human achievement even louder. Human thought has spanned the oceans, moved the mountains, and filled in the valleys. "The human mind is master of nature," they sang.

At the moment the Ice Maiden was watching a group of travelers make their way across a snow field. They were tied together with a heavy rope so they could help each other if one of them should fall into a crevasse as they walked on the slippery ice.

"Vermin!" screamed the Ice Maiden. "How can you be masters of nature?" And she looked away from them, down into the valley where the train was passing.

"Human thought! There they sit, those thinkers, being carried by nature's power. I can see every one of them. Look at them! One alone sits as proud as a king. The others sit in a clump. Half of them are asleep. When the steam dragon stops they will get off and go their way. These thinkers will go out into the world." Again the Ice Maiden laughed.

"Avalanche!" the people exclaimed in the valley.

"Another avalanche, but it cannot reach us," said two of the passengers of the steam dragon simultaneously, for they were two minds with the same thought, as the saying goes. It was Rudy and Babette; and the miller was with them.

"As baggage," he said. "I had to come along because I am necessary."

"I see the two of them," the Ice Maiden said. "Many chamois have I killed. Millions of rhododendrons have I broken and crushed, not even their roots have I spared. I have obliterated them. Thinkers! The power of reason!" And once more she laughed.

"Another avalanche!" cried the people of the valley.

CHAPTER TEN: THE GODMOTHER

In Montreux—one of the towns that together with Clarens, Vernex, and Crin forms a garland around the northeastern shore of Lake Geneva—Babette's godmother was staying. She had come from England a few weeks before, accompanied by her daughters and a nephew. The miller had already visited them and told them of Babette's engagement. When they had heard the whole story of the romance—how it had begun at Interlaken and how Rudy had captured the eaglet—they were so amused and interested that they insisted that the miller must come again soon, bringing both Babette and Rudy with him. And so they had come, for Babette to see her godmother and the English lady to see her godchild.

At the little town of Villeneuve, at the end of the lake, the travelers embarked on a small steamer that within half an hour would bring them to Vernex, just below Montreux. They sailed along the coast that the great poets had sung about. Here on the shore of the blue-green lake, under the shade of a walnut tree, Byron had composed his melodious verses about the prisoner of the dismal castle of Chillon. At Clarens where weeping willows mirror themselves in the waters of the lake, Rousseau had walked dreaming of Héloïse.

Where the Rhone River, flowing from beneath the snow-clad mountains of Savoy, runs into the lake, there is a tiny island. From shore it might be mistaken for a small boat, though it is a mass of rocks. About a hundred years ago a lady had had these rocks encircled by a wall, and earth transported from the mainland; then she had planted three acacia trees. Now these trees were full grown and they kept the little island in perpetual shade. Babette thought that the island was lovely, the most beautiful sight she had seen on the whole boat trip, and she wanted to go ashore. "For surely," she declared, "it must be a delight to be there." But the steamer sailed on and landed its passengers where it was supposed to, at Vernex.

Now they had to walk, up the mountain in the direction of Montreux. The mountainside was covered with vineyards, and around each was a white wall. Between the rows of walls, on which the sunshine played, the three of them made their way. The houses stood in the shade of fig trees; and they passed gardens where laurel bushes and cypress trees grew. The pension where Babette's godmother was staying was halfway between the shores of the lake and Montreux.

There they were given a most hearty welcome. Babette's godmother was a tall, pleasant woman with a round smiling face; as a child she must have resembled one of Raphael's angels, for her white hair now curled about an old angel's face. Her daughters were tall and slender and pretty. Their cousin was dressed from top to toe in white. He had gilded sideburns that were so ample that he could have shared them with three other gentlemen and still have had enough for himself. His hair was also golden; and he immediately turned his full attention to Babette.

Richly bound books, musical scores, and drawings were lying on the large table. The doors to the balcony were open, offering a view of the lake, in whose calm, glossy water the mountains of Savoy with their villages, forests, and snow-covered peaks were perfectly reflected, upside down.

Rudy, who was usually so cheerful, confident, and filled with life, felt out of place. He moved about gingerly, as if the polished floors had been strewn with dry peas. Time seemed like a solid rock that would never be worn down. He felt as if he were on a treadmill, and now someone was suggesting that they take a "promenade"!

The others walked so slowly that Rudy had to take one step backward for every two that he took forward, in order not to get ahead of the company. They were going to Chillon, to that crumbling old castle on the rock. There they would look at the whipping post and at the cells of the condemned; at the stone slabs on which the wretched prisoners slept; and at the trap door through which they were flung to meet their deaths on the iron spikes jutting up through the surf. To see all this is called a pleasant amusement. It is a chamber of horrors that was lifted by Byron's song into the world of poetry.

Rudy felt the horror as he leaned against the castle's massive wall. He peered through a narrow window and looked out over the lake. There was the tiny island with its three acacia trees. He wished he were there, away from the chattering people who surrounded him. But Babette was enjoying herself. She had been much amused.

Later that day, when she was alone with Rudy and the miller, she remarked that she thought her godmother's nephew was "perfect."

"Yes, a perfect ass," said Rudy; and this was the first time that he had said something that did not please Babette. The Englishman had given her a book as a souvenir. It was Byron's *Prisoner of Chillon* in a French translation, so she could read it.

"Maybe the book is all right," Rudy said, "but I don't care much for the fellow who gave it to you."

"He looked like a flour sack without any flour in it," said the miller, laughing at his own joke. Rudy joined in the laughter; he thought that the miller had been both witty and precise.

CHAPTER ELEVEN: THE COUSIN

When Rudy came to the mill a few days later he found the Englishman there. Babette was serving him broiled brook trout. The plate was decorated with parsley, which Rudy felt certain that the girl had picked herself in order to make the dish look as it did when it was served in the finer hotels. Why all this to-do? What did the Englishman want? Why was Babette running back and forth like that? It wasn't necessary at all.

Rudy was jealous and this amused Babette. She wanted to know everything about her lover, his weaknesses as well as his strength. She was so young that love was still a game to her. Yet it must not be forgotten that, though she played with Rudy's heart, he was her happiness, the center around which her thoughts played, and the source of all her joy. The more furious he looked, the more laughter there was in her eyes. She would gladly have kissed the Englishman with the blond hair and the gilded sideburns, just to see Rudy show how much he loved her by stamping out of the room in a rage. She was being neither fair nor clever, but Babette was only nineteen years old. She did not give too much thought to what she was doing, and none whatsoever to the impression that she might be creating on the Englishman, who might well misunderstand and decide that she was more pleasure-loving and frivolous than a recently engaged miller's daughter ought to be.

The mill was situated on the road to Bex, in the shadow of the high snow-covered mountains that the local people call the Diablerets. Nearby is a raging mountain stream whose waters are always foaming and filled with bubbles; but this is not the stream that turns the great wheel of the mill. A smaller one that leaps down the cliff as a waterfall, passes through a stone tunnel under the road and from there across the larger stream in a trough, finally falls upon the paddles of the mill wheel. The wooden trough was almost always filled and often the water overflowed, so anyone deciding to use one of its rims as a short cut to the mill would find that he had chosen a very slippery path. And this was exactly what the Englishman had done.

Guided by the light in Babette's window, and dressed all in white as if he were a miller, he attempted to make his way to the garden by balancing himself on the narrow ledge of one of the sides of the trough. But he had never learned how to hold on where there was nothing to hold onto, so he slipped into the trough and almost fell into the larger stream below it.

Wet to the skin, he climbed the linden tree next to Babette's window; then he started to hoot like an owl, as this was the only bird he knew how to imitate. Babette lifted the curtain and peeped out. She saw the figure in white and recognized him; then she grew not only frightened but very angry. She put out the candle and in the darkness let her fingers make certain that the windows were securely locked.

"Let him howl and hoot to his heart's content," she thought; then it suddenly struck her how terrible it would be if Rudy were in the vicinity.

And Rudy was: he was right below her, in the garden. She heard angry words and shouting. They were going to fight! One of them might even be killed. She had to do something!

Babette opened her window and called out Rudy's name. In her confusion and alarm, she begged him to go away. "You must go away!" she cried.

"So I must go away!" he demanded. "Oh, I see, you had another and better appointment! You are shameless, Babette!"

"You are horrible!" she screamed back. "I hate you! Go away! Go away!"

"You have no right to say that to me!" he called up to her. His cheeks were burning and his heart was burning. He turned and walked away.

"When I love you so much, how could you think such things of me!" Babette was very angry, which was fortunate, for if she hadn't been, she would have been very sad and could not have fallen asleep.

CHAPTER TWELVE: THE POWER OF EVIL

When Rudy left Bex on his homeward journey, he set out for the mountains: high up where the air was fresh and cool, where there was snow, and the Ice Maiden reigned. There the tops of the leaf-bearing trees appear no larger than potato plants. Only the evergreen grows and it is stunted. A few rhododendrons bloomed in great patches of snow. A blue gentian was in flower, and with the handle of his rifle Rudy broke its stem.

Far ahead of him, he spied two chamois. His eyes looked toward them eagerly. For the moment new thoughts banished the old. But the mountain antelope were too far away to attempt a shot. Rudy continued climbing higher to where the only vegetation, even in summer, are a few blades of grass growing among the boulders.

There were the two chamois walking serenely as if Rudy were not there; they were making their way toward a great field of snow. Rudy hurried after them. Suddenly the clouds rolled down from the mountain peaks and engulfed him. He took a few steps and then stopped. In front of him was a wall of stone.

It had started to rain. He felt tremendously thirsty, and though his head was burning hot as though he had fever, his body was cold. He reached for his water bottle, only to find that it was empty; he had forgotten to fill it before setting out. Rudy had never been ill before in his life, but now he knew how it felt to be ill. He was tired and his only desire was to lie down and sleep, but everything about him was soaking wet. He tried to pull himself together, but tiny quivering objects danced before his eyes.

All of a sudden he noticed something that he could remember having seen in this place before. It was a small house, built right up against the side of the cliff. In the doorway stood a young girl. At first he thought it was Annette, the schoolmaster's daughter, the one he had kissed at the dance. No, it wasn't Annette; and yet he felt sure that he had seen her before. Maybe it was the girl he had met near Grindel, the night he returned from Interlaken.

"What are you doing here?" he asked.

The girl smiled. "This is my home. I have a flock to herd."

"Where is your flock? There is no grazing here among the rocks and snow."

The girl laughed. "You seem to know the mountains well; but not far below here there is a meadow. That's where my goats are grazing. I tend them well. I have never lost a single creature. What is mine I keep."

"You talk boldly," Rudy said.

Again the girl laughed. "So do you!"

"Have you any milk? I am so dreadfully thirsty."

"I have something better than milk. Some travelers and their guides passed by here yesterday, and they left a half bottle of wine behind. I am sure they'll never return for it and I don't want it. You shall have it. I am sure you have never tasted any better wine," she added while she poured the wine into a wooden bowl.

"It is good," he agreed. "I have never drunk wine that warmed me so quickly. A moment ago I was freezing and now I feel as if I were sitting before a fire." Rudy's eyes gleamed with new life. All his sorrow and troubles were forgotten, and his natural human desires were aroused.

"You are the schoolmaster's daughter. Come, Annette, give me a kiss," he demanded.

"Yes, if you will give me the beautiful ring you are wearing on your finger."

"My engagement ring?"

The girl poured more wine into his bowl. "Yes, that's the one: that ring and no other." She lifted the bowl to his lips and Rudy drank.

A feeling of power and happiness flowed through his veins. The world was his and only now did he understand how to live. All was created for our sake, for us to enjoy. The river of life was a river of pleasure; you need only let the current carry you to know a life of bliss. He glanced at the young girl who was Annette—and yet wasn't. But neither was she the "phantom" girl, as he called the creature he had met near Grindelwald.

The girl before him had a freshness about her like new-fallen snow and, like the rhododendron, she was in bloom; she moved as gracefully as the chamois; and yet, surely, she had been created of Adam's rib and, like Rudy, was a human being.

He threw his arms around her and looked into her marvelous clear eyes for a second. Only for a second! And how is one to describe, to tell in words, what he saw in that fraction of a moment? What was it that overpowered him: a ghost? Or was it a bit of life that exists in death? Had he been lifted upward or had he been plunged into a deep, death-filled world of ice?

He saw the blue-green glass walls and the bottomless chasm that surrounds them. He heard the sound of water dripping like a thousand bells, and each drop appeared like a tiny blue-white flame. The Ice Maiden kissed him, and the eternal coldness penetrated his backbone and touched his forehead. He cried out in pain. Tearing himself from her arms, he stumbled and fell. Night closed his eyes. But a moment later he opened them again. Evil's performance was over.

The girl was gone. The house was gone. Water was dripping down the cliff. He was lying in the show, shivering with cold. His clothes were drenched and his ring was gone: his engagement ring that Babette had given him. Beside him lay his hunting rifle. He picked it up and pulled the trigger but it did not go off. Nearby in the cleft were heavy clouds that appeared as solid as snow. Inside them Vertigo sat and waited for some powerless prey. There was a noise; it sounded like a boulder falling from the top of the canyon to its bottom, carrying with it everything in its path.

Down at the mill Babette sat crying. She had not seen Rudy for six days. Rudy, who was in the wrong and ought to come and ask for forgiveness, for she loved him with all her heart.

CHAPTER THIRTEEN: IN THE MILLER'S HOUSE

"What a terrible mess these humans make of their lives," said the parlor cat to the kitchen cat. "The engagement between Babette and Rudy has been broken off. She cries all the time and he has probably forgotten her."

"That's too bad," replied the kitchen cat.

"I agree with you." The parlor cat licked her left front paw. "But I won't spend my time mourning about it. After all, Babette can just as well get engaged to the one with the red sideburns. Though we haven't seen hide nor hair of him since the night he tried to climb up on the roof."

The powers of evil have their own rules; they can play with us and within us. This Rudy had learned while he was high up in the mountains, and he had not stopped wondering about it since. What had happened? Had the apparition been something he imagined because he had a high fever? He had never known fever or any illness before. But he had new insight into himself since the night he had judged Babette so harshly. He remembered how wildly his heart had been made to beat by jealousy; like a foehn wind, jealousy had swept through him. If only he could tell Babette his thoughts. If only he could confess to her his temptation and how it had become a deed. He had lost her ring, and because of that loss she had regained him.

Would she make any confession to him? Every time that Rudy thought of Babette he feared that his heart was about to break. So many memories rushed into his mind. He saw her laughing like a happy child. He remembered all the sweet words she had spoken so innocently, so tenderly; and it was as if a ray of the sun had entered his breast and soon his whole heart was full of the sunshine of Babette.

She would make a confession to him; she must!

Down to the mill Rudy went; and the confession began with a kiss and ended with Rudy admitting that he was the sinner. His error had been that he had doubted Babette's fidelity. Such lack of faith was almost unforgivable! Such mistrust was almost disgusting! And his violent passion might have caused a catastrophe for them both. About that there could be no doubt! And Babette preached a little sermon for him. She enjoyed the task very much, and she did it charmingly. On one point, though, she was in perfect agreement with Rudy: her godmother's nephew was a conceited puppy. She would burn the book he had given her, for she wanted nothing ever to remind her of him.

"Well, it is all over," said the parlor cat. "Rudy has come back. They understand each other and they say that in understanding the greatest happiness is found."

"I heard the rats talking last night," said the kitchen cat, "and they decided nothing could make you as happy as tallow candles, unless it was rancid lard. Who do you think is right: the rats or the lovers?"

"Neither one of them," answered the parlor cat. "If you don't take anybody's word for anything, then you never make a mistake."

The event that would bring Rudy and Babette their greatest happiness was not far off: the most beautiful day in their lives, their wedding day.

The ceremony was not to take place in the church in Bex, or in the miller's parlor. Babette's godmother had requested that they be married in Montreux: the wedding celebration at her pension and the wedding itself in the beautiful little church in the town. The miller, who was the only one who knew what the English lady intended to give her godchild as a wedding present, said that he thought this was the least one could do; it was only a trifling inconvenience which the wedding gift would more than make up for. The day was decided upon, and the miller and the young couple planned to go to Villeneuve the night before, so that they could take the boat to Montreux early the next morning, for the two daughters of Babette's godmother wanted to have time to dress the bride.

"If there is to be no party when they come home, then I don't give a meow for the whole wedding," said the parlor cat.

"Oh, but there is going to be a party! The larder is full. There are ducks and pigeons and a whole deer hanging out there. It makes my mouth water just to think of it all." The kitchen cat licked her chops. "Tomorrow they are leaving."

Yes, tomorrow! And that evening Babette and Rudy would sit on the bench outside the mill for the last time as an engaged couple. There was a red glow above the mountains, the vesper bells began to peal. The sun's rays, the daughters of the sun, were singing: "Everything that happens is always for the best!"

CHAPTER FOURTEEN: VISIONS IN THE NIGHT

The sun had set. The clouds rolled down into the valleys along the Rhone. The wind blew from the south: an African wind, a foehn wind that tore the clouds to bits and then was gone. In the stillness that followed, the shattered clouds re-formed themselves and floated between the forest-clad mountains and over the swift turbulent river in the most fantastic shapes; they looked like prehistoric animals:

giant eagles and great leaping frogs. The clouds seemed to sail on the water rather than float in the air. A fir tree that had been uprooted by the storm was carried by the current. The water made whirling eddies in its wake. Vertigo and her sisters were turning and twisting in the on-rushing torrent. The moon casting its light on the snow-covered mountaintops, the dark forests, and the white clouds made everything appear ghostly; nature's spirits were abroad. The mountain folk looking through their windows saw them. In great crowds these phantoms passed in homage before the Ice Maiden. She had come down from her glacier castle; a fir tree was her boat and the waters from the melting ice fields carried her downstream to the lake.

"The wedding guests have come." The message was sent through the air and could be heard in the water.

Visions! Visions can be seen inside as well as out. Babette was having a strange dream.

She was married to Rudy and had been for many years. He was in the mountains hunting chamois, she was at home in their living room; next to her sat the Englishman with the gilded sideburns. He was talking to her. His eyes were tender, his voice was soft. His words seemed to be casting a spell over her. He reached out his hand; she took it and followed him out of the house. They were going downward, ever downward!

Babette felt that her heart was heavy with guilt. She had committed a sin against Rudy, a sin against God. Suddenly she was alone: abandoned. She had to make her way through hawthorn bushes whose thorns ripped her clothes. Her hair was gray. Painfully she turned and looked upward. There on the edge of a cliff stood Rudy. She raised her arms toward him but she did not dare to call his name; nor would it have helped if she had, for what she was seeing was not Rudy but his hat and coat hanging on a cane: a trick the hunters used to fool the chamois.

Babette wept in anguish. "It would have been better had I died on my wedding day—on that day that was the happiest of my life. My Lord . . . my God, it would have been merciful! It would have been a blessing. . . . It would have been best for Rudy and me. No one knows his future." In front of her was an abyss; with infinite pain she threw herself into it. From the depths came a tone of sorrow, as if a string had snapped.

Babette woke; the dream was over and forgotten. Only the memory of having dreamed something terrifying remained. She knew that the Englishman had been in the dream. She had neither seen nor thought about him for months. Would he be in Montreux? Would she have to see him at her wedding? A shadow fell across her delicate face. She wrinkled her brow. But soon she was smiling again and her eyes were bright with happiness. It was a beautiful day. The sun was shining; and tomorrow was Rudy's and her wedding day.

He was already up and waiting for her when she came downstairs. In a little while they would be on their way to Villeneuve. How happy they were. And so was the miller. He smiled and joked; he was a good father and a thoroughly honest man.

"Now we are masters of the house!" said the parlor cat.

CHAPTER FIFTEEN: THE END

It was still afternoon when the three happy travelers reached Villeneuve. After they had eaten, the miller lighted his pipe and made himself comfortable in an easy chair. Soon he was asleep. The young couple went for a walk, arm in arm, out into the town. They followed the main road; on one side were cliffs covered with greenery, and on the other the deep, blue-green lake. The heavy walls and towers of the gloomy castle of Chillon were reflected in the clear water. They saw the little island with the three acacia trees not far away. It lay like a bouquet on the water.

"It must be beautiful over there." Babette felt again the same wish to visit the little island, and this time it was easy to fulfill. There at the water's edge was a small rowboat. There was no one about, so they could not find out to whom it belonged. They would borrow it anyway. The mooring was easily untied and Rudy knew how to row.

The oars slid through the yielding water like the fins of a fish. Water is so strong and yet so pliant; it has a back that can carry great weights, a mouth that can swallow and smile gently. It can portray perfect serenity and yet it has the most horrifying power to destroy. In the wake of the boat was a track of foam. Within minutes they reached the island, which was only just big enough for two to dance upon.

Rudy whirled Babette into the air three times, and then they sat down on the little bench under the acacia trees to hold hands and look into each other's eyes. The setting sun gave a brilliance to everything about them. The pine forest on the mountainside became lavender, as if it were a field of heather in bloom, and higher up, the naked rocks seemed almost transparent. The clouds appeared to screen a fire, and the lake itself was like the petal of a rose. As the shadows from the valleys crept farther and farther up the sides of the snow-clad mountains they became blue-black, while their peaks were still as red as lava. For a moment the scene was like a picture of the Creation, when the crust of the earth—still burning—rose to form the mountains. Never had Rudy or Babette seen such a sunset. The snow-covered Dent du Midi shone like the full moon when it rises above the horizon.

"There is so much beauty and so much happiness," one said to the other.

Rudy in a burst of passion exclaimed, "The world has no more to give me. An evening like this is a whole life. And this is not the first time that I have felt like this; and then, too, I have thought: 'Were my life to end now, how good a life it would have been!' The world is good. This day is over. But a new one will come, and it will be even more beautiful. How great and good God is, Babette!"

"I am so happy," she said, looking at him.

"The world has no more it can give me," Rudy repeated.

The vesper bells rang from the mountains of Savoy and from the mountains of Switzerland. To the west, framed in gold, were the blue-black Jura Mountains.

"May God give you all that is beautiful, everything that you ask for!" she exclaimed.

"He will!" Rudy replied. "Tomorrow you are mine, all mine: my own little, beautiful wife."

"The boat!" screamed Babette.

The little rowboat had loosened its moorings and was drifting away from the island.

"I'll get it," Rudy said. Hurriedly he took off his jacket and his boots, then he dove into the lake and started swimming.

Cold and deep was the blue-green water. It had come from the melting glaciers. Rudy looked down into it. He saw a shining round object roll, twinkle, and wink, as if it were playing. "It must be my engagement ring," he thought, "the one I lost." The ring grew larger and larger until it was a glittering circle and in the center of it was a glacier.

Deep gorges gaped around him. The dripping water played a carillon, while each drop burned with a blue-white flame; and in a single glance he saw a vision that I must use much space and many words to describe. He saw young hunters and young girls: men and women who had been swallowed by the glacier appeared before him alive; their eyes were wide open and they were smiling. He heard church bells chiming from far below, from towns and villages that had long since been buried. People were kneeling in a great church, and mountain streams played the organ, whose pipes were huge icicles. The Ice Maiden sat on the smooth, transparent floor. She rose to welcome Rudy, then she bent down and kissed his feet. A deathly ice-cold quiver like an electric shock passed through him. Ice and fire! From a single touch you cannot tell the difference.

"Mine! Mine!" The cry came from all about him, and within himself. "I kissed you when you were a child. Kissed your mouth. Now I kiss you on your toe and your heel. Now you are mine!"

Silence. The church bells had stopped ringing. The last tone disappeared in the fading rose color of the clouds.

"You are mine!" came the cry from the depths of the lake. "You are mine!" came the cry from the boundless heights.

It is lovely to fly from love to love, from earth into heaven.

A string snapped. A mournful tone was heard. Death's kiss of ice was victorious against corruption. The prologue was over, now the drama of life could begin; discord was absorbed into harmony.

Do you think it was a tragic story?

Poor Babette! Nothing could have been more terrifying, more horrible, than those hours she spent on the island alone. No one knew where the young couple had gone. The evening grew darker. Desperate, she stood sobbing, while above the Jura Mountains a storm was gathering.

Lightning flashed over the mountains and could be seen in Switzerland and in Savoy, one bolt after another. The thunderclaps came so close to each other that one became part of the next. The lightning was as bright as light from the sun, and for brief moments everything was as light as midday and you could see the individual vines in the vineyard. Then came the darkness and it was doubly dark. The lightning came in ribbons, in zigzags, in balls of fire, making strange patterns in the air as it was drawn by the water of the lake. Lightning came from all sides, and the peals of thunder were made louder by their own echoes. On the shore, people were busily pulling their boats up on land. The rain came and everything that could move searched for shelter.

"Where are Rudy and Babette in this terrible weather?" the miller asked.

Babette was sitting with her hands folded and her head bent. Now she was silent, made mute by sorrow, from the screams and moans she had uttered. Inside her a voice said, "Rudy is in the water: deep down as if he were under a glacier." She recalled what she had been told about his mother's death and his own rescue. How Rudy was thought to have been dead when he was carried out of the crevasse in the glacier. "The Ice Maiden has taken him back," she whispered.

Suddenly there was a flash of lightning as blindingly white as snow when the sun shines upon it. Babette looked about her. The lake seemed to be raising itself; its water looked for a moment like a glacier. And she saw the Ice Maiden, standing majestically in shimmering blue-white. At her feet lay the body of Rudy. "Mine!" she cried. And again there was only darkness and the murmuring waters were black.

"It is too cruel," Babette moaned. "Why should he die, just as our day of happiness had come? God, help me to understand! Make my heart lighter. I do not know Your ways. I grope in darkness. I am too weak. I need Your wisdom."

God did lighten her heart. He sent her a thought, a ray of grace. In that moment she relived the dream she had had the night before. She remembered the words she had spoken and what she had wished for Rudy's sake and her own.

"Woe is me! Was the seed of sin in my heart? Would my dream have been my future, had not the string been snapped for my sake? Oh, how wretched I am!"

In the gloom-filled darkness she sat lamenting. In the deep silence of nature, she thought she heard again Rudy say, "The world has no more it can give me." The words had been shouted in joy and now they were echoed in pain.

A few years have gone by. The lake is smiling and its shores are smiling; the vines are heavy with grapes. The steamship, with its many flags flying, sails by, and the sailing ships, like white butterflies, play on the mirror of the lake. The railroad has come. It goes past Chillon and far up and down the Rhone Valley. At every station are foreigners carrying red leather-bound guidebooks under their arms, and when they sit down in the train they read about what they have already seen. They visit the castle of Chillon and, looking out over the lake, they notice the tiny island with the acacia trees. They look it up in their books. They read about a young betrothed couple who, one spring evening in 1856, rowed out to the island; and how the young man met his death. "It was not until the following morning that people on the shore heard the bride's despairing, fearful screams."

The guidebook does not tell what happened to Babette, of her quiet life that was spent with her father—not in the mill, strangers live there now, but in a pretty house near the new railroad station. Many a night from its upper windows she has looked out over the topmost branches of the chestnut tree to the snow-capped mountains where Rudy once played. Often she has watched the sunset, seen the children of the sun go to sleep in their splendor on the peaks, and heard them repeat the tale of the man from whom the whirlwind had stolen a cap: how the wind could take his covering but not the man himself.

The snow on the mountainside has a rose luster, and so does the heart who believes that "God wills the best for us all." But few are so fortunate as Babette, who had it revealed to her in a dream.

61

The Butterfly

THE butterfly wanted a sweetheart, and naturally it had to be a flower. He inspected them. Everyone sat as properly and quietly on her stalk as a young maiden should. The trouble was that there were too many of them to choose from, and the butterfly didn't want to be bothered by anything so fatiguing. He flew over to the camomile flower. She is called by some the French daisy and she knows how to tell the future. Young maidens and boys who are in love ask her questions, and then answer them by tearing off her petals, one at a time. This is the rhyme they usually recite:

> "With all her [or his] heart . . .
> With only a part . . .
> Not lost forever . . .
> She'll love me never."

Or something like that. You can ask the camomile flower any questions you want to. When the butterfly came, he did not tear off any of the petals; he kissed them instead, for he was of the opinion that you get furthest with compliments.

"Sweet daisy, dear camomile flower, matron of all the flowers, you who are so clever that you can see the future, answer me: which of the flowers will be my sweetheart? This one or that one? Please tell me so that I can fly directly over to her and propose at once."

The camomile flower did not answer. The butterfly had insulted her by calling her a matron. She was a virgin and hadn't been proposed to yet. The butterfly asked the same question a second time and a third, then he got bored and flew away to go courting on his own.

It was early spring. Snowdrops and crocuses were still in bloom. "How sweet they are," he remarked. "Just confirmed, but they have no personalities." Like so many young men, he preferred older girls. He flew to the anemones but he found them too caustic. The violets were a little too romantic and the tulips a little too gaudy.

Soon the Easter lilies came, but they were a little too bourgeois. The linden blossoms were too small and had too large a family. The apple blossoms were so beautiful that they could be mistaken for roses, but they were here today and gone tomorrow. "Our marriage would be too short," the butterfly muttered.

He was most attracted by one of the sweet peas. She was red and white, pure and delicate; and was one of those rare beauties who also knows what a kitchen looks like. He was just about to propose when he happened to notice a pea pod with the withered flower at its tip. "Who is that?" he asked with alarm.

"That is my sister," replied the sweet pea.

"So that is what she will look like later," thought the butterfly. "How frightening!" And he flew away.

The honeysuckle had climbed over the fence. What a lot of girls there were, and all of them with long faces and yellow skins. The butterfly didn't care for them. But whom did he like? To find out, you must ask him.

Spring passed, summer passed, and then autumn came. Still the butterfly had no wife. The flowers were dressed in their finery, but they had lost their fresh innocence and scent of youth. As the heart grows older it needs scent, odor, perfume to arouse it; and the dahlias and the hollyhocks have none.

The butterfly lighted on a little mint plant with curly leaves. "She has no flowers, but she is a flower from her roots to the tip of her tiny leaves. She smells like a flower. I shall marry her." And the butterfly proposed.

The mint plant stood stiff and silent. At last she replied: "Friendship, but no more! I am old and you are old. We can live for each other, but marriage, no! It would be ridiculous at our age."

And that is how it happened that the butterfly never got married. He had searched too long for a wife, and now he had to remain a bachelor.

It was late in the autumn. The rains had come and the wind blew down the backs of the willow trees. It was not the weather to be out flying in, especially in summer clothes. But the butterfly was not outside, he was in a room that was kept summer-warm by a stove, where he could keep himself alive.

"But to live is not enough," declared the butterfly. "One must have sunshine, freedom, and a little flower." He flew to the windowpane. There he was seen, admired, and a pin was stuck through him. He was "collected" and that is as much as a human being can do for a butterfly.

"Now I sit on a stalk just like the flowers," he said. "It isn't very comfortable, probably just like being married: you are stuck." And with that he consoled himself.

"Not much of a consolation," said the potted plants who lined the window sill.

"But you cannot trust potted plants," thought the butterfly, "they have associated too much with human beings."

62
❖

The Snail and the Rosebush

AROUND the garden ran a hedge of hazelnuts, beyond it there were fields and meadows, where cows and sheep grazed; but in the center of the garden there was a rosebush in full bloom. Under it lay a snail who was very satisfied with the company he kept: his own.

"Wait till my time comes," he would say, "and see what I shall accomplish. I am not going to be satisfied with merely blossoming into flowers, or bearing nuts, or giving milk as the cows and sheep do."

"Oh, I do expect a lot of you. Won't you tell me when it's going to happen?" asked the rosebush very humbly.

"I must take my time," replied the snail. "Do you think anyone would expect very much of me if I hurried the way you do?"

The following year the snail lay in the same sunny place, under the rosebush. The plant was full of buds and flowers, and there were always fresh roses on it, and each and every one was a tiny bit different from all the others. The snail crept halfway out of his house and stretched his horns upward; then he pulled them back in again.

"Everything looks exactly as it did last year. No change and no advancement. The rosebush is still producing roses; it will never be able to do anything else."

Summer was past and autumn was past. Until the first snow, the rosebush continued to bloom. The weather became raw and cold. The rosebush bent its branches toward the ground and the snail crawled down into the earth.

Another spring came. The rosebush blossomed and the snail stuck its head out of its house. "You are getting old," he said to the rosebush. "It is about time you withered and died. You have given the world everything you could. Whether what you gave was worth anything or not is another question, and I don't have time to think about it. But one thing is certain and that is that you have never developed your inner self, or something more would have become of you. Soon you will be only a wizened stick. What have you got to say for yourself? . . . Aren't you listening? . . . Can you understand what I am saying?"

"You frighten me so." The rosebush trembled. "You have asked me about things I have never thought about."

"I don't think you've ever thought about anything. Have you ever contemplated your own existence? Have you ever asked yourself why you are here? Why you blossom? Why you are what you are, and not something else?"

"No," the rosebush said. "My flowers spring forth out of joy! I cannot stop them from coming. The sun is warm, the air refreshing. I drink the dew and the rain. From the soil and the air I draw my strength. I feel so happy that I have to flower. I cannot do anything else."

"You have lived a very comfortable and a very indolent life," said the snail severely.

"How true! I have never lacked anything. But you have been given much more than I. You are a thinker. You can think deeply and clearly. You are gifted. You will astound the world."

"Astound the world! Not I!" The snail drew in his horns and then stretched them out again. "The world means nothing to me. Why should I care about the world? I have enough within myself. I don't need anything from the outside."

"But isn't it the duty of all of us here on earth to do our best for each other, to give what we can? I know I have only given roses. But you who have received so much, what have you given? What will you give?"

"What have I given! What shall I give!" snarled the snail. "I spit on the whole world. It is not worth anything and means nothing to me. Go on creating your roses, since you cannot stop anyway. Let the bushes go on bearing their nuts, and the cows and the sheep giving their milk. Each of them has their own public; and I have mine in myself. I am going to withdraw from the world; nothing that happens there is any concern of mine." And the snail went into his house and puttied up the entrance.

"It is so sad," said the rosebush. "No matter how much I wanted to, I couldn't withdraw into myself. My branches are always stretching outward, my leaves unfolding, my flowers blooming. My petals fall off and are carried away by the wind. But one of my roses was pressed in a mother's psalmbook, another was pinned on a young girl's breast, and one was kissed by a child to show his joy in being alive. Those are my remembrances: my life."

The rosebush went on blooming innocently, and the snail withdrew from the world, which meant nothing to him, by hibernating in his house.

The years passed. The rosebush had become earth and the snail had become earth; even the rose that had been pressed in the psalmbook was no more. But in the garden rosebushes bloomed and there were snails, who spat and retreated into their houses: the world meant nothing to them.

Should I tell the story from the beginning again? I could but it would be no different.

63

The Silver Shilling

"Hurray! Here I go out into the wide world," exclaimed the newly minted silver shilling. It clinked and rolled and out into the world it came.

It passed through the warm, moist hands of children; felt the cold, clammy palm of the miser; and was kept a whole week by a poor old couple before they dared to spend it. Whenever it got into the purse of a young person it was soon out again. As I have said, it was a silver shilling; and it was made of quite pure silver, with only a very little copper in it. Now it happened that after it had traveled about in its native country for a whole year it went for a trip abroad. By chance it was overlooked in the bottom of a purse, and its owner did not even know that he had it along.

"Why, there is a shilling from home," he said when he finally noticed it. "Well, since it's come this far, it might as well do the trip with me as a tourist." The shilling almost jumped for joy. It was dropped back into the purse, which now was filled with foreign coins, but they came and went, while the silver shilling remained: and this, it felt, was an important distinction.

Several weeks went by. The coin had traveled far, without knowing exactly where it was. The other coins explained that they were in France or in Italy, and mentioned the names of towns, but how could the little shilling have any idea what the place looked like? One really cannot see the world from the bottom of a purse.

One morning the shilling noticed that the opening of the purse wasn't completely closed; and so it moved up there in order to get a glance outside.

This it never should have done, for now it would have to pay the penalty for being curious. The shilling slid out of the purse and into its owner's trousers' pocket. That evening, after the purse was put aside for safekeeping, the traveler's clothes were brushed; and the coin fell out of the pocket and down onto the floor. No one heard it and no one saw it.

In the morning the man dressed and traveled on, but without his silver shilling. It was found by someone else, who put it in his purse where there were three other coins, all ready to do service.

"It is lovely to travel," said the shilling, "to see different people and learn their customs."

But at that very moment someone shouted: "That coin is false! It is counterfeit!" And it is at this point that the silver shilling's real adventures began; at least, so the coin itself seemed to think, for it would always start its story here:

" 'False! Counterfeit!' A shiver went through me. After all, hadn't I been made at the Royal Mint of almost pure silver? Couldn't I clink as a silver coin ought to? Wasn't my stamp genuine? I felt sure that there must be some mistake. The voice couldn't be talking about me; but it was! I was called false and said to be worth nothing. Then I heard another voice say, 'I'll spend it tonight, when it's dark.' And that was to be my future. I was to be spent in the dark, and discovered and cursed in the daylight. 'Counterfeit! Worthless! I must get rid of it,' were the words that always greeted me."

Every time the coin was picked up, it would tremble and quake, for it knew that it was being passed on dishonestly, as a coin of the realm.

"Oh, poor me!" it lamented. "What good did it do me that I was made of silver, and bore a picture of our king, when he wasn't respected there? In this world you only have the value that the world gives you. How horrible it must be to really be counterfeit, to sneak through life knowing that one deserves no better fate. It must be monstrous, for even though I was innocent, I had a bad conscience. Every time I was taken out of a purse I dreaded the moment when I would be looked at. I knew what would happen. I would be rejected, thrown across the counter, as if I were the personification of deceit.

"Once I was given to a poor working woman as payment after a long day of toil. But she didn't know how to get rid of me. No one would accept me. Oh, I was a disaster for the poor woman.

"'I will have to fool someone,' she said, 'even though it is a sin and a shame, for I am too poor to keep a false coin. I can try to pass it off on the rich baker. It won't hurt him because he can afford it.'

"Now I was to give that poor woman a bad conscience," sighed the shilling. "And I thought to myself, 'Could I really have changed so much with age?'

"And the woman took me to the rich baker, but he knew his currency. I had hardly been put down on his counter before I was flung right back into the poor woman's face. I felt a great sadness come over me. I, who had had such a happy youth, confident of my value and my genuineness, now was the cause of grief to others. I became melancholy, as melancholy as a silver coin can be when it is unwanted. The woman picked me up and took me home with her. 'I won't try to fool anyone with you again,' she said, gazing at me with kindness and generosity. 'I shall drill a hole in you so everyone can see that you are counterfeit. . . . And yet, it suddenly struck me that you might be a lucky coin! Just like that, out of nowhere the thought came to me that you were a lucky coin. I'll make a hole in you anyway, but then I will put a string through it and give you to the neighbor's little girl to wear as a good-luck charm.'

"And that was what she did. It isn't very pleasant to have a hole drilled through you, but you can bear an awful lot when you know that the intentions are good. A string was drawn through me and that's how I became a medal and was hung around a little girl's neck. The child smiled at me and kissed me; and I spent one whole night sleeping on her innocent, warm breast.

"In the morning the girl's mother took me between her thumb and her forefinger and looked at me intently; she had her own ideas about what ought to be done with me. She took a pair of scissors and cut the string.

"'A good-luck charm, let's see how much your luck amounts to.' She put me in vinegar, so that I became green; and then she puttied up my hole and rubbed me so that no one would notice that I had a hole. When it grew dark, she took me to the office of the state lottery, to find out how much luck I would bring.

"How horrible I felt! I had a pain in the middle of myself, as if I were about to break in two. At the state lottery office there would be a whole till full of coins both large and small, and every one of them proud of their faces and inscriptions; and there in front of them all, I knew I would be called counterfeit and thrown back at the woman. But it didn't happen. There were so many people buying tickets that I was thrown unnoticed in among the other coins. Whether or not she ever won anything on that lottery ticket, I cannot tell you. All I know is that the next morning I was discovered and humiliated again. Once more I was put aside and then sent on my way to deceive someone else. And it is unbearable to have to play the fraud when you are honest; and I see no reason to deny that I am honest.

"A year and a day went by. I passed from one hand to another, from one house to another. Always cursed, always unwelcome. No one had any faith in me and finally I had no faith in myself, or in the world. It was a difficult time.

"One day I was given to a tourist. He looked so ignorant and innocent that, naturally, he was cheated. He took me for good currency without a glance but, when he wanted to use me, he heard the hue and cry, 'Counterfeit! Valueless!'

" 'I was given it as change,' he said, looking at me carefully. Then he smiled broadly and that was the first time that a face had smiled when it was examining me. 'What are you doing here?' he asked. 'It is a coin from my own country. A good honest silver shilling that has had a hole drilled through it, as if it were counterfeit. That's really funny! I'll take good care of you and see to it that you come home again.'

"Happiness rushed through me when I heard myself being called 'good' and 'honest.' And now I was to go home. Back to my native country again, to that land where everyone knew that I was made of pure silver—almost pure silver, that is—and that the face on my head was that of our king. I would have sparkled with joy if nature had meant for me to sparkle, but only steel can sparkle, not silver.

"I was wrapped in a piece of fine white paper so that I would not have to associate with the other coins and get lost again. I was only brought out on special occasions when my owner met people from his own country, and they spoke well of me and said that I was very interesting. Isn't it funny that you can be called interesting when you haven't said a single word?

"Finally, I was home and my trials and tribulations were over. Life was pleasant again. I was silver and my inscription was authentic. It didn't matter that a hole had been drilled through me to proclaim me as false, because I wasn't and that is all that is important. Don't give up, eventually justice will triumph. That's my philosophy," said the silver shilling.

64

The Teapot

ONCE there was a teapot who was very proud. She was proud of being porcelain. She was proud of her spout and she was proud of her broad handle, for they gave her something to boast about both in front and in back. She didn't talk about her lid, which had been broken and then glued together. There is no point in talking about your shortcomings; others willingly do that for you. The cups, the cream pitcher, the sugar bowl—the whole tea service preferred discussing the mended lid to talking about the fine spout and the strong handle. And this the teapot knew.

"I know what they think," she said to herself. "And I know my own faults, too, and admit them; and that I call modesty and humility. We all have faults, and we all have our talents, too. The cups have a handle and the sugar bowl has a lid, but I have both. And one thing more that neither one of them will ever have: a spout. That is what makes me queen of the tea table. The sugar bowl and the cream pitcher are servants of taste, but I am its mistress. I disseminate my blessings among a thirsting humanity. In my interior, fragrant Chinese leaves are mixed with insipid boiling water."

This was the way the teapot had talked when she was still a youngster. One day while she was standing on the tea table, she was lifted by a very refined and delicate hand. Unfortunately, the refined and delicate hand was also careless. The teapot fell to the floor, and both her spout and her handle were broken off.—We shan't talk about the lid, for that has been mentioned enough already.—The teapot had fainted: there she lay with boiling water running out of her. But the worst was yet to come: they laughed at her—the teapot!—not at the careless hand that had dropped her.

"I shall never forget it! Never . . ." she would mutter to herself when she thought about her youth. "They said I was an invalid and put me in a corner of the closet. But I didn't stay there long; the next day I was given to a beggar woman, who had come to ask for leftovers from the table. I was to know poverty, and the thought made me quite speechless. Yet then and there began what I would call a better life. One is one thing and becomes another.

"I was filled up with earth, which for a teapot is the same as being buried. But inside the earth a bulb was placed. I don't know who put it there, but there it was. I am sure it was meant as a substitute for the Chinese leaves and the boiling water, and to console me for my broken spout and lost handle. The bulb lay in the earth inside me, and it became my heart: my living heart. And I was alive, something I had never been before. Within me were power and strength, and my pulse beat. The bulb sprouted. It was so filled with thoughts and feelings that it almost burst; then it flowered. I could see it. I carried it within me and I forgot myself when I looked at its beauty.

"Oh, that is the greatest blessing, to be able to forget yourself in caring for others. The flower didn't say thank you; I don't think it even noticed me. But everyone admired the flower, and if that made me happy, think of how much happier it must have made the flower.

"One day I heard someone say that the flower was so lovely that it deserved a better flowerpot. They cracked me in two, and that hurt terribly. My plant was placed in a finer flowerpot, and I was thrown out into the yard, and here I lie, an old broken piece of pottery. But I have my memories and they cannot be taken from me."

65

The Snowdrop

IT was winter. The air was cold and the wind was sharp, but indoors it was comfortable and warm, and the flower was indoors. It lay inside its bulb, underneath the snow and earth.

One day it started to rain. The drops of water penetrated the snow and the earth and touched the bulb, bringing a message from the world above. Soon a sun ray found its way down through the snow to the bulb and pricked it.

"Come in," said the flower.

"I cannot," answered the sun ray. "I am not strong enough yet to open your door; but I will be, come summer."

"And when is it summer?" asked the flower, and it repeated its question each time a sun ray touched it. But it was long to summer. Snow still lay on the ground and every night the puddles of water froze.

"Oh, how long it takes, how long," sighed the flower. "It is prickling and tingling inside me. I have to stretch myself, I want to get out, I must! I want to nod good morning to the summer; it is going to be delightful!"

And the flower stretched itself inside the bulb and broke through the thin skin, which the water had softened and the earth and snow had warmed and the sun rays had touched. Out through the earth, under the snow, it came, with a white bud on its green stalk, and its long, narrow, thick leaves that hugged the flower to protect it. The snow was cold but porous; the light came through it and the flower felt that the sun rays were more powerful.

"Welcome, welcome!" they sang; and the flower lifted its head through the snow into the world of light. The sun rays petted it and kissed it so much that it opened. It was as white as the snow with some fine green lines in it. Because of its happiness and because of its humbleness, it bent its head.

"Sweet flower," said the sun rays, "you are fresh and pure, you are the first, you are the only flower. We love you! Your little white bell shall ring that summer has come, that the snow will melt and the cold wind cease to blow. We, the sun rays, shall govern the world and everything will become green, and your little flower shall have company. The lilacs and laburnum will bloom, and last of all the roses. You, little snowdrop, are the first flower, so pure and bright."

It was a great pleasure. The little flower felt as though the air itself sang to it, while the sun rays penetrated its leaves and its stalk. There it stood, so delicate, so fragile, and yet so powerful in all the beauty of its youth. Dressed in its white dress with green ribbons, it praised the coming of summer.

But it was long to summer yet; the clouds obscured the sun and the bitter cold winds blew. "You have come a little too early," they grumbled. "We are still powerful and we will make you feel it. You should have stayed indoors; this is not the time for running about in such finery."

The weather turned bitterly cold. The days that came were so dark that not one sun ray was seen. It was proper weather to freeze to death, for such a little flower. But it had more strength within itself than it had realized. Its faith that the summer, which it longed and cared for, would come had once been confirmed by the warm sun; so there it stood, confident in its white dress amid the white snow, bending its head as the heavy snowflakes fell around it and the cold winds flew above it.

"You are going to break!" screamed the winds. "First you will freeze, then you will wither. Why did you let the sun rays tempt you to bloom? They have tricked you. They have made you a summer fool in winter weather."

"Summer fool," the little snowdrop repeated the words in the cold morning air.

"Summer fool!" shouted some children who had come into the garden and spied the flower. They gave it the same name as the winds had, which was not so strange, for a snowdrop is called a summer fool in Danish.

"It is so beautiful, so graceful. It is the first flower of the year and the only one in the garden." The children said these words, too; and to the flower they felt as sweet as the sun rays had. She was so happy that she did not even feel that she was being picked.

A little child's hand closed around the flower; it was kissed and carried into the house. There in the warm room the snowdrop was put in a glass of water and that was very refreshing. The flower thought that summer had suddenly come.

The daughter of the family was a very sweet girl; she was fourteen and had just been confirmed. She had a friend, a boy; he, too, had just been confirmed, but he was not living at home, he was in the town studying. "He shall be my summer fool," said the girl, and took the little flower and put it inside a folded paper on which she had written a poem. For in Denmark it is a custom that the young people send the first snowdrops of the year to one another, together with a verse. But the letters are never signed, the receiver has to guess who has sent them.

It was very dark inside the envelope, as dark as it had been inside the bulb. The letter was put in the postbox and started on its journey. The snowdrop wasn't very comfortable. Several times it was squeezed, but everything, even the unpleasant, comes to an end.

The journey was over. The letter was opened and read by a young man. He was pleased. He kissed the flower and put it with the letter, down in the drawer of his writing desk. There were many other letters in the drawer, but only one had a flower in it. It was still the first, the only flower, as the sun rays had called it, and that was pleasant to think about. And the snowdrop was given a long time to think about it, for it lay there all summer and all winter. Only when it again became summer was it taken out. But this time the young man was not happy to see it. He crumpled up the poem and threw it across the room. The flower fell on the floor, and even though it was wizened by now, it was a pity that it should lie on the floor.

Still it was better than to be burned, and that was what happened to the letter. Into the stove went all the letters and the poem. What had happened? She had made a summer fool of him, and found another friend. This sort of thing happens quite often.

The next morning the sun shone through the windows and its rays fell on the little dried, pressed snowdrop; it looked as if it had been painted on the floor. The maid who came to sweep picked it up and put it between two leaves of a book that was lying on the table. Again the snowdrop was among poems, but this time they were printed, and they are more important than those that are written by hand, for they have involved expense.

Years went by. The book stood in the bookcase. Every once in a while it was taken down and read. It was a good book, the poems of Ambrosius Stub, a Danish poet well worth being acquainted with.

The man who was reading the book turned a page and then exclaimed, "Why, there is a snowdrop, a summer fool," and then he said more thoughtfully, "A summer fool. Maybe there is a reason why it should lie in this book. Ambrosius Stub was a summer fool too: a jester, a poet. He, too, came too early, before summer; therefore, the sharp winds whipped him and snow and ice froze him. A winter fool, summer's dupe, a joke of nature, out of season; but yet the first one, the only one of the Danish poets who is still summer-young. Yes, little snowdrop, you fit the book, I think someone has put you there for a reason."

And the snowdrop was put back in the book; and it felt both honored and happy to know that it now was a bookmark in a volume of poems written by a poet who was the first to write about the snowdrop; a poet who, like the flower, had stood in the bitter, winter weather with a dream of summer in his soul: a summer fool. The snowdrop interpreted what she had heard her own way, as we all do.

That was the snowdrop's tale.

66

Who Was the Happiest?

"WHAT beautiful roses," said the sunshine. "And all the little buds will soon become as beautiful as they are. They are all my children, I gave them life by kissing them."

"They are my children," said the dew. "Didn't I suckle them with my tears?"

"I should think they are mine," interrupted the rosebush. "You may call yourself godparents. As for your presents, I consider them christening gifts, for which I say thank you."

"My sweet little rose-child!" they all three said at the same time, and wished each rose the greatest happiness in the world. But that was not really possible. Only one rose could be the happiest, as one would also have to be the least happy of all the roses on the bush. But what we want to know is, which would be the happiest?

"I will find that out for you," said the wind. "I travel a great deal and am thin enough to get through the narrowest crack. I know everything inside and out."

Each rose had heard what had been said and every swelling bud sensed it.

Just at that moment a woman dressed in the black clothes of sorrow came walking through the garden. She looked at the roses and then picked one that was not completely unfolded. Just because it was not fully in bloom, she considered it the most beautiful of them all. She carried the flower to the still silent room where only a few days ago her young daughter had played and laughed happily. Now she lay in a black coffin and looked like a marble sculpture of a sleeping figure. The poor mother kissed the dead child and then kissed the rose, before she placed it on the young girl's chest, as if she hoped that the freshness of a rose and a mother's kiss could make the girl's heart beat again.

The petals of the rose shook with happiness. It was as if the whole rose swelled and grew. "I have become more than a rose, for, like a child, I have received a mother's kiss. I have been blessed and will travel into the unknown realm, dreaming on the dead girl's breast. Truly, I am the happiest of us all."

In the garden where the rosebush grew, there worked an old woman; she did the weeding. She had also been admiring the rosebush, but she had especially been observing the only fully unfolded rose among the flowers. One more day of sunshine, one more drop of the pearly dew of night, and its life would be over. Now that it had bloomed for beauty, it might as well end its days being useful, thought the woman. She picked it and put it in an old newspaper with some other flowers she had collected that had, as she said, bloomed their time. When she got home she would mix the rose petals with lavender, sprinkle a little salt over them, and put them in a jar; that was called "making a potpourri."

"I am being embalmed," thought the rose. "That is something that only happens to kings and roses. I have been the most honored. Certainly I am the happiest."

Two young men were out walking in the garden. One of them was an artist, the other a poet. Each of them picked a rose—the one he thought was the most beautiful.

The artist painted a picture of the rose that was so true to life that the rose almost mistook the canvas for a mirror.

"In this way," said the artist, "the rose will live through many, many years, while millions and millions of other roses will have bloomed and died."

The rose heard it and thought, "I am the most highly favored, the happiest."

The poet contemplated his flower and the rose inspired him. It was as if he could read a story on each petal. It was a work of love, a piece of immortal poetry.

"I am immortal!" sighed the rose. "Oh, surely, I am the happiest."

Amid all this array of perfect roses there was one little flower that had a defect. It sat by chance—or maybe good luck—hidden behind the others. The petals on one side were not exactly like the petals on the opposite side, and in the middle of the flower a little green leaf grew. This sort of thing can happen among roses.

"Poor child," said the wind, and kissed the little rose on her cheek. The flower thought it was done in homage. She knew that she was a little different from the others and that she had a green leaf growing in the middle of her flower, but she had never considered it a flaw. On the contrary, she had always thought it a sign of distinction.

A butterfly landed on the rose and kissed each of her petals; it was proposing, but the rose let it fly away without an answer. A grasshopper came; true, he landed on another flower, but it was one quite nearby. He rubbed his legs together and that is a sure sign of love among grasshoppers. The rose that the grasshopper had sat on didn't understand this; but the little rose who had been singled out for special merit, she understood it very well. The grasshopper had looked at her and especially at her little green leaf and in his eyes had been written, "I love you so much that I could eat you up." Greater love no one can show, because that means that truly the two become one. But the little rose did not want to be joined quite so firmly to the grasshopper.

The nightingale sang in the star-filled night. "She sings for me, only for me," whispered the rose with the defect or the badge of merit—all as you look at it. "Why is it always I who am singled out for recognition, and not my sisters? Why was I created so exceptional that I had to become happiest of all roses?"

At that moment two gentlemen smoking cigars came walking past the rosebush. They had been discussing roses and tobacco. They had been told that the smoke from a cigar would turn a rose green, and now the experiment had to be tried. They did not want to take one of the more beautiful roses and that is why they decided on the little rose.

"Again I am the chosen one," she cried. "Oh, I am overwhelmed by the honor, I am the happiest!" The little rose turned quite green, both from the smoke and from being so very extraordinary.

One rose was perhaps the loveliest of them all; she was still a bud when the gardener picked her. She was given the place of honor in the bouquet he made of all the most beautiful flowers in the garden. The bouquet was brought to the young gentleman who owned the house and the garden, and he took it along that evening in his carriage.

The flower was the symbol of beauty amid beauty, for the young man took the bouquet along to the theater. The audience were dressed in their very best, thousands of lamps burned, and music played.

When the ballet was almost finished and the ballerina, who was the most admired dancer at the theater, came out for her last great dance, bouquets fell down on the stage like a rain of flowers. Among them was the bouquet with the rose in it, and the flower felt an indescribable joy as it flew through the air. As it touched the wooden floor, the bouquet seemed to be dancing too. It jumped and then slid along the stage. But in its final fall the rose broke her stem. The ballerina for whom, as homage, it had been picked was never to hold the rose in her hand. A stagehand picked it up, for it had fallen behind the sets. He smelled it and acknowledged its beauty, but it had no stem so he could not put it in his buttonhole. He did not throw the rose away but slid it into his pocket. Later that night, when he returned home, he filled a little liqueur glass with water and put the flower in it.

In the morning it was placed on the little table that stood beside his grandmother's chair. The old woman, too weak to get outside in the sunshine, looked at the beautiful rose and smelled its fragrance.

"Poor rose, you were meant for the rich and famous young girl and instead you have come to a poor old woman. But to her you would only have been one more flower, to me you are as lovely as a whole rosebush," the old woman said, and gazed at the flower with eyes as happy as a child's. Maybe the freshness of the rose brought back to her memories of her own youth, long ago past.

"The windowpane was broken, so it was easy for me to get in," said the wind. "I noticed the old woman's eyes and it is true they were like a child's: expectant. I saw the rose too, in the liqueur glass on the table beside her. Who was the happiest of all the roses? I know, I could tell you!"

Every rose on the bush had her own story and each of them believed herself to be the happiest; and such faith is a blessing in itself. The last rose left on the bush was certain that it was far happier than any of her sisters could have been.

"I have survived them all. I am the last one, the only one left. I am my mother's most beloved, her favorite child."

"I was their mother," said the rosebush.

"No, I was," said the sunshine.

"No, it was I who was their mother," said the dew.

"You all had part in them, and now I shall share the last rose among you." And the wind blew and scattered the petals of the flower over the branches where the dewdrops hung in the morning and where the sun would shine during the day. "I had my part in it, for I collected the stories of the roses and I will tell them to the world. Which one of them was the happiest, can you tell? I won't, I have said enough."

With those words the wind lay down behind the rosebush and the day was still.

67

The Adventures of a Thistle

AROUND the manor house was a lovely garden with very rare and beautiful plants and trees. Guests always expressed their delight and wonder when they saw it. On Sundays, people from the district, and even from the towns, asked for permission to look at the garden, and sometimes classes of school children came with their teachers.

Outside the garden, right up next to the fence, grew a thistle. It was so big, spreading its branches out in all directions, that it could be called a bush. No one noticed it except the donkey who drew the milk wagon. He would stretch his neck toward the thistle and say, "You are so beautiful that I could eat you up." But he couldn't, for the rope with which he was tethered wasn't long enough for him to reach it.

The manor house was filled with guests: members of the most distinguished families in Copenhagen were there. Many of the young girls were beautiful, and among them was an heiress from Scotland. In her homeland she belonged to the very best society, and she was wealthy. "A bride worth winning," whispered many of the young men and their mothers, too.

The young people were meandering on the lawns. Some of them were playing croquet. They walked among the flower beds, and one of the girls picked a flower and gave it to a young man to wear in his buttonhole. And all the other girls did the same. But the Scottish girl went about for a very long time without being able to decide which flower to choose. None seemed to satisfy her. Then she noticed the thistle bush with its bright reddish-blue flowers, growing on the other side of the fence. She smiled and asked her host's son if he would pluck one of them for her. "It is the national flower of Scotland," she explained. "It is portrayed in our coat of arms. Get one of them for me, please."

The young man climbed over the fence and plucked the most beautiful of the thistle's flowers; and was pricked as properly as though he had picked a rose.

The girl put the flower in his buttonhole, and the young man felt deeply honored. The other young men envied him, and every one of them would gladly have exchanged his lovely garden flower for the thistle given by the Scottish girl. But if the son of the owner of the manor was pleased, how do you think the thistle felt? It was as if dew had fallen upon it in the middle of the day.

"I am more than I thought I was," she mumbled to herself. "I undoubtedly belong on the other side of the fence: inside the garden, not outside it. It is strange, the world we live in, and not everything gets the position it deserves. Now, at least, one of my flowers is on the other side of the fence, and that in a buttonhole."

Every new bud that came and unfolded itself into a flower was told the story, for there is no reason to keep good news a secret. Soon the thistle bush heard—not from the chatter of birds or the voices of human beings, but from the air, which knows all secrets and can penetrate locked doors—that the young man who had been given the thistle flower had also gained the hand of the young Scottish girl. It was a good match.

"I have joined them together," the thistle bush said. She was thinking of the flower that she had supplied for the buttonhole. Now there was still another story to tell her offspring. "I shall probably be planted inside the garden," she thought. "Maybe I'll be put in a flowerpot; you get squeezed a little, but it is glorious." And the thistle bush imagined it all so vividly that soon she was convinced that this was her future. "I know it, I shall be planted in a flowerpot!"

She promised every new flower that it would be potted, or be put in a buttonhole, which was an even greater honor. But none of them ever was placed in either. The thistle drank the air and the sunshine during the day and licked the dew at night. She was visited by bees in search of honey for their dowries, and they took the honey from the flowers and left the flowers themselves behind. "Robbers!" screamed the thistle bush. "I wish I could prick every one of you." But it couldn't.

Old flowers hung their heads, withered, and died; but new ones came, and every one was greeted with the same joy and expectation by the bush. "You have come just at the right moment," she would say to each one. "Any minute now we are moving into the garden."

There were a couple of innocent daisies and a plantain who admired the thistle bush greatly; they heard every word she had said and believed them all.

The old donkey who pulled the milk wagon was standing in the ditch. He glanced at the flowering thistle, but his rope was too short, he could not reach it.

The thistle bush gave so much thought to the thistle from Scotland, whom she felt she must be related to, that at last she believed that she, too, had come from that country; and that her parents were probably the thistles that had grown in the Scottish coat of arms. This was a daring assumption, but a great thistle is capable of great thoughts.

"Sometimes one is descended from so great a family that one hardly dares to think about it," said a nettle that grew nearby. She had once heard that, in olden times, cloth had been woven from nettles, and she had never forgotten it.

Summer passed and fall passed, the leaves fell from the trees, and the few flowers that were left had even brighter colors, but less fragrance. The gardener's apprentice sang while he worked in the garden:

> "Uphill and downhill,
> All is God's will."

The young spruce trees down in the forest began to get "Christmas-yearning," although it was only the end of October and there was long to wait.

"Here I stand. No one thinks about me, and yet I was the matchmaker," said the thistle. "First they got engaged and then they were married a week ago. And I am going nowhere because I can't move."

A few weeks went by. The thistle now had only one last flower. It grew on the stem near the root and was particularly large and beautiful. The cold winds blew on it and its color and loveliness faded; finally its pod stood naked: it looked like a silver sunflower.

The young couple were out walking in the garden. They took the path along the fence, and the young woman was looking beyond it.

"The thistle is still there!" she exclaimed. "But now it has no more flowers."

"Yes, it does," her husband laughed. "There is the ghost of one." And he pointed at the silver-colored pod, which had become as beautiful as a flower.

"How lovely it is!" she said. "It should be carved in the frame around our portrait."

Again the young man had to climb the fence and pick a flower from the thistle bush. It pricked him—that was revenge for calling its last flower a ghost. The silver pod was brought into the garden, and from there into the hall of the manor house, where it was placed beside the painting of the young couple. In the bridegroom's buttonhole a thistle flower had been painted. Everyone talked about the flower in the buttonhole and the silver pod whose image was to be carved into the frame. And the air carried the conversation far and wide.

"What adventures I have had!" cried the thistle bush. "My first-born was put in a buttonhole and my last is going to be in a frame. I wonder what is going to happen to me?"

The donkey who was tethered nearby brayed. "Come over here to me, my sweetheart, and I will show you what could happen to you, if my rope were long enough."

But the thistle bush didn't answer. She grew more and more thoughtful. She thought and thought, and at Christmas her thinking bore a flower: "When your children are inside the fence, then a mother doesn't mind being outside herself."

"What a kind thought," said the sun ray. "You, too, will go far."

"Will I be put in a pot or a frame?" asked the thistle bush.

"You will be put in a fairy tale," answered the sun ray.

And here it is!

68

A Question of Imagination

THERE was once a young man who was studying to be an author, and he wanted to become one before Easter; then he would marry and live by his pen. It would be easy, if only he could find something to write about, but no ideas ever came to him. He had been born too late; everything had been thought about and written down before he came into the world.

"How fortunate the people were who were born a thousand years ago," he said. "Even those born a hundred years ago were luckier than I am, for then there was still something left to write about. Everything in the world has been written up; no wonder I can't find anything to write down."

He studied and thought so long and so hard that he made himself ill. No doctor could help him, but maybe the old wise woman could. She lived in a little house where the road entered the pastures. She was the gatekeeper; she lifted the latch for carriages and those on horseback. But she knew a great deal more than how to open a gate. Some say that she knew even more than the doctor, even though he drove in his own carriage and had to pay "rank tax," which only the nobility and the very rich must pay.

"I'll visit her," declared the young man.

Though her house was small, it was nice, if a bit ordinary. There wasn't a tree or a flower anywhere near it. Next to the door there was a beehive—very useful! There was a little potato patch—very useful! There was a hedge of blackthorn bushes; they had already flowered but their berries would be bitter until after the first frost.

"The very picture of our prosaic times," thought the young man, and that, after all, was a thought: a pearl found in front of the old wise woman's house.

"Write it down," she said. "Crumbs are also bread. I know why you've come, you want to be an author by Easter and you cannot find anything to write about. You have no ideas."

"Everything is already written. Our times are not like the old."

"No," she agreed, "they are not. In the old times they used to burn old wise women like me at the stake, and the poets had empty stomachs as well as empty pockets. These times are not only just right: they are the best! It is you who have poor eyes. You cannot see and I doubt if you can hear either. Have you been saying your prayers before you go to bed? . . . There is enough to write about if you can write. You will find, peeping out of the earth with the first flowers, stories enough for your pen. In the running water of the brook or the still waters of the lake there are poems to be caught like fish. All you have to do is to learn to understand, learn to catch a sun ray and keep it in your hand. Now you can try my glasses and my ear trumpet. Pray to God, and stop thinking about yourself."

The last thing was the most difficult, and really more than the old wise woman could demand.

The young man put on the glasses and stuck the ear trumpet in his ear. They were standing in the middle of the potato patch, and the old wise woman picked up a potato and gave it to him. It spoke, told its story: the history of the potato, an everyday tale in ten lines.

What did it tell? It talked about itself and its family: how it had come to Europe as an immigrant and had at first been persecuted and condemned because of misunderstanding and ignorance, until finally its true value, which was greater than gold's, was recognized. "By royal messenger, we were distributed to all the town halls in the country, and our importance was proclaimed. But the people didn't believe it, and they did not know how to plant us. One man dug a hole and dumped a whole bushel of us into it. Another planted us here and there in the garden; he expected that we would grow up like trees and that he would be able to shake down the fruit. We grew, flowered, and set fruit, and then we withered and no one thought that below us in the earth lay that blessed wealth, the potato. Yes, we have suffered; that is, our forefathers have. But if you have any family feeling, then you can feel the suffering yourself. We have a most interesting history."

"That's enough," said the old wise woman, and threw the potato back on the ground. "Now take a look at the blackthorn bush."

"We have family abroad, in the home of the potato," said the blackthorn bushes, "but farther north than they grow. The Norsemen came, steering a westerly course, through storms and fogs to an unknown land, and there—beyond the ice and snowbound coast—they found herbs, green grass, and bushes with deep blue berries the color of grapes. Sloeberries are turned into fruit as sweet as grapes by the first frost. The same will happen to our berries. They called that country Vineland, Greenland, Sloenland!"

"That was a very romantic story," said the young man.

"Yes, but come along." The old wise woman had heard the blackthorn bush's story before. She led the young man to the beehive.

He could see right through it. What a busy place it was! In all the corridors stood bees fluttering their wings in order to keep the air fresh in the great factory: that was their job. Bees came streaming in from the outside. They had been born with little baskets on their legs, which they filled with pollen. The baskets were emptied, and the pollen was sorted and made into honey and wax. The bees flew away again. The queen bee wanted to fly too, but wherever she flew, all the other bees would have to follow; and it wasn't the season for changing hives. Still she wanted to fly, so the wings were bitten off Her Majesty by the other bees, and then she had to stay where she was.

"Come along," the old wise woman said, and tapped the young man on the shoulder. "Let's go out into the road and look at the travelers."

"What a mass of people!" exclaimed the young man. "And each one of them has a story. It's too much for me, we'd better go back."

"No, go straight ahead, right into the midst of the multitude. Look at them, listen to them, and try to understand them with your heart. Then you will find that you have lots of ideas and plenty to write about. But before you go, give me back my glasses and my ear trumpet." And she took both of them away from the young man.

"I cannot see anything!" he complained. "I can't hear a thing."

"Then you can't become an author by Easter." The old wise woman shook her head.

"What shall I do then?" wailed the young man.

"Neither by Easter nor by Whitsun. Imagination can't be taught."

"But what am I to do? I would love to earn a living by serving the muses."

"That's not difficult, that can be arranged in time for the Mardi Gras. Buy some masks and make faces at the poets. Even when you understand them, don't be impressed, just make a grimace, and you'll get paid well enough to feed a family."

"Isn't that amazing," said the young man, and followed her advice. He became an expert at looking down his nose at poets because he couldn't become one himself.

The old wise woman told me his story, and she has so much imagination that she would give it away, if only one could.

69

The Days of the Week

THE days of the week wanted to have some time off so they could hold a party. They were so busy the whole year round, and they were never free, all at the same time; but every fourth year is leap year, when an extra day is added to February, to keep accounts straight.

On this day they would have their party, and since it was in February, when Mardi Gras is, they decided to have a masquerade. They were to dress themselves according to whim and taste. They would eat well, drink well, and in a spirit of comradeship give speeches in which they told each other the truth, both pleasant and unpleasant. The old Vikings used to throw at each other bones that they had gnawed on; the days of the week would throw jests and jokes in an innocent carnival mood.

The twenty-ninth of February arrived and so did the days of the week.

Sunday, who is chairman of the week, came dressed in a black suit with a silk cape. Pious human beings believed he was dressed for church, but the worldly ones knew that he was dressed as a domino and ready for a masquerade. The red carnation he wore in his buttonhole was the red lamp that sometimes is lit outside the theater and shouts: "Everything sold out. Have fun, have fun!"

Monday was a young man, closely related to Sunday, and fond of diversions. He always left his work if there was a parade in the street. "I must hear the music of Offenbach," he exclaimed. "It does not affect my brain or my heart, it goes directly into my legs and then I must dance. I had a little too much to drink last night, and my right eye is swollen from a fight, but after a night's sleep I will be ready to work. Remember that I am young!"

Tuesday is strong, the day of the bull, of work. "Yes, I am strong!" Tuesday agreed. "I am used to work. It is I who ties the wings of Mercury to the merchant's boots. I look into the factories to make sure that the wheels are oiled and the machines are working. I watch the tailor at his table and the joiner at his lathe. I keep an eye on everyone, that is why I am dressed in a policeman's uniform. You might call me Policeday." That was meant as a joke, but then policemen are seldom very good at joking.

"Here am I!" said Wednesday. "I am in the middle of the week, the Germans call me Herr Mittwoch. I am the salesman in the store, the flower standing in the middle of all the other honorable days. If we marched in a row, I would have three days in front and three behind me; the others would be my guard of honor. I am sure I am the most important day in the week."

Thursday came dressed as a coppersmith, with a kettle in one hand and a hammer in the other; they were the symbols of his nobility. "I am of the most noble descent," he claimed, "from the heathen gods. In the northern countries I am named after the god Thor, and in the south after Jupiter. Both of them were masters of lightning and thunder, and I am their heir." And then he hit the copper kettle with the hammer.

Friday was a girl. She called herself Freya, or sometimes Venus, depending upon the country she was in. She was quiet and gentle, according to herself. But this particular day she was dressed in her best and looking very gay, for it is the day when women are free. They can even propose, if they want to, such is the tradition on that day, they don't have to sit and wait for a suitor.

Saturday was dressed as an old housekeeper; she had a broom in one hand and a bucket in the other. Her favorite dish was gruel. She didn't demand that the others eat it, just that it be served for herself, and it was.

All the days of the week sat down at the table. I have made a drawing of it. It could be used as an idea for a pantomime, and how amusing it will be depends upon how well you perform it. I have only written it as a February jest, for the only month that sometimes receives an extra day.

70

The Great Sea Serpent

THERE once was a little fish. He was of good family; his name I have forgotten—if you want to know it, you must ask someone learned in these matters. He had one thousand and eight hundred brothers and sisters, all born at the same time. They did not know their parents and had to take care of themselves. They swam around happily in the sea. They had enough water to drink—all the great oceans of the world. They did not speculate upon where their food would come from, that would come by itself. Each wanted to follow his own inclinations and live his own life; not that they gave much thought to that either.

The sun shone down into the sea and illuminated the water. It was a strange world, filled with the most fantastic creatures; some of them were so big and had such huge jaws that they could have swallowed all eighteen hundred of the little fish at once. But this, too, they did not worry about, for none of them had been eaten yet.

The little fishes swam close together, as herring or mackerel do. They were thinking about nothing except swimming. Suddenly they heard a terrible noise, and from the surface of the sea a great thing was cast among them. There was more and more of it; it was endless and had neither head nor tail. It was heavy and every one of the small fishes that it hit was either stunned and thrown aside or had its back broken.

The fishes—big and small, the ones who lived up near the waves and those who dwelled in the depths—all fled, while this monstrous serpent grew longer and longer as it sank deeper and deeper, until at last it was hundreds of miles long, and lay at the bottom of the sea, crossing the whole ocean.

All the fishes—yes, even the snails and all the other animals that live in the sea—saw or heard about the strange, gigantic, unknown eel that had descended into the sea from the air above.

What was it? We know that it was the telegraph cable, thousands of miles long, that human beings had laid to connect America and Europe.

All the inhabitants of the sea were frightened of this new huge animal that had come to live among them. The flying fishes leaped up from the sea and into the air; and the gurnard since it knew how, shot up out of the water like a bullet. Others went down into the depths of the ocean so fast that they were there before the telegraph cable. They frightened both the cod and the flounder, who were swimming around peacefully, hunting and eating their fellow creatures.

A couple of sea cucumbers were so petrified that they spat out their own stomachs in fright; but they survived, for they knew how to swallow them again. Lots of lobsters and crabs left their shells in the confusion. During all this, the eighteen hundred little fishes were separated; most of them never saw one another again, nor would they have recognized one another if they had. Only a dozen of them stayed in the same spot, and after they had lain still a couple of hours their worst fright was over and curiosity became stronger than fear.

They looked about, both above and below themselves, and there at the bottom of the sea they thought they saw the monster that had frightened them all. It looked thin, but who knew how big it could make itself or how strong it was. It lay very still, but it might be up to something.

The more timid of the small fish said, "Let it lie where it is, it is no concern of ours." But the tiniest of them were determined to find out what it was. Since the monster had come from above, it was better to seek information about it up there. They swam up to the surface of the ocean. The wind was still and the sea was like a mirror.

They met a dolphin. He is a fellow who likes to jump and to turn somersaults in the sea. The dolphin has eyes to see with and ought to have seen what happened, and therefore the little fishes approached it. But a dolphin only thinks about himself and his somersaults; he didn't know what to say, so he didn't say anything, but looked very proud.

A seal came swimming by just at that moment, and even though it eats small fishes, it was more polite than the dolphin. Luckily it happened to be full, and it knew more than the jumping fish. "Many a night have I lain on a wet stone—miles and miles away from here—and looked toward land, where live those treacherous creatures who call themselves, in their own language, men. They are always hunting me and my kind, though usually we manage to escape. That is exactly what happened to the great sea serpent that you are asking about—it got away from them. They had had it in their power for ever so long, and kept it up on land. Now men wanted to transport it to another country, across the sea.—Why? you may ask, but I can't answer.—They had a lot of trouble getting it on board the ship. But they finally succeeded; after all, it was weakened from its stay on land. They rolled it up, round and round into a coil. It wiggled and writhed, and what a lot of noise it made! I heard it. When the ship got out to sea, the great eel slipped overboard. They tried to stop it. I saw them, there were dozens of hands holding onto its body. But they couldn't. Now it is lying down at the bottom of the sea, and I guess it will stay there for a while."

"It looks awfully thin," said the tiny fishes.

"They have starved it," explained the seal. "But it will soon get its old figure and strength back. I am sure it is the great sea serpent: the one men are so afraid of that they talk about it all the time. I had not believed it existed, but now I do. And that was it." With a flip of its tail, the seal dived and was gone.

"How much he knew and how well he talked," said one of the little fishes admiringly. "I have never known so much as I do now—I just hope it wasn't all lies."

"We could swim down and look," suggested the tiniest of the tiny fishes. "And on the way down we could hear what the other fishes think."

"We wouldn't move a fin to know anything more," said all the other tiny fishes, turned, and swam away.

"But I will," shouted the tiniest one, and swam down into the depths. But he was far away from where the great sea serpent had sunk. The little fish searched in every direction. Never had he realized that the world was so big. Great shoals of herring glided by like silver boats, and behind them came schools of mackerel that were even more splendid and brilliant. There were fishes of all shapes, with all kinds of markings and colors. Jellyfish, looking like transparent plants, floated by, carried by the currents. Down at the bottom of the sea the strangest things grew: tall grasses and palm-shaped trees whose every leaf was covered with crustaceans.

At last the tiny fish spied a long dark line far below it and swam down to it. It was not the giant serpent but the railing of a sunken ship, whose upper and lower decks had been torn in two by the pressure of the sea. The little fish entered the great cabin, where the terrified passengers had gathered as the ship went down; they had all drowned and the currents of the sea had carried their bodies away, except for two of them: a young woman who lay on a bench with her babe in her arms. The sea rocked them gently; they looked as though they were sleeping. The little fish grew frightened as he looked at them. What if they were to wake? The cabin was so quiet and so lonely that the tiny fish hurried away again, out into the light, where there were other fishes. It had not swum very far when it met a young whale; it was awfully big.

"Please don't swallow me," pleaded the little fish. "I am so little you could hardly taste me, and I find it such a great pleasure to live."

"What are you doing down here?" grunted the whale. "It is much too deep for your kind." Then the tiny fish told the whale about the great eel—or whatever it could be—that had come from the air and descended into the sea, frightening even the most courageous fishes.

"Ha, ha, ha!" laughed the whale, and swallowed so much water that it had to surface in order to breathe and spout the water out. "Ho-ho . . . ha-ha. That must have been the thing that tickled my back when I was turning over. I thought it was the mast of a ship and was just about to use it as a back scratcher; but it must have been that. It lies farther out. I think I will go and have a look at it; I haven't anything else to do."

The whale swam away and the tiny fish followed it, but not too closely for the great animal left a turbulent wake behind it.

They met a shark and an old sawfish. They, too, had heard about the strange great eel that was so thin and yet longer than any other fish. They hadn't seen it but wanted to.

A catfish joined them. "If that sea serpent is not thicker than an anchor cable, then I will cut it in two, in one bite," he said, and opened his monstrous jaws to show his six rows of teeth. "If I can make a mark in an anchor I guess I can bite a stem like that in two."

"There it is," cried the whale. "Look how it moves, twisting and turning." The whale thought he had better eyesight than the others. As a matter of fact he hadn't; what he had seen was merely an old conger eel, several yards long, that was swimming toward them.

"That fellow has never caused any commotion in the sea before, or frightened any other big fish," said the catfish with disgust. "I have met him often."

They told the conger about the new sea serpent and asked him if he wanted to go with them to discover what it was.

"I wonder if it is longer than I am," said the conger eel, and stretched himself. "If it is, then it will be sorry."

"It certainly will," said the rest of the company. "There are enough of us so we don't have to tolerate it if we don't want to!" they exclaimed, and hurried on.

They saw something that looked like a floating island that was having trouble keeping itself from sinking. It was an old whale. His head was overgrown with seaweed, and on his back were so many mussels and oysters that its black skin looked as if it had white spots.

"Come on, old man," the young whale said. "There is a new fish in the ocean and we won't tolerate it!"

"Oh, let me stay where I am!" grumbled the old whale. "Peace is all I ask, to be left in peace. Ow! Ow! . . . I am very sick, it will be the death of me. My only comfort is to let my back emerge above the water, then the sea gulls scratch it: the sweet birds. That helps a lot as long as they don't dig too deep with their bills and get into the blubber. There's the skeleton of one still sitting on my back. It got stuck and couldn't get loose when I had to submerge. The little fishes picked his bones clean. You can see it. . . . Look at him, and look at me. . . . Oh, I am very sick."

"You are just imagining all that," said the young whale. "I am not sick, no one that lives in the sea is ever sick."

"I am sorry!" said the old whale. "The eels have skin diseases, the carp have smallpox, and we all suffer from worms."

"Nonsense!" shouted the shark, who didn't like to listen to that kind of talk. Neither did the others, so they all swam on.

At last they came to the place where part of the telegraph cable lies, that stretches from Europe to America across sand shoals and high mountains, through endless forests of seaweed and coral. The currents move as the winds do in the heavens above, and through them swim schools of fishes, more numerous than the flocks of migratory birds that fly through the air. There was a noise, a sound, a humming, the ghost of which you hear in the great conch shell when you hold it up to your ear.

"There is the serpent!" shouted the bigger fish and the little fishes too. They had caught sight of some of the telegraph cable but neither the beginning nor the end of it, for they were both lost in the far distance. Sponges, polyps, and gorgonia swayed above it and leaned against it, sometimes hiding it from view. Sea urchins and snails climbed over it; and great crabs, like giant spiders, walked tightrope along it. Deep blue sea cucumbers—or whatever those creatures are called who eat with their whole body—lay next to it; one would think that they were trying to smell it. Flounders and cod kept turning from side to side, in order to be able to listen to what everyone was saying. The starfishes had dug themselves down in the mire; only two of their points were sticking up, but they had eyes on them and were staring at the black snake, hoping to see something come out of it.

The telegraph cable lay perfectly still, as if it were lifeless; but inside, it was filled with life: with thoughts, human thoughts.

"That thing is treacherous," said the whale. "It might hit me in the stomach, and that is my weak point."

"Let's feel our way forward," said one of the polyps. "I have long arms and flexible fingers. I've already touched it, but now I'll take a firmer grasp."

And it stuck out its arms and encircled the cable. "I have felt both its stomach and its back. It is not scaly. I don't think it has any skin either. I don't believe it lays eggs and I don't think it gives birth to live children."

The conger eel lay down beside the cable and stretched itself as far as it could. "It is longer than I am," it admitted. "But length isn't everything. One has to have skin, a good stomach and, above all, suppleness."

The whale—the young strong whale!—bowed more deeply than it ever had before. "Are you a fish or a plant?" he asked. "Or are you a surface creation, one of those who can't live down here?"

The telegraph didn't answer, though it was filled with words.

Thoughts traveled through it so fast that they took only seconds to move from one end to the other: hundreds of miles away.

"Will you answer or be bitten in two?" asked the ill-mannered shark.

All the other fishes repeated the question: "Answer or be bitten in two?"

The telegraph cable didn't move; it had its own ideas, which isn't surprising for someone so full of thoughts. "Let them bite me in two," it thought. "Then I will be pulled up and repaired. It has happened to lots of my relations, that are not half as long as I am." But it didn't speak, it telegraphed; besides, it found the question impertinent; after all, it was lying there on official business.

Dusk had come. The sun was setting, as men say. It was a fiery red, and the clouds were as brilliant as fire—one more beautiful than the other.

"Now comes the red illumination," said the polyp. "Maybe the thing will be easier to see in that light, though I hardly think it worth looking at."

"Attack it! Attack it!" screamed the catfish, and showed all his teeth.

"Attack it! Attack it!" shouted the whale, the shark, the swordfish, and the conger eel.

They pushed forward. The catfish was first; but just as it was going to bite the cable the swordfish, who was a little too eager, stuck its sword into the behind of the catfish. It was a mistake, but it kept the catfish from using the full strength of its jaw muscles.

There was a great muddle in the mud. The sea cucumbers, the big fishes, and the small ones swam around in circles; they pushed and shoved and squashed and ate each other up. The crabs and the lobsters fought, and the snails pulled their heads into their houses. The telegraph cable just minded its own business, which is the proper thing for a telegraph cable to do.

Night came to the sky above, but down in the ocean millions and millions of little animals illuminated the water. Crayfish no larger than the head of a pin gave off light. It is incredible and wonderful; and quite true.

All the animals of the sea looked at the telegraph cable. "If only we knew what it was—or at least what it wasn't," said one of the fishes. And that was a very important question.

An old sea cow—human beings call them mermen and mermaids—
came gliding by. This one was a mermaid. She had a tail and short
arms for splashing, hanging breasts, and seaweed and parasites on
her head—and of these she was very proud. "If you want learning and
knowledge," she said, "then I think I am the best equipped to give it
to you. But I want free passage on the bottom of the sea for myself
and my family. I am a fish like you, and a reptile by training. I am
the most intelligent citizen of the ocean. I know about everything
under the water and everything above it. The thing that you are worrying about comes from up there; and everything from above is dead
and powerless, once it comes down here. So let it lie, it is only a
human invention and of no importance."

"I think it may be more than that," said the tiny fish.

"Shut up, mackerel!" said the sea cow.

"Shrimp!" shouted the others, and they meant it as an insult.

The sea cow explained to them that the sea serpent who had
frightened them—the cable itself, by the way, didn't make a sound—
was not dangerous. It was only an invention of those animals up on
dry land called human beings. When she finished talking about the
sea serpent, she gave a little lesson in the craftiness and wickedness
of men: "They are always trying to catch us. That is the only reason
for their existence. They throw down nets, traps, and long fishing
lines that have hooks, with bait attached to them, to try and fool us.
This is probably another—bigger—fishing line. They are so stupid that
they expect us to bite on it. But we aren't as dumb as that. Don't
touch that piece of junk. It will unravel, fall apart, and become mud
and mire—the whole thing. Let it lie there and rot. Anything that
comes from above is worthless; it breaks or creaks; it is no good!"

"No good!" said all the creatures of the sea, accepting the mermaid's opinion in order to have one.

The little tiny fish didn't agree, but it had learned to keep its
thoughts to itself. "That enormously long snake may be the most
marvelous fish in the sea. I have a feeling that it is."

"Marvelous!" we human beings agree; and we can prove that it is
true.

The great sea serpent of the fable has become a fact. It was constructed by human skill, conceived by human intelligence. It stretches
from the Eastern Hemisphere to the Western, carrying messages from
country to country faster than light travels from the sun down to the

earth. Each year the great serpent grows. Soon it will stretch across all the great oceans, under the storm-whipped waves and the glasslike water, through which the skipper can look down as if he were sailing through the air and see the multitude of fish and the fireworks of color.

At the very depths is a *Midgards-worm,* biting its own tail as it circumscribes the world. Fish and reptiles hit their heads against it: it is impossible to understand what it is by looking at it. Human thoughts expressed in all the languages of the world, and yet silent: the snake of knowledge of good and evil. The most wonderful of the wonders of the sea: our time's great sea serpent!

71

The Gardener and His Master

A FEW miles from Copenhagen stood an old castle with thick walls, towers, and corbie gables. Here lived, in the summertime, a noble family. This castle was the handsomest of all the castles and farms they owned. It was in such good repair that it looked as if it had been newly built. Inside it was both cozy and comfortable. Over the entrance portal had been cut in stone the coat of arms of the family. Rose vines grew up the wall and made a frame around the shield and the windows. A big lawn that was smooth as a carpet stretched in front of the castle; hawthorn bushes, both red and white, grew in the garden, besides beautiful and rare flowers seldom seen outside the hothouse.

The noble family had an excellent gardener. It was a pleasure to look not only at the flower garden but at the vegetable garden and the fruit orchard as well. Near the orchard a small part of the original garden was still to be seen. It was filled with bushes cut in the shapes of pyramids and crowns. Among these stood two big ancient trees. They had but few leaves on them, even in summer; and if one did not know better, one could have believed that all the branches that had been cut off the bushes had been carried by the wind into the trees. But all the little bunches of twigs had been flown up there: they were birds' nests.

From ancient times, rooks and crows had nested there. The two old trees were a city of birds, and the birds were the proprietors. They were the oldest family in the castle, and they felt that they were the masters. They tolerated the two-legged ones that could not fly but had to stay forever on the ground. But human beings did not interest them, even when they came with their guns and frightened them, so they flew out of their trees, screaming with hoarse voices: "Caw! Caw!"

The gardener had often asked his master for permission to have the old trees cut down; they were half dead as it was, and ugly. If they were gone, the birds would be gone too, and one would be spared listening to their screaming. But the master wanted to get rid of neither trees nor birds. He said they had been there from ancient times, and they belonged to the castle.

"Those trees are the birds' inheritance; let them keep it, my good Larsen," he would say. The gardener's name was Larsen—but that is neither here nor there, as far as my story is concerned. "Haven't you enough land, little Larsen? Why do you need to take the birds? If the park isn't big enough, you have a kitchen garden, the orchard, and the hothouse."

And what the master said was true, the gardener had a large domain that he took great pains to keep. His master and mistress acknowledged it, but at times they could not help informing him that they had seen flowers or eaten fruits at the table of friends that were superior to what he could produce. This made the gardener quite sad, for he always did his very best. He had a simple, loving heart and took great pride in his work.

One day his master called him to the castle and told him, in a most courteous but patronizing way, that while dining with some noble friends the day before they had been served some pears and apples so succulent that they and all the other guests had never before tasted their like. The fruits were not native, of that he felt sure, but they ought to be imported; that is, if they could be made to grow here. They had been bought in the biggest greengrocery in the city, and the master wanted the gardener to ride in immediately and inquire what the names of the fruit were and if shoots for grafting could be sent for.

The gardener knew the greengrocer well, for it was to him that he sold, with his master's permission, the surplus fruit and vegetables from the gardens. He saddled a horse and rode to town and asked the greengrocer where the much-praised apples and pears had come from.

"They are from your own orchard," said the greengrocer, and

showed the gardener some of the fruit, which he recognized at once. He hurried back and told his master the good news that the apples and pears he had found so delicious had come from his own garden.

Both the master and mistress refused to believe it. "I don't think it possible, Larsen," said the master. "You will have to get it in writing from the greengrocer before I will believe it."

The gardener rode to town once more, and this time he returned with a testimonial from the greengrocer.

"It is strange, but I guess it must be true," said the master. From then on great bowls filled with pears and apples from their garden stood on the table, and they were proud of them. Crates were sent to all their friends in town, in the country, and even to some in foreign lands. It really was quite exciting, quite an honor; but it had to be remembered that that particular year had been a good year for fruit everywhere.

Some months later the master and the mistress were invited to the king's table. The day after, the gardener was called into the drawing room again. For dessert His Majesty had served some melons, from the royal hothouses, that had been most succulent and tasty.

"You must go to the royal gardener, Larsen, and get some melon seeds so we can grow them ourselves."

"But the royal gardener got his seeds from us," answered the gardener, very pleased.

"In that case, the royal gardener has understood how to grow them. Every one of them was superb," said the master, looking more annoyed than pleased.

"I guess I can be proud of them," said the gardener, "for it will please you to know that the royal gardener had no luck with his melons this year; when he saw ours he asked for three of them for the royal table."

"Larsen! Don't tell me that it was our own melons we ate."

"I am sure they were," said the gardener. "But I will go and ask."

And he did and it was their own melons they had eaten and he got it in writing from the royal gardener.

His master and mistress were both pleased and surprised, and told everyone the story and even showed the testimonial from the royal gardener. Melon seeds were dispatched to their friends, as apples and pears and shoots for grafting had been sent before.

Seeds from the new type of melon were exported. They were

named after the castle, so now its name could be read in French, German, and English. It was all quite unexpected.

"I hope the gardener won't begin thinking too much of himself," said the master to the mistress.

He didn't; but the fame was a spur, he wanted to be one of the best gardeners in the country. Every year he tried to improve some of the vegetables and fruits, and often he was successful. It was not always appreciated. He would be told that the pears and apples were good but not as good as the ones last year. The melons were excellent but not quite up to the standard of the first ones he had grown.

As for the strawberries, they were fine, but berries as big and juicy were served at other tables. The year the worms ate the radishes, no one seemed to be interested in talking about anything else, even though so many other things had grown well that year. It was as if his master felt relieved at being able to point to a failure.

"The radishes didn't work out this year, little Larsen," they would say, and repeat it. "The radishes didn't work out."

Twice a week the gardener took fresh flowers up to the castle. He arranged them marvelously so each color complemented the others; his bouquets were a delight.

"You have taste, Larsen," his mistress would say. "But remember, taste is a gift from God, not of your own making."

One day he arranged in a crystal bowl a water-lily leaf and a strange blue flower as big as a sunflower.

"It is the lotus flower from Hindustan!" exclaimed the mistress. She had never seen anything so beautiful before. The bowl was put where the sun could shine on it in the daytime, and at night it was illuminated with candles. Everyone who saw it found it lovely and rare, and said they had never seen a flower like it before. The young princess, who was both good and kind, was so delighted with it that she was given the flower to take home with her to her castle.

The next day the master and mistress went down into the garden. They wanted to pick one of the marvelous flowers themselves. They looked everywhere, but they couldn't find it. At last they called the gardener and asked him where the blue lotus flower grew.

"We have looked everywhere," they said, "both in the flower garden and in the hothouse."

"You won't find it either place," answered the gardener. "It is only

518   A Treasury of Hans Christian Andersen

a humble flower from the kitchen garden. But beautiful it is, like a blue cactus, though it is only an artichoke."

"I wish you had told us that." The master sounded annoyed. "We thought it was a rare foreign flower. How could we have thought anything else? It is most embarrassing. The young princess was so enamored of it that we gave it to her. Although she is very well versed in botany, she did not recognize it; but then I am sure botany has little to do with vegetables. My good Larsen, how could you bring such a flower up into the rooms of the castle? You have made us appear ridiculous."

The beautiful blue flower from the kitchen garden was banished from the elegant rooms of the old castle. It didn't belong there! The master and mistress excused themselves to the princess and explained that the beautiful blue lotus flower was only a common vegetable. Their gardener was the culprit who had been so impertinent; they had reprimanded him severely.

"Oh, what a pity! How unjust!" exclaimed the princess. "He has opened our eyes, showed us a beautiful flower, where we would never have thought of looking for it. I will order the royal gardener to bring me an artichoke flower every day as long as they are in bloom."

And the royal gardener did; and the master and the mistress told Larsen that he, too, could bring a freshly cut artichoke flower to their rooms every day.

"It is really quite a fascinating flower," they said, and complimented the gardener. "Larsen loves praise, he is like a spoiled child," the mistress said, and the master nodded in agreement.

That autumn there was a terrible storm. During the night it grew worse and on the outskirts of the forest great trees fell; their roots were pulled right out of the earth. The two great old trees that housed the colony of birds did not fare better. Down they came, nests and all. Inside the castle one could hear the angry screams of the birds, and some of the servants said that the birds knocked on the windowpanes with their wings. The master said it was an affliction. The gardener said nothing; he was happy to see the old trees gone.

"Now you are contented, Larsen." The master looked at the fallen trees. "The storm has cut them down for you; the birds have departed for the forest, a part of the old times has gone. Soon there will be nothing left to remind us of it. You, this has delighted; me, it has grieved."

The gardener had a plan—it was an old one he had thought of long ago—as to what he would do with the area where the trees had stood. It was a sunny spot and he meant to make it the most beautiful part of the park.

The trees had smashed the bushes in their fall, and they could not be saved. In the cleared plot of land he now planted all the typical common plants of Denmark, gathered from forests and fields. Bushes, trees, and flowers that no other gardener had ever dreamed of introducing into the park of a castle he planted there. Each got the soil, the sun or shade it desired; he nursed them with devotion and the plants grew and flourished.

The juniper from the heath of Jutland thrived. It rose like a miniature Italian cypress. Near it grew the holly, green in winter and summer. And in front of them were ferns of all different types, like dwarf palm trees. The great thistle, the most despised of all weeds, bloomed with flowers so beautiful that they would have enhanced any bouquet. Not far from them, where the soil was a little more moist, the common dock was allowed to flourish, with its big picturesque leaves. From the fields had been brought great mulleins that looked like giant candelabra. Woodruff, primrose, lily of the valley, the calla, and the three-leafed wood sorrel: all were there; none had been forgotten. It was a marvel to look at.

In the direction of the fields the garden was fenced by a row of dwarf pear trees. They had been imported from France but, having been given plenty of sun and careful nursing, they soon bore fruits as big and succulent as in their own country.

Where the two old trees had stood a flagpole was erected and from its top the white and red flag of Denmark flew. Near the flagpole another smaller pole stood, around which the vines of the hops twisted themselves; in the late summer the sweet scent of their flowers could be smelled far away. In the winter a sheaf of oats hung from the pole; it is an old custom to provide a meal in this way for the birds at Christmas.

"Larsen is getting sentimental in his old age," said the master.

"But he is loyal and true," added the mistress.

At New Year's, one of the illustrated papers from Copenhagen carried a picture of the old castle. One could see the flagpole and the sheaf of oats for the birds. It was particularly mentioned how pleasing it was to see that such an old tradition was kept alive.

"It does not matter what Larsen does," the master remarked. "The whole world will beat the drums for it. There is a happy man. We must be almost proud of having him."

But they weren't really proud of it. They felt that they were the owners and that they could dismiss Larsen if they wanted to. They didn't, for they were decent people, and there are lots of their kind, which is fortunate for the Larsens.

That was the story of the gardener and his master. I have told it, now why don't you think about it.

72

The Professor and the Flea

THERE once was a balloonist—that is, a captain of a balloon—who came to a bad end: his balloon ripped and he fell straight to the ground and was smashed. His son, who had been along on the trip, had parachuted down two minutes before the tragedy. That was the young man's good luck. He landed safe and sound, with invaluable experience in ballooning and a great desire to make use of it; but he didn't have a balloon or any money to buy one with.

He had to make a living, so he taught himself how to talk with his stomach; that is called being a ventriloquist. He was young and handsome, and when he had bought new clothes and grown a mustache he had such a noble look that he might have been mistaken for the younger son of a count. All the ladies found him handsome; and one of them so much so that she ran away from home to follow him. They traveled to distant towns and foreign lands, and there he called himself professor, no less would do.

His greatest desire was still to get a balloon and then ascend into the sky with his wife, but balloons are expensive.

"Our day will come," he declared.

"I hope it will be soon," said his wife.

"We can wait; we are young. Now I am a professor. Crumbs are not slices, but they are bread," he said, quoting an old proverb.

His wife helped him. She sat at the door and sold tickets, which was no fun in the winter when it was cold. She also took part in the act. She climbed into a chest and then vanished. The chest had a

double bottom; it was a matter of agility, and was called an optical illusion.

One evening after the performance, when he opened the false bottom, she wasn't there. He looked everywhere but she was gone. Too
much dexterity. She never came back. She had been sorry and now
he was sorry. He lost his spirit, couldn't laugh or clown, and then he
lost his audience. His earnings went from bad to worse and so did his
clothes. At last the only thing he owned was a big flea. He had
inherited the animal from his wife and therefore was fond of it. He
trained the flea, taught it the art of dexterity: how to present arms
and to shoot off a cannon; the latter was very small.

The professor was proud of the flea and the flea was proud of himself. After all, he had human blood in his stomach, if not in his veins.
He had visited the grand capitals of Europe and performed before
kings and queens, at least that was what was printed in the playbill
and the newspapers. He knew he was famous and could support a
professor—or a whole family if he had had one.

The flea was proud and famous; and yet, when he and the professor traveled, they always went fourth class—it gets you to your destination just as quickly as first. They had a silent agreement that they
would never part; the flea would remain a bachelor and the professor
a widower, which amounts to the same thing.

"A place where one has had a great success one should never
revisit," said the professor. He knew human nature and that is not
the poorest sort of knowledge.

At last they had traveled in all the civilized parts of the world; only
the lands of the savages were left. The professor knew that there were
cannibals who ate Christian human beings. But he was not a real
Christian and the flea not a human being, so he thought that there
was no reason not to go there, and he expected it to be a profitable
trip.

They traveled by steamer and sailing ship. The flea performed and
that paid for their passage.

At last they came to the land of the savages. Here a little princess
reigned. She had overthrown her own parents, for though she was
only eight years old she had a will of her own and was marvelously
charming and naughty.

As soon as she had seen the flea present arms and shoot off his little cannon, she fell wildly in love with him. As love can make a

civilized man into a savage, imagine what it can do to one who is already a savage. She screamed, stamped her feet, and said, "It is him or no one!"

"My sweet little sensible girl, we shall have to make him into a human first," said her father.

"You leave that to me, old man," she answered, and that was not a very nice way to speak to her own father, but she was a savage.

The professor put the flea in her little hand.

"Now you are a human being," declared the princess. "You shall reign together with me, but you will have to obey or I shall kill you and eat the professor."

The professor got a room for himself. The walls were made of sugar cane; if he had had a sweet tooth, he could have licked them; but he didn't. He got a hammock for a bed, and lying in that was almost like being in the balloon he still dreamed about.

The flea stayed with the princess, sat on her hand and on her sweet neck. She pulled a long hair out of her head and made the professor tie one end around the leg of the flea; the other end was fastened to her coral earring.

The princess was happy, and she thought that if she was happy, then the flea ought to be happy too. But the one who was not happy was the professor. He was used to traveling, sleeping one night in one town and the next in another. He loved reading in the newspaper about himself, how clever he was at teaching a flea human accomplishments; but there were no newspapers among the savages. Day after day he lay in his hammock, lazy and idle. He was well fed. He was given fresh birds' eggs, stewed elephants' eyes, and roasted leg of giraffe, for the cannibals did not eat human flesh every day, it was a delicacy. "A child's shoulder in a spicy gravy with peppers is the most delicious dish there is," claimed the princess.

The professor was bored. He wanted to leave the land of the savages but he had to take the flea along; it was his protégé and the supplier of his daily bread.

He strained his power of thought as much as he could, and then he jumped out of the hammock and exclaimed, "I've got it!"

He went to the princess' father and said, "Please allow me to work. I want to introduce your people to what we, in the great world, call culture."

"And what can you teach me?" asked the father of the princess.

524   A Treasury of Hans Christian Andersen

"My greatest accomplishment," answered the professor, "is a cannon which when fired makes such a bang that the earth trembles and all the birds in the air fall down roasted and ready to eat."

"Bring on that cannon," said the king.

But the only cannon in the whole country was the little one the flea could fire, and that was much too small.

"I will make a bigger one," said the professor. "I need lots of silk material, ropes, strings, needles, and thread. Besides some oil of camphor, which is good against airsickness."

All that he asked for, he got. Not until he was finished and the balloon was ready to be filled with hot air and sent up did he call the people together to see his cannon.

The flea was sitting on the princess' hand, watching the balloon being blown up. And the balloon stretched itself and grew fatter and swelled. It was so wild it was difficult to hold.

"I have to take the cannon up in the air to cool it off. Alone, I cannot manage it, I have to have someone who knows something about cannons along to help me, and here only the flea will do."

"I hate giving him permission to go," said the princess as she held out the flea to the professor, who took it on his hand.

"Let go of the ropes, up goes the balloon!" he cried.

The savages thought he said "up goes the cannon," and the balloon rose up into the air above the clouds and flew away from the land of the savages.

The little princess, her father and her mother, and all their people stood and waited. They are waiting still and if you don't believe me you can travel to the land of the savages. Every child there will tell you the story of the flea and the professor. They are expecting him back as soon as the "cannon" has cooled off. But he will never return, he is back home. When he travels on the railroad he always goes first class, not fourth. He has done well for himself, with the help of the balloon, and nobody asks him where or how he got it. The flea and the professor are wealthy and respectable, and that kind of people are never asked embarrassing questions.

Translator's Note

In an age more economical than our own, paperbacks were published first; and then, if they were successful, a bound volume appeared. Throughout Andersen's life his fairy tales and stories were printed in almost leaflet-sized booklets, without binding or illustrations —containing anywhere from one to more than a dozen tales— before they were collected and printed in book form. It is to these booklets that Andersen refers in his notes.

The notes were written for the Danish editions of Andersen's works. Many of his stories appeared in Germany, some in England, and a few in the United States, before they were published in his native land. Although he always wrote his tales in Danish, he was able to supervise the German translations personally.

Preface, 1837: for the Older Readers

NOTHING that I have written has been evaluated so differently as *Fairy Tales, told for children*. A few people, whose judgment I prize, have said that these fairy tales are the most valuable of all my work; while others have remarked that they are of no importance whatever and advised me not to write any more of them. This diversity of opinion, and the silence with which the professional critics greeted these tales, weakened my desire to write again in this literary form. Thus a year has passed before the third booklet follows the second and the first.

While I was engaged in writing something larger and completely different, the idea and the plot of THE LITTLE MERMAID intruded and would not go away, so I had to write this fairy tale.

I feared that if I published it alone it would seem a little too presumptuous, so I decided to place it among a group of tales that I had already begun. The others in this booklet are more children's stories than this one, whose deeper meaning only an adult can understand; but I believe that a child will enjoy it for the story's sake alone: that the plot, in itself, is exciting enough to absorb a child's attention.

The shorter tale, THE EMPEROR'S NEW CLOTHES, is a Spanish story. For the whole amusing idea we must thank Prince Don Juan Manuel, who was born in 1277 and died in 1347.

While talking about these two tales, I will take the opportunity of saying a few words about my earlier stories.

In my childhood I loved to listen to fairy tales and stories. Many of them are still very alive in my memory. Certain of them seem to me to be Danish in origin for I have never heard them anywhere else. These I have told in my own way: where I thought it fitting, I have changed them and let imagination freshen the colors in the picture that had begun to fade. There are four such stories in this volume: THE TINDERBOX, LITTLE CLAUS AND BIG CLAUS, THE PRINCESS AND THE PEA; and THE TRAVELING COMPANION. In Anacreon's poem, as most people know, the fable THE NAUGHTY BOY is to be found.

Three of the stories are entirely my own: LITTLE IDA'S FLOWERS, INCHELINA, THE LITTLE MERMAID.

With the third booklet, the tales become a little volume; whether this will be the only one depends upon the impression this collection makes on the public.

In a little land like ours, the poet is always poor; honor, therefore, is the golden bird he tries to grasp. Time will tell whether I can catch it by telling fairy tales.

Copenhagen, March 1837   H. C. Andersen